Richard Laymon wrote over thi[...] [...]
May 2001, *The Travelling Vampir*[...] [...]
Best Horror Novel, a prize for [...]
shortlisted with *Flesh*, *Funland*, [...] *.....* (Best Anthology)
and *A Writer's Tale* (Best Non-fiction). Laymon's works include the
books of the Beast House Chronicles: *The Cellar*, *The Beast House* and
The Midnight Tour. Some of his recent novels have been *Night in the
Lonesome October*, *No Sanctuary* and *Amara*.

A native of Chicago, Laymon attended Willamette University in
Salem, Oregon, and took an MA in English Literature from Loyola
University, Los Angeles. In 2000, he was elected President of the Horror
Writers' Association. He died in February 2001.

Laymon's fiction is published in the United Kingdom by Headline,
and in the United States by Leisure Books and Cemetery Dance
Publications. To learn more, visit the Laymon website at: http://
rlk.cjb.net

'A brilliant writer' *Sunday Express*

'Stephen King without a conscience' Dan Marlowe

'In Laymon's books, blood doesn't so much as drip as explode, splatter
and coagulate' *Independent*

'No one writes like Laymon and you're going to have a good time with
anything he writes' Dean Koontz

'Incapable of writing a disappointing book' *New York Review of Science
Fiction*

'This is an author that does not pull his punches . . . A gripping, and at
times genuinely shocking, read' *SFX Magazine*

'One of the best, and most underrated, writers working in the genre
today' *Cemetery Dance*

Also in the Richard Laymon Collection published by Headline

The Beast House Trilogy:
The Cellar
The Beast House
The Midnight Tour

Beware!
Dark Mountain*
The Woods are Dark
Out are the Lights
Night Show
Allhallow's Eve
Flesh
Resurrection Dreams
Darkness, Tell Us
One Rainy Night
Alarums
Blood Games
Endless Night
Midnight's Lair
Island
Quake
Body Rides
Bite
Fiends
After Midnight
Among the Missing
Come Out Tonight
The Travelling Vampire Show
Dreadful Tales
Night in the Lonesome October
No Sanctuary
Amara
The Lake
The Glory Bus
Funland
The Stake

*previously published under the pseudonym of Richard Kelly

Savage

and

In the Dark

headline

SAVAGE first published in Great Britain in 1993
by HEADLINE PUBLISHING GROUP

IN THE DARK first published in Great Britain in 1994
by HEADLINE PUBLISHING GROUP

First published in this omnibus edition in 2006
by HEADLINE PUBLISHING GROUP

A HEADLINE paperback

1

0 7553 3177 X (ISBN-10)
978 0 7553 3177 2 (ISBN-13)

Typeset in Janson by Avon DataSet Ltd, Bidford on Avon, Warwickshire

Printed and bound in Great Britain by
Mackays of Chatham plc, Chatham, Kent

Headline's policy is to use papers that are natural, renewable and recyclable
products and made from wood grown in sustainable forests. The logging and
manufacturing processes are expected to conform to the environmental
regulations of the country of origin.

HEADLINE PUBLISHING GROUP
A division of Hachette Livre UK Ltd
338 Euston Road
London NW1 3BH

www.headline.co.uk
www.hodderheadline.com

Savage

From Whitechapel to the Wild West
on the track of Jack the Ripper

THIS BOOK IS DEDICATED
TO BOB TANNER
GENTLEMAN AND SUPER AGENT.

WITH YOUR GUIDANCE AND HELP
I'VE GONE BEYOND WHERE I THOUGHT
I COULD GO.

– ON TOP OF WHICH –
YOU SUGGESTED AT LUNCH A WHILE BACK
THAT I TRY AN ENGLISH SETTING.
SO I DID.
SO THIS BOOK IS YOUR FAULT.

I love my work and want to start again. You will soon hear of me with my funny little games . . . My knife is nice and sharp. I want to get to work right away if I get a chance. Good luck.

Yours truly

Jack the Ripper

from a letter dated 25 September 1888, attributed to Jack the Ripper

God did not make men equal, Colonel Colt did.

anonymous Westerner

Contents

Prologue

Wherein I Aim to Whet Your Appetite For the Tale of My Adventures

London's East End was rather a dicey place, but that's where I found myself, a fifteen-year-old youngster with more sand than sense, on the night of 8 November 1888.

That was some twenty years back, so it's high time I put pen to my story before I commence to forget the particulars, or get snakebit.

It all started because I went off to find my Uncle William and fetch him back so he could deal with Barnes. Uncle was a police constable, you see. He was a mighty tough hombre, to boot. A few words – or licks – from him, and that rascal Barnes wasn't ever likely to lay another belt on Mother.

So I set out, round about nine, reckoning I'd be back with Uncle in less than an hour.

But it wasn't in the cards for me to find him.

The way it all played out, I never saw Uncle William again at all, and I wasn't to set eyes again on my dear Mother for many a year.

Sometimes, you wish you could start from scratch and get a chance to do things differently.

Can't be done, however.

And maybe that's for the best.

Why, I used to pine for Mother and miss my chums and wonder considerable about the life I might've known if only I hadn't gone off to Whitechapel that night. I still have my regrets along those lines, but they don't amount to much any more.

You see, it's like this.

I ended up in some terrible scrapes, and got my face rubbed in more than a few ungodly horrors, but there were fine times aplenty through it all. I found wonderful adventures and true friends. I found love. And up to now, I haven't gotten myself killed.

Had some narrow calls.

Run-ins with all manner of ruffians, with mobs and posses after my hide, with Jack the Ripper himself.

But I'm still here to tell the tale.

Which is what I aim to do right now.

With kindest regards from the Author
Trevor Wellington Bentley
Tucson, Arizona 1908

Part One

Off to Whitechapel
and on to America

Chapter One

The Gentleman, Barnes

It was a lovely night to be indoors, where I sat all warm and lazy by the fire in our lodgings on Marylebone High Street. I had survived the awful tedium of studying my school lessons (needn't have bothered with those, really), the servant had gone off to see her sweetheart, and I was perking up considerable with the help of Tom and Huck, who were hatching wild schemes to help Jim escape from Uncle Silas and Aunt Sally. Tom was an exasperating fellow. He never did *anything* the easy way.

Keen as I was on Mr Twain's book, however, I kept an ear open for the sound of footfalls on the stairs. And I kept not hearing any. There was just the sound of rain rapping on the window panes.

Mother should've been back some time ago. She'd left directly after supper to give her Thursday night violin lesson to Liz McNaughton, who had but one leg due to a carriage mishap on Lombard Street.

Though it was mean-spirited of me, I found myself wishing Liz had kept her leg and lost an arm. Would've put a damper on her violining. That way, Mother would've been spared the chore of paying her a visit on such a rough night, and I would've been spared my worries.

But worry I did.

I could never rest easy when Mother was away at night. I had no father, nor any but the foggiest memory of him, as he'd been a soldier attached to the Berkshires, and was fetched up dead by a Jezail bullet at the battle of Maiwand when I was just a sprout. Growing up fatherless, I had a morbid dread of losing Mother as well.

So while I wondered what had delayed her return that night, I conjured up a whole passel of dreadful fates queuing up to have a go at her. Even in more normal times, she might have been run down by a hansom or attacked by cutthroats, or met some other terrible end. But these were not normal times, what with the Whitechapel murderer lurking about with his knife.

While most of the folks in London knew only what they read in the newspapers, I was quite well versed on all the grim particulars of the Ripper's atrocities due to Uncle William, who worked out of the Leman Street police station. He had not only gotten a first-hand look at two of the victims right where they fell, but he took a keen delight in regailing me (when Mother wasn't about) with gory descriptions of what he'd seen. Oh, his eyes merrily flashed with mischief and relish! I've no doubt he was quite amused at how I must've blanched. However, I was always eager to hear more.

Tonight, awaiting Mother's return, I wished I knew *nothing* of the Ripper.

I told myself there was no reason to fear that he might strike her down. After all, one-legged Liz's flat was no closer to the East End than our own. The Ripper would have to roam far from his usual hunting grounds before coming into our neighborhoods. Besides, it was still too early in the night for him to be out stalking. And he only killed whores.

Mother certainly ought to be safe from him.

But I made my head sore with worrying. By and by, I set the book aside and took to pacing the floor, all in a bother. I'd been at this a while before a door shut down below. That was followed by heavy, staggering footfalls on the stairway. Mother's step was usually quick and light. Curious, I hurried out and peered down the stairs.

There, struggling beneath the weight of Rolfe Barnes, was Mother.

'Mum!'

'Give us a hand.'

I rushed down and took the other side of the rascal. He was soaked to the bone and stank of rum. Though he hardly seemed able to keep his legs beneath him as we wrestled him up the stairs, he mumbled and growled, deep in his cups.

'We aren't taking him *in*, are we now?'

'We most certainly are. Mind your tongue, young man. He might've perished in the street.'

And such a shame that would've been, I thought. But I held my tongue. Barnes had a habit of turning into a brutish lout after he'd taken a few sips, going foul of mouth and mean of temper. However, he'd fought at my father's side in the second Afghan war. The way he told it, they'd been great chums to the bitter end. I always reckoned him a liar on that score, but Mother wasn't about to find fault with the man. From the very start, she'd treated him like a regular member of the family.

Not that she was gone over him. She had the good sense, at least, to reject his amorous advances (so far as I know). Even after declining his marriage proposal some years ago, however, she'd never turned him away from our door.

And tonight, by all appearances, she had dragged him through it.

'Where did you find him?' I asked as we fought our way up the stairs.

'He'd fallen in a heap in front of the Boar's Head.'

'Ah,' said I. The pub was just at the corner. 'He was likely waiting in ambuscade, and fell in his heap when he saw you coming along.'

'Trevor!'

With that, I concentrated on the job at hand.

Barnes grumbled and cursed all the while as we helped him into our flat. Mother responded with murmurs of 'Poor fellow' and 'You're soaked through' and 'You'll catch your death for sure' and 'What shall we do with you?'

What we did with him was remove his coat and settle him

down on the sofa. It fell upon me to remove his sodden boots while Mother took off her own coat, then hurried off to make tea.

I reckon it was her mistake, leaving me alone with him.

My mistake, speaking up.

I spoke up mostly to myself. Muttering, really. I didn't expect a chap in his condition to hear me, much less comprehend.

What I said was, 'Bloody cur.'

Quick as the words left my lips, his fist met my nose and sent me reeling backwards. I dropped to the floor. In the next few moments, Barnes proved himself quite lively for a fellow far gone with drink. He bounded over to me, dropped on to my chest, and pounded me nearly senseless before Mother came running to my aid.

'Rolfe!' she shouted.

He clubbed my face once more with his huge fist. Then he tumbled off as Mother tugged his hair. My mind all a fog, I tried to muster the strength to rise. But I could only lie there and watch while Barnes grabbed Mother's wrist and scurried up. He pulled her to him and struck her face such a blow that it rocked her head sideways and sent spittle flying from her lips. Then he flung her across the room. She fell against an armchair with such force that she rammed it into the wall. On her knees before it, she lifted her head off the cushion and tried to push herself up.

Barnes was already behind her. 'Too good for me, is it?' He swatted the back of her head. 'You 'n' your scurvy whelp!' He smacked her head again and she cowered against the chair, burying her face in her arms.

Barnes clutched the nape of her neck with one hand. With the other, he tore the back off her blouse.

'No!' Mother gasped. 'Rolfe! Please! The boy!'

She tried to raise her head, but he cuffed it again. Then he tugged her underthings down to her waist, baring her back entirely.

I was not so stunned by the several blows that I didn't flush with shame and outrage.

'Stop it!' I yelled, trying to get up.

Ignoring me, Barnes snatched the heavy belt from around his waist. He doubled the leather strap and swung it. With a crack like a gunshot, it lashed my mother's back. She let out a startled, hurt yelp. Across the creamy skin of her back was a broad, ruddy stripe.

He got in two more licks.

I had tears in my eyes as I swung the fireplace poker with all my strength. The iron rod caught him just above the ear and sent him stumbling sideways, the belt still raised overhead in readiness to strike another blow against Mother. He shouldered a wall, bounced off it, and dropped like a tree.

I pranced around for a bit, kicking him. Then I realized he was knocked out and in no condition to appreciate my efforts, so I figured to finish him off. I straddled him, got a good grip on the poker, and was all set to stove in his skull when a shout stopped me.

'Trevor! No!'

Mother, suddenly standing before me, threw out an arm to ward off the blow.

'Stand back,' I warned.

'Leave him be! See what you've done to him!' With that, she fell to her knees at the scoundrel's head and hunkered over him.

I gazed at her poor back. The thick welts were blurry through my tears. Here and there, trickles of blood made bright red threads along her skin.

'Thank the Lord, you haven't killed him.'

'I jolly well *shall*.'

She looked up at me. She said not a word. Nor was a word needed. I hurled the poker from my hand, then stepped away from the still body and wiped my eyes. I sniffed. The sore, wet feel of my nose got me to look down, and I found the front of my shirt soaked with blood. I dragged out a handkerchief to stop my nose from bleeding, then dropped into a chair. I would've liked to tip back my head, but I dared not take my eyes off Barnes.

Mother came to me. She stroked my hair. 'He hurt you awfully.'

'He *whipped* you, Mum.'

'It was the liquor, no doubt. He's not an evil man.'

'Evil enough, I should say. I do wish you'd let me spill his brains.'

'Such talk.' She ruffled my hair in a manner that seemed rather playful. 'It comes of reading, no doubt.'

'It comes of watching him whip you.'

'Novels are wonderful things, darling, but you must remember they're make-believe. It's an easy matter to dispatch a villain in a story. He isn't flesh and blood, you see, he's paper and ink. Spilling a bloke's brains can be rather a lark. But that's not life, m'dear. If you killed Rolfe, it would weigh on your soul like a cold, black hand. It would trouble you all your life, keeping you awake at night and tormenting you every day.'

Well, she spoke in such an earnest, solemn manner that I was suddenly mighty glad she'd stopped me from dispatching Barnes. Though I was sure she'd never killed a person, she knew deep in her heart about the burden of it.

Since that time, I've sent many a fellow to Hell. I've lost more than a trifle of sleep over it. But the greater burdens on my soul don't come from those I killed. They come because I didn't kill some rascals soon enough.

Anyhow, Barnes was still among the breathing. It'd be wrong to polish him off, or so we were both convinced at the time, but I got to worrying about what might befall us if he should wake up.

When her lecture ran down, I got off my chair and said, 'We've got to do something about him, you know? He's likely to be at us again.'

'I'm afraid you're right.'

We both stared at him. So far, he hadn't stirred. But he was snoring a bit.

'I know just the thing,' I said, and hurried off to my room. I returned a moment later with a pair of steel handcuffs, a

Christmas gift from Uncle William who thought I'd make a fine constable one day and wished to whet my appetite for the calling.

Together, Mother and I rolled Barnes over. I brought his hands up behind his back and fastened the bracelets around his wrists.

We stood up and admired our work.

'That should do splendidly,' Mother said.

'Shall I go out and fetch a Bobby?'

Her face darkened. She frowned and shook her head slowly from side to side. 'He'd be carted off to gaol for sure.'

'That's where he *ought* to be!'

'Oh, I'd rather not have that.'

'Mum! He *whipped* you! There's no telling what mischief he'd have done if I hadn't bashed him. He must be dealt with.'

She was silent for a while. She stroked her cheek a few times. She flinched once, probably due to the sorry state of her back. Finally, she said, 'Bill would know what to do.'

I liked the sound of that.

Bill would know what to do, all right.

Give him a peek at his sister's back, and he would deal with Barnes in a most appropriate manner.

'I'll go and fetch him,' I said.

Mother glanced at the clock on the mantel. So did I. It was nearly nine. 'Best wait for morning,' she said.

'He doesn't go on duty till midnight. I've plenty of time to catch him before he sets off.'

'And there's the rain.'

'A drop of rain won't hurt me.' I tucked the bloody handkerchief back into my pocket, rushed across the floor and hefted the poker. 'You keep this at hand, and don't hesitate to use it.'

Nodding, she accepted the poker.

I hurried into my room. There, I snatched up my ivory-handled folding knife – another gift from Uncle. I thought to offer it to Mother. A good sharp blade might be better than a poker for helping Barnes to mind his manners. However, I decided she might be loath to use such a deadly weapon, so I kept it for myself.

And a good thing I did so. Later on, it was to save my life.

When I returned to the front room, Barnes was still snoozing. I got into my coat.

Mother gave me a few shillings. 'Take a hansom, darling.' Then she forced an umbrella on me.

She gave me a hasty kiss.

I said, 'Be careful now, Mum. Don't trust him an inch.'

Then I was on my way.

Chapter Two

I Set Out

From the street, I gazed up at our bright, cheery windows and didn't mind the cold rain on my face. What I minded was leaving Mother with Barnes. I wished I'd bashed him better. He was bound to wake up and Mother, being so good-hearted and forgiving, would take pity on him.

She'd want to ease his distress. Given half the chance, she'd unlock the handcuffs so he could stretch his arms and get comfortable and take a sip of tea, and then he'd be at her again.

She might have a problem finding the key, however, as I had it in my trouser pocket.

I was feeling a bit pleased about that when Mother came to one of the windows. Spying me, she raised a hand and wiggled her fingers. I waved back, never guessing this would be my last glimpse of her for many a year. Then I opened the umbrella and set off at a quick, splashy pace.

It didn't take long to reach the cab rank at the corner of Baker Street and Dorset Street, where my eyes lit on the familiar round figure of Daws. Glad to find him on duty, I hurried over to him. Daws and his horse were both spouting white clouds, the one from a briar pipe turned upside down to keep out the rain, the other from its nostrils as it snorted.

'Master Bentley,' he greeted me, the pipe bobbing in his teeth and shaking out a shower of sparks that drifted down and sprinkled the bulging front of his coat.

'Good evening, Daws. Hello, Blossom.' I gave the horse a solid pat on the neck. 'I'm off to my uncle's, 23 Guilford Street.'

''N' how's Mum?'

'We've had a spot of trouble,' I said.

'Hello. Trouble, is it?' He gave the brim of his top hat a tug. 'Bill's just the chap to set it right, I'd say. Jump aboard.'

I scurried into the cab. It pitched like a skiff in a storm when Daws, at the rear, hurled his bulk into the driver's seat.

'Mind yer teeth!' he called out.

With a snap of the reins, we were off at such a lurch that I was thrown against the seatback. We raced along at an amazing clip. I should've thought Blossom incapable of such speed. Her hooves clamored like cannon shots on the pavement as Daws shouted and cracked his whip near her rump. On more than one occasion, dashing around street corners, we tipped and nearly overturned. It was a rousing ride from start to finish, and I should've enjoyed it greatly if my mind hadn't been burdened with worries about Mother.

When I found us in front of Uncle's lodging house, I leaped to the street before we had stopped.

'Watch yer step!' Daws called. Rather too late.

I wasn't in the puddle but a moment before I regained my feet. With a drippy wave to assure Daws that I hadn't ruined myself, I ran for the front door of Uncle's.

But it was Aunt Maggie who opened to my knocking.

She looked greatly surprised to see me.

'Trevor! And you out on such a night?' She darted her head about, peering into the darkness behind me. 'Where's Catherine?'

'She sent me to fetch Uncle William. We had a row with Rolfe Barnes, and she's home keeping guard on him.'

'Come in out of the wet.' Though in a haste to be off, I followed Aunt's instructions. When dealing with the female breed, I knew even then that explanations wasted a passel more time than simple obedience. They're a thick-headed lot. For stubbornness, they've got mules beat by a mile.

'You're a dreadful sight,' she said. 'You're soaking wet. You'll catch pneumonia for sure. What happened to your face? Oh, dear.' She touched my cheek, which hadn't hurt much up till she started poking at it. 'Barnes did this to you?'

'Yes, and he whipped Mum with his belt.'

Aunt's eyes widened. Her mouth fell open, then closed a bit and she pursed out her lips. 'Oh, Bill will just about kill him.'

'That's what I'm hoping for,' I admitted. And wished she would get around, someday, to calling for him. 'My cab's ready to go.' I pointed it out to her. Daws answered with a cheery wave.

'Bill's not here, of course.'

Of course.

'He's not?'

'Why, no.'

'He hasn't gone on duty yet?'

'He went off *hours* ago. It's this horrid Ripper business, you know. They have him working double shifts so that the poor man's rarely home at all.'

The news didn't perk me up. *Now*, what was I to do?

'Mum wants me to fetch him,' I muttered.

'That's quite impossible, really, I should think. Would you care for some tea and a bite . . .?'

'The cab.'

'Oh, yes. You'd best ride it on home, then.'

'I'm supposed to fetch Bill.'

Aunt Maggie frowned. 'Are you quite all right?'

'I don't much care to leave without him.'

'He isn't here, Trevor.' She said those words very slowly as if speaking to a half-wit.

'Yes. I understand. He's on duty.'

'Quite. Rest assured, however, I'll certainly tell him first thing about Barnes and he'll take the matter in hand.'

'Tomorrow.'

'First thing tomorrow. Now, you hurry on back to Catherine.'

'Yes, ma'am.'

'Yes, ma'am, is it?' With a tilt of her head, she fixed her eyes on me and squeezed them narrow. Studying me out. Though I tried real hard to look innocent, it didn't wash. She nodded to herself. 'I'll have a word with the cabman, if you please.'

I hailed Daws. He climbed down off the hansom and scurried for us nimble and quick, puffing smoke. While I waited, Aunt Maggie hot-footed it into the parlor. I heard her clinking some coins. She came back about the same time Daws showed up at the door and doffed his hat.

'I wish you to return young Trevor here straightaway to his own lodgings,' she said. 'I fear he has other intentions, but you're to mind what I tell you, as I'm paying his fare and giving you a bit of something extra.' She emptied her fist into Daws's hand. 'Ride him to 35 Marylebone High Street, and nowhere else. Is that quite understood?'

'Quite, quite, yes. Not to worry. Back to his mum it is, or I'm no Daws and I am. Yes.'

She gave me a quick look as if choosing a target, then kissed the bruised part of my cheek. 'Now, off with you,' she said.

'Come along, Master Bentley.'

Polite as you please, I bid farewell to Aunt Maggie and hurried off with Daws.

'Could you take me home by way of the Leman Street police station?' I asked.

'Ah, but I couldn't do that. Daws gave his word, he did. His word's his bondage.'

'But you're my friend, aren't you?'

'I'm pleased to think so.' He gave me a swat on the back. 'Now you wouldn't ask your friend to break his word, would you?'

'I suppose not,' I muttered, and stepped aboard.

The cab shook as it did before when Daws climbed to the driver's seat, but this time it didn't bound away with a lurch. Daws clucked and Blossom snorted and we started rolling along. I sat there, having lowdown thoughts about Aunt Maggie. She always had been rather a stick in the mud, and now she'd done her best to spoil my mission.

Well, it just wasn't in me to get carted home like a prisoner.

I'd set out to fetch Uncle William, and that's what I aimed to do.

As John McSween would later say, 'You do what you reckon needs the doing, and damn them that tries to stop you.' Though I wouldn't be meeting up with John for a spell yet, that was just how I felt about matters while Daws was turning the hansom around.

I jumped out. This time, my feet cooperated. I hit the street running.

'Trevor!' Daws shouted.

'Cheerio!' I yelled. With a glance back and a wave, I raced around a corner.

I rather expected Daws to give chase, and he proved me right. Blossom came along at a trot and the cab rattled by, Daws keeping a lookout for me from his perch. Well hidden in the dark of an alleyway, I watched them pass.

Soon, they were gone. And so was Mother's umbrella, which I'd left behind in the heat of my escape. The umbrella was in good hands, however. An honest fellow like Daws was bound to drop it home for me.

Feeling rather proud of my derring-do, I crept out of the alley. A four-wheeler went by, but there was no sign of any hansom, so I returned to Guilford Street and struck out, heading east.

Directly across the road was Coram Fields, and a straight shot up Guilford Street should take me to Gray's Inn Road. There, a turn to the right would lead to Holborn, which I could follow eastward to the area where a map might've proved quite useful if I'd had one at hand.

With confidence born of youth and ignorance, however, I never doubted that I'd somehow find my way to the Leman Street station and locate Uncle William.

Chapter Three

Me and the Unfortunates

And so I set off at a brisk pace for Gray's Inn Road.

I kept a sharp lookout for hansoms. Daws may have given up on me, but I took no chances and ducked out of sight on the rare occasions a cab came rolling along.

Gray's Inn Road led me, sure enough, to Holborn. I scooted along at a fair clip that had me huffing and warm in spite of being soaked to the skin.

Whenever I got an urge to slow down, I pictured Mother alone with Barnes, maybe watching out the window and wondering why I hadn't shown up yet with Uncle Bill. Barnes wasn't likely to harm her, not shackled like he was. He might even snooze along till morning. But Mother would like as not have a rough night of it, anyhow, what with waiting for me. She was bound to worry. And she'd be worrying all the more if Daws should pay her a visit and tell her how I'd dodged away.

By the time Holborn started to be Newgate Street, I'd stopped dodging hansoms. I even gave some thought to hailing one and taking a ride back home. Dang my hide, though, my pride just wouldn't allow it. I'd started off to fetch Uncle Bill, and I aimed to get the job done.

Before I knew it, I was hot-footing it past the Bank of England. I cut across the road, rushed on by the pillars in front of the Royal Exchange, and got to Cornhill.

Cornhill went in the right direction, and I followed it. Pretty soon, I was in foreign territory. Leadenhall Street? I'd never been this far east. But east was where I wanted to go.

So far, there'd only been a handful of people about. But that changed. The farther I walked, the more turned up. They roamed the streets, sat in the doorways of lodging houses, stumbled out of pubs and music halls, leaned against lamp posts, lurked in dark alleys. They were a sorry looking lot.

I saw mere tykes and many youngsters no older than myself. Some just roamed about like stray dogs. Others seemed to be having a good time with their chums, chasing each other and such. Every one of them was barefoot and coatless and dressed in rags. They shouldn't have been out in the cold and rain, but I figured they must have no place better to go.

Some of the grownups wore boots and coats, but plenty didn't. A lot of the women had shawls pulled over their heads to keep the rain off. There were men in hats with brims pulled down as if they didn't want anyone to see their faces. Nobody at all had an umbrella, so it was just as well I'd lost mine.

Even without a brolly, the cut of my duds made me stand out all too much. Heads turned as I hurried by. Folks called out to me. Some came my way, but I picked up my pace and left them behind.

They're likely just curious, I kept telling myself. They don't mean to harm me.

Mother liked to call such folks 'unfortunates'. Uncle Bill, when he had me alone to regail me with Ripper stories, put it otherwise. To him, the unfortunates were 'a godless crew of cutthroats, whores, riffraff and urchins' who dwelled with vermin, carried horrible diseases, and would cheerfully slit a fellow's gullet for a ha'penny.

I figured Mother's view was tempered by the goodness of her heart, while Uncle Bill's was likely jaundiced by the nature of his work, and the real truth might fall somewhere in the middle.

The people all around me sure did look unfortunate, but they couldn't all be ruffians and whores. I'd read enough to know plenty of them worked hard at such places as slaughterhouses, docks and tailoring shops. Some were peddlers, carters and dustmen. They did the hard and dirty work, and just didn't earn much at it, that's all.

As I walked along, however, I couldn't help but get the jitters. Uncle Bill might have a tainted view of things, but that didn't mean he was altogether wrong.

I kept a sharp eye out.

As John McSween would later tell me, 'Look sharp, Willy. You wanta spot trouble before it spots you.'

And what I spotted, just about then, was a gal up against a lamp post. Her curly hair was all matted down with rain. She looked older than me, but not by much. Except for a bruised, puffy eye, she was rather pretty. She wore a long dress and had a shawl wrapped around her shoulders. As I got closer, she pushed herself away from the post and took a step toward me.

I pulled up short.

This might be one of those whores Uncle Bill'd told me about.

I got all hot and squirmy inside.

Figuring the wise move would be a quick bolt for the high ground, I glanced across the street. But over there was a legless fellow propped against a wall. He had a patch over one eye and a bottle at his mouth. He wasn't about to chase after me, but I didn't much relish getting any closer to him than I already was.

So I stayed my course.

The gal walked right up to me. I stopped and gave her a smile that made my lips hurt. Then I did a sidestep, hoping to dodge her. She sidestepped right along with me. She grinned.

'What's your awful hurry?' she asked. I reckon that's what she asked. It sounded, like 'Wot'sur ohfulurry?' Her breath fairly reeked of beer.

'I'm afraid I've lost my way. I'm trying to find . . .' There, I hesitated. It might not do, at all, to let such a person know I was looking for a police station. 'I'm on my way to Leman Street,' I told her. 'Is that far from here?'

'Leman Street, is it? Well, Sue, she'll take you right there, won't she?'

Once I'd figured out what she'd said, I felt my stomach sink. 'Oh, that's not necessary. If you'd just be good enough to *tell* me . . .'

But she stepped right in against my side, took my arm and commenced to drag me along. Mixed with her beery fumes was a flowery sweet odor of perfume that wanted to clog my nose.

'No, it's quite all right,' I protested.

'A young toff such as yourself and you'd be sure to run afoul of the likes of which would do you horrible harm and likely leave you for dead and you shouldn't want that now should you? Sue, she'll see you safely along and we'll get where you're bound to be going by and by.'

'Thank you, but . . .'

'This way, this way.' She steered me around a corner.

We were on a street even narrower than the one we'd left behind. Several of the gas lamps were out, leaving big patches of blackness. On both sides were lodging houses, many with broken windows. Few had lights inside. I glimpsed people in doorways and leaning against walls and roaming about in the darkness ahead of us.

If I had to be in such a place, I was glad to have company.

'What's your name?' Sue asked.

'Trevor.'

'And, Trevor, do you like me?' She pulled my arm so it met up with the swell of her bosom.

Not wanting to offend her, I let it stay.

'You're very kind,' I said.

She gave a throaty laugh. 'Kind, is it? Oh, but you're a sweet young toff and a brave one at that.' She turned her face to me and her beery breath rubbed my cheek. 'Am I a pretty one?'

Her face was only a blur in the darkness, but I easily recalled how she'd looked under the streetlamp. Besides, I would've agreed that she was a pretty one even if she'd looked like the back end of a horse. Just to keep her happy. 'You're quite pretty,' I said.

'You'd like a go at me, now wouldn't you?'

A go?

I wasn't sure what that might entail, but it scared me plenty. My mouth got dry and my heart started whamming so hard I could barely catch my breath.

'It's awfully late,' I said. 'And I really am in quite a rush. But thank you, anyway.'

'Aw, you're such a shy one you are.'

With that, she steered me into an alley.

'No, please,' I protested. 'I don't think . . .'

'Now it won't take any time at all, Trevor, and then we'll be right along on our way.'

Sue was just about my own height. She might've out-weighed me some. But I was strong for my size, and quick. Could've broken away from her, if I'd tried.

Didn't try.

For one thing, I didn't relish losing my one and only guide through dangerous territory.

For another, I didn't want to hurt Sue's feelings.

And then, too, I'd never had a 'go' at anyone. Here was my chance to learn, first hand, what it was all about.

By the time I decided this was neither where I wanted to do my learning nor who I wanted to learn it from, Sue had me pushed against a brick wall.

She unbuttoned my coat and spread it open. Then she commenced to rub me through my shirt. It felt just fine. But that was nothing to when she rubbed me down below. If this was what having a 'go' was all about, I'd been missing plenty. I was all-fired embarrassed, but that didn't count near as much as the rest of the way I was feeling.

Before I knew it, she'd unwrapped her shawl and lifted my hands and planted them smack on her bosoms. There was nothing except thin wet cloth between them and me. I could feel their heat coming through. They were big and springy and soft, with parts that pushed like little fingertips against my palms.

I knew I shouldn't be touching her there. I reckoned it was a sin, for sure, and I might be risking hell.

If Uncle Bill could see me now, he'd tan my hide. Mother would likely faint dead away.

But I didn't care a whit about that.

All I cared about was how good those bosoms felt and how good Sue's hands were making me feel. Nobody'd ever touched me down there, that was for sure.

Whore or not, Sue seemed just then to be the finest human being I'd ever encountered in my whole life.

Then she fetched me up a whack.

A quick, hard punch below decks.

I felt like my guts were exploding up through my stomach.

She scampered out of reach. I crumpled. My knees hit the mud. As I clutched myself, I heard her call out in a rough whisper, 'Ned! Bob!'

In a trice, the three of them were having at me. They trounced me good, but I got in a few licks. I caught Sue a good one on the chin, which pleased me greatly. All around, though, I took the worst of it.

They stripped me of my coat and shirt and shoes. But when they went for my trousers, I hauled out my knife and got the blade open right smart and split open the nearest arm. Don't know whether it belonged to Ned or Bob, but whichever, he let out a howl and scurried out of range.

I got to my feet and fell back against the wall and slashed at the fellows when they tried for me.

They grunted and cursed and leaped away from my blade.

'Come on, y' bloody swines!' I raved. 'I'll rip your guts out! Come 'n' get it! I'll cut y' up for bangers.'

Sue stood back, watching, hanging onto the booty.

I kept ranting and slashing.

Ned and Bob finally gave up trying for me. They backed off, huffing for breath, one of them clutching his gashed arm.

'Well, go in and get him, you fools,' Sue said. 'We ain't got nary a bob off him yet. He's got a pocketful of coins, he does, I felt them there.'

They both looked at her.

'Well, go on!'

The one I hadn't cut took her up on it.

He came rushing at me, growling. He flung out an arm to block my knife. I went in under it. He slammed me hard against the wall.

My blade punched straight into his belly.

His breath gushed out, hot and stinky in my face.

For a while, he didn't move. I felt his blood pouring over my hand, running down my belly and soaking the front of my trousers.

Then he backed away. He slid off the blade. Clutching his stomach, he took a couple of steps. He sat down hard. From the splashing sound, he must've found himself a puddle.

'Bloody hell,' he muttered. 'I've been killed.'

Sue and the other fellow bolted.

I was alone in the alley with the man I'd stabbed. He was making awful sounds. Whining and moaning and crying.

'I'm sorry,' I told him. 'But you shouldn't have come at me.'

'You gone and killed me dead is what you done.'

'I'm awful sorry,' I said. And I was.

He let out a bellow that curdled my blood. I ran. Not out into the street. That's where Sue and her confederate had gone. Instead, I dashed the other way, deeper into the black pit of the alley.

Chapter Four

The Mob

I hot-footed around the corner of a building at the end of the alley and almost ran down a woman standing there under a streetlamp. I thought, for just a blink, that she was Sue. She gave me an awful start.

But I gave her a worse start.

She screamed as I skidded to a stop in front of her.

She was much too large to be Sue.

To her, however, I must've looked just right for Jack the Ripper.

'Murder!' she shrieked, and flapped her hands in the air. 'Help! Murder! It's *him*! The Ripper!'

There I stood, bare to the waist, my trousers bloody, a knife in my hand. Can't say I blamed her much for getting riled.

'I'm not,' I gasped. 'Please.'

Still shouting and waving her arms, she stumbled backward a few steps and fell on her bum. 'Help!' she blurted. 'Murder! Bloody murder!'

Suddenly, she wasn't the only one yelling. From all up and down the street came cries of alarm and rage.

The voices had people with them.

People running toward me.

Plenty of them.

I lit out.

They were coming from both sides, so I raced straight across the street, aiming for another alley. Through all the shouts of 'Murder!' and 'The Ripper!' and 'He won't get away!' and 'He'll get a taste of steel from me!' and 'Kill him!' came the high shrill piping of police whistles.

From the sounds of things, I had three constables after me.

Where in tarnation had they been when I was getting attacked?

I made it into the alley well ahead of the mob and chugged along through the darkness wondering if Uncle Bill might be one of the whistle-blowers, but mostly wishing the sounds hadn't come from so far away.

The folks on my tail had blood on their minds. I reckoned I wouldn't have none left by the time the police caught up.

While I was still running through the alley, I folded my knife and dropped it back into my pocket. That was a good move. With the knife out of sight, I didn't get myself jumped by the excited folks on the next street over.

Before any of them took a notion to grab me, I gasped out, 'Which way'd he go?' I tried to sound like a neighborhood fellow. The words came out, 'Wichwydeego?'

Shoulders shrugged. Heads shook.

'Who?' asked a man with a clay pipe.

'What's going on?' asked a fat woman.

'Didn't you *see* him?' I blurted.

'Ain't seen . . .'

'The Ripper!' I cried out. Then I pointed down the dark, rainy street. 'There he is!'

Several women started yelling and screaming.

'Come on!' I shouted. 'Let's get him!'

I vamoosed without more than a few seconds to spare before the mob came pouring out of the alley. Now, I was at the head of my own little mob. It consisted of four men who were all a bother to chase down the Ripper, same as those behind us, but who didn't figure I was him.

We were fresher than the other bunch. We managed to stay ahead of them. Every now and again, I'd yell 'There!' and point and we'd rush around a corner.

This section of town had corners galore. The streets were short and narrow and twisty, chock full of alleys and doorways and courts and just more corners than you could shake a stick at.

By and by, when it looked clear behind us, I grabbed my side like I had a stitch in it and slowed down. The others looked back at me. I waved them forward. 'Go on,' I huffed. 'Don't let him get away. Went to the right up there.'

They hurried on ahead.

I ducked into the dark under an arch, and not a moment too soon. Along came the other crew. They were looking mighty haggard. One fellow flung up an arm and waved at my crowd. 'We're with you!' he called. 'Get him!'

The whole bunch hurried by. I counted eight of them. Not a constable in the bunch. Not one in uniform, at least. That made me durn glad I'd outfoxed them.

Well, I stayed where I was for a while, catching my wind and trying to figure out a safe move. Returning to the streets didn't seem to be it. Not a few folks had gotten a look at me, and even more had likely heard that the Whitechapel murderer was a fifteen-year-old chap running about shirtless.

I had to get a shirt.

Then I'd be all right.

And I wouldn't be freezing so bad, either.

What with all the action, I hadn't been bothered much by the rain and cold. But the longer I crouched there in the darkness, the worse I felt. Even though the arch kept rain from falling on me, I was already drenched. Before long, I was all a-shiver. My teeth took to chattering up a storm. I hugged my chest and rubbed my goosepimply arms, but that didn't help much.

A shirt was just what I needed.

That and a coat and shoes. And a pair of dry trousers, too.

A magic wand would've come in right handy.

Lacking that, my only recourse appeared to be thievery. I'd already handled the breasts of a whore and stabbed a man, so turning robber didn't seem like any great sin.

Besides, it was necessary for self-preservation.

When it comes down to saving my own hide, I'll do pretty much anything short of betraying a friend. That's a fact. It grieves me to think about some of what I've had to do over the years when it was touch and go with the Grim Reaper. Stealing some duds is about the least awful on my whole long list.

It seemed like a big thing at the time, though.

I'd never stolen anything, up till then. But I sure did need a shirt.

So, finally, I stood up and stretched out my kinks.

Turning away from the street, I crept through the narrow passageway and found myself in the courtyard of a lodging house. The arch wasn't over my head any more, and rain was falling on me again. I figured some of the rooms had to be empty, though. All I had to do was find one and break in.

The nearest door, just to my right, was for room No. 13. That ain't a lucky number, so I passed it by for the moment and scouted around.

A few of the other rooms, further on, had lights glowing dim in their windows. I heard people laughing and carousing in some of them.

But the window just around a corner from No. 13 was dark. It was broken, too, and had a rag stuffed in its hole to keep the weather out. I listened for a while. No sound at all came from beyond the window. That didn't mean the room was empty, but it gave me hope.

I went back to the door and rapped it softly a few times.

Nobody spoke up, so I tried the knob. The way it gave, I could tell the door wasn't locked. But I couldn't shove it open. Figuring it must be bolted from the inside so the room wasn't deserted, after all, I nearly gave up.

Then it came to me that whoever lived there might've used a different door to leave by.

Back at the window, I pulled out the rag. I put my face to the hole in the glass and called softly, 'Hello? Is anybody here?'

No answer came.

I stuck my arm in through the hole, reached around toward the door, and the very first thing I touched was its bolt! Well, this seemed like the greatest luck ever.

Thirteen might be an unlucky number for some, I thought, but not for me.

I slid that bolt back real easy, then pulled my arm out of the window being careful not to get it cut. After that, I stuffed the rag into the hole just like it was before.

I went to the door and eased it open. It didn't get very wide before it bumped something. It was wide enough to let me in, though. I entered and stood still, keeping it open for a quick escape. Nobody let out a cry. About the only sound other than my own heartbeat came from outside. That was the rain smacking down on the stone courtyard and splashing into puddles.

If the room had been much darker, I couldn't have seen a thing. The window and open door let in a trifle of light, though. Enough to let me make out that what the door had bumped up against was a small table by a bed. Not enough to show whether anyone was stretched out on the bed.

Sure hoped not.

Creeping forward, I reached down and felt among the bedclothes.

Probably would've screamed if I'd found a foot there.

But the covers were smooth.

Beside the other end of the bed was another table. There was a chair nearby.

Everything *in* that room was nearby. It was about the smallest room I'd ever seen, and I pitied any person who had to live in such tight quarters. Why, there was hardly enough space for the bed. It was pushed up tight into a corner, and you couldn't even open the door without whacking the table by its foot.

Standing there, I felt like an intruder on someone's misery.

But at least I was out of the rain. Even though the room had a chill, it beat the weather outside.

I shut the door. I was about to slide the bolt home to make sure there wouldn't be any surprise visitors when it came to me that the place didn't seem to have any other way out. That was quite a puzzle. What did the lodger do, reach through the broken window to work the bolt every time she came and went?

It was a she, I was pretty sure of that but didn't know why at first.

Then it came to me. Along with burny smells from the dead fire and some other smells like sweat and beer and some I couldn't put my finger on, there was an odor of perfume that was so sweet it made me feel a little sick.

It smelled the same as what Sue'd had on.

This better not be Sue's digs, I thought. And I could just picture her coming in along with Bob or Ned (whichever rascal I hadn't stabbed in the alley) and the both of them cornering me.

I shut that bolt right quick.

And wondered where I'd hide if someone should show up.

No place at all but under the bed.

I hunched down and made sure there'd be enough room for a fellow my size. There seemed to be. That made me feel a little less trapped, so I tried to stop fretting about who might come along, and started scouting the room.

On the table by the head of the bed were a couple of bottles. I uncorked one and gave it a sniff and went woozy with the stink of flowery perfume. Then I tried the other bottle. It was a lot bigger. It smelled of rum.

Well, rum could turn fellows into nasty drunken louts like Barnes, but Mother had sometimes administered a bit of it to me for medicinal purposes. Shaky as I was with the cold and wet, I was in sore need of such medication.

I took a few swallows real quick. It scorched my throat on the way down and lit up a cozy fire in my belly. The stuff chased off my chills so quick I drank some more. And then some more.

Feeling considerably better, I corked the bottle, set it down and did some more exploring.

What I found next was almost better than the rum.

On the chair was a whole heap of clothing. I picked

31

up the items one at a time, and held them toward the dim light from the window for a better look. There were two big shirts that smelled ripe, a smaller shirt that looked like it might belong to a boy, an overcoat, a bonnet and a petticoat.

Well, this was just about the best luck in the world!

Figuring to keep one of the big shirts and the overcoat, I put everything else back on the chair. And jumped a mile when a woman laughed close by.

'Ain't you the randy one!' she blurted.

My heart stopped cold when I saw the rag get plucked out of the window hole.

Quick as I could, I dropped the shirt and coat on the chair and scurried. As the bolt clacked, I belly-crawled under the bed. The door swung open, letting in a chill and the smell of rain. Then it bumped shut. The bolt slid.

'Ah, Mary, Mary, Mary,' a man said.

This wasn't Sue, at least. But I still didn't relish the idea of getting caught. I tried to hold my breath, and hoped they couldn't hear my heart drumming.

'Now let go for a bit,' Mary said. 'You'll be wanting your coat off.'

'I'll be wanting more than that off you.'

She laughed.

There was a sound like a coat might make hitting the floor. Then footsteps. Someone sat on the bed. A match scratched. In the orange, fluttering glow, I saw the booted feet of the man just beyond my shoulder. The woman was crouched at the fire grate. She had her back to me.

When the fire was going good, she stood up straight and turned around.

'We'll have it cherry and warm in no time at all,' she said.

'I've got to be off in a bit,' the man told her.

That was welcome news.

'We'll be quick then, won't we?'

With that, Mary started to shed her duds. While she worked at them, the man pulled off his boots. Then he swung his legs up. The bed slats moaned a bit, and I knew he must be stretching out.

From my hiding place, I couldn't see any higher than Mary's knees. She stood barefoot on top of her coat and clothes kept dropping to the floor around her. Her legs had a ruddy glow in the firelight. Scared as I was, I got an awful urge to scoot closer to the edge of the bed for a better look at her. I was curious, but mostly I was feeling excited like I'd been with Sue before that gal whacked me.

Long about the time I decided to make my move, Mary came hurrying over to the bed and climbed on.

Those old slats groaned and creaked and pressed against my back. Pretty soon, the bed was shaking and jumping. From the sounds Mary and the fellow made, you'd think they were pitching fits. They thrashed about something fearful. They huffed and grunted and gasped. They both used vile language that doesn't need repeating here. I was just commencing to believe that 'having a go' might entail a fight to the death, but then Mary started in blurting, 'Oh! Oh, yes! Harder! Harder! Oh, yes! Oh, deary! Yes!' If she was being killed, she was liking it. Then she let out a squeal that sounded closer to rapture than to pain.

After that, things settled down. The bed stopped moving. There was some hard breathing as if they'd both tuckered themselves out.

Then the man swung his legs over the side. He got into his boots, stood up and stepped over to the table by the head of the bed. Coins jangled. 'A bit of something extra for you, Mary,' he said.

'And would you care to go again?'

'Gotta be off, I'm afraid.' He bent over his coat and picked it up.

'You wouldn't want me to be going back out on such a night, now would you? And with that murdering fiend about?'

'That's none of my concern.'

'Be a dear. Please. I'm in arrears. I'll *needs* to go out again if you don't give me more.'

'Take care,' was all he said. Then the bolt slid back. A chill gust swept over me, but went away a moment later when he shut the door.

Mary let out a sigh that made my heart ache.

I thought about the shillings in my pocket. I'd fully intended to leave them behind in payment for the rum I'd consumed, for the coat and shirt I intended to take. If she had them now, she might not need to go out again.

She would be ever so grateful.

And I knew I'd feel good for doing her such a kindness.

But I was keenly aware of her lying naked on the bed above me. Though I wanted a look at her, I feared what she might have me do.

Also, how could I make myself known to Mary without giving her a terrible fright? Why, she'd likely scream. I'd already had a narrow escape from those who mistook me for the Ripper. One round of that was enough to last me.

I decided to stay put, and leave the money after she had gone.

That was a decision I'll always regret.

I should've scurried out and planted all my money in her hand and risked whatever screams or shows of gratitude she might have thrown my way.

I should've done whatever was needed to stop her from going out again.

Well, you just don't know what's going to happen in this life, or you'd do a lot of things different.

Even though I wanted to give her that money, I chose to play it safe for myself and stay hidden.

Soon, Mary climbed off the bed. She walked over to her pile of clothes. I kept my eyes on her, hoping for a peek at her good parts, but never saw more than her legs and arms, not even when she bent down to pick up her things.

It was something of a letdown, really.

Though I didn't know it just then, I would be seeing Mary sprawled out naked on her bed before the night was out. And that was a sight such as I wouldn't wish on anyone.

Chapter Five

Bloody Murder

Mary finished dressing and went out the door. I stayed hidden under the bed, figuring she'd reach in through the window hole to shut the bolt.

Well, I waited and listened and wondered what was taking her so long.

Maybe she'd decided not to bother with the bolt. But I was in no hurry to crawl out. If she'd just forgotten, she might come back in a minute or two when she remembered.

Besides, I was feeling pretty good. My fears of being caught had eased off, now that I was alone, and that left me rather weak with relief. What with the fire, the room was warm and toasty.

But I reckon it was likely the rum that kept me pinned to the floor. I'd never imbibed more than a trifle of such stuff before tonight. It had me all lazy and comfortable.

By and by, I figured Mary wouldn't be coming back to bolt her door, after all, and I'd best grab the clothes and make my getaway.

Being so cozy, though, I wasn't eager to move on.

Figured to wait a few more minutes.

Well, I drifted off. Right there under Mary's bed, the warmth and rum and my general tiredness got me.

I believe I slept longer than a few minutes. It might've been more like a few hours.

When I woke up, it was too late to skedaddle.

I hadn't even heard them come in.

A squeal is what woke me up. It came from right above me on the bed. It wasn't at all like the squeal Mary'd let out last time. This one sounded full of shock and pain, but muffled as if her mouth were covered. It ended quick.

35

The bed kept shaking. I heard wet, smacking sounds. And grunts like a man putting a lot of energy behind his work.

Blood started to drip off the edge of the bed and splash the floor beside me. It looked purple and shiny in the firelight.

For a bit there, I tried to believe I hadn't woken up at all and this was just a horrid nightmare. It was too awful to be happening for real. But I couldn't convince myself. I knew it was real.

Mary'd found a fellow and brought him back to the room while I was dozing, and now he was busy killing her.

Couldn't be anyone else but Jack the Ripper himself.

He was butchering her right on top of me.

I wanted to scream, but kept my teeth gritted tight and lay there shivering, the scaredest I'd ever been.

From all I'd heard about the Ripper, he didn't seem like a man at all. More like a creeping phantom or a raging demon out of the pits of hell.

I commenced to pray in my head that he'd finish up quick with Mary and go away.

Pretty soon, he climbed off the bed.

I figured the Lord had answered my prayers.

Wrong.

The Ripper wasn't near ready to leave yet.

What he did was stand in front of the fire. It was burning low, giving off just a murky glow and not much heat. All I could see were his shoes and the legs of his dark trousers. Then he tossed in a waistcoat and shirt. His own, I reckoned. They flamed up. He stood there for a bit as if warming himself, then walked over to the chair where those other clothes were heaped up. He returned to the fire. He added in the bonnet and petticoat. With a good blaze going, he came back to the bed. But he wasn't done adding fuel. He stepped up to the fire again and stuffed in a big blanket.

When that caught, the room fairly lit up and heat came rolling against me.

He got out of his shoes and trousers. He had to bend down

to take off the pants, but didn't get low enough for me to see his face.

Or for him to see mine.

He didn't add his shoes or trousers to the fire.

He came to the bed again, and climbed aboard.

Mary was probably already dead, by then. But he wasn't done with her.

He went to work all over again.

Every now and then, he'd say something. 'Oh, yes' and 'Quite nice, really' and 'Come on out of there, you tasty morsel'. He didn't talk like the East Enders. He talked like a gent. 'I do believe I'll have *this*,' he said. And, 'Off you come, my charming tidbit.'

Sometimes, he chuckled softly.

Sometimes, he seemed to get worked up and breathless.

Throughout it all, there came the most awful wet tearing sounds and lots of sloshing. I even heard him eat something. There were chewy noises, smacking lips, sighs.

It's a wonder I didn't fetch up my supper.

I tried not to listen. I tried not to think about what he was doing to Mary. I tried to keep my mind busy figuring a way to save my own hide.

The knife in my pocket was pressed between my leg and the floor. I could get to it. But even with the weapon in hand, what chance would I have against such a monster? He'd get me for sure if I tried to scamper out from under the bed.

The only thing to do was wait and pray and hope he'd leave without finding me.

I spent a lot of time staring out at the room. There wasn't much to see. If he had a hat and coat, they were somewhere out of sight. His shoes and pants were in front of the blazing fire. The wooden handle of a tea kettle on the grate was burning. Mary's clothes were hanging off the seat of the chair. Her dress draped the tops of her muddy shoes.

I was gazing out at these things, wondering about my chances of making a dash for the window and maybe taking a dive right through it to the courtyard, when a gob of flesh dropped to the floor. It hit with a sloshing splash right before my eyes. It was a dripping red mound with a nipple on top.

When I realized what it was, my head fogged up. My mouth filled with spit, the way it does if you're about ready to toss. I heard a ringing in my ears. Each time I blinked, sharp blue lights flashed around everything. So I shut my eyes, swallowed and tried to pretend I was somewhere else.

I started off pretending I was safe at home, comfortable in my chair and reading *Huckleberry Finn*. By and by, I turned into Huck himself. I was on the raft with Jim, floating along the Mississippi at night, sprawled on the deck and gazing up at a sky full of stars. It was all silent and peaceful, and I felt just grand. I wanted to drift down the river for ever and ever.

I must've been passed out cold.

But then I came to just in time to see the Ripper's feet right beside the bed. He bent down. My heart almost gave out. I figured he was onto me, and any second he'd be yanking me out from under the bed and slitting me open. But what he did was clamp a bloody hand over the breast and pick it up. He didn't have a good enough grip on it, though. It slipped out of his fingers and fell again. This time, it landed on its side and sort of caved in a bit. He used both hands to scoop it up.

He took a couple of steps to the table.

Then he went over toward the fire. He got into his trousers and shoes. When they were on, he walked off to the side where I couldn't see him because my shoulder was in the way. I heard some rustling of clothes, and hoped it meant he was putting on his coat.

There came a sound like creaking leather. It put me in mind of stories that the Ripper was thought to carry a valise like maybe a doctor's bag, that he toted his knife or scalpel in it, and used the satchel to carry off innards from his victims.

Well, he came back to the bed and stood there, near enough for me to reach out and touch his shoes. From the goppy sounds that came next, I figured he was putting something from Mary into his case.

My mouth filled up again. My ears rang. I saw those old blue flashes. But I hung on.

And finally he went to the door. It opened, letting in a breeze that chilled my bare back and made the fire blaze even brighter than before.

The door shut.

I stayed put.

It was a puzzle, what came next.

He locked the door. He didn't reach through the window and slide the bolt, he used a key from the outside. I heard that key scrape its way into the lock, heard a loud clack, and then the key pulling out.

I wondered if he'd found the key on Mary. But if she'd had it, how come she didn't use it instead of reaching through the window for the bolt?

I wondered why I was even bothering my head with such a mystery.

The main thing was, the Ripper was gone.

He might've locked me into the room. That was fine, though. I could get out by the window.

I thought about waiting a while to make sure he wasn't coming back. But what I wanted more than anything was to get shut of this room and all that had happened here.

I scurried out from under the bed, slipping and sliding on the bloody floor. On my feet, I made the mistake of looking back.

There was Mary.

She didn't look much like a person at all, the way she was carved up. It was so awful, if I did any kind of job telling you about it here, you might get so revolted you'd quit reading my book. Besides, I'd feel guilty for putting such pictures into your head. My aim is to inform you and entertain you with the tale of my adventures, not to give you black thoughts or put you off your feed.

Let me just say, the way the Ripper left Mary, you couldn't have figured out whether she was a man or a woman. She didn't have much face, either.

I looked longer than I should've, mostly because it took

me a spell to figure out what the mess on the bed really *was*. When I caught on, I gagged and looked away. But I looked away in the wrong direction, so I saw the stuff on the table. Both her breasts, and a gob of innards.

I started to keel over, but somehow stayed on my feet and stumbled to the window. I shoved it open. Tried to climb out, but fell out instead. The cold and rain cleared my head some. As I picked myself up, I recalled why I'd snuck into the room in the first place. But I wasn't raring to climb back in to fetch any shirt and coat. I saw them on the chair when I pulled the window down, and kept my eyes on them so I wouldn't catch another look at Mary.

Then I ran through the courtyard. The rain quit when I was under the arch. I stopped running, and leaned out far enough to glance up and down the street, scared the Ripper might be there. I didn't see him or anyone else. But the gas lamps didn't give off a whole lot of light, and left plenty of black spaces where someone might be lurking.

All I wanted, just then, was to find my way home without running into more trouble. The last thing I wanted was to meet up with the Ripper. But a close second was getting took for the Ripper myself.

Being shirtless and bloody in the Whitechapel area at an hour like this, I was bound to rouse suspicion in anyone who might see me. That being the case, it shouldn't matter a whit whether I tried to walk casual or raced along like the devil was on my heels.

At least if I ran, I'd be quicker about getting away to somewhere safe.

I stepped out from under the arch. The rain came down on me. While I tried to decide which way to go, I rubbed my hands together until I figured most of the blood was off. Then I rinsed my chest and belly real quick.

Being lost, it didn't matter much which direction I picked.

So I turned to the right and kicked up my heels. I went splashing through the street top speed. So much motion started my head to hurting something fierce, but I kept on chugging.

At a corner, I checked both ways. My heart did a tumble when I spotted some folks off to the left. One was a constable. Nobody let out a shout, though, so maybe I wasn't seen.

Safe past the corner, I wondered if maybe I shouldn't go back and tell the Bobby everything. Just didn't have the gumption, though. First thing you know, he'd be thinking *I* was the one that done in Mary.

And I *was* the one that stabbed Ned or Bob in the alley tonight. Rain or not, there might still be blood on my knife from him. I could throw my knife away. Didn't fancy doing that, however. Aside from it being a gift I prized, it was my only weapon and I might need it.

So I figured my best plan was to keep shut of constables or anyone else.

Well, I rushed around a bend in the road and pulled up short and lost my breath. My stomach dropped down to my heels.

Not that I recognized him. Cramped under the bed that way, I hadn't seen enough: just his legs, his hands when he reached down a few times, his trousers and shoes. There was nothing particular about any such thing.

The fellow walking past the street lamp ahead of me wore a hat and overcoat. Below the hem of the coat were trouser legs. They might've belonged to the pants I'd seen in Mary's room. Looked the same. But dark pants are dark pants. From where I stood, I couldn't see enough of the shoes to know if they were like the Ripper's.

But he carried a leather case like a doctor's bag.

That was enough for me.

I just knew, deep down, this was Jack the Ripper. In my rush to hightail, I'd chanced to take the same route as him, and caught up.

What with the distance and the rain smacking down all around us, he hadn't heard me come around the corner. Or if he did hear, he didn't look back. He kept on walking, and left the glow of the street lamp behind him.

I stood still and watched.

It'd likely take me hours to scribble out all the thoughts

that went through my head then. But they boil down to this: much as I wanted to get away from the Ripper and go home to be and pull the covers over my face, I reckoned as how it was my duty to follow him.

And that's what I did, even though it scared the tarnation out of me.

I was fifteen and wet and cold and terrified, and as I followed Jack the Ripper in those dark morning hours I reckoned I might not live to see the daylight.

But I kept after him, all the same.

Here's the thing.

He was a monster who'd done unspeakable things, not only to Mary but to a handful of other women. He deserved the worst kind of punishment for that. More important, though, there'd be more women falling under his blade if somebody didn't put a stop to him.

Maybe it was chance. Maybe it was fate or the will of God. But somehow, I'd ended up being the fellow with an opportunity to put the quits to his string of bloody murders.

It wasn't a job I could walk away from.

Chapter Six

I Tail the Fiend

My plan was to follow the Ripper to his digs, wait till he'd settled in, and then fetch the police. I sure didn't aim to tangle with him. He'd had a lot more practice in the way of knives, and he was a head taller than me so he'd have me beat on reach. Besides, I was scared witless of him. I'd be doing enough if I just stayed on his trail.

He led me this way and that, picking streets that were mostly deserted. I hung back. I kept off to the side so I could duck into doorways or alleys in case he might take a notion to look over his shoulder.

He acted like he didn't have a worry. He never once checked his rear. I got a side view of his face a few times when he turned corners, but couldn't tell much. Just too dark, and his hat brim shadowed it from the street lamps. All I could see was he had a beaky nose and a weak chin.

I judged as how it might be a good thing to get a close-up look. But I didn't dare have a go at that. Knowing his face wouldn't count for much if I ended up dead for trying.

The trick was to stay alive and not lose him.

After a while, it started seeming like a fairly simple trick. He wasn't being cautious or dodgy. He walked along like a gentleman out for a stroll. I didn't have a bit of trouble keeping my eyes on him.

Though we sometimes walked by other folks, they minded their own affairs. A few gave me odd looks, but none spoke to me or raised any sort of fuss.

I got to pondering what a hero I'd be for tracking Jack the Ripper to his lair. Why, I'd be the most popular bloke in London, in the whole of England, for that matter. Her Majesty the Queen, herself, would likely honor me. Mother, she'd be just so proud . . .

That reminded me of Mother's plight, the reason I'd set out in the first place. Well, I hadn't managed to fetch Uncle Bill, but it didn't seem very important just now. Barnes wouldn't be getting out of the handcuffs. Mother ought to be all right.

What I should do, I decided, was go and find Uncle Bill first thing after discovering the Ripper's lodging place. That way, he'd get in on the glory.

I picked up my pace when the Ripper vanished around a corner. I got him in sight again. he was strolling toward a street lamp, toward a woman who stood there holding on to the post.

She spoke to him. I couldn't make out her words.

He walked over to her.

There was nobody else on the street that I could see.

I went all soft inside and felt like my heart might explode, it was thumping so hard.

He doesn't dare! I thought.

I stood frozen while the woman took his arm and snuggled up against him and they started walking off together.

He'd done two in one night before, so this shouldn't have surprised me. But it sure did. I'd just *known* he would lead me straight to his lodgings and I'd end up a hero.

It wasn't about to happen that way, though.

Mary hadn't been enough for him. He was fixing to butcher this gal, too.

It'd be my fault, if I let it happen.

I dug the knife out of my pocket, pried open its blade and rushed after them.

My father had died in battle. If it was good enough for him, it was good enough for me. I reckoned I might be meeting up with him any second. Eager as I was for the reunion, though, I hoped it wouldn't happen for considerable more years.

I didn't want to die just yet. But I couldn't let this gal get killed, either.

I slowed down a trifle as the distance closed. Pretty soon, I was no more than a few paces behind them. The gal wore a bonnet. Her head was leaning against his shoulder, and her arm was hooked around his back. He had one arm around her. His other swung the leather case along at his side.

They hadn't heard me yet. I was holding my breath. It helped, too, having lost my shoes to the thieves.

It went against the grain to back-stab a fellow.

I went on and did it anyway.

Charged right up behind him and jammed my blade through his coat.

He let out a sharp cry. I tugged the blade out to get ready for another go. Before I could stick him again, he whirled around. His case clobbered the side of my face and sent me staggering. As I fell on my rump, the woman took to screaming. Then she took to her heels.

The Ripper didn't go after her.

I'd saved her.

But matters were looking dicey for me.

I scrambled to get up as the Ripper came at me. He didn't seem to be in any great hurry. He switched the case to his left hand, reached inside the front of his coat, and came out with a knife. Likely the same knife he'd used on Mary.

'You're Jack the Ripper!' I blurted as I got to my feet.

'Am I now?' he asked.

It was the same voice I'd heard on the bed above me.

I backed away into the street and slashed about with my knife to keep him at a distance.

His knife was a damn sight bigger. He didn't swing it at me. He just held it steady in front and looked like he didn't plan to fool around, just ram it through my gizzard and hoist me off my feet with it.

'Give yourself up,' I said, 'or I'll run you through.'

He laughed at that. Can't say I blamed him.

I kept backing away. He kept coming.

I kept hoping he'd topple because of the stabbing I'd given him, but my blade must've hit a place that didn't count for much.

Suddenly, he made his move.

He lunged, thrusting at my belly.

I leaped aside. His blade missed me by a hair, and I whipped mine down. I didn't have any target in mind, just hoped to slash him somewhere, hurt him the best I could. But what happened, I whacked off most of his nose. It came clean off and fell.

He squealed.

Sounded a bit like the squeal he'd torn out of Mary.

He dropped his satchel and clutched his spouting stub and *roared*. The sound of that roar made my heart quake.

I made like a jackrabbit.

It might sound cowardly, but I'd had enough. That roar did it for me. He stopped being a wounded man and turned into the monster that had cut Mary into a faceless, gutted carcass. That had *eaten* her.

I wanted shut of him for good.

And I'll tell you, I didn't feel much like a coward as I raced off. I'd done my duty. I'd saved that woman from him and I'd marked him in a way he couldn't hide.

I figured, if I could only make my escape and live to tell my tale, Jack the Ripper would either disappear forever or end up in gaol next time he showed his noseless face.

I hadn't killed him. I hadn't captured him. But I'd stopped his reign of terror.

That's what I thought, anyhow.

Even though he was chasing after me, I figured he wouldn't catch up. After all, I was young and quick. And I wasn't hurt.

From the sounds of him dashing along behind me, I hadn't lost him yet.

I took a glance back when we were near a lamp, and saw how near he was and shriveled up inside. The knife in his right hand was pumping up and down. He'd lost his hat. His coat had come open, and was flapping behind him. His face and bare chest were black with blood.

He looked like the worst kind of nightmare spook.

I took to yelling for help. Not that I had much breath to do it with. The yelling came out feeble. And nothing seemed to come of it. After a while, I gave up and put all my energy into staying ahead of him.

I dashed down streets and alleys. I plowed around corners. Every so often, something came out of the dark and bumped me. I tripped a few times, but always got up and running again in time to keep from getting killed.

We ran past people sometimes. None was a constable. None tried to help. They all either ignored us or cowered or ran out of our way.

That eager mob must've turned in early.

Well, I'd about had as much running as I could take, but I

kept at it. And so did he. He wasn't about to give up the chase. I wasn't about to let him catch me.

The race seemed to go on for hours. Couldn't have been that long, really, but it felt like it.

And then I dashed out of a space between a couple of warehouses or factories or something and straight across the road from me was the river Thames.

I made for it.

The Ripper was quick on his feet, but how would he be in the water? If he wasn't much at swimming, I'd be in fine shape.

I raced out onto a dock that had some boats beside it. I glimpsed some other boats moored a ways offshore, and saw Tower Bridge off in the distance. The bridge gave me a clue as to where I'd ended up, but where I was didn't count for much. All that mattered was getting into the river ahead of the Ripper, who was clomping along the boards behind me, snorting and growling.

The tide was in, so I figured I wouldn't wind up pounding myself into the sand.

At the end of the dock, I flung my arms out straight and dived, shoving off as hard as I could. It seemed I was in the air forever. Then the river smacked my front. It wasn't much colder than the rain, and I was so hot from all the running that it almost felt good. I kicked along, staying below the surface and fighting my way through the currents. No splashes came from behind me, though I'm not sure I would've heard them anyhow.

Maybe he hadn't followed me into the water.

Or any second he might just grab one of my feet.

I changed my angle a bit to throw him off.

I needed a breath in the worst way, but I stayed under and kicked and paddled with my arms. The knife in my right hand was slowing me down. Figured I might have a call to use it, though, so I kept hold. Wasn't long before my chest felt like it might either burn up or explode, so I surfaced. My head popped out of the water. I sucked in air, and twisted around.

And saw the Ripper.

He was nothing more than a dim shape in the rain and darkness, but the way he was crouched at the edge of the dock, busy working on a task I couldn't rightly see, I figured what he must be up to.

Untying a painter that belonged to one of the dinghies floating by the dock.

He aimed to come after me in a boat!

Didn't seem fair. But I wasn't about to waste any time cursing him or my fate. I swung around and churned the river.

Next time I looked back, he was in a boat and rowing after me.

I took to diving under and changing course. Thought about doubling back on him, but knew I couldn't hold my breath long enough to pull it off. On top of that, I was getting mighty tuckered out from struggling with the currents.

Then it came to me that I might take cover behind one of the bigger boats that were moored nearby.

Even better to board one. Then I might have a chance at bashing him if he tried to climb up after me.

I swam for a sloop that was anchored off to the right. The way it floated there, all dark and quiet, it looked deserted.

That's where I'd make my stand.

The Ripper's dinghy was still a good distance off when I reached up and grabbed the anchor chain. I clamped the knife between my teeth, pirate fashion, and shinned up to the prow. It was no easy trick, but I made it. I clambered over the side and got the deck under my hands and knees. Felt so tuckered I wanted to flop and rest, but the Ripper wouldn't give me any time for that.

I stumbled to my feet and took the knife out of my teeth. As I turned to look for him, a shape came rushing at me.

I didn't have time to say hello or ask for help or duck.

The bloke laid a club across my head.

The night flashed real bright for a bit. Then the deck pounded my knees. Then I didn't feel a thing.

Chapter Seven

On the Thames in the *True D. Light*

It came as a great surprise to wake up at all. If I'd been aware enough to give the matter any thought, I would've concluded that my days of waking up were over for good.

When I opened my eyes, I met so many surprises they pretty much left me dumbfounded.

It was daytime, gray light coming through the portholes of the narrow cabin where I was stretched out.

There was a mattress under me, covers heaped on top of me.

I felt ropes around my wrists and ankles.

The way everything pitched and rocked, it didn't take much figuring to realize I was on a boat. Probably the same boat I'd boarded hoping to fight off the Ripper, the same boat where someone had brained me senseless.

So what had become of Jack the Ripper?

Though my head was aching fierce, I raised it off the pillow for a look around.

The young woman on the other bed wasn't covered. She wore a white night-dress. Her arms were lashed against her sides, her feet bound together. Her head rested on the lap of a man wearing trousers and a heavy sweater and a bandage that masked most of his face. The bulk of the bandage was where his nose used to be.

The bandage was muddy brown in its center with blood that had seeped through and dried.

This was my first good look at the Ripper. Though finding him sitting just a few feet away gave me an awful turn, he didn't appear particularly fiendish in the daylight. His black hair was neatly trimmed, parted up the middle. He had rather dainty eyebrows. His brown eyes were small and close together, while his ears stuck out like big flaps. His mouth wasn't much more than a slit, and had only a trace of lips. What with his thin lips and sunken chin, his upper front teeth stuck out in a way that might've been comical if I hadn't known who he was.

With his right hand, he stroked the woman's hair. The knife was in his left, resting on her belly while he stared back at me for a spell. Then he raised it and gave the blade a twirl in the air.

'Greetings,' he said. He sounded like he had a stuffed up nose.

The woman was wide awake, gazing up at him with weary, scared eyes.

'I've spared your life, you miserable whelp, so I expect your everlasting gratitude.' He said that as if it were a joke.

'Bugger off,' I told him.

He laughed.

The gal darted her eyes over at me.

I sat up. The covers fell down to my waist. I was shirtless. From the feel of the bedclothes, I was trouserless as well.

The Ripper kept his eyes on me. They looked amused.

'You wouldn't like to leave your bunk,' he said. 'There *is* a lady present.'

'And you'd better not harm her, if you know what's good for you.'

She gave me a wild, pleading look as if she hoped I'd settle down and not get myself killed in her presence.

'I shouldn't risk vexing me,' the Ripper said, 'were I in your rather precarious position. I'm quite displeased with you. It would do my heart wonders to peel the hide off your body and enjoy your screams.'

'It did *my* heart wonders to lop off your nose,' I said.

His upper lip twitched. He pounded his left hand down on the gal's stomach. Her wind gushed out and she bucked, half sitting up. He yanked her hair so her head dropped down on his lap again. Her face was bright red as she gasped for air.

'I quite enjoyed that,' he said.

His message was clear. If I should do anything to displease him, he would take it out on her.

'I suppose you have a name,' he said to me.

'Trevor. Trevor Wellington Bentley.'

'What a high-sounding name for a scurvy ruffian.'

I held my tongue.

'Trevor, you *know* who I am, I daresay.'

'Jack the Ripper.'

'Bravo! A keen mind. In plain truth, however, my name is Roderick Whittle. And this dear morsel is Trudy Armitage, a Yank. Trudy has agreed to play the role of Helpless Captive for the duration of our voyage. You have the honor of being aboard her family yacht, the *True D. Light*. Rather disgustingly clever wouldn't you say?'

I chose to say nothing, and just stared at him.

He stared back.

After a bit, he said, 'You led me a merry chase, young Trevor. I was quite set to cut your heart out, you know, but all's well that ends well, as the Bard is apt to say. You rendered me a service, leading me here. Things were getting quite warm for me. I'd been considering the merits of a sea voyage, and you led me to just the proper craft for such a venture. It hasn't the necessary provisions for the trip I have in mind, but it came equipped with crew and captive.' He stroked Trudy's thick brown hair, and smiled down at her.

'They were all set to sail with the tide, Trudy and her groom fast asleep while her father busied himself with final preparations. I was forced to dispatch the father.'

When he said that, Trudy's eyes blinked and watered. Her chin trembled.

Whittle patted her head. 'There, there, no use in crying over Papa. He's with the Lord now – and the fish.'

She cried all the harder, gasping and shaking as the tears rolled down her face.

I felt mighty sorry for her. I knew how hard it was, having a father killed. But that wouldn't be nearly as hard as what Roderick Whittle likely had in mind for her.

She was a pretty thing, no older than twenty. She looked buxom and healthy, broad across the shoulders and hips, with heavy bosoms that bounced around under her nightdress because of how she shook with her crying. I caught myself watching how they moved, and looked away quick.

Not that the sight of them stirred me up. Not after the pair I'd seen in Mary's room.

I watched Whittle stroke her hair.

And feared what might be going through his head.

'Where are we going?' I asked, intending to distract him.

He looked over at me. 'Just now, we're sailing down the Thames. The original destination was to be Calais. Isn't that right, Trudy?'

She nodded and sobbed.

'However, my command of the French language is really quite poor. I'd be quite silly to take up residence where the natives don't speak my tongue. No, such a place is not for me. I rather fancy trying my luck in America, instead.'

'*America?*'

'I'm sure you must've heard of it. The Colonies?'

'That's *three thousand miles* away.'

'Quite. A trifle farther, actually.'

'We can't make a crossing this time of the year!'

'Oh, but we shall certainly have a go at it.'

The man was mad. But that goes without saying when you consider what he'd done to women. I chose not to point it out. Trying to sound calm, I asked, 'Is this boat large enough for such a voyage?'

'How do you suppose it came to our fair isles?'

'We made our crossing in the summer,' Trudy pointed out between sniffles. 'And Michael had . . . Father and I to help him. He won't . . . be able to manage it alone.'

'Which proves my foresight in sparing young Trevor. Have you ever been to sea?' he asked me.

I shook my head.

'Not to worry. You're a quick study, and we have ample cause to know you're agile and strong. We'll give you double duty as my servant and as Michael's hand. No doubt you'll perform admirably.'

I gave it some thought. Though the idea of seeing America appealed to me, going there trapped on a boat with Whittle sure didn't. I wanted more than anything to get home to Mother. By now, she was likely frantic with worry. If I let myself get shanghaied, I'd be on the seas a month and she'd figure me lost forever or dead before I might find any way to let her know otherwise.

Of course, I reckoned I'd never get a chance to let her know a thing.

Trying to cross the Atlantic in November in a boat that couldn't be more than fifty or sixty feet from stem to stern, with only me and a stranger named Michael for its whole crew, we'd probably all wind up blowing bubbles.

If somehow we got lucky enough to survive the ocean trip, Whittle was bound to butcher all three of us the moment we got in sight of land.

Just no way he'd let us go free.

It all looked mighty bleak except for one thing. He aimed to have me help out, and I couldn't do that trussed up with ropes.

I lifted my bound hands out from under the covers. 'When would you like me to start?'

He laughed at that.

'Michael might need help,' I explained. 'You wouldn't want him to run aground or anything, would you?'

'Nor would I want you to jump ship. I'm quite certain of Michael's eagerness to cooperate. He's in love with Trudy, and knows I'll rip her, so to speak, should he vex me. I trust him entirely. At least so long as I keep Trudy within reach of my blade. She means little or nothing to you, however.'

'I don't want you hurting her.'

'I shall, of course, if you cause me trouble. Nevertheless, your heart isn't bound to hers. You might choose to risk her for the sake of your own freedom.'

'I wouldn't,' I told him. To this day, I don't know whether or not I spoke the truth.

I surely was eager to get untied and up on deck where I could dive overboard and swim for shore. But if that meant cashing in Trudy's life . . . well, I just don't know.

But I was spared the need to decide.

Whittle said, 'You'll remain here in the cabin with us until we're well out to sea.'

It wouldn't do to argue. Any kind of fuss from me, and he'd give Trudy a punch, or worse.

I laid back down and worked the covers up around my neck and turned my back to the both of them. Would've been a blessing to fall asleep, but I was in too much turmoil. Besides, my head hurt from the bash Trudy's father had given it.

He'd whacked me a good one, but I'd killed him just as sure as if the knife had been in my own hand. There he'd been, fixing to set sail for France with his daughter and son-in-law, and I'd led the Ripper right to him. It weighed on me. I told myself it was his own fault for knocking me senseless. If he hadn't been so quick with his club, I could've warned him. Together, we might've handled Whittle.

Well, I'd snuck onto his yacht in the wee hours, bare to the waist and a knife in my teeth. He couldn't be blamed for getting the wrong idea. Then Whittle'd rowed up, no doubt with a story about being attacked on the streets by me, and the old man must've allowed him aboard to take me off.

If only I'd picked a different boat, Trudy and her father and Michael, they'd all be on their way to Calais.

I'd done this to them.

For a spell there, I had a mighty hard struggle not to start crying. That would've given Whittle no end of amusement and besides I didn't want Trudy to take me for a sniveling boy.

I wondered if she hated me for bringing the Ripper into her life.

Right then I vowed to save her.

Chapter Eight

Ropes

'Trevor? Trevor?'

A sweet, quiet voice woke me, so I must've fallen asleep after all. Though I knew it wasn't Mother calling to me, just for a bit I thought I was home in my own bed.

But my hands and feet were bound and the bed was bouncing up against me and rocking from side to side. That reminded me, all too quick, of where I was and how I'd gotten there.

Opening my eyes, I rolled over. It was night. The cabin was aglow with murky light from an oil lamp.

Whittle was gone.

Trudy lay under covers, only her face showing.

'Where is he?' I asked.

'He went to the galley for food.'

I could scarcely believe that he'd left us alone. With Michael manning the boat and both of us tied, however, he had no choice but to fetch food himself or starve. I rather hoped he would bring some for us. The mere thought of it was enough to set my dry mouth watering, my stomach growling.

'We've got to do something,' Trudy said.

I sat up, dragging the bedclothes to my chest. They did

little to warm my backside, but this was no time to worry about the cold. Shivering a bit, I gave the cabin a study. It was narrow and just long enough for the two berths, with walls at each end. The wall near my feet had a door in it.

'Where does that go?' I asked.

'Aft,' Trudy said. She sat up, too. Her covers tumbled down to her lap. I could see she was still tied, arms pinned to her sides by ropes wrapped around her middle. 'We're in the forward cabin. The galley's aft.'

'Through that door?'

'There's the head, then the main saloon, then the galley.'

I didn't know what she meant by some of that, but figured she was trying to tell me that Whittle'd gone pretty near to the other end of the boat.

'He quizzed me about our supplies,' Trudy said. 'He wants a hot meal. So he's bound to be away for a while. Come over here and untie me.'

'Well . . .' I said.

'Quick!'

'Is there a way to get *out* of here?'

'We shan't know that until we try. Now, don't argue.'

'I'm not wearing a stitch of clothing, ma'am.'

'Do as I say.'

Some of my sympathy for Trudy leaked away. For a poor helpless damsel in distress, she seemed a trifle bossy.

But I gave it some thought and saw how this might be a chance to save ourselves. It'd be a shame to miss it on account of my modesty. So I swung myself off the bed. I stood up. Cupping my private parts, I hopped across the space between our beds. Before the jumping floor got a chance to throw me down, I dropped to my knees.

The air fairly froze me. I clenched my teeth to stop their clicking, and reached up for Trudy.

The way my hands were bound at the wrists, I had free use of my fingers. I used them to pluck at the knot in front of Trudy. It was tight against her belly. The twisted bundle of hemp felt hard as iron. My shaky fingers picked at it, slipped off, and tried again.

'Use your teeth.'

I pushed my face in against her and clamped my front teeth on the knot. She was nice and warm through her gown. I could feel her press against me when she breathed. I tried to pay her no mind and only think about the job.

The knot gave some.

I kept on tugging. It made my teeth ache, but I could feel it loosen. I pulled my head away and tore at the knot with my fingers until it came open.

Trudy pulled her arms out of the ropes. She flung her covers aside and leaned forward to work on her ankles. While she was busy with that, I gnawed on the knot at my wrists. I undid it some, and got my hands free.

Sitting on the cold wood between the beds, I struggled with the rope around my ankles.

It seemed like some kind of a race to see who'd get done first. But the race was really to get clear of the ropes before Whittle came back through the door.

Not that I had a notion what we'd do once we got ourselves untangled.

Likely as not, we'd only accomplish getting ourselves killed a little quicker than otherwise.

Trudy beat me at getting free. I was still unwrapping my ankles when she stepped down off her bed and rushed to the door. She tried its handle.

'Drat,' she said. 'He locked it.'

'He'd be a fool not to.' I kicked the rope away and got to my feet. While Trudy still had her back turned, I yanked a blanket off my bed and wrapped it around myself. 'We might be able to bash through it,' I suggested.

'He'd hear the ruckus.'

She came toward me. I retreated a few steps, and watched her stretch for something that looked like a trap door in the ceiling. She unlatched it and pushed up against it.

'Where does that go?' I asked.

'It's the hatch to the forward deck.' She shoved again, grunting.

'Let me have a go at it.'

'It's no use. It must be latched topside.'

'Shouldn't Michael be able to open it for us, then?'

She didn't answer that, but commenced to knuckle the hatch with both fists. For a gal opposed to the ruckus of breaking through a door, she was raising a mighty racket.

I doubted it would do much good, though. Even the way we were closed away below the main deck, I could hear all kinds of noise from outside: waves slapping against the hull, sails whapping, the mast creaking, wind whistling through the rigging, all manner of other groans and rattles and clanks. Unless Michael had his ear to the hatch, I didn't hold out much hope of him catching the sound of Trudy's whacks.

But Whittle wasn't likely to hear them, either.

While she kept on punching at the hatch, I knelt on her bed and checked a porthole. It wasn't big enough to squirm out through, so I didn't even try to get it open. But I pushed my face against the glass.

All I could see were rough waves, not a blink of light anywhere from a boat nor shore.

'I don't believe we're on the Thames any more,' I said.

She paused in her banging long enough to say, 'Of course not, silly. We're out in the Channel.'

I sank inside with the news of that. It wouldn't do, now, to jump ship and swim for land.

Trying to perk myself up, I thought how the *True D. Light* was bound to have a lifeboat or dinghy of sorts. That didn't accomplish much in the way of perking, though. Even if we could get outside, Whittle would surely be on us before we could lower such a craft.

I reckon Trudy hadn't thought that far ahead, for she continued thumping the hatch.

She stopped when the boat gave a sudden pitch that banged my forehead against the glass and flung her onto me. She pushed and shoved and got herself off, and stumbled backward and dropped onto the other berth.

I turned myself around.

'He's bound to come back soon,' Trudy said.

'I'm afraid so.'

She shook her head. She sighed. Then she said, 'You'd best tie me up.'

'What?'

'Tie me *up* again.'

'We just finished getting ourselves *un*tied.'

'But there's no way out. We can't let him know we tried to escape.' She flung herself back across the aisle, bent over beside me and snatched up one of the ropes. 'Get off.'

I stood up. With one hand, I kept the blanket on my shoulders. With the other, I grabbed the handle of the hatch to keep myself from being tossed off my feet.

Trudy sat on her bed and stretched out her legs. She reached the rope toward me. 'Be quick about it.'

'No.'

'What did you say?'

'No. I'm not going to tie you up.'

'You'll do as I say, boy.'

It goes against my grain to argue with women. Besides, it's generally a great waste of time. But Trudy was starting to irk me with her bossy ways. I told her, 'If you had no better scheme in mind than hoping we might slip out a door, you shouldn't have insisted that I untie you in the first place. Since we *are* untied, however, we're no longer entirely at Whittle's mercy. We'll have the element of surprise in our favor. And it'll be two against one.'

'Don't be a fool.'

'I say we put up a fight.'

'What do you know? You're a *child*.'

'I fought him once before and made a good showing. It was me who cut off the blighter's nose, you know.'

'And a lot of good that did. If you'd left him well enough alone . . .'

'He would've murdered a woman on the streets. I saved her from his blade.'

'And led him to our boat.'

'I know. And I'm sorry for that. I'm sorry for what he did to your father, too. But he's *Jack the Ripper*! You've no idea what a monster he is. I saw what he did to one poor woman. He must be put a stop to, or he'll do the same to you.'

'He needs me.'

'He'll butcher you.'

'Don't be silly. He doesn't dare kill me, not if he wants safe passage to America. But he'll certainly punish us for getting free of the ropes, so quit your arguing and tie me up.'

I let go the hatch handle and took the rope from her. She pressed her arms against her sides, ready to have herself trussed.

'Lie down,' I said.

'You've got to tie me first.'

'No.'

'Trevor!'

'All right, then!' Though I wasn't keen on being naked again, I needed both hands so I tossed my blanket to the other bed. Trudy turned her head away. Not before giving me a look, however.

On my knees again, I tucked one end of the rope under her arm, then wrapped her around the middle.

'Tighter,' she said. 'He can't know the difference.'

I gave the rope rather a rough tug. She winced. She deserved a little hurt for being obnoxious, but right away I felt bad about it and apologized.

'Shut up and tie the knot.'

'I'd much rather not. Let me leave it undone. I'll cover you up, and you lie down and pretend to be asleep. I'll do the same. We'll wait for just the proper moment, then jump Whittle and throttle him.'

'There'll be no jumping of Whittle.'

I sighed.

I didn't put up any more fuss. I knotted the rope, then

scurried down and bound her ankles. When they were secure, I covered Trudy with the bedclothes.

I hurried over to my own berth and gathered the ropes Whittle had used on me. Feeling a bit down on Trudy, I said, 'Now, of course, I'm supposed to tie myself.'

'Do your feet first. That shouldn't present any great difficulty.'

I swung my legs onto the bed, spread them apart, and dropped one of the ropes between them. Then I drew the covers up over my lap.

'What do you think you're doing?' Trudy asked, her tone snappish.

'I may be a silly child and a fool, thank you, but I'm not a coward.'

'Tie yourself this minute!'

'I have a better use for Whittle's rope.'

The one in my hands wasn't nearly so long as the coil I could feel under the backs of my legs. After dragging the covers to my shoulders, I stretched it across my chest and wound its ends around my hands.

'What are you planning?'

'To have a go at playing Thuggee.'

'What are you talking about?'

'The Thuggee. A cult of fanatical murderers in India who employ the garrote to strangle . . .'

I went mum at the sound of a clacking latch. The door swung open. Whittle came in. He carried a bottle and a steaming pot that had a spoon in it. Clamping the bottle under one arm, he turned around to lock the door.

Secured from this side, it wasn't meant to keep us in but rather to keep Michael out. I supposed he must be keeping all the doors and hatches locked so he wouldn't need to worry about the fellow sneaking below for a try at rescuing Trudy.

He might as well have spared himself the bother. As I found out later, Michael didn't have the grit for such a venture.

After fastening the door, Whittle started to turn around. I shut my eyes before he got a look at me.

'Sit up, deary,' he said in that stuffed voice of his thanks to losing his nose. 'We shouldn't like to have you withering away, now, should we?'

I looked. He was on his knees, facing Trudy. He held the pot near her face. With his other hand, he spooned food into her mouth.

'Quite tasty, I daresay. I don't fancy myself a master of the culinary arts, but this stew is really quite exceptional.'

The odor was delightful. It set my parched mouth to watering again, my hollow belly to grumbling.

He kept shoveling, giving Trudy a few moments to chew and swallow between each spoonful. I wondered if he aimed to save any for me.

It wouldn't come to that, though.

I slipped out from under the covers, swung myself around and lowered my feet to the floor. Trudy, chewing, shook her head at me. Whittle started to look over his shoulder. I sprang. Whipped the rope down past his face. Jerked it across his throat as I rammed against his back. The blow flung a spoonful of stew into Trudy's face. Then he knocked her flat and fell across her chest.

Riding his back, I pulled at the rope for all I was worth. He made choking, gaggy noises. He twisted and bucked under me. He stabbed at my shoulder with the spoon. His other hand dumped the pot down my back. The grub was hot enough to sting, but it didn't hurt enough to make me ease off. I kept on strangling him.

If Trudy'd lent a hand, I might've killed the Ripper then and there and saved the world a heap of grief.

But she was nicely tied because she'd insisted and I'd given in to her.

So she just lay there helpless, leaving the job to me.

Whittle bashed the side of my head with the pot. The world flashed bright, but I held on and kept tugging at the rope. Then he lit into me again and again. I lost count after the fifth bong. But I didn't lose my wits entirely.

Before long, I was sprawled on the floor and Whittle was

sitting on me, wheezing for air, clobbering my face with the bottom of the pot. When he got tired of that, he roped my hands in front of me. He sat quiet for a spell, just staring at me and trying to get his wind back.

'What *shall* I do with you, Trevor?' he finally asked.

I was too dazed to give an answer, but I reckon he wouldn't have heeded my advice, anyhow.

He pulled out his knife.

He tapped the end of my nose with its blade.

'Shall I nip it off?' he asked. His other hand reached around behind him and fingered my private parts. 'Perhaps I ought to make a girl out of you. Which would you prefer, young man?'

'Cut my throat and . . . go bugger yourself.'

That got the swine laughing. 'You're too much fun to ruin,' he said. 'But you simply must be punished. Ah! I know just the thing!'

He put his knife away, climbed off, and lifted me onto my bed. As he worked on tying my feet, he said, 'This will be just the perfect torture for a stout-hearted lad such as yourself. It ought to give you second thoughts, even third and fourth, should you ever take it into your head to tangle with me again.'

He covered me to the shoulders with the bedclothes.

Then he crossed over to Trudy's berth and slapped her across the face.

'Leave her be!' I yelled.

He struck her again.

'I didn't *do* anything,' she cried out. 'It was *him*. It was all *his* idea!'

He gave her a back-handed smack that knocked her head sideways. She didn't say much after that. She didn't fight him, either. She just acted like a big, limp doll while Whittle threw off her covers, sat her up and untied her feet. When he told her to stand up, she obeyed.

He made a loop at one end of the rope, and dropped it over her head. He tightened the loop around her neck.

'Strangulation is most unpleasant,' he said. He glanced at me. 'I know that from recent experience at the hands of young Trevor.'

He passed the other end of the rope through the handle of the hatch above Trudy's head, pulled the slack out of it, then ducked down, hoisting her.

Trudy's arms were lashed fast against her sides, just as I'd left them. Her legs thrashed. Her body, wrapped in the white nightgown, twisted and swung. She let out the most awful retching sounds.

'No!' I cried out. I sat up so fast my head seemed to whirl inside.

'Stay or you'll make it worse for her!' Whittle yelled.

With that, he lowered Trudy until her feet met the floor. She stood there, weaving and choking, dancing about some in order to keep her balance as the boat rocked and bounced.

'That's enough,' I said. 'I'll be good. I promise. Please. Let her be.'

'A promise quickly forgotten once the heat of sympathy has cooled.'

'No! I promise! As God is my witness!'

'Witness this, my friend.' He let the rope fall from his hand. While Trudy staggered about, trying to stay on her feet, he stepped around to the front of her and removed the rope that bound her arms to her sides. He slipped the nightgown off her shoulders, pulled it down her body until it lay in a heap at her feet.

She just stood there, letting him.

I just sat on my bed, watching. He'd said he would make it worse for her if I interfered, and I believed him.

After stripping her naked, he tied Trudy's hands.

Then he grabbed the rope that was dangling from the hatch above her head. He slipped it between her legs, reached behind her to find it, brought it around to the front, gave it a pull that made her yelp and jump, then tied it around the top of her thigh.

'How's that, deary?' he asked her.

64

She answered with a whimper.

He patted her face. 'Steady as she goes,' he said. 'Should you lose your sea legs, I fear you may hang yourself. And such a pity that would be.'

He squeezed past her. He smiled over at me. 'See what you've done to Trudy?'

Well, it was just too much for me and I started to weep. 'Please,' I blubbered. 'Please, let her down.'

'By and by. Perhaps.'

He withdrew the leather belt from his trousers, doubled it, and whipped Trudy's back. She flinched and squealed. She pranced to keep from falling.

I thought of Barnes whipping Mother with *his* belt. And I wished I had finished him off with the fireplace poker, and I wished I had killed Whittle and I prayed for the Lord to strike him dead and I vowed to kill him myself if God let him get away with this.

I cried and pleaded and cursed.

It was all just a blur through my tears. It seemed to go on for hours. I wished it was me instead of her. She looked so beautiful and helpless it just twisted my heart to see the way Whittle lashed her. Each time he struck, she jumped and twitched and cried out. Even in the dim glow from the lamp, I could see red stripes all over her back and rump. A few times, she lost her footing and strangled for a moment before she got the floor under her again.

When Whittle finally lowered his arm, I thought he was done with her. But what he did was turn Trudy around. He commenced to whip her front, laying the belt across her face and arms and breasts and belly.

At last, he put his belt back on.

Trudy hung there, limp and whimpering, shaking all over, shuffling her feet so she wouldn't fall again.

When his belt was buckled, he grinned at me. He winked. 'Now for my favorite part.'

He went up close to Trudy, held on to her hips, and took to licking her.

'Nothing like the taste of blood,' he said.

He spent a long time licking her. He licked her all over, front and back. Then he fell into Trudy's bed, pulled the covers over him, and said, 'Sleep well, my friends.'

Chapter Nine

A Rough, Long Night

I couldn't hardly believe Whittle was just going to *leave* Trudy dangling. I figured he'd get up again, pretty soon, and let her down. But he didn't. He no sooner covered himself up with her blankets than he got to snoring.

What with the cold and the way the boat bounced around, Trudy didn't stand a chance of lasting through the night. It was a toss-up whether she'd freeze to death or hang.

Didn't Whittle care? Even though her life meant nothing to him, it seemed he'd want to keep her breathing just so he wouldn't lose his hold on Michael. Besides that, being the monster that he was, he'd be missing out on a heap of pleasure by killing her this way instead of butchering her with his knife. Didn't make any sense at all.

Well, there's no accounting for the whims of a madman.

I stayed in bed, listening to him snore and keeping my eyes on Trudy. She'd let up on her sobbing. She just stood there, her head up, her legs apart and bent just a bit, her feet shuffling as the floor tried to throw her. The way shadows hid her eyes, I couldn't tell whether she was watching me. But she must've suspected I was looking at her, for she always kept her hands low as if she was worried I might get a peek at what was between her legs.

I'd been in her fix, I would've been holding on to the rope over my head and let folks look where they pleased.

She needn't have bothered trying to cover that part, anyhow, since I got glimpses every now and again when the boat lurched and she couldn't help but jerk her hands up as she stumbled about. I didn't see nothing but a bunch of hair, and it pained me how the rope looked like it was digging up into her.

The sight sure didn't stir me up, and neither did her bosoms which jiggled and shook considerable.

There'd been times when I'd longed something awful for a chance to spy what girls had under their clothes. Why, it used to drive me crazy wondering how it might be, and what it would feel like to touch certain places.

I reckon Sue the whore had a hand in souring my appetite for such things. But nothing like the way Mary soured it, thanks to Whittle. And now here was Trudy, bare as the day she was born and near enough to reach out and touch, and yet I was no more thrilled than if she'd been a fellow.

It was a peculiar business to be worrying about while she stood there at the end of a rope. But the truth is, I felt cheated. Even though I knew it'd only make me feel guilty if I was taking enjoyment out of watching Trudy, I figured it would've been the natural thing.

Maybe I was just hurting too much to appreciate her. After all, my face and head purely throbbed with pain from the drubbing Whittle'd given me. Or maybe it had to do with feeling so awful about the way he'd tormented Trudy – on account of me.

I suspect all that played a part in it, but the main thing was Whittle's work on Mary. She'd been the first gal I ever saw naked, and that was a sight to turn the stomach. I got to thinking Whittle might've put me off women forever.

And I hated him for that. Not that I needed any more reason to hate the filthy swine. The extra bit of hate over how he'd ruined women for me, though, was enough to make me lose caution.

I pushed my covers down and sat up.

'What're you doing?' Trudy whispered.

'Shhhh.' Not that I figured Whittle could hear her through his own snoring.

As I swung my legs down, Trudy shook her head wildly.

'Stay where you are.'

'He'll be the death of us both if I don't kill him.'

'You *can't* kill him.'

'I'll slash his throat with his own knife before he even wakes up.'

'If you leave your berth, I'll scream.'

'What's the matter with you?'

'Look what you've already done to me with your foolishness. It wasn't *you* he strung up and whipped.'

'I wish it had been me. Honest.'

'It wasn't. If you try for him again, there's no telling what he'll do to me.'

'Nothing he won't do, anyway, if he lives.'

'Lie down and be still. I swear to the Almighty, I'll scream if you don't.'

Well, I stretched out and pulled the blankets back on top of me. 'If you hadn't made me tie you up,' I muttered, 'we would've had him. It'd all be over, now. He wouldn't have hurt you like he did do. We'd be sailing back to London this very minute.'

'Hush up and go to sleep.'

'I'll hush up.'

'And go to sleep. I've had enough of your staring at me.'

'I'm only looking out for you.'

'I know what you're doing. You're horrible and nasty. Now, stop it and turn your head away.'

'No, ma'am. I'm sorry. If you'd rather I not see your front side, you might turn around.' I don't know why *she* hadn't thought of that.

'If you must know, I need to see the lamp.' It was by the door past my feet. 'It helps me keep steady.'

'Well, then, stay the way you are. Rest assured, I'm not taking any special enjoyment from the view.'

She muttered, 'Beast,' and then went quiet.

I kept my eyes on her. She kept shifting about. She seemed to know just which way the floor'd tip next, and changed her footing ahead of time. Good as she was, though, I had my doubts she'd be able to keep it up all night – or until Whittle quit his sleeping and unhanged her.

I could see how the cold was getting to her. She'd been goosebumpy and shivering all along. As time went by, though, the shivers got worse till she was fairly shuddering. Her teeth chittered together. She shimmied from head to toe. It put me in mind of exotic Arabian harem dancers I'd read about. Then she got too out of control for any sort of dancer. The way she shook and twitched and jittered about made her look like a marionette – one that had a fellow with an attack of palsy running the strings for it.

All of a sudden, the boat nosed down and pitched Trudy off her feet. She dropped backwards till the noose stopped her. She let out a choke. Her tied hands flew up and grabbed the rope beside her face while she heeled the floor. Just when she almost got herself standing, another lurch of the boat flung her feet out from under her all over again.

Whittle kept on snoring.

A shout might've stirred him up. But I figured he might just let her swing.

I hurled myself out of bed. My bound feet landed on stew. I gave the floor a smart slam, but didn't let that stop me. In a blink, I was on my hands and knees, scooting myself toward Trudy. Tied like I was, I didn't know how to go about saving her.

What happened, though, I pushed right into her kicking legs. After giving me a few thumps, they quit thrashing and used my shoulders for braces. I scooched forward, head between them, forcing them back, and before long Trudy was standing. She coughed and gasped for a spell, but I could tell she wasn't getting strangled any more.

She stood there, shaking and panting, and mashing my head with her knees till I feared my skull might cave in.

'Let go,' I whispered.

'I'll fall.' Her voice had a whiny, scared sound.

Somebody laughed. It wasn't me. It wasn't Trudy.

'Whittle!' I cried out. 'Help us!'

'It's been a jolly fine show. I shouldn't like to spoil it now.'

Had he not been asleep, at all – the snoring a mere ruse?

'Let her down, damn your eyes!'

'Please,' Trudy sobbed.

'You're both doing splendidly without my interference. Carry on.'

I railed at him something fierce and Trudy kept on pleading. Whittle laughed as if thoroughly enjoying himself. But finally he must've grown tired of our voices, for he said, 'Quit your blithering, now, or I may lose my patience.'

'Let her down at once!' I demanded.

I heard a loud clap. Trudy yelped and flinched and near crushed my skull. Then she took to blubbering.

After that, we both kept mum.

We stayed just the way we were. What with my hands and feet tied, I was none too steady. Trudy's grip on my head helped to keep me from going over sideways, and I kept her from falling forward or backward. A peculiar arrangement, but it worked most of the time.

Every so often, we'd take a spill. Then Trudy's commence to choke till I could get back to my hands and knees and she'd latch onto my head again.

The cold made me shake. So did the strain of fighting to stay up. Every muscle in me took to jumping around under my skin. I don't know how a person can work up a sweat when he's freezing, but I sure did, and the air grabbed hold of all that sweat and made it feel like ice.

Would've felt wondrous to crawl back to my bed and get under the covers. Nothing stopped me from doing that except I knew Trudy wouldn't last five minutes if I didn't stay put.

It got so bad I started figuring it might be best to go ahead and let her hang. After all, Whittle was bound to kill her anyhow, sooner or later. If her neck got stretched tonight, it'd only save her from more misery later on.

Never quite convinced myself of that, though, I'm glad to say.

I stuck it out.

By and by, all the cold and aches seemed to go away. I fancied I was home in bed, safe and cozy. I even heard Mother, off in another room, playing sweet music on her violin.

I woke up and thought I *was* home, for I was warm under covers. But the boat was rocking me gently. I opened my eyes, saw daylight, and felt like I wanted to die. Much as I'd hoped to save Trudy, I must've lost my wits and crawled back into my bunk, leaving her to swing. I'd betrayed her. I'd killed her.

I couldn't look, didn't want to see poor Trudy slumped at the end of her rope.

Then I noticed I wasn't tied any more.

Confused by that, I went on and turned my head. Trudy wasn't hung, after all. She was stretched out on her berth, all but her face hidden under blankets. Her face was mighty pale except for bruises and a couple of red marks from Whittle's belt. Her eyes were shut. I could see her eyes sliding around under the lids, so I knew she wasn't dead.

Well, she was such a fine sight I got teary. I hadn't let her die, after all. And neither had Whittle. Sometime during the night, he must've let her down and put us both into our beds. Not that he'd taken pity on us. He had no pity in him. It simply went against his plans to have us turn up our toes when we still had the whole voyage ahead of us.

He wasn't on either bed, so I reckoned he'd left us by ourselves.

I rolled onto my side, flinching and moaning with all my aches, and saw he was gone, all right. He'd shut the door after him. On the floor between our berths were Trudy's nightgown and a lot of stew – dried gravy and chunks of meat and potatoes and vegetables.

The sight of that food set my belly to grumbling.

71

I got down there. My knees hurt fierce. The air chilled me some, though it felt warmer than last night. I plucked up pieces of meat and potatoes and carrots and jammed them in. They were cold. They tasted almighty fine, though I had a rough time working up enough spit to swallow.

After a few mouthfuls, I remembered Trudy. She hadn't gotten much into her before my attack on Whittle, so I reckoned she might be near as hungry as me.

I gathered some grub in my hands and crawled over to her.

She looked so peaceful, asleep like that, I hated to disturb her. Did it anyhow, though, figuring she'd appreciate the food and might not get another chance at some for a while.

'Trudy,' I whispered, close to her face. 'Trudy, wake up.'

Her eyelids squeezed tighter as if she wanted nothing to do with waking up. Then her face scrunched. She let out a few little whimpers.

'Whittle's not here,' I told her.

She opened her eyes and blinked at me.

'You might wish to eat a bit,' I said, raising my cupped hands so she could see the food.

She looked at it, but didn't move.

'I saved it for you.'

'Where is he?' she asked, her voice all quiet and scratchy.

'I hope he's gone to the Devil, but I imagine he's only gone to another room. Are you untied?'

She nodded her head ever so slightly.

'You ought to sit up and eat, then.'

'Go away. Leave me alone.'

Here she was, giving orders again. But she didn't put much pep behind them.

I dumped one hand into the other, then pinched up a chunk of meat and put it to her lips. She kept them shut and shook her head. I rubbed the meat across her lips, greasing them up.

'Stop.'

She sounded so pitiful, I quit. But then her tongue came out to clean off the mess, and she must've liked the taste. She opened her mouth. I put the meat in. She chewed and chewed on it, and made awful faces when she tried to swallow.

'If you want more,' I said, 'you'd best sit up.'

She rolled onto her side, pushed herself up on one elbow, and brought out her other arm to hold the covers against her bosom. She was in a sorry condition. Her shoulders and what I could see of her chest were just as smooth and white as cream where she hadn't been lashed. But Whittle's belt had left little that wasn't dark with purple bruises, or welted, or striped with threads of dried blood. Her neck was rubbed raw from the noose. It was shiny red and oozing. My knees had looked like that, just the summer before, after I went chasing Tipper Bixley across Marylebone High Street and took a spill and scraped them up something awful. I wound up with scabs that lasted to the start of the school term.

Trudy's wrists were bruised and raw, too, but not near as bad as her neck.

I looked her over pretty good while I stuck food into her mouth. I wasn't quite fit as a fiddle, myself, but all that damage on Trudy made my heart ache. I felt so sorry for her. But mostly I felt guilty as sin. I'd done all this to her, just as surely as if I'd strung her up, myself, and given her the whipping.

'I won't let him hurt you again,' I said.

She chewed and swallowed. She looked into my eyes. All I saw in hers were tiredness and pain. She didn't say a thing. She didn't try to boss me or scold me or nothing.

It was just awful.

Whittle hadn't killed Trudy, but he'd sure taken the starch out of her.

When the last of the old stew was gone, she turned onto her back and covered herself to the chin. She stared up at the ceiling.

'Everything will be all right,' I told her.

I knew it was a lie. So did she, more than likely. But she didn't tell me so, just lay still and gazed.

Back in my bed, I licked the stew gravy and grease off my

hands. Then I spent a while licking my wrists, which were pretty much as raw as Trudy's.

I gave some thought to having another go at Whittle. But remembered all of what he'd done to Trudy after my last try.

If I should attack him again and muck it up, she would be the one to pay.

I decided to call it quits and behave.

Reckon I'd lost near as much starch as Trudy.

Chapter Ten

Patrick Joins Our Crew

By and by, Whittle came in. His arms were full of clothes, and he left the door open. 'Good afternoon, my friends,' he said, sounding wonderful chipper. 'I trust you slept well.'

With that, he commenced to split up his bundle, tossing garments and shoes onto our beds.

'You'll have free reign of the ship for a while,' he explained. 'We're anchored at Plymouth, and I've sent Michael ashore for all we'll be needing.'

He stood with his back to the doorway, watching as we sat up and dressed ourselves. He'd brought heavy sweaters for both of us, trousers for me, pantaloons and a skirt for Trudy, along with stockings and shoes. The clothes were too large for me. I reckoned they belonged to Michael or to Trudy's dead father. Michael, I hoped. It didn't set well, the idea of wearing a dead chap's duds. Why Whittle hadn't returned my own trousers to me, which would've fit properly, I didn't know. I allowed I wouldn't make a nuisance of myself, however, by asking.

He watched me cinch the belt tight.

'Should you consider using that to strangle me, please remember what came of your previous mischief.'

'You needn't worry,' I said. 'I'll not attack you again.'

'It will go very hard with Trudy, should you forget yourself.' With that, he patted the handle of the knife at his hip.

Trudy'd managed to get herself dressed, but she just sat on her bunk when Whittle told her to stand. He pulled her up. She hobbled, stiff and moaning, as he ushered her past me. I followed them out of the cabin.

He let her go alone into the lavatory. He shut the door and we waited in the narrow aisle. I saw he'd changed his bandage. The new one was fresh and white, without blood and such leaking through.

'I take it you've grown rather fond of Trudy,' he said.

'I shouldn't like to see her hurt, is all.'

'Such a gallant lad. I was quite impressed with your efforts to save her from hanging, last night.'

'You could've lent a hand.'

'Oh, but I had such a merry time watching.'

'We might have perished.'

He laughed and clapped my shoulder. 'Not allowed, my boy. Nobody dies while I am captain of the *True D. Light*.'

Trudy finally came out, and I got my turn. In a mirror above the wash basin, I took a gander at my face. It was a frightful sight, all puffy, dark with bruises, stained with dried blood. I cleaned off the blood, then sat down to relieve myself. I'd had no opportunity for that since setting off for Whitechapel. Two nights ago? Three? Sitting there, I realized I had no certain knowledge of how much time I'd spent aboard the yacht. I was aware of two nights passing, but others might have been missed while I was asleep or unconscious. Though I'd had little to eat and nothing whatsoever to drink during that period, the toilet proved itself welcome.

Done, I stepped out and was surprised to see that Trudy and Whittle had wandered off. I spotted them beyond a narrow doorway at the far end of a room considerably larger than the one where we'd so far spent our captivity. This, I supposed, must be the main saloon Trudy had mentioned last night.

It had berths along both sides which were more spacious than ours. One looked as if it had been slept in. No doubt, this was where Whittle had spent the night after returning Trudy and I to our beds.

There were cabinets, seats, a table, and even a gas burner which accounted for the warmer air in this section of the boat. Through portholes, I glimpsed other crafts anchored near ours. Thoughts of escape set my heart to pounding, but I pushed them away, fearful of the outcome for Trudy if I should arouse any suspicion or anger in Whittle.

I joined them in the kitchen – or galley, as Trudy had called it. The room was as wide as the main saloon, but not so long. At the far end, a few stairs led upward to a closed door.

The galley was equipped with a stove, a sink with water pumps, counters and cabinets. Whittle sat at a small table while Trudy stood at the stove, preparing ham and eggs.

Whittle gestured for me to sit down across from him. I did so.

'I'll have a dab more tea,' he said.

I filled his cup from the pot on the table, and eyed the cup in front of me.

'Do help yourself, Trevor.'

I poured steaming tea into my cup, and sipped at it.

'Had I known we'd be embarking on this little adventure,' he said, 'I should've asked Elsworth to join us. However, I fear I'll be forced to get along without his services. A fine fellow, Elsworth. What's to become of him? I didn't even find an opportunity to provide him with a reference.'

'Shall we go back for him?'

Whittle laughed. 'I think not.'

'Are you certain you wouldn't prefer to . . . return home?'

'You've made that rather impossible for me,' he said, and lightly fingered the bandage where his nose used to be. 'Besides, I've long had my heart set on America.'

'Why?'

'Just the place for a gentleman of my tastes. Particularly the Wild West, don't you know? Why, with any luck, my various depredations will be laid at the feet of the aborigines, the redskins. They're really quite keen on a wide variety of mutilations.' Whittle put down his cup and leaned toward me, his eyes agleam. 'I understand that they not only scalp their victims, but have been known to skin them alive, dismember them – oh, they have a jolly time of it.' He patted his lips with a napkin. 'Perhaps I'll join up with a band of marauding savages and show them a few new tricks.'

'Perhaps you'll find yourself scalped.'

That set him to laughing again. 'Oh, Trevor, you're marvelous. A fellow of infinite jest.'

I didn't care much for the reference to Yorick. After all, he was dead, nothing more than a skull, when Hamlet made that remark about him. Nevertheless, I judged I ought to count myself lucky that Whittle found me so amusing. It might help to keep me alive, at least for the duration of the voyage.

Trudy brought the food over. She sat down and joined us. We ate in silence for a while. It was wonderful to wrap my teeth around the hot eggs and ham. Trudy merely picked at hers. She seemed just as tired and gloomy as she'd been when I first woke her up.

'Why so downcast?' Whittle finally said to her.

She didn't answer. She just stared at her plate and pushed around a bit of egg.

Whittle smiled at her. Then he jabbed her arm with his fork.

She flinched and tears filled her eyes.

'Speak when you're spoken to.'

She nodded.

'Am I to take it you're not enjoying your voyage?'

'I . . . I'm not feeling well.'

'You *must* take better care of yourself.'

'You're going to kill me.'

'Not at all. Perish the thought. Perish it,' he said again,

and tipped me a wink. 'Even should I face a sudden urge to – how shall I put this tastefully? – *slice* your sweet flesh, why, I should most certainly resist it. I've already explained how important you are to the success of our venture. I must keep Michael cooperative, don't you know? Now there's a stout fellow,' he added, turning to me. 'I doubt he's slept a wink since we set sail, and I'm sure it's been no easy task to skipper this yacht single-handed. He's made quite a fine account of himself, all in all. And, unlike some I might mention, he's given me not a moment of aggravation.'

When we were done with the meal, Whittle set us to work. I pumped a bucket full of salt water at the galley sink, and went off to scrub the stew off the floor of our quarters. While I was busy at that, Trudy washed the dishes.

The scrubbing didn't take long. Whittle carried my bucket topside, going up the stairs and out the door at the rear of the galley. Then he came down and ordered Trudy to bake some loaves of bread.

'We'll be having company this evening,' he told her.

I saw some life come into her eyes. 'Michael will be eating with us?'

'More than Michael, I daresay. He's to fetch along an able-bodied seaman.'

I rather hoped he might fetch along, instead, a troop of constables. Or perhaps a concealed revolver.

'He was all done in, actually. I realized it would be the height of folly to attempt our crossing without an extra hand.'

'It's no less the height of folly,' I said.

As usual, he laughed.

'We'll all find ourselves in Davy Jones's Locker.'

'Full fathom five, is it?'

'Make sport of me, then. You'll be whistling a different tune when we capsize in a gale or fetch up on an iceberg.'

'We should take the southern route,' Trudy said, all at once showing some more interest in matters. Maybe my talk of going down had stirred her up.

'A southern route?' Whittle asked.

'Instead of making our way west, we should sail south to the Canaries.'

'A foul idea.' He eyed me, but I gave no hint that I'd caught on to his word-play.

'This is just the best possible season for it,' Trudy went on. 'We'd have fine, sunny weather for our crossing, and ride the tradewinds and currents all the way.'

'All the way to where, might I ask?'

'To the West Indies.'

'I've no use for the West Indies. Nor for the Canaries. The Canaries! Unless my schooling has been for nought, those islands lie off the coast of *Africa*! And they're in the control of the bloody Spaniards. Isn't that correct, Trevor?'

'Lord Nelson lost his arm there,' I pointed out.

'You see? That's no place for an Englishman. I'll have none of it.'

Trudy knew better than to push him. So she hauled out the flour, after that, and got started on the bread. Whittle stayed with her.

I went into the main saloon. It had a small library. I found a collection of tales by Edgar Allan Poe, set myself down and tried to read. Couldn't manage it, though. Here I'd been a day or two on the rough seas of the channel without so much as a touch of sickness, but trying to keep my eyes on the lines of a story while the boat was rocking ever so gentle put my breakfast in jeopardy. By and by, I gave up.

I just sat there thinking and worrying. When the nice smell of baking bread came along, it made me just so lonesome for home I near cried. Later on, Trudy staggered by. She didn't give me a glance or a word, but went straight to the forward cabin and plonked down on her bed. Whittle went topside.

He was up there for a long spell before he hurried down. He locked the door on Trudy, then said to me, 'Come along. Michael's returning.'

I followed him through the galley and up the stairs, coming out on a section of deck toward the rear of the yacht. I glimpsed the wheel and a passel of instruments. Didn't give them much of a look, though. It was the harbor that caught my eyes. Every sort of boat and ship was moored around us, plenty near enough to reach with a good, quick swim. The shore itself, with all its docks and markets and crowds, was less than a quarter mile off. The water looked gray and cold, but calm.

Well, I was sorely tempted to plunge in. I didn't have a single doubt but that I could make an escape. I'd be free of Whittle for good, I'd miss out on drowning in the Atlantic, I'd find my way home and be safe and Mother'd weep for joy at my return.

And Whittle'd likely open Trudy with his knife.

I told myself he'd do it anyhow, sooner or later.

But if he killed her on account of me . . . I just couldn't stomach the idea of that.

Besides, I judged that sooner or later, one way or another, I might somehow get to save her. Couldn't do that if I jumped ship.

That all went through my head as I went with Whittle to the stern and we stood there waiting for the skiff to reach us.

It had two men in it, so Michael'd found himself a hand for our trip. The broad-shouldered fellow had his back to me. A seam of his sweater was split. A tweed cap, tilted at a jaunty angle, topped his scraggly red hair.

The other sat at the stern, his head down. I took him for Michael, as he looked so thin and beaten-down.

The boat was fairly heaped with a seabag and all manner of bundles and kegs and boxes and sacks.

Whittle called, 'Ahoy!' That caused Michael to lift his head. He looked up at us. He was still a fair piece away, but the distance wasn't enough to stop me from seeing the dull, sorry look on his face. He said something to the oarsman.

That fellow checked over his shoulder. He seemed younger than Michael and not more than a couple years older than myself. His rosy face was rather square, with a wide nose and heavy chin.

'He's up and hired a bloody Irishman,' Whittle muttered.

'Perhaps the fellow's French,' I said.

He glared at me. 'Better that than an Irish addle-head. Blast him!'

As the skiff glided in close, we tossed out lines to Michael and his crewman. Before long, it was tied up snug alongside.

The Irishman smiled up at us and touched a finger to the small brim of his cap.

'And who have we here?' Whittle said, sounding miffed.

'Patrick Doolan, sir,' the fellow answered.

Turning his gaze to Michael, Whittle said, 'Were you unable to find a full-grown man?'

'He's an experienced sailor,' Michael explained, his voice weary. 'And he's eager to go to America.'

'If it's after a strong, hard-working seafarer you are, sir, you'll not find one in these parts the match of Doolan himself.'

Whittle groaned. But he laid off with the complaints, maybe figuring it wouldn't help any to turn Patrick against him.

Both fellows commenced to hand up the supplies, which we piled on the deck all around us. Each time I went back to the rail for another helping, I gave Michael a look. Not once did he have a pistol in his hand for blowing Whittle to kingdom come, so by and by I concluded either he'd had no luck in finding himself a weapon or he'd been too yellow to take any such risk.

I wondered what he might've told Patrick about our plight. More than likely, not a whit. Patrick went about his unloading chores as if he hadn't a care, all helpful and smiley.

Once the skiff was empty, we lowered a ladder over the side for Patrick and Michael to climb aboard. Then we towed the skiff along toward the bow. We hoisted it out of the water, turned it bottom-up and lashed it secure to the deck. Whittle had us tie it down directly on top of the forward hatch. His idea, more than likely, was to make things all the harder for Michael in case he might take a mind to open the hatch and let Trudy out.

Not that Michael had the sand for such a trick. He was shorter on gumption than any fellow I ever ran across.

Why, there wasn't a reason in the whole world he couldn't have fetched himself a pistol while he was ashore buying up supplies and looking for a crewman. If he'd done that, would've been no feat at all to put a ball of lead into Whittle. The man was a monstrous fiend, but not so powerful that a bullet wouldn't have laid him low.

Later on, when we were far out at sea and had a few minutes that the waves weren't trying to kill us, I asked Michael how come he hadn't latched onto a pistol back at Plymouth and filled Whittle with lead.

He gave me just the queerest look.

He said, 'I should've thought of that.'

He wasn't just a coward, but a numb-skull to boot.

Chapter Eleven

Patrick Makes his Play

By the time we got done stowing the gear and supplies, it was night. Trudy had stayed locked inside our quarters all the while. Whittle finally went and let her out, so she could make us supper.

Michael and Patrick both looked mighty shocked to see her. It seems like Patrick hadn't known, till then, we had a woman aboard. I'd gotten used to her battered face and skinned neck, but not so her husband or the Irishman. We'd gathered in the saloon and lit the lamps, so there was plenty of light for them to see her injuries by.

Michael let out a moan and rushed to her and threw his arms around her. She petted his hair and wept.

Patrick watched, frowning and looking confused.

Whittle watched, grinning. I don't know which amused him more, how those two were carrying on or how Patrick seemed so perplexed by such matters.

At length, Whittle said, 'They're husband and wife.'

Patrick nodded. 'And what is it that's befallen the lady, and yourself and Trevor? It's only Michael here that hasn't a bit of injury to him.'

'Young Trevor befell me,' Whittle said, and touched the bandage in the middle of his face. 'I befell Trevor and Trudy.'

Then he told all. He didn't fudge on a bit of it, but explained how he was the very same Jack the Ripper as had cut his way through the East End whores, and how I'd attacked him in the street and lopped off his nose, and how we'd come aboard the *True D. Light* where he'd slit Trudy's father with his knife and taken her prisoner, and how Michael had sailed us single-handed from London to Plymouth, and how Whittle himself had overpowered me and Trudy when we'd tried to mutiny on him, beating us and causing our injuries, and how the aim of it all was to sail for America where he might journey to the Wild West and cut up women all he pleased, like an Indian.

Well, Patrick sat silent, taking it all in. He frowned and bobbed his head and stroked his chin like he was getting a lesson in mathematics, maybe, and was working hard to keep it all straight.

'Is the situation quite clear to you now?' Whittle got around to asking him.

'Is it that you're a foul Devil of a murdering poltroon?'

Whittle smiled, 'Precisely.'

'And is it that you've slain this poor lady's own father and it was your own cruel hands that thrashed her so sorely?'

'Quite.'

'And will you make *this* clear to me?' he asked, drawing a knife from the scabbard on his belt. He was seated on the berth beside me, facing Whittle across the narrow aisle. Course, I'd seen he had a knife all along. Just show me a seaman without one. Whittle hadn't tried to get it off him, either.

Seemed a bit reckless, admitting all his crimes to an armed man – even if the fellow wasn't more than seventeen, and Irish.

Well, when Patrick pulled the knife, my heart commenced to wham like thunder. Michael and Trudy laid off hugging and kissing and weeping so they could watch. Whittle, he sat calmly and didn't even go for his knife.

Patrick pointed his blade at Whittle, shook it at him as he said, 'Will you make it clear to Doolan, here, why he ought to refrain himself from sending you down this minute to the fires of Hell which are surely waiting for you?'

'It's quite simple, really. I've no intention of harming you. You seem a fine, stout lad, and I'm sure you'll be a splendid addition to our merry crew. As for my crimes, I've committed none against you or your kin. You needn't bother yourself about them, really.'

'By all the saints, you're a strange one.'

'Oh, I agree. Strange, but not mad. I'm quite sensible, actually. Quite practical. I'm well aware that, for a successful passage, I must have the cooperation of everyone on board. To insure that, I'll be keeping Trudy close at hand. So long as I'm given no trouble, however, I'll not harm her. At the conclusion of the voyage, I'll take my leave of the three of you and we shall all be free to go about our business.'

'And it's your business to shed the blood of sorry, helpless women.'

'I'm not asking friendship of you, merely your help in seeing us safely across the sea.'

'Kill him!' Trudy ripped out.

I jumped half a mile.

Maybe Patrick had already made up his mind to go for Whittle. Or maybe he'd been about ready to put his knife away. But Trudy no sooner shouted 'Kill him!' than Patrick hurled himself at the Ripper, going for his throat with the blade. Quick as lightning, Whittle blocked Patrick's slash, snatched out his own knife and jammed it into Patrick's belly so hard it hoisted the young chap off his feet and made his cap fly off. Patrick gave out an awful grunt. As he folded at the middle, Whittle sprang up and hung on to him so he wouldn't fall and kept the knife in him and jerked it around some, making Patrick twitch and yell.

I got up quick, thinking to join in, but Whittle fixed me with a look that stopped me cold. Besides, I was too late to help Patrick.

Michael and Trudy, they weren't stirring themselves. They only just stood there, looking sick.

So I sat back down.

'Good lad,' Whittle said. He kept his hold on Patrick and stuck him ten or twelve more times. When Patrick was all limp and saggy, Whittle eased him down to the floor. There was more blood than I'd seen since Mary's room. It was too much for Michael. He heaved and got some on Patrick's head. Trudy just stood there and shook.

Whittle, he picked up Patrick's knife off the cushion.

'The ignorant sod,' he said.

Then he told me to give him Patrick's belt. I crouched down beside the poor fellow. His belt was all bloody so I got my hands red, but that didn't bother me much. I felt awful sorry for him. He looked so lonesome. His eyes were open, and full of surprise and sadness.

I hadn't known him more than a couple of hours, but I'd liked him. Seemed pretty clear to me that Trudy'd got him killed. I allowed I should try not to hold it against her, though.

Well, I got the belt off him and handed it up to Whittle. He buckled it around his waist, then shoved Patrick's knife into the leather sheath.

'I'm afraid we'll simply have to do without his services,' Whittle said. 'Trudy, I'm famished.' With his own bloody knife, he pointed to the galley.

'What about Patrick?' I asked.

'He won't be joining us.'

'Shouldn't we . . . do something with him?'

'He'll keep.'

Well, we left him and all went into the galley. I pumped out salt water and cleaned my hands, but Whittle kept his red. Trudy prepared our meal. There wasn't room for all of us at the table, so I ate on my feet. I had a rough time downing much, for I felt plain miserable about poor Patrick. I could see him sprawled out on the floor if I looked through the doorway. And Whittle wasn't much better of a sight what with his soaked sweater and how he piled food into his mouth with bloody hands.

I forced myself to clean my plate, anyhow. Michael and Trudy did the same, though they both looked a trifle green. Nobody said anything.

When we finished, it was clean-up time. Trudy had the easy job. She got to stay and wash the supper things. Seemed as how she rightly deserved to clean up the ugly mess in the saloon, her being the one that got Patrick killed. That job was given to me and Michael, though.

First off, Whittle told us to lug the body into the forward cabin.

'We'll heave it overboard,' he explained, 'once we're out to sea.'

I could see how it might be a risky business to drop Patrick in the harbor where we might get noticed, so I didn't complain but just grabbed his ankles and lifted. Michael took him by the wrists. We commenced to carry him along. My feet slid around on his blood, but I was careful not to step in any of Michael's mess.

We got him into the cabin and Whittle had us put him on the floor between the berths. This was *our* quarters, mine and Trudy's. I sure didn't relish the notion of spending the night in it, locked up with Patrick's remainders.

Turned out, it didn't come to that. Which should've been a relief to me, but wasn't much of one.

Michael and I, we shared a nasty time swabbing up the

floor of the main saloon. Whittle manned the bucket. He took it topside now and again to dump it over the side.

When he got done, he told Michael we wouldn't sail till dawn. That way, Michael could have a good night of sleep to get set for the voyage. I was to help out on deck.

Well, it came time to turn in.

Time for me and Trudy to get locked inside that tiny cabin along with Patrick.

What Whittle did, though, he told me and Michael to sleep in the saloon. Then he took Trudy along to our usual place, closed the door after they were both in, and locked it.

They were all three shut up tight together in that one little room.

We stared at the door for quite a spell. Finally, Michael sat down at the side of a bunk and hunched over and rubbed his face.

'We'd better get some sleep,' I said.

'He's a madman,' Michael muttered. 'Completely mad. And Trudy . . . oh, poor Trudy.'

'I'm sure he won't kill her.'

'Some things are worse than death.'

'That may be so, but if we bide our time and keep our eyes open for the proper opportunity, we might kill Whittle and save her yet.'

He gave me a sour look. 'It's your fault we're in this fix.'

'I'm terribly sorry for that,' I told him. 'However, we're in it, so we'll simply have to carry on.'

After that, he crawled under the covers. I shut down the lamps, and got into the other bed. I was no sooner stretched out and comfortable than there came a quick, high 'No!' from Trudy. Then Whittle let out just as mean a laugh as I'd ever heard.

That was the start of it.

For just the longest time, all manner of horrid sounds came through the dark from behind that door. Thumps. Shuffles. Whimpers. Trudy pleading and Whittle chuckling. Not a peep came out of Michael. He stayed in bed, but I didn't reckon he was any more asleep than me.

I took a notion to get up and listen at the door. The thing is, I didn't *want* to hear what was going on in there, so I gave up on the idea.

Well, Trudy fetched up a shriek that turned the marrow of my bones to ice. It ended with a hard clap. Next time she came out with one, the noise of it was soft and muffled, so I knew Whittle must've thrown a gag across her mouth. He'd likely done it to keep her from being heard by folks in the boats around us, or even ashore, she was that loud.

The gag quieted her down considerable, but didn't stop the yelps and squeals and howls. Every now and then, Whittle'd say something I couldn't quite make out. And he laughed and chuckled pretty often, like he was having himself a jolly time.

I lay there, trying hard not to wonder what he was doing with her. Couldn't get it out of my head, though, that whatever it was, it included Patrick.

By and by, I plugged my ears. That helped. Somehow, I got to sleep.

Chapter Twelve

Overboard

Come sunup, Michael woke me. I looked at the shut door, and then at him. He had misery all over his face.

'I'm sure he didn't kill her,' I said. 'He wouldn't do that. She's his only hold over us.'

'I don't wish to discuss it,' he told me.

Well, we went up on deck. The morning was cloudy, with a stiff breeze blowing. Seagulls were squawking away, and you could hear folks talking soft on boats all around us while they got ready to haul. It seemed mighty peaceful, but peculiar too. We were on a yacht chock full with madness and death, and nobody had a clue but us.

Michael didn't talk except to give me instructions. Together, we raised anchor and set the sails. He took the helm, and we fairly scooted clear of the harbor.

Later on, he sent me below to fetch coffee and food. No sign of Whittle or Trudy. Their door was still shut. And it stayed that way while I made up a pot of coffee and threw together some bread and marmalade. I used a dull little knife that didn't even have a point on it for spreading the jelly. But it gave me ideas, so I hunted high and low for a decent knife or any other thing that might do for a weapon. I came up with nothing but forks and dull knives. Whittle'd had plenty of time on his own, and must've scoured the galley to get rid of whatever might be turned against him.

I thought to give the saloon a going over, but held off, not wanting to risk it with the door so near. Besides, Whittle wouldn't have left any sort of weapon-like items lying about in there, either.

So I gave up, for the time, and carried our coffee and bread topside. It tasted mighty fine. We were cutting through the waves at a fair clip, the sails all billowed out pale in front of us, and my only care for a while was how to drink my coffee without spilling half of it.

I sort of let on, just in my own head, that me and Michael were a couple of buccaneers setting forth on a grand adventure. We were on our way to the Far Tortugas or the Happy Isles or somesuch, where there'd be warm breezes and long white beaches aplenty and whole scads of tawny-skinned native girls with bare breasts.

But I no sooner pictured those native girls than Mary's breast plopped down on the floor in front of my face, and that led to a raft of other thoughts, just as real and terrible, till there I was again on the Death Boat thinking about what I'd heard last night in the dark.

I saw we were empty, so I went down for more coffee. The door was shut yet. Just the sight of it gave me the fantods.

I didn't linger about, but hurried right up to the deck as fast as I could.

Later on, the coffee got to me. I couldn't bring myself to go below and take care of business. What they called the head was just too near that awful door. I feared it might open up in front of me and I'd have to see what was in there. So I did it over the side.

Michael had me take the helm while he did the same. After he was done, he let me stay and gave me lessons in a tired voice about how to steer and keep the canvas full. It was bully, actually. For a time, I got to forget about the horrors.

Land was still in sight, though a considerable distance off and not much more than a long smudge way out across the water. There weren't any other boats near enough to worry about smashing into. Now and then, the sun peeked out from among the clouds and felt uncommon warm and friendly. I did a fair job of steering us along, and Michael told me so, and I judged he wasn't such a sorry bloke, after all, even if he was a coward.

The whole while, we didn't speak a single word about Trudy or Whittle. They must've been on Michael's mind, though. They were sure on mine, like a heavy black ugliness that I couldn't shake off for more than a minute or two at a time.

The longer they stayed locked away, the worse it all seemed.

They didn't come out, and they didn't. The whole morning went by. Then the afternoon crawled along. I got hungry, but didn't mention it to Michael for fear he'd send me down to fetch food.

Near sundown, just after we'd passed Land's End, Trudy came up through the companionway. She was barefoot, so we didn't hear her. All of a sudden, she stepped out and was right there with us. We both gawped at her, but she didn't so much as look at us. She hadn't on a stitch of clothes. She was blood all over. It was mostly dried and brown. Her hair was caked with it.

She carried Patrick's head along with her, holding it against her belly by its ears.

Just as casual as you please, she walked past us real slow to the stern and dropped the head overboard. Then she stood there, feet spread and arms out to keep her balance on the pitching deck. She stood there and gazed out behind us. Like she was watching for the head to float off in our wake, though it must've sunk like a rock.

We didn't know Whittle was with us till he spoke up. 'Good day, me hearties,' he said, all full of vim and fun.

He gave us a smile. Only his teeth and eyes were white. The rest of his face and the bandage on it were stained with blood. He wore the sweater and trousers from yesterday. They looked stiff.

He just gave Trudy a glance, then swung his head about, surveying the sea. 'I trust you managed swimmingly in my absence.'

'My Lord, man,' Michael said, 'what have you *done* to her?'

Whittle smiled, nodded, and patted Michael's shoulder with a bloody hand. 'You needn't bother your . . .'

Splash!

We all jerked our heads aft. No Trudy.

Whittle muttered, 'Damnation,' Michael stood gaping like an idiot, and I went for the stern. Hanging on to the bulwark there, I studied the water behind us while I kicked off my shoes. I spotted her. Only just her head and shoulders. She was way back, and getting farther off every second. I skinned off my sweater and dove.

The cold water squeezed the breath right out of me. Coming up for air, I heard a call and glanced around. Whittle, at the rear, flung a life-ring after me. It landed short, so I had to lose some time swimming for it. While I did that, I saw Michael turning the boat so it wouldn't get away from us altogether.

With the life-ring tucked under one arm, I went for Trudy again. For a while, she was out of sight and I figured maybe she'd gone under for good. But then a wave picked me up high and I caught a peek at her.

If she'd meant to drown herself, she must've changed her mind. Otherwise, wouldn't she just have let herself sink? I wondered if she hadn't fallen overboard by accident, but then I judged she'd done it on purpose – if not to put an end to her miseries, then 'cause she simply couldn't stand all that blood on her body for even a second longer and had to either bathe it off in the ocean or die trying.

Each time a swell hoisted me, I got a look at her. The space between us shortened, but she was still a good piece off. The cold water stiffened me up something awful. She'd been in longer than me, so we didn't either of us have much time left. I figured it was all up, just about.

Well, then Trudy noticed I was coming after her. She hadn't seen me before, I reckon, on account of the rough waters. All of a sudden, she came swimming straight at me. It wasn't but a couple minutes before we joined up, and she hooked an arm through the ring.

We both hung on it, shivering and gasping for air. She didn't say a thing, not even to thank me. I didn't hold it against her, though. Neither of us was in any shape to talk, and besides, it was just her way not to appreciate a thing I ever did for her.

We clung to that ring like a couple of strangers. Now and then, our legs collided or tangled, the way we were kicking to help the floater stay up.

Each time the waves hoisted us, we got a look at the *True D. Light*. It came circling around real slow, and I didn't hold out much hope of it reaching us before we froze up and sank. But then one time we came out of a deep valley and there was Whittle rowing the skiff toward us.

And wasn't I glad to see him!

By and by, he paddled right up beside us. Trudy let go the ring. She grabbed an oar he held out to her, worked her way along it, and draped herself over the gunnel. The boat near capsized, but Whittle scurried to the other side and it was all right.

She didn't have a trace of blood on her. Not that I could see, and I guess I saw every part of her, pretty near, while she struggled into the skiff and then later, after I was in. I didn't see any fresh wounds, either. She had all the bruises and marks from the whipping and hanging Whittle'd given her, but nothing fresh. So every bit of the blood must've been Patrick's. In its own way, that was almost worse to think about than if the blood had come out of her own body.

Anyhow, froze up as I was, I somehow managed to haul myself into the skiff. We got the life-ring aboard, and then Whittle commenced to row us for the yacht.

I sat in the bow, hunched over and shaking apart. Trudy, she was on the other side of Whittle, lying on the bottom, curled and hugging her knees.

'You gave us an awful scare,' he told Trudy, but he sounded more like she'd given him a jolly show. 'This is rather inclement weather for a swimming party. Did you enjoy it?'

She didn't answer.

Her rump was in easy reach of his foot. He fetched it a smart kick that made her flinch. But she still didn't say anything.

He kicked her again. Then he laughed, and laid off conversation the rest of the way to the yacht.

Michael had reefed the sails, so the *True D. Light* was only moving around because of the currents and waves and such. When we came up alongside, he lowered the boarding ladder. I tossed him the bow line. He tied us up. Whittle climbed the ladder, leaving me with Trudy in the tossing skiff.

She only just laid there.

Michael stared down, all pale and hang-jawed, like Trudy was something strange and revolting.

He was no more use than a neck ache.

'Trudy,' I said, 'you've got to get up. We've reached the yacht.'

She might as well have been deaf.

'Help her,' Whittle called down to me.

It was what I'd aimed to do, anyhow. I couldn't see a way around it. So I kept low and made my way to where she lay. I crouched by her rump. 'Trudy?' I asked. 'Please get up.'

She didn't stir, not even when I put a hand on her cold hip and gave it a shake.

So then I pried her top arm away from her knees and hauled it toward me. She rolled. Her knees swung up and knocked me sideways. The gunnel jammed my ribs. Next thing I knew, my feet were kicking at the sky. Then I hit the ocean head-first.

I tumbled around underwater for a spell, clawed for the surface and banged my head on the underside of the skiff, and finally got to air. I reached for the skiff, but a wave snatched it away so I missed. Before my hand slapped down empty, what do you know if Trudy didn't reach out and catch my wrist.

It must've brought her senses back, knocking me overboard.

Whittle, he was up on the yacht, looking down at us and laughing like he might bust a seam.

Trudy towed me up close, till I could hook my elbows over the gunnel. Then she scooted to the other side to keep things steady. While I hung there, trying to squirm into the boat, she clutched me under the arms and hauled. She didn't let up, but kept pulling even when my head pushed into her breast. She squished me against her and helped me turn over and eased me down.

'Are you all right?' she asked.

I nodded up at her. She frowned down at me. And right then I forgave her everything and was mighty glad I'd worked so hard at saving her.

She crouched over me for a spell, then got up and climbed the ladder all by herself. I followed her up. I had one leg over the bulwark when Michael went to hug her and she slapped him across the face.

He stood there, blinking, and Whittle laughed, and Trudy went down below.

Whittle clapped me on the shoulder. 'You've done splendidly, Trevor,' he said. 'Go down, yourself, and bundle up, before you catch your death.'

He was the cause of all our troubles, but right then I near forgot how much I hated him. I hurried myself down the companionway.

I found Trudy in the saloon, squatting down to light the heater. All a-tremble, she shook out two or three matches trying. While she worked at that, I saw that the door to the forward quarters was open.

I turned away quick, though not quick enough by a long sight. Just a glimpse was too much. Not only Patrick's head was gone. He had no arms or legs, either. More was missing, but I don't aim to tell about that. And what was left of him had been split open and hollowed out considerable.

It made me plain sick to see such a thing. I dropped down onto the bunk I'd used last night, and remembered all the noises that'd kept me awake – Trudy whimpering and screaming and such. Much as I felt sorry for Patrick, I felt a lot sorrier for her. He'd been dead, and shut of the business. But poor Trudy, she'd had to watch and I didn't want to think about what Whittle must've done to her, or made her do.

She got the heater going, then took a couple of towels out of a cabinet and gave me one. I stripped off my wet trousers and socks. We both rubbed ourselves dry. We climbed under our covers, and didn't it feel fine to lay in a warm bed!

I thought to ask her what had gone on last night. Kept mum, though, figuring it wouldn't do her much good to talk about it and she more than likely wouldn't tell, anyhow.

So we just kept quiet.

By and by, Whittle came along with Michael.

'Oh, my God!' Michael blasted when he saw what was past the door. 'What did you *do* to him?'

'Why, I *ripped* him, of course.'

'Where's the *rest* of him?'

'Fish food, no doubt.'

He must've tossed the missing parts out a porthole. If he ate any, like he did with Mary, he didn't let on.

Michael came out with another, 'My God.'

'All the less for you to deal with,' Whittle told him.

'I don't see why *I* have to do it,' Michael whined.

'Would you rather I ask Trudy to clean up the leftovers?'

The way Michael didn't answer, I reckon he would've preferred it that way.

'And poor Trevor's all done in from the business of saving your bride from the ocean depths.'

'I belong at the helm,' Michael said.

'You belong where I tell you. I'm certain the boat will manage itself spendidly until you've finished.'

'Please. It's not . . .'

Whittle, he hauled off and kicked Michael's rump. That sent the fellow stumbling along. I bolted up to see better. At the doorway, Michael lost his feet altogether and, crying out, flopped down right on top of Patrick. He squealed like he'd been stuck, then took to blubbering.

I settled back down and turned my head away, not wanting to watch any more of this. Trudy, she'd pulled the covers over her face when the two first came in.

Pretty soon, Whittle said, 'You see? He's no trouble – hardly weighs more than a dog.'

Michael walked by me, gasping and sobbing.

When he and Whittle were gone, I looked and saw a trail of red drippings and other mess on the floor between our berths. I kept my eyes from wandering into the front cabin.

Pretty soon, along they both came again. This time, Michael carried a bucket and mop.

It was dark by the time he finished cleaning the place.

He never spoke a word to me or Trudy. But he sighed and sniffled considerable.

Whittle let me and Trudy stay warm in our beds till Michael was all done. Then he fetched us fresh sets of clothes. We got up and dressed ourselves. Trudy made supper. We all ate, and then he sent Michael and me topside to get us under way again.

Michael didn't say one thing about any of what had happened that day. He gave me orders and instructions, and that was it.

Once we were sailing along nicely, he turned over the helm to me. He said we'd man the boat in shifts, three hours at a turn. If I should run into any trouble, I was to fetch him quick. Then he went below.

I was glad to be rid of him. I kept my eyes on the compass and sails, and kept us heading in the proper direction, more or less, until he showed up to relieve me.

Whittle and Trudy weren't to be seen. The door to their cabin was shut. I climbed into my bunk in the saloon. Tonight, no sounds came from the other side of that door. And I knew they didn't have Patrick in there with them any more, which was a mighty relief.

Chapter Thirteen

High Seas and Low Hopes

Michael kept a ship's log. I saw plenty of it, for he scribbled on it every day. It didn't say much, mostly just gave our location in degrees of latitude and longitude, which he figured out somehow by using a sextant along with various tables and charts. He tried to figure that stuff out each day at noon if the sun was showing. That wasn't often, let me tell you. But it came out now and again, and we stayed on course.

We were making for New York Harbor, which is where

Michael and Trudy and her father had set out from when they left for England, and Whittle said it suited him fine.

The trip took us thirty-six days and nights and seemed to last about ten years.

It was pretty much the same routine the whole time except when we hit storms. Michael and I took turns at the helm, though it seemed like we spent hours each day fooling with the sails, raising and lowering them because we wanted to keep as much sail flying as we could, but had to reef the mainsail whenever the wind kicked up too hard.

Trudy fixed all our meals. When she wasn't busy with that, she came topside and stood look-out. Whittle shared the look-out duties with her. We all took our turns at it, for none of us was eager to fetch up on an iceberg. We ran into a passel of those, and steered clear of them.

We all got along the best we could, pitching in to help each other, and such.

Trudy stayed cold toward Michael for a spell, holding it against him that he hadn't jumped in the ocean to save her instead of me doing it, I reckon. She never did warm up to me. When she wasn't bossing me around, she acted like I wasn't there at all. She was always civil and meek to Whittle, and didn't once give him any lip.

Michael acted like a whipped dog around Trudy and Whittle both. If he'd had a tail, it would've been drooping between his knees most of the time. He sure knew how to sail the yacht, though. He'd turn into a man again when nobody was around but me and all he had to do was navigate and steer and muck about with the sails or rigging, and give me orders. The dicier it got with the weather, the better he handled himself. Why, you never would've guessed he had a yellow streak at all if you could've seen him skippering us through a gale with waves higher than mountains. Then later on you'd see how a look from Trudy or Whittle made him wither, and you just couldn't believe it.

Whittle, he acted the whole voyage like he was having just the bulliest time ever. He paraded about like Long John Silver himself, a knife on each hip, and hardly a word ever passed his lips that wasn't an 'Aye, matey' or an 'Avast, me hearties' or a 'Shiver me timbers'.

Whereas pirate sorts generally sported an eyepatch, Whittle took to wearing one where his nose used to be. After he'd healed enough to stop bandaging himself, he fashioned a whole variety of patches that he tied onto his face. One day, he'd be sporting a disk of red silk. The next, he might have one made of white lace or leather or velvet or tweed. I don't suppose Trudy had a dress or petticoat or blouse or hat or shoe that didn't wind up with a round hole in it the size of a gold piece. She wore some of those things after Whittle'd been at them, and you could see where he'd gotten the material for this or that nosepatch.

Every so often, when he was feeling ornery or full of mischief, he'd take and pluck his patch up to his forehead and make us sick.

Taken all round, though, he behaved a sight better than I might've expected from the likes of him. He'd come near losing Trudy and me, that first day out of Plymouth. If we'd gone and drowned on him, it would've put an awful wrinkle in his plans. I figure he realized that, and chose not to push his luck. He went ahead and gave us a fair share of thumps and kicks, but he never tormented any of us much – not as I knew about, leastwise.

Each night, he took Trudy into the forward cabin and locked the door, leaving the saloon as sleeping quarters for me and Michael when we weren't taking our turns topside. I never heard much out of her, though. When she'd come out the next day, she didn't look like she'd been strung up or otherwise abused.

Her neck got better slowly. By and by, the scabs fell off and her skin was pink and shiny across her throat.

As for me, I behaved. Plenty of chances came along for me to bash Whittle or shove him overboard, but I always resisted. Whenever a chance showed itself, all I had to do was remember how he'd dealt with Patrick, or how he'd punished

Trudy after I'd failed at garroting him. It was never a sure thing that a bash or push would've put an end to him, so I never dared.

When things got slow and I had time for my mind to wander, I often longed for home. But I grew curiouser, all the time, about America. I'd read a heap of books about the place. It sounded grand, and I allowed what a shame it'd be to travel so far and only just turn around, first chance, and return to home. The plan I hit on was to send off a message to Mother, letting her know I wasn't dead, after all, and then explore around a bit.

I'd no sooner get excited about all that, however, than the glooms would set in. I judged I was bound to end up killed and never reach America. If the ocean didn't swamp us, Whittle'd carve us down to torsos once he stopped needing a crew.

My odds were on the ocean, though.

It never let up. At the best of times, it shoved us up and down and jolted us and pitched us from side to side. At the worst of times, it gave up toying around and did its best to demolish us. While that was going on, you'd never see hide nor hair of Whittle or Trudy. They'd be hiding down below with the door shut tight while Michael and I worked like mad, tied to safety lines so as not to get swept overboard. One of us would wear out our arm on the bilge pump while the other manned the wheel, and sometimes one or the other of us had to climb in the rigging or go up the mast, and wasn't that just the most fun?

There were times my heart near gave out from the fright of it all, when we'd be in that tiny boat at the bottom of a gorge, the waves like cliffs looming over us, and then one would avalanche down on top of us, or almost, but more often than not we'd go sliding up a slope and hang on the crest and go shooting straight down into the next chasm, diving down so steep it seemed we might flip end over end, or strike the bottom so hard the boat would fly all to flinders.

The wind, it'd be shrieking through rigging like a banshee.

Water'd be smashing against us, trying to tear us loose and throw us into the seas. By the time it'd all ease off, we'd be dripping icicles off our noses and hair, and near dead.

We'd get maybe a day or two of normal roughness, and then we'd find ourselves in just such another fix and it's a mighty wonder the *True D. Light* didn't give up and call it quits and fall apart underneath us. But she held together, and so did we somehow.

It's a plain miracle, is all I can say, that we were all still alive to look out and spot land off in the far distance on the thirty-sixth day of our voyage.

Chapter Fourteen

Our Last Night on the *True D. Light*

As Whittle wanted no truck with Customs people or any other brand of officials, he decided we ought to avoid the New York harbor and pick a section of shoreline where we weren't likely to get noticed.

So we hung well off the coast till after sundown. Then Michael steered us into a place he said was Gravesend Bay. We went in behind a jut of land for shelter from the wind and rough seas. There, a couple of hundred yards from the mouth of Coney Island Creek, Whittle had us reef the sails and drop anchor.

Safely moored on the quiet waters, we went below and ate our last meal aboard the *True D. Light*. I didn't have much stomach for food. On the one hand, I was mighty glad to be shut of the ocean at last. It had done its most to kill us, but we'd gotten across alive. On the other hand, though, Whittle'd had uses for us when we were on the high seas. Now, he didn't need a crew or cook or captive. He didn't need us at all. That dampened my appetite considerable.

I could see that Michael and Trudy were worried, too. They fidgeted and picked at their food and didn't say much. Nobody asked what Whittle aimed to do. None of us had the grit, I reckon. Maybe they were like me, and figured talking about it might only serve to give him ideas. Maybe if we just let it lie, he'd forget it was about time to kill us all.

When Whittle finished eating, he patted his lips with a napkin and sighed. He wore a flimsy silk nosepatch that I reckoned had left a good pair of Trudy's bloomers with a hole in them. It kind of drooped in the middle and clung to his tiny nubs at both sides, but puffed out like a sail when he sighed.

'Taken all around, me hearties,' he said, 'it's been a marvelous voyage. You were fine shipmates and companions. I daresay I'll be quite sorry to take my leave of you. However, all good things must come to an end.'

Trudy, she turned a shade of gray and caught her lower lip between her teeth.

Whittle gave her a cheery smile. 'You've nothing to fear, Trudy. Am I so ungrateful as to harm you now that we've reached safe harbor? I may indeed have some mischievous ways about me, but I am not a heartless fiend. I count you as my friend. I count you *all* as my friends,' he added, nodding and smiling at Michael and me. 'We've sailed the vast reaches of the sea together – we band of brothers. And sister,' he added, tipping Trudy a wink. 'We honored few.'

He went on spouting such rubbish for a spell. He laid it on thick as molasses about how highly he thought of us and how grateful he was and how we were his comrades and mates and chums and how he wouldn't even *think* about hurting us in any way. Well, he jabbered on about it till I lost any doubt but what he aimed to kill us all.

Finally, he yawned and said, 'I'm all done in. I suggest we

retire for the night. We'll rise early, for I'm quite keen to be on my way. Just before dawn would seem the best time to set out, I should think. I'll take the skiff ashore, and you three may carry on as you fancy. Make for the city or the warm Carib or Timbuktu, it's all the same to me.'

Trudy was set to clean the supper dishes, but Whittle told her there was no need. Then he led her off.

Michael watched her go. From the look on his face, he figured he was never going to see her again. Not alive, anyhow.

As soon as Whittle shut the door, I said, 'We've got to save her. There's no time to lose.'

In a snap, his face changed. He wiped off his sorrow and hopelessness, and came up looking all superior and scornful. 'Don't be ridiculous,' he said.

'If we don't stop him, he'll butcher her. You know it as well as I do.'

'He'll do no such thing.'

I was plain astonished. Shouldn't have been, though. I'd seen enough of Michael to know he had no spine when it came to dealing with Whittle. 'We can't sit here and allow her to be killed!'

'Don't raise your voice to me, boy.'

'Do you *wish* him to murder Trudy? You saw how he carved up poor Patrick Doolan.'

His face went a bit slack at the reminder of that.

'*I* saw the work he did on a London whore. Why, he just carved her up something awful. He even *ate* parts of her. I heard him do it. He'll do the same to Trudy if we don't stop him.'

'Nonsense,' he muttered.

But I could see he believed me.

'Trudy will be perfectly fine,' he said, 'so long as we do nothing to rock the boat.'

'We might have a go at burning it,' I said. 'If we set a fire . . .'

'Are you mad?'

'I've given it quite a bit of thought.' I told him. It was the truth. Thirty-six days on the Atlantic had given me plenty of time to hatch schemes, for I'd known it would come down to this if we lived through the voyage. 'Once we get the fire going, we'll cry out an alarm. Whittle, he'll come leaping out through the door all in a heat to save himself. He won't care a bit about killing Trudy. One of us will be waiting topside to bring Trudy up through the hatch.'

'The skiff's on top of the hatch,' Michael pointed out. He sounded tired and annoyed.

'Why, don't you think I know that? We move it clear before we light the fire.'

'Whittle would hear the commotion.'

'We'd need to be quite stealthy about it.'

'The hatch may be locked from below.'

'Trudy can handle that.'

'Suppose she can't? Just suppose we're unable to open the hatch, and she's trapped by the fire. And where is Whittle through all this? If he gets past the fire, he'll come topside and then we'll be in a fix.'

I had already considered that. 'We block the companionway door. He might not be able to break through it at all before the fire gets him. And if he does, it should still delay him and give the three of us time to escape in the skiff.'

It was quite a bully scheme, actually. I'm sure Huck Finn would've been proud of me. And Tom wasn't here to ruin it with fancy trimmings. Neither of them were here, except in my head. My only audience was Michael.

While I explained how we'd keep Whittle below with the fire and make our getaway, he simply scowled and shook his head.

'It's too risky,' he finally said.

'It's time for risks,' I told him. 'Unless you're eager to have Trudy cut into pieces, we'd better have at it.'

He only just sat there and kept on shaking his head.

'Do *you* have a plan?' I blurted out.

'The only sensible thing is to leave Whittle be. He promised he wouldn't harm Trudy. In the morning, he'll row ashore and that will be the end of it.'

'It's certain to be the end of Trudy long before that.'

'We've no choice but to trust Whittle and hope for the best.'

'I'll do it myself, then.'

With that, I hurried on over to the stove and grabbed some matches. Michael went after me into the saloon. There, I snatched a book down from the cabinet. It was an Emerson. I'd never had much use for him, anyhow. I tore out pages by the handful, crumpled them and piled them up on the floor between the berths. While I worked at that, Michael pranced around me, fuming and railing at me in a hushed voice so Whittle wouldn't hear. He said, 'Stop this nonsense,' and, 'Don't you dare,' and, 'You'll be the death of us all,' and such. But I went on with what had to be done. I was yanking a cover off one of the bunks when he jumped me from behind.

He hooked an arm across my throat and commenced to choke me. I went wild, thrashing and kicking. I tried to tear his arm clear so I could breathe, but that was no use. I went at him with my elbows, punching them backward. Got in a few good licks. He never let up, though. He kept on squeezing till I thought my eyes might pop out. I saw some dandy fireworks. They went off with crashes like cannons, which weren't cannons at all but my heart thundering.

Well, I allowed I'd had it. Seemed mighty peculiar that I'd gone and gotten myself killed by Michael instead of by Whittle, and all I'd hoped to do was save the hide of his wife.

All of a sudden, I wasn't aboard the *True D. Light* any more. I was standing in an East End alley with my back to a wall, looking at the fellow I'd stabbed. He was sitting in a puddle, hunched over. He said, 'You gone and killed me is what you done.'

I felt mighty sorry for him and wished I hadn't done it.

Then I was on my back, Michael crouched over me and pulling off my belt. All I could do was fight to suck in air. He propped me up and crossed my hands in front and wrapped the belt around me. He cinched it in tight and buckled it. Then he hoisted me onto the bunk.

I lay there, glad to be alive and figuring him for the biggest fool that ever drew a breath.

He should've helped me, not throttled me.

Well, he put what was left of Emerson back into the cabinet. Then he picked up all the paper balls and took them topside, where I guess he pitched them overboard. He didn't want any evidence left around to upset Whittle, I reckon.

When he came back, he bent over me and made sure I hadn't slipped my arms out of the belt. 'Now you lie still,' he said. 'If you give me any more trouble, I'll pound you silly.'

He got under his own covers. But he left the gaslamps burning so he could keep an eye on me.

No sounds came from the other side of the door. If Whittle'd already killed Trudy, he'd been quiet about it and done it so quick she never got a chance to let out a yelp.

Maybe he'd told the truth, though, and aimed to row away in the morning and leave us alive.

But I knew the stripe of Whittle.

Trudy was either dead by now, or soon would be.

By and by, I figured it was too late for doing her any good. Or any harm, either. I felt awful about that.

Trudy'd been bossy and annoying, and hadn't lent a hand the time I had my chance to strangle Whittle. She'd never acted friendly toward me at all unless you count the time she helped me onto the skiff after she'd knocked me overboard. Even still, I never hated her. I only felt sorry for her, mostly, and blamed myself near as much as Whittle for her miseries. I'd saved her from hanging and from drowning, and I might've saved her from Whittle's knife tonight if Michael hadn't stopped me.

Resting there on the bed I still wanted to have a go at saving her. But I didn't see how I could manage it, not with Michael set to get in my way. Besides, I figured Whittle'd already had plenty of time to cut her up.

I decided I might as well write her off and do what I could to save myself.

It didn't take much work to squeeze my arms out from

under the belt. Michael had his head turned toward me. What with the dim light and shadows, I couldn't see whether his eyes were open or shut. He didn't move or raise a fuss, though, so I figured he must've fallen asleep.

After I'd pulled my arms free, I sat up and slipped the belt around to get at its buckle. I unfastened that, then put the belt where it belonged so I wouldn't lose my trousers.

Then I swung my feet down and took off my shoes. My notion, you see, was simply to dive overboard and swim for land. Would've been too dicey, trying for the skiff. But I'd take the life-ring along with me. And my shoes. I was busy tying their laces together so I could hang them around my neck. That's when a key rattled in the door lock.

Right quick, I scurried under my covers and pulled the shoes in with me. I shut my eyes, letting on to be asleep.

The door bumped shut. 'Rise up, maties,' Whittle said, just as cheery as you please. 'The time has come for my departure.'

I yawned and rubbed my eyes. 'Is it morning?' I asked, though I knew it wasn't.

'Why wait any longer? I'm eager to be on my way.'

Whittle stood with his back to the door. He wore his overcoat. It hung open. There was no blood on his sweater or trousers, nor on his face or hands. Both the knives in his belt had clean handles. I took all that for a good sign. It gave me hope, for just a bit, but then I figured he would've stripped naked for the butchery like he'd done that night in Mary's room. He always kept drinking water in the cabin, too, so he might've used it for washing. That sank my hopes some.

Michael sat up and looked at the door.

'Trudy's fast asleep,' Whittle said. 'Her assistance won't be necessary.' With a smile, he added, 'I rather imagine she'll be quite overjoyed when she awakens and learns of my departure. If we're very quiet about the preparations, perhaps we won't disturb her.'

I wished I could believe him.

He hadn't locked the door after coming out, but he stayed

in front of it as Michael and I climbed out of our beds. I'd untied my shoe laces while he was talking, so he didn't catch on that they'd been laced together. I brought them out from under the covers with me, and put them on.

He kept his post at the door and ordered us about, his voice low as if he was being careful not to wake Trudy.

Earlier in the day, he'd loaded a large valise, filling it with clothes and loot. The clothes were mostly Michael's, as he was about the same size as Whittle and the father's duds were too big. The loot was all the money and jewels he'd found aboard the yacht, which was considerable. Michael, Trudy and her father, they'd been rich from the father's hotel business in New York City. They'd brought along tons of money, not to mention a scad of necklaces and earrings and brooches and bracelets and such so Trudy could fix herself up splendid for dress-up affairs. Whittle, he'd spent some spare time during the voyage hunting around for all the valuables. After finding what he could, he'd asked Trudy about hiding places where there might be more, and she'd obliged him by opening up some secret compartments. So he probably had every bit of it, now, in his valise.

Following his orders, Michael carried the case topside and I went up after him, empty-handed. He had Michael set it down by the stern. Then the three of us made our way forward.

It was a calm night, but mighty cold. Not another boat was in sight. A few lights glowed along the shore and inland. I sure wished I was there among them, and judged this might be as good a time as any for a swim.

But I held off, concerned about Trudy. Maybe Whittle hadn't killed her yet.

Maybe, instead of abandoning ship, I ought to have a go at throwing Whittle overboard.

I glanced back at him. He had a knife in his right hand. Not hankering to catch it in my belly, I went on after Michael to where the skiff was secured. Whittle used his knife to cut the ropes. Then he stood back and watched while Michael and I turned the skiff right-side up. We worked at it slowly, being careful not to raise any sound. Trudy was just beneath the deck from us, after all. Being quiet with the skiff seemed like a way to trick our minds into thinking she was only asleep.

We lowered the skiff over the side. Whittle walking in front of me, Michael behind, I towed the skiff by its bow line to the stern.

Whittle told me to tie it. While I did that, he told Michael to pick up the valise. I thought he aimed to have Michael climb down and load it into the skiff for him. But when Michael bent over to grab the handle, Whittle stepped in quick and slashed a knife across his throat. Michael straightened up quick and stood rigid, his mouth wide like he was mighty surprised. Blood squirted out of his ripped neck. Whittle danced out of its way and whirled toward me.

Well, I flung myself backward. The bulwark caught me behind the knees. As I pitched over the side, Whittle reached and clutched the front of my sweater. He tugged at it, trying to pull me up. But the sweater only just stretched, and I kept falling. So he shoved the knife into my belly. Or tried. Its point jabbed the back of my forearm, instead. I gave out a yell and kicked at him and he let got and I dropped headfirst.

My head missed the skiff. But my shoulder fetched it a hard thump that sent it scooting. I plunged down into the cold water between it and the starboard side of the yacht.

I was mighty shocked at how sudden he'd killed Michael and made his play for me. My shoulder hurt like it had gotten clubbed by a cricket bat. My arm hurt, too. And the water plain froze me. In spite of all that, I felt a trifle thrilled that I'd made it overboard alive. I'd gotten clear of Whittle, and that was what counted the most.

The ticket, now, was to *stay* clear of him.

So instead of popping up for air, I swam underwater to where I thought the yacht ought to be. I got my shoes off, then let myself rise, arms overhead. Sure enough, my fingers met the bottom of the hull. It was all slimy, and rough with barnacles. I kept under there, feeling my way around. When I found the rudder, it told me which way to go. I turned myself around and headed the other way.

Whittle likely figured he hadn't killed me. He'd be up there, waiting. So it didn't seem smart to surface where he might spot me.

I worked my way toward the bow, walking my hands along the hull and kicking a bit. The *True D. Light* had seemed awful tiny when we were out in the ocean getting knocked about by giant waves. Underneath it, though, with my air running out, it felt ten miles long. I reckoned my chest might explode before I got to the front of it.

Finally, though, the hull narrowed down to its prow. I let my head come out of the water on the port side, gave a quick look around and didn't see either Whittle or the skiff. After breathing for a spell, I went down again and hid under the hull for as long as I could stand it. Then I came up for another breath and went down again. I must've done that twenty times, till once when I was up for air I heard the splash of oars nearby. Over on the other side of the prow. Well, I ducked under and held my breath forever.

Down there, I couldn't hear the oars. But I judged that Whittle was in the skiff, circling the yacht, scouting for me. Finally, I judged he must've had time to pass the bow, so I scooted over to the starboard side before bobbing up for air. He wasn't in sight.

No sound of oars, either.

I hung there for a while, then peeked around the end of the bow.

There was Whittle, a hundred feet off, rowing for shore.

Chapter Fifteen

On My Own

Whittle was almost to shore when I climbed the anchor chain and crawled onto the deck. If the water'd been cold, the air felt twice as bad. I didn't linger, but scurried along to the stern, keeping low in case Whittle might have an eye on the yacht.

Michael, he was sprawled out and still. Nothing to do for him. He was in the hands of Providence, now. So after a quick look to make sure Whittle hadn't turned around, I hurried below.

The heater was on, but it didn't give off enough warmth to stop my shudders. Real quick, I stripped off my duds and grabbed a towel out of a storage compartment. While I rubbed myself dry, I kept looking at the shut door to the forward cabin. I didn't want to see what was on the other side of it.

With a strip of sheet from my bunk, I bandaged my forearm. Then I put on some dry clothes. Didn't they feel just fine! They were the father's, and awful big on me, but I'd gotten used to wearing the dead man's things for I'd worn this or that of his almost every day of the voyage. I cinched in the trousers with a belt, and turned the cuffs up the way I'd always done. Then I got into his best shoes. Whittle had taken all Michael's spares, except the pair I'd had on when I went overboard. Those were at the bottom of the bay, and I didn't relish the notion of stealing the shoes off his body. So these would have to do, even though they fit loose.

Last, I put on the father's heavy coat.

That took care of getting myself dry and warm. There was nothing left but only to check on Trudy.

111

All tight and sick inside, I went to the door. I knocked on it. She didn't answer, so I rapped harder. Then I called her name a few times.

Nothing.

Well, I took hold of the door handle and tried to make myself turn it. I just couldn't though. Pretty soon, I gave up.

Topside, I searched the dark waters for Whittle and his skiff. They were nowhere to be seen.

So what I did, I raised the anchor and set the mainsail. No easy job, but it beat taking a swim. At the helm, I steered for a piece of shore far away from where Whittle'd been headed.

I picked a long stretch of beach that didn't have any lights nearby. It took a spell to get there, but by and by I ran the *True D. Light* straight up onto the sand. She scraped along and stopped with a rough jolt.

Well, I rushed to the prow, all set to leap off and skedaddle before somebody might show up.

But then I got to thinking about Trudy.

I knew she was dead. But I didn't know *for sure*.

So I hurried down below again, and this time I didn't knock or call her name or give myself time to lose my nerve. I just swung the door open wide and looked in.

Even though I'd seen Whittle's work on Mary, it didn't make me ready for this.

With a yell, I spun around and heeled it, in such a lather to get away that I stumbled as I raced up the companionway stairs and barked a shin. I gave Michael a last look, and allowed he was lucky to be dead.

Then I dashed along the deck to the prow and jumped.

The beach knocked my legs out from under me. I landed on damp, cold sand, picked myself up quick and took just a few running strides toward the distant trees. Then I stopped.

Instead of rushing inland, I headed to the right.

Toward the area where Whittle must've landed his skiff.

All along, I'd reckoned it would take a miracle to survive the voyage. If the ocean didn't kill me, Whittle would do the job with his knife. Now I was clear of them both. Safe on land in America.

But Whittle was here, too.

Much as I wanted to be shut of him forever, it was me who had brought him aboard the *True D. Light*, me who had gotten Michael and the father murdered, me who had failed to save Trudy.

Walking brisk along that beach, leaving the yacht behind with its horrid cargo, I knew it was me who had to track down Jack the Ripper and put an end to him.

Part Two

The General and His Ladies

Chapter Sixteen

The House in the Snow

I hadn't walked far before snow started coming down. Not much at first, but soon the night was just thick with big white flakes so I couldn't see more than a few yards in front of me.

It seemed like a good thing. If Whittle was lurking about, up ahead, he wouldn't have much luck at spotting me through the heavy downfall. Maybe I could sneak up on him.

I grabbed a chunk of driftwood to use for a club, and shoved a few rocks into the pockets of my coat. They didn't amount to much as weapons go. They'd do just dandy, though, if I could catch him by surprise.

Having such things gave me a sense of power that made me realize just how helpless I'd felt during those weeks on the yacht.

It sank in that I was actually free. Not a prisoner trapped aboard a boat. Not a lackey who had to obey orders and watch my step, always worried Whittle would punish Trudy if I didn't behave.

He couldn't hurt her now. He'd done his worst to her. As horrible as that was, it had taken away his only hold on me.

So I wasn't his slave any more. I was myself again, Trevor Wellington Bentley. Free. If I had a mind to do so, I could walk away and likely never set eyes on Whittle again.

If I had a mind to. Which I didn't.

The end of my slavery meant I was free to be a hunter. That was all I cared to be – a hunter of Whittle. I figured I'd stalk him forever, if that's how long it took.

By and by, I got to *hoping* he'd hung around the shore and seen me beach the *True D. Light*. I hoped he'd decided to lay for me. I hoped he might come leaping at me through the falling snow. Just let him. He would catch a couple of rocks in the face for his trouble, and once he was down, I'd bash his head to pudding.

All my eagerness for that skipped out on me, though, when I came to the skiff. The sight of it turned me cold and trembly. I filled my right hand with a rock and twisted around in circles, scared to death he might jump me, wishing the snow would let up so I could see him coming.

When nothing happened, I settled down some and gave the skiff a study. It had been dragged up the sand a few yards beyond the reach of the waves. It was empty except for the oars and a puddle of water that had collected near the stern. The puddle looked black. The snowflakes melted away when they fell on it, but otherwise the bottom of the boat, the bench seats and the tops of the oars all wore smooth, pale mats of snow.

I circled the skiff, looking for footprints. The only ones I found were my own. This near the water, the sand was stiff and hard, so Whittle wouldn't have left much in the way of impressions and what there might've been was hidden under an inch or more of snow.

As he'd left no tracks for me to follow, I put myself in his place and reckoned he had likely headed straight inland. He would want to put distance between himself and the bay, figuring the yacht might be found at daylight. What with the bodies on board, things could get hot for strangers in the area.

That goes for me, too, I realized.

It wasn't a comforting notion.

I put my back to the bay and started to march. Trekking over the dunes, my night in Whitechapel came back to me as clear as if it had been yesterday. The part about getting chased by the mob that mistook me for the Ripper. That had been an awful dicey time, and it had only been luck, mostly, that saved me. Well, I didn't need much imagination to see how I could find myself blamed for the killing of Trudy and Michael.

What if they grabbed me for it? How could I prove it was Whittle, and not me, who'd done such foul deeds? Maybe I'd end up swinging at the end of a rope.

When all that sank in, I allowed I had plenty more to worry about than tracking down Whittle.

The trick was to keep clear of everyone, at least until I could put some miles between me and the *True D. Light*.

It seemed like a mighty fine plan, but it flew all to smash the moment I came upon the house.

What I found, first, wasn't the house but a low stone wall that blocked my way. It stretched out in front of me for as far as I could see through the snowfall. My first thought was to pick one direction or the other and hike around it.

After all, the wall hadn't just grown out of the ground by itself. Someone had built it, and that meant there must be people nearby. I'd aimed to avoid people.

Then I figured that if Whittle'd come this way, he might've seen things different. What if he saw the wall as a sign that a house was close, and went looking for it? Maybe a house was just what he wanted – a place to get out of the weather and warm himself up, maybe have himself a good meal and a sleep. Maybe have himself a high time butchering whoever lived there.

Well, I climbed to the other side of the wall and went searching. I kept an eye out for footprints, but didn't find any. What with the darkness and the heavy falling snow, there wasn't much to see at all. Besides, Whittle'd likely had a good headstart on me. He might've passed through here before the snow'd hardly commenced to fall.

And everybody in the house – if there *was* a house and folks inside it – might be dead by the time I got there.

By and by, I figured there had to be a house. The area was planted with trees and shrubs, some of which gave me an awful start when they sort of loomed up and I took them for Whittle. There were some sheds, too. And a gazebo. And a walkway that only showed because some overhanging limbs kept the snow off its flagstones.

Finally, the house turned up. It looked to be made of stone, and maybe a couple of stories tall. Standing at the foot of the porch stairs, I could only see as high as an upstairs window, and that was dark. There didn't seem to be any light at all coming from this side of the house. The corners of its wall were out of sight.

I checked the porch stairs. The snow on them was thick and smooth, trackless.

I climbed three stairs, then got a sudden case of the fantods, so I backed down.

No point rushing things. The last time I'd gone sneaking into a stranger's digs, that's when I'd gotten mixed up with the Ripper in the first place. Seemed the wiser course to scout around before making up my mind as to whether I ought to try the house.

With that in mind, I headed off to the right. The windows along the ground floor were high enough so I didn't need to duck. They were all dark. At the corner, I turned and made for the front. The windows along this wall were dark, too. A couple of times, I stepped back and looked up. Didn't seem to be any lighted windows upstairs, either.

Well, it stood to reason. If a family was in there, they all would've turned in by now. I hoped they *were* asleep, and not slaughtered.

Whittle was mad, but crafty. Maybe he figured to play things safe, and not mark his arrival in America by killing folks straightaway.

Likely as not, though, he wouldn't look at it that way.

Pretty soon, I came to the front of the house and followed its long porch to the stairs in the middle. By now, it came as no surprise to find the windows dark. From the look of the snow on the stairs, nobody'd climbed up or down them for a spell.

I had a mind to walk the rest of the way around the place, but figured I was only just looking for an excuse to put off going in.

So up the stairs I went. The snow on them squeaked under my shoes. Under the porch roof, I put some white tracks on the floorboards, and stomped one foot to shake the clinging powder off my shoe and sock. The thump of it startled me considerable. I felt like a plain fool. Quiet and stealth were called for, not clean shoes.

A single thump shouldn't have been enough to rouse the household – if anybody was in shape to arouse. And if Whittle was in there, he only would've heard it if he had his ear to the front door, likely as not.

Anyhow, I stood still for a long while. Nothing came of the thump. But I wasn't eager to try the door. I set down my driftwood club and brushed some snow off my hair and coat. Then I bent down for my club, but decided not to take it in with me. If Whittle was inside, I'd have to make do with my rocks. Because he might not be. And I didn't fancy the notion of creeping inside a strange house with a weapon in my hand. I'd had a knife in my teeth when I climbed aboard the *True D. Light*, only to get myself laid into by an innocent chap who took me for a villain.

There's one thing about Trevor Bentley, he doesn't often make the same mistake twice.

So I kept my hands empty, the rocks in my pockets.

The door wasn't locked.

I eased it open and stood for a spell with my head in the crack. There wasn't much to see but only darkness. Nothing to hear but the tick-tock of a clock pendulum somewhere close by. So in I crept, and shut the door real soft.

It was mighty good to be out of the snowy weather. The air felt warm and friendly. It smelled a trifle old and stale like Grandmother's place near Oxford. It smelled of wood smoke, too. From a fireplace, I reckoned. And there was a bittersweet aroma that put me in mind of Daws the cabman. I remembered how he'd kept his pipe upside-down so the rain wouldn't put it out, the night I went to fetch Uncle William, and suddenly I felt mighty lonesome for home.

I would've given just about anything, right then, to be there with Mother.

I told myself this was no time to stand around feeling sorry for myself. This was dangerous territory, after all, whether or not Whittle was lurking about.

Keeping my eyes and ears sharp, I took to snooping about. Part of the time, rug was under my shoes. Other times, it was wooden floor. I moved slow, crouching some, my hands feeling ahead to warn me off collisions. I met up with an umbrella stand, a small table, a lamp, a couple of chairs. I only knew what they were by their feel. Somehow, I missed knocking any over. By and by, I found a newel post and stairway. The stairs seemed to be as wide as I was long.

It seemed smart to explore where I was before venturing into the upper parts of the house. So that's what I did. And before long, I found myself in a parlor. That's where the fireplace was. The fire had burnt itself down to glowing embers, but it gave the room some extra warmth and enough ruddy light for me to see I wasn't blind, after all.

Though the light was faint and left swarms of shadows, I saw right off that the room had walls and walls full of books. Where there weren't bookshelves or curtained windows, there were cabinets or paintings. The place was all aclutter. It had a sofa, and so many tables and lamps and chairs and so on that it seemed more like a storage room than a place for folks to spend their time.

Even though I worried some about what might be hiding in the shadows, I wasn't eager to move on. I stepped over close to the fire, instead, and huddled down to feel its warmth better.

From somewhere behind me, a voice said, 'Chuck another log on there, fellow.'

Chapter Seventeen

The General

Well, I jumped up so quick I near hurt myself, and swung around.

Off in a corner, a match flared. It showed a broad, wrinkled face with white hair curled all around it and a thick, droopy mustache. The old man was sitting in an armchair off to the side a ways. I must've walked right by him on my way to the fireplace.

He sucked the match flame down into his pipe a few times, and puffed out some smoke. 'Get that fire blazing,' he said. 'I only let her burn down because I was too comfy to get up and fool with it.'

He didn't sound like he meant me any harm. He sounded downright friendly, in fact. So I figured there was no good reason to hightail. I turned to the fireplace, moved the screen aside, added some wood onto the andiron, and puffed away with the bellows till the fire took. After putting the screen back where it belonged, I faced the old man again.

'Much appreciated,' he said.

What with the shimmery red light, I could see him better now. He was a husky fellow, all abulge under his flannel nightshirt. A blanket covered his legs. He sat there, looking at me, sucking on his pipe, just as calm as if I'd been invited into his parlor, not snuck in like a thief.

'General Matthew Forrest,' he said.

A General? That might explain how come I hadn't riled him.

'Don't stand there with your maw hanging,' he said. 'Introduce yourself.'

I let out a couple of noises like 'Uhhh, uhhh' while I tried to figure things out. He talked like a Yank, pretty much the same as Michael and Trudy, rather flat and clipped. Just a few words from me, and he'd know by my voice I wasn't any native. Then I'd have an awful piece of explaining to do. What I needed was a good string of lies about who I was and where I'd come from – lies that left out everything about Whittle and the yacht.

'What's the matter, cat got your tongue?'

I nodded, and suddenly hit on a plan. *Cat got your tongue?* Yes, indeed!

I commenced to frown and shake my head and touch my lips. Then I remembered how one of those rascals in *Huckleberry Finn* had let on to be a dummy. He'd wriggled his fingers and such, pretending it was sign language. So I had a go at that.

The General furrowed his brow. He tapped the bit of his pipe against a front tooth. 'I see,' he said. 'You're a mute. Not deaf, however. I knew a fellow name of Clay who suffered from just such a predicament. That was back in '74. A couple of Comanches laid their hands on him, cut his tongue clean off at the root. This wasn't more than half a mile from Adobe Walls. A buffalo hunter happened along, just afterwards, and picked off the savages with his Sharps. Saved Clay, but his tongue was already out. Being reluctant to part with it, he poked a hole in the tongue and wore it around his neck. Before long, the thing dried up like jerky. I hear he ate it, a year or two later on, to stave off hunger after he lost his mount and had to hole up in a cave for a week till the Indians cleared out.'

This General sure was a talker, which suited me fine. He rather put me in mind of Uncle William, the way he seemed to relish his grisly tale.

'I don't suppose the Comanches got yours,' he said.

Shaking my head, I stuck out my tongue so he could see I had one. Then I fingered my throat and let out a grunt.

'A problem with the voice box, eh?'

Nod, nod.

'That's a shame. However, it does give you a certain edge in conversational gambits.'

When he came out with that, I couldn't help but laugh.

'The Lord has seen fit to saddle me with not one but *two* women in my dotage, so your silence is mighty refreshing.'

Two women! That set off alarms in me. What if Whittle'd come in, skipped the parlor and missed the General, but found the gals?

I must've looked anxious and fidgety, because the General waved his empty hand in my direction and said, 'Oh, don't bother about them. They aren't likely to stray down and interrupt us. Once they've turned in for the night, they remain turned in. That's why I've taken to the habit of coming down for a smoke and a drink this time of . . .'

'I fear they might be in danger, sir!' I blurted.

So much for acting mute.

If the General was surprised to hear me talk, he didn't show it. He didn't sit still for a blink, but bounded out of the chair so quick it was amazing. 'Explain yourself,' he said. Turning his back to me, he dropped his pipe on a table and struck a match.

While he plucked the glass chimney off a lamp and lit the wick, I said, 'I followed a murderer tonight. He may've come here.'

The General didn't say a thing. He stepped past me lively with the lamp and snatched a revolver off the fireplace mantel. It was huge.

I bet he knew how to use it, too.

'Follow me,' he said. 'Look sharp.'

We hot-footed it out of the parlor, across the foyer and up the stairs. My heart pounded fierce. I hoped the women weren't dead, as that would be a sorry loss for General Forrest. But I sure hoped we'd find Whittle. Scared as I was of the man, I was keen to see him struck by lead. Five or six slugs in the chest would do him proper.

I fetched one of the rocks out of my coat pocket before we reached the top of the stairs. The General moved fast and silent into a hallway up there. I stayed close behind him. The lamp cast a glow that lit us and the walls on both sides, but left a long stretch of darkness ahead.

A runner on the floor kept our footsteps quiet, but boards creaked plenty. They would creak for Whittle, too, I judged, if he came sneaking along. But that didn't ease my mind much, so I looked over my shoulder every few seconds. When we walked past a couple of shut doors, I worried they might fly open and Whittle'd leap out. But they stayed shut.

The next door we came to, it stood open and the General hurried through. He didn't tell me to stay out, so I followed him, not hankering to be left all alone in the hallway. We rushed over to a big canopy bed. I could tell, right off, that Whittle hadn't been at the woman because the covers weren't thrown off and she wasn't a bloody carcass. Only her head showed. It wore a bonnet.

The General's hands were full, what with the lamp in one and his revolver in the other, so he gave the mattress a jolt with his knee. The woman let out a moan.

'Stir your bones, Mable.'

She mumbled, 'Huh? Whuh?'

'We may have trouble. Get up now and come along, and be quite about it.'

She rolled onto her back, caught sight of me and bolted up fast, clutching the covers to her front. She was a skinny, wrinkled old woman. Some white hair stuck out from under the edges of her bonnet. She blinked and worked her jaw. 'Who . . .? What in heaven's name . . .?'

'Shhhh,' the General said. 'Let's go.'

'Why, I never . . .' she mumbled. But she didn't waste any time. Throwing some sour looks in my direction, she scampered out of bed and shoved her feet into slippers. She wore a wool gown so long she had to hoist it a bit so the hem wouldn't drag the floor.

The General took the lead. I hung back and stayed behind Mable, figuring to guard the rear. She had a bit of a limp, but she moved along spritely.

She kept glancing back like she suspected I might knock her on the head with my rock.

Up the hallway a piece, we rushed into another bedroom.

The gal in this one must've been a light sleeper, for she sat up quick before the General got a chance to call out or knee her bed.

'Gracious sakes,' she said, 'what *is* going on?'

'Nothing at all, my dear,' the General told her. 'Nothing at all.'

She frowned, looking fairly perplexed. She was a fine, pretty woman, maybe ten years older than me, with sleek black hair that hung to her shoulders.

'Nothing?' Mable asked, giving the General a sharp look. 'Why, you've frightened me out of ten years' growth. Something had *best* be going on, you old fool. Who's this *child*? What's he doing in our home?'

'Trevor Bentley, ma'am,' I said.

'He came to warn us of a killer in the house,' the General explained.

'Oh, my,' the younger woman said.

'You stay here and watch the women, Trev.' With that, he headed for the hallway.

'Don't you dare leave us alone with this young rascal,' Mable blurted.

The General, he let on that he didn't hear her. He vanished with his lamp. We were in darkness for a bit. Then a match lit up the young woman. Sitting on the edge of her bed, she touched its flame to a lamp on her night table. She turned the wick up bright, and put the chimney over it, and blew out the match.

Mable went over to the lamp. She picked it up and held it off to her side as if she aimed to pitch it at me. 'I've dealt with my share of ruffians, fellow,' she said. 'Don't tempt me.'

'Settle down, Grandma,' the young one said, not at all snappish but soft and friendly. 'I'm sure Trevor doesn't mean us any harm.'

To show she was right, I tucked away the rock into my pocket.

'There,' she said. 'You see?' She stood up and went to her grandmother, and took the lamp. She set it on the table where it belonged.

She was a head taller than me, and slim and fine-looking. She wore a white nightdress that didn't quite reach to her ankles.

She gave me a smile that warmed me up considerable, then edged on past me and went for the door.

'I shouldn't go out there,' I warned.

She didn't heed that, but stepped out into the hall and looked both ways.

'Sarah, you get back in here this moment!'

Well, she stood out there ignoring me *and* her grandmother. I had to admire her pluck, but I was scared for her. So I heeled it into the hall. I had a mind to grab her and tow her back inside the room. Kept my hands to myself, though. Just stayed beside her.

We both studied the darkness.

I didn't know where the General had gone to, but I sure wished he'd show up quick.

'Come back in here and shut the door,' Mable sang out.

Sarah didn't answer. In a quiet voice to me, she said, 'I do hope Grandpa's all right.'

'I doubt the killer's in the house,' I said. I couldn't be certain, of course. I allowed it was a safe bet, considering Mable and Sarah hadn't gotten themselves butchered. But then again, he might've hidden out in another room for some reason. I figured there was no telling, when it came to Whittle. He might be creeping up on us even as we stood there.

Far off at the end of the hall, light came glowing from a doorway. Pretty soon, the general walked out behind his lamp and revolver. He didn't glance our way. He crossed to another door and entered a room.

'Let's go back inside,' I whispered.

She didn't answer, but just stood and folded her arms across her chest. I could hear her breathing sort of ragged. She was barefoot, and must've been mighty cold. Even though she had on a heavy nightdress, the chilly draft was likely chasing right up under it.

She put me in mind of Trudy, the night Whittle'd left her hanging. I thought about how I'd nearly frozen, myself, trying to brace her up. And then the way Trudy'd looked, dead, pushed itself into my head.

It made me just sick to think about. And it made me figure I could be a gentleman some other time. So I grabbed hold of Sarah's arm and said, 'Excuse me,' while I tugged her into the room. I dragged her clear of the door, let go, and threw it shut.

Old Mable, her mouth dropped.

Sarah frowned at me. 'That wasn't necessary,' she said, and rubbed her arm where I'd squeezed it.

'I'm quite sorry,' I said. 'Really, I am. But I shouldn't want Whittle to lay his hands on you. We're much safer, here.'

'Whittle?' Sarah asked.

'He's a horrid man, so quick with his knife we wouldn't stand a chance. He's likely not in the house, at all, but he might be. I don't know, really.'

'So *that's* what's going on,' Mable said, loud and triumphant. 'I knew it. I sensed it in my bones. A *killer* in the house. Why, he'll rue the day he crossed trails with Matthew Forrest.'

Well, she'd perked up in a way that was plain astonishing. She grinned and rubbed her hands together. 'He's met his match *now*, this Whistle.'

'I certainly hope so,' I allowed.

Sarah didn't seem gleeful like her grandmother. She looked worried. 'He's not as young as he was in the Indian Wars,' she said. 'His hearing isn't what it used to be.'

'Nonsense. His ears are fit as a fiddle. He hears what he wishes to hear, and that's a fact.'

We all stood silent, then, watching the door and listening. I hoped Mable was right about the General's ears. As time went on, though, I got to worrying. The revolver wouldn't do much good if Whittle crept up behind him and slit his gullet. Then Whittle'd be the one with a gun.

I wished I hadn't left the General on his own. I could've watched his back for him.

'Perhaps I should go and help him,' I finally said.

'I'll go with you,' Sarah said.

'Now quit, both of you. Matthew is perfectly capable of dealing with this Whistle character.'

'Whittle,' I corrected her this time around. 'Roderick Whittle.'

'How is it that you know such a man?' Sarah asked me.

Well, things had gone too far for lies to serve much purpose, so I said, 'He brought me from England. We sailed together. He murdered the others on the yacht, but I escaped. He no doubt believes I drowned, or he would've lurked about to have another go at me. As he landed not far from here, I feared he might've come to your house. I crept in, myself, to search for him.'

'You came here to save us?' Sarah asked.

'Yes, ma'am.'

'That was awfully noble of you.'

Her words warmed me up considerable.

'Noble if he's not giving us a pack of lies,' Mable said.

'Grandma!'

'It sounds mighty far-fetched to me. Likely as not, he was fixing to rob or murder us till he ran afoul of Matthew, and then thought better of it and made up this ridiculous story to get himself off the hook.'

'I believe him,' Sarah said.

'Why, you're just like Matthew. You're both just as gullible as can be. It wouldn't surprise me a bit if . . .'

A sharp thump on the door made us all jump. 'Open up.'

It was the General's voice.

And wasn't I glad to hear it! I didn't waste any time, but rushed on over and opened the door.

Chapter Eighteen

Forrest Hospitality

'I've scouted all the upstairs rooms,' the General said as he came in. 'There seems to be no intruder about, but the better part of wisdom says we stick together until I'm convinced he's nowhere in the house.'

'I don't suspect he exists this side of Trevor's imagination,' Mable allowed.

'He most certainly exists,' I said. 'It's quite possible he never came into the house, though. I haven't seen him since he rowed ashore. He may have gone in quite a different direction.'

Old Mable gave me a scathing look as if she'd expected me to come out with just such an excuse.

'It never hurts to err on the side of caution,' the General said. 'Come along.'

Sarah stepped into some slippers. Then she picked up her lamp. I held back, and followed the others into the hallway. We trooped downstairs to the parlor. It was a sight warmer than the rest of the house, and must've felt good to the women.

Mable plonked herself into the General's chair and covered her legs with his blanket. Sarah set the lamp on the mantel. Then she put more wood on the fire. After replacing the screen, she squatted down close to the blaze. 'Oh,' she said, 'it does feel wonderful.'

My eyes had been on her, not on the General, so I'd missed whatever he'd been up to. He took me by surprise when he stepped close to my side. 'Take this,' he said. He gave me a pistol. It was a tiny thing, not much bigger than my palm, with a barrel about three inches long. 'If the killer shows his face while I'm gone . . .'

'Matthew! Don't you *dare*! Take that away from him!'

'Hush!'

'I *never*!'

'This is a good time to start.' To me, he said, 'All you need to do is draw back the hammer, point, and squeeze the trigger. Go for the chest.'

'Yes, sir,' I said.

'You old fool! Don't you put a gun in his hand!'

Well, he acted like he didn't hear her. Taking his lamp and his big revolver, he hurried out of the parlor.

'Matthew!' she fairly squealed. 'Matthew!'

Sarah turned her face away from the fire. 'There's no call to be throwing a conniption, Grandma.'

I took a step toward the old woman, and she flinched up tight. She studied the pistol like it was a rattlesnake. Some drool trickled down her chin.

'You hold onto it,' I told her, and offered it by the handle.

She looked at me and blinked. She blinked a few times at the gun, then at me again. She wiped the spit off her chin. Then she reached out quick and snatched away the pistol.

'I shouldn't know how to use such a thing, anyhow,' I told her.

After that, she sort of slumped down in her chair. She cradled the little gun on her lap as if it were a cup of tea. Maybe she didn't know how to use it any better than I did, but I was more confident than ever that Whittle wouldn't turn up.

He hadn't come to this house, after all. That was a relief, but a disappointment, too. Since he wasn't here, the General wouldn't get a chance to shoot him. He was on the loose, and I wondered how I'd ever manage to track him down.

The longer I stayed, the farther away he was likely to get.

That was heavy on my mind when the General returned.

'The fellow must've bypassed us,' he said.

He saw that Mable had the gun, but he let the matter lie and didn't mention it.

'The thing for us now,' he said, 'is for the rest of you to

turn in. I've taken the precaution of locking the doors. I'll keep on my toes and patrol the house till dawn. Sarah, show Trevor to a guest room.'

'I should be on my way, actually,' I said. 'He's out in the night, somewhere, and the sooner I find him . . .'

'Nonsense,' Sarah broke in.

'Nonsense is right,' added the General. 'I won't have you straying out in the snow.'

'We had the Great Blizzard last winter,' Sarah told me. 'Some four hundred souls perished.

'This is no blizzard, but the snow's coming down heavy. You don't want to be out in it, Trevor. You'd freeze up like a statue.'

I reckoned that was true. And I sure didn't hanker to leave the warm house. I was loath to part from the General and Sarah, too. Mable wouldn't be any great loss. But I liked the other two and they were the first really friendly folks I'd encountered in longer than a month.

Besides, there was slim chance I'd be able to find Whittle tonight.

The General, he took the little gun from Mable. She gave it up without a fight. He handed it to me. 'Keep this with you.'

'Yes, sir.'

Sarah fetched her lamp off the mantel and said, 'Come along, Trevor.'

I bid the others goodnight. Together, we left the parlor and headed for the stairs. 'Do you have a home of your own?' Sarah asked.

'Yes, ma'am. It's nothing like this, of course. Mother and I have a flat in London, England.'

'Just the two of you?'

'There's Agnes, our servant.'

'We've had servants,' Sarah said. With a soft laugh, she added, 'They never stay long. Grandma makes life too unpleasant for them.'

As we started up the stairs, she asked, 'What of your father?'

'He was a soldier. He lost his life at the Battle of Maiwand.'

'Oh. I'm awfully sorry. Your mother is all right, however? She wasn't among those you mentioned who were murdered on the boat?'

'She was safe at home when last I saw her. I left her on an errand, actually. It was something of an accident that I found myself on the yacht.'

'Then she doesn't know what's become of you?'

My throat clogged up when Sarah asked that. All I could do was nod in reply.

'Well then, we shall take care of it first thing in the morning. I've never been blessed with a child of my own, but I can certainly imagine how terribly worried your mother must be.'

I managed to come out with a shaky, 'Thank you.'

We entered one of the rooms just past the top of the stairs. 'I hope you'll be comfortable here. We keep the room tidy for occasional guests – mostly Grandpa's old friends from the Point.'

I saw the big bed, and it looked grand.

Sarah lit up the lamp on the table beside it, then turned around to face me. 'I'm afraid we have no suitable clothing for a young man of your size. How old are you?'

'Fifteen, ma'am. I'll be sixteen next June.'

'You're so dear,' she said. Smiling kind of sad, she reached out and petted my cheek. 'I do hope you'll be in no hurry to leave us.'

My face heated up considerable, what with her stroking it.

'I'm quite glad to be here,' I murmured.

'Goodnight, now. Sleep well. We'll see you in the morning.'

'Yes, ma'am.'

'Sarah. Please call me Sarah.'

'Sarah.'

Leaning forward, she gave my forehead a gentle kiss. Then she turned away and left me alone. Out in the hall, she took a turn to the left, so I figured she was going on to her own room. I hurried over to the doorway and watched her, mostly to make sure she didn't get jumped even though I figured Whittle was far off somewhere in the night.

She just kind of flowed along, all graceful and elegant.

She put me in mind of my mother so much it made me feel peaceful and lonesome, both at the same time.

Once she was safe in her room, I went back to the night table. I set down the little pistol. Then I shucked down to just my sweater, which was dry and hung low enough to keep me decent in case I had to get up quick. I pulled back the bed covers, snuffed the lamp, and climbed into bed.

The sheets were silk. They felt slick, and mighty cold at first. After a spell, though, they warmed up.

The bed was so soft it snuggled against me. Not a bit like my bunk on the *True D. Light*. It didn't bounce and rock and pitch this way and that, either.

I hadn't felt so comfortable in ages.

Nor so safe.

Come morning, I woke on my own. I just lay there a while, nice and warm, mighty glad to be where I was and not aboard the yacht any more. But then I got to thinking about Trudy. That took the pleasure out of lazing in bed.

I climbed out, tugged the sweater down as far as it would go, and stepped over to a window. Well, the sight of all that snow took my breath away. We had snow at home, now and again, but I'd never seen so much of it. None was falling now. It must've come down all night, though, for there to be such a load. It hung all white on the branches of the trees out there, must've been a foot thick on the roofs of the sheds and such, and looked to be knee-deep where it was stacked against the brick wall at the edge of the property. What with the sky clear, all that snow glared so white in the sun that it stung my eyes.

I saw some other houses away off in the distance, and wondered if maybe Whittle'd chosen one of them. It seemed likely. Before the notion could take a good hold on me, though, I quickly reminded myself how the General kept a pistol handy. Maybe that was a common practice in these parts, and Whittle'd gone into a house fixing to do murder and gotten himself killed for his troubles. I hung on to that idea. It helped some, but not much.

I could see a silver of the bay from my window. It was bright blue, with white-topped waves rolling toward shore. The yacht wasn't in sight, of course. I judged it might be seen from a different corner of the house, but it wasn't a thing I wanted to look at, anyhow.

'Good morning, Trevor.'

Startled, I dragged my sweater down, stretching it toward my knees. Then I turned around.

'I hope you slept well,' Sarah said, and walked straight in.

With the daylight, I saw she was even prettier than I'd thought. Her shiny black hair was pinned up, her face rosy, her eyes bright and happy. She wore a dress that looked like green velvet and had white lace around the collar and wrists.

'I . . . I slept quite well, thank you.'

She came walking right at me. Her eyes flicked down at my bare legs. 'You must be freezing.'

I wasn't freezing at all. I was broiling. Sweat was trickling down my sides under the sweater.

'I brought these for you,' she said. For the first time, I noticed she was carrying a robe and slippers. 'They belonged to my father. They're probably too large, but they'll have to do until we can purchase a wardrobe for you.'

She handed over the robe. I had to let go of the sweater. Before it unstretched too far, though, I shook open the robe and let it drape. She crouched in front of me and set the slippers down. I was mighty glad to have the robe hanging betwixt her face and me.

'Try them on,' she said.

I stepped into the slippers. They felt a sight better than the cold floorboards. But they were too big, just as she'd said.

'Is your father away somewhere?' I asked.

From the look of loss that filled her eyes, I wished I hadn't asked. 'He died in battle some ten years ago.'

'I'm sorry.'

'We have much in common, you and I. We both lost our fathers in war. Mine was killed by the Utes at Milk Creek.'

'Utes? Are those Indians?'

She nodded, and stood up straight.

Well, she seemed to be living in the house with just her grandparents, so I allowed I wouldn't ask about her mother.

'Slip into the robe and come along now,' she said. 'I've prepared a hot bath for you downstairs.'

A hot bath!

'Smashing!'

Luckily, she turned around and went for the door. I quickly plucked off the sweater. I got the robe on and tied its belt, then followed her into the hall. We went down the stairway, and she led me toward the rear of the house where I'd never been before. No sign of the General or Mable.

The kitchen was nice and warm with a fire in the stove. Off to one side, a door stood open. We went in, and there stood a tub chockful of water so hot, steam was rising off it.

'I'll go and fetch some of Papa's clothes for you,' Sarah said. 'They'll be too big, of course, but they'll have to do until we get you to a store.'

'Thank you,' I said.

I waited till she'd cleared out. She left the door open, more than likely to let heat keep coming in from the kitchen. But nobody was in sight, so I stripped off and climbed into the tub.

The water near scalded me. It was dandy! I hadn't taken a proper bath since the Wednesday night before I'd set out from home. Not that I'd been a stranger to water in all that time, what with a few dips in the ocean and waves splashing me and getting myself showered by squalls so often. The sea water'd always left me salty and itchy. Every *drop* of water, whether it came from the ocean or the sky, had been just frigid.

So I was mighty glad to be in a tubful of hot water, even if it was sort of boiling me.

I lay there, just enjoying it for a spell. Then I soaped myself down and ducked under to get the suds out of my hair. When I came up for a breath, here was Sarah coming in with a bundle of clothes. The water was murky enough to hide my lower parts, thank goodness.

She put down a pair of shoes, then set herself in a chair with the other things on her lap and took to chatting with me. When she asked if I had any brothers or sisters and I said no, she allowed as how that was another thing we had in common. She'd been the only child of her parents. She went on from there, and told how she'd spent most of her early years in boarding schools because her mother had died of pneumonia when Sarah was only six, and her father had been a cavalry officer always on the move from one outpost to another out west until he wound up in Colorado and got himself killed by the Utes in seventy-nine. Later, she'd lived in Syracuse and taught at a girls' school until two years ago when her grandfather, the General, retired from the army. That's when she moved in here to live with him and Mable.

She said she cooked and cleaned house and did the shopping for them. As much as she appreciated them, however, she admitted she found herself lonesome for companionship of folks nearer to her own age. That's how come she was so glad I'd turned up last night.

I could see how it might wear on a person, spending night and day with nobody about except a couple of codgers. Even *interesting* codgers like the General would likely get tiresome if they were your only company, and I'd already noticed that Mable wasn't much fun at all.

Still, though, it seemed a trifle excessive for Sarah to be enjoying her new friend while he sat naked in a bathtub.

She kept chatting along until my water lost most of its heat and I commenced to shiver. She finally noticed. Maybe my lips were looking blue.

She fetched me a towel, and said, 'You get dressed while I start breakfast.'

She went into the kitchen. I could see her through the

doorway, but she wasn't paying any mind to me, so I climbed out and dried myself. I shut the door and used the toilet, then hurried into the clothes. From the size of things, her dead papa was taller and leaner than Trudy's.

Seemed like I'd never get shut of wearing dead father duds.

After rolling the sleeves and trouser legs out of my way, I joined up with Sarah in front of the stove.

It looked like she only had enough ham and eggs in the skillet for two.

'Where are Mable and the General?' I asked.

'I suppose they're sleeping. I heard Grandpa prowling about the house last night, and he probably didn't turn in until after sunrise.'

'It appears I came along on a false alarm,' I told her.

'Perhaps you were led here by Providence.'

I gave that notion some pondering, and judged she might be right. Taken all around, I was mighty lucky to still be alive. So maybe the Lord had plans for me. Likely, He aimed for me to send Whittle packing south for hell.

If that's what He had in mind, though, He could've done it Himself easy enough by sending the *True D. Light* to the bottom of the sea.

I would've gone down with her, of course.

So maybe there was more to all this than met the eye.

Chapter Nineteen

The Yacht and the Horse

We ate a splendid meal of ham and eggs and rolls, all washed down with hot coffee. It was better than anything I'd tasted in a long time, considering we'd run out of eggs and fresh meat on the yacht after just a couple of weeks at sea. After that, we'd had only flour and potatoes that didn't come out of tins. I'd gotten a mite tired of it all.

I still had my mind on Providence, and was glad He'd sent me here for such a breakfast. I thanked Him in my head. While I was at it, I let Him know I'd appreciated the bed and bath, as well, and allowed He'd done a good job sending me to these people.

When we were done eating, I helped Sarah clear things. Then we stood at the sink together, her washing while I dried. Back home, Agnes had taken care of such matters. I didn't mind helping, however, and Sarah seemed to enjoy the job.

We'd no sooner finished than the General and Mable showed up. The General, he clapped me on the shoulder. 'That killer of yours must've known better and stayed clear of us,' he said.

'We were quite fortunate, then,' I told him.

'Fortunate.' Mable huffed. 'Never *was* such a scoundrel, in my opinion.'

If she wished to take a hike through the snow, I thought, I could show her a couple of bodies that might change her tune on that account. But I kept mum.

'We ought to alert the authorities,' the General said, 'so they can keep a look-out for him.'

'Trevor and I might take care of that while we're in town.

He's in sorry need of new clothes, and we want to cable his mother in England so she'll know he's safe.'

'Nonsense!' Mable blurted. 'Send him off. We've got no use for him.'

'He's a child, dear,' the General told her.

'He's all alone in this country,' Sarah added, 'without a soul to look after him. Except us. The Lord guided him to our door.'

'Don't you go *Lording* at me, girl.'

'Trevor did us a fine service,' the General said. 'He came here to give us a warning. Besides, he seems a fine fellow to me.' He gave my shoulder another slap. 'Young man, you're welcome to remain under our roof for as long as it pleases you. So long as you behave yourself.'

'Thank you, sir.'

'I'll be *switched* if I'll have this rascal . . .'

'And you'll treat him *friendly*, dear, or I'll have to put you out in the snow.'

Well, she sank down on a chair and glowered at me.

Sarah took to fixing breakfast for the two of them.

By and by, I escaped and went upstairs. The General's talk about notifying authorities had unsettled me some. What with a couple of bodies in the yacht and nobody around to blame but me, I feared I might find myself in a spot of trouble.

At the end of the hallway was a window. I peered out. Down below were the rear grounds of the house, along with the trees and gazebo and such I'd roamed through last night, and the wall. Everything was piled high with snow. The sun had gotten itself swallowed by clouds, so the snow wasn't glaring white any more, but gray and gloomy.

Off beyond the wall, the land sloped down to the shore of the bay. I didn't see foot tracks anywhere. I looked to where the skiff should have been, but couldn't spot it. Likely as not, the snowfall had buried it.

Then I scanned along the beach to the right and braced myself. My heart took to pounding up a storm. I didn't much *want* to see the *True D. Light*, but that's what I'd come to the window for. I rather expected to find her crawling with local folks and constables.

The snowy beach stretched alongside the waves for about half a mile that I could see. Nobody was there.

The yacht wasn't there, either.

I stood peering out the window, searching this way and that, puzzling over the mystery, and then I spotted a ship far out on the rough, slate-colored water.

The sight sent a cold wind blowing through my bones.

I knew she was the *True D. Light*.

It must've been low tide when I beached her.

I hadn't bothered to drop anchor or reef the mainsail.

So now she was flying along with her sail full of wind, carrying Trudy and Michael on a journey to nowhere.

I got goosebumps all over.

Quick as I could, I rushed downstairs to the warm kitchen and live people.

We left the General and Mable to their breakfast. Sarah fetched me a pair of boots and leather gloves, a heavy coat and a hat. More of her dead father's things. She got bundled up, herself. Then we went out the front door and trudged across the snow to the stable.

It was on the left side of the house, where I hadn't seen it till now. It was plenty big. We hauled at the double doors. When they came open, they shoved swaths across the snow.

I looked in.

All of a sudden, I remembered the pistol the General'd given to me last night. It was still on the table by my bed. I felt a proper fool for leaving it there.

The stable wasn't exactly dark inside, but it wasn't bright by a long shot.

Sarah started through the doorway, but I grabbed her arm. She frowned at me – not like she was angry, only curious. 'What is it?' she asked.

'I shouldn't like to think that Whittle might be hiding in there.'

'He'd be silly, don't you think, to spend the night in a cold stable with a house so handy?'

How could I argue with that?

Still, though, I felt right jittery and kept my eyes sharp as we went inside.

I let go of her arm. She took hold of mine, though. Spite of what she'd said, she must've been worried.

We stopped before going in too deep, and looked around.

The place smelled like hay, mostly, but had a few other aromas that weren't so sweet. Near the front were a couple of carriages, one fancier than the other, and a sleigh that had two rows of seats. The walls of the place were all hung with tools and tack.

We walked in farther, to where the horses were. There were stalls to hold four of them, but the gate of the last stall stood open.

Sarah pulled up short and let out a quiet gasp. 'My Lord,' she said. She didn't release my arm, but dragged me along beside her. We hurried past the first three stalls. The horses, seeing us, snorted and snuffled. White plumes blew out of their nostrils.

The fourth stall was empty.

Sarah gazed into it, breathing hard, puffing out clouds of white. 'He's taken Saber,' she murmured. 'Wait here. I've got to tell Grandpa.'

She let go my arm and rushed off.

I wasn't keen on being left alone, but she was hardly out the doors before it came to me I needn't worry about getting jumped by Whittle. He'd come along last night, after all. It had been a mighty narrow call for the General and the women, for he must've been tempted to take over the house. He'd chosen, instead, to pinch a horse and light out.

It spooked me some, knowing he'd been here. But he was likely miles and miles away, by now. Any chap who would filch a horse on a snowy night, when he had a chance to hole up in a nice warm house, aimed to do some hard traveling.

In a way, it was good to know we were safe from him. It troubled me, though, that he'd gotten away. I had half a mind to grab a horse and chase after him.

More than half a mind, really.

It was what I ought to do.

But with such a headstart, and any direction to choose from except toward the water, he'd be near impossible to run down. Besides, there I would be in a strange land in the dead of winter, no money, no clothes but the borrowed ones on my back. And the folks here, they'd been awfully good to me. Making off with one of their horses would be a dirty play, and give Mable reason to bully the General and Sarah.

If all that weren't enough cause to hold me off, there was knowing that I'd miss out on my chance to cable Mother. She deserved to know, straight away, I wasn't dead after all.

So I gave up the notion of chasing after Whittle.

It seemed I was letting down everybody he'd killed, especially poor Trudy, but I judged I owed more to the living. The dead weren't likely to appreciate my efforts, anyhow.

Well, that led me to thinking about those Whittle hadn't killed *yet* – the ones he'd be butchering down the road a piece unless I stopped him.

They complicated things considerable, and I commenced to figure maybe I'd better take a horse, after all. By then, however, it was too late.

Sarah came striding along, frowning. She didn't have the General with her.

'Best not to tell him,' she said. 'If he finds out Saber's been stolen, he'll saddle up and ride off, and he won't come back empty-handed. He's too old for such shenanigans, but that's exactly what he'd do.'

We could go together! I thought.

Before I got my mouth open to suggest it, Sarah said, 'The way his health is, I doubt we'd ever see him again. But would that stop him? No, I hardly think so. Why, he would rather die and leave Grandma a widow than allow a horsethief to get away from him.'

'He's certain to learn the horse has gone missing,' I pointed out.

'We'll leave the stable door open. Saber always did have a feisty nature. He's run off before. I'll simply explain that he was here when we set out for town. That won't throw Grandpa into such a tizzy as if he takes a notion that Saber's been stolen.'

Sarah wasn't just pretty, but had a sharp mind to boot. It bothered me that she was given to such trickery, but the way she had it figured, she was deceiving the general for his own good.

I told her the plan was quite clever.

She opened the gate of a stall that had a huge gelding inside named Howitzer. The name was embroidered in gold on his blue blanket. After pulling the blanket off him, Sarah walked him toward the front of the stable. There, I helped harness him to the sleigh.

Outside, snow was drifting down.

'Perfect,' Sarah said. 'It'll cover Saber's tracks.'

Well, Saber had no tracks that needed covering, as he was long gone. What Sarah meant was that the snow might hide the tracks Saber *would've* made, if he'd been here this morning and wandered off.

We stuck to her plot, and left the stable doors open.

Then we both climbed into the sleigh. Sarah sat down close against me and spread a blanket across our laps. Then she picked up the reins, gave them a shake, called out, 'Gee-yup,' and off we went.

Sarah steered us away from the house. We glided past trees and a fountain with no water in it but that had a statue of Bacchus, who was sticking a grape in his mouth and wore nothing except for snow heaped here and there, and looked to be freezing.

We stopped at the wall's front gate. It was shut. Whittle must've taken time to dismount and close it after him, so folks wouldn't catch on he'd been here.

'I'll see to it,' I said as Sarah reined in.

'Leave it open a bit for Saber,' she told me, still keeping her mind on our ruse.

I hopped into the snow, swung the gate wide, and waited while Sarah 'gee-yupped' Howitzer then 'whoaed' him once they'd gotten to the other side. I left the gate standing open some, rushed ahead and climbed into the sleigh. It felt good to have the blanket on my legs again.

After we took a turn to the right, Sarah clucked a few times and Howitzer commenced to trot along at a smart pace. We fairly flew over the snow, the wind and flakes in our faces.

'Would you care to take the reins?' she asked.

'Smashing.'

I took the leather straps from her and gave them a shake. Howitzer checked over his shoulder, let out a snort of white steam, then faced the front again and kept on trotting. His hooves thumped quiet through the snow. The only other sounds came from him huffing, and the sleigh runners hissing along, the harness creaking and jangling, and bells on the harness tinkling out real merry.

It was all just uncommon peaceful.

'We'll be to Coney Island in no time,' Sarah told me, and gave my thigh a pat under the blanket. She smiled at me. Her cheeks were ruddy, her eyes moist from the weather. 'It's a shame you didn't arrive in the summer. People come from miles around. It's just so lively and gay.' She squeezed my leg. 'If you stay, you'll see for yourself. You *will* stay, won't you?'

Stay till *summer*? The notion stunned me. I didn't know how to answer, and wished she hadn't asked. By and by, I said, 'I shouldn't like to impose on your hospitality.'

'You'd be doing us a great favor. You could help with the chores and keep me company. We'd have a wonderful time.'

'It sounds splendid, really,' I told her. 'If it weren't for Mother . . .'

'I know. I'm sorry. You must miss her terribly.'

'I rather imagine she should like me home with her.'

'Does she have the means to pay for your return voyage?'

The question knocked me flat.

'The means?' I asked, though I knew precisely what she meant.

'Financially.'

My hesitation was all the answer Sarah needed.

'No matter,' she said. 'Stay on with us, and we'll pay you a wage. That way, you'll be able to purchase your own ticket home, and not work any hardship at all on your mother.'

She said it kindly enough, but it let the wind out of my sails, anyhow. All along, I'd known that getting home to England would be no easy trick. Most of the time, though, I'd been so worried about getting killed by Whittle or the ocean that I hadn't given much thought to the problem. When I'd considered what to do on the slim chance I survived, I'd always figured I'd find a way to get back, somehow, sooner or later.

Sarah's offer seemed to be the solution. All I needed to do was stay on long enough to earn the ship's fare. That sure seemed better than asking Mother to scrape up the funds. I reckon I should've felt mighty grateful. Instead, though, I had this kind of trapped feeling.

'It seems like a fine idea,' I finally said.

'Wonderful. We'll let your mother know of your plans.'

'You don't suppose Mable will object, do you?'

'Oh, she may whine and complain a bit. But we won't let that bother us.'

Well, by this time we'd left behind the few houses I'd been able to spot from my bedroom window. More came along, though. They got smaller, closer together. Pretty soon, they fairly lined the road. There were some street lamps, too, and I could see a town up ahead.

This looked to be the main street. Sarah took the reins from me, and slowed Howitzer. We went gliding past a few other sleighs, and some folks on horseback. I gave all the horsemen a study, not really figuring any of them was Whittle, but checking on them just the same.

Plenty of people were on foot, going and coming from various markets and shops and public houses. A good many of the establishments appeared to be shut, but some were open.

Just on the other side of a big hotel, Sarah pulled off to the side. We climbed down, and she wrapped the reins around a hitching post. I followed her onto a boardwalk and into a shop called Western Union. Nobody in there but us and a fellow behind the counter.

'I'd like a message sent to England,' Sarah told the chap.

'That's what I'm here for,' he said, real chipper. He slipped a form across to her and slapped a pencil down on it. 'Give me the name and address of the party she goes to. Put that right there.' He pointed to a space at the top of the form. 'Message goes here. And down here, I'll need your name and whereabouts if you'll be expecting a reply. We'll deliver it to you the day she comes in, if you live hereabouts.'

'We reside at the Forrest house,' Sarah told him.

Hearing that, he grinned. He had an upper tooth gone, right in front, and the remainder of his choppers looked just about ripe to folow its example. 'You're the General's granddaughter, then. And who's this young man?'

'He's our house guest from London,' Sarah told him.

'Trevor Bentley,' I said.

Sarah passed the paper across to me. I penciled in Mother's name and the address of our lodging on Marylebone High Street, London W1, England. While I puzzled over what to tell her, the fellow said, 'She's pay by the word, so you want to be brief.'

Well, they stood there waiting, so I wrote quick. 'Dear Mother, shanghaied to America, safe now. Will work for General Forrest and earn my fare home. Hope you are well. Your loving son, Trevor.'

Sarah handed it over to the fellow. After she paid him, he allowed we might get an answer in two or three days if the party chose to make a prompt reply. Said he'd have a boy deliver it to the General's house.

Then we were off. I felt mighty good about getting that cable sent to Mother, and thanked Sarah for it.

'It ought to lift a terrible burden from her heart.'

When she said that, I choked up some. My eyes watered, but I turned away so she wouldn't notice.

We waited for a rider to pass, then hurried across the street and went into a general store. It seemed we were in there forever, Sarah picking out this and that for me. We ended up with a whole passel of things – everything from a toothbrush to boots and house slippers, socks and longjohns and trousers, shirts and sweaters and a waistcoat, a jacket, even a nightshirt and robe. The whole pile cost her a bundle of money. But she hadn't more than got done paying for it than she hauled out her purse again and bought us each a licorice stick, a copy of the New York *World* for the General, and a sack of chestnuts for Mable.

We hauled our load on back to the sleigh, and it was a good thing there was only the two of us, or we never would've managed to fit it all in.

We boarded, and Sarah turned us around and we started heading back out of town.

She said, 'I hope we're not forgetting anything.'

I shook my head, even though I remembered we'd told the General we would stop at the constabulary and give information about Whittle. No point in reminding Sarah, though. If she'd forgotten, that suited me.

I couldn't see how it mattered. The *True D. Light* had carried off Michael and Trudy, so there weren't any bodies to account for. And Whittle, he likely hadn't stopped riding yet and wouldn't ever be showing up anywhere close to this town. So I didn't see any advantage, at all, to telling on him. It might only serve to stir up trouble for me.

When we got back to the house, the General forgot to ask if we'd gone to the authorities. He was too much in a frenzy about Saber getting loose. The three of us went outside and hunted high and low for the horse, till by and by the General allowed we ought to give up. Saber'd run off before, he said, and would probably wander back in his own good time.

I knew better, of course, but didn't set him straight.

Chapter Twenty

Christmas and After

Two days before Christmas, a boy from Western Union came along with a telegram. It read, DEAREST TREVOR MY HEART IS FULL WITH NEWS THAT YOU ARE WELL STOP I LONG TO HAVE YOU HOME STOP WRITE TO ME AND STAY SAFE STOP I MISS YOU STOP ALL MY LOVE MOTHER

The message made me miss her something awful, so I sat down straight away in the General's study and wrote a long letter to her.

I scribbled on about what had happened to me after going to fetch Uncle William, and brought her all the way up to the present, telling her what nice people Sarah and the General were, and how I'd be working here at the house until I could afford a return ticket. Of course, I made no mention of a few items. Figured she was better off not knowing about me and Sue in the alley, or how I'd stabbed the whore's confederate, or about me hiding under Mary's bed when Whittle killed her, or even how he'd killed everyone on the boat except me. Knowing such matters wouldn't likely ease Mother's mind any.

I did tell her that Jack the Ripper was Roderick Whittle, and how he'd chased me to the Thames, and how I'd been his prisoner until we reached the shores of America where I escaped from him. She could pass the information on to Uncle William, and he could let the news out to everyone. It'd come as a great relief to the authorities – not to mention the East End whores – that Jack the Ripper would no longer be prowling the streets.

The next day, Sarah and I rode into town again. She sent me into the store with some money to purchase tobacco for the General while she took my letter to the post office for me.

The day after that, Christmas happened. It only made me sad, mostly. I longed more than ever to be at home. It had always been a jolly time, with parties and caroling, a great feast at Uncle's house with goose and plum pudding and such, and getting ambushed under the mistletoe by folks I'd never let kiss me otherwise. We always had a Christmas tree on the parlor table all bright with tapers and fancy doodads. I wondered if Mother had put up a tree this year without me there, and thought how lonesome she must be. She wouldn't be getting my letter for a few weeks, but at least my cable must've perked her up some.

Christmas was pretty much like any other day at the Forrest place, only gloomier. We didn't even have a tree. According to Sarah, the General and Mable were down on Christmas because they had no family except her and didn't enjoy being reminded of the fine old times they used to have.

The General sat around morose in the parlor, smoking his pipe and drinking rum till he fell asleep at midday.

Mable, she went for a walk and disappeared. Sarah and I had to go out hunting for her. We found her about halfway to town, crouched down a ways off the road, digging in the snow. She gave us kind of a scatter-brained look and said she was aiming to pick some posies.

We loaded her onto the sleigh and took her home. Sarah told me this sort of thing had happened a few times before. Every now and again, the old lady would slip a cog and wander off. 'It's her age,' Sarah explained.

Back at the house, we tucked Mable into bed. The General was still snoring in the parlor. We hadn't gotten any chance to eat, so Sarah set to work on making some chowder.

We ate by candlelight in the dining room, just the two of us. Sarah could see I was feeling low, and tried to cheer me up. She poured us some red wine, and we 'Merry Christmased' each other and sipped at it. The wine tasted sweet and sent a warmth through me. But it put me in mind of the rum I'd drunk in Mary's room, and that reminded me of things that didn't improve my mood any.

After the chowder was gone, we kept sitting there and drinking the wine.

By and by, Sarah told me she'd be back in a minute and I should stay put. Feeling plain miserable, I helped myself to another glassful. Well, along she came hiding one hand behind her, and knelt beside my chair. I scooched it away from the table, and turned it toward her. 'Close your eyes, Trevor,' she said. I shut them. When she told me to open, I looked and she was dangling a gold watch in front of me by its chain. 'Merry Christmas,' she said.

My throat clutched and my eyes watered up. I couldn't say a thing. She put the watch into my hand and I studied it. The timepiece was blurry, so I had to blink before I could make out the crossed revolvers engraved on its case.

'It's . . . grand,' I finally managed to stammer out. 'Thank you ever so much.'

'It belonged to my father,' she said. 'I want you to have it.'

'I shouldn't . . . really.'

'Certainly you should. You'll never know how much joy you've brought into my life. You must keep it always.'

'I . . . I do wish I had a gift to give you.'

'You might give me a kiss.'

With that, she uncrouched some. Hands on my knees, she leaned forward and turned her cheek to me. I kissed it. Then she faced me and looked me in the eyes.

'I know you miss your mother awfully,' she said. 'I do wish you *could* be with her, on this day especially.'

I nodded, and wished the tears would quit running down my cheeks.

'I doubt I'll ever be blessed with a child of my own,' Sarah went on.

'Oh, certainly you . . .'

She touched a finger to my lips. 'If I *did* have a son, I hope he would be as fine a young man as yourself.'

Then *she* took to weeping.

She sank to her knees and crossed her arms on my legs and

buried her face and gasped and sobbed. I set my new watch on the table.

'Don't cry,' I said. 'It's all right.'

She kept at it. I patted her back and stroked her hair. Finally, she stood up. She straightened her dress and sniffled a few times. 'I'm sorry,' she murmured. 'I don't know . . .' And suddenly she was bawling all over again, even harder than before.

I got to my feet and put my arms around her.

We stood there, mashing each other tight, both of us sobbing to beat the band.

It took a while, but we finally got worn out and stopped our crying. We didn't let go of each other, though. It felt mighty comfortable to be hugging her, even though I knew she wasn't my mother and she knew I wasn't her son.

When we unclenched, she tried to smile. Her face was all red and slick with tears, her eyes ashimmer. She looked just lovely. 'Aren't we the silly ones, though?' she said. 'Carrying on that way?'

I didn't know what to say. Sarah brushed the tears off my cheeks with her fingertips. Then she kissed my mouth, real gentle and sweet.

Not long after that, I went on up to my room and turned in. Taken all around, it had been a mighty strange Christmas. I spent a while puzzling over things, but my head was all foggy from the wine and before I knew it I was asleep.

Sarah woke me up the next morning with a kiss. She took to doing that every morning. Each night she'd come into my room at bedtime. We'd usually chat a spell, then she'd kiss me goodnight and go on her way.

In between, we looked after the General and Mable. I helped prepare meals, clean the house, and care for the horses. About once a week, Sarah and I went into town. We took the sleigh sometimes, or a carriage when the road was clear. There in town, we always bought supplies and a copy of the *World*, and Sarah always fixed us up with licorice sticks. Sometimes, when the weather was good, we wandered over to the beach.

A boardwalk was there, with all sorts of shops and booths and bath houses and pavilions and rides and such, but they were shut down for the winter. Sarah, she never failed to go on considerable about what a bully time we would be having there, come summer.

The way my savings were stacking up, a dollar each week, I could see I'd still be around through summer, and likely for a few summers more. I didn't know how much a boat ticket for England might cost, but it had to be dear.

Well, my spirits sank some whenever I thought about it. Mostly, though, I was fairly happy to be where I was. Sarah treated me real good. The General, he seemed to like having me around. Even old Mable warmed up to me. She bossed me something frightful, but didn't get snappish too often.

There were times when I went for whole days without giving a thought to Whittle. I figured I was safe, and he was far away somewhere. For all I knew, he might've gone and gotten himself killed. I sure hoped so.

Every time we came back from town with a new edition of the *World*, though, I hunted through it. I checked each story, half afraid I'd find one about a butchery and know Whittle was up to his old tricks.

There were murders aplenty reported in that newspaper. Folks were forever getting themselves shot or bludgeoned or strangled or stabbed. For a while, though, I didn't find anything that looked like Whittle's work.

It was the middle of January when I came across a story about a woman 'of low character' named Bess who was found 'unspeakably mutilated' in a place called Hell's Kitchen. That sure set my heart to thundering. But I read on a bit, and the paper said a fellow named Argus Tate had been nabbed for it.

As the weeks went by, I found half a dozen more stories about women getting cut up. More often than not, it happened in Hell's Kitchen or Chelsea. I didn't tell Sarah why I was interested, but asked her about those places and she said they were in Manhattan, across the East River from us. When she let out that they were only just fifteen or twenty miles from us and you could cross the river by a bridge or boat, I felt rather squirmy inside.

You could get there in a *day*. Whittle could get *here* in a day.

Of course, it might not be him that was killing those gals. That's what I told myself. I had to tell myself that, because otherwise it'd be my duty to go after him. I allowed I'd stay where I was unless I knew for sure it had to be Whittle over there.

I kept on checking the newspaper, and always hoped nothing would turn up to make it Whittle for certain.

My studies of the *World* didn't take much time. In between chores and trips to town and such, I trekked through a good many of the books in the General's parlor. I read a heap of Shakespeare and Charles Dickens and Stevenson and Scott. I had a go at some tales by Edgar Allan Poe, but gave up quick on those, for they reminded me of when I'd tried to read one on the *True D. Light* and gotten woozy. I wanted no truck with anything that put me in mind of that yacht or Whittle.

The books I liked best were those about America. I read plenty of Mark Twain, and even got to finish *Huckleberry Finn*, which I'd left hanging the night Mother dragged Barnes home drunk and I set off to hunt for Uncle William. I read all the *Leatherstocking Saga* by Cooper, and bunches of stories by Bret Harte. They gave me an awful hankering to see the Mississippi and the great forests and plains and mountains, and gold fields and the like. I longed to travel and have adventures.

Every now and then, I took a notion to light out for the West. I dreamed about it, but knew I was meant to stay with the Forrests until I could earn enough money for my return to England.

Besides, I heard tales from the General that made me glad to be safe in the civilized East.

After my goodnight kiss from Sarah, I often crept downstairs to the parlor and sat for hours with the General. We'd sit in front of the fireplace, him smoking his pipe, both of us taking sips of rum, and he'd talk on and on about his times with the Army.

He told me about West Point, and about Civil War battles, but mostly he liked to talk about his experiences during the Indian Wars.

Back on the yacht, Whittle had gone on considerable about going West and joining up with savages. If he'd had a chance to chat with Matthew Forrest, though, I reckon he might've sung a different tune. For one thing, most of the Indians were already killed or tame by now. For another, they did things to white men that would've made any reasonable chap eager to stay clear of them.

The General went on considerable about such horrors. I don't know if he just enjoyed trying to shock me, or if he *had* to talk about them. Maybe it was both.

Scalping seemed like a frightful thing, but that wasn't the worst of it.

Whenever the Indians had a chance to work on dead men, they stripped them naked and not only scalped them but packed them full of arrows and cut off their heads and arms and legs and privates and scattered such things about. It sounded just as bad as what Whittle'd done to Mary and Trudy.

The redskins didn't usually do such things to women, though, so Whittle had them beat there. They mostly hung on to the white women, and abused them, and kept them for slaves.

The General told me the two main rules of Indian fighting: don't let the heathens capture your women, and don't let them take you alive.

When women were at risk, you had to kill them. If it came down to one bullet left, and you had a choice of whether to plug an Indian warrior or your wife, why there wasn't any choice to be made. You shot your wife in the head.

He told me about a time when it looked as if the Sioux and Cheyennes might overrun Fort Phil Kearney, so the soldiers put all the women and children inside the magazine and left an officer with them who was supposed to touch off the powder and blow them all to smithereens rather than let the Indians take them alive. Fortunately, it didn't come to that.

He said the worst thing, next to letting them get their hands on women, was to let them take *you* alive.

One thing they liked to do was to strip a fellow naked and stake him out on the ground. Then they'd build a fire by one of his feet. When that foot was good and crisp, they'd cook the other, and then the legs and arms. They took their time about it, too. When they finally got tired of it all, they'd build a fire on the poor chap's chest and that would finish him.

Another favorite sport was to hang their captive upside down over a low fire. The head would cook real slow. By and by, though, it'd explode.

Sometimes, a white man would get turned over to the squaws. The General clammed up about what manner of games the squaws played on their prisoners, so I judged it must've been a sight worse than what he *had* told me. That was hard to imagine, though.

The upshot was, you'd rather be dead than captured.

If things got nip and tuck, you always saved your last bullet for yourself.

He told me about a time he found himself and his troops surrounded. He had a revolver for himself, but plenty of the others didn't. They only had rifles, so before the Indians came whooping down at them, every one of them tied a string around his rifle trigger and put a loop at the other end. That way, when it came down to the last round, they could put the rifles' barrels to their heads and use the toes of their boots to pull the triggers. Well, they got out of that scrape all right, but the General said it was common, when he came upon a massacre, to find whole passels of men who'd shot their own women and children, and followed it up with a bullet for themselves.

It made me sick to hear about such things, and to think about them afterwards. Putting a gun to your own head seemed mighty extreme, but for a man to shoot his wife and children or anyone else he loved – it made me shudder.

One time, I asked the General how he felt about it. He took a pull on his pipe, and let the smoke out slow, then said, 'There are many fates worse than death. Slow torture at the hands of the red man, that's one of them. Another is to lose those you love. A bullet in the brain-pan is quick and merciful next to either of those circumstances.'

I never told him about Trudy. But I spent considerable time worrying my head about the way she'd ended. Getting done by Indians was no worse than how Whittle'd butchered her. I took to feeling guilty about saving her life. If I'd let her hang or drown and not been so quick at jumping to the rescue, she would've been spared from his knife. The trouble is, I'd *known* it. Even while I'd been working to save her those times, I'd known she might be better off dead. But I'd gone ahead and saved her anyhow.

Maybe I didn't have it within me to do otherwise. But after hearing all the General had to say about saving a bullet for the woman, I knew I'd done wrong.

Chapter Twenty-one

Losses

Early in April, on a rainy Tuesday afternoon, Mable went roaming off. She'd pulled such stunts five or six times before, always sneaking out of the house when the rest of us were busy. On this particular day, the General was snoozing by the fire and I stayed in the kitchen to keep Sarah company while she baked cookies. It wasn't till the cookies were done and we carried out a plate so the General and Mable could enjoy some hot ones that we noticed she'd gone missing again.

It always fell on me and Sarah to go hunting for her, as Sarah didn't want the General out in the weather for fear he'd come down with pneumonia or such. Besides that, he never worried much about his wife's disappearances.

I came back to the parlor after a quick search of the house and shook my head. 'She seems to have gone off,' I said.

Sarah winced.

The General swallowed a mouthful of cookie and said, 'Yes. There's been a palpable, refreshing silence for the past hour or so. My eardrums have greatly appreciated the respite.'

'Grandpa!'

'Oh, now, no need to worry your head about Mable. I believe she only takes her little jaunts for the fun of being retrieved.'

'It's *pouring* outside.'

'The rain'll do her good. She hasn't bathed in a fortnight.'

That was on account of me, I reckon. Sarah'd woken me up a couple weeks ago and after giving me my morning smooch, she'd said a hot bath was waiting for me. It had gotten to be a fairly regular thing. Every few days, she would prepare my bath bright and early so I could have it before the General and Mable got around to stirring. I'd go down and soak, then by and by she'd come along with coffee for both of us. She'd sit on her chair near the tub, and we'd have a nice chat while we sipped. Later on, she'd come over and scrub my back for me.

I'd found the business a trifle embarrassing the first few times, but that passed as I got used to it. Then I got to where I really looked forward to those baths.

Sarah took her baths on the days between mine. When she finished, she'd come into my room all fresh and rosy from the heat, her hair still damp. I always stayed in bed and waited for her.

It usually ran through my mind, while I was waiting, that maybe I could head downstairs and take coffee to *her*, and stay and chat and maybe wash her back for her. The notion made me feel a bit squirmy. It also put my mind at ease, though, for the way I got stirred up by thinking about Sarah in the tub made it clear Whittle hadn't ruined women for me, after all. I purely longed to go down and visit her, but I felt guilty about it. After all, Sarah was some ten years older than me and often put me in mind of Mother, so it didn't seem right.

I let her go on bathing alone, figuring if she wanted me to join her, she ought to ask.

It bothered me considerable that she never asked, but allowed she must have her reasons, so I never let on that our bathing ritual seemed a mite one-sided and unfair. Besides, whenever I *imagined* her asking, it wrecked my nerves so bad I judged I'd likely turn down the invitation.

Anyhow, on that particular morning two weeks before Mable wandered off into the rain, I put on my slippers and robe and hurried downstairs. Sarah had gone on ahead of me. I figured to find her in the kitchen, starting the coffee. But she wasn't there, so I waltzed on into the bathroom.

Mable must've thought the bath was meant for her.

She'd beaten me to it, but not by much. She wasn't in, yet. With one foot on the floor, she was holding on to the edge of the tub while she swung her other leg over the side. Of course, she didn't have a stitch of clothes on.

She hadn't seen me. I should've stepped out quick and silent, but I didn't.

Not that I took any pleasure from the sight of her. Not by a long shot. But I was so surprised to find her climbing into my tub that I just stood there, gaping.

Her face was all dark and wrinkled like old wood. So were her hands. But the rest of Mable, mostly, was white except for a passel of blue veins and looked maybe thirty years younger than her face. She was so skinny her bones showed through her skin. The way she was bent over, her breasts dangled. They were long and rather flat, and hanging so low the nipple of one rubbed the rim of the tub.

160

I saw all that pretty quick, and then I noticed her scars. When I saw those, I gasped. Must've been fifteen or twenty of them, though I never got a chance to count. Puffy pink scars, each about an inch long, on her rump and down the backs of both her legs. I'd pretty much gotten used to Mable's limp, but seeing all those nasty scars made me realize why she hobbled.

Well, the gasp gave me away.

Mable looked over her shoulder and let out a frightful squeal. I hot-footed into the kitchen. Safe outside the door, I called in, 'I'm frightfully sorry, Mable.'

'You'll *be* sorry when I lay my hands on you. Land *sakes*! A woman can't bathe in her own house! Sarah! SARAH!'

Sarah rushed into the kitchen. She saw me standing there flustered. Then she fetched a glance at the open bathroom door. Then her cheeks colored considerable and her mouth dropped. 'Oh, my,' she said.

Mable must've heard her. 'You get in here right *now* and shut the door! That horrid child's been *spying* on me!'

Sarah went into the bathroom and closed the door. I heard Mable rail on at her for a spell, and Sarah talking soft and reasonable, explaining the mistake. By and by, Mable settled down and Sarah came out.

She met my eyes. She was blushing fierce. 'It's all right,' she told me. 'In the future, we'll both need to be more careful. It must've been horribly embarrassing for you.'

'I do hope Mable will forgive me.'

'I made it clear that you had no intention of spying on her, and that the bath was intended for you.'

'I never . . . meant to look at her.'

'Oh, I know, I know.' Smiling a bit sadly, Sarah stroked my hair. 'After all, you've had every opportunity to spy on *me*, if your inclination leaned toward such things. You've never done that, have you?'

'Why, no. Certainly not.'

'I'm sure you haven't,' she said, but the look she gave me was uncommon peculiar and set my face burning. Pretty soon, she said, 'You'd best have your bath another day.'

Then we went over to the sink, and Sarah pumped water into a pot. I added some wood to the stove, working up my courage, then asked, 'What happened to Mable's legs?'

She hoisted an eyebrow.

'I only glimpsed her for a blink, really, but . . .'

'Grandpa's never told you about that? All those nights you sneak downstairs and talk with him till all hours?'

I hadn't known Sarah was aware of all that. She'd done some spying herself, apparently.

'What happened to her?' I asked.

'If Grandpa hasn't told you, perhaps he'd rather you not know.'

'I suppose I might ask him about it tonight,' I said.

'Don't you dare. For heaven's sake, Trevor.'

'I won't, then.'

She set the pot of water on the stove to heat it. I figured she'd had her say on the subject of Mable's legs, but then she led me to the table and we sat down.

'It happened just after the end of the Civil War. Grandpa had been reassigned to a post in the West. He and Grandma were traveling there, just the two of them on horseback, when they were ambushed by a war party of Apaches near Tucson. Before they knew what was happening, Grandpa was shot off his horse. An arrow took him in the shoulder. When he fell, he struck his head on a rock. The blow rendered him unconscious, so he was completely unaware of all that happened afterward. I believe he's never forgiven himself for that, though it certainly was no fault of his. That's likely why he hasn't told you the story. He's never spoken a word of it to me, either. I only know about it because I once asked my father about Mable's limp. I've kept it secret from Grandpa that I know, and you must promise to do the same.'

'I promise,' I told her.

'What Mable did, she saw that Grandpa was down so she leapt off her mount and ran to his side. The way Papa told it, arrows were flying all about her. None hit her, though.'

'The Indians likely wanted to take her alive,' I said.

'That's exactly what Papa told me. And it seems to be the only reason they weren't both killed that day. What Grandma did, though, she drew out Grandpa's service revolver and emptied it at the Apaches. She got one of them, too. Then she was empty, and the savages were closing in. Fortunately, her shots were heard by a squad of cavalry patrolling nearby. She didn't know that, though. Besides, the soldiers were still a distance off. Grandma didn't have time to reload, so she dragged Grandpa across the ground to a hole in the rocks. It was like a cave. She shoved him all the way in, but there wasn't quite room enough for both of them. She wedged herself into the rocks as best she could. Her legs and . . . hindquarters . . . wouldn't fit. I guess the Indians had plenty of time to rush in and drag her out, but they didn't do that. Instead, they stayed back and poured arrows into Grandma. They made a game of it. The way Papa told it, they were prancing about laughing and whooping it up and sailing arrows into her when the soldiers came riding in and scattered them.'

Well, that story changed my outlook on the General and Mable both. I could see why he'd never told me about it, and why he always went on the way he did about Indian tortures and how you had a duty to save your women even if it meant killing them. He must've seen it that he'd failed Mable. The Apaches hadn't taken her off, but they'd damaged her considerable, and the fact it didn't turn out worse was only due to luck. The whole thing made me feel sorry for the General, and like him all the more.

As for Mable, I never again looked on her as an obnoxious old nuisance, and felt rather ashamed for ever thinking bad thoughts about her. It was just bully, picturing her crouched at the General's side, blazing away at the redskins. Then she'd dragged him to safety, even though he was near twice her size, and caught a heap of arrows in the backside for her troubles. She was a heroine to me after I found out about all that.

163

Of course, I couldn't let on that I knew. But I treated her extra nice from that time on. More than likely, she laid it down to my blunder of barging into the bathroom, and figured I was trying to win myself back into her good graces. That wasn't it, though. The reason I turned so friendly was simply because I admired her awfully for the gumption she'd shown against the Apaches.

When the General mentioned that she hadn't bathed in a fortnight, I knew it had to be on account of me. It weighed on me some while I got into my slicker and hurried off to the stable with Sarah. I wanted to be Mable's friend, and not someone who gave her troubles.

We harnessed Howitzer to one of the carriages and set off in the rain toward town. That was the direction Mable always took when she wandered off. There'd usually been snow on the ground, the other times, so we'd worried about her freezing up. We'd always found her in time, though, and she'd never seemed the worse for wear. I figured she could handle some rain, so I wasn't much concerned.

Not till I saw her.

Mable was sprawled face down by the side of the road, on a stretch between their place and the house of the nearest neighbor. Even from a distance, I could see she wasn't moving. But I couldn't see the puddle till we reined in Howitzer and jumped down and ran to her.

It wasn't much of a puddle, actually.

No more than a yard around and a couple of inches deep. But it had drowned her.

Or maybe it hadn't, and she'd keeled over dead and her face just *happened* to land in the water.

Either way, Mable was dead.

I hunched down and rolled her over. She tumbled, all loose, like she didn't have any bones. Her face was gray with muddy water. The rain cleaned it off, and fell into her mouth. Her eyes were open, staring. The raindrops splashed on her eyeballs, but she didn't blink.

'Oh, dear Lord,' Sarah murmured.

She closed Mable's lids, and then I picked up the poor limp body. Mable's been a bit shorter than me, and skinnier. It surprised me, how heavy she felt. I managed, anyhow, and took her to the carriage and put her down across the rear seats. We climbed aboard, then turned for home.

We didn't say a thing. We didn't cry or carry on, either. I wasn't feeling any particular sorrow, just then. Mostly, I felt rather afraid and sick, and guilty we hadn't gotten to Mable in time to save her. And I dreaded how the General would take to the loss of his wife.

Much as he always complained about her, I didn't suppose he'd be glad to have her gone.

We left the carriage in front of the porch. Sarah, she went in ahead of me. I followed, holding Mable's body. We found the General in the parlor.

He rose from his chair. His mouth dropped open, then shut again. Not speaking a word, he stepped over to us and put a hand on Mable's cheek.

'I'm so sorry,' Sarah told him, her voice quivery.

'I appreciate your bringing her back to me, dear.' He gave me a sorry glance, nodded, and took the body from my arms. 'I'll put her to bed,' he told us.

We both just stood there, silent, while he carried her away. I heard the fire crackling and popping, heard the stairs groan under the General's slow footfalls.

Pretty soon, along came the gunshot.

We both jumped.

I looked quick at the fireplace mantel. The General's revolver was there, where he always kept it.

Sarah and I raced upstairs.

I knew what we'd be finding, but we had to go and see for ourselves, anyhow.

In the room, Mable and the General were stretched out side by side on their bed. It almost looked like they'd laid down for a nap, except for the bloody mess on the headboard behind the General.

He was holding one of Mable's hands.

His other hand hung over the side of the bed.

I didn't see any gun.

But he had a string looped around the toe of his right house slipper.

I stepped past the end of the bed. The string dangled down from his foot to a rifle on the floor, where it was tied to the trigger. The rifle must've been thrown off him by the recoil.

Chapter Twenty-two

Mourning and Night

Sarah was their only surviving relation, but the General and Mable had a passel of friends she had to notify. About thirty of them showed up, mostly old men, some with their wives in tow. Just about all the men came in full dress uniform. They looked just splendid, sabers hanging at their sides, chests full of medals.

A service was held at the local Methodist church. One old fellow after another stood up front and eulogized the General and Mable. They had some mighty fine things to say about the couple.

When it came time to pay our last respects, we all lined up and filed past the coffins. Mable, she was rouged up pretty good and looked peculiar, but she was dressed in a fine satin gown like she was on her way to a party. The General looked ready to escort her there. A military ball, maybe. He was decked out in his uniform. He had more medals than most of the mourners put together. He'd shot himself through the mouth, so he didn't have any holes that showed.

I tucked one of his briar pipes into the coffin with him.

Sarah, she kissed each of her grandparents on the forehead.

They were planted in a graveyard behind the church. A powdered lady wearing more rouge than Mable, sang 'Nearer My God to Thee' and then a skinny little soldier who looked older than dirt raised a bugle to his lips and played 'Taps'. It was a sunny afternoon, but we all watered the grass something awful.

When that part was over, everybody came to the house. There was more food laid out than I'd ever seen in one place. We all ate, and the men got liquored up. Later on, some of the folks cleared out. Others stayed on, though. Some servants Sarah'd hired for the occasion made up guest rooms for them.

There wasn't a bedroom left for me, so I figured I'd settle down in the parlor. A drunk with a white beard down to his belt buckle snored on the sofa. I sat in the General's old chair. Its cushions were all sunken in from him.

The snoring wouldn't let me fall asleep, so I just sat there missing him and Mable, and wishing I'd known them better. By and by, I lit up one of the General's pipes. I figured he wouldn't mind. Back when he was alive and we'd sat up talking, he'd offered to let me smoke one. I'd always turned him down, but now I wished I'd smoked with him. When the pipe died out, I fetched the General's bottle of rum. That stuff always had a way of making me doze off. So I took a few sips of it, judging I'd need some help if I was to get any sleep at all.

I tucked the bottle out of sight quick when Sarah suddenly wandered in. She came silently through the parlor, her hair down and gleaming, her white nightdress ashiver with the firelight, floating soft around her. She looked just lovely.

Leaning down over me, she whispered, 'You don't want to spend the night in a chair.'

'It's quite all right, really.'

'I know a better place,' she said, and took my hand.

She hadn't brought a lamp along with her, so after we left the parlor we had to navigate our way in the dark. She kept hold of my hand, and didn't utter a sound as we climbed the stairs and started down the hallway.

I figured there must be a spare room, after all. But she led me to hers. She let us in, then shut the door real easy so as not to make a sound. Over by the bed, her lamp was burning.

'This should be much more comfortable for you,' she said in a hushed voice.

'It's *your* bed,' I told her.

'It's roomy enough for both of us.' With that, she went to it and stepped out of her slippers and climbed aboard. She pulled the covers over her, then scooched to one side. 'I brought in your nightshirt,' she said. Taking out an arm, she pointed to a chair by the wall. My flannel nightshirt was neatly folded on top of it.

Well, I didn't hanker to strip down in front of Sarah even if she had been a regular visitor during my baths. Those times, I'd been sitting in a tubful of water. So I doused the lamp before getting out of my funeral duds and slipping into the nightshirt.

I eased under the covers and lay on my back, close to the mattress edge so as not to bother her. The rum I'd drunk made my head a trifle foggy, but I felt so strange about being in the same bed as Sarah that I was wide awake. My heart wouldn't slow down, and I was shaking some even though the bed was warm and cozy.

By and by, Sarah's hand snuck over and found mine. She gave it a gentle squeeze. 'I'm so very glad you're here,' she whispered.

'This is vastly more comfortable than a chair, isn't it?' I said.

'You're all I have, now.'

When she said that, I feared she'd take to weeping. But she didn't. She rolled over warm against my side and said, 'Hold me. Please.'

So I turned and hooked an arm over her back, and she snuggled against me. 'It'll be all right,' I told her. I wanted to cheer her up. More than that, though, I needed to talk and take my mind off the feel of her. Sarah's head was tucked against the side of my neck, her breath tickling me. The way we were stretched out, she was pressing me tight all the way down to our knees. There wasn't a thing but our nightclothes between us. Her skin was hot through the cloth. I could feel every breath she took, and even her heartbeats.

'It'll be all right,' I said again, stroking her back. 'You'll see.'

Right off, I could tell that talking wouldn't do the job. I bent myself away from her and hoped she hadn't noticed the reason for it.

'Why,' I went on, 'I imagine you'll find yourself a husband in no time at all and you'll have a whole houseful of children.'

'If only that were so.'

'Just wait and see.'

'It's too late for me, Trevor. I'll never marry. I'll be an old spinster.'

'Don't talk that way. Why, I should think there must be *fifty* men in town who fancy you. There's Henry at the general store, for one. And the chap who owns the pharmacy. I could see just by how they . . .'

'I'll be twenty-seven years old, come October.'

'That isn't *old*. Besides, you're beautiful. I've not seen another woman in the whole town who could hold a candle to you, in the way of looks.'

'You're so sweet, Trevor.' She kissed the side of my neck. It sent shivers down to my toes.

I tried not to think about that.

'If you should set your mind to it,' I hurried on, 'I've no doubt but that you could find yourself married before summer. No doubt at all. I'll help you. We'll pick out a fine chap for you, and . . .'

Her mouth got in the way. She gave me a kiss, but it wasn't the usual kind – brief and gentle. With this one, she mashed her lips against mine. Her mouth was open and wet, and she was breathing into me. It wasn't a way I'd *ever* been kissed before.

While our mouths were locked together, she took to squirming so that her body rubbed against me. I couldn't help but squirm, myself.

I'd never felt so fired up and strange. The nearest thing was my time with Sue in the alley, but she'd been a stranger and more my own age and we'd had more clothes on and she wasn't half as pretty as Sarah. Sue'd been after my money and such, too, whereas I didn't actually know what Sarah was after.

Taken all around, I felt tight and hot and fit to bust, but awfully confused and ashamed, too.

It went on for a spell, but finally Sarah unclenched me. I thought she was done. I felt awful disappointed, but mighty relieved, too. I wiped my mouth dry and fought to catch my breath.

She wasn't done, though.

She sat up and threw the covers off us. That was fine, for it had gotten mighty warm underneath them. But then she shucked off her nightdress. I could see her plain in the moonlight from the windows. Her skin looked pale as milk, and shadows smudged her face.

Kneeling beside me, she started to slide my nightshirt up my legs. I took her by the wrists.

'You'll be so much more comfortable without it,' she whispered.

I felt rather panicky, and searched for a way to call her off. 'The house is simply jammed with people,' I said, and suddenly wondered how come she'd waited for tonight, as we'd been alone in the house for a few days, ever since the bodies had been taken away. Maybe she'd needed this long to work up the gumption. Or maybe she'd only brought me in here to sleep, and hadn't planned on getting so friendly. 'What if someone should walk in?' I asked.

She answered that by climbing off the bed, crossing over to the door and turning the key in its lock. 'Now we're safe,' she said. 'We'll have to be careful when we leave the room tomorrow, is all.'

She came walking back to the bed. She crawled on, but this time she didn't kneel beside me. Instead, she straddled me down near my knees. I could feel the sides of her legs touching my skin. Her thighs were spread wide, and looked smooth as cream. She was dark where they came together. From seeing Trudy, I knew the dark place was hair. Above that, she was all pale and slender, a dot of shadow at her navel, and dark at the tips of her breasts. Her breasts were bigger than Trudy's, bigger than they looked when Sarah had clothes on.

She lifted my hands toward them and leaned in. Her breasts were almost out of reach, but not quite. She guided my hands over them. They were warm and moist, and I'd never touched anything so smooth. Not even satin or velvet or silk. The nipples didn't feel smooth. They were rumpled and puckered, with springy centers that stuck out. But something about them stirred me up even more than her smooth parts.

'You've . . . never been with a woman . . . have you?' she sort of gasped out.

'Not . . . in this manner.'

'Squeeze.'

I squeezed. Sarah writhed and moaned. But we were both sweated up pretty good by then, so my fingers slid around when they tightened on her breasts and it put me in mind of Whittle trying to pick up Mary's breast off the floor, and how it was all bloody and slipped out of his hand. Before I had a chance to stop myself, I jerked my hands back as if they'd gotten scorched.

Sarah flinched as if I'd struck her. 'Trevor?' Her soft voice sounded confused, hurt.

'I'm awfully sorry,' I said.

She said it again. 'Trevor?' All forlorn.

'They're lovely bosoms. Truly.' To prove it, I reached out for them. But my hands stopped short. I brought my arms down to my sides. 'It's not at all your fault,' I murmured.

She gazed at me for a spell, not saying anything. Then she

171

swung her leg clear and tumbled off. She rolled onto her back, pulled her pillow down and covered her face with it.

She just lay there sprawled in the moonlight, silent, motionless except for her breathing. Wasn't long, though, before she commenced to sob and whimper. Her misery just tore at my heart. But the way her breasts shook filled my head with more thoughts of Whittle. I couldn't help it, and even pictured him crouching over Sarah, slicing them off, cupping them up in his hands.

I hadn't laid eyes on him for months, yet here he was, tormenting me and Sarah both.

She'd had too much grief already. She didn't deserve this. I shut my eyes to keep them from her breasts, and stretched my arm across her belly and patted her side. She went stiff for a bit. Then she took hold of my wrist. I reckoned she was about to hurl it away, but all she did was hang on. Her belly kept jumping under my arm.

Finally, she calmed down. She sniffed and let out a sigh. Through her pillow, she said, 'Oh, Trevor. You're such a dear. Will you ever forgive me?'

'Forgive you? For what?'

'For making such a fool of myself.'

'You've done no such thing.'

She let go of my wrist. But I kept my arm across her and caressed her side.

'I'm not . . . I've only been with a man but once. And that was eight years ago. Ever since then, I've always behaved . . . like a lady. Until tonight.'

'You're a splendid lady,' I told her.

'Little better than a slut,' she said. This time, her voice wasn't muffled. I opened my eyes and saw that her head was turned toward me, the pillow hugged to her breasts. 'You had every reason to be disgusted.'

'Oh, but I wasn't. Not at all. Quite the contrary.'

'You needn't fib to me.'

'I found it all quite wonderful until . . .'

'Until?'

'Well . . .' It wasn't something I much cared to tell her about. My mouth got dry, and I could feel myself blushing all over.

'Please,' she said.

'It's rather unpleasant. Sickening, actually.'

'Trevor, tell me.'

There seemed to be no way around it. So I decided to tell her the truth. 'I'm afraid I've had some rather rum experiences in the matter of ladies' chests.'

She huffed out some air. It sounded very much like a sort of laugh. '*What?*'

'Whittle. Remember the murderer I told you about when I first arrived?'

'The man who stole Saber.'

'Yes. Whittle. He cut the breasts off two women. I saw them afterwards.'

'Dear Lord!' she gasped.

'When I . . . squeezed yours . . . I couldn't help but remember.'

'Oh, my Lord. Oh, Trevor.'

'So you see, it wasn't you.'

'You poor thing.' With that, she rolled toward me. I turned onto my side, and we hugged each other, the pillow soft and thick between our chests. She kissed me, but it wasn't like before. It was gentle and sweet and motherly.

Right off, I knew I preferred the other sort.

What with the covers off and still being sweaty, I started to feel cold except for where the pillow was and where our bodies touched. Sarah didn't have a stitch on, so it must've been worse for her. I couldn't stir myself to fetch up the blankets, though, because it felt so peaceful to be laying with her that way.

I was glad I'd told her the truth. Now she knew I hadn't found anything wrong about *her*. There was more to it than only that, however. When you've got a dark secret, it doesn't seem quite so terrible after you've talked about it. Especially if the person you've told is someone as sweet as Sarah.

I took to thinking about the way things had gone for a while there before Whittle'd ruined it all.

By and by, I said, 'Of course, yours are still attached.'

She asked, 'What?' in that surprised, amused way she had.

'Your bosoms.'

'Yes, they are.'

'Perhaps if I should . . . become accustomed to them.'

'What?'

'Perhaps they wouldn't put me off.'

'I see.'

'Shall I have a go at it?'

She didn't answer, but I felt the pillow slide away. She tucked it under the side of her head. 'I'm to be your cure?'

'I do hope so,' I said.

She laughed softly, but then caught her breath when I curled my hands over her breasts.

That night, I got accustomed to attached ones. Whittle stood in my way for a while, but finally he skulked off and there was only just me and Sarah in that room. I held and caressed and squeezed those breasts of hers. I lifted them and shook them. I rubbed my face all over them. I felt their nipples press my eyelids. I licked and kissed and sucked.

Hardly got a good start on them before Sarah tugged the nightshirt off me.

She thrashed about and whimpered and moaned and hung on to my hair and gasped out my name over and over again.

We wrestled about considerable.

We were all over each other, touching everywhere, and I didn't feel shy once.

Then I found Sarah on top of me. Next thing I knew, her mouth was jammed against mine and her breasts were mashed to my chest and she took hold of me below decks. But not with her hands. I felt myself sliding into a tight, juicy place where I wasn't sure I ought to be. It felt bully, but Sarah acted like she was in pain, and that rather scared me so I tried to get out.

'It's all right,' she gasped.

'I'm hurting you.'

'No. No. It's where . . . I want you.' And then she shoved down and I went all the way in so far and deep it seemed I was getting swallowed up by her.

Well, I'd been feeling for a while like I might just bust. All of a sudden, that's exactly what I did do. I tried to pull out quick so as not to mess her, but she clutched my rump and wouldn't let me. I couldn't get out. I couldn't stop, either. Nothing to do but let it happen right inside her. The way she twitched and yelped while I unloaded, I figured she was even more upset than me.

When it stopped, I felt so embarrassed I wanted to die.

'I'm so awfully sorry,' I said.

She kind of relaxed, sinking down on me and panting like she was all tuckered out. She rubbed her cheek against mine, her hair making my face itch, her breath hot on my ear.

'I didn't mean to do that,' I told her.

'What?' she whispered.

'You know. *Do* that. *In* you.'

'It was wonderful.'

'But I've . . . gotten you full of yuck.'

She laughed softly, jiggling. 'It's not yuck, darling. It's your love. You've filled me with your love.'

'Was that . . . *supposed* to happen?'

'Oh, yes. Oh, yes.'

Well, that came as a considerable relief.

She went on kissing me. By and by, my love commenced to leak out of her. It syruped me up, and turned cold. But I didn't mind, for Sarah was heavy and warm and acting like I'd done her just the most wonderful favor of all time.

I felt pretty much the same about her.

Chapter Twenty-three

Fine Times

Before you know it, we both got stirred up again and had another go-round. This time, I took the top. I rather knew what to expect, so I wasn't scared. The only surprise was that it didn't end so quick. I got plenty of chance to plunge about and appreciate things.

After we finished, we pulled the blankets over us and snuggled.

'I love you so much, darling,' she whispered.

'You're simply smashing,' I said.

She laughed softly, her sweet breath caressing my face.

'I only wish we'd had a go at this months ago,' I told her.

She laughed again, then squeezed me hard. 'We couldn't, of course. Not with Grandma and Grandpa in the house.'

'They needn't have known.'

'I couldn't bring myself to take the risk. They would've thrown you out of the house. Besides . . .'

She didn't go on, so I asked, 'Besides what?'

'I . . . feared that I might frighten you off. I couldn't bear the thought of losing you. That's what I thought I'd done tonight, lost you. When you pulled away from me.'

'It was only Whittle.'

'The cure seems to have worked.'

'Splendidly.'

'We'll have such fine times together.'

In the morning, I dressed and crept out of Sarah's room without being spotted by any of the visitors. Later in the day, the last of them departed.

The house was empty, but for the two of us.

We didn't talk about last night. We didn't carry on, either.

But I could tell she hadn't forgotten about it. She acted different. She hardly ever took her eyes off me, and stayed a lot closer to me when we were doing chores and such. She touched me considerable, but not in any needful way – more like how she might touch her best friend. Also, she couldn't stop talking. She chatted on and on about this and that, and laughed at near everything I had to say.

I felt mighty grown-up and happy, though I got a bit nervous at times, wondering what was to happen next.

After our evening meal, we went into the parlor. She had me sit in the General's chair. Then she filled one of his pipes with tobacco. She lit it up, smiling at me as she sucked the flames down into the tobacco. When it was going good, she handed it to me. She sat at my feet and leaned back against my legs. I puffed away. Every now and then, I reached down to stroke her hair and she'd turn her head and gaze up at me.

The only light in the parlor came from the fireplace.

It all seemed uncommon peaceful and nice.

When the pipe went out, Sarah got to her feet and hauled me up. Humming a slow, peaceful tune, she started to dance with me. We stayed right in front of the fire. There wasn't much room, what with all the furniture, so we more or less kept to the same place, hanging on to each other and turning in circles.

It was cozy and a bit exciting, the way we held each other and glided about and sometimes kissed.

She hummed one tune after another. After five or six of them, she began to unbutton my shirt while we danced. We fumbled about and undressed each other and kicked our duds out of the way. After that, we went on dancing just like before. Only it felt quite different.

She was all smooth warm skin against me, sliding and rubbing. Sometimes, we danced far enough apart so our fronts hardly touched at all, just the tips of her breasts brushing my chest and me prodding her belly a bit. Other times, we mashed ourselves together. The hand I had on her back drifted down, and I took to holding her rump, which was ever so soft but flexed up firm with every step. She did the same to me.

Eventually, we gave up on the dancing part. We stood there squirming and kissing and caressing each other till we couldn't hold off any longer, and ended up on the rug in front of the fireplace.

We went upstairs after we were done, and had a fine time in her bed, and then fell asleep.

In the morning, she woke me with a kiss as she'd done so many times before. I opened my eyes to find her leaning over the bed, wearing her nightdress. 'Your bath is ready, dear,' she said.

She'd brought my robe and slippers into her room. She walked out, the same as she used to do. I put on the robe and slippers, went downstairs, greeted her in the kitchen, and got myself into the tub.

Like always, she brought the coffee in. I sat in the tub, sipping mine, while she took her usual seat nearby.

'We'll be going into town today,' she said. 'I need to see our attorney about a few matters.'

'An attorney?'

'He'll be turning over the estate to me.'

'The house?'

'Oh yes. The house, everything. I'm Grandpa's only heir, of course. He was very well off. Not that *he* earned a great deal. But he'd inherited a considerable sum from the family.'

'I'm quite glad to hear that. So then, you'll be able to continue on without financial worries.'

'None at all.'

I considered asking if she might raise my weekly pay a trifle, now that she was coming into a certain amount of wealth. That would've appeared greedy, however. Besides, such a request would only serve to remind her that I aimed to book passage for England if I could ever afford to do so.

Sitting in the bathtub with my coffee, I wished I hadn't thought about returning home.

I was not at all eager to leave Sarah.

Still, England was home and I sometimes missed Mother terribly.

I worried about her. She hadn't responded to any of the several letters which I'd posted to her during the past months. I'd received no message whatsoever other than the quick response to my cable just before Christmas.

It was perplexing, disturbing.

At times, I wondered if something terrible had happened to her. That seemed unlikely, however. Uncle William and Aunt Maggie no doubt knew my whereabouts and would've let me know if Mother had met with some sort of tragedy. But why hadn't she written to me? It seemed quite unlike her, and a day rarely went by that I didn't puzzle over the situation.

'Is something troubling you?' Sarah asked. I reckon my worry showed.

'It's Mother again, I'm afraid.'

She frowned and shook her head. 'You *should've* received a letter from her by now. It's strange.'

'I do hope she's all right.'

'Oh, I'm sure she's fine.'

'Then why hasn't she written?'

'She probably did. Maybe her letters were misplaced. Such things happen. You shouldn't let it upset you.' With that, Sarah set her cup aside. She came over to the tub, knelt behind me, and rubbed my shoulders. 'Any day now, the postman will come by with a letter from her. You'll see. But the main thing is, she knows you're in good hands.'

'I am that,' I said, and looked over my shoulder to smile at Sarah. My worries about Mother faded out, right quick. Sarah didn't have her nightdress on, any more. 'I say!' I said.

She laughed and kissed me. 'Never you mind,' she said, and took to soaping my back. I was used to that, but liked it all the more knowing she'd stripped down. When she finished my back, she reached around with both arms and slicked my front, which she'd never done before. Not just my chest, but my belly, too. Then lower down. She had to lean in pretty good for that. She nibbled the side of my neck while she was at it. Sent shivers all through me. And so did watching her hands. They were up to their forearms in the water, one sliding the soap bar while the other rubbed and stroked me.

'You are a thorough wench,' I said.

'One can't be too clean.'

'And does that apply to you as well?' I asked. Before she had a chance to answer, I scooped up water with my coffee cup and flung it over my shoulder. She let out a squeal that turned into laughter. Then she grabbed both my shoulders, pulled me backward and shoved, scooting me down till my head went under.

I came up gasping and blinking, just in time to watch Sarah swing a leg over the rim of the tub. She climbed right in with me. Kneeling between my legs, she took away the cup and handed the bar of soap to me. 'Finish the job you started,' she said, and laughed some more.

I was mighty glad to oblige her.

I soaped her up good, using both hands and taking my time about it. By and by, she quit laughing. She breathed heavy and moaned, and took to guiding my hands around. I'd been working mostly on her breasts, but she didn't want her southern section neglected, so she took my hands down there. After a bit, she was in an awful frenzy. I could say the same for myself, actually.

She didn't wait to rinse, but sprawled atop me, all sudsy and slippery.

Well, that came to a quick, wild finish. But we didn't stop. We carried on, thrashing and tussling and flopping about, taking breathers now and again to soap up places we might've missed earlier, soaping some of the same places, too, then commencing to splash around and join up all over again. It's a wonder nobody drowned.

The water was cold by the time we climbed out.

There was near as much on the floor as in the tub.

We dried each other with towels. Then I stayed and mopped the floor while Sarah made breakfast in the kitchen.

After the meal, we dressed and went out to the stable. There, we harnessed Howitzer to the carriage and headed off. Sarah let me handle the reins, as she knew I enjoyed it. That left her to hop down and attend to the gate. After closing the gate, she rushed over and checked the mailbox. I longed to see her reach inside and pull out a letter from Mother, but she returned empty-handed. Climbing aboard, she shook her head. 'I'm sorry,' she said.

'Perhaps the postman hasn't arrived yet,' I told her, though I knew it was already past noon. Back when the General was alive, Sarah had usually brought the mail to him before he'd finished breakfast. Though he and Mable ate much later than us, they'd get done by around eleven. So the postman had certainly come along by now, but with nothing to leave.

'Maybe tomorrow,' Sarah said.

Disappointed, I got us rolling.

Sarah stared at me, looking rather solemn. Pretty soon, she said, 'Shall I buy you a ticket for England?'

The merest whisper of a breeze could've knocked me over when I heard those words. I gawped at her.

'I'm able to afford it now, you know. Would it make you happy?'

'Do you mean it?' I blurted.

'Of course. If that's what you want.'

I gazed at her, struck dumb with surprise and gratefulness. The sun was out, shining on her face. She looked so beautiful it made my heart sore.

Much as I longed for home, the notion of going away from Sarah all of a sudden filled me with a sick, lonely feeling.

I'd been keen on Sarah since the moment I first saw her, the night I warned the General about Whittle and we stormed into her bedroom. It was likely Christmas night that I fell in love with her. After that, I would've been sorry to part with her. But now, what with all that we'd done since the funeral, I could hardly bear the thought of going off and never seeing her again.

'Would you come along with me?' I asked.

'What would your mother have to say about that?'

'I'm sure she'd be quite fond of you. You could stay with

us. I'd show you all of London. We'd have a ripping good time!'

She shook her head. 'It's nice to think so, but ... the difference in our ages. Your mother would be appalled. *Everyone* would be appalled.'

'They needn't know that we're more than chums.'

'We'd have to behave like strangers. We couldn't so much as hold hands or kiss, much less dance or share a bed ... or bathe together.'

'Why, we would find times for such things.'

'No. I'm afraid not.'

'But Sarah!'

'It would be too horrible for both of us.'

'But how can I leave you?'

'I haven't *ordered* you to leave. I'm simply offering you the opportunity. The choice is yours.'

'I can't go without you.'

When I said that, her eyes watered up. She stroked my cheek and kissed me. 'You may change your mind, someday.'

I shook my head.

'If ever you do, tell me. We'll buy the ticket for you. Next week, next month, next year. You may grow weary of me, you know.'

'Never,' I said.

Soon after that, we reached the outskirts of town. Sarah gave me directions to the attorney's office, which turned out to be in his home. Before climbing down, she handed me a wad of money and told me I should go on and buy our supplies. She would find me when she was finished with the legal matters.

I left her, and headed for the markets.

I had a fair idea what we needed in the way of food and such, and set to gathering it. But my mind was all ajumble. Had I done the proper thing, refusing her offer? I felt as if I'd betrayed Mother. I felt, too, that Sarah had somewhat let me down. After all, she *could* go with me.

The more I puzzled over it, though, the more I saw she

was right. Should she come with me, we'd be forced to keep apart. It would be awful.

So it came down to stay or lose Sarah, and I'd made my choice to stay. Bad as I felt about Mother, though, pretty soon I eased my mind about that. If Sarah hadn't offered to buy me a ticket home, why, I would've been staying anyhow. At least for several more months. The trick was to keep on saving my money till I'd earned enough for the passage home, and study the situation then.

I was feeling fairly comfortable about things by the time I'd rounded up our food and supplies. I loaded them into the carriage. Sarah hadn't returned yet, so I read the *World* while I waited for her.

Chapter Twenty-four

Slaughter

The story that changed everything wasn't in the issue of the *World* that I read while waiting for Sarah to return from the attorney's office. I turned from page to page, and gave little thought to Whittle.

We went on about our lives, both of us mighty pleased and content. The next couple of weeks were smashing. We bathed in the mornings, and danced in the evenings. Between all that, we ate our meals and cleaned the house, worked on the grounds, took horseback rides, had picnics here and there, went into town for supplies, and generally had a fine time at whatever we were up to. It was wonderful even when we only just talked. Sometimes, we did nothing except sit about and read. Taken all around, we couldn't have been much happier.

But then came the day we returned from town and I settled down for a look at the newspaper while Sarah sat nearby with a book of poems by Elizabeth Barrett Browning.

The story I ran across went like this:

TOMBSTONE ROCKED BY SAVAGE MURDERS

Tombstone, Arizona Territory, infamous for its history of gunslinging desperados and marauding Apaches, was stunned on 22 April by the early morning discovery of Alice Clemons (42) and her two daughters, Emma (16) and Willa (18), brutally slain in their room at Mrs Adamson's Boarding House on Toughnut Street.

According to the *Tombstone Epitaph*, the three women met their fate at the hands of person or persons unknown sometime during the previous night. They were found by the maid at 9:00 the following morning, whereupon the unfortunate woman swooned at the grisly sight.

All who viewed the scene were shocked beyond measure. 'The room looked like a slaughterhouse,' averred Dr Samuel Wicker, who went on to say that all three women had been most horribly butchered and dismembered. Said Deputy Marshal Frank Dunbar, 'I've seen a few white men who got themselves carved up near as bad by the Apache, but these were ladies. Whoever done this is a monster, pure and simple.'

In addition to numerous unspeakable mutilations committed upon Mrs Clemons and her daughters, it has been reported that all three were scalped. This has led some to suspect that they did, indeed, fall victim to one or more renegade savages. Since the surrender of Geronimo to General Miles nearly three years ago, the citizens of Tombstone had experienced little or no difficulty with the redman. They had considered such troubles to have come to an end, and many are filled with dismay at the possibility that murderous Indians may be lurking in the area.

Not so Deputy Dunbar. 'A white man did this,' Dunbar avowed. 'He left bootprints in the blood. You don't catch many redskins shod in boots. He had a long stride, too, that puts him around six feet tall. If you don't count the likes of Mangus Colorado, your basic Indian's usually a short fellow.'

Be he redman or white, the vicious assailant remains at large and no witnesses have come forward with information about his identity. The people of Tombstone, so accustomed to acts of bloody violence, remain shaken by the unthinkable nature of this outrage perpetrated in their midst.

When I read that story, I felt like the world had caved in on me. I sat there stunned, my breath knocked out.

'What is it?' Sarah asked, looking at me.

'Whittle.'

She shut her book and leaned forward. 'What? They've caught him?'

I could only shake my head.

She set her book aside, came over to me, and took the newspaper from my shaky hands. 'Which piece . . .?'

'Tombstone.'

She stood there, reading. Then she knelt in front of me, put the paper on the floor, and rested her hands on my legs. 'It might have been anyone,' she said.

'No. It was Whittle. I *know* it.'

'You can't know for certain.'

'He's doing precisely what he planned to do – go out west and cut up women. He even considered that his butcheries might be mistaken for the work of Indians. He hoped he might join up with a band of hostiles. And show them a few of his tricks.'

Sarah rubbed my legs gently while she gazed at me. 'You're not responsible for him. None of this is your fault.'

'I should've gone after him.'

'You did what you could, darling. You came *here* to save us from him. It would've been foolhardy for you to venture out again that night in the snow, and it was too late to chase after him by the time we found that he'd stolen Saber.'

'That's when I should've left.'

'No.'

'If I'd borrowed a horse and pursued him . . .'

'He was hours away by then. It would've been hopeless.'

'Hardly hopeless,' I told her, feeling just miserable. 'The man's got no nose. I could've asked about, tracked him down. I couldn've *got* him. But I didn't even have a go at it. I didn't want to have a go at it. I was safe and comfortable here.'

'Here is where you belonged, Trevor. I know how you feel, but it's never been your duty to stop him.'

'I don't know about duty,' I told her. 'But I had opportunities to kill him and failed. It's my fault he boarded the *True D. Light*. It's my fault he murdered the folks aboard her. It's my fault he ever came to America at all. Trudy and her family, and those Clemons women in Tombstone, they'd be alive today if it weren't for me. I've no doubt Whittle has killed others, too. Many others. Probably a whole string of gals between here and the Arizona Territory. They likely just didn't make the *World*, or I missed the issues that told of them. Maybe I did read about some of them, but talked myself into thinking it hadn't been Whittle's work. But this time, I can't deceive myself. Nobody but Whittle could've done this business in Tombstone. I'm afraid I must go after him.'

Sarah didn't say a thing for quite a spell. She only just held my legs and gazed at me real solemn. Finally, she said, 'It's no wonder that Grandpa took to you. You're so very much like him. Duty. Honor. Set the wrongs of the world aright, or die in the attempt.'

'I'm not the one who'll do the dying. That'll be Whittle's job.'

'Your mind is set, then.'

'I don't want to leave you, Sarah.'

'You *won't* leave me. Do you truly think I would let you go journeying off on such a campaign without me?'

That was the second time in a couple of weeks she'd thrown astonishment into me.

'You're joking,' I said. I knew she'd meant it, though.

She gave my legs a hard squeeze. Her eyes were afire with excitement. 'We'll go together. It may take a few days to make preparations. We'll need to close the house . . . hire a caretaker . . . set our finances in order . . .'

'But you're a woman,' I pointed out.

'I am indeed. I am also a Forrest, from a long line of soldiers and adventurers.'

'It's likely to be quite dangerous.'

'Whatever the dangers, we'll face them together.'

'I should do this alone.'

'Indeed?' She hoisted her eyebrows. 'You wouldn't return to England without me. Now you're suddenly eager to journey west alone? Why, the only difference is the direction of travel.'

'Going to England would not have put you in harm's way.'

'You would rather leave me here to fend for myself?' she asked.

'I'm afraid so. Yes. You'd be safe here.'

'I'd be lonely,' she said. 'I'd be destroyed. There would be nothing here for me except an empty, forlorn house. You *are* my life, Trevor. So what if we travel into danger? Better to face any peril, and perish if it should come to that, than to stay here without you.'

'It isn't that I *want* to leave you behind.'

'I know, darling. I know.'

Reaching out, I stroked her hair. 'I've seen what Whittle does to women. If he should lay his hands on you . . .'

'We won't allow that to happen.'

Part Three

Bound for Tombstone

THREE

Part Three

Bound for Jamestown

Chapter Twenty-five

Westering

We aimed to travel by rail, as that was the quickest way to cross such a distance.

So on top of making arrangements for the house, Sarah figured she had no choice but to sell off the horses. She knew that her attorney, Mr Cunningham, might be interested in them, so we went to his office together.

He was a heavy, cheerful fellow who put me in mind of old Daws, the cabman. That made me a bit lonesome for home, but the glooms couldn't stand up against all the excitement I had inside me.

After making up our minds that we'd hunt down Whittle together, Sarah and I had both found ourselves caught up in the thrill of it all. We knew it was a grim mission full of hazards, but that didn't seem to matter near as much as knowing we were about to set off on an adventure together.

Well, she explained to Mr Cunningham that she intended to escort me to Arizona Territory so I could join up with my father, a cavalry major stationed at Fort Huachuca, which wasn't too far from Tombstone. She could've made him a general, but I reckon she didn't want to lay it on too thick. She told him that she aimed to shut down the house and hire a caretaker. Then she asked if he might like to purchase the three horses.

Well, the upshot was that he offered to look after the horses instead of buying them. That way, they'd still be Sarah's when she got back from the trip. He also said he knew just the fellow to take care of the house, and would gladly handle the matter of hiring him.

Next, we went to the post office. There, Sarah arranged to have her mail forwarded to General Delivery in Tombstone. I mailed a letter to Mother, in which I told her about making a trip west and said she could write to me in Tombstone. I didn't mention that Sarah'd be with me. Nor did I say a thing about going in pursuit of Whittle, figuring she'd only fret if she knew the truth.

Done at the post office, we headed for the bank. Sarah loaded up on money.

That finished our town business. For the next couple of days, we set the house in order. Mostly, we cleaned and covered the furniture and got rid of perishables and such. When that was pretty much taken care of, we packed for the trip.

We wanted to travel light, so we didn't use trunks. I fit all my duds into just one valise. It took a couple more to hold Sarah's outfits. We figured to leave behind everything but our clothes and toilet articles. And weapons. Sarah slipped the single-shot pistol and some extra ammunition into her handbag. I threw the General's army revolver, holster, and a passel of spare bullets into my valise. We chose to leave the rifle behind. It wouldn't fit in our luggage. Sarah allowed we wouldn't want to be lugging it about, but I suspect she didn't want it around because of her Grandpa using it to shoot himself.

Mr Cunningham had hired a fellow name of Jim Henderson to look after the house. Henderson had dropped by a few times to talk with Sarah, and she'd arranged for him to ride us to the railroad depot in town.

It was the first day of May, sunny and warm and breezy, that we set out. At the station, we bid farewell to Henderson. Then we went to a ticket window and Sarah paid our fares to Manhattan. The train hadn't arrived yet, so we waited out on the platform with some other folks. Most of them didn't have any luggage at all. Others had little more than what they might need for an overnight stay. I don't suppose any of them were about to start on a journey as great as ours. I was so excited I could hardly sit still.

By and by, along came the howl of a whistle. I rushed over close to the tracks, and saw our train. It chugged around a bend in the rails, smoke belching from its chimney, just monstrous and wonderful. As it roared closer, I could feel the floorboards shaking under my boots. The engineer waved down at me from his high window, just as such chaps used to do when I was back in England standing by the tracks to enjoy the thrill of a passing train. I waved back to him. A moment later, the locomotive rolled by, clanking and hissing steam, followed by the coal car and a string of passenger carriages.

After they groaned and squealed to a stop, I went back to Sarah. A porter took our baggage, and we climbed aboard. Sarah let me have the window seat. Though I'd ridden many times on the underground and even gone by rail on holidays with Mother, I'd never felt near the thrill that coursed through me when this train commenced to chug along and leave the station behind.

I met Sarah's eyes. With a smile, she gave my hand a squeeze.

'Here we go,' she said.

After that, I kept my face pretty much mashed to the window.

It was glorious: the country, the bridge over the East River, the towers of New York City. But my aim here isn't to run along about all that; it's to tell you the story of my adventures.

The way I see it, an adventure is someone else's mishap.

Nothing much happened in the way of adventures for a spell, so I'll scoot along with my narrative and get to it rather quick.

What we did was change trains at Grand Central Terminal, then ride west toward Chicago in a Pullman car. The trip was bully. We spent plenty of time talking, meeting friendly people and such. We ate fine meals in the dining car, and slept at night in berths with hanging curtains. Whenever I could, I watched out the windows.

We sped along through towns and forests and mountains, crossed bridges over deep canyons and river gorges that gave me the sweats with notions of derailing, and raced across valleys where we zipped past farms and villages.

The nights were glorious. I spent many an hour in my berth, hidden away in darkness behind the heavy curtain, peering out at the moonlit land, wondering about the lives of all the strangers out of sight beyond the lighted windows of farmhouses and homes along the tracks. I'd just lay there, watching everything slip by while the train rocked me gently, wheels clickity-clacking over the rails, whistle sometimes letting out long, mournful hoots.

It was awfully peaceful, but it often gave me a peculiar empty feeling. A longing for I didn't know what.

Sarah wasn't the cause of it, I know that. She had the lower berth, directly under me. At night, I'd wait a while and then poke my head out the curtain. When the coast was clear, I'd climb down and join her. We had some smashing times, but we had to be quiet about if for we had let on to the other passengers that I was her servant. They would've been mighty shocked to see me sneaking down to her bed.

We never got caught, though. By and by, I'd kiss her goodnight and climb back up to my own berth, where I'd lay awake and gaze out the windows and feel strange all over again.

Before you know it, we arrived in Chicago. We spent the night in a fine hotel on the shore of Lake Michigan, returned to the depot the next morning and boarded a train that would take us south to St Louis.

After leaving Chicago behind, we went through just the flattest land you'd ever hope to see. Except for a passel of small towns with more grain elevators than you could imagine, there was nothing to look at but miles and miles of fields as far as the eye could see. Once in a while, there'd be a farm house and barn and silo off in the distance, but that was about it.

Finally, we came to the Mississippi River. It took the breath right out of me. Here was the *Mississippi*! Mark Twain's river! We got closer and closer to it, and then we were above it on a bridge. I'd never seen the beat of it. I couldn't believe I was here, gazing down at the very same river where Mark Twain had been a steamboat pilot, where Tom Sawyer and Huck Finn and Jim had gone swimming and rafting. I couldn't see a paddlewheel, but there were ships aplenty, and I even spotted a couple of kids fishing off a canoe. I just hankered something awful to be down there with them.

Maybe I'll come back someday, I told myself.

And that's when it struck me why I'd been having those strange spells of longing. Because I was only just speeding along on the rails, glimpsing so many new places I'd like to explore, so many strangers I was never likely to meet. Glimpsing them and passing by, leaving them all behind.

There wasn't any way around it, though. Not if I wanted to reach Tombstone and track down Whittle.

Well, we stayed one night in St Louis, so Sarah took me to a restaurant on the shore of the Mississippi. Before returning to our hotel, we roamed along the river bank for a while. We watched boats drift by, all lit up in the distance, the sounds of voices and laughter floating soft across the water, sometimes the wail of steam whistles. It was just grand. I wanted to stay forever, but the wind stiffened and pretty soon a storm came along, chopping up the river and pouring rain down on us as lightning bolts split the sky and crashed all around. Drenched, we hot-footed it back to the hotel.

The next morning, the sky was clear again. We boarded a train that would take us across Missouri and Kansas to Denver, Colorado.

For days and nights, we headed west across the vast plains. Beyond the windows, I saw herds of cattle. And *cowboys*. When I saw my first cowboy riding his horse along a dusty trail near the tracks, I knew we'd reached the Wild West. The notion excited me something awful. But it scared me a bit, too, for it came as a reminder that we were traveling closer each minute to Whittle.

We were still a long way from Tombstone, though. We hadn't even reached Denver yet, and from there we'd have another few days riding south to El Paso. That would only take us into Texas, and we'd *still* need to travel farther west before getting into the Arizona Territory and finding our way to Tombstone.

Even if Whittle was still there, which I greatly doubted, we wouldn't be arriving for near a week after leaving Denver. So I tried to calm down and not think about him, and just fill myself with the wonders of rolling through the American West.

I saw cowboys aplenty. I kept a sharp lookout for them, and never got tired of seeing more. Now and then, I found myself hoping the train might get stopped and robbed by the likes of Jesse James. He'd gotten himself back-shot by a scoundrel name of Bob Ford six or seven years ago, so I knew we didn't stand much chance of enjoying a run-in with the James Gang. But I reckoned there were other outlaws available to have a go at us, and rather fancied myself plucking the General's revolver from my valise and engaging in some gunplay with them.

While I was on the lookout for cowboys and hoping for a hold-up, I caught sight of my first Indian. He sat astride a pony at a crossing, and looked just fearsome, feathers in his headband, face painted red, wearing a blue army jacket and leather leggings. What with all I'd read about the savages, and what I'd heard from the General and Sarah, my insides just squeezed up with fright. I was all set to make a grab for the revolver. But he didn't have a weapon that I could see. And the train was moving along so fast that he was out of sight in just a second or two.

I saw quite a number of Indians as we went along. None scared me like the first one, though. Some were mighty old, and some were squaws, and some were kids. Mostly, they looked rather poor and pitiful. It was hard to picture such creatures on the warpath, massacring settlers, taking scalps and torturing their captives.

Well, the Indian wars were over. They'd been beaten. At least that's what the General had led me to believe. He hadn't been quite correct on that score, as I was to find out later on, but that's a matter I don't aim to get into, not here.

By the time we pulled into Denver, I'd gotten fairly used to seeing both cowboys and Indians. They didn't thrill me quite as much as they'd done at the start, but I was still awfully excited about finding myself in the West.

We spent the night at a hotel near the depot. Early the next morning, we boarded the train that was to carry us south to El Paso, Texas.

Whenever we changed trains, we always found ourselves mixed in with a whole new bunch of passengers. We'd chat a bit with some of them, Sarah explaining that I was her servant. By and large, they seemed like decent folk.

This time, one of the passengers in our car was a man name of Elmont Briggs.

The trouble was ready to start.

Chapter Twenty-six

Briggs

At just about the same time the conductor yelled 'All aboooard', Elmont Briggs came striding up the aisle. He appeared to be heading for the seats behind us, but stopped quick when he spotted Sarah.

She raised her face to see who was standing there.

For a spell, they stared at each other.

The fellow looked perplexed, but awful glad to see her. He was probably about Sarah's age, and had a face so pretty it looked downright girlish. It was clean-shaven, with reddish lips, a pert little nose, big blue eyes and pale brows. His wavy golden hair hung clear to his shoulders. I wondered if he might be a gal after all, even though he was dressed like a man. He was all decked out in shiny boots, black trousers and coat, and had a string tie around the neck of his shirt. A woman wasn't likely to dress in such a fashion. Besides, his chest looked flat. Then he spoke, and his low voice removed my doubts.

'Libby Gordon!' he proclaimed. 'I don't believe my eyes.'

'Pardon me?' Sarah said.

'It's *me*. Elmont Briggs.'

'I'm pleased to make your acquaintance, Mr Briggs,' she told him, sounding a bit amused. 'But I'm afraid . . .'

'You don't remember me? Yale? Class of '84. You accompanied James Bellows to the . . .'

'My name is Sarah Forrest,' she explained. 'I've *never even been* in Connecticut, much less accomapnied a James Bellows to *any*thing. Obviously, you've mistaken me for this Libby person.'

'You're not Libby Gordon?' he asked, tilting his head to one side.

'No, indeed.'

'But . . . the resemblance is uncanny. Remarkable. I'm dumbfounded.' Frowning, shaking his curly locks, he said, 'Please accept my apologies for intruding in such a bold fashion.'

'It's quite all right.'

I figured he would move on, now. But he stayed put.

The train started moving, though. As usual, it took off with a sudden lurch. Elmont staggered sideways. Even though he didn't seem to be in much danger of falling, he caught hold of Sarah's shoulder.

'Woops,' he said. Then he let go of it and grabbed the

corner of her seat back. 'I only met Libby once,' he explained. 'I've never forgotten her, however. One does not forget such a vision of beauty. When I spied you sitting here ... Such a shock. Such a delightful shock. But an error.'

Sarah's face was turned away, so I couldn't see how she was taking all this.

Elmont's eyes shifted over to me. He curled his lips. It was suppose to be a smile, I reckon, but it looked a mite sour. 'And would this fine young man be your brother?'

'My servant, Trevor.'

'You're traveling alone, then?'

'With Trevor.'

'I should very much like to join you. Perhaps we might sit together.'

'Perhaps you should shove off,' I told him.

Well, his pretty blue eyes bugged out and his face got scarlet. Sarah's head swung around. She looked as out of sorts as Elmont.

'Trevor!' she whispered.

'He's after my seat,' I snapped. *He's after you*, is what went through my mind.

'Is your boy always this impertinent?' Elmont asked.

'Bugger off,' I told him.

And Sarah slapped me across the face.

'What's the *matter* with you!' she snapped.

I just sat there, my cheek hot where she'd smacked it. The cheek didn't hurt much, but I felt like I'd been kicked in the stomach.

I felt a whole lot worse when Sarah stood up without saying another word and followed Elmont up the aisle.

She'd never struck me before. She'd never even spoken harshly to me. I doubt there were ever two people who got along any better together than me and Sarah.

Now, she'd not only struck me but gone off with Elmont. She stayed with him, too. For a long, long time. Leaving me there alone and miserable. Couldn't she see that Elmont was a cad? What was wrong with her? How could she fall for his flattery like that? How could she abandon me? What if she doesn't come back at all, and takes up with him?

I almost got up to go looking for her. But I didn't relish the notion of seeing them together. They might be laughing. They might be holding hands. Or worse.

It sickened me to think about such things.

I couldn't stop it, though. I pictured his lips on her mouth, his hands exploring her body and sneaking under her clothes. In my mind, she didn't simply allow him such liberties, but led him along. And touched him in return.

I told myself they wouldn't dare. People would see. But the car wasn't particularly crowded. If the seats across the aisle from them were empty . . .

Well, she finally came back. She gave me a sharp look, then sat down.

'How could you speak to him that way, Trevor?'

'How could you go off with him?'

'He's a very nice man. You had no call to abuse him. You were awful.'

'I doubt there ever *was* a Libby Gordon. The cur took a fancy to you, that's all. He's a bloody liar.'

'You're acting like a child.'

Well, her slap hadn't stung me any more than those words did. I couldn't speak at all for a spell. Then I said, 'I'm a child and he's a man, is that it?'

'Don't be ridiculous.'

'He looks like a woman.'

'Stop it! For heaven's sake, Trevor.'

'Why did you go off with him?'

'I had little choice after your atrocious behavior. I can't *believe* you spoke to him that way. I've never been so embarrassed. What in the world possessed you?'

'I don't like him. Not one whit. He's a smooth-talking philanderer, that's what he is.'

'Ridiculous. You should be ashamed of yourself. Not only did you mistreat him, but you've misjudged him as well. The poor man lost his wife and child to smallpox last year.'

'I doubt it.'

'You're being impossible.'

'I shouldn't trust a word he breathes. He would quite obviously tell you *anything* in order to win your sympathies. Can't you see his intentions?'

When I said that, Sarah quit scowling. She gazed into my eyes, and pretty soon she smiled. Leaning against me, she whispered, 'Why, Trevor, you're jealous.'

'Not in the least.'

'You are!' She patted my leg. 'Oh, dear. What am I to do with you? Elmont's nothing to me. I've no feelings at all for him except as a friend.'

'He's after more than your friendship.'

'How can you say such a thing?' she asked, still talking soft. 'You don't know the man.'

'I know he intends to have you.'

'I hardly think so. If that is his intention, however, he'll be disappointed.'

Well, I wasn't feeling quite so down any more. Though it disturbed me that Sarah considered Elmont a 'friend', it seemed clear I hadn't lost her affections to him.

After a while, she said, 'I'm so sorry that I struck you, darling.'

'It didn't hurt.'

'Will you forgive me?'

'Of course.'

Then she whispered, 'You won't stay away from my bed tonight?'

'Why, I hardly think so.'

With my mind eased considerable on the score of Elmont Briggs, I took to watching out the window. In the early evening, however, came the chime of the dinner bell. 'Now don't get yourself into a tizzy again,' Sarah said. 'I asked Elmont to join us at our table.'

'Splendid,' I muttered.

'Please be nice to him.'

'I'll have a go at it.'

'Remember, you're supposed to be my servant. We can't have him suspecting the truth.'

We waited until most of the other passengers had cleared out of the aisle, then left our seats. Elmont was a few rows behind us, alone. When he saw us approaching, he stood up and gave Sarah a warm smile. The smile cooled some as he turned it on me, but I bobbed my head and said, 'I do hope you'll forgive my earlier rudeness, Mr Briggs. You bore such a remarkable resemblance to a scoundrel I once knew . . .'

Sarah gave me a sharp glance, so I shut my mouth.

'I accept your apology,' Elmont said.

He took the lead. The dining car was some distance back. At the end of each car along the way, Elmont would pull open the door for Sarah. Once she was outside in the noisy vestibule, he'd leave me holding the door, hurry around her, and get the next one. Which he always managed to shut while I was still between cars. He was mighty irritating.

The way Sarah let him get away with it, I got to feeling like she didn't care, one way or the other, if I was left behind. So I let it happen. When we finally came to the dining car and Elmont slammed the door in my face, I just stayed put. I stepped to the edge of the steel grille that covered the coupling, held on to the safety chain there to keep my balance, and stared off at the wooded hills. They were mighty pretty, what with the sun sinking low, but I was in no mood to enjoy the view.

I aimed to wait for Sarah to come along and fetch me.

But she didn't.

Having too fine a time with Elmont, no doubt.

It was windy and cold out there between the cars, so by and by I went on in.

Sarah and Elmont were seated across from each other at one of the dinner tables, Sarah talking away to him and looking happy. When she saw me, she waved me over to join them. 'What kept you?' she asked.

'I stopped for some fresh air,' I explained, feeling mighty let down.

'Where I come from,' Elmont said to Sarah, 'we don't eat with the help.'

'You're certainly an endearing chap,' I told him.

'Nor do we allow back-talk.'

'Behave yourself, Trevor, or I *shall* send you off.'

'Yes ma'am.'

After that, I kept mum. The waiter brought our meals along. I ate and watched Elmont, and listened to the conversation. He was just ever so charming. I reckon he and Sarah'd already found out plenty about each other, as they'd spent so much time together earlier. They didn't fill me in on what I'd missed, but I managed to figure out that Elmont was on his way to California, where he'd gone in with his brother to buy a fancy hotel on the beach at Santa Monica. To hear him talk, he was loaded down with money.

He invited Sarah to come and visit him there when she finished the visit with her father at Fort Huachuca. I had to smile at that, but Elmont didn't notice.

Sarah's father at Fort Huachuca?

I reckon she didn't consider Elmont *much* of a friend, not if she'd been telling him stretchers like that.

Though it amazed me that she'd fibbed to him, I was glad.

She allowed that she might consider a trip to Elmont's hotel, but maybe she didn't mean it.

I doubted he *owned* such a hotel.

The way it looked, lies were flying as thick as the gravy on my beef.

I knew what they were covering up, on Sarah's part.

As for Elmont's lies, I could only guess. The way I figured things, he didn't want Sarah to know he was using the last of his inherited wealth to ride the rails in search of a rich, available woman. And she was it.

Of course, I might've been wrong.

Maybe it was just my jealousy doing the thinking for me.

That's how I saw him, though.

I don't know that Sarah was smitten by him, but she sure did hang on his every word like she'd never encountered a fellow more fascinating and amusing. You could see he was aware of it, too. He had victory in his pretty blue eyes.

Matters turned worse after the meal. He invited Sarah to play cards with him in the parlor car. I started to follow them there, but Elmont said to me, 'I don't believe the lady will be requiring your services.'

'Go ahead and run along,' Sarah said.

Run along?

I heated up considerable. But I allowed that causing a row wouldn't help my cause any. It'd only serve to peeve Sarah. Besides, the way I felt betrayed by her – again – I wasn't particularly eager to keep her company. If she preferred a swine like Elmont over me, maybe she deserved him.

I cast a poison glare at Elmont, then went on my way.

Back in my usual seat, I sat alone and boiled. I tried to tell myself that Sarah was only just being kind to the man. But it wouldn't wash. In spite of what she'd said about considering Elmont no more than a friend, I'd seen enough to figure she was uncommon fond of him.

I had some awfully mean thoughts about her.

It got to seem like she'd only taken up with me in the first place was because I was handy. I was living in her house where she could get at me whenever she pleased. My age hadn't mattered much to her, then. And maybe the various men around town simply hadn't appealed to her, one way or another. I wasn't quite what she wanted, but I'd *do*.

Maybe she'd lied all along about loving me.

Maybe she'd lied about a whole heap of things.

She sure had told some stretchers to Elmont. And to every other passenger we'd spent any time with during our travels. Well, those fibs were understandable. We couldn't very well give out the truth about the two of us. The same goes for deceiving her attorney, Mr Cunningham, and any number of other folks.

Taken all around, though, she'd lied to just about everyone I'd ever heard her talking to.

Even the General.

Sitting there by my dark window, I recalled the time that Saber got hooked by Whittle. Instead of trying out the truth on her grandfather, Sarah'd come up with a fancy story about the horse running off on its own. We'd even left the stable doors and the front gate open to make it look good.

The more I thought about Sarah, the more it seemed like she never spoke the truth if she could come up with a lie that'd serve her better.

No telling how many lies she'd foisted off on me.

Why, I never could understand how a beautiful woman like Sarah was as unlucky with men as she'd always claimed. There she'd been, carrying on about how *old* she was and likely to end up a spinster – husbandless, childless, alone and pitiful.

Maybe she'd only said those things to win my sympathy.

She'd probably been with half the men in Coney Island, and thrown over each of them when a new fellow struck her fancy. The same way she was throwing me over for Elmont.

I felt like I'd been swindled.

For a while there, I plain hated Sarah and wished I'd never gotten tangled up with her. But then I got to thinking about all the fine times we'd had. The memories just carved me out hollow. Not the memories themselves, I reckon, but the notion that all the good things with Sarah were behind me.

Just for the sake of torturing myself even more, I hauled out the gold watch she'd given me at Christmas. I opened it up and saw she'd been gone for nearly two hours. Then I snapped it shut and stared at the crossed revolvers engraved on its cover. *You'll never know how much joy you've brought into my life*, she'd said.

She'd brought plenty into my life, too.

Suddenly, I felt just rotten for all the mean thoughts I'd been having about her. She'd had good reasons for most of the lies I'd heard her tell. For all I knew, she'd never lied to me. Maybe she truly did love me, and loved me still. So what if she was spending time with Elmont? Why, I'd spent hours and hours with the General. The old man had fascinated me, but I sure hadn't *fallen* for him.

That eased my mind some, but not for long.

Elmont wasn't the General. He had designs on Sarah. He aimed to have her.

Even if all they did was play at cards and enjoy each other's company tonight, he was busy working on her. And he'd be having more chances tomorrow. And the day after that. On his way to California (if that's where he was really planning to go), he'd be traveling along our route and making sure he rode in the same trains as Sarah for the rest of the trip until we reached our destination at Tucson. Days from now.

I tried to tell myself that Sarah was bound to see through his smooth ways, sooner or later.

Maybe he'd make a try for her, and she'd spurn him and that would be the end of it.

But maybe he'd make his try, and she'd welcome it. After all, he was a man – not a child. Maybe Elmont was just the sort of fellow she'd always hoped to meet.

My thoughts were in a terrible whirl, so I was glad when Freemont the porter came along to make up the beds. After he was done, I went to the lavatory at the end of the car. I used the toilet, washed up and brushed my teeth, then walked down the curtained aisle.

I'd hoped Sarah might've come back while I was gone. Her berth was empty, though. I climbed into mine, got into my nightshirt and packed my clothes away.

Then I lay there in the darkness. The night outside didn't interest me. The gentle rocking of the train didn't soothe me. Nor did the regular clickity-clack of the wheels. When the horn hooted now and again, it sounded as mournful and lonely as my heart felt.

By and by, I got to wondering if Elmont had already managed to win Sarah's heart. I wondered if he'd already won her body, as well.

They might be together in his berth.

That notion hadn't more than entered my head when the

curtains parted and Sarah looked in at me. I reckon I was glad to see her, but I felt tight and sick inside. .

'I do hope you enjoyed yourself,' I said.

'Are you still in a mood?' She sounded weary.

'Oh, not at all. I'm quite delighted you prefer Elmont's companionship to my own.'

She reached in and stroked my cheek. 'I suppose I shouldn't have stayed away so long . . .'

'But you simply couldn't bring yourself to part company with Princess Charming.'

'For heaven's sake, Trevor.' She let out a long sigh, then backed away. The curtains fell shut.

I stewed for a spell, wishing I hadn't spoken to her that way. When you feel like you might be losing someone you love, though, you get rather crazy. You don't act sensible. You turn mean and wild, and make things even worse.

Well, I heard Sarah come back and settle into her berth.

I figured this was my chance to make matters right.

I waited a bit, then stuck my head out the curtains and checked the aisle. It looked like a long narrow canyon walled in by swaying shrouds, dimly lit by the gas lamps at each end. Nobody was in sight.

I climbed down to Sarah's bed. She pulled back the covers to let me in, but I just knelt on the mattress beside her.

My heart was pounding so hard I almost couldn't breathe.

'What *is* the matter with you?' she asked.

'Elmont Briggs.'

'You've no cause to be jealous. You're in my bed. Elmont is not in my bed.'

'Has he kissed you?'

'My God, Trevor!'

'Has he kissed you?' I asked again.

'Don't be ridiculous.'

'With his pretty red lips?'

'Do you honestly think I would allow him such liberties?'

'Would you?'

'You're talking nonsense. Now hush.' Reaching out, she

slipped her hand beneath my nightshirt. It glided all warm up my leg and gently took hold of me. 'I don't want to hear another word about Elmont.'

'I need to use the toilet,' I said.

Before she could say anything, I started to back my way through the curtains. She gave me a soft squeeze, then let go.

'Hurry back,' she said.

I started toward the rear of the car, wondering why I'd left her. It wasn't that I had any urge to use the toilet. That was just the first excuse that popped into my head. What I needed was to get shut of Sarah for a few minutes and settle down. Maybe take some fresh air. Clear my head and try to get Elmont out of it before going back to her and maybe saying things I'd have cause to regret.

When I walked past the curtains shutting off Elmont's area, an awful frenzy came over me. I had a notion to reach in and grab him. I wasn't quite sure which berth might be his, though. Would've been awful to intrude on a stranger. So I went on along to the back of the car, tugged the door open and stepped outside.

I wasn't the only one there.

Another fellow stood between the cars, his back to me, the wind tossing his long curly hair.

Elmont Briggs himself.

He hadn't looked around yet to see who'd come through the door. I should've gone back inside, returned to Sarah and savored knowing it was me, not Elmont, in her bed.

But I was just fifteen, and had more gumption than sense.

'I say,' said I. 'If it isn't the one and only Elmont Briggs.'

I had to pretty near shout so he could hear me over the noise of the wheels.

He turned around slow. He had a cigar between his lips, its tip glowing red in the wind. When he saw me, he plucked it out. He jabbed the air with it, pointing at me. 'Sarah's boy.'

'I'm nobody's *boy*, Elmont.'

'Has she sent you to fetch me?'

I stepped up closer to him. And sorely wished I had my

clothes on. I was barefoot, my nightshirt blowing about like a woman's dress, the cold gusting up under it. I couldn't help feeling somewhat at a disadvantage. This was no way to be dressed when confronting a scoundrel.

'Speak up, boy. Does Sarah wish me to join her?'

'You're to stay away from her.'

'Am I?' He showed me his teeth. They looked gray in the darkness. I reckon he was smiling. Then he poked the cigar between them and gave it a puff.

I slapped the cigar out of his mouth.

He grabbed the front of my nightshirt, hauled me up against him and smashed his knee into my belly. The blow picked me clear off my feet. When they came down on the grille again, he was rushing me backward. He shoved me into the guard chain. Then he let go, ducked down and grabbed me around the legs. I couldn't do much more than catch hold of his hair before he hoisted me over the chain and pushed.

Chapter Twenty-seven

Farewell to the Train and Sarah

My grip on Elmont's hair didn't save me. Some came out in my hands, is all.

Then I was plunging headfirst, flapping and kicking, feeling the breath of the speeding train against my back. Time seemed to drag awful slow. It gave me plenty of chance to wonder what I might land on and whether I'd get myself cut in half by the wheels. I even had a chance to see my body sprawled out dead by the tracks, my nightshirt up around my chest. Seemed awful, making an indecent spectacle of myself that way.

Figured I might have time to arrange the garment, but I was still considering it when I struck the ground.

Not headfirst, though, thank the Lord. It was my back that hit. If my wind hadn't been knocked out already by Elmont's knee, the landing would've done it. I smacked down hard, but that wasn't the end of it. I bounced, and the ground was so steep it flung my legs up and somersaulted me. I tumbled and rolled for quite a spell, and finally came to a stop in some soft grass.

I lay sprawled there, hurting all over but happy to be alive. While I fought to wheeze some air into my chest, the clatter of the train faded down the tracks. Nobody must've seen me go overboard except Elmont, because it didn't stop. Pretty soon, the whistle tooted a farewell to me.

When I was able to breathe again, I got to my feet. I felt a trifle wobbly, so I didn't go anywhere but just stood where I was.

At the bottom of the railroad embankment. The high slope loomed over me, all rocks and weeds and bushes. From where I stood, I probably couldn't have seen the train even if it had still been there. All that remained of it was a distant rumble and some ragged tatters of smoke black in the moonlight.

Turning around slow and careful, I saw nothing except woods. Not a road or a house or a human being, nor the glimmer of a campfire.

I wasn't frightened, though.

I hurt too much to feel fear or much of anything else besides my hurts. My bones ached. My hands and knees burned, and so did parts of my back and rump. I'd been scuffed and scratched up considerable during my fast trip down the slope.

The nightshirt was clinging to my back. With dew, I hoped. I shucked off the shirt and held it out under the moonlight. It was shredded some. It looked mighty filthy, but I could only see a few dark spots that I took for blood. The better part of the dampness was dew, which came as a relief.

I put the shirt on, then made my way up the embankment. It wasn't a pleasant journey in bare feet, but a sight less distressing than the quick trip down it. When I got to the top, I sat on a rail to brush the grit and pebbles off my feet. The rail still felt a bit warm from the train going by.

The tracks stretched off into the distance, gleaming like silver.

I wondered what Sarah was thinking right then. She was likely all warm and snug in her bed, worrying about how come I was taking so long at the toilet. Maybe figured my supper hadn't agreed with me.

It was me who hadn't agreed with Elmont.

I could've kicked myself for knocking that cigar out of his mouth. Now he was riding along the rails with Sarah, all pleased with himself for removing a certain impudent servant boy.

With me out of the way, no telling what he might get up to.

He'd probably no sooner chucked me over the side than he'd gone looking for her.

No. Wouldn't do that. Too wily.

He'd want Sarah to fall asleep and not catch on till morning that I'd gone missing. Then he'd be at her full time.

It got me angry and miserable thinking about such things. Pretty soon, I realized I wasn't helping the situation by sitting on a rail. So I got up and started after the train.

The cinders hurt my feet. The wooden ties weren't a whole lot better. So I took to walking along the smooth iron of a rail. The only trick was keeping steady. Every so often, I'd fall off and do more damage to my feet.

But I kept at it. There was bound to be a depot up ahead, and likely a town. Just a matter of getting there. Of course, it might be twenty miles off. Or fifty. So long as I followed the tracks, though, I'd reach it sooner or later.

I tried to tell myself that Sarah'd be there waiting for me. The only chance for that was if she got worried and searched the train and figured out I was nowhere aboard. She might do just that. She sure wouldn't be able to get the train to come back for me, but she was bound to make it stop at the first station and let her off. Then she'd be shut of Elmont, and we'd be joining up again soon as I found the depot.

More than likely, though, Sarah'd drifted off to sleep. It'd be morning before she realized I was gone. By then, the train would be a few hundred miles south.

It was mighty depressing to contemplate.

But I judged things would turn out. All I needed to do was stick with the tracks, keep on heading for Tombstone, and we'd find each other by and by.

Unless Sarah decided to take up with Elmont, give up on me, and head off for parts unknown with the scoundrel.

That was out of my hands, though.

I tried not to worry my head about such things. The trick for me was just to keep on walking and find civilization.

The rail had been warm at first. But it cooled off pretty quick. Before long, it felt like ice under my feet. The wind picked up, too, and turned nippier by the minute. It slipped clean through my nightshirt, and tossed it about, and rushed up underneath it.

Finally, I took to shaking so bad and my feet were so numb that I fell off the rail every third or fourth step. I gave up on the rail, and hobbled along on the gravel and cinders and wooden ties. They weren't near as cold as the iron. My feet thawed out enough to let me feel every sharp thing they stepped on.

What I did was rip off my long sleeves and bind them around my feet. That helped some. I kept on going. No matter how far I trudged along, though, the tracks just kept on stretching out empty ahead of me and I never saw a thing except forests on both sides.

I allowed I'd likely freeze up stiff before I ever came to the next depot.

At last, I went down the embankment. It was mighty rough on my feet and hindquarters, but I got to the bottom. There, the wind wasn't so bad. Couldn't feel it much at all once I'd made my way into the trees and burrowed into the moist leaves. The ground was hard and lumpy. I still felt cold and miserable. But I fell asleep, somehow.

Morning improved matters considerable. I woke up to find warm sunlight shining down on me through the tree-tops. It felt so fine I just lay there, soaking up the heat and listening to the birds sing. Other than the birds and some bugs humming about, I heard a breeze rustling the leaves and a sound I couldn't quite place. It was a rushy noise like a strong wind. It didn't gust and fade like wind, though. It whushed along steady.

All of a sudden I knew it must be a river.

And me with my mouth as dry as sand.

I stood up quick, forgetting about my aches and pains. Right off, they reminded me of themselves. I let out a yowl. The way my feet felt, I might've been one of those fellows the General told me about – one of those captives who got staked down by Indians and had his feet toasted. The rest of me wasn't much better off. I stood there hunched over like a cripple. That didn't get me any closer to the water, though.

Finally, I straightened myself up. I turned toward the sound of the stream, and started to move. The first few steps were pure torture.

The pain was rather like a plunge in frigid water, shocking and horrid for a bit, but not so bad after you'd gotten used to it. Pretty soon, the pain eased off some.

I hobbled along, dodging tree trunks, ducking under low limbs, taking the long way around thickets and boulders and deadfalls in my way, sometimes pushing on through bushes that scratched my legs and snagged my nightshirt. Before long, I was breathless and pouring sweat. My nightshirt felt like it was pasted to my skin. The sleeves came off my feet a few times, and I had to stop and fix them before I could go on. Other times, I stopped for no reason other than to wipe my face and catch my wind.

At last, though, I came to the river.

What a grand sight! A lane of water thirty or more feet

across, curling and tumbling its way over a bed of pale rocks. It was mostly shadowed by the trees, but here and there it shimmered with patches of sunlight.

I stood on the bank, gazing down at it, so struck with admiration that all my torments seemed to vanish.

This was *my* river. I'd trekked through the wilderness and discovered it. Me, Trevor Wellington Bentley, a lad from London. Like Natty Bumpo or Daniel Boone, I'd made my way over the trackless, uncharted land of the American frontier to find a secret wonder.

Battered as I was, I felt just bully.

It seemed as if nothing in the world existed except me and the woods and my river.

The rocks along the shore hurt my feet, but not my mood. Pretty soon, I stepped into the clear, rushing water. It was almighty cold! So cold I swear my feet hissed and steam curled off them. But they felt a whole lot better.

Crouching down, I scooped water into my mouth. One handful after another. It was the sweetest liquid that ever passed my lips. It was magical nectar. I felt like I was drinking mountain tops and sunlight and shadowy glens and a chill wind from the forest.

When I couldn't hold any more, I waded along through the currents. With every step, my stomach sloshed. I kept close to shore, and didn't stop till I came to one of the sunny places.

Hanging on to a boulder, I untied the sleeves and shook them out. I washed them, spread them out on the rock to dry, then did the same with my nightshirt.

The water froze me up frightful when I plunged in. It put me in mind of when I'd dived into the ocean to save Trudy. I hadn't thought about her much in recent times, and wished she hadn't snuck up on me now. A whole passel of bad memories started running through my head.

But they didn't last long. When I stood up and breathed the fresh air and saw the pale blue sky and the green trees and the river running along, all the horrible things didn't stand a chance. I was alone in the wilderness, nobody around to cause me troubles or worry.

The water didn't seem so cold any more. It felt soothing on my scrapes. I stayed in it for quite a while, paddling about and floating. Tom Sawyer himself likely never had a better time on the Mississippi than me in that river. I wished there was a Jackson Island where I could camp – but of course I had nothing to camp *with*. Even if I'd had matches for a fire, I had no food to cook on it.

My stomach, which was bruised on the outside from Elmont's knee, felt rather empty on the inside. That didn't worry me much, though. I allowed I could always find *some-thing* to stave off starvation, one way or another. I'd worry about it later.

For now, I was mighty content.

I gathered my footwear and nightshirt, which were already dry, then waded over to a flat slab of rock hanging out from the shore. I climbed onto it and sprawled out. The sun warmed me up. Soft breezes with just a touch of coolness brushed along my skin.

I felt uncommon lazy. Everything seemed pretty near perfect, except I got to wishing Sarah was here with me. We could swim in the stream together, and lay out on the rock to dry. I got an awful hankering to see her stretched out in the sunlight, all bare and wet and shiny. See her and feel her and so on.

Well, of course we'd never get together again if I didn't start moving.

I was loath to stir myself, though. It would be a shame to leave my river. I wished I had a raft or canoe. Then I could just float along peaceful, take a drink whenever I got the urge, jump in to cool off when the sun got too hot, and have a fine time. That'd be a blessing for my feet, too.

But I had no raft or canoe, and didn't see how I could make one.

I could follow the river, hike along its shore or wade and swim if the terrain got too rough. That notion struck my fancy, and I nearly decided to have a go at it. But there was no way to judge where the river might take me.

Part of me didn't much care where it'd take me. I could just roam along forever, exploring. But mostly I wanted to join up with Sarah the quickest way possible, and that meant returning to the tracks.

I took one more swim. While splashing about, I wondered if there might be a way to carry some water with me. Of course, I had no container. I drank as much as I could hold, and pondered the problem.

The General once told me how the Apaches could carry around a huge load of water, enough to last a small party of warriors for days. What they'd do was kill a horse and take out its small intestine. They'd clean it out the best they could, then fill it up. When they had yards and yards of gut fit to burst with water, they'd wrap it around a horse they hadn't killed yet, and be on their way.

Well, I didn't have a horse available. I'd spotted some squirrels and gophers and such, but didn't hold out much hope of catching one. Besides, the whole notion seemed a trifle gory for my taste.

Thanks to Whittle, I'd seen my share of intestines. I wanted no more truck with such things.

But I did hit on a plan, thanks to the General's story. After wrapping the sleeves around my feet, I soaked my nightshirt real good. Then I didn't wring it out or put it on. Instead, I draped it loose over my shoulders.

I started on my way, not at all happy to leave the river behind, but hoping it wouldn't wander far from the tracks so I might be able to find it later, if need be.

It was hot work, trudging back through the woods. The water in my nightshirt stayed cool for a while, and felt good the way it dribbled down my skin. Pretty soon, though, it turned so warm I couldn't tell the difference between the water and my sweat.

Finally, I came to the embankment. I scurried up, sorely missing the shade of the woods. The sun felt like fire, and the breezes had traveled elsewhere. I wished I'd just stayed at the river.

All burning and breathless and drippy, I stumbled onto the flat ground at the top of the slope. And sat on a rail. And squealed and leapt up when it scorched my rump.

After a wait to catch my breath and allow the pain to fade, I unslung my nightshirt and tipped back my head. I reckon I squeezed quite a lot of river water into my mouth. It was mixed with dust and sweat, but did wonders for my thirst. In my head, I gave thanks to the General for giving me the idea.

When I couldn't wrestle any more water out of the night-shirt, I put it on and started following the tracks. I'd learned my lesson, and stayed off the rails.

They were so shiny in the sunlight that they hurt to look at.

I walked between them, keeping my eyes on the gravel and cinders. I kept my ears open for trains, too. Another was bound to come along, sooner or later. For all I knew, several might've gone by while I was away. I probably would've heard them, but maybe not.

Anyhow, I didn't hanker to get run over. And maybe I could even get one to stop and pick me up.

The farther I walked, the surer I got that a train would whistle in the distance. From behind me. I'd turn around and wave my arms. It'd toot for me to clear out of the way, but I'd stay put so the engineer didn't have any choice but either to put on the brakes or splash through me. In my head, the train always stopped with a few feet to spare. The engineer and fireman, they leaped down to shout at me, but I acted quite meek and polite, explained my situation, and they settled down and asked me aboard. They gave me a ride to the next station, and there stood Sarah on the platform, thrilled to pieces and weeping for joy as I ran to embrace her.

It was a splendid daydream.

I played it out quite a few times in my head. Even improved on it, having the train approach from the front, heading north, with Sarah riding in the locomotive to keep a lookout for me.

Reality came back to me, though, when I spotted a bridge in the distance.

A bridge meant a gorge. A gorge might mean water. Maybe this was a place where my river cut across to the other side of the tracks. I was mighty cooked by then – wet on the outside and dry on the inside. The river was precisely what I needed to set matters right.

I hurried along smartly, eager to get there.

By and by, the rushy sound of water came along. This just had to be my river!

But I stopped dead, just short of the bridge.

The rail on my left was almost where it belonged. But not quite.

Chapter Twenty-eight

Desperados

The spikes meant to pin the rail down firm had all been yanked and scattered about. The rail was off to the side by half a foot.

The next train to happen along would wind up chewing earth. If it had much speed at all when it derailed, it'd likely pitch over and plunge into the gorge.

That's the first thing that ran through my mind. The second thing was how to stop the train in time to save all the lives certain to be lost in such a catastrophe.

I doubted my ability to repair the damage. The only other choice was to hurry up the tracks and have a go at stopping the train. But what if it came from the other direction?

I never got to thinking about the third thing. What it would've been, of course, was that somebody had *done* this to the rail.

Before I reached that stage of my thoughts, however, a gunshot barked. I jumped. And looked up from the rail to see a horseman charge up out of the gorge alongside the bridge. He came galloping straight at me, waving his pistol.

I chose not to bolt. After all, the only escape seemed to be a dive off the embankment. That was likely to bang me up considerable. And the fellow might shoot me. So I stayed put and raised my arms.

He slowed his horse to a trot, and reined it in just in front of me.

This was the closest I'd been to a real cowboy. Of course, I judged he wasn't an actual cowboy, but a desperado instead.

Not that he looked especially desperate. Other than the revolver in his hand, there was nothing fearsome about him. He wasn't ugly. He wasn't much bigger than me. He had a weathered, dirty face with a few days' worth of whiskers, and didn't seem to be much older than twenty. He was frowning, but not in an angry way. More like he was confused and rather amused.

Not saying a word, he gave his reins a shake. He walked his horse around me in a slow circle, studying me while I turned around to study him.

He was all decked out in a big hat with its brim turned up, a red neckerchief the size of a bib, and a bandolier chock full of cartridges that hung across his chest from one shoulder. His dusty old shirt was dark with sweat. Around his waist, he wore a belt with holsters on each side. The holster at his left hip was empty. The one on his right held a six-gun with its handle to the front. The holsters were tied down around the legs of his leather chaps. His boots had silver spurs that looked too fancy for the rest of his outfit.

After circling me a couple of times, he halted his horse and said, 'You fall outa bed or what?'

'I was thrown from a train, actually. I had a bit of a row with a fellow, and he chucked me overboard.'

'How come ya talk funny?'

'Do I?'

'Yup. You some kind of an easterner?'

'My home's in London, England.'

A corner of his mouth turned up. 'I'll be durned,' he said.

'Trevor Wellington Bentley,' I introduced myself, and held my hand out toward him.

Instead of shaking it, he touched the barrel of his revolver to the brim of his hat. 'Chase Calhoun, here.'

'Pleased to make your acquaintance, Mr Calhoun.'

'Well, don't get *too* pleased. I reckon I'll have to shoot you.'

All of a sudden, I felt mighty short of breath. But I managed to say, 'I do hope that won't be necessary.'

'Thing is, Willy, you got in the way. Me and the boys, we're fixing to hold up the express.'

He wasn't alone, then. That didn't come as any great surprise. Working the rail loose would've been a big job for just one man. I figured the rest of his gang must be waiting in the gully.

'You'll be causing a terrible wreck,' I explained.

'We can't rob the train without we stop it first.'

'You might send one of your compatriots up the tracks to wave it down. Otherwise, there's bound to be an awful loss of life. Women and children. I shouldn't like to have that on my conscience.'

'Well, you won't.' With that, he aimed the revolver at my face and thumbed back the hammer.

'I might be of some use to you,' I said.

'Don't see how.'

'I could ride with your gang, perhaps. I could run errands, perform chores, cook for you. I make quite a fine pot of coffee, actually. Why, there's no end to the things I might do to help. I might care for your horses. And I'm really quite an amusing chap. Why, I sailed across the Atlantic with a cutthroat worse than any ten train robbers, and he spared my life for no other reason than he didn't want to lose the enjoyment of my company.'

It was a stretcher, but I would've said just about anything to stop Chase from pulling the trigger.

'You sure run on,' he said.

'You seem like a fine fellow.'

'You're all right, too, Willy. I won't get no pleasure outa plugging you, but . . .'

'You certainly don't *look* like an Indian lover.'

He hadn't looked fearsome before. When he heard me say that, though, his face twisted ugly. 'Say your prayers.'

'If you shoot me, that's exactly what you are. No better than a bloody *Indian* lover.'

'My *folks* was massacred by the Sioux, boy!'

'And my best friend was General Matthew Forrest of the Fifth Cavalry.'

The hammer dropped.

Real slow, hooked by Chase's thumb.

'You knew General Forrest?'

'We were great chums. He took me into his home. I was present at his deathbed. Until last night, I was traveling in the company of his granddaughter, Sarah.'

'Well, let's see what the boys have to say. Move along.'

He rode alongside me as I walked to the edge of the gully. The bridge crossed a river, just as I'd figured. Over by the shore, the 'boys' were waiting. Chase dismounted, and led his horse down the slope, which wasn't steep enough to give me much trouble.

His gang stood by their horses and watched us come. Four of them, not counting Chase. A couple of them pointed at me and said things I couldn't make out, and laughed. The other two didn't seem amused.

'This here's Willy,' he said when we got close.

'Trevor, actually.'

'Whatcha wearing there, Willy?' asked one of those who'd pointed. He looked not much older than me. I found out later he was Chase's kid brother, Emmet.

221

'I was thrown from a train last night,' I told him.

'He's from England,' Chase said. 'Allows as he's a friend of Matthew Forrest.'

'General Forrest?' asked an older fellow named John McSween who had a big, droopy mustache that had some gray in it.

'I saved his life,' I said. Another stretcher, but I figured it couldn't hurt my cause.

'Don't see how the General'd *need* a lad the likes of you to save him,' McSween said.

'Why, a scurvy coward tried to back-shoot him on the streets of Coney Island,' I said. 'I called out a warning, and Matthew whirled around and emptied his revolver into the cad. Dropped him like an old boot, he did. Matthew presented me with a gold watch to show his gratitude. I would show it to you, but it's with the rest of my possessions aboard the train.'

'What're we gonna do with him?' Emmet asked his brother.

'Well, I was fixing to shoot him down, only then he took to claiming how he's a buddy of the General.'

A huge, red-faced fellow named Breakenridge said, 'Buddy or not, we can't chance him. He's had a good look at us.'

'I told him my name, to boot.'

'I reckon that settles it, then,' said a weasel-faced fellow with red hair. They called him Snooker, and I never learned his true name. 'I'll do the honors.' He pulled a Winchester out of his saddle holster and worked its lever.

Before he could swing the barrel my way, McSween clapped a hand on his shoulder. 'Hold your water there, pal. I rode with Matthew Forrest. This lad saved his hide, he's aces with me.'

'I don't reckon he's ever even *met* your General,' Emmet said. 'He knows he's in a fix. Likely just a pack of lies.'

'Can you prove you ain't lying to us?' Chase asked me.

'I could tell you how his wife, Mable, saved him from the Apaches and caught a dozen or more arrows in the backside for her troubles. She walked with a limp to her dying day.'

'She's passed on?' McSween asked.

'Yes, I'm afraid so. Matthew, too.'

'I'm right sorry to hear the news.' Turning to Chase, he said, 'I don't see as how it'd be right and proper to shoot this lad. He ain't fibbing. Mrs Forrest sure enough had a hitch to her gait. The story went, she got it fighting Indians when her and the General got ambushed.'

'I'd be honored to join the gang,' I said. 'You wouldn't need to split the booty with me.'

'We don't have a mount to spare,' Chase explained.

'Well,' said McSween, 'I reckon he might double up with me. Either that, or we oughta let him go on his way.'

'Where you trying to get to, Willy?' Chase asked.

'Tombstone. I was traveling there with Sarah Forrest . . .'

'Tombstone! Why, that's clear down in Arizona Territory. You won't get there riding with us.'

'It's a mite far to hike with nothing but rags on your feet,' McSween said.

'Actually, I was simply hoping to reach the next railroad depot.'

'How come we don't let him stay with the train?' McSween suggested. 'They'll get it running again, by and by. He can ride on along with it.'

'He knows us,' Snooker whined.

'I won't betray you. You have my word as a gentleman on that. However, I'm afraid the train won't be fit to take me anywhere. As I explained to Mr Calhoun, it's likely to be demolished in the crash.'

They all glanced about at each other.

'That's what he told me, all right,' Chase said. 'He seems to believe it'll run smack down into the gorge, here.'

'What does *he* know about such business,' Emmet muttered, scowling my way.

'We've derailed four trains already,' Chase said, 'and never a one of them crashed much.'

'Have you ever done it this close to a gorge?' I asked him.

'I'm afraid the lad has a point,' McSween said. 'Perhaps we

ought've pulled the rail a hair farther off from the bridge. If she comes along under a full head of steam, who's to say but what she *won't* sail down here? We don't wanta be the ones to cause a wreck, you know.'

'They'd make it mighty hot for us,' Chase agreed.

'What we oughta do,' McSween said, 'is ride on up the tracks a distance and yank a rail there.'

'I'm sure it would save a number of innocent lives,' I said.

Snooker commenced to complain, and Emmet took his side. But Chase put an end to the protests when he pulled a watch from his shirt pocket. 'The express'll be along in fifteen, twenty minutes. We ain't got time to fool with another rail. What we'll do, we'll post Willy down the tracks so he can try and wave her down. She might brake for a boy in a nightshirt. That'll slow her down enough so she won't go over the edge.'

'He'll warn 'em, Chase.'

'I trust that he won't,' McSween said, giving me a friendly nod.

I nodded back at him.

Chase mounted up, then reached a hand down for me. I grabbed hold, and he hauled me up behind him. I lost the sleeve off one foot and had to squirm and kick some to get myself aboard. What with my state of dress, it caused considerable amusement for the audience below. Emmet and Snooker hooted and whistled and made remarks. McSween handed the sleeve up to me so I could put it on later.

I hung on tight to Chase as the horse carried us up the slope. I had saddle bags under me. They were leather, and hot from the sun, so they didn't feel good against my skin.

But I didn't mind the discomfort much. I was rather pleased with myself, actually. I'd managed to hang on to my life. It looked like the train might not crash, after all. And riding sure did beat walking.

I had my arms around Chase's waist. I gave some thought to going for his guns. They were in easy reach. If I was quick enough, I might be able to disarm him. Make him climb down. Then I could take his horse on up the tracks, meet the train and prevent the robbery altogether.

Why, I'd be quite a hero. I judged the railroad would likely be so grateful I might get a free ride all the way to Tucson.

I couldn't bring myself to try it, though. Too risky. But also, it seemed too lowdown. I didn't care at all for the rest of the gang, but I rather liked Chase and McSween. They'd put their trust in me. It just wasn't in me to do them dirty.

By and by, Chase said, 'I reckon this is far enough.' He halted his horse and helped me to the ground. 'Have a try, Willy. But if she stops and you tell on us, folks are likely to end up dying. You'll be one of 'em.'

'I'll simply explain that I need a ride,' I told him.

Then he trotted off, raising dust. I tied the sleeve around my foot. By the time I got done, Chase was almost to the bridge. I watched until he rode down the slope and vanished.

More than likely, nobody had an eye on me. I was no longer in the clutches of the outlaws. And I figured they weren't likely to hunt me down if I took a notion to race down the embankment and hightail into the woods. I'd be shut of them, and free.

It wouldn't hurt them any.

Sure would hurt the folks aboard the express, though.

Besides, I'd be missing my chance to see a gang of real desperados rob a train.

So I stayed there by the tracks.

Pretty soon, a whistle tooted way off in the distance.

Chapter Twenty-nine

The Holdup

The train slid around a far-off bend, its chimney chugging out black smoke that hung above the whole train, thick near the front, spreading out some over the freight and passenger cars, rising higher and thinning out behind the caboose. In the distance as it was, the whole string seemed to be moving rather slow and quiet.

It got quicker and noisier, the nearer it came.

Pretty soon, the ground took to shaking under my feet.

I stayed between the rails and waved my arms. Well, the whistle howled and howled like it was shouting at me to get out of the way. The engineer, he leaned out his window and flapped an arm at me. Yelled, too, but I couldn't hear him.

The train kept on thundering closer and tooting.

Then it screeched. Steam hissed and spit from the locomotive, throwing out white clouds down low to the tracks. Sparks sprayed up from the wheels as they skidded over the rails.

I could see it wouldn't stop in time to miss me, so I jumped clear. Not a second later, the sun was blocked out by the great engine. I covered my ears to save them from the awful noise. Things got hot for my legs, but it didn't hurt too much. All wheezes and squeals, the train slowed to a halt.

I'd done it!

The engineer and fireman both jumped down. They came striding back past the coal car. They didn't look any too pleased.

'You hoping for an early grave, son?' the engineer asked. He was an older fellow dressed in overalls and a tall, striped hat.

The other fellow, the fireman, didn't say a thing. He stood

in front of me with his fists planted on his hips, scowling. He was red and dripping sweat. He had more muscles than any man I'd ever seen before. His face had muscles.

'I'm afraid I fell from a train last night,' I said.

'You *fell*?'

The fireman shook his head. His eyes were squinted so narrow I wondered how he could see with them.

'Actually, a bloke picked me up and *tossed* me.'

The fireman grinned.

If I'd had any notion to warn these fellows they were on their way to a stickup, I lost it when I saw that grin.

'My fare was paid all the way to El Paso,' I explained. 'I should be most grateful for a ride.'

The engineer rubbed his chin and looked at my feet.

'Please, sir.'

After letting out a sigh, he said, 'I s'pose we can give you a ride to the next station, anyhow. Seeing as how we've already gone and stopped. I had half a mind to keep moving, but you looked so set on flagging us down, I suspicioned the bridge might be out. How's the bridge?'

'I shouldn't say that it's out. However, it did seem rather rickety. You'd be well advised to proceed with care.'

I heard somebody huffing up behind me, and turned around. It was the conductor, a little fellow, holding his cap down tight as if to keep the wind from stealing it. There wasn't any wind, but he didn't let the lack of it interfere. The gold chain of a watch swayed across the front of his waistcoat. One side of his jacket was swept back behind the revolver holstered on his right hip.

'What have we here?' he asked, giving me the eye.

'Take him on back with you,' the engineer said. 'He claims he got chucked from the southbound last night.'

'Natty attire,' said the conductor.

'Hurry,' the engineer said. 'We're losing time.'

With a crook of his finger, the conductor gestured for me to follow him. 'I'm much obliged,' I called to the other two, then hurried after the little man.

We were still walking along the right of way when the whistle blasted. A wave of rattles and clanks came running down from the front. The passenger car beside us jumped forward with a lurch. Then the one behind it did the same. Pretty soon, the whole string was creeping along.

The conductor stepped a bit closer to the tracks. We stopped and waited while the train picked up more and more speed. It still wasn't going particularly fast, though, when the caboose rolled by.

The conductor almost let it pass, then caught a handle and hopped onto the steps of the rear platform. As he scooted up, I grabbed hold and swung myself aboard.

We entered the caboose.

'Take a seat,' he said. I pulled a chair away from the cluttered desk, but he snapped, 'Not there. What's the matter with you?' Then he pointed me to a bench across from a potbelly stove.

I sat down on it. 'I'm much obliged for the ride,' I told him.

'Ain't my doing. I got work to do, so keep your mouth shut.'

'Yes, sir,' I said.

He sat at the desk and started working on some papers. And near fell out of his chair when all of a sudden the train braked. 'What in the nation!'

Glaring at me like it was my fault, he popped to his feet.

I shrugged, all innocent.

'What's going on?'

'I've no idea, really.'

Well, he rushed over to a window and poked his head out. Then he cried, 'Damn!' He shoved back from the window, snatched out his sixgun, and pointed it at me. 'You dirty bastard, you tricked us!'

'Don't shoot! Please! I'm not one of them.'

Some guns went off. The conductor, his eyes almost jumped out of his head. I've never seen a fellow so red in the face.

He thumbed back the hammer and let it drop.

I judged I was dead.

The hammer landed with just a clank, not a blast. I didn't wait for him to try again, but leaped off the bench and struck his gun hand. Not a moment too soon. I hadn't more than whacked it when he got off a shot. The noise slapped my ears, but the bullet missed me. I threw a punch into his belly. His air whooshed out, and he tumbled back against a wall. Slammed it pretty hard.

I twisted his hand till he dropped the gun, then used both my fists to lay into him. He didn't seem to have much fight left, but I was sore. I kept on pounding him. 'I'm *not* with them,' I shouted while I punched. 'I *told* you that! Damn your bloody eyes!' Punch punch punch. 'And yet you tried to *shoot* me!' Punch punch punch. 'You'd no reason to *do* that!'

I went on railing at him and hitting him. But pretty soon I realized he wasn't in any shape to appreciate my efforts. I stepped back away from him, and he slumped to the floor and didn't move.

I picked up his revolver and aimed it at him. I had half a notion to shoot him. After all, he'd done his best to kill me and it was only pure luck that he hadn't put a slug in my chest. But then I got hold of my temper.

I was in enough trouble without plugging a railroad conductor. He'd mistaken me for one of the robbers, and I reckoned I could expect the same judgement from the engineer and fireman.

If I stuck around.

He got stirred up some when I commenced to strip off his duds, so I laid the barrel across his head. After that, he didn't give me any more trouble. I shucked off my nightshirt and the ragged sleeves I'd been wearing on my feet. Then I got into his trousers, socks, boots and shirt. They fit snug, but I reckoned they would have to do for now.

I buckled his belt around my waist and holstered the gun.

He was moaning some by the time I finished. I restrained myself, however, and didn't clobber him again.

I emptied out the pockets, not wanting to steal what I didn't need.

He was still stretched out on the floor when I rushed out the rear of the caboose. I jumped to the ground. The gang was near the front of the train. They all had bandannas pulled up to hide their faces, but I could tell one from the next because of their sizes and duds and such. I just caught a glimpse of Chase and McSween and Breakenridge as they climbed into the side door of a car.

Emmet, mounted, held the reins of all the horses. My friends the engineer and fireman were sprawled on the ground by the tracks, Snooker keeping them covered with his Winchester. He and Emmet were both watching the passenger cars, likely prepared to shoot at anyone who tried to interfere. They saw me coming. I waved to show I didn't mean any harm.

Between me and them were four passenger cars, most of the windows open. Nobody seemed foolish enough to poke his head out, but I heard a lot of commotion from inside while I hurried along, There were angry voices, scared voices, a few folks crying and taking on like they figured they'd be getting themselves massacred.

I'd gotten past three of the cars when somebody stretched an arm out a window of the one ahead of me. The hand had a revolver in it.

Snooker and Emmet were both looking the other way, trying to see what was happening in the express car.

Ran through my head to shout a warning.

Judged it wouldn't help much.

I shouted, anyhow, but didn't leave it at that. All Emmet and Snooker got time to do was glance in my direction. By then, the conductor's sixgun was already in my hand. I let fly at the passenger's arm.

This was my first try with a firearm. When it went off, it near jumped out of my grasp. Of course, I missed the target. My bullet went high and knocked a hole through the upper part of the window. But I might as well have hit the arm, for it dropped the gun and jumped back out of sight, never firing a shot.

Emmet, he gave me a curious look with his head tipped sideways. Snooker winked at me.

I hurried along and picked up the passenger's revolver. It was a Colt .45 Peacemaker, the same as the conductor's. I holstered it, and shoved the conductor's gun under my belt.

Then I hurried on and joined up with Snooker and Emmet.

'Dang!' Snooker said. 'Ain't you the one!'

'Yeah,' Emmet said. 'Thanks.' Unlike Snooker, he didn't seem too friendly.

I couldn't help but smile.

In just the course of a few minutes; I'd been shot at, I'd beaten the conductor senseless, robbed him, and fired at a passenger. All those things shook me up considerable. So did knowing I'd joined in on the side of the outlaws. But I felt mighty pleased with myself, anyhow.

'I'm delighted I was able to help,' I said. 'The conductor was kind enough to loan me his weapon.'

Snooker laughed from under his bandanna. 'Appears he loaned you a sight more than his iron.'

'He was quite generous, really.' I stepped past the two prisoners and nodded toward the express car. 'May I?'

'See what's taking so long,' Snooker said.

So I climbed aboard. Just in time to see Breakenridge fetch the strongbox a kick. He looked even bigger than I remembered him. Big and burly as a bear, but his kick didn't even shake the safe.

'Take more'n your boot,' McSween allowed.

'Well, *shitfire!*'

Chase had the drop on a fellow who looked scared and had a bloody hand clamped over his mouth. 'Didn't hardly recognize you, all dressed up.'

'I was forced to subdue the conductor.'

'Good for you, Willy!' McSween said.

'We've run into some trouble here,' Chase explained. 'The messenger, he won't open the box for us.'

'Can't,' the fellow said from behind his bloody fingers.

'That's what he claims. Says it's a through-safe, locked in Denver and can't be opened till El Paso.'

'I don't reckon he's lying,' McSween said.

'Hey!' Breakenridge called from somewhere in the dark near the front of the car. 'Here's the ticket.' He came back with an ax. 'Stand clear, buddies!'

We gave him some room. He hefted the ax over his shoulder and swung it down. It chopped against the safe with a terrible clamor, and bounced off. The door stayed shut. The blow did little more than leave a scratch on the box's steel top. He had another go, with the same result.

'Too bad it ain't made out of logs,' McSween said.

Breakenridge paid no attention, but gave the box about ten more licks. He might've kept at it all day, but the ax handle finally broke. The head flew up and whistled past Chase's face.

'Lord sakes!' Chase blurted.

'We ain't getting into it,' McSween said.

Breakenridge gave it another taste of his boot, then flung the ax handle off into the darkness.

'We might take the safe with us,' I suggested. 'Given enough time, we should be able to . . .'

'Tried that once,' Chase said.

'Let's just see what we can get off the passengers,' McSween said. 'Better than going off empty-handed.'

Chase jabbed his gun into the express messenger's chest. 'You stay here. Poke your head out, and we'll oblige you by blowing a hole through it.'

'Yes, sir,' he said between his fingers.

We all climbed down. Breakenridge, who was winded and sweaty from his labors with the ax, slid the door shut.

Chase explained the situation to Snooker and Emmet.

'We could've got in it easy if we'd only just brought us along some dynamite,' Snooker said, sounding whiny.

'Right,' Chase told him. 'And got our own selves blowed to Kingdom Come.'

'Farney never knew what-for about the stuff. He was the stupidest ass to ever . . .'

'Don't speak ill of them that's gone,' McSween said.

'He wouldn't *be* gone if . . .'

'Well, we don't *have* dynamite, so leave it lie. Let's just gather up what loot we can from the passengers and be on our way.'

'I want in on it,' Emmet said.

'You stay with the horses,' Chase told him.

'Let *him*,' Emmet said, nodding at me. 'I always gotta mind the horses. It ain't fair.'

'We didn't come here to shoot people,' Chase said.

'I won't shoot a soul!'

'So long as a soul doesn't happen to cough behind you,' McSween said.

That brought him a sharp glance from Emmet.

'Y'all gonna hold that against me forever? It just ain't fair. No fair! All I ever get to do any more is hang on to the reins and wait around while everybody else has the fun.'

'Give the boy another chance,' Breakenridge said.

'A feller already tried to plug us out a window,' Snooker added. 'Willy took a shot at him and . . .'

'Missed,' Emmet said.

'Got close enough to scare him off. But what I'm saying, we don't know but what we might run into a feisty passenger or two. If it comes down to gunplay, couldn't hurt none to have Emmet along.'

Chase seemed to think it over for a spell. Then he nodded his head. Looking at me, he said, 'You'd have to watch our prisoners here. Think you can handle them?'

'I managed the conductor, and he had the benefit of a firearm.' I patted the handle of the revolver I'd taken off him.

'You might have a call to shoot one of these fellers,' McSween said. 'Have you got the sand?'

'They'll either lie still, or meet dire consequences.'

'Good enough for me,' Chase said. 'All right, Emmet. But

mind your weapon. Nobody's to get ventilated without he pulls down on us and asks for it.'

'You got my word.' Looking mighty happy now, Emmet climbed down off his horse and handed all the reins to me.

Then the whole gang hurried off on foot. They stayed in a cluster, talking among each other, then split up alongside the first two passenger cars. When they were in position, they pulled their revolvers. All at the same time, they rushed up the stairs. Chase and Emmet entered the lead car, front and back. McSween and Snooker went in the front of the next, Breakenridge the rear.

They hadn't more than got inside when gunshots thundered. Some folks shrieked and others commenced to bawl. Then I heard Chase call out, 'This is a hold-up, friends. Settle down. We don't aim to hurt you. We don't want nothing but your money and watches. Just hand 'em on over to my pal when he comes by. We'll get done right quick, and you can be on your way.'

I didn't suppose they'd be on their way any too soon, not with the rail out. From where I stood, though, I could see that the engine had stopped short of the ruined section of track, and hadn't derailed at all.

'You're starting down a hard road, son,' the engineer said.

I looked down at him, sprawled there on the ground beside the fireman. They both had their heads turned, their eyes on me. Neither of them made a move to get up, but I switched the load of reins into my left hand and unholstered the Colt.

'You don't want no part of these doings,' the engineer told me.

'If I'd taken no part in these doings, sir, your train would presently be a heap of debris at the bottom of the gorge. It was my idea to flag you down.'

'If that's the case, I'm mighty grateful.'

'Your conductor took me for one of the outlaws and tried to shoot me down.'

'That's no call for you to turn to a life of crime, son. I ain't asking you to let us go or nothing of the sort. All I'm saying is you shouldn't ride off with this bunch. You ride with outlaws, you'll wind up eating lead or swinging at the short end of a rope. That's a plain fact. What you wanta do is bid 'em a fare thee well and stay here. We'll see to it you get a fair trial.'

Up till he mentioned the fair trial, he near had me.

'I do appreciate your concern, sir. However, I'd rather prefer to take my chances with the gang. They haven't shot at me once, whereas your law-abiding conductor never gave me so much as the benefit of a doubt before he fired upon me.'

'You're making a bad mistake, son.'

'Perhaps. Now you lie still and leave me in peace.'

'Leave him in peace,' the fireman said. 'He's a dead man, but just don't know it yet.'

'Shut your mouth.' I pointed my Colt at it. He grinned, then rested his face on his crossed arms.

Pretty soon, Chase and Emmet trotted down the stairs from each end of their car. Emmet had his gun in one hand, a valise in the other. He hadn't gone in with the valise. I wondered if it might be full of loot.

It looked a lot like Whittle's leather bag. Whittle's loot hadn't been money and watches, but parts taken from Mary.

Watching Emmet and Chase hurry on to the third passenger car, I remembered myself walking along the street so long ago on that cold, rainy night in Whitechapel. Following the Ripper. It came to me how, if I'd only just let him go and not rushed in to save that whore, I never would've found myself standing here in league with a band of robbers.

If I'd let him go, the whore'd be dead. But Trudy and her father and Michael, they'd likely still be among the living. I never would've met up with Sarah. I wondered if the General and Mable might still be alive, but judged they wouldn't be. Me being at the house probably hadn't done them any harm. But Sarah wouldn't have traveled west if not for me, so whatever might come of that would be my fault. Whatever Briggs might do with her.

The ladies in Tombstone, and whoever else Whittle

might've killed in America, they wouldn't be dead if it weren't for me. Maybe more women in London would be, though.

Finally, it ran through my head that it was me who'd caused the train not to derail and crash. If I hadn't interfered with Whittle that night, I'd be home with Mother right now and the train would likely be a heap of rubble at the bottom of the gorge, all sorts of passengers broken up and dead.

It was enough to make me dizzy, thinking about all the folks whose lives had either been saved or lost, or only just changed considerable, for no other reason than because I'd taken a notion to follow Whittle and stop him from butchering just one whore.

It's mighty confounding, in life, how so much good and harm can get set into motion by just a single lad who only meant to do the proper thing.

Now, I'd thrown in with a gang of outlaws.

I couldn't see much good coming of that, but it sure beat the notion of standing trial.

Anyhow, I waited, bothering my head, but not completely lost in my thoughts. I stayed aware enough to make sure my prisoners behaved and the horses stayed put, and to kind of watch the train. Chase and Emmet weren't in the third passenger car for long when the others jumped down and hurried along to the last car before the caboose. I was too busy with my other thoughts to wonder about the conductor. He never showed his face, though.

When the bunch started heading back, all the deep thinking deserted me. They had my full attention. They carried three satchels among them, so they must've done rather well. They walked slow, keeping their eyes on the windows till they got past the passenger cars.

'Any trouble?' Chase asked me.

'Not at all. And you?'

'It went slick as grease.'

They emptied the satchels into their saddle bags, then took their reins from me and mounted up.

McSween brought his horse over close to me. 'You done a

fine job, Willy. Climb on aboard.' He reached down to give me a hand.

'Don't do it, son,' the engineer warned. He seemed a good fellow who wanted to save me from a bad end.

Emmet laid a bullet into the dirt no more than an inch from the engineer's nose. It threw up dust into his eyes.

I grabbed hold of McSween's hand. He swung me up behind his saddle.

As we galloped toward the bridge, every last one of the band pulled his gun and took to firing into the air. They shouted out whoops and banged away at the sky. Hugging the steed with my knees, I unlimbered both my Colts and let fly.

It was simply bully!

But part of me was listening and counting.

The sixgun I'd taken off the conductor, it fired four times.

Chapter Thirty

Shooting Lessons

We went charging to the bottom of the slope and didn't stop when we came to the water, but raced downstream, staying in the shallows near the shore. We splashed along right quick for a while, then slowed and took it easy.

McSween and I were at the rear. Some of the others were laughing and talking up ahead, but what with the rushy sounds of the water and the hoofs plopping and such, I couldn't make out a thing they said.

We must've put quite a few miles between us and the train before we finally rode up onto the bank and dismounted. I untrapped my feet from the tight boots, waded into the water and helped myself to a drink while the others tied their horses to some bushes and pulled off the saddle bags.

By the time I joined them, they'd dumped the loot into a heap. They were sitting on the ground, busy separating the watches from the money. I sat down by McSween.

Well, looked like they had enough watches to open up a shop. They had a good big pile of coins, too, and a bundle of greenbacks.

'It don't appear we've struck it rich,' Breakenridge said.

'Should've let *me* try the messenger,' Snooker said.

'I stuck my iron through his teeth,' Chase told him. 'If he could've opened up the safe, he would've.'

'Poor fellow wet himself,' McSween said, and commenced to roll a smoke. After he got it fired, he offered his makings to me.

I thanked him, and took him up on the offer. The others got busy counting the money and didn't notice how I fumbled about with the tobacco pouch and paper. Otherwise, they'd have had a good laugh on my account. It required quite a bit of work, but I finally had myself a crooked cigarette with tobacco leaking out its tip.

McSween, who'd been watching the count, looked over at me. He only glanced at my cigarette, then plucked it from my mouth. Just as nimble as you please, he flipped it open, took his pouch and tapped in some more tobacco, then tongued the paper, rolled it, tightened it up and smoothed it out.

I was in the midst of saying, 'I'm more accustomed to a pipe,' when he poked the remade smoke between my lips.

'There you go,' was all he said. Then he lit it for me.

'Thank you so much,' I said.

We sat there and smoked. By and by, the others finished counting. All together, they'd taken a total of $985.36 from the train passengers.

'Well,' McSween said, 'it's better than we done last month at Pueblo.'

'Just by a hair,' Chase said.

'We had to divvy up that eight ways,' Breakenridge pointed out. 'This time, we only got the five of us.'

I wondered what had become of the other three. Maybe they'd simply moved on. But maybe they'd been shot or captured. Had Farney been one of them – the fellow who'd blown himself up with dynamite? I didn't think I ought to ask.

'Six,' McSween said.

Breakenridge gave me a surly look. 'He ain't one of us.'

'I don't see it that way, Meriwether,' McSween told him.

Breakenridge bristled. It appeared he didn't care to hear what must've been his Christian name. But he kept his mouth shut. Big and powerful as he was, he apparently knew better than to tangle with McSween.

'What do you say, Chase?'

'You needn't give me any,' I spoke up. 'It's quite all right, really.'

'Seems to me,' Chase said, 'the kid deserves a cut. He handled the conductor for us, tended to the horses, kept the prisoners from acting up.'

'Took a shot at that damn hot-head passenger,' Snooker added.

'And missed,' Emmet put in. He did like to remind everybody of my poor aim.

'He done fine,' Snooker said.

'We'll cut it six ways,' Chase said. And that's what they did. I ended up with $150.00. I did some calculating and judged I'd been shorted to the tune of about fourteen dollars, but I didn't let on.

This was far and away more wealth than I'd ever had in my whole life.

McSween picked out a watch for me. It wasn't near as fine as the one Sarah'd given to me, but I accepted it.

'What'll be done with the other watches?' I asked.

'We'll sell 'em off when we get to Bailey's Corner,' Chase explained. 'We got a feller there gives us a good price on 'em.'

'Bailey's Corner?' I asked.

'That's about a week's ride from here,' McSween told me. 'We'll head on down there and kick up our heels.'

'Whooee!' cried Snooker, who apparently fancied the notion of kicking up his heels.

McSween slapped my shoulder. 'We'll fix you up good, Willy. Get you outfitted proper.'

'Smashing,' I said.

After that, Chase dumped all the watches into a saddle bag. I got back into the tight boots. Then we mounted up and rode across the river. We left it behind us, and pretty soon we left the woods behind us, too. Hour after hour, we rode along over rocks and dusty yellow earth that glared with the sun, hardly a tree anywhere to give us shade. The only things that seemed to grow out here were cactus and scraggly little bushes. They were mostly in blossom, it being May.

May or not, the sun felt almighty warm. Nor was my seat behind McSween's saddle too comfortable, particularly as my bum had gotten itself scuffed up the night before. Aside from that soreness, I ached in my legs and all up my back from riding so long. I was hungry, too. These fellows hadn't eaten since the time I'd joined up with them.

I took to thinking that the life of an outlaw had its drawbacks. Would've been a lot easier on these fellows to take regular jobs as store clerks or such, instead of tackling robberies so they had to spend their time on horseback riding mile after mile.

But they'd sure made themselves a load of money for their troubles. So had I.

My pockets were just stuffed to the brim with greenbacks and jangling coins.

I didn't feel quite right about my new wealth. After all, it had been stolen from folks who'd likely worked hard to earn it. I didn't see a convenient way to return it to them, though. It might as well be in my own pockets, instead of split around among the others in the gang.

Besides, I judged that I deserved some recompense. It

might be looked upon as repayment for the favor of saving all those folks from a nasty crash. Not only that, but one of those law-abiding folks – the conductor – had tried to murder me. I hadn't even done a thing wrong. But did that stop him? No, sir. I'd be dead with a bullet in my chest if his gun hadn't misfired. I figured $150.00 was about fair pay for playing target for that rascal.

By the time I had it all parsed out, my regrets about the money seemed foolish. Taken all around, maybe I deserved more than what I got.

I still do feel that way, mostly. I can't bring myself to feel ashamed of taking my split. It was wrong, of course. But my conscience has plenty of awful doings to work on without fretting over what I gained from a robbery that wasn't my fault, anyhow.

Sometime late in the afternoon, a jackrabbit made the mistake of showing itself. It no sooner hopped into view from behind a bush than Snooker leaped from his horse, whipped out his Winchester, and tried to draw a bead on it. The hare was pretty far off by the time Snooker fired his first shot. His bullet *whinged* off a rock. His next kicked up dirt. Well, that rabbit dodged four shots. But the fifth threw it tumbling. Snooker yelled, 'Whooee!'

'Fine shot!' McSween called to him. 'Reckoned you'd get it right if you tried long enough.'

The remark didn't seem to bother Snooker. He just grinned, then slid his rifle into its boot, swung himself onto his horse, and galloped out to where the hare lay on its side. His horse hadn't even stopped moving before he hopped off. He hit the ground at a run, snatched up his prize, leaped into his saddle and came racing back toward us, whooping and hollering and swinging the dead critter over his head by its ears. When he got closer, you could see blood spraying out. It sprinkled Snooker considerable, but he didn't pay it any mind.

I figured the hare was meant to be food, and Snooker would want to dismount and clean it. We'd all have a chance to get off the horses. I was mighty eager to stand on my own feet and stretch and take a rest from the misery. But Snooker joined up with us and we kept on riding.

He cleaned his game, sure enough. But he stayed in his saddle to do it, holding the hare off to the side and carving away at it with his knife. Watching the guts drop out and fall to the ground, I was put in mind of Whittle. I turned my head away and studied the back of McSween's shirt.

By and by, Emmet shouted, 'Mine! I got it!'

He went racing after another rabbit, reins in his teeth, his hands full of iron. He blazed away just twice. His first slug tore off half the critter's head. His second, fired at near the same instant, took it in its rear and knocked it sideways.

It was the most splendid bit of shooting I'd seen up to that time.

'Astonishing,' I muttered.

'Seen worse,' McSween said.

'I certainly wish *I* could shoot in such a manner.'

'Well, ask him real sweet, and maybe he'll show you a thing or two.'

I decided to do precisely that.

Later in the afternoon, we stopped near a creek where a stand of cottonwoods grew and there was some grass. Chase sent me off to gather firewood while the rest of them saw to their horses. When I returned with an armload, they were arranging their saddles and bedrolls under the trees. McSween said I could borrow his saddle blanket for the night. So I took that and spread it out to air.

I hadn't more than laid it on the ground when McSween called to Emmet. 'The lad here purely admires your talent with the Colts. You oughta take him over yonder and learn him a few tricks.'

My face heated up. But I said, 'I'd be quite grateful.'

Emmet, he grinned. 'You think I'm good, do you?'

'Quite the best I've ever seen.'

'You're a regular John Wesley Hardin,' Snooker said.

'I can sure outgun you any day of the week with both eyes shut.'

'If you could slap leather as good as you flap your gums, you'd be a wonder to behold.'

At that, Emmet took the opportunity to slap leather. Both guns seemed to jump into his hands. They came up cocked and ready. But he didn't let the hammers drop. He just grinned at Snooker, who hadn't gone for his at all.

Snooker's hand had darted to his face, not his holster.

Pulling his fingertip out of his nose, he studied what he'd found up there and said, 'You beat me fair and square, you little booger.'

Emmet laughed, lowered the hammers with his thumbs, and holstered the weapons. Then he squatted down, felt around inside one of his saddle bags, and came up with a box of ammunition. 'Come on along, Willy,' he said.

The others stayed behind. We walked down along the creek a ways. Then Emmet stopped and nodded toward a dead stump on the other side, about thirty feet off. 'Watch here,' he said.

After setting the box of cartridges on the ground, he stood loose, arms hanging at his sides, and stared over at the stump. 'That's an hombre there that's fixing to poke me full of lead. Now, I just can't count on him missing. From what I've seen, most fellers can't shoot any better than you do, but I can't *count* on that, you see? So I wanta plug him before he gets to take a crack. That's what the quickdraw's all about. As a general rule, the man that clears leather and gets off the first shot's gonna be the one that walks away. Here goes.'

Emmet snatched out both his Colts. In a flash, they came up cocked and level and spat lead. His bullets thunked into the stump, throwing out little clouds of dust and wood.

'Ripping!' I said.

'They don't come much better,' Emmet told me.

'Have you been in actual gunfights?'

'Why, I should say so. I've killed four men.' He seemed right proud of the accomplishment.

Not wanting to appear the complete novice, I said, 'I've killed one man, myself.'

He narrowed an eye at me. 'You?'

'Oh, yes, quite. A bloke had a go at me in London, and I dispatched him with a knife.' Actually, I was never certain the man had died, but he'd told me he would. That seemed good enough for the purpose of bragging.

The way Emmet looked at me, he couldn't figure out whether I was lying or not. But he said, 'A knife won't do you no good at all out here. Any man that's worth his salt packs iron and ain't afraid to use it. You gotta be quicker than the next guy, or you just won't last. And you gotta hit what you aim at.'

He stepped aside, then nodded at the stump.

I let my arms hang, the way I'd seen him do. Then I went for my Colts. The one in the holster came out clean, but I had a spot of trouble with the one in my belt. By and by, I got them both up and cocked. I pulled the triggers. The hammers clanked.

Emmet snickered.

'Ain't *you* the gunfighter?'

My face heated up something awful. 'I'm terribly sorry.'

'Terribly dead, that's what you'd be if that was more than an old dead tree over there.'

'I'm afraid my irons are empty.'

'I noticed that.' Laughing some, he picked up the box and opened it. 'You don't hardly need two Colts just now. You'll be lucky to handle one good enough to count.'

'Yes, sir,' I said. I jammed the conductor's pistol down my belt, then helped myself to some ammunition.

Then stood there with my sixgun in one hand and cartridges in the other. Stood there and stared at them and sweated.

Emmet grinned at me. 'What're you fixing to do with 'em?' he asked.

'Slip them into the gun, is it?'

'That's the idea.'

What I did, I took a cartridge between my thumb and finger and tipped the barrel up and puzzled over the matter. I'd handled the General's weapons, but I never had occasion to load them. I simply didn't have a clue as to how I might go about it. Sliding a round down the muzzle didn't seem the proper way. The bullets had to get into the cylinder, somehow. I was still trying to figure it out when Emmet suddenly commenced to split his sides.

He acted like he'd never seen anything funnier. He laughed so hard he couldn't stand up straight and his eyes filled with tears. Every now and then, he'd gasp out a word or so. An 'Oh, Lord!' or a 'Never in my born days!' or a 'Wish the boys was here!'

The boys *wasn't* here, and mighty glad I was for that.

Though I suspected they'd be hearing about me.

Emmet went on busting himself with gaiety and tears while I worked on my problem. He was still at it when I found a little door behind the Colt's cylinder. It opened sideways, and showed me a used shell. I shook that one out and replaced it with a fresh round. Then I turned the cylinder and repeated the trick. I put in six cartridges and shut the door.

Emmet hadn't noticed at all. He'd worn himself out. He was bent over, holding his knees and gasping when I fired into the air.

The noise jerked him up straight. He gazed at me. His red, wet face grinned. Then he applauded.

'I'm not a total dunce, really,' I said.

Shaking his head, he rubbed his eyes and took some deep breaths. Finally, he said, 'Now that you're loaded . . .' and then wheezed and took on again. Finally, he got control of himself. 'Let's see . . . let's see if you can hit anything. Oh . . . they do work so much better . . . with bullets in 'em.'

Well, I stuck my arm out straight, pointed my Colt at the stump, and pulled the trigger. The gun blasted and jumped. Through the ringing in my ears, I heard a quiet thud. A puff exploded off the stump.

I'd hit it dead center!

'I say!' I blurted.

Emmet looked at me and wiped one of his eyes. 'Only thing is, you took all day to do it.'

I holstered the Colt, rubbed the sweat off my hand onto the leg of my trousers, then tried for a quickdraw. I snatched the gun up quick. It no sooner cleared leather than I thumbed back the hammer. I brought the barrel up fast, pointed it in the general direction of the stump, and let fly.

My bullet sang off a rock just to the right of the stump.

Emmet, he didn't laugh or say a word.

I had another go. This time, I hit the stump.

Twice more, I unlimbered that Colt with all the speed I could muster and got off my shots. Both of them poked holes in the target.

Emmet looked at me, frowning some.

I took a deep breath, feeling pleased with myself and more than a trifle surprised. The air smelled strong with gunsmoke. It seemed a fine aroma.

'I did rather well, wouldn't you say?'

'You ain't hopeless,' he told me.

I reloaded, slapped leather, and pounded another hole into the stump. Out of six tries, I only missed twice.

Emmet didn't seem particularly happy about my progress. He watched me, narrow-eyed, while I loaded up again. When I finished and holstered my weapon, he stepped over so we were shoulder to shoulder, both facing the stump across the stream. 'On the count of three,' he said. 'One. Two.'

He said, 'Three,' and I pulled. So did he. His Colts blasted, and the roar of them was still in my ears when my shot followed. His slugs smacked the stump not more than a blink or two before mine did the same.

Then he eyed me again. 'I don't much like getting my leg pulled, kid.'

'Pardon me?'

'Acting like you ain't got the first notion how to handle a sixgun . . . like you didn't know how to *load* the damn thing. Making a fool outa me the way you done.'

Seems like I was *forever* getting myself wrongly accused of this or that.

'Why, I've never fired a weapon before today, much less had an occasion to fill one with bullets. Never.'

'Bullsquat.'

'It's the honest truth.'

'You've had your laugh on me.' He put away his Colts, then picked up the ammo box and headed back for camp.

I caught up with him. 'Actually, I apprenticed in gunmanship under no less than Wild Bill Hickok.'

That got him to look at me. 'There you go again. He's been sleeping in sod since seventy-six.'

Some calculating showed me I was no more than about two when Hickok died.

'I'm a spot older than I look,' I told Emmet.

That got him to laugh.

'Who really showed you?' he asked.

'No one but you, actually. I never in my life fired a shot until this very day when that fellow stuck his arm out the train window.'

He gave me a puzzled look. There was some wariness to it, but not much anger.

'I'm not having you on,' I said. 'Believe me. If I'd known what I was about, I most certainly wouldn't have humiliated myself in the matter of loading bullets.'

He took to smiling again when I reminded him of that. 'Land, I've never seen such a thing.'

'I suppose you'll tell everyone.'

'It's just a shame they wasn't there to see it for themselves.'

Chapter Thirty-one

My First Night in the

Outlaw Camp

Back at the camp, a big pot of stew was bubbling on the fire. The smell set my mouth to watering.

McSween was busy stirring the mixture, Chase bringing in some more firewood, Snooker cleaning his Winchester, Breakenridge resting on the ground with his back propped up by his saddle, busy at nothing.

'How'd it go?' McSween asked.

'Well,' Emmet said, 'we had us quite a time.'

'Glad to see nobody's wounded,' McSween said.

'You all sure missed a show,' Emmet announced.

With everybody looking on, he drew one of his Colts and plucked a cartridge from his gunbelt. 'This right here's how Willy went to load up,' he said. Holding the pistol in front of his face, frowning and sticking his tongue out a corner of his mouth as if he were trying very hard to think, he poked his bullet into the muzzle. 'I say,' he said, mimicking the way I talk, 'isn't this how it goes, really?'

'No!' Snooker squealed. 'Did he?'

Well, I hadn't and Emmet knew it. But I judged he might like me more if I didn't spoil his fun.

'Sure as I'm standing here.'

Snooker and Breakenridge, they both whooped it up considerable. Emmet, too, though not as hard as he'd done in the first place. 'Yep!' he went on. 'Just what he did!' Chase didn't laugh, but sort of grinned with one corner of his mouth and shook his head at me.

McSween glanced my way, then looked around at the others. He didn't seem amused, but rubbed his whiskery cheek. 'Well,' he said, 'no call to make sport of the lad. He didn't know no better.'

'It just beats all!' Snooker blurted.

'Well, that's what *I* reckoned,' Emmet said, calming down some. 'But then he figured out where the bullets go, so I picked myself up off the ground and watched him try to shoot.'

'Hope you took cover,' Snooker said.

Emmet gave my arm a squeeze. 'Show 'em, Willy.' With the pistol in his other hand, he pointed to a tree off beyond the campsite. 'See if you can put one in there.'

'Don't plug the horses,' Snooker said.

The horses, they were way off to the other side, and not in any danger at all no matter how bad a shot I might be, unless I turned halfway around.

But I didn't figure I *was* a bad shot. Quite the contrary. I was feeling just brimful of talent.

'Hold on, there,' Breakenridge said. He wanted to be standing up so he wouldn't miss the fun.

While he got to his feet, Snooker made quite a show of scampering around behind me. 'Think I'm safe here?' he asked.

'Quit your funnin' the lad,' McSween told him. He unsquatted and turned to watch me.

They *all* watched me.

'Are we quite ready?' I asked.

'Just take her easy,' McSween said. 'Spite of what Emmet likely told you, quickest draw in the world don't matter worth a hill of beans if you miss what you're aiming at.'

'Don't blow your toes off,' Snooker warned.

I pulled and fired. Bark jumped off the tree trunk.

The laughing stopped.

'I'll be,' McSween muttered. 'That's some mighty fair work, Willy.'

Emmet said, 'I learned him real good, huh, boys?'

'Where'd you learn to shoot like that?' Chase asked me.

'Over by the creek.'

'He claims he never fired a gun till today,' Emmet explained.

'That the honest truth?' Chase asked.

'Yes, sir,' I said.

'Jesus wept,' Breakenridge said.

'Just don't let it swell your head up,' McSween told me. 'There's a whole lot more to life than being handy with a sixgun. Not that it don't help. But it can get you into scrapes if you don't watch yourself careful.'

'McSween knows plenty about scrapes,' Chase said, and sounded serious.

'That's a fact.'

'I don't suppose I'm quite good enough to start taking on real gunfighters,' I said.

'Glad to hear you say it,' McSween said. 'And you're right. You got loads of natural talent, looks like, but what you gotta do is hone your skills. And learn what you can from those of us that's been around.'

'Thank you. I'd like to learn whatever's necessary.'

McSween and Chase, they'd treated me fine pretty much from the start. But after my demonstration with the Colt, the others warmed up to me. All of a sudden, I was no longer an outsider. They talked to me and joked with me, just like I'd been with the gang forever. It made me feel welcome and happy.

Long about dark, the stew finished cooking. McSween scooped out gobs of it into tin cups, and we all sat around the fire to eat. The rabbit parts were mixed in with beans and onions. A morsel of food hadn't passed my lips since the previous night aboard the train, so I consumed the stew with great relish.

I can't recollect ever enjoying a meal more than that one. Not only did the hot stew taste wonderful, but I was among five new friends who were actual western desperados – actual train robbers. Me. Partnered up with a gang of outlaws.

Good fellows, even if they did ride on the wrong side of the law. Good fellows who figured I had the makings of a gunfighter.

For a while there, I forgot about all my aches and worries. I hardly felt like myself at all. Trevor Wellington Bentley seemed like a stranger I'd left behind. I was Willy. A hard-riding ruffian good with a Colt, caught up in a grand adventure. It was ever so bully!

After we got done eating, I volunteered to take the pot and cups down to the creek. I went off by myself and cleaned them. The night was lovely, all atwinkle with stars, a full moon glinting silver on the water and making all the rocks and bushes look like they were brushed with milk. The creek gurgled along, quiet and peaceful. I could hear the boys talking off in the distance. Some birds were warbling. A coyote howled.

I don't know as I'd ever been quite so happy to be right where I was.

When the supper things were clean, I set them on a rock and dried my hands. I stretched. I filled myself with air that smelled a bit of woodsmoke. Then I snatched out my Colt. Didn't fire, though. The night was too calm for gunshots. I didn't want to stir up the boys, either.

The iron felt heavy and good in my hand.

I holstered it. 'Don't make me ventilate you, hombre,' I whispered. 'Go for your iron, and you'll be sleeping under sod.' The hombre in my head didn't listen to reason. I slapped leather. 'Pow!'

Well, I was having myself a fine time, so I kept at it for a while. By loosening my belt so the holster didn't hang so high, I was able to draw faster. Each time I pulled, though, the gun lifted the holster off my leg a bit. I could see why Emmet and the others tied theirs down. What I needed was a rawhide thong, but I didn't have one.

Not wanting the others to catch on that I'd been practicing, I tightened up my belt again before gathering the utensils and heading back to the fire.

They were passing around a bottle of whiskey. I took my place by McSween's side. He handed me the bottle, and I swigged some, then passed it over to Chase.

'Emmet tells us you killed a feller,' McSween said.

'Only one,' I said, recalling that Emmet had claimed four for himself. 'And you?'

'None that didn't ask for it.'

'Mine asked for it, I reckon. He attacked me, and I did no more than defend myself.'

'Did the law take after you?' Emmet asked.

'Indeed, I found myself pursued by Bobbies and an awful mob. If they'd caught me . . .'

'What the tar are them Bobbies?' Snooker wanted to know.

'Why, they're constables. Policemen.'

'So they had a posse on your tail,' Chase said. 'Been in the same fix our own selves from time to time. How'd you get shut of it?'

'I nipped into a courtyard and hid.'

'This was over there in England?' McSween asked.

'Yes, sir. If I hadn't stabbed that bloke, I'd be there still.'

'So you lit out?'

'Actually, I ran afoul of Jack the Ripper.' None of the boys acted like they'd ever heard of him, but they seemed mighty interested in my tale. So I plugged on, only taking breaks to hear all the things they had to say and to answer questions and to swallow some whiskey whenever the bottle came around.

I explained how the Ripper'd skulked about the East End, murdering whores. Then I told how, after escaping from the mob, I'd taken shelter in Mary's room. How I'd been right there under her bed when the Ripper butchered her. I told about following him afterwards and attacking him.

'That showed a heap of gumption,' McSween said.

'Why, I couldn't allow him to slay the poor woman. I only wish I'd killed him then and spared the world from further woes. If I'd had a Colt in my hand, he'd be in Hell where he belongs.'

I told about stabbing him in the back, and how it hadn't appeared to damage him much at all. The boys took on quite a bit over my removal of Whittle's nose. But they settled down and listened as I described the chase and my plunge into the Thames.

About then, Breakenridge fetched a new bottle from his saddle bag, and we started in on it. I was feeling mighty fine.

After I explained what happened to Trudy's father, Snooker allowed the old man got no worse than he deserved. 'He shouldn't've busted your head, Willy boy.'

'It goes to show what comes of making wrong estimations in regard to another feller's intentions,' McSween added.

I went on with my story, telling about our trip to Plymouth, the death of the Irishman, then about our voyage across the Atlantic. Why, the boys seemed purely spellbound as I told of how we fought our way through rough seas and those terrible storms.

I was just full of myself and liquor and the joy of having an audience that hung on my every word. I was in rare form. But I got the yacht all the way to Gravesend Bay before I realized I hadn't mentioned much of anything about poor Trudy – only that she'd been aboard and cooked for us. Nothing about the ways Whittle had tormented her, or how she'd been the one to throw the Irishman's head overboard, or how I'd saved her those times from hanging and drowning.

I hadn't left such things out of my story on purpose, They'd simply stayed inside me. And I was glad of that.

Some of the fun leaked out of me when I recalled all that had happened with Trudy, and how she'd ended.

I drank some more whiskey, almost dropped the bottle, but caught it in time. Then I handed it over to Chase.

'We were anchored offshore, that night. I was quite sure Whittle wouldn't let us live. I knew we had to take drastic steps if we were to save Trudy. Michael, however, wanted no part of it. The bloody coward.'

I do have some recollection of calling Michael a bloody coward.

Then it was suddenly morning. I found myself wrapped in a blanket near McSween, sore all over, my head just afire with agony. I grabbed my head to keep it from coming apart. That helped some.

It wasn't quite sunup yet. The others were still snoozing away.

I lay there with my pains and tried to think back. I couldn't remember turning in. For a while, I couldn't remember anything at all that had happened after coming back from the creek and sitting down by the fire. Then bits and pieces started showing themselves. Pretty soon, I recalled what had gone on up till I reached the part in my story where I called Michael a bloody coward.

Beyond that, it was all blank.

Had I passed out? Or had I gone on with my tale? For a while, my worries hurt more than my head, for I feared what I might've told about me and Sarah.

It didn't feel good at all, lying there, so I sat up. My boots were by my head, along with my belt and holster and both guns. I sure couldn't recall taking them off.

Over on the other side of them the grass was matted down with once-used stew. Had I done that?

I checked my clothes. If I'd lost my supper, at least I'd gotten none on me.

Oh, I felt a proper fool.

My mouth was so dry I could hardly swallow, so I got into the boots and went over to the stream. I drank till I couldn't hold any more, then washed up and sat on a rock and hung on to my head.

I had half a notion to wander off, for I sure didn't look forward to facing the boys.

I stayed there even after I heard their voices.

Finally, I worked up my nerve and went back to the camp.

McSween had the fire going. He looked at me and smiled. 'Glad to see you ain't dead, Willy.'

'I rather wish I were.'

'Know how it is.'

I appreciated McSween's kindness. Chase came along, and didn't make sport of me, either. Emmet and Snooker and Breakenridge, however, had themselves a fine time at my expense. I felt too sick to care much. From their comments, I gathered that my story hadn't progressed much beyond telling how I'd beached the yacht and gone along the shore looking for Whittle. I'd got a bit rowdy, at that point, and jumped to my feet and yelled, 'Show your face, you bloody cur! I'll put a slug where your nose use to be!' Then I'd pulled my Colt, dropped it, bent over to pick it up, and would've fallen into the fire except that Chase leaped and caught me.

In spite of my ill health and humiliation, I was mighty glad I'd passed out and never had a chance to blather about me and Sarah.

Well, I survived all the joshing the boys handed out. With some breakfast in me, I felt a spot less sick. But then it came time to mount up. I took my usual place behind McSween. We left the camp behind, and I commenced to experience the most frightful agony as the horse rocked and swayed under me.

By and by, I thought I might lose my breakfast. So McSween let me climb down and walk. Right away, I felt better. The way the horses ambled along, I had no trouble at all keeping up with them. My boots pinched, but not too bad. Every so often, I'd give my feet a rest and ride for a spell. Mostly with McSween, but also with Emmet and Snooker. I couldn't stay on any of their horses for long, thought, without feeling woozy. Then I'd jump down and walk some more.

The day seemed to drag on forever.

Finally we stopped and made camp. By then, I wasn't feeling horrible any more, just sore and headachy. Emmet and Snooker tried to talk me into some shooting, but about the last thing I wanted was to hear gunfire. 'I'd rather not, really.'

'There'll be plenty of time for practice,' McSween said, 'when Willy ain't feeling so poorly.'

So they let me off the hook.

After supper, we sat around the fire and the boys passed around a bottle of whiskey. When it came to me, I took one whiff and winced. The others drank, though.

They asked me to go on with my story. Actually, I would've preferred to hear about their adventures, but they insisted, so I went ahead.

I told about finding Whittle's skiff, hiking through the snow and sneaking into General Forrest's house. McSween, he'd been a trooper in the General's command, and asked a passel of questions about him. I talked considerable about the General and Mable, but didn't say much about Sarah. Only that we got to be friends, and how, after the deaths of her grandparents, I'd stayed on as her servant until I read about Whittle in the newspaper and we headed west.

Not a word about our baths or dancing or any such thing.

Even though I mostly kept mum about Sarah, I took to missing her something awful. I tried not to let it show.

When it came time to tell about Briggs, I had to bend the truth considerable. Otherwise, they would've seen it was jealousy that got me into trouble. I let on that Briggs had been rude and ornery to Sarah, and pestered her till I had no choice but to deal with him. Finally, it came to getting myself tossed off the train.

'The next day, I climbed on back up the hill and followed the tracks. I thought Sarah might disembark, don't you know, once she discovered that I'd gone missing. Perhaps she would be waiting for me at the next station down the line. But then I met up with you chaps. I haven't a clue what to do next, actually, other than ride along with you.'

'We're pleased to have you, Willy,' Chase said.

'You've all been mighty good to me.'

'Seems to me,' McSween said, 'like you've got business elsewhere.'

'I do hope to find Sarah.'

'You don't wanta be showing your face around no railroad depots,' Chase said. 'Not for a spell, leastwise.'

'No, I should think not.'

'Not unless you're looking for a chance to use your Colts on something more lively than a stump,' Emmet said.

'You ain't likely to find her, anyhow, walking the rails,' McSween told me. 'By now, your Sarah's either turned around and headed for home, or gone on down the line figuring you might catch up to her at Tombstone.'

'Least if she hasn't been interfered with by that Briggs feller,' Chase added, which didn't make me feel any better.

'I reckon Tombstone is where I need to go. Even if Sarah's not there, it seems the best place to start my search for Whittle.'

'Well,' McSween said, 'you can't go nowhere till we get you a horse. Best thing's to stick with us till we get to Bailey's Corner. You can buy a good mount there and rig yourself up for the hunt.'

Chapter Thirty-two

Dire Threats

The next day, I got my horse.

I'd been taking turns riding double with some of the boys, and was mounted behind Emmet when he pointed and said, 'Over yonder.'

I leaned sideways and looked past him. Off to the right, at some distance, a pair of horsemen were headed in our general direction. These were the first strangers we'd come across since lighting out from the train.

Emmet reined in, and the rest of the boys caught up with us.

'Not enough of 'em to be a posse,' Breakenridge said.

'If we had a posse after us,' Chase said, 'it wouldn't likely be coming from the east.'

This talk of posses unsettled me some. Nobody's mentioned, until now, that we had any reason to worry about such things.

'Don't matter who they are,' McSween said. 'Thing is, there's only just the two of 'em.'

McSween took the lead, and we headed for the strangers. When we got within hailing distance, he waved his arm and called out, 'Howdy, boys!'

One nodded. The other touched a finger to the brim of his hat. They were riding side by side, going slow as if they weren't in any rush to get somewhere. From the looks on their faces, they were neither glad to meet us nor unhappy about it. They didn't rightly have expressions, at all. They just watched us approach.

The older of the two was a slim fellow with grim eyes and a mustache that was just as black as his outfit. His hat was black, same as his string tie and frock coat, trousers, gunbelt and boots. I didn't care at all for the looks of him.

The bloke he rode with wasn't just younger, but heavier. He looked as if the heat didn't agree with him. His face was red and sweaty, his shirt collar open, his tie hanging loose. He had a black coat like his friend, but it was tied down behind his saddle.

I wondered if they might be a pair of preachers or undertakers, dressed in black that way.

If it'd been up to me, I would've passed them by.

But McSween rode straight toward them. 'Hate to be a bother,' he said, 'but you boys look like you've got a horse to spare.' The last word wasn't out of his mouth before a Colt was in his hand, cocked and pointed at the skinny fellow.

Emmet, Chase and Breakenridge all pulled at once. On both sides of me, hammers went *snick-clack*. Snooker took a while to come out with his Winchester. He worked its lever and shouldered it.

Both the strangers hoisted their arms.

'Climb on down,' McSween said.

They dismounted and stood beside their horses. Each had one hand in the air, the other holding reins.

'Willy, get on over here.'

I slid off the back of Emmet's horse and walked toward the two fellows. The way they glowered at me, I rather shriveled up inside. But then their eyes turned to McSween as he swung to the ground. He stepped in front of them, one at a time, and took their pistols. They never said a word to him. The fat one, his chin was trembling. The mean one looked like he wanted to bite McSween.

After collecting their sidearms, McSween fetched their rifles out of the saddle scabbards. He handed one of the Winchesters to me, then toted the other weapons over to a thicket of prickly bush and tossed them in among the nettles.

Coming back, he said, 'Let's have your boots off, friends.'

They sat on the ground and tugged their boots off.

'Try 'em on, there, Willy.'

'I'd rather not, actually.'

'Go on, now. You need a pair what fits, don't you?'

Well, this didn't seem a good time to argue the matter, so I gathered the boots. I sat down with my back to the fellows so I wouldn't have to look at them, then pulled off the boots I'd taken from the conductor. I tried on the new ones. The first set felt too tight, the second too loose. The loose boots belonged to the fat chap. They felt a sight better than what I'd been wearing, but I had no wish to keep them on. They were hot and juicy inside so I felt like my feet were sliding about in swamp slime.

So I yanked them off and shook my head. 'They're altogether too large,' I said, and got into my old familiar boots.

'Well, that's a shame,' McSween said.

I carried the boots back to their owners and dropped them.

'Too bad, friends,' McSween told them. 'You lost out on a sale.'

'A sale?' the fat guy asked.

'Why, we ain't here to rob you. Nosirree. Willy here, he'll pay you fair and square for what he needs.' After saying that, McSween checked the horses over pretty good. He looked inside their mouths, ran his hands down their legs, studied their hoofs, and such. Then he came around front and said to the thin fellow, 'He'll give you eighty dollars for your mount, friend. Throw in an extra ten for the tack, and ten for the Winchester. Willy, you owe the man a hundred dollars.'

I wasn't eager to do it, but figured I hadn't much choice. So I counted out my money. I stepped closer to the man, who was still on the ground with his legs stretched out. He just glared up at me. I tossed the money at his feet.

'You take my horse, boy, and I'll kill you sure.'

A chill started to rush through my bones, but then I flinched as a couple of gunshots bashed the silence. The slugs missed him. They kicked dust onto the legs of his black trousers.

'You best watch your tongue, mister,' Emmet said. I looked up at him in time to see smoke drifting away from the muzzles of his Colts.

McSween drew his own pistol. Crouching, he aimed it at the fellow's face and thumbed back the hammer. 'You wanta take back them words?'

'Take 'em back, Prue,' the fatty blurted. 'They'll shoot us both sure.'

'It's *my* horse.'

'No call to threaten a boy's life,' McSween told him. 'He's my buddy. You look like the sort to follow through on a thing like that, so I reckon you either repent your words or die right here.'

'Prue! Good God, man!'

Prue, he looked fit to bust. Not scared at all, but just in a rage, all red in the face, his breath hissing through his gritted teeth.

'What's it gonna be?'

Prue took to nodding.

'What's that?'

'I take it back.'

'How's that?'

'*I won't kill him.*'

'I don't reckon I believe you. Goes against my grain, though, to shoot a man down in cold blood. So I'll tell you this. Listen good. We ain't taking nothing we ain't paid for. We're leaving you a horse and your weapons. No law says we gotta, but it wouldn't be right to do otherwise. You keep that in mind. We treated you fair and square. Now, if you or your pal take it into your heads to come after us, know this. Next time I catch sight of either one of you, I'll figure you come to make good on your threat to the lad. Lead'll fly. It's that simple.'

After having his say, McSween unsquatted and holstered his gun. He led the horse forward between the two men. While I held the reins, he unloaded the bedroll, saddle bags and such so we wouldn't be taking anything we hadn't paid for.

Then I mounted up and slid my new Winchester into its scabbard.

I was awful shaken by the whole affair, but it did feel good to be sitting up high in the saddle of my own horse.

We rode off at a trot. I wanted to dig my heels in and light out fast, but the others just weren't in that much of a rush. Except for me, Snooker was the only one who even looked back to keep an eye on those fellows.

They were watching us. Not even heading for the bush to retrieve their guns.

Well, I reckon they were too smart for such a play.

If they'd fired just a single shot, I've no doubt at all but what McSween would've wheeled around and led the gang in a charge.

The pair was still in sight when we slowed our horses to a walk. Me and Snooker were at the rear. I rode over closer to him and said, 'Do you reckon they'll be coming after us?'

'Never can tell. I'd rest a sight easier if McSween'd shot

'em. Now we're gonna have to watch our backsides.'

'They don't seem at all worried, do they?' I asked, nodding toward the others.

'Them rascals is nothing we can't handle. Just gotta watch they don't take and bushwack us. If they do that, though, they'll wind up dead. We ain't a bunch of gals, you know.'

'I rather suppose you've dealt with worse rascals,' I said.

He gave me a weasely grin full of sharp, yellow teeth. 'None that's still above ground.'

'Who's the best of the lot?'

Patting the stock of his rifle, he said, 'Why, I reckon I could knock the left eye out of a gnat at a hundred yards in a sandstorm. Chase and Emmet, they're mighty sharp with their sixguns, though they can't hold a candle to McSween. You take Breakenridge, now, he's having a lucky day when he can hit the *air*. But I once seen him get shot twice by a card sharp, then lay one punch that turned the bastard's head clean around backwards. They never bothered to untwist him, either. Saw him in his casket.'

'Which side up?' I asked.

Snooker laughed. 'Face and ass!'

'You're having me on.'

'It's the plain truth, just ask Breakenridge.'

I thought I might pass on that, as Breakenridge wasn't one for talking much and generally seemed rather solemn. 'Is that how he came to be on the wrong side of the law?'

'Oh, he got himself acquitted on that one. A fair fight, you know. The way I hear it, he was just a kid in Missouri when he laid an ax into his schoolmaster on account of the fellow called him a name. Went home to fetch it, first. Then came along with it and chopped him up right there in front of everyone.'

'I say,' said I. 'What did the schoolmaster call him, do you know?'

'Called him Meriwether.'

'But that's his name, isn't it?'

'He don't care to be reminded of the fact.'

'I heard McSween call him that.'

'Well, I reckon McSween can call him anything he likes.'

'They're great chums, is it?'

'Not hardly. They only just tolerate each other. But Breakenridge, he knows you don't fool with McSween.'

'That dangerous, is he?'

'Only if you rile him.'

'He seems quite friendly, really.'

'Oh, he's as sweet as pie, mostly.'

'Is he the leader of the gang? I'd rather assumed it was Chase, but . . .'

'Chase pretty much runs things. But he don't run McSween. It'd been up to Chase, I reckon we would've let them fellers alone, back there, and you'd still be riding double. Looks to me like McSween took a notion you oughta have a horse of your own, that's all. He thinks highly of you, Willy.'

Well, it didn't come as a surprise to hear that, but it made me feel mighty good.

'With a friend the likes of him, you ain't got much to worry about. He'll look after you and see no harm comes your way.'

Later on in the day, McSween broke off from the rest of us and rode to the top of a hill. Up there, he raised a pair of field glasses to his face. He studied the direction we'd come from.

I met up with him at the bottom. 'Are they after us?' I asked.

'Didn't see no sign of 'em. I spect they knew better, though I wouldn't trust that one feller no more than a rattlesnake.'

'What if they should come?'

'Be some gunplay.'

'Perhaps we shouldn't have taken the man's horse.'

'He acting up on you?'

'Not at all. He's quite fine, really.' I patted the horse's neck, and he glanced back at me and nodded like he appreciated the kindness. 'I just don't want any troubles to come of it.'

'Don't worry yourself about that, Willy.'

The rest of the boys had started moving again. We rode along behind. McSween didn't seem in any hurry to catch up with them.

'Got a name for him?' he asked.

'I should imagine he already has a name.'

'Has he whispered it to you?'

I laughed.

McSween rolled a smoke. He lit it up, then handed his makings across to me. I'd had some practice since my first go at it, back when we'd divied up the loot. So I made myself a smoke that wasn't too crooked or leaky. I lit up, and passed the makings back to him.

'You oughta give him a name,' he said.

'He doesn't feel as if he's actually *my* horse.'

'Why, sure he is. You paid for him fair and square. All you're missing's a bill of sale. Fraid I didn't think of that. If it'd make you feel better, I'll do you one up myself when we make camp. We'll let on like I sold him to you. Not that anyone's likely to raise a fuss about it.'

'Other than the owner, do you mean?'

'You heard what I told him, didn't you?'

'Yes.'

'Well, I don't say such things but what I mean 'em.'

'So you'll actually shoot him if you ever see him again?'

'That's the long and short of it, Willy.'

'What if he sees you first?'

'You sure do worry your head over things.'

'I shouldn't like to see you get shot.'

'Many a man has tried.' He flicked his smoke away and pulled off his hat. While he held that in one hand, he stroked his mustache with the other. Then he gave his long hair a few flings with his fingers. 'You see all this-here silver?'

Both his mustache and his hair were mostly black, but streaked with plenty of shiny strands.

'Know what it is, Willy?'

'Gray hair, is it?'

'Silver. Precious silver. It's the pay you get for staying alive.

The longer you go without getting perforated by various rapscallions and Indians – or scalped – the more you collect. All you gotta do is take a gander at a man's head, and you can get yourself a fair estimate of his worth. You see much silver up there, you know he ain't easy to kill.' He flapped his hat back down onto his head. 'What I'm getting at, you shouldn't be spoiling your good times fretting about me. What're you gonna call your horse?'

I gave it some thought. 'Perhaps I ought to name him Meriwether.'

When I said that, McSween laughed harder than I'd ever seen him do before. He didn't take on like Emmet over my reloading, gasping and weeping, but he sure did laugh up a storm. After he'd settled down some, he said, 'That's purely rich, Willy. Don't you do it, though. That old boy's a mite touchy about his name.'

'How does General sound?'

'After Matthew Forrest? I reckon he'd be right proud.'

'General it is, then. Howdy, General,' I said. The horse bobbed his head up and down as if he liked the new name.

Once I'd named him, he did seem to be more mine. I suddenly felt fonder of him just because of it. I knew I'd actually stolen him, no matter what sort of light McSween wanted to put on the doings. But I told myself that General was better off with me. Just by looking at the previous owner, you could see he had a mean streak. I had no doubt but what he'd mistreated General whenever he got the chance. So I pretty much stopped feeling bad about stealing him, though I never got past worrying that the fellow might come after us.

By and by, it came to me that I was all set up, now, to travel on my own. I had myself a horse, a rifle, two pistols, a bit of money. No reason, really, not to bid the gang farewell and head for Tombstone to seek out Sarah and Whittle.

I just wasn't eager, though, to take that step. Partly, I reckon, it was for fear I might run afoul of the pair we'd robbed. I didn't hanker to be alone if that should happen. Thing is, I didn't hanker to be alone at all.

So I figured to ride along with the boys, at least till after we got to Bailey's Corner.

For the next few days, we kept an eye on the territory to our rear. Nobody appeared to be following, though.

Each evening, after finding a place to camp, Emmet and I wandered off for shooting practice. He gave me some rawhide to tie down my holster, and that helped considerable. I got quicker on the draw, and my aim improved.

A couple of times, I asked McSween to come along with us. He never did, though, until the final evening before we rode into Bailey's Corner.

'You've come along real good,' he said after watching me pull and fire. 'That feller Whittle, he's gonna rue the day he crossed your trail.'

'If I'm ever able to find him, perhaps.'

'I've got half a mind to join you for the hunt,' he said.

'Do you?'

Emmet gave McSween a look as if he figured the chap had gone daft.

'Yup. Half a mind.'

'That would be smashing!'

'Fact is, I used to be a fair hand at tracking redskins. Might be I could help you run down this Whittle and put him to rest.'

'Why on earth you wanta do such a thing?' Emmet said.

'Not much sport in robbing trains.'

'It's what we *do*.'

'Seems like maybe I've done enough of it for a spell. It'd feel good to take a rest from it and get in on a good chase.'

Chapter Thirty-three

Trouble at Bailey's Corner

Nothing more was said about McSween's notion to help me track down Whittle. I got to worrying, later on that night, about whether he'd meant it or not. After the others had turned in and McSween was standing first watch, I crawled out of my blanket and went looking for him.

We'd been posting lookouts ever since we took Prue's horse, as a precaution against ambush. There'd never been any sign of Prue or his friend, but McSween had said we shouldn't count them out. 'It's when you quit watching for trouble,' he said, 'that it most always sneaks up on you.'

It took me a few minutes to spot him. He stood in a shadow between two high, moonlit boulders off beyond the campsite. He had his back to me.

I was trying to walk quiet, mostly as it was night and I didn't care to disturb the stillness. So sudden it shocked me, McSween whirled around and grabbed iron.

'Don't shoot!' I whispered. 'It's me!'

'I *know* it's you. If I was fixing to shoot, it'd be done with by now.' He holstered his Colt. 'You got a lot to learn, Willy, or you ain't likely to grow no silver.'

As I walked closer to him, he said, 'Many a feller's died before his time for no better reason than he walked up behind the wrong man. I knowed a marshal in Tucscon shot his best friend dead in just such a manner. Heard him sneaking up, turned and let fly. Put three slugs in his buddy and only just saw who he'd killed by the muzzle flashes.'

'That's awful,' I said.

'Happens plenty. What you wanta do is keep your distance and call out, make sure he knows who you are.'

'Yes, sir.' After a bit, I asked, 'How did you know it was me?'

'Them tight boots you got on. Your gait's got a hitch to it 'cause of how they pinch your toes.'

'You must have frightfully good ears.'

'They've had a share of practice. So how come you're up and about?'

'Will you actually help me to search for Whittle?'

'I might do just that very thing.'

'It would be splendid.'

'Well, I spent some time down there, know the territory. Ran with Al Sieber and his boys back in eighty-two. That's when we took on Nan-tia-tish. Then it was Geronimo and Nachite raising hell. Chased them all through creation. I reckon there ain't a canyon or a cactus between Fort Apache and the Torres Mountains that I ain't met up with, one time or another.'

'I'm not familiar with those places, actually.'

'You don't need to be, 'cause I am.'

'Have you been to Tombstone?'

'Many a time.'

'You'll be able to help me find it, then?'

'Why, sure. Lead you straight to it. She's a far piece west of here, then a ways south. Shouldn't take more than a couple of weeks to get there, once we start out.'

'When shall we start?' I asked.

'Let's just wait and see. We wanta spend us some time at Bailey's Corner and live it up some, you know.' He smiled, pale teeth showing under his mustache. 'You don't wanta start off on a long journey with too much cash weighing you down. It'd only serve to tire the horses.'

'Will the others come with us, do you suppose?'

'That'll be up to them. Much as I'll likely miss the boys, I reckon we'd be better off shed of 'em. First thing you know, they'd be hankering to pull a holdup. We don't want none of that. Can't hunt a man proper if you gotta keep a lookout for lawmen and posses and the like. It'd only serve to interfere with business. Sides, they'd slow us down.'

'I'd hate for you to leave them on my account,' I said.

'High time I pulled out. I been putting it off too long already.'

'Then, you're not doing it only because of me?'

'Let me tell you a thing or two, Willy. Chase is the only feller in the bunch that has a lick of sense. Them other three, any one of 'em could end up dragging us all into some kinda mess. Breakenridge, he's got a temper so hot he'll kill a man for looking at him sideways. Emmet's got an itch to swap lead with any feller that gives him half an excuse. Snooker's got himself a streak of yellow that makes him worse than either of 'em. He's a back-shooter, and he ain't particular who he does it to. You ride with boys like that, you always gotta watch 'em and try to keep a rein on 'em, but sooner or later they're gonna draw you into some mighty deep trouble. I been with this bunch for a couple of years, now, and we been lucky. But luck has a way of petering out on you. Best to get shut of 'em.'

When I think about what happened later, it seems funny – in an awful sort of way – that McSween said such things just the night before we went into Bailey's Corner. He'd sure been right about luck petering out. But he couldn't have been more wrong about Breakenridge or Emmet or Snooker being the cause of our trouble. McSween himself was the one who brought it down on us all. Because of me.

Prue and his friend must've been tracking us the whole time after we 'bought' the horse. They'd been smart enough to keep well out of sight, so we never saw hide nor hair of them, nor suspected they were on their way. They didn't show up until our second night in town, and they showed up with help.

We were having us a farewell supper at the Silver Dollar Saloon, drinking beer and eating steaks, all sitting together around a corner table. I was feeling mighty fine. I'd had a good sleep the night before in a hotel bed, I'd had two baths and a haircut, I'd been eating good meals for the better part of two days, my wealth had increased by fifteen dollars due to the sale of the stolen watches, and I was decked out in a brand new outfit.

I was mighty proud of my outfit. The whole gang, except for Breakenridge, had helped me pick it out the day we got into town. Dressed up the way I was, I felt just like one of the boys.

I wore a pair of dandy boots that didn't pinch, spurs that jingled every time I moved my feet, comfortable trousers, a blue shirt like McSween's, a leather vest, a red bandanna that dropped around my neck, and a splendid beaver hat. The pride of my new gear was a gunbelt with a big silver buckle, loops across its back for ammunition, and holsters at each hip. Both holsters had tie-downs. They held the Colts I'd acquired at the train.

I knew I looked bully. Quite the desperado. But I near choked on my last swallow of steak when Emmet said, 'We gotta make sure Willy don't ride outa here tomorrow a virgin.'

Snooker let out a whoop. 'Let's take him on over to Sally's!'

Last night, they'd all gone to Sally's, but I'd let on that I had a bellyache, and got out of it. It hadn't been much of a lie, for the notion of 'visiting the ladies' had indeed turned me queasy.

'I'd rather not, actually,' I said.

'Feeling poorly?' Emmet asked.

'Why, there ain't nothing to it,' Snooker said. 'No call to be scared.'

'I'm not at all scared,' I protested, though such talk was giving me an awful case of the fantods. In my head, I found myself back in that East End alley with Sue the whore. Much as I'd been thrilled by that encounter – up till she attacked me – the notion of taking up with another person of her sort upset me considerable. 'I'd rather not, is all.'

'He's plumb terrorized,' Emmet said.

'Oh, leave him be,' Chase told him.

'Gals isn't nothing to be scared of,' Snooker went on. 'They's just the same as fellers, only they got nicer parts.'

'It can be a mite trying, first time around,' McSween said.

I judged he was coming to my aid, but then he disappointed me. 'What we'll do, we'll have Sally fix you up with a sweet young thing that'll treat you right.'

Once again, Sue came to mind. I shook my head.

'It don't *hurt*, you know,' Emmet said.

'I'm quite aware of that,' I blurted. 'Me and Sarah . . .' Well, I shut my mouth quick. But not quick enough.

'You and Sarah?' Emmet asked. 'The General's daughter?'

'Granddaughter,' I corrected him.

'Well, shooey,' Snooker said.

'If that don't beat all,' McSween said, smiling some.

My face felt like it was burning up. 'I'm quite fond of her, really,' I muttered. 'I shouldn't like to . . . have a go . . . at someone else.'

'Don't wanta betray her, is that it?' McSween asked.

'Why, she don't ever have to know,' Emmet said.

'Still . . .'

Snooker said, 'I bet she's gone and taken up with that feller on the train you told us about, anyhow.'

That remark changed my embarrassment to anger. 'Bugger off,' I snapped.

Snooker's eyes got wide. 'What's that?'

'Let's settle down, boys,' Chase said.

'What'd he say to me?'

'Bugger off and sod you.'

'*What?*'

'Are you deaf?'

'Willy,' McSween said, real low.

Snooker leaped up from the table so fast his chair fell over backward. Other folks in the saloon stopped what they were doing and turned to watch us. 'Why don't you and me step outside, kid?'

I jumped up, myself, figuring to accommodate him.

McSween was next to spring to his feet. 'Now the both of you quit.'

Snooker jabbed a finger at me. 'He cussed me, John! I got every right to . . .'

'What makes you guess he cussed you?'

'Why . . . he . . . I don't rightly know *what* he said, but it was a cuss.' Glaring my way, he asked, 'Weren't it?'

'Bloody right.'

'You see?' he asked McSween.

McSween didn't answer. What he did was yank both his Colts and let fly.

'*Jesus!*' Snooker yelled through the explosions.

But the bullets weren't aimed at him.

Someone cried out.

I turned my head in time to see Prue, pistol in hand, stumble backward with a shocked look on his face and three holes in his white shirt. On both sides of him were men with badges. As they went for their guns, Snooker spun around and pulled. Emmet shouted and blazed away from where he sat. I snatched out my own Colts. Though I loathed the notion of killing a lawman, I knew I had to help my friends. Before I got the chance, both lawmen flopped to the floor without ever firing a shot. Only Prue's fat friend was still standing. He'd been shielded for a spell by Prue's body, which knocked into him as it pitched backward. Now he was raising a double-barreled shotgun. About seven or eight slugs all punched him at near the same time. It was an awful thing to watch. They smacked holes all over his belly and chest, one poked through his throat, and another broke his front teeth and sent blood spouting out his mouth. His shotgun went off, and would've blasted the floor except that Prue's face was in the way.

The roaring quit. I looked around and saw nobody who appeared ready to join the fight. The other folks in the saloon were mostly flat on the floor or crouched under tables.

When I turned to check on the boys, I could hardly see them through the clouds of gunsmoke. They were on their feet, hands full of iron, glancing this way and that as they stepped clear of the table.

McSween, reloading, said, 'I reckon we wore out our welcome.' The way my ears rang, I almost couldn't hear him.

'Anybody else wanta try us?' Emmet yelled.

Nobody answered.

McSween holstered a gun just long enough to drag some money from his pocket. He tossed the greenbacks onto the table to pay for our meal, then drew again.

Chase led the way out, me and McSween backing ourselves through the doors to watch those in the saloon.

A few folks were gathered on the walk, but they rather shook their heads at us and kept their hands a safe distance from their holsters. We stepped down to the street. A few horses were tied at the hitching post there, and I figured we might take them and hightail.

That wasn't what the others had in mind, though.

I stayed with them. What we did was walk across the street toward our hotel. I kept figuring we'd get shot at by someone, but not a single soul tried. We made it clear to the other side of the street without any gunplay, and walked into the hotel.

'What are we *doing*?' I asked McSween.

'Clearing out.'

Apparently, however, none of the boys was in any big rush to get on with it.

We got some wary, curious looks in the lobby, but no trouble.

Then we were up the stairs and going into our rooms. Mine was shared with McSween and Breakenridge. As soon as McSween got a lamp burning, we set to gathering our gear. I heard some yelling from outside the window. My mouth was parched, my heart thumping fit to explode. But McSween and Breakenridge seemed mighty cool as they stuffed this and that into their saddle bags.

We stayed together in the room until all three of us were ready. Saddle bags draped over our shoulders, bedrolls roped across our backs, Colts holstered and rifles in our hands, we stepped into the hallway.

Nobody there.

A couple of minutes passed, then the others came out of their room.

'Reckon there's a back door outa here?' Chase asked.

'The front door suits me,' McSween said.

I shriveled cold.

Just as calm as you please, McSween and Chase strode side by side to the head of the stairs and started down. I kept next to Emmet, behind them. Breakenridge and Snooker followed us, watching the rear.

That stairway seemed just endless. It was all I could do to stop my shaky legs from giving out.

We didn't see nobody at all in the lobby.

McSween and Chase didn't hesitate for a blink, but stepped right out the front door.

Well, we paraded straight down the middle of the street. It was empty except for us and the horses and carriages along both sides. But it seemed that everyone in town had their eyes on us. Doorways and windows were packed with silent watchers.

I heard some horses shuffling their hoofs, snorting, letting out a whinny now and again. A piano was playing a lively tune nearby. Off in the distance, a dog was yapping. Other than that, about the only sounds came from us – our boots thumping soft on the dusty street, our spurs clinking, the leather of our gear squeaking and groaning.

It was a mighty long walk.

I judged that, any second, a volley would roar out and we'd all be dropped in our tracks.

Didn't happen, though.

Finally, we came to the livery stable at the far end of town. The proprietor, a fellow named Himmel, had seen us coming and had already sent his boys to fetch our horses. McSween settled accounts with him. Then we spent just forever, it seemed, fumbling about with our bridles and saddles and such. McSween finished before me, and mounted up. While I worked at tightening General's cinch, he sat up there high on his saddle and rolled himself a smoke.

I tied down my saddle bags, tied down my bedroll and slipped my Winchester into its boot. By the time I got done and climbed aboard, the others were all mounted and waiting for me.

We rode out onto the street.

What came next shouldn't have surprised me, not after what I'd seen of the gang so far.

There we were, at the very end of town. We had no reason at all to ride in the opposite direction.

That's just what we did, however.

McSween dug in his spurs, pulled both Colts, and charged, spitting lead at the night. For a cautious man proud of his silver hair, he sure had himself a keen interest in gawdy exits.

We all followed him, yelling and blazing.

If we were shot at, I never heard the gunfire through all our own commotion.

We were still on our saddles, none the worse for wear, by the time we left Bailey's Corner behind us.

Chapter Thirty-four

The Posse

The hard way we rode, only stopping now and then to let the horses catch their wind, I judged that the boys didn't figure we were in the clear.

Finally, I had to ask. I put the spurs to General and caught up with McSween. 'Do you reckon they're coming after us?'

'That's a good bet, Willy,' he said, looking over at me. 'You know them two lawmen that was fools enough to side with Prue? They was town deputies. I don't know the one, but the other was James Brewer, brother to the sheriff, Ike.'

'Well, where was *he*, then?'

'Ike? Don't rightly know. I gave him all kinds of time to take a crack at us. Wanted him to try, but he never showed. Sure would've been a blessing to kill him then and there. Way matters stand, we gotta figure he'll lead a posse after us.'

'What are we to do?'

'Whatever we gotta.'

We kept on riding through the night. I spent plenty of time remembering how the train engineer'd tried to talk me out of joining up with these boys, and wished more than once that I'd heeded his warning. It was far too late for that, though. In the course of a week, I'd helped rob a train, I'd stolen a horse, and I'd stood with the gang in a shootout that left four men murdered. I was no better than an outlaw, myself. And now McSween judged we had a posse coming for us, so I figured I might end my life just as the engineer had predicted, either shot or swinging from a rope.

It made me feel plain sick to think about.

I kept looking back over my shoulder. Behind us was nothing but moonlit desert.

Maybe a posse *won't* come, I told myself.

I couldn't take much comfort from hoping that, but I did finally calm down. What helped my nerves was knowing I was with the boys, and they weren't likely to let any posse have its way with them. No, sir. I wouldn't be getting myself shot or hanged long as I stayed with McSween and Chase and Emmet and Snooker and Breakenridge – and the engineer be damned.

My optimism lasted till just after dawn.

That's when we halted near the top of a rise and spotted the cloud of dust a few miles to our rear. I couldn't see anyone back there, just dry washes and piles of rock, cacti and stunted trees, and all that blowing yellow dust.

'Aw, shit,' Snooker said.

Chase glanced at McSween. 'Fifteen, twenty of 'em?'

'Least twenty, I'd say.'

'Aw, shit,' Snooker said again.

'Who'd think a town that size,' McSween said, 'could come up with that many fellers eager to get their toes turned up?'

'Reckon we oughta split up?' Chase asked.

Oh, I didn't care for *that* notion. Not one whit. Goosebumps went scurrying up my back like a troop of spiders with icy feet.

'It'd thin 'em out,' Breakenridge said. 'I'd sure rather have four or five on my tail than all of them.'

McSween commenced to roll a smoke. After giving it a lick, he said, 'We put our heads together, maybe we can figure us a *better* way to thin 'em out.' He lit up. Smoke curled away from under his mustache as he smiled. 'Get my drift?'

He offered his makings to me.

Dry as my mouth felt, it would've likely caught fire if I'd had a go at smoking. I shook my head.

'Are you saying we ought to attack them?' I asked.

'Seems a fine idea to me,' he said.

'Jesus wept,' said Breakenridge.

Chase gazed off at the dust cloud, which seemed to be closer to us already, and rubbed his chin. 'Let's do it,' he said.

'Hot damn!' Emmet blurted.

Snooker and Breakenridge didn't appear to enjoy the notion, but they didn't speak against it.

'How you doing, Willy?'

We sat atop our mounts, all by ourselves, waiting.

'Not at all good, actually.'

'Can't say as I blame you,' McSween said. 'Not feeling too spry myself, if the truth be known. Sorry we pulled you into this.'

'It was my own choice.'

'My own blamed fault. I just knowed I should've plugged Prue and the fatty back when we took the horse. Just gave 'em credit for more sense than they turned out to have.' He lifted his bandanna and mopped some sweat off his forehead. 'This is what comes of having a generous nature.'

'It is a shame they showed up when they did,' I said.

'You never know. At least we ain't got them to worry about no more.'

'I'd rather have dealt with those two on my trail than a whole crowd.'

He laughed softly. 'Well, there ain't gonna be a crowd much longer.'

I looked over my shoulder and was glad to see that the gap between the piled boulders was still empty. The low thunder of hoofbeats sounded louder and louder.

'What you might wanta do,' McSween said, 'is dig in your spurs and light out.'

'That's what I *intend* to do.'

'It's right now I mean.'

'Now?'

'That's what I'd like you to do, Willy. Go on and skedaddle. No point in you being in on this. At the best, you'd only bloody your hands. At worst, you'd end up killed. Go on, now. We'll handle this here posse. Things work out, I'll catch you down the trail.'

'I'm not a bloody coward,' I told him.

'Why, I know that.'

'It's only because of me that we *have* this posse after us.'

'That's no call for you to stick with us.'

'It's all the call I need,' I said, talking quite a heap braver than I felt.

'Reckon it's too late, anyhow,' McSween said.

I was still watching the gap. It was still empty. But now the thunder was so near I almost thought I could feel the air quaking.

'This is it, Willy,' McSween said. He shouldered his Winchester and thumbed back its hammer. 'Ride fast, keep low, and shoot straight. And God be with you.'

'You, too,' I told him. It came out no louder than a whisper.

A lone horseman rode through the gap. His head was turned. He seemed to be talking to someone behind him, though he was too far off for me to hear his voice. McSween's rifle spoke. The fellow pitched backward. His horse reared.

He fell off, but one of his feet got hung up in a stirrup. The horse scampered to the right, dragging him.

'Hightail!' McSween yelled.

We didn't linger. We hunched and dug in and bolted.

From behind us came shouts. 'There!' and 'Bastards!' and 'Get 'em!'

It was Whitechapel all over again, a mob after my blood, only this time they had guns.

They blasted away at us.

Bullets whinged off rocks, buzzed past my head. I kept an eye on McSween racing alongside me low in his saddle with the wind shoving his hat brim up. He didn't look like he'd been hit yet. So far, I'd been lucky, too. I figured a slug was on its way toward my back. I waited for it to whack me, but all I could feel was General dashing like mad, the hot wind rushing into my face so quick it wanted to choke me.

The mouth of the pass hadn't seemed like more than a stone's throw away when me and McSween had picked our spot to wait for the posse.

But that stone's throw seemed more like a mile now that the mob was on our tails, spitting lead.

I wished I hadn't been so eager to play bait.

None of the others had volunteered for the job, however, and I'd figured McSween shouldn't have to go it alone.

Even though it *was* his own daft idea.

'You don't never wanta try this trick on the redskins,' he'd said. 'Why, hell, it's *their* trick. You take your white folks, though, they fall for it every time.'

I'd neglected to ask him how many redskins got themselves shot dead while leading their pursuers into such traps.

At long last, we galloped between the boulders at the mouth of the pass. The gunfire slackened off a bit, so I raised my head and glanced about. I didn't see hide nor hair of the boys up there among the rocks. What if *they'd* lit out? The notion shook me. But I reckoned they weren't the sort to pull such a dirty stunt.

I took a chance and looked back. Here came the posse, two

at a time, racing at us down the narrow pass, only the pair in front firing. The rest had quit shooting so they wouldn't hit their own.

Me and McSween kept riding just as fast as our mounts could carry us.

The boys kept waiting.

If they were here.

Suddenly, puffs of smoke bloomed on the canyon walls as four guns crashed and four men tumbled off their horses.

McSween cut to the left. Rifle in hand, he hurled himself to the ground and dashed behind a clump of rocks. I reined in General, snatched out my Winchester, and leaped down to join him.

He was already scurrying up the slope. I followed, rather hoping it might all be over before we found a proper perch.

It sounded horrid. The canyon just roared with gunfire. Horses squealed and whinnied. Men shouted, cried out.

They came to kill us, I told myself.

Too soon, McSween picked himself a rock. It was big enough for both of us. We rose up behind it and shouldered our rifles.

Down below was mayhem. Dead men. Dead horses. A few fellows rode breakneck for the mouth of the pass in a panic to escape. Others stayed. Of those that stayed to fight, some simply crouched in the open and returned fire, some scampered up into the rocks, some hunkered down to take shelter beside their fallen mounts, and a few rode in their saddles, shooting this way and that as their horses wheeled and bucked.

McSween's rifle deafened my ear. One of the men on a circling, snorting horse keeled over sideways.

I levered in a cartridge myself and sighted in on a fellow who was squatting next to a dead man. He'd lost his hat. He was bald. His head was down while he worked at reloading his pistol.

I spent a fair amount of time lining him up in my sights. It beat looking at the carnage. McSween kept on firing quick.

The way I judged matters, my fellow was just a lawabiding citizen doing his duty. Maybe he was a shopkeeper, or the like. Maybe he had a wife and children. If I shot him, I'd be no better than a murderer. On the other hand, I wanted McSween to figure I was doing my level best to help the situation.

So I eased my barrel over some, took aim at his weapon, and squeezed the trigger. Missed. My bullet raised some powder off the shirt of the dead man.

My fellow finished reloading. He looked up toward me and McSween, swung his pistol toward us, and caught a slug in his forehead from McSween's rifle.

I didn't feel too sorry about it, but was glad I hadn't been the one to kill him.

With him dead, I had no choice but to search out another target.

The only fellow still moving down there had a wounded leg and was hobbling toward a skittish horse. Just as he got to it, he fell. But he latched a hand on to one of the stirrups. The horse lit out for the mouth of the pass, towing him. It was a big white stallion. I levered a round into my chamber and aimed toward the man's feet. I figured to try for one of his boot heels. But then there wasn't any point, for the stallion caught lead. It stumbled sideways and stepped on him. It missed him when it toppled over. Before the man could move – if he had it in him to move – he got smacked by three or four slugs.

After that, the shooting stopped. The quiet seemed mighty unnatural. Other than the wind and the ringing in my ears, all I could hear were the cries of wounded men and horses.

We climbed down to the bottom of the pass. All of us did, that is, except for Breakenridge. Snooker'd been near him on the slope, and said he'd been killed.

Keeping our guns ready, we wandered among the fallen. It turned out there were nine dead and seven wounded. Ike Brewer, the town sheriff, was among the dead.

We disarmed the wounded to avoid surprises, then

gathered enough horses for them. Those too hurt to ride, we tied aboard their saddles. We sent them through the mouth of the pass, figuring that the few who'd escaped from our ambush would likely see to them.

When they were gone, we climbed up a slope and found Breakenridge. A bullet had gone into his right eye, and he was awful to look at.

Nobody seemed particularly upset about the loss of him. He hadn't been the friendly sort, after all. If the others felt the same as me, they were mostly feeling glad it was him instead of themselves that had gotten killed.

It took four of us to tote him down to the bottom. Snooker held our rifles for us. I helped out by lugging one of Breakenridge's legs. He was huge and heavy. We were mostly all worn out by the time we got done.

We spent a while rounding up our horses. Then we hoisted Breakenridge up across his saddle, and tied him so he wouldn't fall off.

We rode south out of the pass.

Early in the afternoon, we unloaded Breakenridge in a dry wash and covered him with rocks. Chase read some words over him from a Bible he took from his saddlebag. Then we split up what was left of Breakenridge's loot. We kept his horse as a spare, and rode on.

All through the day, we kept a watch behind us. There was no sign that the remains of the posse was coming after us. McSween allowed it was a good thing we'd shot Ike in the ambush, as he'd been a stubborn fellow who wouldn't have given up. The way he saw it, the rest of the bunch likely figured they'd got off lucky, and were hurrying on back to town with the wounded.

I hoped he was right about that, but not because I was scared of the posse. It would take more than whatever handful had survived the trap to do us any harm. I just hoped they wouldn't show up because I didn't want any more of them to get killed.

I was feeling mighty lowdown and miserable about the

slaughter back at the pass. We hadn't any choice to speak of. It was them or us. But there just wasn't a way to put it in a light that eased the burden. I hadn't shot anyone, but I'd helped bait the trap. And the posse never would've come after us if we hadn't stolen Prue's horse. It all stemmed from that.

Four men in the saloon and nine at the pass, and Breakenridge – not a one of them would've gotten killed if I hadn't made a choice to ride with the gang.

Fourteen men.

That got me to thinking how Trudy and her father and Michael had also died on account of me. No way I could blame myself for the General and Mable, but they'd taken me into their home and they'd ended up dead, too.

It seemed like nobody was safe around me, like I carried a curse that got folks killed.

Just a matter of time, I judged, before my curse would wipe out McSween and Chase and Emmet and Snooker.

If I stuck with them.

Much as I wanted McSween to help me track Whittle, I finally made up my mind to ride out alone. I sure would miss him. But I'd miss him more, and take on a new load of guilt, if he came along and got killed for his troubles.

I didn't let on about my plan. During supper that night, the boys discussed splitting up. Chase and Emmet figured they'd go east in the morning, Snooker said he thought he'd head up to Denver, and McSween allowed as how he and I would make for Tombstone. I acted as if that suited me.

Later on, we all turned in except for McSween, who had first watch. I lay in my blanket, waiting. When it came my turn, I pretended to be asleep. McSween knelt and shook my shoulder. 'Time to play sentry, Willy,' he whispered.

I yawned, rubbed my eyes, and gave him a good show of waking up. McSween crawled into his blanket while I pulled my boots on and strapped on my gunbelt.

'Come sunup,' he said, 'we'll hit the trail for Tombstone.'

'Splendid,' I said, and felt badly about how he might feel in the morning when he saw I'd lit out.

I wandered off past the others. I climbed a pile of rocks and sat down at the top, figuring to wait an hour or so. The sky had clouded up. With the moon and stars hidden away, there wasn't enough light to see much. That would work to my advantage when it came time to sneak into camp for my things.

Sitting up there, darkness everywhere, I soon found that the notion of riding off alone had lost some of its appeal. It was a mighty big wilderness. A fellow might lose his way. Worse, a fellow might run afoul of thieves or cutthroats. Or Indians? The Indian wars had ended, so everyone said, but that didn't mean every last savage was accounted for.

I hadn't worried about such things while I'd been with the boys; I'd always had them to rely on. In a while, I'd be leaving them behind.

I can take care of myself, I thought.

But it would be a blessing to have McSween at my side.

There was really no call to sneak off without him.

Then I thought, if I don't get shut of him, I'll get him killed. I don't want him to die on my account like all those others.

By and by, it came time for me to go if I was going.

I stood up.

Fire spit at me from off in the dark. A boom pounded my ears. A slug nipped my side. Startled more than hurt, I took a quick step backward and my boot found nothing but air. Crying out, I fell. Rocks jabbed and poked me as I tumbled down. I kept figuring one might split my head open, but that didn't happen.

I came to a stop on my back, my legs hoisted up by a boulder. The ground under me shook with pounding hoofs.

Earlier that day, I'd felt sorry for the poor folks we'd ambushed. Now, I suddenly wished we hadn't let a single one of them get out alive.

McSween had said they wouldn't come. Not with Ike dead. But he'd been wrong.

And somebody'd *shot* at me.

From beyond me came shouts of alarm from the boys. They were mixed in with the thumping of hoofs and war-whoops that came from our attackers.

I kicked my legs down and got to my knees as a bunch of horsemen charged through a break in the rocks, their guns ablaze.

I patted my sides, figuring I must've lost my Colts in the fall. But they were snug in their holsters. For just an instant. Then they filled my hands.

I shot two blokes out of their saddles straight away.

Then McSween got hit. I saw him in the muzzle flashes, both his pistols blasting as slugs smacked his chest, knocking him backward. At least three men caught his lead and dropped from their horses before he went down.

I don't believe I witnessed the ends of Chase or Emmet or Snooker.

My eyes weren't watching for them.

My eyes were on the horsemen as they dashed this way and that, yelling and firing, some riding at me with their guns aroar.

I used only my right hand, as I'd had little practice with my left. I never moved my legs at all, but stood there at the edge of the campsite, aiming and firing. When my hammer came down on a used shell, I dropped that gun and switched to the other.

Before you know it, that one ran out, too.

I went to reload, and thought it strange I hadn't been killed yet. I just hoped I could get it full of bullets and take down a few more of the bastards before they got me.

But when the cylinder was full and I raised my arm to continue killing, I couldn't find a target.

I fired once, anyhow, to scatter the horses.

As they hurried off, the moon came out. Its pale light came down. In front of me, shrouded by drifting gunsmoke, was a field of twisted bodies.

They weren't all dead.

Some men lay there, writhing and moaning.

I checked on them. They weren't McSween or Chase or Emmet or Snooker.

I shot them.

At daybreak, I covered my friends with rocks. I read out loud from Chase's Bible.

I let the men from the posse lay where they'd fallen. There were eleven.

I set all the horses free except General. I gathered money, food and ammunition, as there was no advantage to leaving such things behind. Then I saddled up General and rode out.

Part Four

Plugging On

Chapter Thirty-five

Ishmael

The wound I'd taken in my side while standing watch didn't amount to much, just a gouge across my ribs. More than once, I wished whoever'd taken the crack at me had been a better shot.

I knew I wasn't fit to go on living.

The third or fourth night after the shootout at the camp, I decided to blow out my brains. It seemed a proper way to stop myself from doing more harm in this world.

I'd built a fire, which was only to keep me warm as I hadn't cooked a meal or eaten much of anything since the shooting. I sat down beside it and put a Colt to my head. Then it seemed maybe I ought to leave a letter behind.

A letter for who, though? Mother? Sarah? Neither of them was ever likely to see my last message, left out here in the middle of nowhere.

Maybe somebody would find it, sooner or later, and send it along. I couldn't count on that, though. Every day, I'd been riding west, putting my back to the sunrise and heading for the sunset, and not once had I met up with a human being. That suited me. But it didn't allow much hope of anyone finding my note.

What would I write in it, anyhow? That I was the curse of death to everybody I met? That I'd turned bad and killed men? Wouldn't serve any useful purpose for Mother or Sarah to know such things. Better to let them go on wondering what had become of me than to weigh them down with the grim truth.

So I gave up the notion of leaving a message.

I thumbed back the hammer and was all set to squeeze the trigger when General gave a snort.

The sound reminded me that he was hobbled for the night. He would die if I went and shot myself without releasing him first.

I only aimed to kill myself, not General.

So I holstered my gun and went to him. He looked over his shoulder. 'You'll be quite better off without me, chum,' I explained, and gave his neck a pat.

Then I crouched down and untied the hobble.

'Get on, now.' I smacked his bum. He trotted off a bit, stopped and looked back at me.

It was no concern of mine. He was free. He could stay or go, as he chose. I judged he'd move on once I'd finished putting a slug into my brain pan.

I walked back to the fire, sat down, and drew my Colt. As I pulled back the hammer, I remembered how the train conductor had tried to shoot me dead, only his gun had misfired.

It hadn't been a bad round, as it had gone off just a while later when I was riding away with the boys, shooting at the sky.

I'd counted the misfire to be a rare piece of luck.

I didn't look at it that way now. It had been the worst kind of luck, leastwise for the gang and the men that came after us in the saloon and the chaps of the posse. All those fellows were dead because of one misfire.

Well, it wasn't likely to happen twice.

And if it should, I had me four more chambers full of bullets in the one gun, five in the other. (Emmet had taught me not to travel about with a round under the hammer, and only to load that chamber for target practice or troubles.) There wasn't enough luck or magic or whatever in this world to stop them all from doing their job.

A miracle wouldn't be saving me this time.

I judged the misfire *had* been a miracle, of sorts. Pretty much as if I hadn't been meant to get killed.

Pondering over that, I saw how I'd squeaked by and survived dicey situations over and over again ever since the night I set out for Whitechapel.

There was the ocean, which should've either swallowed me up or froze me solid long before I ever reached the shore of America.

There was Whittle, who'd butchered so many folks but not me.

Getting chucked off the train by Briggs could've been fatal, all by itself.

Chase had threatened to shoot me. I gave that some thought, though, and allowed it shouldn't count. He'd likely been joshing, and never actually intended to do such a thing.

The conductor, though, had certainly had a go at me and failed.

Not a bullet had touched me during the gunfight at the saloon. Of course, I don't believe that Prue or the others got off a single shot, so maybe that shouldn't count, either.

But the posse men had taken a great many cracks at me, particularly when McSween and I were leading them into the ambush.

Later on that night, a fellow had creased my side. If he'd been half good with his gun, he would've killed me sure.

All that made for quite a string of close shaves, but then I'd come through the massacre at the campsite without taking a hit. Mighty perplexing, when you consider I only just stood there and didn't take cover and the bullets flew so thick and everyone but me bit the dust.

Just call me Ishmael.

I lowered the Colt onto my lap and gazed at how its black steel gleamed in the firelight.

'And I only am escaped alone,' I whispered.

Had to be a reason.

Had to be a reason I'd survived such a passel of narrow calls.

The reason had to be Whittle.

I was meant to live long enough, at least, to put him in the ground.

That's how I figured it, anyhow.

And that's how come I decided not to shoot myself, that night, after all.

Chapter Thirty-six

Strangers on the Trail

Once I made up my mind to go on living, I still didn't feel any better about being the cause of so many deaths, but I did all of a sudden find myself hungry.

General had wandered off, so I had to chase after him. I brought him back to camp and hobbled him. Then I cooked myself up a pot of beans.

When I got done chowing them down, I set up the tin can and some sticks on the rocks around the fire. Then I stepped back, pulled and fired.

My first shot knocked the tin flying.

I holstered and drew and went for the sticks.

When that gun was empty, I practiced with the other. Left-handed. It came out clumsy for a spell. More often than not, I hit my fire or bounced my bullets off the rocks. But I got better, by and by.

Blazing away, I remembered a chap the boys used to call Willy. Willy'd considered it a great adventure to ride with desperados, smashing fun to slap leather and fire away at stumps and sticks and cans and such.

I found myself rather missing Willy.

He was dead.

He'd died with McSween and the rest of the gang.

He'd died young, and never got the chance to return home to his mother or to find his sweetheart, Sarah.

Tough break, that.

I don't rightly know who I missed more, Willy or McSween.

McSween, I reckon.

I used up a whole lot of ammunition, taking turns with both hands, and killed me a heap of kindling.

Then I turned in.

The next morning, I came upon a wagon trail. It appeared to be leading west. I was tempted to stay clear of it, for I didn't relish the notion of meeting up with travelers. But the trail would be a sight easier on General than the rough terrain we'd been crossing. We'd make better time on it, and it was bound to take us somewhere.

Seemed a better way to find Tombstone than if I just kept to the trackless wilds and hoped for the best.

So we took it.

Soon enough, some travelers came along. I spotted a couple of horsemen riding toward me. While they were still a good piece in the distance, I gave some thought to steering General off the trail so as to avoid them. But then I judged it might rouse their curiosity. Better just to act natural and pass them by.

Funny thing was, much as I wanted to be clear of these two strangers, I didn't feel any fear of them. Not even when they were close enough for me to see how ornery they looked. One had a pinched, pointy face that put me in mind of Snooker. The other had a droopy eyelid. Both had the same sort of lazy, smirky ways in how they stared at me.

'Howdy,' I said, and touched the brim of my hat.

'Howdy back,' said the bloke with the droopy lid. I nudged General to go around him, but he raised a hand. 'Hold her up there.'

I did as he asked. Then I dropped the reins over the saddle horn to free my hands. 'Yes sir?' I asked.

The one with the pointy face laughed. 'Yes *sir*. Ain't he got manners?'

'He's pretty, too. Just as pretty as a girl.'

'I betcha he *is* a girl!'

They appeared to enjoy the bit of wit.

'You got titties in there?' The one winked his bad eye in the direction of my shirt, and grinned. 'Give us a peek.'

'Ride on, fellows.'

'Why, she's shy.'

'I'm shy on patience,' I said.

'Now you be nice. Angus and me, we haven't had us a girl in near a month.'

'And she was ugly.'

'Ugly but willing.'

They both laughed.

'I'm not a girl,' I said.

Well, they glanced at each other and laughed all the more.

'That don't make no difference,' Angus of the half-mast lid finally said to me. 'Know what I mean? Now, you just climb down off your horse, there, and get shed of them duds.'

I didn't move.

'You do what Angus says!' snapped the other.

'If you'd like me to oblige,' I said, 'you'd best fill your hands.'

All of a sudden, they turned uncommon serious.

They glanced at each other, silent and smirkless, then turned their faces toward me.

'Have a crack, chaps,' I said. 'Or ride on.'

They both spent some time studying me out. I saw their eyes flick about, taking in my holstered Colts, the torn and blood-stained side of my shirt, my hands resting atop my thighs, and my face. They took quite a spell on my face.

Then Angus said, 'We didn't mean nothing, mister. Only just having us some fun.'

The other bobbed his head. 'We'll just be moving along. Adios, now.'

They split apart and rode past me.

I turned General around, as I didn't aim to get back-shot.

Angus and the other rode off slow at first, neither one of them glancing back. Then Angus, he put the spurs to his horse. His friend did the same, and they both hightailed.

I rode on, puzzling over matters. It seemed odd the way they'd backed down. What seemed odder, though, was that I didn't feel much of anything. They'd had it in mind to use me like a woman, I reckon. But I hadn't been scared, the whole time. Nor had I felt any relief when they'd given up the notion and gone away.

Comes right down to it, I'd just as soon have shot them both.

I didn't *wish* I'd shot them, though.

I just didn't care, either way.

Late in the afternoon, a covered wagon turned up. It was heading west, same as me, but going so slow that I was bound to overtake it.

A blanket draped the rear opening, so I couldn't see how many or what manner of folks the wagon had in it.

Whoever they might be, I wanted no truck with them.

I figured to ride by quick, and urged General to a trot.

But when we came alongside the wagon, I saw how its canvas side was painted up with pictures of red bottles floating this way and that among words that said:

DR JETHRO LAZARUS
PURVEYOR OF THE WORLD RENOWNED
GLORY ELIXIR
'Good for what ails you.'

There was plenty more to read, so I slowed General down to an easy walk.

Toward the rear was a notice that said you could buy one bottle of the Glory Elixir for a 'mere dollar'. Toward the front, it said:

GLORY ELIXIR
GUARANTEED TO VANQUISH
whooping cough
palsy
sour stomach
boils
feminine complaints
arthritis
runny bowels
gangrene
rattlesnake bite
gaseous embarrassments
dropsy
dizziness
DEATH

The Glory Elixir's list of cures rather amused me till I saw that final one. Death. That one took me by surprise and took the fun out.

I put my spurs to General, figuring to get shut of such nonsense.

As we hurried by, I took a gander sideways at the driver. He was all alone at the front.

'Say there, young fellow!'

'Good day,' I said, and left him behind.

'Cowards die many times,' he called after me.

Well, I didn't rightly know what he meant by that. And I judged he could call me a coward if he pleased. What got me to rein in General was that I recognized the words.

As the wagon rattled closer, I met the old man's eyes and said, 'The valiant never taste of death but once.'

He smiled real cheerful. 'A man of learning. Delighted to make your acquaintance. Dr Jethro Lazarus, here.'

'Trevor Bentley.'

'Who hails, no doubt, from the land of the Bard.'

'Quite true,' I said.

'Would you care to join me at the helm?' He patted the seat beside him.

Well, he looked peculiar but harmless, a heavy chap with a red nose and white beard, his head topped with a bowler hat that had two white feathers swooping up from its band, one at each side. Golden hoops hung from his ears. He wore a leather shirt that shivered all over with fringe. It was cinched in around his huge belly by a beaded belt. He didn't wear a pistol, but a rather large knife was sheathed at his hip. His trouser legs were tucked into high moccasins that nearly beat his shirt for all their fringe.

I judged the sensible thing might be to stay out of his reach.

Besides, a blanket draped the opening behind him, so I couldn't see into the wagon. No telling who might be back there, laying low.

'I'll keep to my mount, but thank you for the offer.'

'I'm on my way to Tucson, myself,' he said. 'What about you?'

It didn't seem wise to tell him my plans. 'Just touring about, I reckon.'

'Beware the heathen, barren place of lawless men and savage race.'

'Not Shakespeare, is it?'

'Lazarus.'

'You're a poet, then?'

'Poet and purveyor of the Glory Elixir.'

I wanted no truck with his Glory Elixir, so I asked, 'Did you encounter a pair of rascals, earlier?'

He let out a soft chuckle.

'I do hope they did you no mischief.'

'They beat a quick retreat at the sight of my friend, Buster.' He reached down by his feet and hoisted a shotgun. Its barrels were cut off short, just in front of the forestock. 'Buster.'

I half expected him to point it at me, but he stowed it away.

'Buster's sent many a miscreant to glory,' he said. 'When he gets done with them, they're well beyond the aid of my Elixir.'

I couldn't help but smile at that. 'Doesn't it vanquish death, then, after all?'

'Why, it most surely does, Trevor. However, the vital revivification of the deceased is greatly impeded by the destruction of his anatomy. That is to say, it don't work worth spit if I've blown off the bastard's head.'

Now that I'd been hauled into this talk of death and the merits of Lazarus's flim-flam Elixir, it all didn't seem so grim. 'If a bloke's anatomy wasn't destroyed some,' I allowed, 'he wouldn't likely be dead in the first place.'

'All depends, my friend. Depends on how much is intact and how much is demolished.'

'If a chap's dead, he's dead. This Glory Elixir of yours won't change that.'

'There are more things in heaven and earth, Horatio . . .'

'I might look like a fool, Dr Lazarus, but I don't regularly think like one.'

Well, he pulled back on the reins and halted his team.

'I tell you what, Trevor. Just suppose I give you proof, right before your very eyes, that my Glory Elixir has the power to raise the dead?'

'Reckon I'd purchase a bottle,' I said, shaking my head. He couldn't prove any such thing, and I knew it. Still and all, as he climbed down and I followed him toward the rear of the wagon, I found myself wondering whether I could backtrack to the place I'd buried McSween and the boys. And I wondered if they were shot up too much for the Elixir to work on them. Then I wondered if I should buy enough to raise the other eleven. That'd be the proper thing to do, but I judged they might try to shoot us all over again, and then I took a mind to kick myself for allowing such thick-headed notions. No amount of Glory Elixir could fix any one of those fellows.

Be that as it was, I'd worked up a powerful curiosity to see the old fellow's proof.

He let down the gate at the back of his wagon, then crawled in under the blanket. The wagon shook some as he scurried about inside. Then came a scrapy, dragging sound.

'Lend me a hand,' he called from inside.

I dismounted. By the time I got done tying General to a bolt at the back of the wagon, the blanket was abulge with Lazarus. He jumped to the ground, hauling at the end of a wooden box. A pint bottle of Elixir was standing atop the box, its red fluid sloshing about.

He stopped pulling, grabbed the bottle, and tossed it to me. Then he went on dragging. More and more of the box slid into sight.

'What have you there?' I asked, though I could sure see what it looked like.

'A casket. Be a good lad and take the other end.'

Chapter Thirty-seven

Lazarus and the Dead Man

My curiosity shrank some. I didn't hanker to see what might be inside the casket. But I slipped the bottle into my pocket and did as he asked. When I got close, I had to hold my breath so as to avoid the sickening aroma in the air.

My end of the box was so heavy I near dropped it, but I managed to hang on until we got it lowered into the dust behind the wagon. Then I stepped back a few paces to get clear of the odor.

The hard work must've tuckered out Lazarus, for he sat down on the casket. He plucked a kerchief out of his trouser pocket and mopped his brow.

'You have a corpse in there, do you?' I asked.

He answered with a wink.

'Be a good lad and pass me the Elixir,' he said.

I handed over the bottle. He uncorked it, took a swig, and sighed. 'Good for what ails you. Have a drop yourself,' he said, and held it toward me.

I shook my head. 'I reckon I'll move on. I've seen my share of dead folks.'

'Nothing to fret yourself over. He's in passable shape. He don't even stink much, long as you stand upwind. It was only two days ago I cut him down.'

'Cut him down?'

'He's a fellow who threw a long rope and wound up at the end of a short one.'

'Threw a long rope?'

'A rustler. Cattle. Only his luck ran dry, and he was strung up by the ranch hands that nabbed him. I arrived upon the scene purely by happenstance, in the very nick of time to watch him swing. It was a stroke of wonderful good fortune. Very difficult, you see, to find a healthy subject for revivification.'

He took a few more swallows of the Elixir. 'A lynching's just the thing. If a fellow's hanged proper from a gallows, you see, his neck gets itself snapped. Stretched considerable, too. That's if he don't drop too far and get his head popped off altogether. Either way, the fellow ain't fit. I've brought back a few that had their necks busted, and they pretty much put off my customers, how they stumbled about with their heads all wobbly. But you take a feller that's gotten lynched, he's generally been choked to death so his neck's in fine shape. That's how it went with this one. Choked. Strangulated.' He rapped his bottle against the top of the casket. 'Right off, I knew I had to have him. The ranch boys didn't want me to take him, as they preferred to let him dangle as a lesson for others of his ilk. But I paid them a dollar, and they allowed me to cut him down.'

Lazarus raised the bottle again, took one more sip, then corked it. Smiling at me, he said, 'This fellow here, he'll be dandy once he gets a taste of the Glory Elixir.'

'I shouldn't think so.'

'Shall we give it a try?' Lazarus stood up. He handed the bottle to me.

The lid was only just laid across the top of the casket, not nailed down. The old man bent over it and took hold of the edges. I figured if I aimed to skedaddle, now was the time. I just stood there, though. He had me hooked. I knew he couldn't bring a corpse back to life, but I sure wanted to see how he played out his bluff.

Then he frowned at me and straightened up again. 'Only one problem,' he said.

'Indeed, I should think there might be at least one.'

'I've been fixing to save this fellow for demonstration purposes after I got him to Tucson. I can't lose him now for just one sale.'

'Then you wish me to buy more than one?'

'A revivification oughta be worth five bottles.'

'I'll purchase ten if he's truly dead and he comes back to life.'

'That'll cost you ten dollars. Are you traveling with enough?'

His question put me off even more than the prospect of seeing a dead man inside the casket.

I suddenly knew the name of his game.

He had no intention of revivifying the corpse.

He hadn't been inside the wagon for long, but long enough to slip Buster into the box alongside the body.

'I have ten dollars to spare,' I said.

'You sure?'

'Open it up.'

'By and by,' he said. 'We have one other small matter requiring discussion.'

'Yes?'

He toed the casket. 'Like I say, I aim to use him at Tucson. He won't do me no good at all, alive and kicking. So I don't want you causing a fuss when it comes to rekilling him.'

'Certainly not,' I said.

301

'I'll need to strangulate him, you see. It won't be a pretty sight.'

'It's quite all right with me,' I said, knowing it wouldn't come to that.

'What I'm saying, Trevor – don't get overly fond of him.'

'Not likely,' I said.

He bent down over the casket again. As he shoved the lid off, I switched the Elixir to my left hand, dropped my right to my sixgun.

Lazarus didn't reach inside, so I didn't pull.

I stepped closer, holding my breath to keep out the awful stench.

No sign of Buster.

Just a dead man.

A skinny chap who didn't look to be much older than thirty, wearing boots, dungarees, a dirty plaid shirt and a noose. The noose was loose around his neck, the looped bundle of the hangman's knot resting atop his chest and the cut end of the rope dangling off to the side. His neck looked as if it had been polished with boot black. His tongue was black, too. It stuck out from between his teeth. His face had a nasty grayish color. There were pennies on his eyes to hold the lids shut. I was relieved to find his eyes covered, but thought it a spot peculiar that the pennies hadn't fallen off, what with how the casket had gotten jostled about.

Lazarus gave each penny a flick. They skittered away and rolled about the bottom of the box. The eyes stayed shut.

'Would you care to do the honors?' he asked.

I shook my head, and handed him the bottle of Elixir.

Lazarus uncorked it with his teeth. He spat out the cork. It missed the dead man's face.

'You might prefer to stand back, Trevor. These fellows can get awful frisky.'

I was happy to oblige. I stood back and breathed again. the stink was still there, sour and sweet at the same time, but if I moved any farther off, I wouldn't be able to keep a close watch.

I stayed ready, just in case Lazarus had tucked Buster out of sight underneath the corpse.

The first thing he did, he tucked the black tongue inside the fellow's mouth where it belonged. He pulled down on the jaw to make a bigger target, then commenced to pour Elixir out of the bottle. Some of it missed, splashing the gray lips and running down the whiskery cheeks. But some found its way into the mouth. I saw that his teeth were gray, which seemed a mite peculiar. But then the Elixir dyed them red.

Lazarus quit pouring.

The dead fellow just laid there.

I took myself a deep breath, then held it and stepped up close. Standing directly above the corpse, I could see a little pool of Elixir down there inside his mouth. It didn't appear to be going anywhere.

He gulped.

I flinched and jumped back.

With a whiny noise, he sucked in air. Then he let it out with a loud sigh.

He licked his lips, then opened up as if he hankered for another dose.

Lazarus obliged him.

The fellow's Adam's apple bobbed up and down. He swallowed just as fast as Lazarus could dump Elixir in.

'That should do him.' Lazarus uncrouched himself and rushed backward.

I moved away some, and breathed again.

I didn't rightly know what to make of all this, but I was sure keen to see what would happen next.

What happened next was, the fellow let out a squeal that made my hair rise. Then he bolted up, buggy-eyed and wheezing, grabbed the edges of his box and leaped to his feet. He looked down at himself. He glanced at Lazarus, then at me. Then he cried out, 'Whooooeeee!' and commenced to clap his hands and prance about on the floor of his casket. 'I'm saved!' he yelled. 'Lordy, Lordy, I'm *saved!*' Well, he hopped over the side and bounded toward me, weeping and laughing.

I was just too shocked and perplexed to get clear of him in time. He grabbed me and hugged me and kissed my cheek. And didn't he stink! I shoved him off, and he went skipping over to Lazarus and gave him a slew of hugs and kisses.

Lazarus acted more friendly toward him than I'd done. I reckon he was used to such doings. Instead of trying to free himself from the creature, he hugged him and patted his head. 'No call to take on,' he said. 'You're fine. You're just fine, young man.'

'I was *hung*! I was dead and *gone*!'

'You've been revivified,' Lazarus explained, giving him another hug. 'You've been returned to the land of the living with the aid of my patented Glory Elixir.'

'Glory Elixir?'

'Good for what ails you.'

'Glory! Glory hallelujah!' He broke away from Lazarus and I feared he might come after me again, but instead he dropped to his knees and hoisted his arms into the air. He gloried and hallelujahed for quite a spell.

He was still at it when Lazarus stepped around him. He walked toward me, looking solemn and thoughtful. 'You've witnessed the miracle,' he said.

'Witnessed something.'

He laid an arm across my shoulders and led me toward the wagon. 'It's truly a wondrous thing to behold, the restorative power of the Glory Elixir. It revives the dead! Just imagine the curative miracles that such a fluid works on the living, such as yourself. Why, with *ten* bottles at your disposal, I've no doubt but what you'll find yourself fit as a fiddle for a century at the very least.'

We stopped at the rear of the wagon, and he climbed in.

While Lazarus was out of sight, I turned my attention to the other fellow. He was still on his knees, but he'd quit acting strange. His face had the same dingy gray hue as when he'd been dead, which was odd. Now that he was breathing again, seemed like his skin should've taken on a healthier color.

When he saw me looking at him, he smiled.

'How'd you like being dead?' I asked.

'Not much,' he said.

'If you don't care for it, you'd best hurry off. Lazarus aims to rekill you.'

'Trevor!' Lazarus shouted from inside the wagon.

'I thought he ought to know, actually.'

The revived fellow wasn't smiling any more. But he wasn't lighting out, either.

'You'd best skedaddle,' I warned him.

He just stayed kneeling there.

Lazarus crawled backward, dragging a wooden box out through the blanket. 'Why'd you want to tell him such things?' he asked. He sounded a trifle peeved.

'Well, don't worry yourself. He's still here.'

After climbing down, Lazarus called to him, 'The lad's joshing you.'

'Oh, I know that, Jethro.'

Dr Jethro Lazarus rolled his eyes heavenward. Then he pulled a bottle from the box, just as if nothing had gone amiss. 'There's one,' he said, and handed it to me.

'You *told* me you intended to rekill him,' I said.

'Don't mean *he* has to know it.'

'He'll know it quickly enough when you have a go at throttling him.'

'I'll make it quick and painless.'

'Tell you what, I'll make it quicker.' Well, I swung around and tossed the bottle into my left hand and slapped leather with my right.

Lazarus yelled, 'No!'

His buddy yelled, 'Don't!'

Then my Colt was blazing, blasting up dust all around him. He sprang to his feet. He dodged about.

'Hold still!' I shouted.

He froze and reached for the sky.

'Please! Don't! Don't shoot!'

'No call to fret,' I told him, and took careful aim at his chest. 'Dr Lazarus'll revive you.'

Lazarus chuckled. 'I do believe we've been found out.'

'He's fixing to plug me!'

Shaking my head, I holstered the Colt.

The dead fellow looked quite relieved. He came toward us, watching me careful. Along the way, he dug a hand into a pocket of his trousers and dragged out a sort of rodent by its tail. It looked as flat as if it had gotten stepped on. He gave it a fling and it thumped into the casket. 'How'd he catch on?' he asked Lazarus.

'You called me by my name, dummy.'

'It was more than that,' I said, rather pleased with myself. For the first time since the big shootout at the camp, I didn't feel horrible. I found myself smiling. 'Why, do you two frauds actually *fool* folks with your game?'

'More often than not,' Lazarus said.

His partner came up to us. Even without the dead critter, he didn't smell any too fresh. 'I'm Ely,' he said, and stuck out his hand.

It was the same hand he'd used to rid himself of the rotten carcass, so I didn't shake it but touched the brim of my hat instead. 'Trevor Bentley,' I said.

'Glad you didn't poke me full of lead. Care for a licorice?' He dug into his other pocket and came out with a stick.

It put me in mind of Sarah, and how we always ate just such candy when we visited town. I felt a little pull of sadness, but that passed as I realized Ely'd used the licorice to blacken up his tongue and lips. It had darkened his teeth, too. I'd seen they were gray, which hadn't seemed right. Death shouldn't do that to a man's teeth. I hadn't caught on, though.

'No thank you,' I told him, not wanting any truck with something he'd handled. 'I don't wish to turn my tongue black.'

They both laughed some at that. Ely tore off a piece of licorice and commenced to chew.

'Bootblack on your neck, is it?' I asked.

Lazarus clapped me on the shoulder. 'You're too quick for the likes of us.'

'And how is it you made your face such a color?' I asked Ely.

'Ashes,' he said. He licked a finger in spite of it being one that had plucked the dead thing from his pocket, and took a swipe at his face. A path of gray came off. He had ruddy skin underneath. He grinned like he'd shown me a secret of the universe.

'You two blokes certainly went to a fair piece of trouble on my account.'

'A sale's a sale,' Lazarus said. 'No hard feelings, I hope.'

'Well, you put on a lively show. Did you try it out on that pair of rascals that came along before me?'

Lazarus shook his head. 'I'm afraid we missed the opportunity. They rode up on us too quick. Had a chance to spot Ely.'

'You don't travel along in the casket, then?' I asked the deceased.

He grinned, chewing and showing me his licoriced teeth. 'Gets a mite close in there.'

'I should think so. A mite smelly, too.'

'Oh, Ely don't mind the smell.'

'Nope,' he said, and bit off another piece of licorice.

'You two certainly do beat all.'

'Now,' Lazarus said, 'how many bottles of the Glory Elixir do you suppose you might like to purchase?'

I still held a bottle of the stuff. I shook it, and watched the red fluid slosh about. 'What's it made of?'

'Secret herbs and spices from the Far East, guaranteed to . . .'

'Quit having me on, now.'

'Gin and cherry syrup,' Lazarus said.

'Is it, now?' Well, I believed him. I uncorked my bottle, took a sniff, then drank some. It tasted mighty fine and sweet, scorched my throat, and heated up my stomach. 'And what does it cure, actually?'

Lazarus laughed. 'Sobriety.'

Though I had a vivid recollection of my bout with a hangover following too much whiskey with the boys, I judged that some Glory Elixir might be a fine thing to sip now and again. But then I figured Ely might've had a hand in filling the bottles. Real quick, I lost my thirst for the stuff.

'Suppose I pay you a dollar for the show, and you keep your Elixir?'

Lazarus scowled and rubbed his beard. Pretty soon, he said, 'I tell you what. You keep your dollar and ride along with us. Scout up ahead. Then you let us know quick when someone's coming along so Ely can get himself set for a demonstration. We'll pay you handsomely for your services, give you ten cents on every bottle sold. How does that appeal to you, Trevor?'

I gave it some thought, then said I'd do it.

I went on over to General, mounted up, then waited while they loaded the casket into the wagon. It was good to be out of smelling range of Ely.

When they got the wagon moving, I rode on ahead.

They were quite a pair of rascals. They'd livened me up considerable with their antics.

For a while there, I aimed to follow the plan and scout ahead for them. It'd be a treat to see them have a go at tricking some folks.

I figured I might travel with them all the way to Tucson. They seemed like good company, if you don't count Ely's aroma.

I could see how we might get to be chums.

But chums of mine don't last.

If I stayed with them, they were bound to end up dead. Same as everyone else.

So I chose to spare them.

I was some distance ahead of their wagon by then, so all it took was to quicken General's pace. By the time I looked back, they were out of sight.

Chapter Thirty-eight

I Get Jumped

Later on that same day, another wagon came along. This one had a man and woman up front and a boy about my own age riding a mare alongside. I considered warning them not to be fooled by Lazarus and Ely, but chose to let them look out for themselves. If they were fools enough to fall for such a swindle, they deserved it. Besides, I judged it'd be lowdown of me to ruin business for those two chaps.

All I did was say 'Howdy' as I rode by. The woman acted like I wasn't there at all, but the man and boy watched me close as if they feared I might be a desperado looking for a chance to gun them down.

Lazarus and Ely weren't likely to have much luck with this crowd.

Nobody else came along. When the sun got low, I put some distance between me and the trail. I found a sheltered place in a dry wash. After seeing to General, I did some shooting practice. Then I made myself a fire and cooked up a can of beans.

Now that I'd regained my appetite, the beans didn't seem altogether satisfying. They filled me up, but I had an awful hankering for fresh meat.

After supper, I felt like having a smoke. Didn't have any makings, though. They were back at the old campsite with the rest of McSween's things.

I turned gloomy, remembering McSween.

So I pulled a whiskey bottle out of my saddle bag. It had belonged to Breakenridge. I'd taken it, along with the gang's ammunition and money and some other supplies, even though I hadn't the heart to take McSween's tobacco and paper.

I uncorked the bottle and worked on it. It didn't have the good, sweet taste of the Glory Elixir. But it had never been touched by Ely, either, so that was a clear advantage.

The whiskey didn't perk up my spirits much.

I quit while I still had my wits about me, and turned in.

The next day, I returned to the trail. I still had a hunger for fresh meat, so I kept my eyes open.

There were birds about, magpies and hawks mostly, but a gunshot was likely to blow such a thing to smithereens if I was lucky enough to hit one. McSween had told me once that rattlers made good eating, but not a one showed itself. I figured that was for the best, as I wasn't keen on the notion of chowing down a snake.

I did spot a few gophers or prairie dogs. They'd poke their little heads up out of holes, I'd dismount and have a crack at them with the Winchester, miss, and go on my way again.

It was starting to look like I'd be eating beans from here to the next town. But then, long about noon, I caught sight of a jackrabbit as it hopped away from behind a boulder about fifty yards off.

I lit out after it.

The critter led me a merry chase, but I closed in, slapped leather, and shot from the saddle. My first bullet knocked its brains out.

Feeling mighty pleased with myself, I dismounted and fetched my knife. It had been Snooker's knife, which he'd always worn on his belt. I carried it in one of my saddle bags as I hadn't figured out a good way to wear it, what with having holsters at both hips.

Anyhow, I unsheathed the knife and gutted the hare and cut off its head and skinned it. I couldn't see much advantage to waiting, so I built a fire and cooked it up on the spot. It smelled just splendid as it sizzled away. By and by, the outside turned a lovely golden brown. I took my meal off the fire, then had to wait for it to cool down.

I ate the hare right off the spit and it tasted simply delicious.

When about half was gone, I judged it'd be a fine thing to save some for supper. So I wrapped the remainder in a cloth and put it into a saddle bag along with my knife.

Then I climbed onto General and we headed back for the trail.

We were almost there, passing through a gap between some boulders, when my head got clobbered. Whatever it was thumped me solid through the crown of my hat and shook my brains. I couldn't see anything but red as I tumbled sideways and bounced off some rocks. After I hit the ground, my vision came around in time to let me watch General prance so as not to step on me.

I tried to sit up, wondering what had struck me. Just then, someone leaped off the top of a boulder and landed in my saddle.

General, spooked, reared up on his hind legs. The stranger yelped and pitched backwards, boots kicking at the sky, and came crashing down on top of me. My air blew out. The wound in my side felt like it burst open.

The rascal sat up quick, so I snatched a handful of shaggy hair and tugged. Out popped a grunt that sounded like it came from a boy no more than seven or eight years old.

I'd been attacked by an *urchin*?

It crossed my mind that he seemed mighty big for his age – more my own size. But I had no doubt he was a child. So I figured I shouldn't shoot him unless I had to.

Instead of going for my gun, I kept him held down atop me by the hair and used my right hand to punch him in the side. He grunted and flinched each time I struck a blow, but that didn't slow him down. He squirmed and twisted and finally sailed an elbow into my side. It found my wound.

The pain turned me weak so I lost my grip on his hair and he went to sit up. I grabbed for him, but only caught shirt. He wasn't ready to let that stop him. He strained against it, groaning. I heard a rip and the shirt came down off one shoulder. Then my arm got knocked away by an elbow and he scurried off me.

Without a glance back, he stumbled to his feet and made a dash for General, who was watching us from just beyond the gap.

I sprang up and gave chase.

'Stop or I'll shoot you!' I yelled.

He didn't stop.

I didn't shoot.

I just didn't have it in me to plug a kid. Besides, I was quicker on my feet and gaining on him, so it wasn't called for.

He was still a few strides short of General, yellow hair all abounce, shirt flapping behind like a cape, when I dived and caught him around the legs. He went down hard, breath whumping out. We both skidded through the dust. General scampered clear.

But the kid wasn't done yet. He squirmed and kicked, got his legs free, and smacked a boot heel into my head.

Well, that pretty much shredded my temper.

'Damn your bloody eyes!' I shouted and grabbed the boot that had kicked me. On my knees, I gave it a rough pull. It didn't come off, but dragged him closer. Then I twisted that boot. Crying out, the kid flipped over onto his back.

If you're a sharp reader, it won't come as any surprise to find out that the kid was no boy at all.

I wasn't reading about the situation, though. I was living it, and let me tell you, I couldn't have been any more surprised if he'd turned out to be a circus monkey.

For a while yet, I still thought I'd caught a boy.

He no sooner rolled onto his back than I dropped his boot and charged ahead on my knees, all set to pulverize this kid who'd attacked me and obviously aimed to steal my horse. But the way the shirt was sprawled open, I couldn't help but see he had what appeared to be a pair of smallish bosoms.

I'm not always a quick study.

What I thought, just for a bit, was that the lad had a deformity. Maybe he was some brand of freak or he had himself a disease that made him swell up in such a fashion. I'd once read in a book about the bubonic plague, which caused people to grow lumps on their bodies. Maybe what this kid had were buboes.

That notion gave me pause, for I didn't relish catching a dose of the plague.

My pause was all she needed.

She couldn't go anywhere, as her legs were trapped under me, but she bolted upright and swung a fist into my face.

It knocked me off to the side.

We tussled in the dust, me too stunned to put up much fight, and next thing you know, she was on top of me. She sat across my hips, unleashing a flurry of blows that battered my face considerable.

She had a savage look on her face. It was a pretty face, though, and I decided she likely *was* a girl, after all. So those were breasts, after all. Not deformities or buboes. They were sweaty and bouncing about as she lit into me, but I couldn't work up much interest in them.

Girl or not, she had to be stopped.

I tried to go for my guns, but her legs were in the way.

Finally, I managed to catch her wrists. They were slippery, but I held on. She jerked her arms in a frenzy, huffing and grunting. 'Quit it!' I shouted. 'Stop! I'll . . . have to . . . hurt you.'

'Hurt *me*?' She rather sneered it out, then pulled her wrist up and bit my knuckles.

I yelped and let go. Before she could take another swing at me, though, I threw my fist at her chin and got lucky. As her head snapped sideways, I bucked and shoved her. She tumbled off me. I scrambled to my knees and pulled a Colt and pointed it at her face.

'Don't you move!' I gasped.

She was propped up on her elbows, ready to have another go at me. But when she saw the gun, she sank back down onto the ground and lay there, panting for breath. Blood trickled from a corner of her mouth.

Her shirt hung wide open. Her tawny skin glistened in the sunlight. I could see reddish smudges on her side where my punches had landed.

Her blue dungarees had gotten pulled clear down past her hips during the fight. Some gold hair curled out over where they buttoned shut.

I reckon she saw how I was studying her, for she hiked the trousers up to her waist and shut her shirt. 'You think you're gonna meddle with me . . . you better think again. You'd have to shoot me first.'

'I've every right to shoot you,' I said. 'You tried to nick my horse.'

'Well, he's all yours.' She propped herself back up again with her elbows. Her shirt slipped open some. She checked to see how much. It left a bare strip down the middle of her chest and hung off the sides of her belly, but it kept her breasts covered so she didn't fool with it. She was still breathing hard. She blinked sweat out of her eyes, and stared at me.

'You don't need to go on lying there,' I told her.

'It gives me less room to fall if you kill me.'

I couldn't help but let out a laugh when she said that. The laugh made my head hurt worse. I felt around up there and found quite a bump above my right ear.

My whole face felt tight and sore from the drubbing she'd given me. I checked my right hand. It had a passel of dents from her teeth, but she hadn't broken the skin.

'You sure did me some damage,' I said. 'But I don't suppose I'll kill you.' I holstered my weapon, then added, 'Just leave my horse be.'

'You aim to let me go?' she asked.

I didn't rightly know *what* to do with her.

While I gave it some thought, she sat up. Didn't get off the ground, though. She crossed her legs and watched me.

'Can't let you go,' I said. 'You're no better than a horse thief.' I couldn't help but recollect that I was the same. 'Besides, you bashed me about quite a bit.'

'No more than what you bashed me.' With that, the back of her hand rubbed a dribble of blood off her chin. She frowned at it, then showed it to me. 'You see?'

'I took quite the worst of it, actually.'

'You sure do talk peculiar. Anybody ever tell you that?'

Well, that set me to blushing. 'There's nothing at all peculiar about how I talk, thank you.'

'Oh yes there is. What are you, a Yankee?'

'I come from London, England.'

Her eyebrows went up. 'I'll be danged,' she said. 'An Englishman. If that don't beat all.' Her eyebrows came back down, and she was suddenly frowning. 'I didn't do that to you, did I?'

'What?'

'Your side there.'

I raised my arm and looked down at where the posse bullet had ripped my shirt. The cloth was bright with fresh blood. 'It was healing up quite nicely before you ambushed me.'

'Someone go at you with a knife?'

'It's a gunshot wound.'

'Let me see,' she said, and got up. I watched her close, wary of tricks. On her feet, she tried to fasten her shirt. Its buttons were gone, though, so she pulled it shut and tucked it into her trousers. Then she came on over to me.

'You'd best behave,' I warned her.

'I just wanta see.'

Well, I wasn't fool enough to pull up my shirt and give her a chance at my Colts. So I took them both in my hands, then raised my arms.

She stopped straight in front of me. Her eyes were level with my own, and green as emeralds. I hadn't seen them up close like this. They were so sharp and clear they gave me a squirmy feeling inside.

'You sure are a caution,' she said.

'I don't intend to get myself ventilated by a girl.'

That brought a smile to her face. I saw her lips were dry and cracked. There was a cut at one corner, which I judged must've been caused by my fist. The cut had a drop of blood on it. Her teeth were straight, and shiny white.

'I ain't ventilated a soul all day,' she said.

Then she took hold of my shirt with both hands. It was pretty much untucked from the fight. She hauled out the remainder and hoisted it up. Bending over some, she peered at my wound.

'Why, it's only a scratch, mostly. I bet you just walked too close to a thorny bush.'

'They must have rather big thorns where you come from.'

'Don't they just,' she said. Then she leaned in closer and blew on my wound, which I knew to be more of a furrow than a scratch. Her breath felt pretty good. She did it again.

'What are you doing there?' I asked.

'You picked up some grit and it don't wanta blow off. You got some water, I'll clean it for you. Otherwise, you might just fester up and die.'

'I shouldn't like that to happen.'

'Well, go get your water.'

She let my shirt fall and stepped back. She had a look of mischief in her eyes, so I judged she was up to one trick or another. 'Wait here,' I said. Then I holstered my guns and hurried off to fetch General.

I gave some thought to making the girl come with me. More than likely, she had no intention at all of cleaning off my wound, but aimed to light out.

I rather hoped she might do just that. Run off and hide. I didn't know what to do with her, anyhow, if she stayed. She had already caused me a spot of trouble. The sooner I could get shut of her, the better.

So I took my time going after General. He'd wandered off a piece. I found him nibbling some leaves off a bush, and let him work on it for a while. Watching him, I had a mind to mount up and ride away. If I did that, I'd be clear of the girl whether or not she'd decided to vamoose. Only problem was, my hat had gotten knocked off when she clobbered me off my saddle and I didn't aim to leave it behind.

Besides, I was curious.

Maybe I was more than that.

The hat was the excuse I gave myself, though.

After a while, I took the reins and walked General back through the rocks. Along the way, I found my hat and picked it up. Its crown was caved in some, but the dent popped right out when I gave it a poke. I knew better than to wear my hat, what with the sore lump on my head, so I hung it over my saddle horn.

A few more steps took me past the rocks. The girl was leaning back against a boulder, arms folded across her chest.

'You didn't dodge off,' I called. Didn't quite know how I felt about that.

'Where would I go?' she asked.

'You aren't afraid of me, then?'

'Oh, that beats all.'

'Perhaps you ought to be, you know,' I said, and lifted down my water bag.

'You're *just* a boy.'

'Used to be one.'

She watched me come toward her. Even though she didn't smile or smirk, she had a sassy look about her face. 'And how old *are* you?' she wanted to know.

'How old are you?'

'I asked you first.'

'Older than you, I suppose.'

'Ha.'

'I'm nineteen, going on twenty,' I told her.

'You're a liar's what you are.' She reached out and grabbed the water bag. 'I bet you're no more than thirteen.'

'Eighteen,' I said.

'More likely twelve.' She unplugged the pouch, tipped back her head and commenced to gulp down my water.

She had a tiny, pale scar under her chin. Her neck was smooth and shiny, same as the skin that showed between the edges of her shirt. Staring at those places, I all of a sudden lost my urge to squabble with her.

'Actually, I'm closing in on sixteen.'

She lowered the pouch and smiled. 'That sounds more like the truth.'

'It is the truth.'

'Truth is, I've got you beat. I'll be seventeen come October.'

'So you're sixteen.'

'Older than you by a country mile. Go on and take your shirt off.'

She helped herself to another swig while I started to work on the buttons. 'What's your name?' I asked.

'What's yours?'

'Trevor. Trevor Bentley.'

'Mighty hifalutin.'

I finished with the buttons and pulled my shirt off. 'I told you mine,' I reminded her.

'Give.' She wiggled her fingers at my shirt.

I handed it to her. She bunched up the tail and soaked it with water.

'What sort of name *should* I have?' she asked. She pushed herself off the rock, stepped closer to me, and reached the wet cloth toward my wound. 'Pick up your arm.'

I raised my arm, forgetting to take my Colt with it. By the time I caught the mistake, she was already patting the cloth against my raw gouge. She was gentle about it, too. With both her hands full, she'd have trouble going for either of my guns, so I tried not to worry about it.

'You want me to guess your name, then?' I asked.

'Bet you can't.'

'Rumplestiltskin.'

She laughed softly. 'Yep. You got it on the first try. That's Rump for short.' She stopped swabbing my wound and gave the shirt to me.

As I put it on, she stepped back and slipped the strap of my water bag over her shoulder.

'Saw you cooking up a jackrabbit,' she said. 'You give me some, I'll tell you who I am.'

'You've already told me, Rump.'

'You don't wanta see me shrivel up and die,' she said, and walked on around me.

Here we go again, I thought, figuring I might have to

throw her down. But she didn't try to mount General. Instead, she gave my horse a few pats, then opened the saddle bag and pulled out the remains of my hare. Turning around, she smiled and said, 'Much obliged.'

'That's my supper.'

'Not any more, I reckon.' She unwound the cloth I'd wrapped it in. 'Or are you gonna shoot me?'

'Do you always do just as you please?'

'Pretty near.' She bared her teeth and ripped a chunk out of my hare. Her eyes closed. She chewed a few times and sighed. Then she tore off another chunk and worked on it. Some juice dribbled down her chin. She wiped it off with the back of her hand, then opened her eyes and said, 'Mighty fine, Trevor.' Her words came out sounding thick and mushy. 'It's gonna be a pure pleasure riding with a feller that's such a good cook.'

'You have a notion to ride with me, do you?'

'Name's Jesse. Jesse Sue Longley.'

Chapter Thirty-nine

Pardners

'Which direction are you traveling?' I asked, figuring this might let me off the hook.

'None in particular,' said Jesse Sue Longley.

'Why, you must be going *to* somewhere.'

'Ain't going *to* anyplace. Just *away* from where I been.'

'Where's that, then?'

'That's my nevermind.'

'It's my nevermind if you aim to ride with me. What is it you're running away from? Have you got someone after you?'

Her eyes narrowed. 'Nobody's after me. What about you? How'd you get yourself shot?'

'That's *my* nevermind,' I said.

She smiled. 'Looks like we're even, huh?'

'Looks that way. Far as I know, though, I'm in the clear. Those who caused my troubles aren't looking for me.'

'I can say the same,' she said.

Mine were all dead. From Jesse's manner, I couldn't help but wonder if maybe hers were dead, too. Instead of putting me off, the notion made me feel like we had more in common.

'Where is it that you don't want to go?' I asked.

'Only just Texas.'

'Well, that's not where I'm going.'

'I knew that. I saw you on the trail. You was heading the wrong way for a feller bound for Texas. Not as it would've mattered if I could've nabbed your horse.'

'How'd you get out here, at all, without a mount of your own? Did you walk the whole way, or . . .?'

'Do I look like an addlehead?'

'Not at all.'

'I should say I'm not. No, sir.' She dipped her head down and brought it up sharp as if agreeing with herself rather fiercely. Even though she had a frown on her face, something in her eyes stayed amused – like she was up to some brand of mischief. She'd pretty much had that same glint in her eyes all along. It seemed fitting the times I knew she was having me on, but times like now it didn't rightly belong there and seemed peculiar – as if she carried a secret knowledge inside that maybe set her apart from whatever was actually going on.

'I had me a horse,' she said, 'till yesterday when a dang rattler spooked him and he threw me. He run off, and I ain't seen him since. Sorriest excuse for a flea-bitten nag I ever *did* see. Lost him, and everything I owned but the clothes on my back. Lost me a good Sharps rifle,' she added, as if that were an especially sore point.

'A spot of bad luck, that.'

'Worse luck for the rattler.' A grin came up, matching the usual gleam in her eyes, and she patted her tummy.

'You *ate* it?'

'Killed it first. Stove in its ugly head with a rock.'

'The same as you did to me?'

'Well, your head ain't so ugly, and I didn't stove it in.'

'You certainly had a go at it, didn't you?'

'I only just meant to knock you off your saddle,' she protested. 'If I'd aimed to kill you dead, you'd be stretched out in the dust before now.'

'I doubt that.'

'Not me.' She bent over, hitched up a leg of her dungarees, and snatched a knife out of her boot top. It was just about the biggest knife I'd ever seen, the blade near as long as my forearm. She tapped its point against my chest. 'This here's my Bowie knife,' she said.

I gazed at it, and felt myself shrink and get cold here and there. She'd had that awful weapon all along. If she'd used it instead of the rock, she could've split my head open. She hadn't even gone for it when we were fighting hard on the ground, and there'd been moments when she'd had the chance. She'd *chosen* not to pull it and gut me.

'Why didn't you use it?' I asked.

'Makes a terrible mess,' she said, and slid it back down into her boot. Standing up straight in front of me, she lost her smile. 'I didn't have any call to kill you. I just needed a horse to ride on.'

'I'd be pleased to have you ride along double with me,' I told her.

'Much obliged,' she said.

She gave me the water pouch. I took my hat off the saddle horn and hung the pouch there by its strap. I needed both hands to mount General, so I put my hat on and winced as it squeezed the lump on my head. Then I reached down. Jesse took hold of my hand, and I gave her a tow as she swung up behind me.

'Mind?' she asked.

Before I could inquire what she meant by that, she plucked the hat off my head. 'Lost mine down a canyon two days back,' she explained.

'It seems you've lost a good deal.'

She slapped my shoulder. 'Gained more than I've lost, pardner.'

I let her wear my hat.

She slipped an arm around my waist, and we rode on over to the trail. It was strange, having a girl behind me, hanging onto me, sometimes brushing up against my back. I rather enjoyed it, actually.

After I'd seen that Bowie knife, I couldn't help but trust her. I couldn't help but like her, too. She was tough and had more gumption than any gal I'd ever run across. Even though she'd tried to steal General and she'd hurt me some, I judged she must have a good heart or she would've cut me open.

She was awful pretty, too.

I took to feeling glad she'd jumped me.

Maybe we'd stay together all the way to Tombstone.

But by and by she said, 'I sure could do with a smoke.'

The words were rocks that crushed my joy.

'I haven't any makings, I'm afraid.'

'Too bad.'

Too bad. Quite.

She's bound to end up as dead as McSween, I thought. Dead as everybody else who's crossed my trail.

There was only one way to save Jesse. I had to get clear of her, and soon.

But I'd told her she could ride with me, and the notion of going against my word didn't set well. Besides, it wouldn't be right to leave her alone in the wilderness without a horse and supplies. So I was stuck with her, at least for now.

Glad to be stuck with her, too, though it worried me.

I'll just have to see that she *doesn't* get killed, I told myself.

The trick was to keep her alive, and let her stay with me till we came to a town or met up with some folks who might be willing to take her off my hands.

We rode on and on. Sometime late in the afternoon we came up behind a buckboard pulled by a pair of mules. It was still a ways off when I saw it had a boy in the back, a man and a woman in the driver's box. This looked like an outfit that might not mind an extra passenger.

The kid was maybe eight years or nine years old. He sat amidst of a jumble of luggage and supplies, so I judged the family likely had food to spare. I couldn't see how they might object to taking Jesse along if I paid them for their troubles.

But it didn't seem right to foist her off on these folks without warning, so I said, 'I should think this family might be pleased to have your company. Perhaps we'll ask if they'd be willing to let you travel with them.'

She didn't answer. Pretty quick, though, she smacked the back of my shoulder.

'Say, now!'

'Dirty sidewinder.'

'You'll be better off.'

'I'm just fine right here, thanks all the same.' Then she fetched me another smack.

'Quit that.'

'You ain't gonna drop me off with a passel of strangers. Get it outa your head.'

We were just drawing up on the buckboard, the kid waving, the man and woman in front both turning around to see us, when Jesse called out 'Gee-yup!' and gave General a whap on the rump. He took off with a lurch. I had half a mind to pull in the reins, but instead I let him trot on until we'd left the bunch a ways behind us.

General settled down to a walk.

'I don't see why you had to do that,' I said.

Jesse didn't talk for a spell. Finally, she said, 'I thought you and me was pardners.'

'You'd be better off with those folks.'

'How do you know that, Mister Smarty? How do you

know the pa – if that's what he even is – don't take a horsewhip to his wife and boy eighteen times a day just to exercise his arm?'

'It wouldn't have hurt to have a talk with them. They might've been quite friendly.'

'How come you're so all-fired hot to throw me off on someone else?'

'I don't care to see you hurt.'

'You fixing to hurt me?'

'Why, no. Certainly not. The problem is, you're likely to *get* hurt if you stay with me. You just won't last, not unless you get clear while there's still time.'

'Why's that?'

'I don't know, actually. But I've left behind me an awful string of dead folks.'

'You got a sickness?'

'Nothing more than bad luck.'

'Well, that eases my mind. You near had me scared. I saw a feller caught himself a dose of the rabies, one time. He took to cavorting down the street all wild-eyed and slobbering. You never seen such a sight. He went to bite old lady Jones, and Sheriff Hayes dropped him stone cold dead. That was in El Paso three years back. Saw it happen with my very own eyes. They say it was a dog bite. You get yourself bit by a rabid hound, you might just as well cash in your chips then and there. That's what I'd do, blow out my own brains and call it quits. You don't want to make a fool outa yourself, foaming all over tarnation and snapping at folks so they have to shoot you.'

'You won't catch rabies from me,' I told her.

'When was the last time you got yourself bitten?'

'Earlier today, actually.'

She let out a laugh and slapped my arm, but not hard. 'Smarty.'

'I do hope I won't commence to slobber and snap.'

My hat suddenly got shoved down onto my head. 'Ow!'

'You better wear it for a spell. The sun's getting to your brain.'

I lifted it some so it wouldn't squeeze my bump. We rode on for a while, then Jesse said, 'So what was it that killed off such a string of folks?'

'Mostly guns and knives.'

'But you ain't the one that done 'em in?'

'I didn't kill my friends. But plenty of them ended up dead on account of me, so it's much the same thing.'

'How'd you manage all that?'

'It's rather as if I led them into trouble, you see. Not that I did such things on purpose. But those folks got killed, anyhow. I'm afraid the same might happen to you.'

'Well, don't go worrying about me.'

'I can't avoid it, actually.'

'You won't get me killed, so quit bothering your head about it. When my number comes up, it won't be on account of you. It'll be my own dang fault. You can bet on that.'

'It *shall* be your own dang fault, quite right. It'll be your stubborn ways. I've warned you fair and square.' I turned General and looked back down the trail. The buckboard was still a distance off, but getting closer. 'You ought to reconsider.'

'Nope. I'd a sight rather take my chances with your bad luck, which I don't believe anyhow, than join up with them folks.'

'You claimed you're not addleheaded.'

'That man, he'd take after me. It's what men do.'

'He's married, Jesse.'

'That ain't likely to stop him. He'll just bide his time till he can get me alone, maybe tonight when his woman's sleeping or maybe he'll just go and try me right in front of her eyes. Some fellers ain't particular who watches.'

'You're daft.'

'I know what I know. It'll happen, sure as you're sitting there. And then I'd be forced to give him a taste of my knife. More than likely, the widow'd lose her head when she saw how I'd carved her husband. Wouldn't matter that he was no good and better dead. He was her husband and the father of her boy, so she'd throw a fit and grab a gun and shoot me. Then *I'd* be killed. And you know what? Every last bit of such a sorry business would be all *your* fault for passing me off on these folks.'

I twisted around on the saddle and gazed at her. She looked grim, but had the usual spark of mischief in her green eyes.

'When was it now,' I asked, 'that you kissed the Blarney stone?'

'What're you getting at?'

'I've rarely heard such malarkey.'

'Malarkey?'

'Outrageous nonsense.'

'You just don't know nothing at all.'

General stepped off the trail without any urging from me as the buckboard closed in on us. But he needn't have bothered. The fellow with the reins brought his mules to a stop in time to miss us, even if we hadn't moved.

'Vahs iss dee problem?' he asked. I'd run into a German or two back home and took him for one because of the odd and spitty way he talked.

Before I could answer, Jesse said, 'No problem.'

He scowled at her. He looked like a hard man. Maybe Jesse hadn't been far off the mark with her notion that he enjoyed taking a horsewhip to his family. The gal beside him kept her head down as if she was bashful. She wore a white linen bonnet. I couldn't see her face at all. The boy in the rear of the wagon watched us, but kept mum.

'Iss dis your sister?' the fellow asked me.

'She lost her horse,' I explained. 'I've been giving her a ride.'

'Allzo,' he said, whatever that meant. One of his dark eyebrows climbed up his forehead. 'Vee take dis froyloyn. She komm mit, yes?'

At that, the gal raised her head. Her face was all ablush. She was working her lower lip between her teeth and she stared at Jesse with a jittery look in her eyes.

Well, then she shook her head just a bit. It wasn't much of

a shake, but enough so the man noticed it. He spat some words at her. They didn't make any sense at all to me, but she cringed and dropped her head.

Now that she was taken care of, he gave me a sly grin and said, 'Vaht vant you for her? I give you dee five dollar, yes?'

'I don't reckon so,' I said.

'Nine?'

'He wants to *buy* me, Trevor.'

'She isn't for sale,' I said.

'But yes. Vee feel?'

Jesse snapped, 'Nobody lays a hand on me, you damn polecat!'

Scowling fierce, he lurched to his feet there in the driver's box, jabbed a finger at her and hissed, '*Shee*son!'

The word wasn't out his mouth before I had a Colt in my fist.

He gave it a glance, frowned some, then came back at me with his oily grin. 'Ten dollar?'

'Bugger off,' I said, then wheeled General around and put in the spurs. We galloped on down the trail till a rocky bend put the buckboard out of sight.

Pretty soon after we'd slowed down to a walk, Jesse pushed her head against me. Her hair tickled the back of my neck. 'Sure glad you didn't sell me off to that pig,' she said.

'I wonder if he might've gone up to twenty.'

She bumped her head against me fairly solid. A bit later, I heard a few sniffles. It crossed my mind she might be crying, but that didn't seem likely. Not Jesse.

Just in case she might still be worried, though, I said, 'You can ride with me for just as long as you like. I won't try to give you away again. Or sell you, either.'

She leaned more of herself against my back and wrapped both her arms around my middle. She gave me a squeeze, then said, 'See that you don't.'

Chapter Forty

The Damsel in Distress

Later on, we came to a shallow creek that crossed the trail. Even though we still had some daylight left and could've gone on, it usually doesn't hurt to camp by water. I'd had no trouble yet with running low. It was dry country, though. If we moved on, no telling when we might run into another place with good water.

Other folks were likely to have the same notion. I didn't want company, and figured Jesse felt that way, too, so we followed the creek north till we were a good distance from the trail.

We found a fine spot that had high piles of rock on two sides, and even a few scrawny trees. They'd give us shade till the sun went down, and block out some of the wind that usually stirred up cold at night.

As I unsaddled General, Jesse said, 'You just stay here and don't you dare come looking for me. I'm going upstream for a spell.'

She wandered off. I stayed where I was, finished removing all my gear from General, set down the sack of oats for him, and groomed him while he ate. When I got done, Jesse still wasn't back yet. I let General wander down to the creek, but didn't follow him.

The reason Jesse had warned me off, I judged, was so she'd have privacy for bathing. It stirred me up some, thinking about that. I took a notion to climb the rocks and spy on her. It seemed like a lowdown thing to do, though. Besides, she might catch me at it and get riled.

So I hauled my saddle into the shade under a tree and leaned back against it to make myself comfortable. A soft breeze was blowing. I closed my eyes and listened to the birds. It was uncommon peaceful and nice. I might've drifted off to sleep except that my mind wouldn't let go of Jesse.

I kept remembering how she'd looked when we were fighting, her shirt open as she threw punches at me. And how she'd looked later, sprawled on the ground. She might be in the creek right now without a stitch on. It was almost more than a body could stand.

I pictured how she might look, all bare and wet. Quite a bit slimmer than Sarah, not near as curvy, more like a boy. I wondered what her breasts might feel like. They weren't near as large as Sarah's. They'd looked like they might be hard, but then I recalled how they'd jiggled some while she swung at me. So they couldn't be terribly hard. Likely not as soft as Sarah's, though.

I recalled my first night in Sarah's bed, and how she'd cured me of being put off by breasts. Then I was thinking about the other fine times I'd had with Sarah. There'd been the dancing and the baths and all those other times we'd ended up having at each other. But there'd been the rest of it, too. Trips into town, horse rides and picnics, and the pure pleasure of just being with her – talking or reading, doing chores or sharing meals.

Pretty soon, I was missing her something terrible.

If only I hadn't seen that story about Whittle in the newspaper, we might still be at the house.

That set me to thinking about our railroad trip, and I got angry remembering Briggs. If that no-account hadn't thrown me off the train, we'd be together yet.

But he had thrown me off.

And I'd joined up with the gang.

It seemed likely that I would never see Sarah again. No telling where she might've gone to, by now. Maybe she'd traveled on to California with Briggs. I sure hoped not. But if she was fool enough to get pulled in by the likes of him, she deserved no better.

It made me feel ornery, thinking that way about her. I told

myself she was too good for him, too smart for him. What she'd probably done was turn around and gone home to Coney Island. I hoped so.

That way, I would be able to find her again after I'd finished my business with Whittle.

Except I won't, I thought.

Till now, I hadn't given it much real thought. But I'd known, way in the back of my mind, that me and Sarah were finished. It finished between us the night I shot down those posse men.

After that, I was no longer fit for her.

Sarah and even Mother herself were good women. I was no better than a murderer. Best for all concerned if I never saw either one of them again.

I judged they'd be better off without me, anyway, on account of how they'd likely end up killed.

The same went for Jesse. But I was stuck with her.

I recalled how she'd put her arms around me there on the trail after we'd left the German behind. It seemed clear she was growing rather fond of me. I couldn't deny that I'd gotten fond of her, too.

She was full of gumption and her sassy ways appealed to me. Even if she'd been an ugly thing, I wouldn't've enjoyed her company. But she was awful pretty. Too pretty.

If I didn't watch out, I might find myself purely infatuated with her. That wouldn't do, at all.

I won't allow it, I told myself.

I'll only take her as far as the next town.

I won't spy on her. I won't touch her. I won't even think about her being a girl.

She's just someone who needs a ride.

My job's keeping her alive long enough to leave her behind.

After making up my mind about that, I felt somewhat better about the situation. I felt pretty near gallant. Jesse was a damsel in distress, me a knight determined not to lose my heart to her and only to fulfill my mission of delivering her to a safe haven.

With that settled, I figured it might be time to rouse my bones and start a fire. So I opened my eyes, and there was Jesse watching me. She sat nearby in a patch of sunlight, barefoot, arms resting across her upraised knees. Her ankles were wet. Water dripped off the cuffs of her dungarees. Her blue shirt was damp and clinging to her. It wasn't tucked in, but she'd used her belt to hold it shut around her waist. Her face glistened with specks of water. Her short hair wasn't fluffy any more, but lay against her head in thick, golden loops. A few of those hung across her brow. Two on the sides curled down in front of her ears and came to points.

In short, she looked wet and fresh and altogether splendid. She looked so fine it put a lump into my throat.

I could see it wouldn't be an easy task to keep my wits and not take a powerful liking to her.

The gleam in her green eyes and how she smiled didn't help at all.

Sitting up, I said, 'You could get yourself shot, you know, sneaking about in such a manner.'

'Bunkum,' she said.

'There was a lawman I heard about, he ventilated his best friend when the bloke walked up behind him unannounced. It happens all the time, actually.'

'This must be my lucky day.'

'I'm quite serious.'

'Well, next time I find you sleeping, I'll be sure and pelt you with a stone.'

'I wasn't asleep.'

'Then you should've heard me coming. Ears no better than that, it's a wonder you've lasted.' A drop of water slid off one of her curls. It trickled down her eyebrow, so she wiped it away with the back of her hand. 'So then, you were playing possum.'

'Not at all,' I protested.

She narrowed her eyes. 'You were up in them rocks having a gander at me. Saw me coming back, so you scampered on down and let on like you'd spent your time dozing.'

A blush heated my face.

'Ah-ha!' She didn't seem angry, but pleased with herself for finding me out.

'I did no such thing,' I said.

'No call to fib about it.'

'It's the truth, Jesse. But you go ahead and think what you wish. I'd be quite a wealthy chap if I had a dollar for every time I've been wrongly accused of this and that. It's as ordinary as daylight.'

'Liar. I seen you.'

'Did not.'

'Did, too.' She pointed a thumb over her shoulder at the rocky height behind her back. 'Right up there. So you might just as well fess up.'

All of a sudden, the bottom seemed to drop out of my stomach. I jumped to my feet, pulled a Colt, rushed past Jesse and went charging up the slope.

'What in tarnation?' she called after me.

I paid her no heed, but raced upward, leaping higher and higher, my mouth gone dry, my heart thudding fit to bust. I wasn't so much scared as outraged. Some bloody scoundrel had gone and spied on Jesse. He'd watched her bathe in the creek. No telling why he hadn't gone on down and attacked her. Maybe he aimed to bide his time and take us by surprise later on. Well, he wouldn't get the chance.

I bounded over the top of the rocks, all set to shoot him dead.

And that's just what I would've done, but he wasn't there.

I wandered about, searching behind every rock, peering into crevices, circling around the few tangles of mesquite thick enough to hide a man. By and by, I judged he must've skedaddled.

From my perch, I had a mighty fine view of the creek. Anyone up here would've had just such a fine view of Jesse. I was in a fit to shoot him. But he wasn't down by the creek, nor hurrying down the slopes. I studied the low land all around us, but couldn't spot him or any horse other than

General. There were hiding places everywhere, though. Dry washes, boulders, jutting heaps of rock, cacti and bushes and a few stunted trees. Not many places for concealing a horse, though a man on foot could disappear in any of a thousand places.

I might've stayed up there longer, hoping he'd show himself, but then it came to me that I'd left Jesse alone.

What if he'd circled around?

What if he'd jumped her?

Quick as I could, I hurried along the top of the rocks till our camp came into sight. There stood Jesse, arms folded across her chest, gazing up at me. And wasn't I glad to see her!

Before starting down, I scanned the area. Nobody appeared to be lurking about. I could see the wagon trail off in the distance, but nobody was in sight on it.

'He got away,' I called, and commenced to make my way toward the ground.

'Who got away?' Jessie asked.

'The bloody cur that *spied* on you!'

She frowned some. 'He wasn't you?'

'Certainly not. Did he look like me?'

'Well, I didn't see him up close. He was only just peeking down outa the rocks.'

'We'll have to keep a careful watch,' I said, and leaped to the ground in front of her. 'I shouldn't have let you go off by yourself. That was a bad mistake.'

'Well, nothing come of it.'

'Not this time. From now on, we'd best stay together.'

'I need me some private times, Trevor.'

'What you need is me standing guard. No telling where this fellow might be, or what's on his mind. I don't aim to see you attacked or killed for the sake of your modesty.'

'I can take care of myself, I reckon. Just let me take along your Winchester, I'll get along dandy.'

I couldn't see a good argument against that. She ought to be fairly safe, armed with the rifle. 'Perhaps that'll do,' I told her. 'We ought to stay together, regardless, unless you're fixing to . . . bathe or the like.'

'Sounds good to me.'

She got into her socks and boots. Then we roamed about the area, gathering stray bits of wood and roots for our fire. I kept my eyes open for the stranger, and also for game. Neither appeared.

Jesse seemed uncommon quiet the whole time.

After we made our fire, she kneaded some flour into dough, jammed wads of it onto sticks, and cooked them over the flames while I heated up a pot of beans.

After we finished our meal, we took the pot and spoons over to the creek. That's when I noticed how still and quiet things seemed. The air had a yellowish cast to it. Looking off to the west, I saw that the sun was gone behind somber mountains of cloud.

'Do you suppose we'll have a storm?' I asked Jesse, who stood nearby with the rifle.

'Could be. Just as likely not. Doesn't appear as how they get much rain in these parts.'

We didn't pay it any more mind. I cleaned off the pot and spoons. Afterward, we spent a while scouting about to gather more fuel. When it got too dark to see, we quit that. We led General back to camp, and I hobbled him so he wouldn't go wandering off too far during the night. Then we sat down by the fire.

Jesse still wasn't talkative. Pretty soon, I asked, 'Are you worried about that chap you saw in the rocks?'

'You might say that.'

'He hasn't shown himself yet. Why, I suppose he dodged off long ago. All the same, we'll need to take turns standing watch. Can't have him sneaking up on us while we sleep, you know.'

'Oh, he ain't likely to sneak up on us.'

'One can't be too careful. It's when you're least expecting trouble . . .'

'I never did see him, Trevor.' She flung a stick, rather

briskly, into the fire. It hit and tossed up a spray of sparks. 'I didn't see nobody. I only just let on.'

I gaped at her, flabbergasted.

'That's the way of it. I'm right sorry I went and got you so worked up about him.'

'He wasn't there at all?'

'Nope. I figured sure you must've climbed up top to goggle at me and you'd fess up once I claimed I saw you.'

'I *told* you I'd done no such thing.'

'Well, who'd admit it?'

'I'm not one to go about lying.'

'Me neither. Not as a general rule. But I wanted to catch you out.'

'Why should I *care* to goggle at you?' I blurted.

'You know why.'

I certainly did know why, but I wasn't about to admit it. So I kept mum.

By and by, Jesse said, 'I seen how you look at me, Trevor Bentley.'

My face heated up, but I doubt it was noticeable in the firelight. 'Malarkey,' I said.

'I don't blame you none for it. You're just a feller. They can't help that sort of thing.'

'You're roaming up the wrong trail, Jesse.'

She narrowed her eyes at me, and a corner of her mouth turned up. 'Why, you can go on denying it till your face turns blue, I know what I know.'

'Seems to me that you hold quite a high opinion of yourself.'

'I sure do. That's a fact. A mighty high opinion. That's how come I don't allow myself to get jumped on by every lowlife sidewinder that takes a fancy to me.'

'I've *not* taken a fancy to you.'

'Sure have.'

'Am I a lowlife sidewinder, then?'

'Don't reckon you are.'

'Thank you kindly, ma'am.'

'That don't mean I'll let you jump on me.'

'I've no intention of jumping on you, actually. You're the one who's done all the jumping on folks, so far.'

She let out a soft laugh. 'Long as you leave the jumping to me, we'll get along fine.'

We went quiet after that, and just sat there watching the fire for a spell. Then the wind kicked up, so Jesse fetched my blanket. She brought it back, sat down beside me, and wrapped it around both of us. I scooted closer to her and our arms touched. That earned me a wary glance.

'Quite sorry,' I said.

'Oh, never mind. It ain't your fault I'm touchy.'

'Whose fault is it, then?'

'Chester Frank and Charlie Gunderson and Jim Dexter, I reckon. Bobbie Joe Sims and Karl Williams, Bennie Anderson, Danny Sayles, Hank Dappy, Ben Travis, Billy "One-Eye" Cooper.' She took a deep breath, then went on, 'Randy Jones, Ephram and Silas Henry, Reverand Haymarket, Jack Quincy. Did I mention Farley Hunnecker?'

'I don't believe so.'

'Well, then, Farley too. And Gary Hobbs, Dix Talman, Robert E. Lee Smith, a dimwit called Grunt – I never caught his real name. Then there was "Sweet Sam" Bigelow and . . .'

'By Jove,' said I. 'How can you recall such a string of names?'

'You ain't likely to forget the names of such swine.'

'What did they *do* to you?'

'It ain't what they did, it's what they *tried* to do.'

'Every *one* of those chaps?'

'There's more. You didn't let me finish.'

'They *all* tried to . . . have a go at you?'

'One way or another. See, I didn't have no one to look out for me. I reckon that was partly the trouble. My ma, she passed on when she gave birth to me, and my pa was a damn drunk. He tried me a few times himself, but I learned him better.'

'Your own father?'

'He was just as low as the rest of 'em. Lower than most. But it was Clem Catlow that was the last straw. Clem was big as a tree, a boxer. He rode into town to fight Irish Johnny O'Rourke, one of our local boys, and KO'd Johnny in the first round. Same night, he followed me when I went to walk home. I worked in the kitchen there at the Lone Star Steak Emporium on Third Street. Anyhow, he stumbled along after me and sweet-talked me some. I gave him a piece of my mind, but he wasn't one to be put off. Finally, he took hold and hauled me into an alley. I says to myself, "It's him or me." I'm a mighty tough scrapper.' She looked at me and hoisted an eyebrow.

'You are that,' I said.

'But I knew I weren't no match for Clem Catlow. One good whack, and he'd likely knock my head crooked. I yelled and begged, but it weren't no use. He threw me down and took to ripping off my duds, so I had no choice but to kill him.'

Just when she said that, thunder rumbled through the night. It sounded some ways off, but we frowned at each other.

'You *killed* him?' I asked, whispering as if to keep the storm from hearing my voice and coming after us.

'Tore him up with my Bowie knife. Let me tell you, it was no easy job squeezing out from under him afterwards, either. But I managed it. Then I ran on home and got my things together and saddled up Pa's horse and lit out.'

Chapter Forty-one

The Gullywasher

'I stabbed a man myself,' I told her. 'It was in an alley, too.'

Jesse looked at me. 'No,' she said.

'Yes, indeed. He and others had a go at robbing me. Then I was pursued by a mob and . . . Why, I would be in England yet if not for that.'

'Ain't it strange? I'd still be in El Paso, I reckon, except for taking my knife to Clem in that there alley. Looks like you and me are two of a kind.'

'I suppose we are.'

Smiling, she bumped her shoulder against me.

Along came another grumble of thunder. It sounded closer than the last.

'Tell me more,' Jesse said.

'I should hardly know where to start.'

'Start at the start. We got all night.'

I gave it some thought, then commenced my story where it rightly began, with Mother bringing the drunken Rolfe Barnes into our flat. When I told about him laying into her with his belt, Jesse let out a hissing noise. 'I know just his kind,' she said. She seemed quite pleased about the way I'd bashed him with the fireplace poker, but allowed as how I should've finished the job.

I plugged along with my tale. Jesse seemed mighty interested, and asked questions about this and that and made comments. All the while, the thunder got noisier and closer and lightning sometimes brightened up the sky. Still, the rain stayed away.

I came to the part about Sue, but didn't let on that she was a whore. According to me, she was simply a stranger who offered to guide me to Leman Street. I told how she'd led me into the alley.

'And you went along with her?'

'I hadn't any choice, actually.'

'What'd you suppose she aimed to *do* in there?'

'It might've been a shortcut, you know.'

'Sounds to me like you were looking to have yourself some good times.'

'Not at all!'

'You got no call to lie, Trevor.'

Right then, the sky lit up bright as noon. Thunder crashed. Rain came pouring down on us. We leaped to our feet, hoisted the blanket over our heads to keep us dry, and rushed over toward the rocks. Along the way, I snatched up my saddle bags and Winchester.

Earlier, I'd spotted a place where a big flat slab jutted out. We raced up a bit of a slope to get there, ducked under the overhang, and huddled down with our backs against a rock wall. I propped up the rifle by my side, hugged the saddle bags to my chest. I was wearing my sixguns. Jesse was wearing my hat. What we'd left out in the weather was my saddle, bridle, bedroll, water pouch, and some other odds and ends that we shouldn't be needing till after the storm.

With our feet pulled in, we were out of the rain. But it gushed down on both sides of us, and in front. Our campfire flickered a few times. Then the last of the flames were pounded out, and all I could see were a few pale wisps getting whipped away by the wind. After that, there was nothing to see except shades of darkness.

There sure was plenty to hear, though. Water splashed down from the overhang so loud we might've been hunkered behind a cataract. The wind wailed and howled like a banshee coming for the dead. Somewhere out in the darkness, General was stomping the ground and letting out frightful squeals and whinnies.

I purely ached to help him. There was no place to give him shelter though. He'd just have to get by the best he could.

The rain was only water, after all, and not likely to hurt him any. He ought to survive if he didn't get struck by lightning or panic so bad as to hurt himself.

Still, it pained me to hear him carrying on. He was mighty spooked.

In a lightning flash so bright it stung my eyes, I saw General rear up on his hind legs. The way I'd left him hobbled, I feared he might pitch over. But he came down safe just as the blackness shut him off from sight.

A roar of thunder came next, so heavy and loud it shook the air.

I gave some thought to rushing out and cutting General loose. I could borrow Jesse's knife, or dig my own out of the saddle bag. But then I judged he would run off and we might never see him again.

Jesse stirred beside me. I looked at her. She was just a dim shape, but I could see enough to watch her take off my hat and set it atop her upraised knee. Just about then, a flash lit her up. She turned her head and smiled at me. She rolled her eyes upward. She said something, but a cannonade of thunder killed her voice and the dark came back.

After the thunder stopped, she shouted, 'Don't this beat all!'

'I do hope it doesn't last!' I yelled back at her.

It wasn't much use, trying to talk.

By and by, she snuggled closer against my side and slipped an arm down low across my back. She rested her head on my shoulder.

If it hadn't been for the horrid noises of the storm and knowing General was out there scared half witless, I might've found myself rather pleased to be huddled with Jesse in such a fashion. As it was, I couldn't work up much interest. I was just too nervous about the chaos raging around us.

But she did feel good and warm where she pressed against me. I put an arm around her, and that felt even better.

As bad as the storm was, we were safe and mostly dry. Lightning couldn't hit us. Nothing at all could hurt us, I judged.

Except for what might happen to General, there was no call to be fidgety about our predicament.

Much as I tried to tell myself that, however, I couldn't get shut of a nasty feeling of dread that had me cold and shaky inside.

'Are you scared, Trevor?' Jesse asked. Her face was near enough to mine that I could hear her plain in spite of the noises.

'Are you?'

'I asked you first.'

'What's to be frightened of?'

'You're all a-tremble,' she said.

'Not at all.'

'Are, too. Is it the storm?'

'I'm not afraid of any old storm.'

'You ain't scared of *me*, are you?' She reached over and patted my stomach.

'What are you doing?' I asked.

'Not a thing. Don't get worked up.'

All of a sudden, my bum was wet. A chill scurried up my spine.

Jesse and I gazed at each other in the darkness.

'Uh-oh,' she said.

I slapped my hand down at the ground beside me. It splashed up water.

This didn't make a lick of sense. We were on a slope. Not much of a slope, to be sure, but enough of one so we shouldn't have water rising around us.

'It's me for the high ground,' Jesse said, jamming my hat onto her head.

As she scurried out from under our shelter, dragging the blanket after her, I grabbed hold of my Winchester and saddle bags. Then I plunged through the curtain of water spilling off the ledge and was drenched in a blink.

On my feet, I swung around and spotted Jesse. She was already in the clear, perched on a boulder off to the right. I waded toward her, water sucking at my boots, and climbed up some rocks till I got up there beside her.

341

'A real gullywasher!' she yelled.

'We ought to . . .' My voice went dead as an awful roar filled my ears. The roar wasn't thunder. I didn't know what it might be, but I didn't like it. 'What's that!' I shouted.

'Flash flood?'

'We'd best . . .'

'What about General?' she yelled.

Before I could think to answer, Jesse threw down the blanket, slipped the Bowie knife out of her boot and leaped off the boulder. I knew just what she aimed to do – cut the hobble so General could make his escape. It was what I should've done myself, but she'd beaten me to it.

Now she was gone. I couldn't see or hear her. There was just the darkness and the downpour and the awful noise roaring closer. I dashed up to some higher rocks, threw down my rifle and saddle bags, dropped my gunbelt, and hurried back to where Jesse'd jumped from. Just as I got there, lightning ripped across the sky.

In its jittery glare, I spotted General a few yards off. He was up to his elbows in the swirling dark flood. The flash lasted just long enough to let me see Jesse burst up out of the water beside him, raising her Bowie knife.

Well, I leaped as the dark came back. Landed on my feet and commenced to trudge through the currents, reaching out for Jesse and shouting her name. Not that she could hear my puny voice through the bedlam of thunder and that *other* noise which sounded like a locomotive barreling toward us.

Just when I wondered if I could ever reach her, the water suddenly went down. Splendid! I thought, feeling it slip away till it wasn't more than ankle-deep. I splashed on ahead, got brushed by General as he bolted past, and then collided with Jesse. We both went down splashing, her on top.

She pushed herself off me. I sat up. Another flash of lightning came along just then. I saw her bending over, hair in her face, shirt drooping open. She reached for me with one hand while the other pushed the knife into her boot. And then a wall of water loomed up behind her.

'No!' I yelled.

I didn't see it smash Jesse, for the lightning quit. I darted my hand toward where she'd been, touched something that might have been her hand, then got myself slammed down by the monster wave. It shoved me along the ground, picked me up, tumbled me head over heels, scraped me against the rocks, bounced me off this and that. Fearing my brains might be dashed out, I hugged my head with both arms. Not a bit too soon, either. I'd no quicker covered up than a blow numbed my elbows and jammed my arms together so tight I thought they might crush my head.

I didn't know it just then, but the mighty wave had hammered me into the rocks not very far from our shelter – head first into a narrow gap.

It was a nice bit of luck, though I hardly considered it so at the time. I figured my arms were busted and I *knew* I was trapped. My arms and head were wedged in tight, the water piling over me, pushing at me, twisting my legs and shoving me up as if it aimed to snap my spine. Of course, I couldn't breathe. But that seemed like a minor problem, as I judged the wave would likely break me to pieces before I could ever find the opportunity to drown.

Then it quit trying to kill me.

Like a grizzly deciding to chase after tastier prey, it let go and raced off.

As the water receded, I sucked in a chestful of air. My knees came down on something solid.

Without the wave ramming at my back, it didn't take much work to squirm myself free. That's when I saw the blocks of stone with the gap between them, and realized how lucky I'd been. If the gap hadn't caught me, no telling where I might've been swept off to.

It didn't seem likely that Jesse'd met with the same brand of luck.

The moment she entered my head, I forgot about all my hurts. I got to my feet, rather unsteady, and turned around to look for her. The rain was still coming down in a deluge. What with that and the dark, I couldn't see a thing below me.

Pretty soon, though, the sky lit up. Where we'd been camped was a wild, surging river. All but one of the trees was gone. I caught a glimpse of the rocky slopes just before the lightning blinked out. No sign of Jesse.

The thunder took a while in coming, so the storm seemed to be moving on.

Off in the distance was the freight train noise same as I'd heard when the bloody wave was approaching. I was all set to scamper for higher ground, but then noticed that the roar was fading, so stayed where I was and waited for another lightning flash.

When it came, I looked again for Jesse on the rocks. If she was there, the short burst of brightness didn't give me enough time to spot her.

So I took to searching.

I was none too steady on my legs. They didn't hurt as much as my arms, but they were awful sore and wobbly. The rocks were slick and, except when lightning came, I couldn't see where I was going. I fell a few times, and once even tumbled down into the water. Didn't quit, though. Kept at it, searching low and high, criss-crossing the slope time and time again. Finally, there was no more point. Jesse was gone. That huge damn wave had carried her off.

I climbed on up to where I'd dropped my guns and saddle bags. They were high enough that they hadn't gotten swept away. I strapped on my belt, then just sat there in the rain.

Jesse hadn't been with me even one full day.

Chapter Forty-two

The Body

Some time during the night, the rain stopped. I didn't notice when it happened, though I never did fall asleep. Just sat there, mulling over Jesse, hating it that I hadn't grabbed her before she could jump down to cut General free, remembering how she'd looked just before the wave took us, remembering *everything* about the hours she'd been with me, and all the while missing her, aching for her to be alive and come back.

Over and over again, I pictured Jesse under water, trying to fight her way to the surface but always being towed down deeper by the rough current, running out of breath so her lungs burned, getting hurled along, tumbled, smashed against rocks, torn asunder until she was dead. Even after she was dead, the flood wouldn't leave her be, but rushed her limp and broken body down through the endless desert beyond where I could ever find it.

A few times, that night, I heard Jesse call out my name. But I knew it was only the wind howling its agony through the night, and not Jesse at all.

Once, she came to me. She sauntered out of the dark, hair shaking in the wind, shirt flapping behind her, a smile on her face and a merry spark in her eyes. 'Can't get rid of me that easy,' she said, and my heart swelled up with joy. Then a bolt of lightning ripped through the clouds and I saw she wasn't there at all and I wept.

That wasn't the only vision I had that night. In the other, I was carrying her dead body in my arms. All the region's kites were swooping down at us. They were going for her eyes, her lovely green eyes, no longer alight with mischief, but flat and dull. As my arms were full, I couldn't fight off the buzzards.

One of the big, stinky things finally perched on her chest, so I bit off its head. I left the carcass in a heap on top of Jesse as a warning to the others. They stayed away, and finally Jethro Lazarus came down the trail in his wagon. He was just the man I'd been looking for. I hailed him, and said I needed to buy a bottle of the Glory Elixir. 'Sold my last bottle no more than a hour ago,' he explained. I cried out, 'No!' Lazarus grinned and shook his head. 'You had your chance to buy some, lad. It's all your fault.' I shrieked, 'No!' again and slapped leather and shot him.

Except I didn't shoot Lazarus. My slug whinged off a boulder no more than six feet in front of me and I wasn't lugging Jesse's body along the trail, at all. I was sitting in the rain, all by myself among the rocks.

Those were the two visions I had that night. They weren't dreams or nightmares, as I was awake when they came to me. After getting over the upset about each of them, I took to wondering what they might mean. They might be omens or premonitions, maybe. But I didn't rightly believe in such malarkey. More than likely, they meant nothing. They were only just my mind going sour on me from too much weariness and grief.

It wasn't till the sun came up that I noticed the rain had stopped.

The sunlight put a new slant on things.

I took a notion that Jesse might not be dead, after all. *I'd* survived the flood. Maybe she'd lived through it, too. It was a slim chance, and I knew it. But even if she had perished, as seemed likely, I needed to hunt for her, bury her decent if I could find her body.

Getting myself off the ground was no easy trick. Some of me was numb, the rest ungodly sore. But I made it to my feet, then stretched this way and that to get the kinks out. I felt like somebody'd taken a sledge hammer to my elbows and shoulders. They were stiff and achy, and I swung my arms around until they limbered up, then practiced drawing my Colts a few times. Once I got my arms working decent, I bent over low enough to pick up my saddle bags and rifle.

Then I turned around and gazed down the slope. Our campsite was dry except for a few puddles which mostly seemed to be in holes where the trees had been uprooted and carried off. The rocks we'd used for a fire ring were gone, along with every trace of burnt wood and ashes. The flood had also carried off my saddle, bridle, bedroll, everything.

Nothing moved down there.

I called out Jesse's name. She didn't answer. I called it out again and again, but the only sounds came from the breeze and a few birds and the creek rushing by.

The creek, off beyond the rocks, looked more like a river now. It was swollen up to ten times its regular size, rough and muddy, sweeping bushes and sticks along toward the south.

I commenced to climb down, groaning some with each step, and was about to jump from the bottom boulder when a whinny came through the quiet.

It was the sweetest sound I could've heard just then, other than Jesse's voice.

It came from the left, so I snapped my head sideways. The pain in my neck fetched a wince out of me, but I had to smile at the sight of General off in the distance. He was no more than a hundred yards away, nibbling the leaves off a bush.

I got about halfway there before he noticed me, nodded and whickered and came wandering over. He seemed no worse the wear for the last night's near miss. After greeting him with some fond words and pats, I swung my saddle bags across his back and led him over to a rock. Using that to give me some height, I had little difficulty climbing onto him. With my rifle in the crook of one arm, I gripped his mane with my other hand and turned him toward the water.

We followed the shore, me calling out Jesse's name and studying both sides of the river. The sun was starting to heat things up, so steam drifted off the damp ground and the water. The mist wasn't thick enough to hide much. It rather gave me the creeps, though. What with the stillness, the limbs and such rushing by on the dirty river, the dead critters here and there along the banks and the white shroud hanging over it all, I felt like I was riding through a wasteland fit for a nightmare.

The flood seemed to have killed everything it met. I came upon the remains of birds, snakes, gophers, and even a three-legged coyote, all of them washed up along the shore. They had flies buzzing about them. A buzzard was working on the coyote.

Once, a dead burro glided by on the river.

Much as I wanted to find Jesse, I took to dreading the notion. She was bound to be dead, same as all these animals. I didn't care to see her that way. It was my duty to keep on looking, though. Mostly, I hoped I might beat the buzzards to her body.

Soon after the mist burned off, I spotted a pair of white legs sticking up out of a tangle of tree limbs at the other side of the river. The sight made me want to curl up and die.

The tree was still in the water, but jammed tight among some rocks. All I could see of the body was its legs. They were bare, which made me wonder what had become of Jesse's boots and dungarees. Maybe they'd been tugged off by the currents, or maybe she'd had time to pull them off so they wouldn't sink her. One leg pointed straight at the sky. The other hung sideways at the knee.

The look of that broken leg made it all worse, somehow. Bad enough she was dead, but it pained me even more to see how she'd been ruined.

As she was across the river, I figured I was likely to drown trying to reach her. Didn't much care, though. I couldn't ride off and leave her there. If I got drowned, so be it.

I stopped General upstream a ways, dismounted, and shed my clothes. Then I raced into the water. It splashed up, wrapped around my shins, and climbed higher until I couldn't run any more, but only trudge along. It was a mite chilly, though not cold enough to bother me much. The current shoved at me. I was near halfway across and still on my feet when a branch came scooting along. I had to backstep to keep it from hitting me. As it slid by, I grabbed hold and let it tow me downstream till I was just above the caught tree. Then I let it go and got sucked down. I was shoved and tumbled for a bit. When I finally got my feet planted firm on the bottom and stood up, I found myself just below the tree. The water was no higher than my waist.

Leaning into the current, I worked my way back to the snagged tree. Its trunk was half submerged. I hung on to the top side of it and stood in the water, catching my breath and trying not to look at the legs. I could see them out of the corners of my eyes, though, off to the right. Even after I was breathing easy again, I stayed put. I just didn't want to do what had to be done.

Finally, I judged as how waiting wouldn't make it any easier.

So I boosted myself up onto the trunk and crawled along its top, crawled straight for the legs and couldn't help but look at them. They were scratched and bruised. They had an awful bluish-gray color. The leg that dangled sideways from its knee was the closer of the two, and made me wish I could've come from the other side.

The body was stuck in the fork where the trunk branched out. It was caught at the waist, actually. More than just her legs were out of the water. Those parts had been out of sight, hidden by some branches, until I'd climbed onto the trunk. I wished I couldn't see them now, but there was no way around it.

They put me in mind of the time I'd walked in on old Mable about to climb into the bath tub. I was seeing what I shouldn't. Shame got mixed in with all the other miseries I was feeling.

Jesse'd been mighty riled yesterday about the notion that I might've spied on her at the creek. I'd hankered to do just that. Now, here I was. And here she was.

The sight of her private areas made me feel sick and sad and guilty.

The tuft of hair down between her legs was dark, not shiny

gold the way I'd imagined it might be. Her rump was heavier than it had seemed when I'd watched it through the seat of her dungarees. Close up, she didn't look near as good as I'd supposed.

All at once, I caught on to how I was studying her and how I was disappointed she didn't *look* good. If I'd felt lowdown before, now I was no better than a snake.

A sidewinder, that's what Jesse would've called me.

I got to my feet so quick I almost fell on her, but found my balance in the nick of time. Standing with one foot on each side of the fork, I bent over picked up the broken part of her leg. It felt wobbly, the skin tight and cool. Holding that leg by its ankle, I reached out and caught hold of her other ankle.

I brought her legs together and gave them a pull. But she was still wedged in tight. I had to move in closer, stepping out along the branches. I had to hug the legs against my chest and push with my body. It was horrible. I was naked. I couldn't keep my own legs together and still keep my footing, so I had to shove at her with my chest and belly and couldn't help but rub her with my lower parts. I sure did wish I'd kept my trousers on.

I shoved and tugged upward and finally she came unstuck, so quick I wasn't ready for it. All of a sudden, she jumped upward. I yelped and let go of her legs and waved my arms and pranced, but it was no good. I tumbled sideways through a thicket of limbs and plunged head first into the river.

Before the current had a chance to rush me away, I grabbed a chunk of rock on the bottom. That halted me till I could plant my feet.

Just as I started to stand up, something pounded against me and knocked me down again. I knew it might be Jesse, so I flung my arms around it. As soon as I pulled it in against me, I knew it was the body, all right. I had it by the waist, and felt its back against me.

As we got rushed along, I kept heeling the bottom, trying to stop us with my feet. But we kept being towed along backward. I reckoned I might drown if I didn't let go of her so

I could break the surface and find a breath. I just couldn't do it, though. Figured I'd rather drown than lose her.

That's how it might've ended, too, but somehow we got swept toward the shore. Just when my chest felt ready to explode for want of air, my bum slid over some rocks and sunlight heated my face.

I scurried out from under the body, wheezing, blinking to clear the water from my eyes, and grabbed hold of her under the armpits and stumbled backward, dragging her toward the shore.

That's when I saw her breasts. I was hunched over, staring straight down at them. The first thing I thought was that they'd swollen up huge from soaking in the river so long. I also figured the water – or death itself – had leached the color out of them. These looked as if they'd never been darkened by sunshine, whereas Jesse's had been pretty near as dark as her face.

The hair on the head of the corpse didn't seem right, either. Too dark and straight and long.

Still, I figured this had to be Jesse. I was only just troubled by her odd appearance.

I bent lower and looked at the face. I was seeing it upside-down. It was an awful shade of purple and the lips looked almost black. The mouth was drooping open. The eyes were shut, but one lid was rather sunk in, as if it had no eye underneath it.

I studied the face, *knowing* this was Jesse, trying to find something familiar about the hideous visage.

All of a sudden, ice chased up my back.

I cried out, 'Yeeah!'

I dropped her and staggered back a few steps, shocked, appalled. I'd been hauling at a stranger!

Not a stranger, exactly.

But not Jesse.

The German's wife.

The river started to swing her away. I sure didn't want to touch her again. Not this awful dead thing that wasn't Jesse. I wished I'd never handled her at all.

But I'd brought her along this far, and it didn't seem right just to let her go. So I splashed after her and grabbed an arm and commenced to pull her toward shore.

It gave me an awful case of the fantods, touching her. Now that she wasn't Jesse.

When I almost had her ashore, I squealed out another yell. For she wasn't alone.

In her other hand, she held the hand of a boy. The kid who'd been riding along behind her in the buckboard. Her son, more than likely.

She'd had him all along, must've. Even when she was pinned, legs up, in the fork of the tree. He'd been under there, clutched in his mother's dead hand.

It was purely amazing and awful.

I dragged the woman, and she kept her grip on the boy. They both came out of the river and onto the dry rocks.

Neither one of them wore a stitch of clothes. Neither did I, for all of that. But I knew how come I was naked.

I sat nearby, gazing at them, wondering. Trying to figure out what had happened to their clothes, but mostly imagining how their final moments must've been, the mother clinging to the boy's hand as they both got carried to their deaths by the monster wave.

I wondered what had happened to her eye. A stick had likely poked it in. I hoped she was already dead when that happened.

The boy didn't appear to be banged up or maimed, but I didn't get near enough to study him. I wished I'd never seen him or the woman.

I gave some thought to burying them. It seemed the decent thing to do. Pile some rocks atop them, maybe. If I went to do that, though, it'd mean getting in close and seeing more of them. I'd already seen more of these two than I could hardly stand.

Besides, there was no telling where the man might be. He was probably as dead as this pair. I scanned about. There was no sign of him or his wagon or his team. They'd likely been swept far off downriver. But suppose he'd lived through it? He might come wandering along and find me, naked as the day I was born, mucking about with his woman and boy. And me with my guns across the river.

Wasn't worth the risk.

He'd seemed like a mean sort of bloke, and I didn't hardly know these people anyhow. They meant nothing to me, and they weren't likely to notice, one way or another, whether I covered them over or not.

I got to my feet and brushed the grit off my bum.

Then I bent down and took a stone in each hand and walked over and set them down on either side of the woman's head. Much as I wanted shut of these two, I just couldn't leave them sprawled out bare and dead for the vultures that were sure to come.

I roamed about the shore, gathering more stones and hauling them back and setting them down beside the woman. I figured I would start with her, and get to the boy afterwards.

I hadn't been at it more than a few minutes, though, when I happened upon my own beaver hat. The sight of it, resting atop a boulder off in the distance, just about knocked my breath out. I rushed over and picked it up, then searched around for Jesse and called her name.

She didn't answer.

Alive or dead, she was nowhere to be seen.

I put the hat on my head. It hurt me some where she'd clobbered me with the rock the day before, and suddenly I just had to find her. It was foolishness to waste time covering a couple of strangers while Jesse was somewhere, maybe dead and needing a burial, maybe alive and hurt and needing help. Bloody foolishness.

So I ran to the river and waded in.

Chapter Forty-three

I Find Jesse

Though the current was still quite swift, the water never rose much above my waist and I was able to stay on my feet all the way to the other side.

I raced along the shore to where I'd left my duds, got into them quick as I could, strapped on my gunbelt, picked up my rifle and saddle bags, then hurried on over to General, who was having himself a drink, and climbed onto him. It was tough to do, what with a rifle in one hand and him without a saddle, but I flung myself aboard, grabbed his mane and hauled his head around. Then I dug in my heels and we were off at a gallop.

Why the all-fired rush, I'm not quite sure. Somehow, it was on account of finding my hat. It had been on Jesse's head, last time I'd seen her. It made me reckon she might be nearby, though there really wasn't a good reason for believing any such thing. Nearby, and needing me. I had to find her straight away. Every second mattered, or so it seemed to me though I'll be blamed if I know why.

General fairly dashed along the river bank, hooves thundering, mane afly. We hadn't made such speed since the time we were with McSween, the posse giving chase. That time, though, I'd had a saddle under me. Now all I could do was hang onto his mane one-handed and grip his sides with my legs and hope for the best.

What with the rush and the way it all jarred me, I couldn't get much of a look at the shores. It crossed my mind that we might race past Jesse and leave her behind. The notion didn't worry me, though. I simply knew we'd find her, and soon.

And it happened just that way.

The river took a turn to the east, and we no sooner galloped around a bluff near the bend than straight in front of us was a buckboard overturned with its wheels in the air and Jesse sitting on the ground, leaning back against it.

Alive and watching me come.

Golden hair, golden skin agleam in the sunlight.

Wearing her boots and dungarees, and no shirt.

I wanted to let out a whoop, but anger and alarm got mixed in with my joy.

Her legs were tied together at her ankles. Her arms were stretched overhead, roped to the wheel rim.

Nobody else seemed to be about.

I pulled General to a halt, leaped down and rushed for Jesse. 'Where is he?' I asked.

'Went off to hunt for his family.'

'Keep a lookout.' Crouching, I propped the rifle up against the buckboard. Then I reached for the top of Jesse's boot, figuring to use her knife on the ropes.

'He took it off me. Don't reckon I'd be in this fix if I still had my Bowie knife.'

With a glance over my shoulder, I saw that General had wandered off a piece. My knife was in the saddle bags across his back. Not wanting to waste time, I commenced to pluck at the bundle of knots by Jesse's wrists.

'Figured you was drowned,' she said.

'I thought the same of you.'

'Came right close to it. Grabbed ahold of a tree and rode it like a raft.'

'Was it the German who got you?'

'Varmint found me sleeping. He's got himself a Henry. Poked me awake with it. Figured I'd slice him anyhow, so I went for my knife and he jammed the damn muzzle halfway through to my backbone.'

'Bloody swine,' I muttered. The last of the knots came loose. Jesse squirmed her hands out of the coils while I backed away toward her feet.

Smack in the center of her belly, just under her ribcage,

her skin was bruised bright red and purple from the muzzle of the Henry rifle.

She lowered her arms. She rubbed her wrists.

'How long has he been gone?' I asked, and started on the knots between her boots.

'I ain't been keeping track of the time, Trevor.'

'What did he do to you?'

'Brung me here, what do you think?'

'Did he hurt you?'

'Oh, he was just as gentle as a lamb on Easter Sunday. What's the matter with you? Sure he hurt me.'

'He took your shirt?'

'The flood got that off me. If it hadn't, he would've. Put his hands all over me, the dirty snake.'

The last bit of knot was too tight. I couldn't work it loose with my fingers, so I hunched down low and went at it with my teeth. The feel and taste of the rope put me in mind of when I'd chewed Trudy's knots aboard the yacht. I suddenly remembered all that had happened to that poor woman, and how useless I'd been when it came to saving her.

Jesse broke into my thoughts, and I was glad to have them stopped. 'The damn sidewinder was happier than a thirsty tick on the hind end of a hound dog. Should've seen how he pawed at me. Put his damn mouth all over me, too, once he had me tied good. Don't know how come he didn't go on and do the rest of what he wanted. Just stopped and grinned and said, "Vee haff you later, yah? I must Eva and Heinrich find."'

The knot came apart in my teeth. I unhunched and pulled at the rope.

'Then he wandered off downstream,' she said.

'He should've gone upstream,' I said. 'That's where they are.'

'You seen 'em?'

'They're dead.'

'That oughta suit him. I reckon he aimed to shoot his wife, anyhow, if she wasn't drowned. He was looking mighty peculiar and sly when he went off.'

I flung the rope away and stood up. 'We'd best light out before he . . .'

Jesse made a quick grab for the Winchester. Just as she shouldered it, a gunshot blasted the stillness. A section of one spoke on the wagon wheel exploded, throwing splinters into her hair. I was whirling around grabbing iron when she fired.

Her bullet took out the German's knee. He was standing in the open about forty paces south of us, levering a fresh round into his Henry. The slug smacked his trouser leg and drilled through. Blood splashed out. He squealed and lurched backward. When he came down on the hit leg, his knee folded.

That's when my first bullet hit him. It punched his forearm. The stock of his rifle jumped and knocked him in the chin. His head flew back. He flung out his arms. The rifle started to fall. I put a bullet into his stomach. He was still up, but going down fast. Before he hit the ground, I laid three slugs into his chest. He landed flat on his back and jerked about and shuddered. Then a rifle went off behind me. The bullet got him under the jaw. He flinched and went still.

Turning around, I found Jesse was standing, the Winchester at her shoulder as she worked the lever. She sighted in on the German, but only just stood there and didn't fire. By and by, she lowered the rifle. She looked at me. Her green eyes were wild and fierce, and didn't show a bit of the fun that had nearly always been there before. She took a deep breath. When she let it out, I could see her shoulders tremble some.

'Are you all right?' I asked.

She nodded. Then she clamped the rifle stock tight under her arm. It rather flattened the side of her breast and pushed the whole mound outward a bit. The sight stirred me up. I didn't let on, though, and looked away quick.

We walked over to the dead German. We stood above him and gazed at him, not saying anything. I went about reloading. My hands shook.

'You'll need a shirt,' I said.

'You shot his full of holes.' Jesse squatted beside him, set down the rifle, and pulled her Bowie knife out of his belt. She shoved its blade down the side of her boot. Then she commenced to unbutton his shirt. It was drenched and red. 'Reckon I can wash off the blood.'

'You can wear mine, if you like.'

'This one'll do me fine.'

After the buttons were open, I wrestled the body up and slumped it forward over its outstretched legs. I held it that way while Jesse pulled off the shirt. Then I let it down. We went to the shore and Jesse crouched on a rock and scrubbed the shirt.

I watched her.

We'd just killed a man. I'd just spent a good part of the morning with the dead woman and her son.

I'd spent the night figuring Jesse was dead.

But here she was, alive and washing the blood off a shirt.

I felt rather dazed and sick, sore with pains all over my body.

But standing there, watching Jesse, I felt quite wonderful. Her dungarees hung low on her hips. Her moist back glistened in the sunlight. It was smooth and slick, though scratched and bruised here and there. The bumps of her spine pushed out at her skin. Her shoulder blades slid about. Some damp ringlets of hair curled against the nape of her neck. I could see the side of one breast, and watched how it jiggled just a little as she worked. Sometimes, the nipple brushed against her knee.

When she finished, she stood up and shook open the shirt and raised it toward the sky. The worst of the blood was gone. Only some rusty stains remained. 'Good enough,' she said. Turning around to face me, she swept the shirt behind her back and pushed her arms through its sleeves.

'You don't mind wearing a dead man's shirt?' I asked, knowing how it was. I'd spent a lot of time in the clothes of dead men.

'After what he done to me – and what he was *fixing* to do? I *like* it.'

She fastened the buttons. The shirt was far too large for

her. As she went to roll up the sleeves, she looked down to study herself. Her skin showed behind the bullet holes. The nipple of her left breast poked out through one of them. When she saw that, she laughed. 'Shoot,' she said. 'Reckon we better trade off, or you'll wear out your eyes staring at me.'

'That one's quite fetching, actually.'

With a playful smirk, she showed me her fist. 'Give,' she said.

So we both shucked off our shirts and traded. The German's was wet and cool. It felt good on my hot skin, but gave me a squirmy feeling.

I followed Jesse back to the body. She took the dead man's belt. It had cartridges in loops for his Henry and his revolver, but no holster. His Colt was tucked into a front pocket of his trousers that was lined with leather. Jesse cinched the belt around her waist, checked to see that the revolver was loaded, then pushed it down under the belt at her left hip, butt forward for a cross-draw.

'Too bad he don't have no hat,' she said.

'I'll let you wear mine.'

She looked up at it, squinting against the sun. 'Where'd you find that?'

'Oh, it washed ashore.'

As I reached for it, she said, 'No, you keep it on your own head. I already lost it once for you. Anyhow, I've got me an idea.'

She pulled her knife and slit a leg of the German's trousers all the way up the side. She cut it off from around his thigh. Being none too careful, she gashed him once. The blade opened a raw pink furrow in his skin.

She sliced and tore at the cloth, getting it to the proper size, then wrapped it around her head and tucked in the loose end. When she finished, the bundle of checkered cloth atop her head resembled a turban.

Still, she wasn't done with the German. She pulled off his boots, checked inside them, and tossed them aside. Then she went through his pockets. She found a folding knife, a handful of coins, and a leather pouch.

'This is for you,' she said, and tossed the knife to me.

She kept the money.

She opened the pouch. Inside was tobacco, cigarette papers and matches. She grinned up at me. 'Let's have us a smoke.'

She got to her feet. I picked up both the rifles and we wandered over toward the buckboard.

'Are they dry?' I asked.

'He never got his feet wet,' Jesse said. 'Told me as how he was up in the rocks when the flood hit. Carried off everything but him.'

We sat down and leaned back against the wagon. Jesse rolled herself a cigarette. She passed the makings to me, and I did the same. She waited for me to finish before striking a match, and used it to light both our smokes.

She drew in on hers, and sighed. 'What ever come of all that there bad luck you was telling me about, Trevor?' The glint was in her eyes again.

I was sure glad to see it. I felt uncommon fine to be sitting there next to Jesse, having a smoke, nobody about who might cause us harm, the sky cloudless and blue.

But I reckoned there'd be trouble ahead.

'I shouldn't be calling the flood *good* luck. Not this morning's business, either.'

'Whatever befalls you is good luck if you come through it kicking. We come through it right handy, appears to me.'

'We lost everything.'

'Didn't lose General. Nor your saddle bags and guns. Didn't lose each other, either.' She reached over and gave my leg a pat. 'Fact is, we gained us a good Henry rifle and a fair .45, a folding knife, a handful of change, and some fine smokes. A gunshot shirt, too,' she added, and nudged my side with her elbow.

'We lost my water bag,' I told her.

'That don't amount to much.'

'It'll amount to quite a good deal if we try to carry on down the trail.'

'You sure are a worrier, Trevor Bentley.'

'It helps me stay alive.'

'We'll do fine, long as we stay here. I'm too tuckered out for travel, anyhow.'

'I didn't sleep all night, myself.'

'Let's get us some shut-eye.'

'Now?' I nodded toward the body.

'Oh, he ain't likely to cause no trouble.'

'He'll draw scavengers.'

'Then let's get shut of him.'

After finishing our smokes, we went over to the German and dragged him by his heels to the river. We waded out a few paces, then let him go. The current sailed him off.

We washed our hands and returned to the buckboard. We hefted it up on its side. All the cargo was gone, but that came as no surprise.

We gave the wagon a shove. It crashed down on its wheels. One wheel was busted before we started and another gave out when it fell. They were both at the rear, so the wagon had quite a slant. But it was dandy for our purpose. We crawled into the shade underneath it and stretched out.

Me and Jesse, side by side.

We lay there and looked at each other for a spell. She eased an arm over and took hold of my hand.

We were safe. We were together. I figured we had some tough times ahead of us, but everything seemed just fine right then.

I drifted off to sleep.

Chapter Forty-four

Mule

Waking up, I was all hot and groggy and felt like I'd been asleep for a month. Jesse wasn't beside me any more. That worried me and cleared my head. I rolled over and crawled out into the blazing sunlight.

Not only had Jesse gone missing, but so had the Henry rifle.

I figured she might've wandered over to cool off at the river. General was there, taking a drink. But I couldn't see hide nor hair of Jesse.

At the shore, I looked up and down the river.

No Jesse.

Nobody else was in sight, either, which came as a relief. We sure didn't need any more trouble, not after all we'd been through.

More than likely, she'd taken the rifle to do herself some hunting.

I got shed of my hat, gunbelt and boots, but kept my shirt and pants on so they'd get wet and keep me cool for a while afterwards. Besides, I didn't fancy being naked on account of Jesse might come back and see me that way.

Then I waded into the water. It wasn't racing along furious any more, and had shrunk down considerable to where it was only about three times as wide as it had been before the storm. Nothing dead appeared to be drifting my way, so I had a drink. After that, I swam and floated about, enjoying the coolness.

I'd just climbed onto a rock, figuring it was time to go searching for Jesse, when the bray of a mule caught my ears.

It came from downstream.

The mule wasn't in sight yet, but the sound made me think it must be hidden by the outcropping about fifty yards south of me. Fearing there might be more than a mule, I ran for my gunbelt. No sooner was it buckled around my waist than the mule hobbled into view. Behind it walked Jesse, prodding it along with her rifle.

The mule was having a rough time, grunting and braying as it struggled forward on three legs. It kept its left foreleg off the ground. The way the hoof wobbled, I judged the poor mule's leg was broken at the knee.

I got into my boots and hat while Jesse nudged the mule closer along the shore.

'Look what I found us,' she called.

'He won't do us much good, being lame,' I said.

'I don't aim to ride him,' she said. 'This old boy, he'll keep us in meat for a week.'

'You want to *eat* him?'

'Gotta put the thing out of his misery, anyhow. No use letting him go to waste.'

I couldn't come up with any good argument against that.

We stood him close to the water's edge. Then Jesse shot him in the head. I was glad she didn't ask me to do it. I'd plugged my share of men, but they'd all been fixing to kill me or my friends. This mule hadn't done any harm. I felt sorry for it. From the look on Jesse's face when the mule dropped, she wasn't too happy, herself, about shooting it.

After setting the rifle down, she commenced to roll up her sleeves. 'You go on and build us a fire.'

She pulled the Bowie knife out of her boot and knelt down beside the carcass.

I hurried off, glad to get away. Instead of scrounging about for bits of wood, I broke up some of the buckboard. Jesse still had the German's tobacco pouch with the matches. She was up to her elbows in blood, though, so I fetched matches out of my saddle bag. I found Snooker's big knife in there, too, and used it to split some kindling.

I made a neat pile of wood, and fired it up.

The notion of eating mule didn't set well with me. But meat was meat. While I watched the flames rise, I recollected that General Forrest had told me how the Apaches were more inclined to eat horses than ride them. They had an appetite for mules, too. According to him, though, they weren't above eating rats. He sometimes called the Apaches 'gut-eaters'. That didn't speak well for their taste in vittles, but I allowed as how I'd rather eat mule than rat just about anytime at all.

With such thoughts in my head about the Apaches, I suddenly recalled their trick of using horse guts for storing water.

The flood had taken our water pouch.

We couldn't leave the creek behind if we didn't have us a way to carry water. It ran from north to south, so following it wouldn't get us any closer to Tombstone.

We might head upstream, find the trail and wait for strangers. Somebody was sure to come along, by and by. Then we'd need to borrow, buy or steal a container.

It seemed a mighty roundabout and dicey way to handle the problem. Better, by a far sight, to avail ourselves of the mule's innards.

I picked up my knife and went on over to where Jesse was busy carving. She'd already cut us a couple of steaks off the critter's flank, and was slicing long, thin strips off the thigh.

'We'll have us these tonight,' she said, prodding one of the steaks with her knife, 'and jerk the rest.' She nodded, quite pleased with herself. She had a smear of blood across her brow. I reckon she'd rubbed a hand there to deal with an itch.

Not being any too eager to commence my task, I helped her cut some more strips.

When we had quite a passel of them, we carried all the meat on over to the fire. We ripped a plank from the buckboard, cut it into a few long poles, and fashioned them into a rack. With that in place, we draped the strips rather high over the fire to let them smoke.

Back at the creek, we washed up. Jesse didn't seem aware

of the blood on her forehead, so I dampened the front of my shirt and wiped it off.

Looking me in the eyes, she reached up a wet hand and smoothed some stray hair across my brow. Then she curled the hand behind my neck, eased me closer to her, and kissed me on the cheek. My face heated up. I felt myself go all mushy inside.

I had a good notion to take her in my arms and have a go at kissing her mouth, but she stepped away quick and said, 'Reckon we oughta float the mule down the stream before it ripens on us.'

My wits were still rattled. I just gaped at her.

She swung out a hip and tipped her head sideways and studied me. She had a frown on her face, but her eyes gave it away that she was amused, not annoyed. 'What's the matter with *you*?'

'Not a thing, actually.'

'You never been kissed before?'

'Not by you.'

'Well, don't let it spoil your day. Come on, now, let's send the mule off to join the German. Then we'll cook up them steaks and . . .'

'I'd prefer to eat first. We've already washed our hands, after all.'

'Won't take a minute. Then we'll be shut of the thing.'

'I'm afraid there's a rather messy job that needs to be done before we dispose of the mule. It's likely to ruin my appetite.'

'What're you talking about?'

'We can fashion a water bag out of the guts.'

She only just stared at me, scowling.

'I know it's rather appalling, but if we clean the intestine properly . . .'

'Where'd you ever come up with such a notion?'

'The General once told me about it.'

'Your *horse*?'

'No, certainly not. General Matthew Forrest, an old Indian fighter. It was a trick the Apaches used.'

'Sure wish *I'd* thought of it.'

She was just full of surprises. 'You think it's a good idea, then?' I asked.

'It's just bully, that's what I think. You're right, though. We oughta eat before we settle down to meddle with the thing's innards.'

With that, we headed on back to the fire. The strips hanging in the smoke had already darkened some. Their drippings fell into the flames, popped and sizzled. Mule or not, the aroma set my mouth to watering.

I added some wood to the fire. Then we cut a couple of sticks from the side of the buckboard, whittled points on the end of each one, and poked our steaks onto them. Jesse held both the steaks over the flames while I removed the whiskey bottle from my saddle bag.

It was about half full.

I held it up for Jesse, sloshed the whiskey around, and watched her smile.

'This should help the steaks go down a spot better,' I said.

Then I sat on the ground and took over my own share of the cooking. It wasn't long before the slabs of meat were good and rispy on the outside. We swung them away from the flames, waited till they quit smoking, plucked them off their sticks, and commenced to rip into them with our teeth.

If I hadn't known my steak was mule, I would've known anyhow that it sure wasn't beef. It was tough and stringy and had an ornery flavor.

After a couple of mouthfuls, I was mighty appreciative of the whiskey.

I took a swallow and offered the bottle to Jesse.

She used one hand to take the steak away from her mouth. With the other, she wiped the grease and soot off her lips and chin. Looking at the bottle, she chewed real hard for a spell. She rolled her eyes upward, and kept on chewing.

I grinned. 'How's supper?'

'I've eaten worse,' she judged, her voice a bit muffled. After a grimace and a swallow, she took hold of the bottle.

'This is better than rattlesnake?' I asked her.

She had herself a sip, and gave the bottle back to me. 'Didn't say that.'

We both took to laughing. Then we ate more mule and drank more whiskey. The more whiskey I drank, the better the mule tasted. Not that the critter ever did quite reach the stage where it gave me any great pleasure in the eating.

I was glad to swallow the last of it and be done.

'What we should've done,' I allowed, 'was spare the mule and eat the German.'

Jesse laughed so sudden and hard that it sprayed her last mouthful into the fire. I looked on, mighty pleased with myself till she commenced to choke. Then I pounded on her back. She took turns coughing and laughing for a while. When she finally got herself under control, her eyes were teary, her nose running. I fetched the bandanna out of my pocket. It was still moist from my swim in the creek. She used it to clean herself, then stuffed it into a pocket of her dungarees.

'Didn't want it back, did you?'

'Consider it yours,' I told her.

'You dang near killed me.'

'I'm bound to kill you sooner or later,' I said. 'I gave you fair warning yesterday, didn't I?'

When I said that, it took some of the fun out of matters. Not just for me, but for Jesse as well.

She looked at me somber. 'You're a good man, Trevor Bentley. Don't go running yourself down that way. Now let's go and gut ourselves a mule.'

'Let's finish the whiskey first.'

We passed it back and forth a couple of times. When it was empty, I held it up and said, 'I don't suppose this will hold enough water to suffice us on the trail.'

'If you've got a few more like it.'

'Only the one, I'm afraid. Though I did have an opportunity to purchase ten bottles of Glory Elixir a couple of days back.'

'Glory Elixir?' she asked, getting to her feet.

'Good for what ails you.'

Then I told her about my encounter with Dr Lazarus and Ely while we went over and got to work on the mule. She seemed to enjoy the tale, and telling it helped take my mind off our ghastly task.

Not that it was all that ghastly for me.

Jesse took it upon herself to slit open the mule's belly and haul out the guts. Mostly, I stood guard. I wasn't exactly worried that intruders might come along, but keeping watch gave me a reason to avert my eyes from the mess.

The few times I did look, it put me in mind of poor Mary in her Whitchapel digs and poor Trudy the way she'd been the last time I saw her on the yacht. What with all my other troubles, it had been some time since I'd given much thought to Whittle.

I wondered how many more women he'd butchered since those luckless ladies in Tombstone. And where was he now? And how was I to go about tracking him down?

It wouldn't be an easy trick, but I judged there was no advantage to worrying about it. For now, what mattered was to take care of a day at a time and get us safe to Tombstone.

'How much of this do we want?' Jesse asked.

I figured it was time to join in. We cut off two sections of intestine, each about a yard long, and stretched them out along the ground. They looked like a pair of slimy fire hoses.

We mashed them flat to empty them, then laid them across a rock by the creek.

After shucking off our boots and socks and rolling up our trouser legs, we picked up the guts and waded in.

We held them under the surface so water flowed in one end and out the other. Kept them under for a long time. When we judged they were as washed out as they were likely to get, we tied a knot at one end of each and filled them up till they were swollen and heavy. Then we twisted them shut at the other end and lugged them back to the fire. With short pieces of the rope that the German had used to tie Jesse, we bound the twisted ends.

We hefted the bloated tubes onto the buckboard, stepped back, and grinned at each other.

'Looks like we got us traveling water,' Jesse said.

'I'm quite surprised it worked, actually.'

Chapter Forty-five

No Rain, Storms Aplenty

The sun went down while we packed some innards back inside the mule and dragged it to the water. We watched it float off toward the south, then washed ourselves and the knives. We carried our things back to the fire.

We added some more wood and sat there, warming our bare feet.

'It's a shame we drank up all the whiskey,' I said.

'We can have us a smoke.'

So we rolled cigarettes and used a brand from the fire to light them up.

'Hope it don't rain,' Jesse said.

Rain seemed mighty unlikely, so we had us a small laugh about her quip. Then we just sat quiet for a spell, enjoying our smokes. When our feet were dry, we got into our socks and boots. I broke some more wood off the buckboard to keep the fire going. Jesse took the whiskey bottle over to the creek and came back with it full. We passed it back and forth.

I watched as she unwrapped the turban from around her head. She folded it, then rubbed her scalp and fluffed up her hair, which shone all golden in the firelight. 'You never got to tell me about that feller you knifed in the alley,' she said.

Then she pulled the hat off my head. She stuffed her cloth inside, and set my hat aside. 'Let's hear all about it.'

It seemed like days ago that I'd commenced the tale of my adventures, only to get stopped by the downpour. It seemed like years ago that I'd been led by Sue into that East End alley. I spent a few moments collecting my memories, then took up the story where I'd left it off last night.

This time, we didn't have any storm or flashflood. Nothing interrupted. We sat by the fire, sometimes adding wood to it and sometimes having a sip of water, while I talked and talked. I didn't stop with the fight in the alley, but went on and told about taking refuge in Mary's digs, about Whittle and the ocean voyage and my escape from him at Gravesend Bay. I gave Jesse pretty much the same version as what I'd told McSween and the boys around the campfire that time I drank myself into a stupor and fell down. I went easy, though, telling about the murders. I only said Whittle'd cut the women's throats, and didn't let on about the way he'd butchered them.

She asked questions now and again. Mostly, she just listened. About the time I had me and Sarah on the train heading west (of course, I didn't tell her that we'd been more than friends), Jesse stretched herself out along the ground and rested her head on my lap.

'Shall I quit now?' I asked.

'Nope. Just getting comfortable.'

So I plugged on, lying considerable about the trouble with Briggs, but coming back to the truth once he'd pitched me off the train. I told how I'd met up with the gang and got pulled into the robbery, all about 'buying' General and the shootout at Bailey's Corner, how we'd led the posse into a bushwhack, and finally about the attack on our camp.

'Nothing much happened after that,' I finished, 'until you came along and brained me.'

'I sure am sorry about all your friends,' she said. 'That was a mighty hard thing. But you oughta not go blaming yourself. McSween's the feller that took General.'

'Only on account of my needing a horse. If I hadn't chosen to ride with the gang . . .'

'Blame Briggs, then. He's the snake that chucked you off the train. Or put the blame on Whittle. You got no call to be ashamed of anything you done, Trevor. Why, you'd still be home in England and wouldn't none of it have happened except you took on Whittle to save that gal. The one he was fixing to kill on the street there. That's how I see it, leastwise.'

'I see it that way myself, sometimes,' I told her.

'It ain't rightly your fault Whittle killed them folks on the boat. Nor even that you shot up the posse. Those boys aimed to kill you, plain and simple. Wasn't no better than murder, how they rode in and shot up the gang. The wonder's that you lived through such a passel of close shaves.'

'I just wish none of it had happened at all.'

That was sure the wrong thing to tell Jesse.

She opened her mouth, but didn't say anything. She just gazed up at me, her eyes shiny with firelight.

'What?' I asked, a bit slow at seeing my mistake.

She shook her head, then got to her feet and stomped off toward the creek.

I went in the other direction and relieved myself, wondering what had put the burr under Jesse's saddle. She'd turned as chilly as the night air, and it didn't make a lick of sense.

Back at the fire, I looked around and spotted General. I recalled how I'd nearly lost him and Jesse both in the flood on account of hobbling him, so it seemed best to leave him free. He wasn't likely to wander far.

By and by, Jesse came along.

'We oughta break up some more wood and keep our meat smoking,' she said. 'Sides, gonna be a cold night less we keep the fire up.'

So we commenced to rip some more planks off the buckboard and hack them to pieces with our knives.

'It's a shame we lost our blankets,' I said.

'Well, you only lost the dang things cause you was fool

371

enough to leave home. Should've stayed there with your ma.'

'Oh?'

'Yep. You would've gone and missed out on every last one of the nasty mean things that's come your way.'

'Oh,' I said. Now, I was commencing to catch on to the nature of the problem.

'Yep.'

We carried our loads of wood over to the fire and dropped them into a heap.

Jesse wiped her hands on the front of her shirt.

'I don't regret *every*thing,' I said. 'I'm quite glad that I met you.'

'That so? Well, you oughta just keep it in mind when you go to wishing you'd stayed home. How do you reckon I feel, you say such things? And after I gone and kissed you, too.'

When she said that, I stepped right up to her and put my arms around her and pulled her close against me and kissed her on the mouth. I rather expected her to shove me away. She didn't do it, though. Instead, she moaned and squeezed me tight. I couldn't rightly believe my luck. I was actually holding Jesse in my arms, kissing her mouth, and she wasn't fighting me off. It was bully.

But then Sarah came into my head. I took to feeling guilty. She'd given herself to me, heart and body. And here I was, taking up with the first pretty gal who'd come my way.

She's more than just a pretty gal, I told myself. She's Jesse Sue Longley.

I might never see Sarah again, anyhow.

Besides, she seemed like part of my past, part of the life I'd left behind when I took up with the outlaws. She'd never met the train robber, the horse thief, the murderer. The boy she'd known was dead and gone. She'd likely have no use for me.

With Jesse in my arms, I had no more use for Sarah, either.

Best to forget about her.

Jesse pulled back and looked me in the eyes. 'What's troubling you?' she asked.

'Nothing at all.'

'Don't you fib to me. What is it?'

I just shook my head. I tried to hug her again, but she held me off.

'Time we got us some sleep,' she said.

'But Jesse . . .'

She didn't say anything, but pulled the German's pistol out of her belt. Stepping past me, she fetched the folded trouser leg from inside my hat.

'I don't kiss liars,' she said, and lowered herself to the ground by the fire. She set the Colt nearby, then eased herself down on her side and tucked the cloth mat under her head to use as a pillow.

Well, I was feeling too riled to sleep. I sat across the fire from Jesse and stared at her.

'I'll keep watch,' I said.

'You don't need to watch *me*.'

'I'm no liar, Jesse.'

'That so.'

'If you must know, I had to do some thinking about Sarah Forrest.'

'Stead of me.'

'Because of you. I needed to set matters right in my mind. You see . . . we were somewhat more than friends. I lived with Sarah for several months, and after the General and Mable were gone, we . . . we rather took up with each other. That's all.'

'That's all, huh?'

'I'm sorry.'

'Betcha wasn't sorry when you was bedding her.'

'I'm sorry now.'

After a while, Jesse said, 'Where you reckon she's at?'

'She might be anywhere. Maybe she returned to her home in New York.'

'Maybe she's waiting for you at Tombstone.'

'It doesn't matter, actually. I don't want to see her again.'

Jesse was silent for a spell after that. She lay motionless, curled on her side, an arm tucked under the pad beneath her head, her eyes open and staring at me from the other side of the fire.

Finally, she said, 'Don't go and throw her over on account of me.'

'You're not the reason. I made my decision before you ever came along.'

'That so.' She said it calm and snide.

'Bloody hell!'

'No call to curse.'

'You're enough to drive a person daft!'

'It ain't me that had my way with Sarah.'

'And I suppose you're just as innocent as the day you were born? You told me yourself about all the blokes who've had *at* you.'

'Didn't a one of them *get* me.'

'That so,' I tossed back at her.

'Yep. And I aim to keep it that way.'

With that, she shut her eyes. It was just as good as if she'd walked away.

I had half a mind to throw a stick at her. The other half wished I was hugging her. She was just the most infuriating woman that ever crossed my path.

My plan, from the start, had been to get shut of her at the first opportunity.

The sooner the better, I thought. All she does is make me crazy.

But the notion of parting with her made me feel cold and empty inside. I recalled how miserable I'd been after the flood, thinking her dead, and my joy when I found her.

Found her hogtied by the German.

Hadn't been for me, he would've had his way with Jesse for sure. She wouldn't be so high and mighty after that, and hold it against me about Sarah. Maybe I shouldn't have been so quick to rescue her.

Well, thinking such a thing made me feel awful lowdown, so I took it back and judged I was glad I'd saved her in time.

I wanted to stop thinking about her altogether. Sleep ought

to do that. So I added more wood to the fire, then unstrapped my gunbelt and stretched out. The ground felt mighty hard. The fire kept the cold off my front, mostly, but it was no use at all for warming my backside.

Maybe we should've skinned that mule and made us a blanket from its hide.

The mule was long gone, though. No advantage to bothering your head about what you might've done different.

I lay on my side, curled close to the flames, and commenced to ponder all the things I might've done different if only I'd known what was to come.

It all ended up with this – from the time I'd set out for Whitechapel on that night so long ago, any different sort of move that might've saved me or the others from grief would've likely changed the direction of my life so that I never would've turned up where I was when Jesse bounced the rock off my head.

Maybe that would've been for the best, I told myself.

Didn't believe it, though. I judged I'd go through it all again for the chance to join up with Jesse.

I must've fallen asleep, for I woke up. It was still night. Colder than before. So cold I was shivering. What must've stirred me awake was Jesse adding wood to the fire. She was crouched at the other side of it, taking sticks from the pile and feeding them to the flames. She wasn't looking at me. I kept mum and shut my eyes. And pretended to be asleep even when she lay down behind me and snuggled in close and wrapped an arm across my chest.

I was purely astonished by her behavior.

It came into my head that this might not be happening at all. Maybe I was having myself another fantasy, like those last night. Or maybe it was a dream.

Jesse sure felt real, though.

Her warmth seeped through my clothes. Her breasts pushed against my back. I could feel her heartbeat and every breath she took.

By and by, she kissed the nape of my neck.

'Possum,' she whispered.

Rolling over, I hugged her and kissed her mouth.

She didn't let me kiss her much, though. She said, 'Don't get no funny ideas, Trevor. It's just too dang cold over there by my lonesome.'

'I see,' I whispered.

'Don't make me use my Bowie knife.' The warning was no sooner out than her lips covered mine.

She was likely joshing about the knife.

I didn't want to risk riling her, though. We kissed and squirmed some, but I took care to keep my hands from straying anyplace that might offend her.

Later on, she lay still with her face buried against the side of my neck.

She seemed to be asleep.

But then she murmured, 'This ain't working out.'

'What have I done?'

'It ain't you, this time. It's the ground. I just can't find me a way to . . .'

'Here, then.' Holding Jesse against me, I rolled onto my back. 'How's this?'

She didn't answer at first. She lay still, then shifted about some. She gently pushed my knees apart and eased her legs down between mine. Her hands curled over my shoulders. She lowered her face against my cheek.

'Am I squishing you?' she asked.

'Not at all.'

'This is real nice.'

It was and it wasn't. Her hair made my face tickle so I had to scratch now and again. Her chin felt like a rock digging into my collar bone. But those were minor bothers. It was wonderful to feel her stretched out atop me, heavy and warm. A spot *too* wonderful, actually.

Before you know it, a certain part of me commenced to push at Jesse.

It upset me considerable. But Jesse didn't speak up or slap me, so I judged she must be asleep.

I quit stroking her back, squeezed my eyes shut, and tried to make my problem go away.

Jesse moaned a couple of times. She squirmed, which didn't help at all. By and by, though, she lay still and commenced to snore.

I went through a mighty rough spell, what with the way she felt on top of me and knowing she was asleep – and all the temptations that ran through my head. But I kept a tight rein on myself. Somewhere along the way, I fell off to sleep.

Chapter Forty-six

We Carry On

When morning came, I woke to find Jesse sprawled out beside me. She lay on her back, an arm across her eyes to block the sunlight.

I took a quick look about. The fire had died. The mule meat above it had shrunk considerable and dangled from the rack like several lumpy, leather belts. General was standing motionless, head down, a few yards beyond the rear of the buckboard. No sign of any intruders.

Satisfied that all was well, I turned toward Jesse again and crossed my legs and studied her.

She looked peaceful and beautiful, spite of her mouth hanging open.

A warm breeze made her hair stir ever so slightly. It wasn't blowing enough to move her shirt. Her shirt had gotten itself twisted around her somehow. It was drawn tight against her chest. With every breath she took, her breasts seemed to strain at the cloth.

Lower, some of the buttons had come open and her shirt was spread apart, leaving her belly bare all the way down to where her dungarees hung about her hips.

It made me hurt to see the awful bruise. It had a dark ring in the center from the muzzle of the German's rifle. Around the ring was a purple smudge. I was glad we'd killed the varmint.

Below the bruise, Jesse's skin looked smooth and velvety. It was spread over with a golden fuzz too fine to see at all if you didn't look close. You didn't need to look close to see the locks that curled out from under the waist of her dungarees. They gleamed as they swayed in the breeze.

I had an urge to kiss the wound, to caress her, to run my hand over her silken belly, ever so lightly. I wondered if I should be able to feel the fuzz. I rather ached to touch the curls and slip my fingers through them.

But caution won out.

She was bound to pitch a fit if she should wake up to find me pawing her.

Afraid that temptation might overcome prudence in the long run, I stole to my feet, picked up my gunbelt and hurried on down to the creek. I pulled off my boots and waded in.

I spent a while swimming and floating, then sat on a rock to let the sun dry me. I felt just bully.

And better yet when Jesse crept up behind me. Far as I knew, she was still asleep. All of a sudden, she wrapped her arms around me, pressed herself against my back, and kissed my ear.

'Whoever you are,' I said, 'you'd best not let Jesse Sue Longley catch you.'

'Why's that?'

'She's the jealous sort. And quite the scrapper. If she should find you chewing on my ear, she'd likely bash you senseless.'

'Chewing, huh?'

So then she did take to chewing on my ear. It felt mighty

strange. I got all goosebumpy, and squirmed until she quit.

'Ain't mule,' she said. 'But tasty.'

Holding on to my shoulders, she stood up. 'How's the water?'

'A trifle chilly. Rather refreshing, though.'

Jesse stepped around to the front of the rock. She had left her boots behind, the better for sneaking up on me, no doubt.

'Should I leave?'

'No call for that,' she said, and jumped into the creek. She waded out till the water was waist deep, then turned and smiled. 'It's right nice,' she said, sinking down. After ducking her head, she cupped some water to her mouth and drank. 'Don't take a notion to come in,' she warned. 'Just stay where you are and keep an eye out for strangers.'

I checked about. Nobody in sight. When I looked again at Jesse, she had her shirt off. She was crouched low so that the water covered her almost to the shoulders. It was fairly clear, though. Below the surface, everything looked shadowed and wavery.

She mopped herself with the shirt, then draped it over her back and flung the sleeves around her neck so she wouldn't lose it.

'Would you like me to hold that for you?' I asked.

Instead of answering, she sank down, filled her mouth, then came up and squirted at me. The spout fell short. It splashed the rock in front of my crossed legs.

'I say! Don't get me wet! I may have to come in and throttle you.'

'You stay where you are, Trevor Bentley.'

With that, she took off her dungarees. She held them off to the side. The current lifted them, stretched them out, filled their legs.

'Don't lose them, now.'

'If I lose 'em, I'll have to take yours.'

I laughed. But my laughter rather got caught in my throat as Jesse's free hand commenced to rub at her body. I thought it might be best to look away. But Jesse knew I was here, knew

I was watching, and had glanced down often enough to know what could be seen through the water.

Obviously, she didn't object to my watching.

She watched me watch, her eyes all bright with their mischief.

A game of sorts. Perhaps a test. Or maybe nothing of the kind. Perhaps she'd simply grown to trust me, to care for me enough that she no longer felt it necessary to bathe in private.

Below the water, her body was blurred and shimmery. Still, I could see her hand gliding up and down her legs, then delving between them before she went about cleaning behind herself.

All the while, she watched me.

When she finished washing, she stayed crouched down, her chin just touching the water. 'Am I as pretty as your Sarah?' she asked.

Right then, I couldn't pull a picture of Sarah into my head. Didn't need to, though. 'Oh, yes, quite. You're far more beautiful.'

'Figured,' she said, and nodded.

'You're also considerably more conceited.'

'That so.' A grin came up that near-about split her face. 'Too bad. It's me you're stuck with, pardner.' Laughing some, she struggled back into her trousers. Once they were fastened, she stood up and waded toward me, her shirt still drapping her back, its sleeves around her neck like arms ready to choke her.

She gleamed in the sunlight. Water dribbled down her skin. Her breasts bounced and shook ever so slightly. They had goosebumps, and the nipples stuck out proud. Drops of water fell off them as she climbed onto the rock in front of me.

Kneeling there, she smiled with just one side of her mouth. 'Watch you don't wear out your eyes.'

'What do you expect me to do with them?'

'It ain't polite to stare.'

'And is it polite to parade about . . . shirtless?'

'Feels good. If I was a feller, I don't reckon I'd wear one much at all. It's all cause of the dang tits.' She scowled down at them. 'You're lucky you ain't got any.'

This was some of the most peculiar talk I'd ever heard. Not that it surprised me much, as it came from Jesse.

'Gotta keep 'em covered all the time . . .'

'Not that you do so.'

She shook her head and kept frowning at them. 'They're only just *me*. Same as my face or hands. I don't all the time gotta wear a mask and gloves, do I?'

'It's different.'

'That's for durn sure. It beats me why, though. Shouldn't oughta be, do you think?' Before I could come up with an answer, she plugged on. 'They're a plain nuisance. Men always gawping at 'em. Grabbing if they get half a chance. That damn German went and *sucked* on 'em. How come he didn't latch onto my shoulder instead? Or my forehead?'

'I don't exactly know, Jesse. It's that there's something rather splendid about breasts.'

Saying the word set me to blushing fierce.

'Well, it don't make a lick of sense.' She pushed against her breasts, mashing them against her chest. 'How's that?'

Lucky hands, I thought. But kept mum, judging she might not appreciate a remark of that caliber. Besides, I doubt that any comment at all could've squeezed through my throat at that moment. I was flustered and stirred up something awful.

She jerked her hands away and the breasts came springing out. They looked a bit red.

'Sometimes,' she said, 'I've got half a notion to cut 'em clean off.'

Whittle's work slammed through my mind. 'Bloody hell!' I blurted. 'Don't you ever say that!'

She gaped at me, startled. 'Land sakes! What's the matter with you? I was only just joshing.'

'There's nothing at all funny about it!'

'Settle down, settle down.' She took hold of my shoulders, looked me in the eyes. 'What is it? Trevor?'

I shook my head.

'Tell me. We're pardners, right?'

'It's Whittle. He . . . he didn't only cut their throats. The women I told you about. He carved them up terribly. And . . . and he cut off their breasts.'

Jesse's hands tightened on my shoulders. She didn't say anything, but just knelt there in front of me, hanging on. By and by, she leaned closer until her forehead met mine. 'I'm ever so sorry I said such a thing,' she whispered.

'If he should ever get his hands on you . . .'

'He won't.'

'He'd cut yours off. Then you'd get your wish.'

'It ain't my wish. I was only just joshing.'

I lifted my hands to Jesse's breasts. I held them gently, feeling their chilly wetness, their slickness and weight, the press of their nipples. She didn't stop me. Instead, she eased herself lower against my hands. Then she kissed my lips.

'We ain't never gonna kill Whittle,' she finally said, ' 'less we hit the trail.'

Then she kissed me again, leaned back and unwrapped the shirt sleeves from around her neck. Reaching high up behind her, she pushed her arms into the sleeves.

As she fastened the buttons, I realized what she'd just said. '*We* aren't going to kill Whittle,' I told her. 'It's *my* duty, and I won't have you involved in such an enterprise.'

'That so.'

'Quite.'

We got to our feet, climbed down from the rock, and Jesse watched while I strapped on my gunbelt.

'You ain't going nowhere without me,' she said.

'Eager to get yourself butchered, are you?'

'You might just need me, you know.'

'I don't need you dead.'

'Same goes both ways. How you think I'd like it, you went off and got yourself killed? I'll *tell* you how I'd like it – not much. So I'm sticking with you. Better get used to the notion.'

Well, I could see no advantage to arguing. With most

women, you might as well try to argue with a stump. And Jesse was worse than most that way.

'Whatever you say,' I told her.

She gave me a look so I knew she wasn't fooled. But there was more to her look than that. It seemed to say, 'Just you go ahead and *try* going after Whittle without me.'

Back at our campsite we gathered up the strips of jerky. We each chewed on a piece while we wrapped the rest in a rag and tucked it into one of the saddle bags. It didn't taste near as ornery as I figured it might, but chewing so hard made my jaw sore. We washed it down with water from the whiskey bottle.

After that, Jesse cut the traces off the buckboard. She mucked about for quite a long spell, and managed to fashion a bridle for General.

We slipped it over his head, then harnessed the swollen tubes of water onto his back with more straps from the traces. When those were in place, there wasn't room for more than one rider. But we didn't have much choice in the matter, as we needed the water.

We strung the two rifles together with a rope tied around the stock of each, and hung them across General's back.

Finally, I put on my hat and Jesse wrapped the German's trouser leg around her head like before.

She mounted up.

We started off northward alongside the creek, me walking.

I felt rather sorry to leave our camp behind. Never mind we'd killed the German there. It was the place where I'd found Jesse alive, against all odds, where we'd worked together and solved a passel of problems, where we'd quarreled and settled differences, where we'd laughed and kissed and held each other, where we'd become somewhat more than 'pardners'.

It was our place by the creek. Its upside-down buckboard was still in sight when I already took to missing it.

But we couldn't stay there forever.

Whittle was waiting for me.

He would always be waiting for me, giving me no peace, until I'd found him and put him down.

We knew the flood had washed away the trail, so I sat by the creek while Jesse rode in search of it. I felt mighty lonesome and jittery after she was gone. I worried and worried.

By and by, I noticed a tree off beyond the other shore. Its stump was jammed into a familiar nest of rocks. It was the very same tree where I'd found the German's wife and boy, though the water'd gone away and left it on dry land.

The sight of it turned my insides cold. I wished I hadn't recognized it. But there it was.

I turned my eyes away quick before they could search out the bodies that I'd left on the bank downstream. I knew they were there somewhere. Sure didn't want a look at them.

At last, Jesse came riding back.

I was mighty glad to see her.

'Found it!' she called. 'Still a ways off.'

We followed the creek for a while longer.

By and by, we crossed to the other side and caught up to the trail about a hundred yards farther west. That much of it had gotten itself swept out by the flood.

We followed it, taking turns riding General, sometimes both of us walking to give him a rest. When we got hungry, we ate jerky. We satisfied our thirst, and General's, with water from one of the gut tubes. Neither the food nor the drink was much to brag about, but it took care of our needs.

The first day, we didn't meet up with any other travelers. To keep it that way, we made our camp a good distance from the trail. The next day, we met a man from Bisbee who'd come up by way of Tombstone. He caused us no trouble, but told us how to get to Tombstone, and we were glad to hear that our destination was only sixty or seventy miles off.

For the next three days, we made our way in the direction he'd told us. We managed to shoot some game so we had a few meals other than mule jerky, we found enough fresh water to keep our gut bags full, and we encountered more travelers but no trouble.

Jesse didn't shuck off her shirt again, the whole trip. Not in front of me, leastwise. I reckon she kept it on so I wouldn't be reminded of Whittle.

I thought about him plenty, anyhow. The nearer we got to Tombstone, the more he crept into my head. If Jesse'd skinned off her shirt a few times, I likely would've spent a heap less time worrying about him and more time feeling good. But she didn't, and I stayed clear of the topic.

We never did get us a blanket. We managed to keep warm at night, anyhow, snuggling together on the ground. Even though Jesse didn't allow me to take liberties with her, not even to touch her as I'd done by the creek, the nights were quite wonderful.

I got to wishing we wouldn't find Tombstone, at all.

But long about sundown of our third traveling day after meeting the Bisbee man, we looked down from a rise and found a town sprawled in the distance, maybe no more than five miles off.

'I reckon it's Tombstone,' Jesse said. Then she slid off General's back, stretched, and rubbed the seat of her dungarees.

We stood side by side, gazing at the far-off town. There wasn't much to see. A pattern of streets, rows of buildings near the middle and a bunch of other buildings scattered about the area. It was too distant for us to make out any of the people there.

Jesse stopped gazing after a while. She handed the reins to me and wandered over to a rock, where she sat down with her back to the town. She unwrapped her turban. She used it to wipe her sweaty face.

'Well,' she said, 'looks as how we made it.' She gave me a rather grim, one-sided smile. 'What'll we do when we get there?'

I led General closer to her, and found myself a rock. It felt all-fired good to sit down after so much walking. 'We'll have ourselves a splendid meal in a restaurant,' I said.

Her smile brightened some. 'Tired of mule?'

I made a snorty 'Hee-haw,' and she laughed.

'What I'm hankering for's a bath,' she said. 'I could use some fresh duds, too, before I sit down to a meal.'

'I'll buy you a fine dress.'

'Buy a dress, and you can be the one that wears it. Ain't gonna catch me in any such getup.'

'I'd certainly like to see you in one.'

'Ain't about to, so you'd best forget it.'

'You are a woman, you know.'

'None of my doing. I'd a sight rather be a man.'

'I'm quite glad you're not one.'

'Oh, I sure do know that.'

I flustered some when she said that, but I was so hot and sweaty she likely couldn't notice. 'Well, I don't aim to *force* you into wearing a dress.'

'Couldn't if you tried.'

'I suppose you'd take your knife to me.'

I expected a snappy retort, but instead she frowned down at her boots. 'I wouldn't cut you,' she muttered. 'You oughta know that.'

'I know.'

She hung her head and rested her elbows on her legs.

'Are you all right?' I asked.

'Nope.'

'What is it?'

She shook her head.

'Jesse?'

She looked up at me. Her green eyes were awful solemn.

Going all soft and squirmy inside, my throat tightening on me, I hurried over to her. She stood and I took her in my arms. She held onto me tight. 'What's wrong?' I asked. 'What is it?'

'Oh . . . everything.'

'*Every*thing?'

'Can't we . . . stay here? I don't wanta . . .' She shook her head.

I held her and patted her. 'We'll stay here. Maybe not *here*. We'll find ourselves a good spot to camp. We won't go into Tombstone. Not tonight. All right?'

She nodded.

'We don't need to go into Tombstone at all,' I said. 'We'll just ride on by, tomorrow, if that's what you want.'

She kept holding onto me for a spell, then eased herself out of my arms. She put her hands on both sides of my face. She gave my lips a gentle kiss, then gazed into my eyes.

'We'll go in,' she whispered. 'Tomorrow. But I just ain't ready for it yet. Not yet.'

Part Five

The End of the Trail

Chapter Forty-seven

Tombstone Shy

We made our camp in a dry wash on the north side of the rise so we couldn't see Tombstone. Jesse was uncommon quiet, maybe embarrassed by the way she'd backed out of going into town, or maybe it was just that she had too much on her mind in need of sorting out. Whatever, I didn't press her.

We sat by a small campfire, and ate our jerky in silence.

When we finished, we kept on sitting there. I opened my mouth time and time again, figuring to ask her what the trouble was. Each time, though, I thought better of it.

She was on the other side of the fire, and sometimes gave me strange looks through the smoke.

Finally, I said, 'I'm not actually eager, myself, to ride into Tombstone.'

'You're only just saying that.'

'It's the honest truth.'

'What about that-there fine meal in a restaurant?'

'Oh, I should like that. And I daresay you should enjoy having a bath and new clothes.'

'But not a dress.'

'Certainly not.'

'So how come you ain't eager?' she asked.

'I don't quite know, really. It would be different, I suppose. I reckon I've just gotten used to traveling with you. I hate for that to end. There'd be other people about. We wouldn't be alone together. It just wouldn't be at all the same. I like things the way they've been.'

Jesse stared at me for a bit, then got up and came around to my side of the fire. She sat on the ground beside me, leaned against me and put an arm around my back.

'You'd have yourself a real bed,' she said.

'In a hotel. Where the wind wouldn't freeze us up and make you lie with me to keep warm.'

'Maybe I'd lie with you anyhow.'

'Would you do that?'

'Maybe. Long as you behaved.'

'Tombstone might be all right, then.'

Jesse went quiet again, but not for long. 'Maybe you'd rather have Sarah in the bed with you.'

'Jesse!'

'Well? You ain't thought about it, *I* sure have. She might just be in town there, waiting for you. What'll you do, then? Give me the boot?'

'No! Good grief! That's what you've been fretting about, is it?'

'I know you claimed I'm prettier, and all, and how you're done with her, but you might just see things different when you're face to face. Maybe you forgot how pretty she is. Maybe you'll remember, right quick, and remember a few other things, besides, like how it was to be *with* her. You been *with* her, Trevor. You ain't never been with *me*.'

I looked at Jesse.

'Don't you get no funny ideas, buster!'

'You're the one who brought it up, actually.'

'Well, put it right outa your head. I'm gonna stay pure for the man that marries me, or die trying.'

'Perhaps I'm that man,' I said, my heart all of a sudden bashing fit to explode.

'And perhaps not. Just perhaps you'll run into your fancy Sarah tomorrow and that'll be it for Jesse Sue Longley.'

'That won't happen,' I said.

'I reckon we'll find out, soon enough.'

'She's nowhere *near* Tombstone.'

'It's where you were heading with her.'

'That was before I got pitched off the train. For all she knows, I might be dead. You're daft if you think she made the rest of the trip and she's waiting around in town for me to pop in.'

'That's where I'd be,' Jesse said.

I pondered on that for a while, and judged Jesse was right. She *would* go on, hoping I'd finally make my way to Tombstone. *She* would. Jesse. But I had strong doubts about Sarah. Mostly because of how Sarah had taken on with Briggs.

'I'll be mighty surprised if she's there,' I said.

'Like I said, we'll find out tomorrow.'

'Even if she is, there's no call for you to fret.'

'So you say.'

'If it worries you so, why don't we put the town to our backs and head elsewhere?'

'How we gonna track down Whittle if we don't go in and ask around? It's where we gotta go if we're gonna pick up on his trail.'

'I doubt he *has* any trail to pick up, actually. It must be two months since he murdered those Clemons women. He likely dodged off long ago.'

'He didn't bolt straight outa London.'

Indeed, he'd continued his grisly work in the East End for more than two months, and might've kept at it longer if I hadn't mucked him up. 'That was quite a different situation,' I pointed out. 'London's a great metropolis with vast crowds of people and hundreds of streets and alleys. A bloke might duck around a corner and disappear forever. *Whittle* might've gone on forever there. But not in a town like Tombstone. Why, he was lucky he didn't get himself caught. Especially being a stranger there, and without a nose. I doubt he stayed in town long enough to see the sunrise.'

'Maybe,' Jesse said. 'Maybe not. He'd have no call to run off if nobody saw him kill them gals. He might just be in town this very minute.'

'*That's* why you wanted to stay out!' I blurted, having her on a bit.

'That ain't why, and you know it.'

'You've got Whittle and Sarah both down there, just itching to have a go at me!'

'Whittle don't worry me none.'

'Well, he ought to.'

'I hope he is down there in town. We can have us a race to see who's first to pump him full of lead. With any luck at all, maybe we'll catch your Sarah in the crossfire.'

That last was an ornery thing to say, but it plucked a laugh out of me. I locked my arm around Jesse's head and clamped it tight and gave her a few gentle punches in the belly. Then she slipped her head free, flung herself against me and bowled me over sideways. I didn't struggle much except to swing my boots clear of the fire. While I concerned myself with that, she got me onto my back and straddled me. With her knees, she pinned my arms to the ground. I was still laughing, spite of her weight on my chest.

'I always knew I could take you,' Jesse gasped.

'You've got me.'

'Yup.' She gave a bounce that made the air grunt out of me. 'Gotcha right where I want you.'

'Delighted to be here,' I said.

At that, she backhanded my face. Not so much a slap as a pat. 'Don't get crude, Trevor.'

'I meant nothing crude. Not at all.'

She fetched my face another whap, a bit harder than the last. 'Did too.'

'You're the one that's put me between your legs!'

'Ah-ha!' She whacked me again.

So I kicked up my legs, swinging them up till I hooked her shoulders with my boots, and flung her backward. She let out a whuff when she slammed the ground. I scurried up right quick, knocked her knees out of my way, and dropped down flat atop her. She squirmed under me, laughing fit to bust.

Instead of pinning her arms, I used my hands to dig into her sides. She fairly squealed. She bucked and thrashed and grabbed at my hands, trying to hold them off.

'Quit!' she blurted between her squeals. 'You quit!'

'Gotcha right where I want you!'

'I mean it! Quit, now! 'Fore I bust a seam!'

'Have at it.'

'Trevor! I'm gonna wet!'

So I quit. Jesse spent a while giggling and gasping underneath me, but she finally settled down.

By and by, she said, 'It's downright mean, tickling a body.'

'Meaner than slapping?'

'I didn't hurt you.'

'I didn't hurt you, either.'

'You dang near split my gut.'

'Shall we call it even, then?'

'Give me a kiss.'

Well, that suited me. So I lowered my mouth to hers, fixing to kiss her real sweet, and she gave my lip a nip.

'Ow! Bloody hell!'

'Now, we're even.'

'Bloody hell! You *bit* me!'

'Ain't the first time.'

I licked my lower lip and tasted blood. 'You made me bleed!'

Smiling, she nodded. 'Don't fret about it none. I ain't got the rabies. Not as I know about, leastwise. Did I ever tell you about that feller down El Paso way that . . .?'

'You told me.'

'Let me kiss your hurt and make it better.'

'And give you another go at chewing on me?'

'I *said* we're even. Don't you trust me?'

'You've got some mighty peculiar ways about you, Jesse.'

'That may be. But we're pardners, ain't we? You can't trust your pardner, who *can* you trust.'

'Do you promise not to bite?'

'Word of honor.'

So I eased my face down toward hers, not quite knowing what to expect. What she did, she slipped out her tongue and licked the blood off my lip. Then she raised her head off the ground and kissed me, just as soft and gentle as you please.

Pretty soon after that, I rolled off her. We lay on our sides, holding each other.

I felt ever so peaceful and contented. But it didn't last. Before long, I took to feeling all hollow and achy inside. This was to be our last night on the trail. Tomorrow, we'd be riding into Tombstone. No matter what else might happen, it would mean the end of our times together in the wilderness. Our times alone, just her and me.

It would all be over.

Things would be different, starting tomorrow, and I didn't want that at all.

I might never again find myself stretched out on the ground by a campfire, holding Jesse in my arms.

It gave me the fantods, thinking about such things.

And it didn't make a lick of sense, really. We'd still be together in Tombstone. But I couldn't shake it out of my head that our fine times together were just about over.

I squeezed Jesse tighter, and she did the same to me.

'It'll be all right,' I whispered.

'Glad you think so.'

'Still fretting about Sarah?'

'It ain't only just her.'

'Whittle?'

'I just don't want to lose you,' she said. 'I've got me some bad feelings about tomorrow.'

'We don't need to go in straight away,' I said, and suddenly felt like whooping with joy. '*We won't go in at all!* We'll head on somewhere else. Perhaps we'll have a go at Tucson.'

Jesse's fingers curled into my back. 'I don't know,' she murmured, but I could tell she liked the notion. 'What about Sarah? What about Whittle?'

'They aren't likely there, anyhow.' Even as I said that, I realized I didn't quite believe it. I was lying to myself, lying to Jesse. They *might* be in Tombstone. And I realized then that Sarah and Whittle were the two reasons I wanted no truck with that town. The *only* reasons, when it came smack to the truth. 'I want nothing to do with either of them,' I said. 'I want nothing to do with anyone except you, actually.'

'Oh, Trevor,' she murmured, and brushed her cheek against mine. 'You can't just let on they don't exist. I can't either. We've gotta face 'em. Might as well be tomorrow, if that's what's meant to be.'

'If it's meant to be, then there's no call to go rushing after them.'

'It don't seem right.'

'Do you *want* to go into Tombstone tomorrow?'

I felt her head shake.

'It's settled, then.'

Jesse didn't say anything for a while after that, and I thought she might be asleep. But then she raised her face off me and brushed her lips against my mouth and whispered, 'I sure do love you, Trevor Wellington Bentley.'

'Not as much as I love you, Jesse Sue Longley.'

'That so?'

'That's so.'

'Well, at least you didn't sell me to the German.'

Then she kissed me again and pretty soon I rolled so she was stretched out on top of me, the way we'd taken to sleeping every night since the flood. We lay still, not saying anything more. All my bad feelings had gone away, dragged off by my decision to stay shut of Tombstone. I heard the fire crackling and popping, heard a coyote howl off in the distance, heard Jesse's breathing close to my ear. Before you know it, I was asleep.

In the morning, we had us one more discussion about Tombstone. Jesse wondered if we ought to go on in just long enough to outfit ourselves with another horse, some equipment and supplies. I allowed as how such things would make our trip a sight easier. We'd only need to spend an hour or two in town, then we could be on the trail again.

We agreed to do it.

Jesse mounted on General, me walking, we made our way

around the rise and headed for Tombstone. Going straight toward where we'd decided to avoid.

Even though neither of us wanted to go there.

We'll only be in town for a bit, I told myself. Even if Sarah *is* there, seemed likely we wouldn't run into her. And Whittle, he'd probably hightailed the night he killed the Clemons women.

In my head, though, it worked out otherwise.

In my head, we no sooner started down the main street of town than Sarah popped out of a doorway and her eyes lit on me. All surprised and joyful, she called out my name and ran to me and threw her arms around me. Wept and lavished kisses on my face as Jesse looked on. So then I had to shove her off me and say something like, 'Stop it, Sarah. Please. I'm afraid another woman has . . .' Just what *would* I say? If she was there, it meant she hadn't given up on me. It meant she still wanted me for herself. Whatever I might say or do, short of giving up Jesse (not a chance of that), was bound to give her loads of pain. I wanted no part of such a scene.

Nor did I want a showdown with Whittle. Not in the streets of Tombstone, not with Jesse nearby where he might get ahold of her. Much as I told myself he was long gone, I knew there was a chance he might be there. Maybe he'd found himself a job, or maybe he was living high and mighty off the loot he'd stolen from the *True D. Light*.

My common sense told me he wouldn't be there. For that matter, he might not even have been the bloke who murdered the Clemons women. Sarah wouldn't be there either.

That's what my common sense said.

But my stomach told me different.

We were on the trail leading into Tombstone for near a mile when I finally said, 'Hold up, there, Jesse.'

She halted General and turned her head toward me.

'This isn't at all where I want to go,' I said.

'I ain't looking forward to it much, myself.'

'So then, why are we doing it?'

She shrugged her shoulders. Then her face lit up with a big smile. 'How many days to Tucson, you reckon?'

'Long as it takes.'

She turned General around.

We put our backs to Tombstone.

I quickened my pace to catch up, and felt like I was leaving all the grief of the world behind me. I felt so chipper that I actually ran for a while, and left Jesse behind until she put her boots to General and trotted up beside me.

'Don't go and wear yourself out,' she said.

'It's a grand morning! Smashing!'

It sure is peculiar how things work out. If we'd gone on into Tombstone that day, we would've missed Barney Dire. We might've avoided Whittle altogether.

Instead, by turning away from town, we started down a path that would lead us straight into Whittle's lair.

Chapter Forty-eight

Apache Sam

'Hello the fire!' came the voice out of the darkness.

I'd shot us a jackrabbit that afternoon, so we hadn't needed to gnaw on mule jerky for our supper. We'd just finished eating it when the man called out.

It startled us both considerable.

I snatched out my Colt. Jesse put a hand on my knee to settle me down.

'Tell him to come on in,' she whispered.

'Step along into the light where we can see you,' I called. 'Don't let me see any iron in your hands.'

'If you're fixing to plug me, I'll just go on my way and leave you be. I ain't looking for no trouble.'

Jesse called, 'You're welcome to come in and set.'

'Thank you kindly, miss.'

With that, Barney Dire led his horse into the glow of the firelight. He held his reins in one hand. He held the other hand up, open to show it was empty. That one was short two fingers, the ring finger and pinkie.

'I seen your light,' he said. 'Hope you don't mind me joining you.'

'Long as you behave,' Jesse told him.

'I most generally do,' he said. 'I ain't the violent sort, Lord knows – though I run up against it now and again, much as I hate such doings.' He tied his reins to a tall cactus over near General, then sauntered closer.

Though he had a voice that made him sound like quite a large fellow, he was so pint-sized that he appeared half-lost inside his duds. Everything he wore looked too big for him. The brim of his hat was as wide as his shoulders. The bandanna hanging around his neck looked the size of a tablecloth. His vest hung down so low it draped the butt of his sixgun. His chaps flapped about his legs like a couple of sails.

Even his thick, dark mustache looked like it belonged on the face of a man twice his size.

He was all creaking leather and jingling spurs as he stepped to the other side of the fire and sat down.

With a sigh, he said, 'Much obliged. Name's Dire. Barney Dire.' He touched the brim of his hat.

'I'm Trevor,' I said. 'This is Jesse.'

'Pleased to make your acquaintance, folks.'

He had a rather calm, friendly manner about him. His eyes, shiny in the firelight, had a bit of humor or mischief that put me in mind of Jesse. Though it seemed smart to remain cautious, I went on ahead and holstered my Colt.

'I'm afraid we haven't any food to offer you,' I said. 'We just now finished eating all we had.'

'Less you've got a hankering for some mule jerky,' Jesse told him.

Barney laughed and shook his head. 'Nope, reckon I'll pass on the offer. Much obliged, anyhow. Just figured to set awhile and jaw with you folks. My old horse, Joey, ain't much for conversation.'

'It can get lonely, traveling alone,' I said.

'Well, there's worse things than lonely. I'd a sight rather run on my own than get saddled with a sourpuss. Or with a gal, if you'll beg my pardon, Miss Jesse.'

I gave Jesse a glance, and saw she was smiling. 'What's your problem with gals?' she asked.

'Why, they're generally a sorry lot. All the time bossing and whining. Not as I'm saying *you're* any such nuisance.' He tipped a wink at me.

'Jesse's quite all right, actually,' I said.

She laughed.

'First thing you know, they're after you to settle down. Don't want you having no fun, seems as how they look at things. Why, they raise a fit if you have yourself a drink or a chaw, and they treat your friends ornery. If they could, I reckon they'd lock you up and never let you out, 'cept when it suited them, and that'd only just be to work chores.'

'I say,' said I, 'you do have a rather low opinion of them.'

'Been married to two of the critters. They was both fine gals till we got us hitched. First thing you know, they up and changed on me. Seems like they was both of 'em cut out to be penitentiary guards.'

Jesse laughed.

'Not as I'm saying *you're* any such,' Barney told her.

'Thanks kindly.'

'You gonna hitch up with Trevor here?' he asked.

'Why, I don't reckon he's likely to ask, now that you've filled his ear with such manure.'

That got Barney to chuckling softly. 'Well, you're both mighty young yet. Not more than children by much. There ain't no call to rush into such a tricky game as marriage.

401

How'd you two throw in together, if you don't mind me asking?'

'Jesse had a go at stealing my horse.'

She blurted, 'Tell the whole world, why don't you!'

'Well, you didn't get it, did you?'

'Only just because I took it easy on you.'

'I got the drop on you!'

'I kept my knife to myself.'

'Settle down, folks,' Barney said. 'Lord alive, I didn't aim to start up a war between you. We don't want no bloodshed here.'

'He started it,' Jesse said.

'I did not.'

'Did too.'

'This is what comes,' Barney broke in, 'of poking my nose into matters that don't concern me. I'm right sorry I asked. Somebody oughta cut it off for me so's I'll stop sticking it where it don't belong. Already missing enough parts, though.' He held up his hand to show us which parts he meant. 'Got 'em shot clean off in Phoenix back in eighty-four. Minding my own business, too. Just having myself a beer when a couple of hotheads down the other end of the bar took to throwing lead and a stray slug found me. Took off both my fingers clean as a whistle.'

'I had it figured,' Jesse said, 'that one of your wives took a knife to you.'

'Ain't how it happened. Not that you're far off the track, though. My first wife, she took after me with a knife every time I came home with a snootful. Got me some scars to show for it, but she never got off a piece of me. Not for lack of trying. I'm small, but quick.' He held what was left of his hand close to the fire and studied it. 'Nope, it wasn't Aggie carried off my fingers. Just a dang bullet.'

'Does it cause you much trouble, being without them?' I asked.

'Oh, I get by. They don't amount to much. Knew a feller got his thumb shot off. Caused him a *sight* of bother, as he was in the midst of gunplay when it happened. Couldn't cock his sixgun, what with his thumb on the ground. He went to drag back the hammer with his teeth, but never got to finish. The same rascal that shot his thumb off plugged him full of holes while he still had the hammer in his chops.' Barney wiggled his own thumb. 'You're better off losing just about any old part than your thumb. I'd a sight rather lose a couple fingers. Comes right down to it, a feller can get by minus an ear or an eye better than a thumb.'

'I bit off a feller's ear, once,' Jesse said.

I looked at her, surprised.

'Well, I did.'

'You never told me.'

'There's a heap I've never told you.' Leaning forward, elbows on knees, she grinned across at Barney. 'It was a sidewinder name of Hank Dappy.' That name sounded vaguely familiar. I judged it might be one of those she'd reeled off the time she was telling me about all the rascals who'd had a go at her. 'He jumped me – fixing to have some high times on account of me being a girl, you know. Well, I bit his ear clean off. You should've just seen him, how he cried and carried on. Well, he chased after me. Went raving as how he'd take his ear back and stick it up my you-know-what.'

I didn't know what, exactly, but didn't speak out.

'I allowed as how that was likely to pain me some, so I didn't aim to let him get his ear back. He was just about to catch me, so I turned around and plonked that stinky old ear of his into my mouth and ate it whole.'

'Jesse!' I blurted.

'Well, I did.'

Barney gazed across the fire at her. He looked purely astonished. 'Ain't you the spitfire!' he said. 'My Lord!'

'And did you swallow it?' I asked.

'Why, sure. Dappy, he was so flummoxed he stopped dead in his tracks. Reckon he figured I was a crazy woman, so he took to his heels and that was the last I ever seen of his mangy hide.'

Barney, grinning under his mammoth mustache, shook a finger in my direction. 'You'd best watch yourself with this one, young feller. She'll be having pieces of you.'

Not to be outdone, I spoke up and said, 'I once cut off a bloke's nose, myself.'

'Why, you pair of rascals are *meant* for each other. Did you gobble it up?'

I shook my head.

'She's got you beat, then. Won by a nose.'

We all spent some time laughing over that. Barney rocked back and forth some, holding his knees. After we'd settled down, he said, 'Now how came you to cut off the nose of this feller?'

'He was trying to kill me, actually. And I him. I was rather hoping to give him a fatal wound, you see, but his nose intercepted my knife.'

'Took it clean off, did you?'

'Indeed. It fell to the street.'

'Should've eaten it,' Jesse said, and gave my ribs a knock with her elbow.

'I was rather too busy trying to save my skin.'

'I once saw me an Apache squaw that'd lost her nose,' Barney said. 'Sure didn't help her looks none. Which is why they done it to her. Any time as you see yourself a squaw that's had her nose sliced off, you know she got herself caught fooling with a feller that weren't her husband. Lets everybody see what brand of woman she is. It's plain as the nose off her face.' Barney chuckled softly and shook his head.

'It seems a trifle extreme,' I said.

'That's Apaches for you. They're the downright extremest sons a bitches that ever walked the dirt. And they ain't particular who they butcher. I've seen such things as give me the night sweats.'

'Sure glad we ain't gotta worry about 'em,' Jesse said.

'Who ever told you that?' Barney asked.

'Why, they're all either killed off or cooped up on reservations.'

'I understand that Geronimo and his band are prisoners in Florida,' I put in.

'That don't mean there ain't renegades skulking about. One's been raiding these parts fairly regular. They figure it's Apache Sam, a Chiricahua that run off from the San Carlos reservation a while back. He's killed a heap of white folks, past couple of months. Creeps up on 'em in the night, murders whatever feller might be about and carries off the women. Does such manner of butchery on the women as would curl your hair.'

When I heard that, my heart commenced to pound like thunder. 'Are they quite sure it's an Apache?' I asked.

'Ain't no white man with the stomach for such doings.'

'He's been seen, though?'

'Not by any folks as lived to tell the tale. They found his hideout, though. Got himself a cave no more than a day's ride from here. Heard all about it from a feller this morning. Seems a week ago, maybe longer, a prospector tumbled onto the cave. Had himself a stroll inside, and what he found was dead women. Eight or ten of 'em, all carved to pieces and moldering. Some was fresher than others, and one appeared as how she'd only got killed just the day before. That prospector, he figured it had to be the work of Apache Sam. So he made tracks to Tucson. They got up a posse, and he showed 'em back to that-there cave. The feller I met, he'd been with the posse. Went in that cave with the rest, and what he saw near unhinged his mind. He couldn't take no more, and lit out. When I seen him, he was still a mite green.'

'And it was just this morning that you spoke with him?' I asked.

'A shade before noon, I reckon.'

'And when did he leave the posse behind?'

'Oh, not long after sunup. The way he told it, the posse got to the cave after dark last night. Didn't go in, though. Figured to keep an eye on it and wait till morning. See, they had no idea if the redskin was in there. Hoped he might show up so they could take a crack at him, and save themselves the bother of searching for him in the cave. Well, he didn't do them the favor. So they went sneaking in at first light. The feller I met, he took one look at them gals and vamoosed. He allowed as how they was the worst sight that ever met his eyes, and the stink would've choked a maggot.'

'And did they find the Indian?' I asked.

'If he was there, he was keeping outa sight. What I hear, though, it's a ripsnorter of a cave. The kind of place where a body might lose himself forever, pretty near. Now I just don't know if they aim to have a try at hunting him out.'

'Do you suppose the posse's still there?'

'Wouldn't surprise me none. I was them, I wouldn't go and waste my time. They won't never find him if he's in there. Injuns are that way, you know. Slippery boogers. If he's got a mind to, he could likely pick 'em off one at a time, they go hunting him in a cave. Best thing'd be to hide around outside and see if he don't put in an appearance, sooner or later. That's how I'd work it. But then, I ain't the reckless sort. You put a bunch of fellers together like in a posse, they can get mighty brave. Start to figuring it's the other guy'll catch what-for, not their own selves. Sides, don't none of them wanta look yeller front of their pals. So they'll do the dangdest things. I reckon they'll hunt all over that cave till they either run short of supplies or get themselves whittled down to nothing.'

'You say the cave's only one day's ride from here?'

It wasn't me who asked that. It was Jesse.

I looked at her. She looked me back, and one of her eyebrows gave a little upward jump.

'A mite close for comfort, huh?' Barney said.

'Sure is,' she told him. 'Whereabouts is it, so we'll know to keep clear?'

'Up on the north slope of Dogtooth Mountain. That's what the feller told me. Where you folks heading off to?'

'Tucson,' I said.

'Well, I'll give you a steer so you stay clear of Dogtooth, then. Up yonder about a mile, you'll hit a fork in the trail.

Either way you go at the fork, you'll get to Tucson by and by. You wanta take the branch that veers off to your right, though. Stick to that one, and you'll miss Dogtooth by more'n ten miles. Take the other – that's the one I rode in on – and it'll lead you through a pass at the very foot of that-there mountain.'

'So we go right at the fork,' Jesse said, nodding.

'That'd be the safe way. Not as you can count on a few miles of distance to keep you safe from that Apache. Ain't no saying where he might be. That cave's only just a place he's been at from time to time. And fairly recent. You ask me, though, he don't live there. Don't live nowhere particular. Just stays on the move. He could be a hundred miles off, right now. Or he might be near enough to hear us talk.'

'I sure hope not,' Jesse said.

'Well, I reckon he'd best watch himself, he's creeping up on us. You'd likely bite his ear off.' Barney laughed.

'I've had my fill of ears,' Jesse told him, and he laughed harder.

After that, we stayed by the fire and talked about this and that for a spell. There was no more talk, though, of such matters as Apache Sam or the posse or cave. By and by, Barney asked if we'd mind him keeping us company till morning. 'Safer all around,' he said.

'You're welcome to stay,' Jesse told him. 'Long as you behave.'

I had no objections, either. He seemed a fine, trustworthy chap. Besides, my mind was too troubled by what we'd heard about Apache Sam to be bothered by Barney's presence.

He spread his bedroll on the other side of the fire. Jesse and I stretched out beside each other. What with him right there, neither of us was eager to snuggle up in our usual manner.

'You ain't got yourselves no blankets?' he asked.

'We lost them in a flood some time ago,' I explained.

'Well, you're welcome to make use of my saddle blanket if you can stand the aroma.'

So he fetched it. We thanked him and spread it over us.

Still, we didn't snuggle up. Not for a while. When we heard Barney snoring, though, we rolled toward each other and hugged.

'You reckon it's him?' Jesse whispered.

'Who?'

'Who you *think*? Whittle. You reckon he's Apache Sam?'

'It shouldn't surprise me at all, actually.'

'Same here. You wanta be in on it, don't you?'

'If he's there, I reckon the posse'll get him.'

'Not if they're looking for a redskin. We gotta go on up to Dogtooth and set 'em right. If we don't and he gets clear, it'll be our own faults.'

'I suppose that's so,' I whispered. Then I yawned and shut my eyes. 'We'll see about it in the morning,' I murmured.

Chapter Forty-nine

Off to Dogtooth

Much as I wanted to join up with the posse and be in on the kill (if Whittle was holed up in the cave), I sure didn't want Jesse to be anywhere near that place.

She would wind up carved and dead, I was just sure of it.

Yet no amount of talking was likely to persuade her against heading for Dogtooth Mountain, come daybreak.

While I laid there beside her under Barney's blanket, feigning sleep and working my head over the matter, I hit upon a plan.

What I'd do is keep still for a while. Wait for Jesse to be

408

fast asleep. Then I'd sneak away, walk General off a distance, mount up and race off. Jesse wouldn't catch on till morning that I'd lit out. By then, I'd already be at the mountain or pretty near it.

A dirty trick to run off on her that way, but it'd keep her out of Whittle's range.

What might she do, however, once she figured out that I'd dodged off without her? She'd be spitting mad, of course. But would she take off after me on foot? Or would she talk Barney into giving her a ride? They might both come after me. I'd have a great headstart on them, but they might show up at the cave too soon, anyhow. Of course, Barney might want no part of pursuing me. If that happened, would Jesse have a go at stealing his horse? Just no telling what she might do.

It crossed my mind that I could take Barney's horse, Joey, along with me. Or just chase it off. That'd be too lowdown, though, and likely to start a whole new passel of troubles.

I would leave Barney's horse right where it was.

I no sooner settled that in my head than I took to worrying about Barney himself. How did I know that he could be trusted? With me gone, he might decide to have himself a good time with Jesse. She would likely kill or maim him if he tried such a thing, but what if he took her by surprise? She was tough, but not invincible. The German had proven that.

Well, I finally came to the conclusion that leaving Jesse behind wouldn't be a clever move.

We'll just steer clear of Dogtooth Mountain tomorrow, I decided. No matter how Jesse argues, I'll stand firm. That posse can have its go at Whittle without us.

Might not be Whittle anyhow.

Now that I'd decided the proper way to handle the matter, my mind eased off and let me relax. By and by, I fell asleep.

I woke at sunup and Jesse was gone.

At first, I figured she'd wandered off to scare up some firewood or maybe answer a call of nature.

Sitting up, I had a look at Barney. He was still busy snoring.

A horse gave a snort, and I swung my eyes over to where we'd left Joey and General tied to some cactus.

Joey was still there.

Alone.

Well, I jumped to my feet, all of a sudden scared. Looking about, I saw my Remington propped against the rock where it belonged. The Henry rifle wasn't there. And one of the water tubes had gone missing too. I scanned off into the distance, all around, but didn't spot Jesse or General.

I called out anyhow.

My yell startled Barney awake. He bolted up, gun in hand. 'What the tar!'

'Jesse lit out for the cave! Blast her!'

He scrunched his leathery face, looking as puzzled as if I'd spoken in a foreign tongue.

'She took my horse and snuck off in the night.'

'What's that you said about the cave?'

'It's where she's going! Bloody . . .!'

'Why in the notion'd she wanta go *there*?'

'Because she figured I'd keep her away from it.'

Still scowling, Barney used the muzzle of his Colt to scratch himself above the ear. 'What's she want at the cave?'

'It's just her way of making sure I wouldn't go there without her. Or not go there at all.'

'You gone and left me behind, Trevor.'

'I need to borrow your horse.'

'No you don't.' He spoke calmly. He eased the muzzle away from his head and pointed it in my direction.

'I'll pay you for him. I've got quite a good deal of money.'

'Ain't got much use for your money. But I got a heapa use for Joey.'

'It's your fault, you know. All your talk of Apache Sam. Why, you even told her where to go!'

Barney still looked mighty perplexed. But he looked wary, too, and kept his revolver ready in case I should have a go at him or Joey. 'You trying to say she's rode off to join the hunt for that danged Apache?'

'Exactly!'

'What is she, touched?'

'We've got to stop her.'

Barney shook his head. Then he stood up, jammed the huge hat down atop his head, and holstered his sixgun. 'This is what comes,' he said, 'of taking up with women. If it ain't one brand of trouble, it's another.'

I rode along behind Barney and his bedroll, sitting astride his saddle bags and other gear. I carried my own saddle bags across my thighs. The Winchester was slung across my back by a rope. Barney kept his horse at a trot that bounced me about considerable.

'I sure am obliged to you,' I said after a spell.

'Don't go and thank me till I've gotten you to Jesse.'

'I'll be most happy to pay you for your troubles.'

'No call to part with your money.'

'I'd like to do *something* for you.'

'Well, now. I'm a feller that enjoys a good story. Suppose you tell me why she's so all-fired eager to go chasing after Apache Sam?'

'It's not Apache Sam she's after. When you told us last night about the bodies being found in the cave, we both realized the culprit was likely not this Apache at all, but Jack the Ripper. I came out west intending to hunt him down and kill him. He's the bloke whose nose I cut off.'

'Aim to finish the job, huh?'

'No woman's safe, so long as he's above ground. He murdered at least five in London. The last was a sorry wench named Mary. I was there in her digs, hiding beneath her bed, the night he butchered her.'

'Now how came you to be hiding under some gal's bed?'

'It was the fault of Rolfe Barnes, actually. Mother teaches violin, you see. She'd been off giving a lesson to One-Legged Liz . . .' And so it began.

As we were likely to be on the trail all day and Barney appeared to relish the story, I didn't hurry it along. I recounted in great detail the whole course of my misadventures. I ran with the truth about all that had happened in London and aboard the *True D. Light*. It wasn't till Sarah Forrest entered the tale that I took to fudging some. The omissions there forced me to bend the truth in regard to Briggs. Then I felt disinclined to tell about running with the outlaw gang, as that would've shown me for a horse thief and a murderer.

Instead of meeting up with the gang after I was pitched off the train, I told Barney that I'd walked to the nearest town, found myself a job there washing dishes in a restaurant, and worked at that till I was able to buy a horse and supplies and set off for Tombstone.

By and by, I got back to the truth. I told him about Jesse ambushing me, and how we'd thrown in together. I told him about the flood. About the German capturing Jesse, and how we'd shot him. About the uses we made of the mule. And finally I got us to where we'd decided against going into Tombstone, after all.

'Jesse feared that Sarah might be there. You know women.'

'That's the plain truth.'

'As for me, I figured that I'd rather give up on my notion to chase after Whittle than to put Jesse at risk. I'd seen what he did to Mary and Trudy. Just couldn't allow that to happen to Jesse. Anyway, we allowed as how we might find him in Tombstone – or at least get ourselves an idea as to where we might start looking. But I didn't want Jesse to have a hand in it, and she was mighty determined to stick with me, no matter what. So I judged the best course was to stay clear of Tombstone and forget Whittle. It was a great relief, actually. But then you came into camp last night with your story about Apache Sam.'

'Makes me right sorry I opened my yap.'

'If you hadn't come along,' I said, 'we likely would've run into Whittle one way or another, anyhow. It's rather as if it was all meant to be that way.'

'One thing's sure. That Jesse of yours, *she* means you to finish the job. That girl's a caution.'

'She's got more sand than sense,' I said.

'Oh, I reckon she knows what she's doing.'

'What took y'all so long?' Jesse called from her perch on a boulder at the foot of Dogtooth Mountain.

It was late afternoon. I'd been walking, the past few hours, so as to give Joey a rest.

'Blast you, Jesse!' I shouted.

She smiled down at us. 'No call to get riled there, Trevor. Howdy, Barney.'

'Howdy yourself, Miss Jesse.'

'Hope you folks didn't wear yourselves out.' With that, she stood up and turned her back to us. She dropped out of sight for a spell, then came walking around from behind the boulder with General in tow. In spite of the cheery words she'd thrown at us from up above, she had a rather sheepish look about her. To Barney, she said, 'Mighty kind of you to show Trevor the way.'

'Saved his feet some, I reckon.' He smiled at me. 'You can thank me, now. Gotcha to her.'

'I'm very grateful. Thank you ever so much.'

'Well, I heard me a good story outa the deal. You two take care, now.' He touched the brim of his hat.

'You're not leaving?' I asked.

'Yep. Done what I aimed to do. Got no room in my plans to hunt after Apache Sam or Whittle or none of their ilk. I always figured it's a sight more healthy to shy away from trouble than to go looking for it. So it's *adios*, kids. Try and keep alive.'

He wheeled Joey around and trotted off.

'Thank you again!' I called after him.

He gave his hat a wave in the air. Then the trail curved around behind some rocks and he was out of sight.

I turned to face Jesse.

'Now don't you look at me that way,' she said. 'I only just did what I had to. Surprised you didn't think of it first and take off on *me* last night.'

'I thought of it,' I admitted. 'But I had more sense than to *do* it. That was mighty lowdown and ornery.'

'Well, it worked. You're here and so am I. How'd you get Barney to come along?'

'He was quite willing to help, soon as I explained what you'd done. He said you must be touched.'

'I just didn't aim to get left out, that's all.'

'I wasn't aiming to leave you out.'

'Was, too. I know you, Trevor Bentley. Ain't no way you would've struck out after Whittle without you got rid of me first.' She jammed her hands onto her hips and shoved her face at me. 'Am I wrong or am I right? You tell me, now.'

'I wouldn't have dodged off and left you alone.'

'Don't go saying I left you alone. You was with Barney.'

'I wouldn't have left you with Barney, either. I wouldn't have left you, at all. We're "pardners", remember? Partners stick together.'

She let her hands drop away from her hips. Her head lowered. Voice soft, she said, 'Well, I knew you'd come along.'

'I didn't want you anywhere near this place.'

'I know that.'

'It's only 'cause I care so much about you.'

'I know.'

Reaching down, I took hold of her hands and gave them a squeeze. She raised her head. Her eyes looked awfully solemn.

'I don't want Whittle getting you,' I said.

'Well, that goes both ways. I don't want him getting you, either, but you need to face him down. If you back out and call it quits, you won't never feel right about yourself. I don't want that for you. And I don't wanta be the cause of it. You turned away from Tombstone on account of me.'

'That had to do more with Sarah than . . .'

'It had mostly to do with Whittle, and you know it. You figured you'd rather give up on him than take a risk of me getting hurt. Well, I went along with it yesterday. But that was selfish. That was me wanting to keep you from Sarah, even if it meant you had to call it quits on your hunt for

Whittle. It was wrong. For the both of us. I'm just almighty glad Barney came along so we'd get a chance to do the right thing.'

'What if it *is* Apache Sam up there?' I asked, tipping my head toward the mountain looming above us.

'Then we'll help the posse kill Apache Sam. After he's taken care of, we'll start after Whittle. We'll go back to Tombstone, if that's what it takes. But we'll pick up his trail, one way or another, and follow it till we've run him down. You and me. Together.'

'I don't know,' I murmured.

'What's not to know?'

'I don't want you getting killed, Jesse. I shouldn't be able to stand it.'

She gave my hands a squeeze. A corner of her mouth turned up, and a glimmer of her usual mischief came back into her eyes. 'I ain't easily killed,' she said. 'Nor are you, either. We'll be fine and dandy.'

'I do hope so.'

'You worry too much, Trevor Bentley.'

'McSween once told me that very thing. He's dead.'

Jesse leaned forward a bit and kissed my mouth. 'Come on,' she said. 'We've got us a cave to find.'

Chapter Fifty

Troubles in Monster Valley

I tossed the saddle bags across General's back. I filled my hat with water from the mule-gut bag, and let him drink some. We strung both rifles together and draped them over his back so we wouldn't need to lug them ourselves. Then we led him along the trail.

By and by, we came upon a trail going up the mountain. It was steep, and hitched its way back and forth up the rocky slope. I'd had some experiences with such switching trails, and didn't look forward to it.

'Must be the way up,' Jesse said.

'Are you sure you want to do this?'

She didn't say a thing, but threw me a smirk. Then she commenced to slog her way up the trail.

I followed, leading General by the reins.

Soon, Jesse stopped and pointed down at a pile of manure. 'The posse came this way, all right,' she said.

'Was it headed up or down?' I asked.

'It's a heap of dung, Trev, not a Western Union telegram.'

'Then what makes you say it was dropped by the posse?'

'It was dropped by a horse. Posses ride horses, don't they?'

'So do Bible salesmen, don't they?'

'You watch yourself or I'll sling it at you.'

As we continued to plug our way up the trail, we came upon several more collections of manure. Obviously, they hadn't all been left behind by the same horse. So I judged that Jesse was right: the posse had come this way. More than likely, anyhow.

I sure hoped that the horses had made their deposits on the way down. I hoped that the posse had finished its business

416

at the cave and departed. Taking the bodies of the women with them. Taking Whittle's body, too. Or Apache Sam's, if he was the culprit. I hoped that we would find nothing above us but an empty cave.

According to books I'd read, caves were supposed to be cool and pleasant, even where the weather outside is boiling hot. I hoped the books were right.

Even though the sun was low, it hadn't lost much of its heat. The sweat fairly poured off me. Jesse's shirt was wet and clinging to her back. We both huffed considerable, but we didn't stop. A cave sounded like just the trick for cooling us off.

Well, the trail went up and up, and so did we.

Every now and again, we stopped to rest and drink. We drank from the whiskey bottle in General's saddle bag. When it went empty on us, we filled it with more water from the tube of mule gut that was roped to his back. The tube was quite full. Jesse explained that she had filled it up that morning at a stream.

We rested often, but not for long. We had to add more water to the whiskey bottle twice.

At last, the trail took us over a summit of sorts. We ran into a good stiff wind that felt mighty good. Halting, we studied the area ahead.

We weren't at the top of the mountain. In front of us, the ground dropped off into a sunless, shallow valley, all rocky and bare, not a tree or bush growing anywhere. The valley was all aclutter with boulders and columns and high heaps of rock, chock full of narrow passes. An army might've been hiding down there out of sight.

Nobody *was* in sight. Not a man, not a horse.

There was no sign of a trail, either.

Beyond the gloom of the valley, the upper region of the mountain stretched itself into the sunlight. It didn't have just one peak, but seven or eight. A couple of them stuck up taller than the others, so they rather looked like fangs. I could see why the mountain had gotten itself called Dogtooth.

'Where's that cave at?' Jesse asked.

'Somewhere across there, I should think.' I nodded at the valley.

'Sure is a nasty piece of land,' she said.

'The valley of the shadow of death.'

'Don't go getting odd, Trevor.'

'Looks like a place where monsters might lurk.'

Jesse gave me a jab with her elbow. 'Quit that. Ain't no monsters down there. You're giving me the fantods.'

'Sorry,' I said, and took the bottle out of the saddle bag. We each drank some water.

As I tucked the bottle away, Jesse pulled out the revolver that she'd taken off the German. She thumbed open its port and turned the cylinder until it showed an empty chamber.

We'd both been keeping only five rounds in our guns, leaving a chamber bare under the hammer to avoid mishaps. While I watched, Jesse dug a cartridge out of her pocket. Her hand trembled some as she plugged it into the cylinder.

I added a sixth round to each of my Colts, then holstered them again.

Jesse kept hers in hand. She started down the slope toward that awful valley.

'Perhaps I ought to take the lead,' I suggested.

'Don't see as it matters,' she said. 'We're as likely to get jumped from behind as the front.'

Or from above, I thought.

I let Jesse stay ahead of me as we made our way down. I judged as how that was for the best, actually. If I took the front, I'd have General between me and Jesse. I wanted no obstacle in the middle to block my field of fire. If it should come to that.

We left the wind behind. And the sunlight. Even before we reached the floor of the valley, my back felt all aprickle. The nape of my neck crawled.

'I must say I don't care for this.'

'How'd Whittle ever find himself such a place?' Jesse asked.

'If it's only Apache Sam, shall we leave?'

She glanced over her shoulder and cast a smile at me. It was as nervous a smile as I'd ever seen on her.

All too soon, we found ourselves at the bottom of the valley. I stayed close to Jesse's back as we made our slow way in among the rocks. They walled us in. They loomed over us. They stood in front of us, blocking our path so we had to go around them.

Except for our footsteps and General clomping along behind me, all I could hear was the wind gusting about. Sometimes, it made a whishy noise like a rushing stream. Other times, it seemed to moan. The sounds of it surrounded us. But stayed high and far away. The wind never came down to where we were. There, the air was still and hot.

It seemed a bit unnatural, actually.

As I followed Jesse through the labyrinth, I couldn't help but think about Whittle bringing his victims through such a strange, forbidding place.

And no birds sing.

He'd likely kept them alive till he got them to the cave. It plain sickened me to imagine the terror they must've felt.

In front of me, Jesse froze.

'What?' I whispered.

'Shhh.' She pointed her gun at the ground a yard ahead of her.

I heard the snake before I saw it. A soft chh-chh-chh. Silence. Another chh-chh-chh. I spotted it. A rattler. So near the same speckled, dirty gray color as the rocks that it was the next thing to invisible. But there it was, as long as my arm, twisting its way across our path.

General must've noticed it then. He gave out a startled snort and backed up. I gave the reins a tug. He stopped, and groaned in a manner that near sounded human.

Jesse thumbed back her hammer. The cocking sound was so loud it seemed almost to echo.

'Don't shoot,' I whispered.

She held fire. A moment later, the snake vanished beneath a lip of rock.

We both kept our eyes on where it had gone, and hurried past it.

I said to Jesse's back. 'Let's not shoot unless we're attacked.'

'I don't aim to get snakebit to spare your ears.'

'It's not my own ears that concern me. I don't like the notion of announcing our whereabouts.'

'Then you best hope we don't meet up with no more rattlers.'

I watched for more as we continued along. And I couldn't help but listen, too. Now that I knew the sound they made, I heard it here and there – off to one side or the other, behind us, in front of us, sometimes even above. It played on my nerves, particularly the notion of a snake dropping down on us from the rocks as we walked by.

It got to be almost more than I could stand. I switched the reins to my left hand and filled my right with iron. Much as I was loath to unsettle the dead quiet with gunfire, the good solid feel of the Colt was comforting. Jesse heard me cock it. She looked over her shoulder at me and smiled.

'Don't shoot unless you're attacked,' she said.

'They're *everywhere*,' I whispered.

'Pretty near.'

Everywhere, but out of sight. I heard them, but couldn't see them. That made it all seem worse, somehow.

Next thing you know, our way forward got blocked by a great boulder. The way to the left was shut off tight. Our only course was to make a turn to the right and pass through a gash in the rocks. It looked like a rough-walled corridor, twice our height and not much wider than our shoulders. It appeared to stretch on for about thirty feet before it opened up.

Jesse turned away from it and studied General. 'I reckon he'll fit,' she said.

'I doubt the posse came this way.'

'There's likely a passel of better routes through this dang mess, but nobody gave us a map. Do you want to turn around and go back the way we came?'

I recalled all those rattlesnakes we'd left behind, and didn't care to give them a second go at us. So I answered Jesse with a shake of my head.

'Look sharp, now,' she said. Raising her gun barrel as if she expected to be leapt on from above – by snake or by madman or by Lord knows what brand of creature – Jesse entered the narrow gap.

I went in after her, leading General and watching him over my shoulder. He seemed mighty reluctant to put himself into such tight quarters. He snorted and tossed his head. 'Easy boy,' I said. 'Easy.' He came on, but didn't appear at all happy about the matter.

The passage was wide enough for General, but not by much. Our tube of water, draped across his back, rubbed against a wall and tore. Water went splashing out of it.

'Damnation,' I muttered.

'What?' Jesse asked.

'There goes our water.'

She looked around at us and grimaced. The water was still pouring from the ruptured gut. But I had no way to get past General and stop the gusher, short of climbing over his head.

All me and Jesse could do was stand there. Pretty soon, the side of the tube that still held water dragged its way down between General and the rocks. It fell with a plop. I ducked and peered under General's legs. I could've crawled beneath him and fetched out the tube, but there wasn't any advantage to that. It was empty and flat.

'At least we've got some in the whiskey bottle,' Jesse said.

'It won't last long.'

'There'll be water at the cave.'

'Will there be?'

'I don't reckon the posse come here without a pretty good supply.'

I judged she was right about that.

'We'd better keep moving,' she said. Turning away, she continued through the gap.

'Come along, fellow,' I urged General, and gave a pull at

the reins. He groaned at me. Sounded quite like a dog, as one might sound if you threatened to steal its bone. But he came along.

I kept my eyes on him, trusting Jesse to warn me of any trouble from the front. Our rifles still hung from General's sides by a rope across his back. And my saddle bags were up there. They seemed to be clear of the nearby walls, however, and in no great danger.

We were about halfway through the gash when General went daft. His eyes bugged out, his ears twitched forward, he squealed and reared. My arm near got wrenched off before I lost hold of the reins. I leaped forward to stay away from his kicking hooves. One knocked my hat off. I stumbled and fell. On his hind legs, General tried to twist himself around. For a while, he was stuck, his belly shoved against one rock wall while his rump was jammed into the other. He thrashed about awful. His front hooves clamored and threw off sparks. He screamed fierce. The rifles and saddle bags skidded down his back. As I got to my feet, hoping to help him somehow, he managed to tear himself loose. He fell, forelegs giving out, muzzle smacking the rocky ground. But he picked himself up right quick and scampered for freedom.

I gave chase, shouting. But General was in no mood to listen. He dashed out the way we'd come, and kept on running. Before you know it, he vanished around a bend. I quit racing after him. While I tried to catch my wind, the noise of his hoofbeats faded out.

'Bloody nag,' I muttered. I felt just about ready to cry. I kept it in, though, and headed on back into the gash.

At least General hadn't run off with our saddle bags and rifles. Jesse, crouching, opened one of the saddle bags. She pulled out our water bottle. It was half empty, but unbroken.

'He's gone,' I said.

'Must've been the snakes,' she said. 'I figured he'd kill himself sure.' She returned the bottle to the saddle bag, and draped the leather pouches over one shoulder.

'We'd best go find him,' I said.

Jesse shook her head. 'Ain't much chance of catching him. Gonna be dark soon, and no telling where he's off to. He might not stop till he's off the mountain.'

'I shouldn't like to lose him altogether,' I said, my throat tight.

'I know.' She looked rather miserable, herself. 'He's a good old boy. We'll find him.' She squatted by the rifles and commenced to pick at a knot. 'What we'd best do right now, though, is try and hook up with that posse. We ain't got much water. We can go hunting for General come daylight.' She got the knot undone, slipped the rope off the stock of my Winchester, and lifted the rifle up to me.

I took it. She made a sling out of the rope and hung the Henry down her back. Then she stood up and drew her revolver.

'I wish we'd never come up here,' I said, picking up my hat. 'We've lost our horse and most of our water. We're surrounded by rattlesnakes. We're lost. Whittle's likely lurking nearby. Or Apache Sam. Things have gone all to smash.'

Jesse hoisted an eyebrow at me. 'You should've stayed home in London, I reckon.'

I saw her trap and dodged clear of it. 'Not at all. I'm quite glad we're together, you know. I only wish we were together elsewhere.'

'Well, Trev, you play the cards you're dealt. This ain't the best hand, but it's what we've got. Now, let's go and find us that posse.'

Chapter Fifty-one

Ghastly Business

Night was near upon us when we came upon the posse. After losing General, we'd gone through the gash in the rocks, found ourselves in a clear area that gave us a view of the mountain peaks, headed that way, circled around some boulders and climbed a slope and squeezed through another tight gap.

We heard some rattlers along the way, but not many. Those we heard stayed out of sight.

As we came out the other side of the gap, we ran into the posse.

There were eight or nine men and about that many horses. They were spread about a clearing in front of the cave entrance.

Alive was one horse, tied to a stand of rocks off to one side.

Alive were also a fair number of buzzards, but they scattered when we showed up. Some perched themselves on rocks and others sailed around overhead, all of them likely hoping we'd leave so they could get back to their meals.

We stood motionless at the edge of the clearing.

'My God,' Jesse whispered.

Mostly, I felt numb. But part of me stayed alert, and I scanned the area to make sure whoever'd done the massacre wasn't in sight.

As one horse had been spared, I judged it likely belonged to the killer. So he was somewhere about. The horse, a pale palomino, was saddled. It glanced our way and took a few steps. When it moved, I heard its shoes on the rocky ground. So it was shod.

'Whittle,' I whispered. 'An Apache wouldn't have shoes on his horse.'

'Unless he stole it off a white man,' Jesse said.

I gazed at the carnage. The gloom of dusk wasn't dark enough to hide much of it.

'Whittle did this,' I said.

I knew for sure, and it had to do with a sight more than the shod horse. The killer had done more than slay the men and horses. He'd mucked about with them.

He'd dismembered a good many of them. The head of a horse had been placed between the legs of a naked man, its mouth on his private parts. All the men were naked. Some had been disemboweled, their entrails strewn about. (The buzzards had likely played a role in that.) Two fellows had been stacked up and arranged in such a way as to suggest they were busy at an unnatural act. The heads of four had been removed and set atop various rocks. The privates had been cut off some of the bodies. The severed arm of one chap had been thrust up the hindquarters of a dead horse.

The clothing and weapons of the dead men were nowhere to be seen. Except for four boots. Those were on the feet of a dead horse.

The atrocities were unspeakably savage, but showed a vile sense of humor.

Only Whittle, I judged, could've committed such acts.

Was he inside the cave? Was he skulking about, sneaking toward us?

'Let's take cover,' I whispered.

Backing off, we ducked behind a low boulder and leaned forward against it. Jesse slipped the saddle bags off her shoulder. She slung the Henry off her back.

We both cocked our rifles and rested them atop the rock, aiming toward the cave entrance.

'You were right about monsters,' Jesse whispered.

'The man's a fiend,' I said.

'But how'd he manage to kill them *all*?'

'He's quite clever, really,' I told her. 'And they were here looking for an Indian. He likely tricked them somehow.'

'Maybe he ain't alone.'

'I don't know.' I glanced behind us. Nothing back there except the maze of rocks. So I turned to Jesse and said, 'Whittle by himself is enough to worry about. There's only one horse, though.'

'If he don't know we're here, we can bushwhack him when he goes to ride off.'

I gave Jesse a nod. She bumped me gently with her shoulder.

Soon, night was upon us.

The dark was kind, actually, as it shrouded the scene of the massacre. We could still see the dim shapes out there, but not all the ghastly particulars. The buzzards were nowhere in sight. Whittle's horse was a light enough color so we could keep our eyes on it. The mouth of the cave looked like a patch of black in the gray wall of the mountain.

I couldn't figure any way for Whittle to get from the cave to his horse without us spotting him.

The trick was simply to wait him out.

Then shoot him down.

'Keep your eyes open,' Jesse whispered after a spell. She rested her rifle on the boulder, then crept backward. I glanced at her a couple of times to see what she was about. She pulled our bottle from the saddle bag and shook it. 'Thirsty?' she asked.

'We haven't much left.'

She popped the cork and took a few drinks. Holding the bottle out to me, she said, 'Water's no problem. Did you see all the canteens and water bags on them nags out there?'

'They might be empty,' I said, and took the bottle.

'They ain't empty, Trevor.' She sounded a bit annoyed. 'Landsakes, but you worry.'

'They may have quite a lot of water in them,' I admitted. 'But I shouldn't care to venture over and fetch any.'

'I will.'

'No, you won't.'

'You can keep me covered. Not as he's out there, anyhow.'

'We still *have* water,' I pointed out, and shook the bottle at her.

'Well, there ain't much. We oughta get more now, before the trouble starts.'

'What trouble? We'll simply ventilate him when he goes for his horse.'

'You never know. Anyhow, it's good and dark right now. Moon ain't even up, yet. This'd be the best time to go out there.'

'We needn't go out there at all.'

'You just stay here,' Jesse said. 'Make sure I don't get jumped. Maybe I can find us some good food and smokes while I'm at it.'

'Jesse.'

She popped up. I reached, grabbed hold of her sleeve and tugged it hard. With a ripping sound, the sleeve tore off at her shoulder. It came sliding down empty, so I snatched her wrist and yanked her to the ground.

'You're *not* going out there!' I gasped.

'Look what you done to my shirt!'

'Stay here.'

She reached a hand toward me. I shoved the bottle into it, then leaped out of range. I rushed around to the front of the boulder, filled my right hand with a Colt, then halted and looked back. I waited till Jesse showed herself and hefted her Henry. She shook her head at me.

I turned away and walked into the massacre. Even though the moon wasn't up yet, there was enough starlight to see by. Not that I knew quite where to look. I wanted to keep my eyes on the cave, but feared what I might step on.

I walked toward the nearest horse. It had no head. Two of the posse men blocked my way – those that were sprawled one atop the other, feet at both ends, heads between each other's legs. I tried not to look at them, and gave them a wide berth. When I crouched over the horse, I found that it had fallen onto the canteen that hung from its saddle horn. But I pulled hard, and worked it free. I gave it a shake. Water sloshed about inside. There didn't sound like much, though.

Slinging that canteen over my shoulder, I set off for another horse. This was the horse wearing boots. Just behind it, one of the severed heads sat atop a stack of rocks. I couldn't see whether or not the eyes were open, but seemed to recall that *all* the heads had open eyes.

I glanced about at the other three heads. Every last one of them seemed to be staring at me.

I quit looking at them, and circled around to the far side of the horse. This one hadn't fallen onto its water bag. Crouching, I lifted the strap off the saddle horn. And heard a low grumble. Shivers raced up my back. I looked around quick. Another grumble. From the head just behind me. Well, it *couldn't* have made such a noise. It had no body attached, but simply rested atop a waist-high pile of rock.

As I gazed at the head, my skin all aprickle, it suddenly rolled forward. It did an odd bit of a somersault, face first, the ragged stump of its neck swinging toward the sky. I let out a gasp and sprang up as it dropped off the edge. It clomped the ground. It rolled straight at me.

I was in such a state that I dang near shot it. But I held fire and danced out of the way. Just as the head was about to bump into the horse's saddle, a coyote dashed out from behind the rocks, snatched it up by the face and scampered off with it.

Well, I'd had enough, and raced for our hiding place. I dropped down behind the boulder, all breathless.

'Good job,' Jesse whispered.

'Bloody hell.'

She rubbed the back of my neck. After a while, she took the canteen and water bag from me and shook them. 'We're all set, now. All we gotta do is bide our time.'

She resumed her position, leaning forward against the boulder with her rifle at her shoulder. Once I was able to breathe right, I picked up my Winchester and joined her.

Nothing seemed to be moving, in among the dead. The coyote must've skedaddled.

Now that the sun had been down for a spell, the night was

taking on a chill. There were likely a passel of bedrolls and blankets on the horses. I judged I'd rather freeze, though, than go out and fetch any such thing. So I kept still about them.

By and by, Jesse whispered, 'Maybe he ain't *in* that cave. He mighta rode off before we ever got here.'

'Why's the horse there, then?'

'Could be he just didn't kill it. No telling why.'

'It might not be his,' I admitted.

'What we oughta do is take a look in the cave.'

'Are you daft?'

'Beats waiting. If he's inside, that's where he's likely gonna stay. Least till morning. If he aimed to ride off tonight, he woulda done it by now.'

'No reason *we* can't wait till morning,' I said. 'Whenever he pops out's fine with me. In fact, it would be considerably easier to pick him off come daylight.'

'It'd be *easier* if he's asleep.'

'He might not *be* asleep,' I pointed out.

'Well, he might not be in there at all. But if he is, he ain't likely to stay awake all night. We oughta go and sneak in, see if we can't catch him snoozing. We can fill him with lead before he gets his eyes open.'

I gazed off at the cave's black opening. It was a narrow slot, not much wider than my shoulders, too low to walk through upright. We'd need to duck down and go in one at a time.

If we went in at all.

Spite of Jesse's logic, I wasn't at all eager to embark on such a venture.

'What do you say?' she asked.

'I say we wait him out. We go walking into that cave, we're likely to get ourselves killed. Whittle might have his eyes on us right now. He might just be hoping we'll try such a thing, so he can get his hands on us. And his knife.'

Jesse looked at me and shook her head. 'Well,' she finally said. 'All right.'

'I just don't see any call to rush into danger when we might simply wait here and shoot him from ambush.'

'Okay. If that's how we're gonna play it, though, we might as well get some shut-eye. You wanta go first? I'll keep watch.'

'And have you dodge off to the cave without me?'

Jesse's teeth showed, gray in the darkness. 'I don't aim to do that.'

'It's not at all funny.'

'I'm scared half witless, Trevor. I wanta get this done, and it won't be done till Whittle's dead. But I sure ain't so dim as to go after him by my lonesome. What do you take me for, an addlehead?'

I couldn't be sure whether or not she was having me on. But I saw no advantage to arguing. 'I'm not at all sleepy, anyhow,' I told her.

'You don't trust me, do you?'

'It's not that. How do you expect a person to sleep when . . .'

The words died halfway out as somebody heaved a scream.

Chapter Fifty-two

Whittle's Lair

Jesse clutched my arm.

We gaped at each other through the darkness as the scream shivered through the night and died.

'My God,' Jesse murmured.

'It came from the cave, didn't it?' I asked.

'He's got a gal in there.'

'Where'd he get a *gal*?'

'Who knows? It don't matter.'

A cave was no place for a rifle, so I left it resting atop the boulder. I shoved myself away and got to my feet. Jesse did the same. 'Stay here,' I snapped at her. 'I mean it! You stay here!'

She pulled her sixgun. 'Let's go.'

'Jesse!'

'Go! That gal ain't gonna last forever.'

I took off running for the cave entrance, but Jesse was on my heels. So I made a sudden stop. As she bumped me from behind, I brought my arm forward, all set to drive my elbow into her. That was bound to let her wind out, and I figured to follow up my elbow with a blow to the face and put her out of action.

Couldn't do it, though.

Much as I wanted to stop Jesse from following me into the cave, the notion of causing hurt to her made me hold off.

She gave me a shove. 'Hurry!'

So I dashed toward the cave, Jesse at my back. And wondered if I was doing her any favor by *not* bashing her senseless. Then I judged that leaving her alone out here might be worse than letting her stick with me. This way, at least she'd be where I could watch over and protect her.

We reached the mouth of the cave. I went in first and hunkered down. Much as I wanted Jesse to be shut of this business, it was mighty good to hear her breathing hard behind me.

I expected to see nothing. But away off in the distance was a fluttery glow such as might come from a small fire out of sight beyond a bend.

Only dark between us and that glow.

Needing the use of both hands, I holstered my Colt. When I commenced to make my way forward, Jesse grabbed hold of my shirt collar. I crouched low to spare my head, and walked slow and careful, keeping my arms stretched out in front of me.

I hadn't taken more than five steps when another scream came. It tore through the darkness. It seemed to make the air tremble as it passed over me. A scream of horrid pain.

'What's he *doing* to her?' Jesse whispered.

Well, my mind filled in plenty of pictures. 'God only knows,' I whispered. I judged he was likely skinning her alive.

But she's not dead yet, I told myself. We might be in time to save her.

It was slow going, though. Every few steps, the cave tricked me. It either put a barrier up to send me stumbling, or dropped its floor out from under me. Sometimes, Jesse's grip on my collar stopped me from falling. Other times, we both went down in a jumble. I banged myself up again and again, but neither of us let out a peep, and we kept moving.

The cool air of the cave now held a faint odor of corruption. I recalled what Barney Dire had told us about the stink, and judged we must be getting near to Whittle's collection of dead women. With each step I took, the odor grew worse.

The shimmery orange glow of light wasn't more than maybe twenty feet away when a third scream came along. Though it made my teeth ache, I was glad to hear it.

Hang on, lady!

The source of the light was still out of sight around a twist in the cave, but I could now see well enough to watch my step. I drew both my Colts. Jesse let go of my collar.

'Careful now,' she whispered.

'Keep behind me,' I warned, then stepped around the bend.

What greeted my eyes wasn't what I'd expected. I was ready to see the grisly array of bodies – and they were there, scattered about the large chamber, dismembered and spoiling, some propped up against the walls, some stacked together in unspeakable arrangements of carnal acts, some simply sprawled on the floor. They were all lighted up by a passel of torches standing here and there among the rocks.

Whittle hadn't cut off their heads, but he'd lifted their hair. Likely to make it look like the work of an Indian. Their scalps hung like banners from staves all about the chamber. Other staves held different trophies. Some had hearts stuck on top of them. Some had breasts. Some had parts I couldn't recognize.

But what I'd expected to see wasn't there – Whittle busy at work torturing a live woman.

Whittle wasn't in sight. Nor was any woman who wasn't already quite dead.

Had he somehow detected our approach and spirited her off? Perhaps the screams hadn't come from this chamber at all, but from the depths of the cave beyond it.

I stepped forward, entering the chamber, forgetting about Jesse until she came to my side. I looked her way as she groaned. Her wide eyes were taking in the scene of horrors. Her mouth was shut tight, lips pressed together in a hard line.

'I wish you'd stayed out,' I whispered. 'You shouldn't be seeing such things.'

'Where is he?'

'I don't know. Perhaps through there.' With one of my guns, I pointed out a dark cavity at the far end of the chamber.

We started toward it. To get there, we had no choice but to walk through the midst of the bodies, the staves with their hideous prizes, the torches.

We came upon a great heap of clothing. While I had noticed it before, I'd been too stunned and confused by the rest of the scene to give it much mind.

As we approached it, however, the notion struck me that Whittle might be buried within the pile. Hiding there, waiting for the proper moment to spring out and have at us. I halted and gave a nod to Jesse.

We trained three revolvers on the mound of garments. Then I commenced to scatter it, booting things this way and that. Near the top were men's duds – no doubt those taken from the posse. Mixed in among the shirts and vests and boots and trousers and longjohns were gunbelts, sixguns, rifles and knives. They all flew about as I kicked. Soon, the pile shrank down to dresses and petticoats and such.

'I don't reckon he's in there,' Jesse whispered.

She was likely right, but I waded in anyhow, stomping and kicking.

'By Jove, that *is* you!'

The merry voice, so familiar though I hadn't heard it for months, resounded through the chamber.

'Trevor Wellington Bentley! Is it possible? And in the company of a lovely young damsel! How utterly thoughtful of you to bring me such a gift!'

Whirling about, I tried to spot him.

Jesse did the same.

'Put down your weapons,' he called, sounding quite pleased with himself. 'I should hate to shoot either of you and ruin the sport.' A gun blasted, its explosion crashing through my ears.

The bullet struck neither of us. I didn't see what it hit, for my eyes were drawn to the muzzle flash.

'There!' Jesse gasped.

'Yes, here,' said Whittle. 'Now drop your firearms.'

He was forty paces away, his back to the rock wall, his front all but concealed behind the corpse of a woman. One arm was wrapped across its bare belly, hugging the body against him. I'd spotted this one before. The crown of its head was black and pulpy. The lips were cut away so its bared teeth seemed to grin most hideously. Nothing but holes remained where the eyes belonged. Both breasts were off. The torso was split open from throat to pelvis. I'd glimpsed this maimed horror before and averted my eyes fast, never suspecting that it might be shielding Whittle.

While one arm clamped it across the belly, the other jutted out straight from above the shoulder, pointing a revolver our way. Whittle's face showed beyond his gun arm. I couldn't see much of it, though.

'What've you done with her?' I asked.

'With whom do you mean?'

'The one who screamed.'

'Ah, *her*. Rushed to her rescue, did you?' With that, he let out a shriek. It sounded for all the world like a woman crying out in the throes of hellish agony.

434

'Quit it!' I yelled.

The scream trailed off into laughter.

'You knew we were out there?' Jesse asked.

'Oh, quite. Of course, I had no *idea* that one of the interlopers was my old mate, Trevor. And what would your name be, my dear?'

'None of your nevermind.'

Whittle chuckled. 'I'll get it out of you later. For the present, it will suffice for you both to drop your firearms.'

Jesse glanced at me, then turned her gaze toward Whittle.

'Shall I count to three?' he asked.

Jesse yelled, 'Three!' and let fly.

I followed her example.

Side by side, we blasted away. I used both Colts at once. Our sixguns roared, and Whittle's spat back. I reckon his aim wasn't up to snuff, for neither of us went down. Ours were nearer the mark. He would've been a dead man for sure if the woman hadn't caught most of our slugs. They smacked into her chest and shoulders. They punched holes through her arms. They gouged her sides. But they couldn't get past her and find Whittle.

Jesse's gun went silent. I gave her a glance. She was commencing to reload.

Whittle fired again, and the bullet zipped past my ear.

I turned all my attention back to him, determined to kill him before my Colts ran dry.

All that actually showed was a bit of his face, so I raised my aim and went for that. It ducked out of sight just as I fired. My bullet slammed through the gal's upper teeth. The next pounded her brow and knocked her head back. The one after that ripped out the side of her neck and Whittle cried out. I thumbed back my hammers and squeezed my triggers. Instead of blasts, there came only quiet clacks.

Whittle shoved the body away from him. As it pitched forward, we faced each other for just a moment. Through the drifting shrouds of gunsmoke, I saw that my last shot had gouged his cheek. Other than that, he seemed unharmed. He wore a black satin nosepatch.

He didn't raise his gun at me, so I judged it was out of ammo. He only had the one. An empty holster hung at his hip. His chest was crossed by twin black belts, each holding a sheathed knife. They looked to be mighty big knives. Knowing Whittle, the knives came as no surprise. But the shiny star pinned to the front of his frilly white shirt surprised me considerable.

A badge!

I saw all this in just the blink of an eye, and then Whittle was dodging off to the side.

I whirled toward Jesse, shouted, 'Get him!' and then realized she was still busy thumbing rounds into her Colt.

When I spotted Whittle again, he was racing hellbent for the end of the chamber.

But not the end that would take him deeper into the cave.

The end that led out.

I holstered, dropped to my knees and scurried about the scattered clothes and such until I wrapped my hands around a revolver. I cleared its leather and swung it round.

I got off a shot that kicked sparks off the cave's wall near Whittle's shoulder. Before I could fire again, he vanished into the darkness. I emptied the gun after him, anyhow, hoping I might catch him with a ricochet. He didn't cry out, though. I judged they'd likely missed him.

I threw down the borrowed revolver. 'Bloody hell!'

'Don't fret,' Jesse said, sounding mighty calm. She, too, was gazing toward the place where he'd disappeared. 'We'll get him.' She snapped the loading port shut on her Colt. 'You might wanta reload, your own self, before he comes back shooting.'

It was when I went to stand up that I noticed Jesse'd been hit. The left leg of her dungarees was all ashine with blood and clinging to her. The hole was high on her thigh. My insides went all cold and shaky at the sight.

'He *got* you!' I gasped.

'Well, I reckon I'll live. I'll tend to it. You go on ahead and load up.'

My hands shook so frightfully that I had a rather difficult time of it. Also, I kept an eye out for Whittle and watched Jesse while I worked at emptying out the used shells and plugging fresh rounds into my cylinders.

What Jesse did was to sit down among the dead folks' clothes and pull the knife from her boot. Using that, she cut the leg off her dungarees. It put me in mind of the time she'd cut off the German's trouser leg to wear on her head. She'd gashed him some, but she didn't gash herself. Her hand was just as steady as you please.

Seeing the hole in her thigh, I dropped a couple of cartridges.

She turned her leg. It had a second hole on the outer side of the thigh, about three inches from the one in front. Blood was running out of both.

'It ain't still in me,' she said.

'That's good, isn't it?' I asked, feeling awful trembly and weak.

'Well, I'd a sight rather have one hole than two.' Looking up at me, she smiled.

I found the cartridges that I'd dropped, stuffed them into the cylinder, checked both guns to be sure they were fully loaded, then slipped them into my holsters and stepped over Jesse's legs. I crouched down beside the shot one.

'Does it hurt awfully?'

'Well, it don't feel good.'

'Watch for Whittle, and I'll bandage you.'

Nodding, she gave her knife to me. Then she leaned back. Braced up on one elbow, she lifted her revolver and rested it on her belly. She turned her head to keep a lookout.

'We near had him,' she said.

'I took a piece out of his face.'

'Too bad that's all.'

I snagged up a calico dress with faded flowers on it. After some cutting and ripping, I had it in pieces. I folded one into

437

a thick patch and pressed it gently against her wounds. It was large enough to cover both of them. I held it there for a bit.

She'd taken off the leg of her dungarees quite high up. Our positions were such that I couldn't help but view a region, overhung by fabric but plainly visible, that took out my breath. A flood of heat rushed through me.

I looked away quick and lifted my hand off the pad. It had a pair of red dots, but wasn't soaked.

'You don't seem to be bleeding terribly,' I muttered.

'Reckon he'll ride off and leave us?'

'I doubt it.'

'Hope you're right. I'd hate to see him get away.'

'I just hope *we* get away.'

With a long strip from the dress, I commenced to wrap the pad into place. Jesse eased her other leg aside so it wouldn't be in my way. That pretty much bared her center entirely. I tried not to look, but couldn't help myself. I did manage not to touch her there, though my hands got mighty close while I worked at winding the cloth around her.

She must've known what I could see, but she didn't complain or try to cover herself.

I felt lowdown for looking. But not so lowdown as to quit it. We were trapped inside a cave and surrounded by women in the most awful states of dismemberment and rot, Whittle was likely fixing to kill us, and Jesse was gunshot. Yet there I knelt, sneaking peeks and feeling like I might just explode with the thrill and wonder of it all.

After giving the strip of dress several turns around her thigh, I tied it secure with another piece.

'All set,' I said, and found Jesse staring at me.

The torches gave off plenty of light for me to see she had the old gleam in her eyes. 'You'd best take your mind off my southern parts and put it on Whittle.'

I blushed so fierce my skin near caught fire.

I stammered something, trying for a denial.

Jesse sat up. 'No call to fret about it. Give me back my knife.'

I handed it to her. She leaned forward, hitched up the cuff of her remaining pantsleg, and slipped the blade into her boot.

'Perhaps you should carry it in the other boot,' I suggested.

'The other boot ain't got a sheath sewed inside.'

'Still, it would be easier to retrieve.'

'That leg's ruined enough without getting knifed.'

'Will you be able to walk?'

'Reckon we'll find out soon enough.'

I got to my feet and held out a hand to her. When she took it, I hoisted her upright. She gasped and cringed. But she didn't go down.

'You can let go of me,' she said.

I did so, and stepped back. After a quick check to be sure that Whittle wasn't lurking at the front of the chamber, I turned my eyes to Jesse. She took a couple of steps. Though she winced with each of them, she stayed up.

I stared at her. She was sure a sight. Standing there with a sixgun in her hand. Her hair all a mess but golden in the torchlight. Her left arm and leg both bare (except for the bandage around her thigh). Her skin moist and shiny. Her shirt tails hanging out. The one leg of her dungarees hitched up over the top of her boot with the handle of the knife sticking out.

'Whatcha staring at now?' she asked.

'You look glorious.'

She reached down and touched the bandage. 'Well, you got me into a dress. Reckon now I'm a regular Becky Thatcher.'

'Becky Thatcher?' I asked, surprised and pleased.

'Ain't you never read about her and Tom Sawyer? They ended up in a cave, same as us.'

'I know them well,' I said.

Jesse fingered the opening in her dungarees, apparently to check that she was properly covered. 'Whittle, he makes their Injun Joe look like a piker.'

'We're quite better armed than Tom and Becky.'

She nodded. 'Let's go and kill him.'

Chapter Fifty-three

The Final Showdown

'Let's do some figuring first,' I said. 'He's bound to be waiting for us, you know.' I went to Jesse's side. She leaned against me, and I wrapped an arm across her back.

'That's a sight better,' she said. 'Now what've we got that needs figuring? Only just one way out. He likely *is* laying for us, but he ain't much of a shot.'

'He got you, didn't he?'

'We was pretty sizable targets, and he still missed four outa five.'

'He likely only hit *you* by accident, anyhow.'

'We was *both* shooting at him.'

'He wants you alive, Jesse. You know ... so he can ... muck about with you.' I hated to tell her that, what with the remains of Whittle's handiwork all around us. But she needed to know the way of things.

Instead of looking troubled by the revelation, she smirked. 'Well, if he only hit me with a stray meant for you, he's a worse shot than I reckoned. We oughta just charge on ahead and blast him down.'

'That's a terrible idea.'

'I'll go first.'

'Are you daft?'

'You said your own self that he don't wanta shoot me. Not sure as you're right about that, but ...'

'Anyway, there's no telling where he might be. We won't be able to see anything at all in the dark part.'

'We could take us a torch.'

'And light ourselves up for him?'

'Well, you got a better idea? Maybe we oughta just stay

here and wait for him to die of old age. Course, my blood might all leak out while we're at it.'

We both looked down at her leg. Thick as the bandage was, some blood had already seeped through it.

I didn't know much about bullet wounds, but it seemed to me that Jesse ought to be lying down and keeping still. Give her blood a chance to quit running out. She wasn't about to do any such thing, though. Not while Whittle still needed killing.

'What we need,' I said, 'is a good trick.'

'One that'll get us through him?'

'Or lure him to *us*. Like the way McSween and I led that posse into the ambush, something along those lines.'

'He ain't likely to fall for any brand of tricks. He's a tricker, himself. Look how he got us in here with his screaming.'

That reminded me. 'Did you see that he was wearing a badge? Letting on to be a lawman?'

'Maybe he *is* a lawman.'

Whittle a lawman? Odd as the notion seemed, I judged it was possible. Perhaps he'd actually led the posse up here to hunt down Apache Sam. That would go a long way toward explaining how he'd managed to kill the whole bunch. It's easy to kill folks that trust you.

'Perhaps he is above being tricked,' I admitted.

'We oughta just go. We'll play the hand that's dealt.'

'This isn't a card game, Jesse.'

'Well, I'm gonna fold if we don't do something quick. And I ain't bluffing.'

'Whittle!' I shouted toward the black opening. 'Whittle!' He didn't answer.

'Jesse's hit! You shot her in the leg.'

'Trying to trick him with the truth?' she whispered.

'You can have her!' I called. 'What'll you give me for her?'

Still, no answer came. But I figured he could hear me, figured I'd caught his interest. Not as he was likely to believe a word that came out of me.

'Give me your gun,' I told Jesse.

She looked at me odd, but handed it over.

'I've taken her gun!' I called out. 'I'm throwing it away.' I tossed it some distance. It struck the rock floor with a clatter, and skidded.

'Trevor!' she whispered, scowling.

'That was her sixgun, Whittle! She's unarmed, now. You can have her. For a hundred dollars. Whittle? Do you hear me?'

'It ain't gonna work,' she whispered.

'You've seen how beautiful she is! I only want a hundred dollars for her. She's worth a good deal more than that. Imagine the fine times you'll have with her.'

'Trevor!'

'Stripping her down to the skin. Having your first looks. Before you start cutting her.'

'Quit it.'

I suddenly lurched behind her. She staggered, but I caught her up and hugged her to me, my left arm across her chest. My right hand shoved a Colt in her ear.

'Damn it!' she blurted.

'Come and get her, Whittle! She won't be much good if I kill her. You'll want those honors for yourself, won't you? You'll want to carve her up slow, a little bit at a time. That's why your brought all *these* gals here, isn't it? So you could work on them at your leisure? So you could savor their torment? So you could enjoy the sight of them thrashing about, bleeding and sweating? So you could hear their screams?'

To Jesse, I whispered, 'Scream.'

'I don't know how.'

'*Do* it. *You're* my hand. You're all the cards I've got.'

'Just stop all this.'

'*Scream.*'

She did it. And a mighty fine scream it was. Whittle himself couldn't have done any better. Her shriek hurt my ears and made me cringe. Even after she stopped, it echoed on through the cave.

'Did you like it, Whittle?' I called. 'Did it heat you up? There's more where it came from. With all your talents for torture, you might have her screaming like that for hours. But you won't have the opportunity. Not unless you come out and pay me. Dead gals don't scream. Dead gals don't squirm and plead. You're about to miss out on the time of your life, 'cause I'll be putting a bullet through her head if you don't come out and buy her off me.'

'Such an amusing lad,' Whittle said from the darkness ahead.

At the sound of his voice, my heart gave a jump. I'd intended him to hear. I'd hoped he would answer. But it came as a shock when he actually spoke out. Maybe I'd hoped, deep down, that he'd considered himself lucky to escape from us, fled the cave and hightailed aboard his horse.

'Are you ready to pay?' I asked. 'Or shall I put a bullet through her head?'

He laughed. 'Come now, Trevor. I know you far too well. You would sooner die yourself than shoot that sweet morsel.'

'She's little more than a stranger I met on the trail,' I told him. 'I've no use for her.'

'Do you take me for a fool? Shoot her? You, who attacked me for the sake of an East End slut? You, who froze through half a night aboard the yacht to prevent Trudy from hanging? You, who leaped into the sea to save her from drowning? Though it was quite apparent that you disliked her from the start? Please. This is so obviously a primitive ruse to lure me into the light.'

'Believe what you will,' I called, and thumbed back the hammer of my Colt. 'Show yourself, or I'll blow her head off.'

'Proceed,' he said.

'Take that outa my ear,' Jesse muttered. 'He ain't falling for it.'

'Listen to her,' Whittle said. Mimicking Jesse, he added, 'I ain't falling for it.'

I kept the gun to her ear. 'I'll count to three,' I told Whittle. 'It's your play.'

'Take care you don't shoot her by accident. Poor lad, you've already put several bullets into one darling tonight. She wasn't alive to notice, of course. But it *was* such a shame. She was quite fond of you, really.'

He made little sense. Still my stomach went cold.

'I rode into Tombstone recently to deliver a prisoner. I've become a Deputy U.S. Marshal, did you know that? Deputy John Carver. John Carver, Jack the Ripper. Clever, what? And fancy, *me* a lawman.' He laughed. 'A marvelous job, actually. It allows me splendid opportunities for travel. I've quite the knack for pursuing felons, you know. However, the job also gives me the liberty to pursue a fairer game.'

'What happened in Tombstone?'

I didn't ask that. I was too full of shock and dread for words. It was Jesse who put the question to him.

'Why, a sweet thing recognized my horse. Seems I'd stolen it from her grandfather's stable.'

Sarah!

'Quite the spirited wench, she was. She had a go at shooting me down in the very streets of Tombstone. Naturally, I prevailed.'

'You killed her?' Jesse asked.

'Oh, not at the time. My bullet merely knocked her senseless. Fortunate, that, as it prevented her from speaking out against me.' He chuckled. 'I simply explained that she was wanted for harboring a fugitive bank robber, and bustled her out of town. Being an officer of the law does have its privileges, you know.'

As I heard all this, I took to trembling fitfully. Fearing an accidental discharge, I turned my gun away from Jesse's head.

'You can't imagine my surprise, Trevor, when she spoke of you. I was rather certain that you'd drowned in Gravesend Bay. You'd not only survived, but captured the fair creature's heart. It's there on a pike to your left, by the way.'

Though my mind reeled, I kept my eyes on the dark where Whittle lurked. One of Jesse's hands gently pressed my leg.

'Oh, she told me so much about you. She was just full of fascinating news. In fact, I've a bit of news for you. She confessed that she interfered rather heartlessly with your mail. She loved you dearly. Not wisely, as they say, but too well. It seems that she chose not to post several of the letters which you intended for your mother. And she intercepted those that your mother sent to you. In the end, she rather regretted that she'd done so. In the end, I daresay, she regretted quite a lot. Most particularly, that my bullet hadn't killed her outright on Toughnut Street.'

I struggled not to believe Whittle. But his words gave me no choice.

'She was quite the most entertaining of my ladies. Indeed, she also proved the most useful. Ironic, that. I do relish life's amusing little ironies. That she who died under my knife should save me from the bullets of the chap she loved most.'

That hideous thing – that scalped and mutilated carcass – was Sarah?

'You bloody fiend!' I yelled.

He laughed. A merry cackle that echoed through the chamber.

'You'll not get your knife on *this* one!' I yelled, and threw Jesse to the floor of the cave. As she fell asprawl on the scattered clothing, I swept my revolver down at her and fired twice. With each shot, she flinched and cried out.

Whittle shouted, 'No!' through the roar of the blasts.

He rushed out of the dark, raising his sixgun.

'She's better dead than in your hands!'

'Damn you!' He took aim at my head.

I got off my shot first. It took him in the left shoulder, turning him so his bullet missed me clean. He was staggering sideways when my next struck his chest. It ripped the leather of a knife scabbard, and sang off the blade. But the blow knocked him off his feet. As he fell, I put a round into his stomach. He grunted. He landed on his bum.

I stepped over Jesse's motionless body, halted, and leveled my Colt at his face. At the satin patch covering the remains of his nose, actually. Then I thumbed back the hammer. 'This is for all of them,' I said.

He flung himself sideways as I fired. My slug splashed his right eye. His head was turned at the moment, though, so it didn't drill through to his brain but only took out a corner of his socket.

He hit the ground screaming. And firing.

Already, I was slapping leather with my left hand. I pulled my second Colt. Before I could bring it into play, my arm was struck. Felt like a club had pounded it just below my shoulder. The gun dropped from my hand. I ducked quick, trying to catch it with my right as bullets sizzled past me. And catch it I did.

As I swung it up, a bullet smacked my *right* shoulder.

I lurched backward, tripped over Jesse's legs, and fell. My head thumped the rock floor.

Next thing I know, Whittle was looming above me, pointing his revolver at my face. He looked frightful. His right eye was a runny gorge. Half his face was masked with blood. He'd lost his nosepatch, so I saw the pulpy scar tissue in the cavity between the nubs of his nostrils. He was sobbing. Blood and drool dribbled off his trembling chin. His left hand was clutched to the hole in his belly.

'See what you've done to me!' he whined.

'Less than you deserved,' I said.

'I'm not finished yet, you scurvy bastard.' He threw his gun away. Whimpering and moaning, he hunched down over me, grabbed the front of my shirt, and hoisted me up till I was sitting. 'I'm not *finished*! Not quite *yet*! Watch! Watch the Ripper at work! He loves his games!'

Stumbling backward, he swept one of the huge knives from its sheath. He stood up straight. A belch came out of him and sent a gout of red flopping out his mouth.

With more energy than I gave him credit for, he jammed a boot under Jesse's hip and sent her rolling onto her back.

I looked this way and that, hoping to spy either of my revolvers – *any* revolver. None was in reach, so I tried to shove myself up to my feet as Whittle dropped across Jesse's hips.

Grunting, wheezing, blood flowing down his chin, he glared at me with his single eye. 'You've never . . . seen the . . . Ripper at play!'

'She's dead!' I yelled. 'Leave her be!'

He ran the blade beneath her shirt. With an upward jerk, he sent the buttons flying. He used the tip of his knife to fling each side of her shirt away, laying her bare to the waist.

I got my feet beneath me. I leaned forward, hoping to stand.

'Splendid set,' he gasped, spraying blood on her face. 'Which . . . which shall I . . . have off . . . first?'

'I'm right partial to them both,' Jesse said.

She grabbed his wrist, pinning the knife down flat between her breasts. Her other arm swung up and chopped the gleaming blade of her Bowie knife across the Ripper's throat.

Chapter Fifty-four

Wounds and Dressings

The blood just leaped out of Whittle, slopping onto Jesse while he sat atop her and made gaggy sounds. Then she jabbed his side to tumble him off.

I crawled toward her.

Whittle's knife still lay on her chest. She tossed it away, then blinked blood out of her eyes and looked at me.

I keeled over.

I woke up once while Jesse was tending to my wounds. My shirt was off. She had me propped up some, a pile of clothes under my back. My left arm was already wrapped tight. She was straddling me, her knife clamped between her teeth as she used both hands to rip apart somebody's shirt that she held up in front of her.

With a popping sound, the fabric split. She hadn't taken time yet to clean herself. Her face and chest gleamed with Whittle's blood.

I passed out again.

By and by, I came around. I was still sitting up against the piled clothes. Now, both my wounds were bandaged. The cave seemed darker than before. I judged that some of the torches had likely burnt themselves out.

Jesse was gone.

I called for her, but she didn't answer.

Worried, thinking that perhaps she had passed out, herself, I looked about as much as I could without trying to twist my body around. Whittle was sprawled nearby, dead as all the folks he'd murdered. I glanced at several of his victims. Had no choice in the matter, as I was hoping to find Jesse. While I did that, my eyes lit on Sarah.

She was facedown where he'd flung her.

The pain from my wounds was nothing next to the agony I felt, looking at her. My poor Sarah. A scalped and gutted carcass. Not only butchered by Whittle, but gunshot many times by me and Jesse. Ruined beyond recognizing long before we ever battered her with our slugs.

My beautiful Sarah, come to this.

She hadn't run off with Briggs, after all. She'd traveled on to Tombstone in hopes that I had survived my fall from the train and would come to her. She'd tried to take on Whittle by herself. And ended here – spending her final hours, or days, suffering the most unspeakable of tortures.

All on account of me.

She had loved me, and died for it.

It didn't matter a bit that she'd cut me off from Mother in

regard to our letters. No doubt, she'd feared losing me. A small betrayal, really.

I'd betrayed her in a far more grievous manner when I gave my heart to Jesse.

At least Sarah had been spared the knowledge of that. She'd died believing that I loved her still.

I suddenly let out a sour laugh that sent pains flashing through my body.

Indeed! It must've been a great consolation to her, believing in my love while Whittle was at her with his knives. What a trifling thing, the affections of a boy. When one is in the lair of a madman. When the body is afire with torment and death is certain.

With every cut of the knife, she should've wished that I'd never roamed into her house, that I'd been cast out into the blizzard the night of my arrival, that she'd never taken me into her arms or into her bed – certainly that she hadn't ventured west with me to search for Whittle.

She should've died cursing my very existence.

All of them should have done so. All of those who crossed my path or Whittle's, and died because of it, ever since that bitter night in London so long ago when I led him to the *True D. Light*.

At least *he'll* kill no one else, I told myself.

We finished him. Jesse and I.

My eyes lit upon a revolver some distance beyond my feet. I wondered if I had the strength to fetch it. A single bullet through my head, and nobody else would ever die on my account.

The last time I'd considered such a move, I'd held off because Whittle still needed killing.

I hadn't any such excuse, now.

Do it, I thought. Do it now, before you drag Jesse into some brand of trouble and get her killed. You near got her killed already. She'll never be safe till she's shut of you for good.

I stared at the Colt, but didn't go for it.

Shooting myself seemed the proper thing to do, and I felt rather lowdown and selfish for wanting to stay alive. Folks were likely to die because of it, and Jesse might be one of them. The thing was, spite of everything, I found that I had a keen desire to keep breathing, no matter what may lie ahead.

There were bound to be rough patches and narrow calls. There were bound to be tragedies. Heartaches and such. But I judged all that was just part of the game. It was the game that counted. Playing the hand that's dealt, as Jesse would say. But dealing a few yourself, too. And savoring the surprises and joys that come along the way.

I judged I would likely have use for both my Colts in the days and years to come – if I survived my wounds. But I knew all the way to my core that I would never again be tempted to use one on myself. They were meant for protecting me and Jesse. They were meant for sending varmints on the downward road.

With such thoughts working through my mind, I forgot to worry about where Jesse'd gone off to. But by and by, along came a sound of bootfalls on the rocky floor. I looked toward the opening at the front of the chamber. A yellowish glow shimmered in the darkness.

Then Jesse limped her way into sight.

She held a torch in one hand. Her golden hair sparkled in its light. Her face gleamed. She was huffing considerable. Saddle bags hung over one shoulder and a canteen swung by her side.

She was all decked out in a yellow calico dress. It was buttoned to her throat, had a frilly lace collar, long sleeves, and a skirt that draped her to the ankles. The gunbelt strapped around her hips, sixgun jammed in at one side, looked quite out of place and strange.

When she saw me looking, she halted and stood up straight.

'Well,' she said, 'don't wear out your eyes.'

'Jesse Sue Longley.'

'That's me.'

'In a *dress*?'

She started moving again, limping closer and grimacing. 'My other duds was in tatters, anyhow. 'Sides, you been hankering to get me into such a getup.'

'You look . . . just bully!'

'It's a mighty confining garment. Makes me feel like a ninny, too. I only just put it on cause of you being shot. You ain't bound to see me in another such rig till the next time you catch lead.'

She stood the torch upright in a nook, then hobbled over to me and sat down. 'How you feeling?' she asked.

'Reckon I'll live. For a while, at least.'

'Gotcha something here to ease the suffering.' She slipped the saddle bags off her shoulder and pulled out a flask. As she popped its cork, she said, 'Found us some food and smokes, too, but nothing'll beat whiskey when you've got holes in you.'

She passed me the flask and I took a few swallows. As the whiskey went down, a pleasant heat seemed to spread through me.

'I'm right sorry about your Sarah,' she said.

My throat tightened so I couldn't drink any more. I gave the flask back to Jesse. She went shimmery as I watched her head tip back. I blinked, and a couple of tears ran down my face.

'At least Whittle'll never get you,' I said, my voice shaking.

She lowered the flask and looked at me. 'He'll get no one ever again, Trevor. You and me saw to that.' Reaching out with one hand, she brushed the tears off my cheeks. 'You drilled him good, pardner.'

'You didn't do at all badly yourself,' I told her. 'For a dead gal.'

A smile lifted one corner of her mouth. 'You hit me, you know.'

'I did not.'

'You sure did.' She handed the flask to me, then commenced to unfasten the buttons of her dress. When they were open down to her waist, she slipped the garment off her

451

shoulders and pulled her arms from its sleeves. She scooted herself around to face me. Her chest was bound, just below her breasts, by a narrow strip of cloth. It held a small patch of cloth to the side of her ribcage. She united it, peeled away the pad, and pointed at a raw nick. The wound was at just about the same place on her as where the posse bullet had creased me, so long ago. It wasn't near as bad as mine, though. Not really more than a deep scratch. 'Told you so,' she said.

'I did that?'

'Your second shot.'

'I'm awfully sorry,' I said, painted to see that I'd hurt her.

'Well, I reckon you had to make it look good.'

'I never meant to *hit* you.'

She raised her arm high and craned her head down to look at the injury. 'It ain't much, is it?'

I forgot to answer. With her eyes turned away, it gave me a chance to study something other than her wound. She'd found the time to clean the blood off her skin. Her breasts looked as smooth as velvet except for their tips, which were dark and puckered and pointing at me.

I didn't look away fast enough. She caught me. 'Trevor Bentley.'

'They're only *you*,' I said, pleased with my quick thinking. 'No different, actually, from your shoulders or face.'

'Liar.'

But she didn't turn away or cover herself, so I had lots of time to appreciate the view while she placed the pad atop her little wound and tied it in place with the cloth strip. After finishing with the bandage, she struggled into the sleeves and pulled the dress up.

'We'd best leave pretty soon,' she said. 'We got us a good, bright moon for our trip down.'

'Is the horse still there?' I asked.

'Yep. I gave him some water. He's a mite skittish, what with the stink and the dang coyotes sneaking around, but he ain't run off yet. Let's rest a bit and put some chow into us before we head out there.'

We had a few more sips of whiskey, then ate hard rolls and beef jerky that we washed down with water. When she finished with the food, Jesse rolled cigarettes and we had us a smoke and more drinks.

The whole time, she never bothered to fasten the buttons of her dress. As it was rather chilly in the cave, I judged she'd left them undone to keep my spirits up. Mighty thoughtful of her. The strip of bare skin down her front helped take my mind off my wounds and other bad things. Every so often, when she leaned certain ways, I caught glimpses inside that warmed me up better than the whiskey.

'We'd best get moving now,' she finally said. She swung the saddle bags over one shoulder, hooked the canteen strap over the other, then struggled to her knees. 'You gonna be able to walk?'

'You're the one with a shot leg.'

'It'll hold out if you will.'

I found that neither arm worked as it should, and moving them sent awful pains through me. I couldn't use them to push myself up, so Jesse had to lend a hand. She stopped in front of me, clutched both my sides just under the armpits, and hoisted me up.

As I came off the floor, I went dizzy, staggered, and would've fallen except that she held me steady.

By and by, I was able to stay on my feet without her.

'I need my Colts,' I told her.

'Aim to do some shooting tonight?' she asked. But already, she was hobbling along to fetch them. There were several revolvers scattered about, but she knew which belonged to me. She grimaced both times she crouched to pick them up, and I felt badly about making her do it. Needed my guns, though, and couldn't get them myself.

She came back to me, her face all sweaty from the pain.

'Sure these are the two you want? All this weaponry, there's likely better to be found.'

'They suit me fine,' I said.

She tucked one down the front of her belt, then emptied

the shells out of the other. Stepping in close, she put her arms around me. I felt the heat of her body, the push of her breasts, the tickle of her hair against my cheek as she worked with one hand to take fresh rounds from the loops at the back of my gunbelt. Then she stepped back and plugged them into the cylinder.

She dropped that Colt into my holster, pulled the other and sent its shells falling. Once again, she snuggled in while she removed ammo from my belt loops. She was still at it when I kissed the side of her face.

Figured that would fetch me a remark. I was wrong, though. Instead of making a smart quip, she went and kissed me full on the mouth, ever so gentle and sweet. She didn't quit very soon, either, but kept her mouth to mine for the longest time. Her breathing filled me. I let my eyes drift shut, and felt as if Jesse was melting into me.

When she eased away, I near fell over. She braced me up with a Colt and a fistful of ammunition.

'Steady, pardner,' she said.

Pretty soon, she let go of me and finished loading my weapon. She holstered it for me. 'Reckon you'll need a shirt. The ones we wore in ain't much good.'

She commenced to wade through the clothes and weapons and such, searching.

It struck me that one of the dresses scattered about on the chamber floor had likely belonged to Sarah. None looked familiar, though. I hoped that the dress Jesse wore wasn't Sarah's, but judged that it wasn't. Jesse was shorter and slimmer than Sarah, so the dress wouldn't have been such a good fit. Perhaps Sarah's was the dress that Jesse'd used for bandages, and parts of it were even now wrapped tight around the thigh of the woman who'd taken me from her.

'Here you go,' Jesse said, and I was mighty glad to have my mind turned away from the track it'd been following.

She held up a shirt that was dark with dried blood.

'Nope,' she said, and dropped it. 'Ripped too bad.'

Continuing with her search, she picked up quite a few

more shirts, one at a time, groaning some with the pain and effort. They all looked quite bloody. A couple had rents in the back. None had any bullet holes at all. One didn't even have a tear in the fabric.

The shirts showed how Whittle must've murdered the posse. He'd killed the men with his knives. Likely dispatched them one at a time in the cave's darkness, and hauled them outside afterwards.

While I pondered over that, it came to me that few of the dresses or petticoats or other female garments were soiled with blood. Whittle must've stripped the gals naked before laying into them. That came as no great surprise, actually.

I could wear a dress and stay shut of strangers' blood if I didn't mind looking like a girl. But the notion didn't thrill me much.

'That'll be fine,' I said when Jesse picked up still another shirt.

'It's awful bloody.'

'They all are.'

She held it up toward the light of a torch. 'Well, least this one ain't torn.'

'He must've slit that poor bloke's throat.'

A corner of her mouth turned up. 'Same as I done him.'

She helped me into that shirt. While it was still open, she ran her hands all over my chest and belly and sides. The caresses felt just splendid. Too soon, she quit and pulled the shirt together and buttoned it all the way up.

'We'd best get moving,' she said.

She took a few steps backward, watching me as I had a go at walking. Then she fetched the torch that she'd used during her earlier venture outside. With the torch raised high, she led us to the front of the chamber.

There, I took a quick look back at the array or horrors. At the carved bodies. At the scalps and such on pikes. At Whittle, sprawled out dead. Finally, at what was left of Sarah. I hated to leave her in such a place. There was no way to take her with us, though.

One thing I've learned, the dead don't need help. They call for some grieving and often need vengeance, but not much else. It's those still alive who matter.

And so I turned away and followed Jesse toward the outside.

Chapter Fifty-five

The Downward Trail

The coyotes scampered off, silent and eerie, when we came out into the moonlight. Jesse tossed the torch aside. It fell near a headless body, casting light on the ghastly work done by Whittle and the other beasts.

We staggered on, and reached the tethered horse. Jesse patted his neck and spoke gently to him.

Was this Matthew Forrest's horse, Saber? Quite likely.

I recalled the morning, so quiet, so lovely with fallen snow, when Sarah and I had entered the stable and discovered that Saber had gone missing. And how we had plotted together to deceive her grandfather. It seemed so long ago. It seemed almost as though a different fellow, not myself at all, had been the one to conspire with her.

Yet this must be Saber. Here, standing before me.

Quite suddenly, the many miles and months between that morning near Coney Island and this night somewhere in the Arizona Territory shrank down to nothing. It *had* been me, not a different fellow at all. It might've been yesterday when Sarah and I gazed into the empty stable stall.

Everything felt like yesterday. Standing there among the carnage while Jesse swung the saddle bags onto Saber's back,

I quite fell apart. I bawled like a child. For Sarah. For McSween. For all of those who'd crossed my path and died. Even for strangers butchered by Whittle, as every victim this side of the Atlantic had died on my account. Maybe I cried for some I'd killed my own self, though certainly not for him.

Jesse took me into her arms. 'It's all right,' she whispered. 'It's all right.'

'It's awful,' I blubbered. 'So many. So many dead.'

'I know.'

She held me for a long while. At last, her embrace and caresses soothed me down. She brushed the tears from my cheeks. She kissed me. 'You ready to go?'

I nodded.

She led Saber through the savaged remains of man and horse. At the boulder where we'd set our ambush, she tied our rifles together. She slung them over Saber, just in front of the saddle, then looped the straps of two canteens and the water bag over the saddle horn.

Holding the reins with one hand, she climbed atop the boulder. She lifted her long skirt, bunching it up so high I glimpsed the bandage around her thigh, then stepped into a stirrup and swung her wounded leg over the saddle.

I climbed the boulder. As Jesse snuggled the horse in close, I heaved a leg over his back and rather leaped with my other. Risky work, having no use of my arms. But Jesse stopped me when I started to fall off the other side. Her arm struck where I was gunshot on the left, and I yelped. But at least she saved me from a nasty tumble. I squirmed about until Saber was square between my legs.

'You okay?' Jesse asked.

'I've been better, actually.'

'Same goes here. You ain't gonna fall off, now, are you?'

'Hope not.'

'You can't hold on at all?'

'Not with my arms.'

She started Saber walking. Instead of heading away, though, she turned him around. Steered him into the midst of the bodies. There, she dismounted. She limped over to a dead horse, fetched a coil of rope off its saddle, and came back. She made a loop at one end of the rope, swung it about a few times, and lassoed me. Stepping up close, she raised the loop beneath my arms, then slipped it tight around my chest.

At the boulder again, she hoisted her skirt and climbed aboard the saddle. She wrapped the rope around herself. When she finished, we were bound together, only enough slack between us so I wasn't quite mashed against her back.

'That oughta hold you,' she said.

'It'll be a spot awkward if we need to climb down.'

'I don't aim to take us nowhere the horse can't carry us,' Jesse said. 'We just gotta find where the posse came in.'

She set Saber to moving at a slow walk. By and by, we found a gap that was wide enough for us. In we went, leaving behind the cave, the ghastly clearing, Sarah and Whittle and all the other dead.

It was mighty good to be going away from such things.

I figured we were lucky to get out alive.

And lucky to have a horse. Not that the bouncing about felt good. It shook me up considerable, and never gave me a rest from the pain. But this sure beat walking. No telling how we might've faired afoot. Not well, likely. But if we rode on steady and didn't get ourselves lost in the maze, we ought to be down off the mountain before sunup. From the trail at the base of Dogtooth, we'd be less than two days from Tombstone. We'd likely get there sometime tomorrow night.

I judged we could both last that long. Then we'd find ourselves a doctor and get patched up proper, and have no more business but to rest and recover.

The trick was to stay aboard Saber.

On a level trail, that wouldn't have been much of a problem. But our course through the rocks was rough. We not only had to wind this way and that and sometimes back out of dead ends, but every so often Saber had to charge up a steep place.

The first time that happened, it took me and Jesse by surprise. I yelped and pitched backward. I tried to reach for her, but my dang arms wouldn't move fast enough. The rope jerked taut, pretty near tearing Jesse out of the saddle. She cried out with pain, but clutched the pommel in time to stop us both from smashing to the ground.

At the top of the grade, she reined in Saber. Then she hunched over. I put my face against her back, and felt how she was twitching.

'This won't do,' I told her.

She didn't answer.

'You'd best let me down. I'm fit enough to walk.'

She sniffed. 'You stay where you're at,' she said, her voice tight and shaky. 'We'll get by.'

'That must've hurt you terribly.'

'I ain't gonna have you walking.' Slowly, she unhunched herself and sat up straight. 'Next time, I'll give you a warning. Just lean up against me tight as you can.'

So that's how we played it. Enough moonlight made its way down through the narrow walls of rock for her to see ahead of us. Usually. And usually, she gasped out 'Lean!' just before Saber lunged up a slope or leapt across a gully. We'd both duck forward and come through it fine. Sometimes, though, he surprised us.

No less than eight more times, on our way across that damn valley, Saber took unexpected jumps or clambered up night-shrouded slants in such a way that I was thrown backward against the rope. Each time, my fall was stopped by Jesse. It's a pure wonder that she was able to hold on, again and again, as the rope tugged so savagely at her chest. But hold on she did.

She rarely cried out, though the pain must've been terrible.

By the time we finally came out of the valley and halted before starting our descent down the mountain, my back was so abraded by the rope that it burned near as bad as my bullet holes. I felt blood sliding down beneath my shirt. Jesse's chest, I knew, could be in no better shape than my back.

I leaned forward against her. She was bent over the pommel, shuddering and sobbing.

'I'm so sorry,' I gasped, weeping myself for her torment and bravery.

I longed to wrap my arms around her.

And did so, though the pain almost drove me senseless.

My hands met warm, slick blood.

'Oh, Jesse,' I murmured.

She sat up a bit. Her trembling hands found mine and pressed them to her. She sniffled. After a while, she lifted my hands. She crossed them at the wrists, then eased them inside the open front of her dress and held them to her breasts. I pushed my face against the side of her neck. Later, I kissed her there.

We stayed that way for a long while, Saber shuffling beneath us but going nowhere. Off in the east, the horizon was going pale with the approach of daylight.

Jesse finally sat up straight and took a deep breath. 'Reckon your hands ain't useless, after all.'

I realized that I was caressing her with them. 'They're all right for this, anyhow,' I said.

'Lord, that was a hellish ride.'

'You were bully.'

'I sorta kept a lookout for General. Maybe we'll find him down below.'

'Maybe.' I couldn't bring myself to care a whole lot, one way or the other.

'Least we didn't run into no rattlers,' she said.

'Matters were dicey enough without them.'

'Well, we're likely past the worst of it. Downhill won't be a problem.'

'Before tomorrow morning, we ought to be in Tombstone.'

'Not if we sit up here all day.' She let go of my hands. They fell. I gasped and flinched. She caught them by the wrists. 'I'm sorry. Lord.'

I hissed through my teeth for a spell. Then said, 'Quite all right.'

Jesse gently lifted them, reached around, and eased them down on my lap.

'Ready?' she asked.

'Take it slow and easy.'

She clucked her tongue and Saber started down the steep, narrow trail. It was easy going. All we had to do was lean back some and keep our balance, and Saber took care of the rest.

As we descended the mountainside, the sun came up, spreading its rosy glow across the desert. A glorious thing to see. And wonderful to feel its warmth after the rather chilly night.

The morning was lovely, and ever so quiet and peaceful. There seemed to be no other sounds than Saber's hoofs thudding on the trail, some birds calling out, bugs buzzing and chittering. Every so often, I heard the quiet chh-chh, chh-chh-chh of rattlers. Though they unsettled me some, they sounded far off, and I didn't let them ruin how good I felt to be riding down that trail with Jesse in front of me, her hair all agleam in the sunlight.

Sore and stiff as I was, I did feel good. It was the fresh, new morning. It was being with Jesse. It was knowing that my hunt for Whittle was over.

Jack the Ripper would never harm another poor soul.

Jesse and I had the world before us, all splendid and bright. After Tombstone, after recovering, we would be free to go on about our lives together. Of course, I would ask for her hand in marriage. More than likely, she'd accept. Maybe she'd even stoop to wearing a gown for the wedding, and I wouldn't need to get shot again before seeing her in another dress.

We weren't a great distance from the foot of the mountain, and I was busy entertaining myself with thoughts of having Jesse for my wife, when Saber bellowed out a frightful scream and reared up. I flew back till the rope stopped me. Jesse cried out. Though jerked so roughly I feared her spine might snap, she stayed in the saddle. I hung from her as Saber scurried backward on his hind legs, staggered and stepped off the trail. Squealing, forelegs kicking at the sky, he dropped into space.

'No!' Jesse yelled.

She leaped sideways, hurling us both off Saber's back, no doubt hoping we might land on the trail.

But we fell short. The slope struck us. Down it we tumbled. It was frightfully steep. It flipped us this way and that, all the while drubbing us with its rocky wall. Tethered together, we crashed against each other as we rolled. My weight pounded Jesse against the mountain. The back of her head clubbed my brow and cheeks and nose. Over and over we went.

As we plummeted, I somehow hugged her to me and clung to her with what little strength I possessed in my feeble arms.

On we tumbled, skidding and rolling, battered by rocks, torn now and again by brambles as we crashed through them, only to be gouged and hammered by more rocks.

Then we went off a ledge.

I was on top of Jesse as we plunged straight down. I twisted myself about in hopes of turning us over so that I might be first to crash against whatever might wait for us below. But I failed. All too soon, we slammed the earth, Jesse's body saving me from the brunt of the impact. My face hit the back of her head. Darkness swallowed me.

When I regained my senses, I found myself sprawled on Jesse's back. I raised my throbbing head. A mat of her hair lifted with it, glued by blood to my face. It peeled away as I looked about.

We had come to rest at the foot of the mountain. Saber lay nearby, dead, a buzzard plunging its beak into his vitals.

Was Jesse also dead?

I spoke her name, my voice dry and rough. She didn't respond.

My arms were trapped beneath her, one hand flat against her belly, the other higher. With it, I felt the rope that bound us together. And her skin. Her skin was sticky with blood. I lay very still, all my thoughts on that hand, hoping to detect the throb of Jesse's heartbeat.

I felt nothing.

Perhaps my hand was too low, too far from her heart. Or

perhaps it was so ruined by my many injuries as to be rendered incapable of finding so small a throb.

I tried to move my hand higher. All I gained for the effort was a burst of pain from my gunshot and battered shoulder.

'Jesse!' I gasped. 'Jesse, wake up! Please!'

She didn't answer. She didn't stir at all.

'You're not dead!' I blurted. 'You're not!'

At that, I quite lost my wits. I bucked and thrashed until my arms came out from under her, and kept at it. Finally, I managed to turn myself over. I lay there, gasping and whimpering, the sunlight blazing in my eyes, my back to Jesse's back.

I sat up, straining against the rope. Jesse came up with me. Lunging forward, I got to my knees. Then to my feet, quickly ducking low and bouncing till I jarred Jesse higher on my back.

I commenced to walk. Stagger, actually.

A few steps towards Saber. I needed a canteen. The buzzard flapped off. But I turned away. How could I fetch a canteen? How, with arms all but useless? How, with Jesse hung on my back?

So I stumbled past Saber, and found the trail.

The trail would lead us ... where? Somewhere. Away. Where we could rest and get better.

On and on, I trudged.

Jesse's head wobbled against the side of my neck. Her arms hung behind mine, and all four swayed like the limbs of a lifeless beast. Her legs swayed, too. I couldn't see them, but often felt the heels of her boots bump against the backs of my legs.

I liked the feel of that.

The bump of her boots. As if she was alive and giving me playful kicks.

On and on, we made our way together down the trail.

Now and then, I fell to my knees. But I always made it back onto my feet again, and struggled onward.

Near sundown, we came upon a covered wagon stopped by the side of the trail.

I couldn't make it that far.

My face met the dust.

Sprawled out under Jesse, my mind half gone with weariness and agony and grief, I tried to call out for help.

When I opened my eyes, I was seated, propped up against a wagon wheel. Jesse was stretched out on the ground, just beyond my feet.

Her face was bloody, her dress a tattered ruin. It was primly spread over her legs and its front was buttoned shut, but her poor skin showed through a score of rents. Her hands were folded together atop her chest.

The wagon wheel shook against my back as someone jumped down out of the rear.

A big old man, white-bearded, his head crowned by a bowler hat with white feathers rising from both sides like jackrabbit ears, Fringe trembled all around his shirt and knee-high moccasins as he bustled toward Jesse, a bottle of red fluid in his right hand.

I knew him.

'Dr Jethro Lazarus, at your service. We meet again, Trevor, my lad!'

Crouching by Jesse's head, he clamped his teeth around the bottle's cork, popped it, and spat it toward a nearby cactus.

'We'll have her fit as a fiddle!' he called, and winked at me.

'Is she . . . alive?'

'Dead as a doornail, sorry to say. But don't fret.' He hoisted the bottle toward me and gave it a shake. 'Glory Elixir. Good for what ails ya.'

'Howdy there,' Ely greeted me, coming into sight from somewhere near the wagon's front, all gawky and grinning. He flapped a hand in my direction.

He looked so . . . chipper.

Dead. Jesse was dead. *Dead as a doornail.*

Of course, I'd feared as much.

I stared at her. My 'pardner'. My love.

I'd known it would come to this, if she rode with me.

Lazarus pried open Jesse's mouth.

'All set to watch the miracle of the Glory Elixir?' he asked me.

All the Glory Elixir under heaven wouldn't be enough to bring Jesse back to me. And I hated the old fraud for playing out his game.

'Just leave her be,' I muttered.

'Leave her dead? When I, Dr Jethro Lazarus, am possessed of the mighty revivification powers of the Glory Elixir? Prepare yourself for the miracle of miracles!'

'Hallelujah!' Ely shouted, and clapped his hands.

Lazarus poured Glory Elixir toward Jesse's mouth. Some splashed off her bloody lips and chin, trickled down her cheeks. But not all of it. Plenty found its target.

And Jesse coughed.

Epilogue

Wherein I Wind Things Up

Jesse and I talked it over considerable, later on, and judged she'd likely never been dead at all. That's our opinion, and even Lazarus confessed he hadn't been sure, one way or the other, when he gave her that dose of his Glory Elixir.

Though a flim-flam artist down to the soles of his moccasins, Lazarus claimed to be an actual doctor. He had surgeon's tools to prove it, and did a fine job with them when he went into me for the bullets.

He and Ely spent most of the evening patching us up. Ely stank considerable, but we didn't complain.

Jesse was in awfully poor shape. Among her many injuries, she had a split on her forehead, and underneath it a lump the size of an egg. It had likely come from the last part of the fall, when she crashed to the ground face-down. She stayed out cold after choking on the Elixir, and didn't wake up till late the next day. Then she was too dizzy and weak to move under her own power.

Lazarus and Ely seemed in no great rush to press on. For a week, we all stayed put at their wagon by the trail. They took the casket out of the wagon, and we slept in there at night.

They tended to us like a pair of nervous mothers. They cleaned us, fed us, saw to all our other needs, and poured Glory Elixir into us every chance they got.

By the end of the week, Jesse and I were both on our feet. We were still banged up and hadn't a lick of strength between us, but we were eager to move on.

We moved on with Lazarus and Ely, riding in their wagon. And got to Tombstone.

Jesse entered the town inside the casket. I didn't like the notion, but she'd insisted. She'd also insisted that she lay in that casket by herself, saying to Ely, 'You just keep that dang stinky varmint outa here, pal!'

After a crowd gathered, Lazarus and Ely dragged the casket out and set it onto the ground. Lazarus was in fine form, expounding on the miraculous healing powers of the Glory Elixir. Soon, he threw the lid off. Jesse, stretched out in the pine box, her face still cut and scabbed and bruised and swollen (with some fake blood added to improve her appearance), her dress soiled and torn, looked so ruined and dead that the sight of her made my heart sore.

Then Lazarus dumped some Elixir into her mouth.

She slurped it down, groaned, and came to life so spry it was purely astonishing. I was dumbfounded, watching her. She cried out 'Glory hallelujah!' as she sprang from the casket, then acted like a nitwit and hobbled out and hugged just about everyone. She hugged me, too. I was the only chap she kissed. She had a grand, merry sparkle in her eye.

Afterward, Lazarus allowed as how he'd never sold so much Glory Elixir at one show.

Well, Jesse had put Ely out of his job. He didn't seem to mind, though.

We joined up with that pair of flim-flam artists and traveled south with them.

Down in Bisbee, we got married. It was Lazarus's idea to make it part of the show. Jesse figured it was a bully notion. So she no sooner got herself revivified than her eyes lit on me and she limped over and threw her arms around me.

'Marry me!' she cried out.

'But we don't actually know each other,' I claimed.

'Don't matter! I been dead and now I'm alive, thanks be to the Glory Elixir! You're a handsome feller! I've gotta have you!'

The crowd went plumb wild, and likely would've carted me out of town on a rail if I'd denied her wish.

So I agreed to have her.

So they sent someone off to fetch a preacher.

Jesse climbed inside our wagon. A while later, out she came. The fake blood was gone from her face. And the nasty old tattered dress was gone, too. In its place, she wore a splendid white wedding gown that she'd bought after our Tombstone show. The crowd just oohed and ahhed like they'd never seen anything so glorious.

I'd never seen anything so glorious, myself. She was still banged up some, but looked ever so beautiful.

Pretty soon, along came the preacher.

And marry us he did.

The whole situation was a sight peculiar. But we had us a grand time, and Lazarus sold enough Elixir to keep the Bisbee folks fit as fiddles for at least a century.

We all of us partied and whooped it up till late into the night. Then Lazarus and Ely showed us to a hotel room, and left us there by ourselves.

We had a passel of aches and scars and the like, but didn't let them hold us back.

On the bed with Jesse, kissing her, feeling her skin against mine, and finally at last joining up with her – it was all so much finer than I'd ever imagined.

We spent the rest of the night in the room. And all the next day. And all the next night. Food and drink were brought to us. We slept part of the time. Mostly, we didn't.

But it came time to move on.

We found Lazarus and Ely in a saloon, surrounded by other folks who'd been present at the revivification and the wedding. Another party ensued.

Finally, around dusk, the four of us made our rather drunken way to the wagon, boarded it, and set off for parts unknown.

We figured to make the wedding a regular part of the show. But that's getting past the rightful end of our story. *Adios*, folks. Carry on.

In the Dark

THIS BOOK IS DEDICATED TO
BRIDGET ANN
THE KANGAROO ISLAND GIRL

Thanks for the letter and photo.
My regards to Roy and Long John Silver.

Your address went missing.
Please write again.

Chapter One

Jane Kerry noticed the envelope when she stepped behind the circulation desk. Her first thought was that it didn't belong on the seat of her chair. She hadn't put it there. Had it fallen from the top of the desk? She wondered if someone might've lost it, and whether it contained anything of importance.

She ignored the envelope as she checked out half a dozen mysteries to old Agnes Dixon. Agnes was one of her regulars, a retired school teacher, and the first person to make Jane feel really welcome in her new job as head of the Donnerville Public Library.

While they chatted in quiet voices, a few more people drifted over to the circulation desk. Others wandered out the door. As usual, the library was beginning to empty with the approach of its nine o'clock closing time.

The envelope.

Jane slipped a dated card into the pocket of Agnes's last book – a Dick Francis – flipped the cover shut, and set it atop the woman's stack. Even as she said, 'That's one of his best,' she took a small step backward. Feeling the push of the seat's edge against her right buttock, she reached down without looking. She fingered the envelope and picked it up.

'Hi,' said a teenaged boy who looked vaguely familiar. 'I'd like to get this, please.'

'Sure thing.'

He pushed a book toward Jane, cover open, and held out his library card for her. She took it with her left hand.

She brought her right hand up and glanced at the envelope. Handwritten in the center, in black ink, was one word:

JANE

What?

Me?

She felt mildly surprised and perplexed, and a little bit anxious.

What could it be?

At least the envelope apparently hadn't been lost by anyone, so she wouldn't need to worry about trying to catch its owner.

She tossed it back onto the seat, and returned to business. She tried to focus entirely on the patrons, getting to know them better, hoping to show them that she was friendly and always ready to help in any way possible.

The mysterious envelope didn't preoccupy her thoughts.

Instead, it lingered just off to the side where her mind seemed to glance at it from time to time, and wonder.

An invitation? A greeting card of some kind? A love letter or poem from a secret admirer?

A complaint?

Maybe a bit of hate mail from someone I shushed.

Could be anything, she told herself. Don't worry about it. You'll find out as soon as everybody's cleared out.

'If you like that one,' she told a pony-tailed girl, 'we've got a lot more by the same author.'

As the girl thanked her and headed for the door, Jane swept her eyes over the remaining people. Quite a bunch. Maybe six still lined up, a few on their way out, a dozen others scattered about the main reading room. No telling how many might be upstairs in the stacks. Nobody in sight seemed to be paying any special attention to her.

Whoever left it will probably stay behind to see if I open it.

Hope he's cute.

Don't hope for cute, she told herself. Just hope he's not a weirdo.

By the time Jane was done checking out books, only a handful of people still lingered in the reading room. She recognized most of them as regulars. They all seemed busy with their own projects. Don, her assistant, was making his way among the tables, gathering up books and periodicals that needed to be put away.

She checked her wristwatch.

Ten till nine.

She picked up the envelope again. Holding it at waist level so that the desk would hide it from the view of anyone who might be watching, she flipped it over.

As she'd thought, nothing on either side except the handwritten JANE.

The envelope looked clean and unrumpled.

Its flap was sealed.

From the envelope's thinness, she supposed that it contained nothing more than a sheet or two of folded paper.

She picked at a corner of the flap, tore it upward, thrust her forefinger into the small hole, and worked her finger along the seam, ripping upward.

As she tore at the flap, she lifted her gaze. Nobody appeared to be watching.

Looking down, she removed a folded sheet of paper from the envelope. Lined, three-hole paper of the sort that students use for filling their looseleaf binders. It was folded into thirds. She could see the raised, dark scribbles of the handwriting on the other side. And a darkness within. A darkness caused by an extra layer of paper. Paper the size of a bank check or a dollar bill.

Somebody sent me money?

Suddenly, she felt like an idiot.

This was not a message from a secret admirer. Nor was it a threat. This was nothing more than payment for a lost book or an overdue fine.

Jane felt silly. A little relieved. And a little disappointed.

She unfolded the paper.

Inside was not a bank check, but a stiff, unwrinkled fifty-dollar bill.

Must've been a mighty *expensive* book, Jane thought.

She moved the bill aside and read the handwritten note:

Dear Jane

Come and play with me. For further instructions, look homeward, angel. You'll be glad you did.

Warmest Regards,
MOG
(Master of Games)

Jane read it again. And again. Then she looked around. The few people who remained in the reading room were paying no attention to her.

'We'll be closing in about five minutes,' she announced.

She refolded the note around the fifty-dollar bill and tucked it back inside the envelope.

'Don, would you come here for a minute?'

The lanky graduate student hurried toward her. He looked worried. Or guilty? 'Is there a problem, Miss Kerry?'

Jane shook her head. 'I don't think so.' She raised the envelope. 'Did you happen to see anyone put this on my chair?'

He rolled his eyes upward as if an answer might be written on the ceiling. Then he shook his head. 'No. I don't believe so.'

'Anyone hanging around the circulation desk when I was away from it?'

Again, he shook his head. 'Not that I noticed.'

She shook the envelope. 'This isn't from *you*, is it?'

'Me? No. What is it?'

Jane hesitated. How much should she tell him? She'd known Don for a couple of months, and she didn't *really* know much about him. Only that he'd been a part-time helper at the library for a year before her own arrival, he was going for a PhD in English literature at the university across town, that he was single and lived in an apartment a few blocks from the library. She also knew that he was agonizingly shy and apparently had no social life.

Maybe he's trying to start one up with me, she thought, by way of a mysterious message and a chunk of money.

'It's an anonymous letter,' she said, and decided not to mention the fifty dollars.

His eyes widened. 'From a secret admirer?'

'Not exactly.'

His jaw dropped. 'Not a threat, I hope!'

'No. Just a . . . strange sort of message. But you haven't seen anyone wandering around with an envelope like this, or acting in any way furtive near the circulation desk?'

'I certainly haven't.' He eyed the envelope. 'May I?'

'Thanks, but . . . I don't think so.' Seeing the dejected look on his face, she added, 'It's rather personal.'

'Personal?' He suddenly blushed. 'Oh. Well. Never mind. If I'd known it was personal . . .' He grimaced and shook his head. 'I'm sorry.'

'Don't worry about it, Don. Really.'

'I . . . may I have your permission to leave? I haven't quite finished picking up, yet, but . . . I'm not feeling especially well. My stomach.' He pressed a hand against it.

'Sure. Go on ahead.'

'Oh, thank you.' He scurried around the end of the circulation desk, entered the office, reappeared moments later with his briefcase, gave Jane a cramped smile and a wave, and hurried for the library doors.

'Hope you feel better,' she said.

Then he was gone.

Jane wondered if she'd had a hand in causing his sudden illness.

Not unlikely. After all, she was his boss *and* a woman, on top of which she had almost (but not quite) accused him of perpetrating the anonymous letter. Plenty to give a person of Don's temperament a nasty case of upset nerves.

Describing the letter as 'personal' had apparently been the final straw.

Shouldn't have told him that, she decided. The thing isn't what you'd normally call personal. Didn't ask my income, didn't get sexy.

It's not personal, it's just plain screwy.

She glanced at her watch. Five after nine. 'We're closing up, now,' she announced. 'Time to hit the streets, folks.'

When the last was gone, she locked the front doors and returned to the circulation desk. She knew that she ought to go upstairs, make sure nobody was lingering in the stacks, and turn off the lights. She wasn't eager to do it, though. Neither she nor Don enjoyed that particular task. Just too creepy up there when you went alone.

Too quiet. Too many shadows. Too many hiding places.

Just plain spooky.

But made a great deal worse because you knew about old Miss Favor, the librarian, Jane's predecessor. She'd died up there. Dropped dead from a bad heart. Dropped dead while she was alone, closing for the night. And there she'd remained until morning when a part-timer had opened the library and discovered her body. According to Don, a rat or two had 'been at her.' He knew the unlucky worker who'd stumbled onto Miss Favor. 'Oh, she was totally freaked out. Totally. She hasn't set foot in this library ever since.'

The upstairs stacks weren't so bad in the daytime. They weren't so bad at night, either, as long as a few people were up there searching the shelves or working at the study carrels. But they were usually deserted when you went up at closing time.

Through some sort of unspoken acknowledgement of their mutual fears, Jane and Don had fallen into the habit of accompanying each other on that special job. It helped. A lot.

But tonight, Jane would need to do it alone.

Thanks a heap, Don.

Well, there was no hurry.

Back behind the circulation desk, she picked up the envelope. She removed the note and the fifty-dollar bill, and studied them both.

She had rarely seen any denominations higher than twenty dollars. The fifty seemed a bit alien. On one side was a portrait of President Grant, on the other a rendition of the U.S. Capitol. She supposed it was real.

She also supposed that she was meant to keep it. After all, the thing had come in an envelope with her name on it.

Why would anyone want to give me fifty bucks?

Was it supposed to be a gift? she wondered. Or maybe payment for some real or imagined services?

Payment in advance?

Cute, she thought. Maybe now he expects something from me. Figures I've taken the money, so I owe him.

That's what he thinks.

She read the note again:

Dear Jane,
    Come and play with me. For further instructions, look homeward, angel. You'll be glad you did.

Warmest Regards,
MOG
(Master of Games)

The 'come and play with me' sounded sort of like the eager request a child might make. *Will you come out and play?*

Of course, 'come' was also a rather vulgar euphemism for an orgasm. 'Play with me' also carried some strong sexual implications. Maybe this was an invitation – payment enclosed – to mess around with its sender.

He wants to fuck me.

The idea blasted away Jane's composure. Anger, humiliation, fear, revulsion, and an unexpected surge of desire seemed to hit her all at once, stealing her breath, making her heart race, surging heat through her body.

'The bastard,' she muttered. Here's fifty bucks, now come and play with me.

Maybe that isn't what he means, she thought.

And maybe it is.

She suddenly looked up. She turned her head, scanning the entire room.

She saw nobody. What she saw were countless hiding places: in among the rows of bookshelves, down low behind

481

the tables and chairs, behind any of the several shoulder-high card catalogs, behind the photocopy machine.

In front of my desk.

She pushed her feet against the rung of her chair and raised herself off the cushion. Hands pressed against the desk top, she leaned forward and gazed past the edge.

Nobody there.

She settled down onto her seat again.

I oughta get out of here, she thought.

Then she thought, How dangerous can a guy be if he's giving me fifty bucks?

Also, he must be familiar with literature. The 'look homeward, angel' business was definitely an allusion to the Thomas Wolfe novel – one of Jane's favorites.

She read that part of the note again. 'For further instructions, look homeward, angel.'

Further? He sees this note as the initial instruction. He has more for me. Maybe the *further* instructions will be given face to face.

Maybe not.

Maybe I'm supposed to go home and look in my mailbox for the further instructions. Look homeward. Maybe I'll find an envelope with another note inside – and and another fifty dollars.

Maybe I'll find it in the book.

Tucked inside a copy of Look Homeward, Angel.

The library's copy, if not checked out or misplaced, should be on a shelf in the fiction section.

In the upstairs stacks.

I need to go up there anyway, she reminded herself. I'll just take a quick look at the book.

What if he's waiting for me there?

Chapter Two

Jane folded the note around the fifty dollars and tucked it back inside the envelope. Her hands were trembling. She felt a little crawly in her stomach. As she walked into her office, she wondered if she *really* planned to go upstairs all by herself when there was a real possibility that the author of the note might be lurking there.

What am I *supposed* to do, leave?

Leave without shutting off the upstairs lights, without making sure everyone has cleared out? No way.

She crouched beside her office desk and slipped the envelope into her purse. Then she stood up. From the top drawer of the desk, she took her switchblade knife.

She'd found the knife a day before her seventeenth birthday, while hiking in the woods near Mount Tamalpias. The point of its slim, three-inch blade had been buried in a redwood trunk. She'd worked it loose and kept the knife.

It made quite a nice letter opener.

She released the lever at the base of the blade, then folded the blade into the handle, where it clicked into place.

If I need to take something like this with me, she thought, I shouldn't be going at all.

She looked at the office phone.

Call the police? That'd be very cute. Explain that somebody gave me fifty bucks, so now I'm afraid to go upstairs and turn off the lights.

They'll think I'm a weenie.

Bringing in the cops over a matter like this would be foolish. But she tried to think of a friend she might ask to come over.

Hello? I'm a little bit spooked about going upstairs here at the library, and I was wondering if you'd maybe like to come over and keep me company? Shouldn't take more than five minutes.

She did have a few friends who would be quick to respond if she called – but none who lived in Donnerville. Most of them lived at least an hour away. She certainly couldn't ask any of them to drive out here on such a lame pretext.

And it really *is* lame, she told herself. For one thing, this Master of Games character might be long gone. For another, he's probably harmless.

Maybe nothing but a twerpy kid. MOG, Master of Games. Sounds like the brainchild of a nerd who's spent too much time playing Dungeons and Dragons, or something.

Well, she thought, we'll soon find out.

For better or worse.

Just in case of worse, I've got my trusty knife.

On her way out of the office, Jane rubbed the switchblade against her right thigh, trying to slip it into her pocket. Having no success, she looked down. She was wearing her denim skirt, not her culottes. The culottes had pockets, but the skirt didn't.

Her only pockets were on the front of her blouse. The white blouse, big enough to be comfortably loose, had a large pocket on each side of the chest. As she headed for the staircase, she unbuttoned the flap over the pocket on the right, lifted it, and dropped in the knife.

The plastic handle bumped against her breast. It turned sideways as it slid downward. From the tip of her breast, it fell to the bottom of the pocket. It hung there as if caught in a hammock, swaying back and forth as she walked.

Terrific, Jane thought. She'd forgotten how *enormous* these pockets were.

The damn knife won't do me a lot of good if I have to spend five minutes fishing it out.

She was already at the fire door, so she went ahead and pushed it open. The lights in the stairwell were still on. The bulbs gave off enough light to illuminate the stair treads. Just fine for safety. But they were dim and yellowish.

Not exactly cheerful.

I really should get them changed, she told herself. Just buy some new ones myself. Might help the dismal atmosphere in here.

While I'm at it, have the stairs de-squeaked.

Every one of the old wooden stairs groaned or creaked or squawked as she climbed.

This is a regular spookhouse. Why did I ever take this job in the first place?

Cut it out, she told herself. The job's just fine.

Right. It's the building *that sucks.*

As Jane arrived at the landing, halfway up, the swinging bottom of her pocket reminded her that she wanted to retrieve the knife.

Get it now, while the getting's good. If you wait till you need it . . .

I won't need it, she told herself.

Lord, I hope not.

Continuing to climb, she shoved her fingers down into the pocket. Her thumb didn't go in with them, but she didn't think she would need its help.

She worked her fingertips between the knife handle and the bottom of her pocket (felt like some sand down there – where'd that come from?) and began to raise the knife. Having no grip on it, she could only bring it up by sliding it against the underside of her breast.

As she set her foot on the top stair, the door burst open and a man charged at her.

She yelped, flinched, reached for the banister.

The man gasped, 'Whoa!'

As Jane grabbed the banister with her left hand, her right squeezed the knife in her pocket.

She felt the hard nub of its button sink down.

Uh-oh!

She dropped the knife as the blade sprang from its handle. It whipped up against her nipple while she stumbled backward and the man skidded to a halt and clamped a hand on her shoulder.

The hand stopped her, held her steady.

'I'm sorry,' the stranger blurted. 'Are you okay?'

Jane nodded. She tried to catch her breath. Her heart was thudding quick and hard. Her nipple tingled and burned. She looked down, half expecting to find the pocket of her blouse soaked with blood.

No blood.

But half an inch of shiny steel point jutted out from the side of her pocket.

The stranger looked at it, too. Then he met her eyes and said, 'Are you sure you aren't hurt?'

'I'm all right.'

'You didn't cut yourself, did you?'

He's talking about my boob! Man!

'It sort of felt like it, but I don't see any blood.'

He still held Jane's shoulder.

She wanted to get away from him, wanted to hold her hurt, wanted to check the damage. 'Were you on your way down?' she asked.

He nodded, but didn't take the hint. 'I shouldn't have been in such a hurry. Afraid I didn't realize it'd gotten so late. You're the librarian, aren't you?'

'That's right.'

'Coming up to shoo me out?'

'I didn't know anyone was up here.'

'I'm really sorry.' He released her shoulder, turned around and opened the door for her.

'Thanks,' she said.

She expected him to head on down, but he followed her out of the stairwell. She looked back at him.

He gave her a smile that looked friendly and a little sheepish. 'Do you mind? Maybe I could help you pick up, or something. I hate to leave you alone up here. Especially right after I've arranged to scare the daylights out of you.'

Jane knew she shouldn't trust him. What was he doing up here after closing time? He might even be the man who called himself MOG. But nothing about him seemed threatening. He looked very normal: his hair slightly unkempt;

his clean-shaven face attractive but not handsome in any striking way; his shirt and jeans casual but neat and clean.

For the first time, Jane noticed that he was carrying a book. It must've been in his left hand all along.

A very thick book.

The nape of her neck began to crawl.

Look Homeward, Angel. Has to be. Can't possibly be anything else.

'What's that?' she asked.

The stranger raised the book. '*Youngblood Hawke*. Wouk? I've been meaning to read it for . . . too late to check it out tonight?'

'No. No, that's fine.' She released a shaky breath. 'You can either stick around, or wait downstairs. This'll only take a couple of minutes.'

'I'll walk along with you, if that's all right.'

'Fine.'

From the stairwell door, an aisle stretched the length of the room. To the aisle's right, study carrels lined the wall. To the left stood row after row of bookshelves that reached to the ceiling. The stranger stayed at Jane's side, but half a pace behind, allowing her to lead the way.

Except for their footsteps and the creaking floorboards, there was silence.

'Was anybody else up here?' Jane asked.

'Just now? I don't think so, but I was reading. I tend to block everything out when I'm in a good book. Want me to grab these?' he asked, gesturing toward several books that had been left at one of the carrels.

'They can wait till morning. Thanks, though.'

'Welcome. My name's Brace, by the way.'

Jane looked over at him. 'It's what?'

'Brace. Brace Paxton.'

Deciding not to question him about his unusual name, she went ahead and introduced herself. 'I'm Jane Kerry.'

'I thought it might be James Bowie.'

'Are you a wise guy, Brace Paxton?'

'Sorry. But maybe you oughta take that knife out of your pocket. I'd hate to see you trip and fall with it open like that.'

'Me, too, actually.' Halting, she turned toward the gap between two rows of shelves. Her back to Brace, she delved into the pocket of her blouse. 'It's a switchblade,' she explained. 'That's how it opened. Its safety thing doesn't work.'

Carefully, she fingered her nipple through the fabric. It felt a little tender, but the pain had faded away. The blade must've given her no more than a harsh, stinging flick. 'I was trying to take it out when you rammed through the door, and I pushed the button by accident.'

'Hope it didn't do any damage.'

A blush spread sudden heat through Jane. She quit fingering her breast and reached deeper into the pocket. 'I guess I'm fine.' She curled her fingertips underneath the knife handle.

'Be careful taking it out.'

'I'm trying to be.'

This is a lousy idea, she thought. He can't see my hand, but he sure knows where it is. Next thing you know, he'll be offering to help.

'If I'd been keeping better track of the time,' he said, 'none of this would've happened.'

'No harm done.'

'I'm glad we met, though.'

Wish I could say the same, she thought. Then she said, 'Well, thanks.'

She tightened her precarious grip on the knife. Then she pushed her knuckles against the pocket, bulging the blouse away from her body to put her breast out of harm's way, and drew the knife upward, sliding its blade free of the slit. 'There. Got it.' She turned around and showed him the weapon.

'You're sure you aren't hurt?'

'I'm fine.' She folded the blade shut.

'Where'll you put it, now?'

'Guess I'll just carry it.'

They continued on their way down the aisle, Jane checking between the rows of shelves, Brace walking slowly beside her.

As they made their way toward the end of the room, Jane realized she was growing more and more tense. At first, she wasn't sure why. Then she knew.

Because they were almost to the Ws.

Should she check for *Look Homeward, Angel*?

Why not?

She'd spent enough time reshelving books up here to know the exact location of the Thomas Wolfe novels. She would be walking right past them.

What about Brace? she asked herself.

If you don't want to do it in front of him, you'll have to go all the way downstairs with him, usher him out, then come back up here by yourself.

Or wait till tomorrow.

She couldn't wait, just couldn't.

'Maybe I'll pick up something for myself,' she muttered, then sidestepped out of the aisle. She found herself facing shelf after shelf loaded with hardbound novels. She crouched down. Wolfe was lower still – level with her knees.

'Are you going for Wouk?' Brace asked.

'Wolfe.'

'*Bonfire* boy, or . . .?'

'Thomas.'

She spotted two copies of *Look Homeward, Angel*, followed by an empty space, after which was a single copy of *The Web and the Rock*, another open space, then two copies or *You Can't Go Home Again*.

Jane pulled out a copy of *Look Homeward, Angel*. Elbows on knees, she opened the book and flipped through it.

'That's just about my favorite book of all time,' Brace said.

'It is?' She looked up at him.

Her heart thudded hard.

What the hell.

'Did you leave a note on my chair tonight?'

'Huh?'

489

'Master of Games?'

Frowning, he shook his head. The confused way he looked, Jane might've been speaking jibberish.

'The what?' he asked.

'Are you the one who left the note?'

'What note?'

'I mean, it's all right. I'm just curious, okay? It's not very often I get mysterious notes with money in them.'

'I don't know anything about any note.'

'You don't, huh?'

'What sort of note?'

'"Come and play with me? For further instructions, look homeward, angel?" *That* sort of note. With a fifty-dollar bill in it?'

He looked mystified. 'It wasn't from me. If I *had* a fifty-dollar bill, I wouldn't be giving it away.' A smile suddenly lit his face. 'Well, maybe to *you*. If you needed it very badly. Maybe.'

If this is Mog, Jane thought, he's got an odd way of lying.

'Okay,' she said. 'Maybe it wasn't you.'

'Anything in the book there?' he asked.

She returned her attention to the novel, riffled through its pages, and made sure that nothing was hidden in the dust jacket. As she slid it back into its place on the shelf, Brace said, 'I think that's another copy . . .'

'I know.' She dragged the second copy forward. Even before lifting it from the shelf, she spotted a strip of white paper protruding from its top like a bookmark.

'There y'go,' Brace said, sounding pleased.

Jane opened the book. Tucked into its gutter was an envelope.

The envelope looked identical to the one she'd found downstairs on her chair. Even her handwritten name looked the same.

She plucked it out and shut the book.

'Woops,' Brace said.

'What?'

'Maybe it was there to mark a passage.'

'You *sure* you don't have anything to do with this?'

'Honest. Just trying to help.'

'Did you notice the page number?'

'No. Sorry.'

'Neither did I. Well, maybe it won't matter.' She returned the book to its shelf and stood up.

The envelope was sealed.

'Want me to leave?' Brace asked.

'No, that's all right, I already told you everything about the other one.' She looked at him. 'You're *sure* you don't have anything to do with this?'

'Pretty sure.'

'Only pretty sure?'

'Almost a hundred per cent sure.'

'You mean, like you don't want to rule out that it might've been done behind your back by one of your alternate personalities?'

'That's about right.'

'Okay. Well, here goes.' She thumbed the button of her switchblade. The knife jumped slightly as the blade sprang out and locked. She slipped its tip under the envelope's flap and slashed the top seam.

To free her hand, she reached forward and set the knife on the edge of a bookshelf. Then she spread open the envelope. Inside was a folded sheet of lined paper. She removed it, unfolded it, and pursed her lips.

'Whoa,' Brace said. 'Looks like you've earned a raise.'

Jane slipped the hundred-dollar bill aside and read the handwritten message aloud.

'"My dear Jane, Congratulations! You've taken your first, minor step on the road to fun and riches. More is waiting. Do you have the will to proceed? I hope so. At midnight, horse around. You'll be glad you did. Yours, MOG."'

Chapter Three

When Jane finished reading the note, Brace said, 'Looks like the game's still on.'

She nodded. She felt *awfully* strange.

'You don't have any idea who's doing this?' Brace asked.

'No idea at all.'

'He's generous.'

'Let's get out of here,' Jane muttered. She tucked the message and money back into the envelope, then picked up her knife. 'Keep your eyes open, okay? He might be up here.'

'Hope so. Maybe he'll give *me* a hundred bucks.'

'As long as that's *all* he does . . .'

Brace stayed at her side as she walked the remaining length of the aisle, turned around and headed back. He said nothing. He seemed watchful and tense.

He's worried, Jane realized. That was good. It confirmed her own take on the situation: anyone who would write such notes and give away that much money to a stranger was certainly abnormal – possibly dangerous.

You'd think he might want to see my reactions.

Is he watching us? Hiding up here?

If he was lurking in the stacks, however, he succeeded in staying out of sight. And he made no sounds. Jane only heard herself and Brace as they walked the old, noisy floorboards.

Maybe he's waiting in the stairwell.

She grew more tense as they approached the stairwell door. Moving ahead of her, Brace opened it. Nobody leaped out. While he waited, Jane stepped over to the panel of light switches. She flicked one after another, dropping sections of the room into darkness until no light was left except for the glow from the stairwell.

Jane hurried over to Brace. It was good to have him holding the door open for her.

Instead of starting down the stairs, she waited for him to shut the door.

'Do you want me to go first?' he asked.

'If you go first, I'll have to take up the rear.'

'Ah.' Smiling slightly, he shifted *Youngblood Hawke* into his right hand, took Jane gently by the forearm with his left, and turned her around.

'I hate this sort of thing,' she said as they started down the stairs.

'What sort of thing?'

'Feeling spooked. Being afraid somebody might jump out at me. I'm not usually such a chicken.'

'You have every right to feel nervous. I'd be pretty shaken up, too, if somebody was sending me anonymous notes. Money or no money, it's weird.'

At the bottom of the stairs, Brace let go of Jane's arm and swung open the door.

She hurried into the bright lights and kept moving, wanting to put distance between her back and the stairway to the stacks. When she heard the door bump shut, she whirled around and smiled at Brace. 'Thanks for the moral support,' she said.

'My pleasure.' He raised the novel. 'Will you let me check out the book? I know we're past closing time, but . . .'

'Happy to.'

She took up her position behind the circulation desk. Brace stepped to the other side.

'I really am grateful,' she said as he slid the book toward her.

He handed over his library card, 'What are you going to do about midnight?' he asked.

The question made Jane's stomach go cold. She shook her head. 'I don't know. I'm not even sure what I'm *supposed* to do.'

'Horse around.'

'Whatever that means.' She slid the book back to him, his library card on top.

Brace tucked the card into his wallet, then glanced at his wristwatch. 'Not quite nine-thirty yet. You've got a while to figure things out.' He met her eyes. 'I'd be glad to help. Do you need to be anywhere right now, or . . .?'

'What do you have in mind?'

'Maybe we could go to a restaurant, or something?'

She stared at him.

She liked his looks. Especially his eyes. They seemed warm and friendly, intelligent – and they looked like the eyes of someone who had known many troubles but had never forgotten how to laugh.

He had the looks of a good and decent man.

But she hardly knew him at all. She wasn't sure she *wanted* to know him. He seemed all right, but he might be the man behind the peculiar notes. For that matter, he might be a rapist or a killer. You just never knew. Even if he was harmless, he could turn out to be jealous and possessive enough to make her life miserable, or a womanizer who would get what he could and dump her. He might be none of the above, but already married.

All sorts of ways for Jane to get hurt – or worse – by this guy.

Then again, she thought, he might be just what he seems. *Figure it one chance in a thousand.*

'A wedge of pie,' he said. 'A cup of joe, and thou.'

Her small cough of laughter took her completely by surprise.

'What do you say?' Brace asked.

'Sure, why not?'

At Ezra's, a block from the library, they sat at a corner booth and Brace plucked two menus out from behind the napkin holder. He handed one to Jane. 'Hope you don't mind if I order a full meal. Do the same, if you'd like. It's on me.'

'What happened to the wedge of pie and cup of joe?'

He grinned. 'I only said that for effect. Thing is, I skipped my supper tonight.'

'On purpose?'

'Forgot about it.'

'You forgot to *eat*?'

A waitress came to the table. Jane ordered a Pepsi and chili-cheese fries. Brace ordered a bacon cheeseburger, seasoned curly fries, and a root beer.

When the waitress was gone, he said, 'I suddenly got this bug to read *Youngblood Hawke*. Does that ever happen to you? There's some book or author you've always wanted to try, and all of a sudden you *have* to?'

'Oh, yes. Sometimes, I need an 87th Precinct fix. Or I get a sudden a craving for a Travis McGee. And there are times I feel like I can't get through the night without reading a Hemingway story.'

'Really? Unusual tastes for a woman. But I did have you pegged for a book nut.'

'Must've been quite a leap, considering I'm a librarian.'

Brace laughed. 'Takes one to know one. I teach lit. over at D.U. Anyway, I got the urge to read *Youngblood Hawke*, so I went over to the university library. Their only copy was checked out, so then I tried the B. Dalton – no luck – the Waldenbooks – no luck. Finally, I gave your library a try. Success! I grabbed the book and hurried over to the nearest carrel to start reading. Thus did I miss my supper.'

'And thus did you miss closing time.'

'My powers of concentration are awesome. And often a pain in the rear. Give you an example. I picked up an F. Paul Wilson novel at an airport gift shop last Christmas. I was supposed to fly home to spend the holidays with my family. While I was waiting for the jet to start boarding, I began to read the book there in the waiting area by the gate. A very *crowded* waiting area. When I came out of the book, the crowd was gone. So was my flight.'

She saw the glint in his eye. 'You're kidding.'

'It's the truth. Stuff like that happens to me all the time.'

'But that's awful!' she gasped, trying not to laugh.

'Oh, everything balances out. Tonight, for instance, my little problem introduced me to you.'

'Lucky you.'

'You're quite an improvement over your predecessor.'

'You knew her?'

'Oh, yes. Old Phyllis Favor. An awful thing.'

'Her death?'

'Her life.'

Jane laughed. 'That's *terrible*.'

'You never met her, did you?'

'No, but . . .'

'I know people who stayed away from that library because of her. Real book-lovers, too. Including myself, when I finally couldn't stomach any more of that woman. I've seen her make people burst into tears by the way she *looked* at them. Not a nice person, may she rest in peace.'

'I've heard she was . . . unpleasant.'

'The earth is a far a better place, now that she's beneath it.'

Jane tried not to laugh, but couldn't stop herself. 'And you seemed like such a *nice* man.'

'People are often mistaken that way.'

The waitress arrived with their food and drinks. When she was gone, Brace lifted his glass of root beer toward Jane. 'Here's lookin' atcha, Madame Librarian.'

She raised her Pepsi and winked at him.

And wondered if she had ever before in her life winked at anyone.

For the next few minutes, she sipped her drink and forked chili-cheese fries into her mouth and watched Brace devour his burger and fries. He didn't say anything, just ate and looked at her and sometimes smiled. From the expressions on his face and his occasional moans, he seemed to be relishing every moment.

Done, he wiped his mouth with a napkin. He sighed. 'Good eatin'.'

'Would you like to polish off my fries?' She had plenty left. She pushed the container toward him, but he shook his head.

'Gotta watch my figure,' he said.

Jane blushed. She couldn't help it. Brace was slim and trim and looked as if he didn't need to lose an ounce. Jane was the one who should be watching her figure, who'd been neglecting it for way too long. She hadn't allowed herself to grow *fat*, but the extra weight and lack of exercise had thickened her, softened her.

Enough so that Brace's mention of 'figures' had triggered the rush of heat. With her fair complexion, a blush never failed to turn her face bright red. Brace couldn't help but notice it.

'So,' he said, 'what do you want to do about your mysterious friend?'

'I'm not sure,' she said, surprised that he'd made no comment on the blush. You *are* a good guy, she thought. 'I guess I'm pretty curious. Who is he? Why is he doing it?'

'He or she,' Brace said.

'It *might* be a woman.'

'Of course, he doesn't call himself "*Mistress* of Games."'

Jane nodded. 'So it probably *is* a man.'

'A man with money to spare.'

'Yeah. Jeez. Fifty bucks. I mean, I'm not exactly rich. To me, that's a lot of money. It's a pair of decent shoes, or a week's worth of groceries. It'd pay my telephone bill for a couple of months.'

'He gave you a *hundred* and fifty.'

'I *know*. Fifty in the first envelope, a hundred in the second. Which means he *doubled* the amount the second time around. What if I find the third envelope, and he's doubled things again? There might be *two* hundred in it. Or even three, if he doubles the whole amount instead of just the previous installment.'

'Or there might be nothing,' Brace said.

'What do you mean?'

'Maybe there isn't a third envelope. Maybe you'll figure out where it's supposed to be, go there looking for it, and he's waiting for you.'

'Yeah.' Though she was aware of that possibility, she didn't like hearing it spoken. The words, especially coming from Brace, seemed to give the idea more weight. 'If he wanted to jump me,' she said, 'he could've done it in the library.'

'I was there. And you left with me.'

Jane suddenly smiled. 'Ah! But at the time he left the message telling me to "horse around" at midnight, he couldn't have known I'd be leaving with you. Which means he never intended to attack me in the library.'

Brace nodded.

The waitress came to their table. 'Will there be anything else, folks?'

'I'd like a cup of coffee,' Brace told her. 'How about you, Jane?'

'Sure.'

As the waitress walked away, Jane shivered slightly though the restaurant was warm. She was nervous, but excited. She had goosebumps. She pressed her thighs together. She wanted to rub her arms, but that might draw Brace's attention.

The waitress returned quickly with two mugs of coffee, and set them down in front of Jane and Brace.

Brace raised his mug. He blew a soft breath at its top. 'So you're fairly sure you want to go ahead with this?' he asked.

Jane shrugged. Her shoulders trembled slightly. Her shivers didn't seem ready to go away. *Just don't get any worse, or Brace'll notice.*

'Is that a maybe?'

'More of an "I think so."' She gritted her teeth to stop her jaw from shaking. She hadn't attempted to drink her coffee yet. She didn't dare lift the mug. Not while she felt like this.

Brace took a few sips from his. He watched her closely, concern in his eyes. 'Are you okay?'

'Just a little nervous. *Very* nervous, as a matter of fact.'

'I know a great way to get over it.'

'How's that?'

'Choose not to play the game. Keep the money you've gotten so far, and forget about going after any more.'

You're probably half right. There'd still be the problem of you.

I could follow the same advice with Brace, she told herself. Choose not to play. This thing with him doesn't have to go anywhere. It can end right here.

A corner of Jane's mouth twitched. 'Quitters never prosper,' she said.

'You want to go ahead with it?'

'I have to, don't I?'

'You do *not* have to,' Brace said. 'All it would take is a decision against acting on the second note.'

'But then I'll never know what might've happened.'

'Do you think it's worth the risk?'

She grimaced and rubbed her chin. Her fingers felt like ice. 'I guess so. Up to a point. You know what they say: nothing ventured, nothing gained. I wouldn't want to get hurt, though. You know? I don't want to get myself ... attacked by some lunatic. It wouldn't be worth it, not for a couple of hundred bucks. But maybe this guy *isn't* a lunatic.'

She picked up her mug. It shuddered, coffee sloshing up its sides but not quite spilling over the brim. With the help of her other hand, she managed to bring the mug under control. As she took a drink of the coffee, she met Brace's eyes.

'You won't have to go alone,' he told her. 'Okay? If you want to follow through, I'll go with you. I'll do whatever I can to protect you.'

She set down her mug, but didn't let go of it. 'That'd help,' she said.

Brace reached forward. He lowered his hand down onto Jane's left wrist, wrapped his fingers around it, and gently squeezed. His hand felt warm. It didn't tremble at all.

'That'd help a lot,' she added. She could feel her tremors and chills subsiding.

Because he's touching me? she wondered. Or because he's coming with me?

'I wouldn't be able to *guarantee* your safety,' he said.

'So when do we ever get guarantees?'

'When we buy a wristwatch.'

She smiled. 'When we buy *anything* from L.L. Bean.'

Brace laughed softly. He squeezed her wrist again. 'Feeling better?'

'A little bit.'

'Anyway,' he said, 'we have no reason at all to believe that your mysterious Master of Games has any intention of harming you.'

'I know, I know. But if it's not something like that, why *is* he doing it?'

'Could I have a look at the notes?' He let go of her wrist. It was warm where he'd been holding it, and now it felt bare and cool.

Jane turned aside. Her purse stood upright on the seat cushion, close to her hip. She reached into it and pulled out both the envelopes. She passed them to Brace. He studied the outsides of the envelopes. Then he plucked out the folded sheets of paper. He removed the fifty-dollar bill and the hundred-dollar bill, and handed them to Jane. 'Why don't you go ahead and put these in your wallet?'

'Should I?'

'They're yours.'

'Guess so.'

While she searched her purse, found her wallet and slipped the money into its bill compartment, Brace unfolded the two notes and held them side by side.

Jane dropped the wallet back into her purse. 'So, what do you think?'

'Same paper, same handwriting, same *mind* behind the notes. On the surface, it all seems fairly straight-forward. He calls himself Master of Games, and these notes are basically instructions to the player.'

'Me.'

'You. In the first note, he invites you to play the game with him. The fifty dollars is the hook, of course. With money like that coming to you out of the blue, you can't help but be intrigued. He's hoping it'll be enough to tempt you into giving his game a try. Your instruction is to "look homeward, angel."

The clue is fairly ambiguous, but not at all difficult. He wanted to make things easy for you, I think. He wasn't trying to confuse you, just get you to play along.'

Jane nodded. She liked Brace's interpretation of the note. It agreed with her own view of it.

'To encourage your participation, he writes "You'll be glad you did." That's a hint that there's more money waiting for you up ahead. The guy keeps his promises, doesn't he?'

'He came through with the money. I'm not sure how glad I am about it, though.'

'Glad enough to continue playing.'

'I guess so.'

'Okay, the second note congratulates you. "You've taken your first, minor step on the road to fun and riches. More is waiting."'

'So there's a lot more money ahead.'

'But to get it, you may need to take some *major* steps.'

'I can quit any time I want to, right?'

'That's sure how it looks.'

She laughed softly, and without any humor. 'It's crazy. Why's he doing it? And why me?'

'He doesn't say.'

This time, she had humor in her laugh. 'I know *that*, dingus.'

'Why do *you* think he's doing it?'

'Who knows?' she said. 'He's probably just a harmless twit with nothing better to do.'

'Might be.'

'I guess just about anything is possible. But I'll never find out what's going on if I quit now. And I'll miss out on all those riches. You, too.'

'The riches are for you,' Brace said.

'I'll share.' She smiled and shrugged. 'I'd probably quit right now if I had to go it alone. How about this: whatever we find tonight at midnight, we'll split fifty-fifty?'

'The money doesn't matter to me.'

'Really? What are you, already rich?'

501

'Oh, not hardly. It doesn't concern me, though.'

'What does concern you?'

'You.'

That one knocked most of Jane's breath out. Her face felt crimson. 'What do you mean?' she asked. Her voice sounded strange to her, muted and husky.

A corner of Brace's mouth tilted upward. 'I'd rather be your friend than your business associate.'

'You won't take *anything*?'

The other side of his mouth tilted up. 'Your undying gratitude will be sufficient recompense, my dear.'

She broke into laughter.

Brace grinned and drank his coffee.

After Jane had settled down, he said, 'The thing now is to decipher the clue. "At midnight, horse around."'

'I don't suppose he means the obvious.'

'The obvious?' Brace asked.

'You know, horse around. Like monkey around, goof around, mess around, *screw* around.'

'We might try it and see if an envelope turns up.'

Jane knew she was blushing. She tried to laugh. 'Hey, come on.'

'I'm sorry. Forget I said that, okay? Anyway, I think you're right. The sort of horsing around that you're referring to is an activity, and he's probably trying to give you a location.'

'Someplace where there's a horse,' Jane said.

'I don't imagine he's trying to send you into the countryside to hunt out stables or a farm. This horse is probably here in town someplace.'

'And not necessarily a *real* horse,' Jane added. 'Maybe just a place with "horse" in its name, like the White Horse Inn, or . . . we could check the telephone directory and see what we can find.'

'I don't think we'll have to hit the reference sources just yet. I think I might know where he wants you to go.'

Chapter Four

After leaving Ezra's, they walked back to the library parking lot. 'Why don't we take my car?' Brace said. 'No point in both of us driving.'

'Fine,' Jane said, and followed him toward an old Ford near the end of the lot.

She felt jittery. Climbing into a car with Brace might be a big mistake. She'd decided to risk it, however, even before he had made the suggestion.

Because she agreed with his theory that the campus statue was probably where they would find the envelope. The campus was two miles from Ezra's, a fairly long walk but a quick drive, and she could think of no good reason to insist that they go in separate cars.

Only one reason existed: climbing into Brace's car would amount to surrendering control to him. If he turned out *not* to be the good guy he seemed, Jane could be letting herself in for a world of pain.

She *wanted* to trust him, though. She liked him, and hated the idea that he might be a threat.

Also, she figured there was at least one logical reason to trust him: if he had evil intentions, he could've nailed her earlier, when they were upstairs together in the library's stacks. A perfect place for an assault, but he'd behaved just fine.

There's no reason not to trust him, she reminded herself as she waited for Brace to unlock the passenger door.

Except for the fact that he's a guy.

He opened the door, then ducked in and began to clear the seat of books, magazines, file folders, and loose papers. 'We could take my car,' Jane suggested.

'No, that's all right. This'll just take a minute.'

'You aren't used to passengers, huh?'

'Sort of a loner.'

Oh, that's a wonderful sign.

She surprised herself by saying, 'Oh, great. I'm about to get in the car with a loner.'

'Don't be afraid, my pretty.'

'Very funny.'

'Sorry.' He stepped backward with the materials clutched to his chest. 'Could you open that?' he asked, nodding at the rear door.

She opened it. Brace leaned in and dumped his collection onto the back seat. 'All set,' he said. He gestured for her to sit in the passenger seat.

Jane climbed in, and he shut the door for her. While he walked around the front, she leaned over and unlocked the driver's door. He pulled it open and climbed in.

'Excited?' he asked.

'A little, maybe. Mostly just nervous.'

He started the car, put on the headlights, and began backing out of the parking space. Jane pulled the safety harness down across her chest and lap. She latched its buckle into place by her hip, then wondered if she might be safer without it. If she needed to make a quick getaway . . .

Hey, cut it out. I'm trusting him, remember?

'I hope it's where it's supposed to be,' Brace said.

'What do you mean?'

'The statue. I haven't actually *seen* it since the thing was banished from the quad. I know where they originally *put* it, but who knows?' The headlights swept across the rear of Jane's parked car, then left it in darkness. She turned her head. Her little Dodge Dart looked dreary sitting all by itself in the lot.

'How long ago did they get rid of it?' she asked.

'Ah . . . three years ago? Right, three. I was one year away from tenure, so the administration threatened to give me the bounce if I didn't shut up about it.' He checked the street, then pulled out, turning right. 'I didn't shut up about it. They kept me, anyway. They kept the statue, too, but safely tucked out of sight so it wouldn't offend anyone.'

'If they found it so offensive, why didn't they melt it down, or something?'

'They almost did. There were suggestions that it should be destroyed and recast into a giant peace symbol, for one thing. Fortunately, the scupltor was an alumnus. Also, there were a few of us who argued that history might be unkind to those who went around destroying works of art because a ludicrous political trend happened to make the subject matter unpopular. They finally compromised and hid it. Just hope it's still there. It's possible that the statue was moved or destroyed or something after the controversy finally died down.'

'If that's the case,' Jane said, 'it obviously isn't the horse we're looking for.'

'It's the most obvious one, though.'

'Not if it's gone.'

Brace looked at her and nodded. 'It'd *better* be the Crazy Horse statue. The only other horse I know about is in front of the Safeway market and goes up and down when a kid drops a quarter in its slot.'

'We might have to give that one a try.'

'Let's hope we get lucky with the statue,' he said.

Brace parked on the street in front of Jefferson Hall, the humanities building. 'This is about as close as we can get in the car,' he explained.

They climbed out.

'Where is it?' Jane asked.

'The other side of campus,' Brace said as they started walking. 'Just this side of Mill Creek. There's a fenced-in area where the maintenance crews keep equipment and things. That's where it's *supposed* to be. More than likely, it hasn't gone anyplace. The thing's a monster – took a construction crew with a giant crane to move it there in the first place.'

On their way through the campus, they encountered several students. Some were alone, while others walked with friends. All of them recognized Brace and spoke to him. Some even stopped and chatted.

'You're pretty popular around here,' Jane said as they reached the far side of the quad.

'It's you they're curious about.'

'So I noticed.'

'Hope you'll forgive the fellows who drooled.'

She laughed. 'Nobody drooled. A couple of those *gals* looked ready to kill me, though.'

'You'll be okay. Just don't turn your back on them.'

She looked behind her. The students who'd stopped and talked were no longer in sight. Nobody seemed to be nearby, or approaching, or watching from a distance. 'I wonder where *he* is,' she said.

Brace turned around. His eyes narrowed as he scanned the walkways and trees and shadows.

'He must be watching,' Jane said. 'He must be. Otherwise, what's the point?'

'I don't know.'

'He *must* be watching.'

'He wasn't in the stacks,' Brace reminded her.

'He might've been. You know? Just because we didn't find him doesn't necessarily mean he wasn't there. Maybe he had a good hiding place.'

'It's possible, I guess.'

'You're *not* him, right?'

Smiling, Brace raised his right hand. 'Honest Injun.'

'Oooo. I heard that.'

'Sorry. I'm evil – the demon who thought it wasn't a sin to call our team the Warchiefs.'

'I don't think *that's* so bad. Warchiefs. It's not like calling them the Redskins, you know? But I'm not so sure about Crazy Horse as a mascot.'

'He was great. You should've seen him, galloping down the sidelines at the football games. And the statue . . . it's magnificent. You'll see.'

'Hope so.'

'We're almost there,' Brace said. He left the walkway and walked on the grass, leading Jane toward the side of a low building.

Though Jane had been on campus a few times, she had never done much serious exploring of the university grounds. She was aware of the wooded area behind the buildings on the western side of the quad, but she'd never ventured into it.

You're about to do it now, she told herself.

She didn't much care for the idea.

Mill Creek was back there someplace.

She had probably noticed a few things from the park on the other side of the creek. Storage sheds? A greenhouse? She couldn't really be sure what she'd seen. Mostly, she remembered seeing thickets and trees. She clearly remembered that the area had seemed desolate and gloomy.

'This is where the statue is?' she whispered, nodding toward the darkness ahead.

'Back behind the science building. Can't see it from here.'

'Terrific.'

'Don't worry.'

'You know what?' she whispered. 'I'm not so sure we oughta keep going. I mean, it's pretty stupid. We don't know what this guy wants.'

Brace halted and turned to face her. She wished she could *see* his face. In the darkness, it looked like a gray smudge. He took hold of both her hands. 'You don't really want to quit, do you?'

'No, but . . . it's getting scary again. We really *should* quit. It's stupid not to.'

'I tell you what. Suppose I go on ahead and check out the statue?'

'What am *I* supposed to do?'

'Go back to where the lights are and wait for me. You should be safe there.'

'And let you do the dirty work?'

'My pleasure, ma'am.'

'No way. What if it's some sort of a trap?'

'All the more reason . . .'

'Oh, sure. I can't let you get hurt, or something, on account of me.'

'Should we give it all up?'

'No, but . . .'

Brace squeezed her hands. 'Let's go ahead, then. Money or not, it'd be a shame to come all the way out here and not get to see Crazy Horse. Especially since I risked my job to save him from oblivion.'

'Okay.'

He let go of one hand, but held on to the other as he turned around and led Jane deeper into the trees behind the building. Her heart was pounding very hard.

Nothing's going to happen, she told herself. We'll find the envelope or we won't, and that'll be it. Nobody's going to ambush us.

In a loud voice that trembled only slightly, Jane announced, 'If any shit *does* go down, the game is over. I'll quit. End of his fun with me. So he'd better think twice before he pulls anything cute.'

'That's telling him,' Brace said.

'I meant every word of it.'

'Do you think he's near enough to hear what you said?'

She felt a tremor slide up her spine. 'Jeez, I sure hope not.'

Brace laughed softly.

'I'm glad you find me amusing. Maybe I should hire out for parties.'

'If you want to know the truth,' he said, 'I think this whole business is great. It's like you and I have teamed up for a treasure-hunting adventure. There's mystery, suspense, excitement, untold riches in the offing, the possibility of danger and romance . . . It's wonderful, in a way.'

Possibility of romance?

With me?

Who do you think *he means?*

Jane blushed. She was glad that Brace couldn't see it in the darkness.

'If he murders us under the statue of Crazy Horse tonight,' she said, 'we can die happy in the knowledge that he gave us a few such precious moments.'

She heard Brace laugh again.

Then he halted. Jane stepped closer to his side. She felt his arm brush against her. 'The light's off,' he whispered.

'What?'

'There's supposed to be a spotlight on the gate. For security.'

'Where?'

He pointed straight ahead. Squinting through the darkness, Jane found a vague shape that she supposed might be a high, chainlink fence beyond the trunks of several trees. She couldn't see through the fence. Nor could she see a gate.

'That's where the statue is?' she asked. 'In there?'

'That's where they put it.'

'Are you sure there's supposed to be a light?'

'It's always on at night. I mean, I don't keep track of it, but I've seen it often enough when I've been around campus after dark. You can see it from the quad when you walk past the science building.'

'And tonight it's out.'

'I don't see a light, do you?'

'No.'

'I'd say our friend has been here,' Brace said.

'Yeah,' Jane muttered. 'And added a little darkness to the game.'

Chapter Five

'How are we going to get in?' Jane asked as they approached the fence.

It reminded her of fences she had sometimes seen around tennis courts: as high as a one-story building and drapped on the inside with tarps.

'I can't climb over that,' she said.

'Sure you can.'

'Well, I'm not *going* to.'

He laughed. 'Me neither. But there might be another way to get in.'

They passed a corner of the enclosure, and walked along the front. Here, moonlight found its way through breaks in the trees. It showed broad, double gates at the center of the fence, and a lane of asphalt that led away toward the quad. Fixed high on the fence was the spotlight Brace had mentioned. It was apparently aimed down at the asphalt directly in front of the gates. A curve of its fixture glowed with moonlight, but its bulb was dark.

'Might've just burnt out,' Brace said as they walked closer to the gates.

'I bet he climbed up there and unscrewed it a little.'

'Whatever, it's just as well. I wouldn't want to be fooling around back here with that light shining on us.'

Jane had hoped the gates would give her a view inside the fenced area, but now she saw that they, too, were hung with tarps. 'Somebody sure doesn't want people looking in,' she muttered.

'It's probably to avoid tempting the students.' Brace stepped toward the padlocked chain that was wrapped around the center posts of the gates, binding them together. He crouched slightly and lifted the padlock. Then he began studying the chain. 'The last thing the college needs is for some guys to break in and boost a tractor mower or some Porta-potties, or . . . all *right*!' He moved his hands together, and the chain parted.

'How . . .?'

'Someone clipped one of the links.'

'I wonder who.'

Unwinding the chain, Brace said, 'Maybe he figured you'd give up if you had to climb over the fence.'

'He was right.'

Brace let the chain and padlock fall to the ground. He

pulled at the gate on the right, and it swung toward him. 'Just slip in,' he whispered.

Jane hesitated. 'Could we go to jail for this?'

'Only if we're caught.'

'I mean it.'

'We'll be all right. For one thing, we aren't the ones who cut the chain. For another, I'm on the faculty. I'd have some explaining to do, that's all. Probably.'

'I wouldn't want to get you fired.'

'You won't. In, in.'

Jane sidestepped through the narrow gap. Brace followed, then quickly pulled the gate shut.

The surrounding fences and the high limbs of trees just outside the enclosure blocked out much of the moonlight. Jane could only see dim shapes – some black, others in grays of varying darkness. The shape directly in front of her was apparently the tractor mower Brace had mentioned. Off to the right was something that looked like a golf cart. And a bird bath. And half a dozen Porta-potties standing all in a row near the fence.

Her heart gave a lurch when she spotted the man.

He stood absolutely motionless just in front of the nearest toilet. Though his figure was vague in the darkness, he seemed to be naked.

'Brace!' She pointed.

Brace looked at the man. 'Don't worry,' he whispered. 'I know him.'

'You *know* him?'

'It's Dave.'

'Who's Dave? What's he doing here? Why's he *naked*?'

'Dave the statue. Michelangelo's David. A miniature reproduction. They stuck him away last year after a coed brought a sexual harassment lawsuit. She alleged that walking by him on her way to class was offensive and stressful.'

'Oh. Okay. I was afraid it was . . . him.'

'I don't think he's in here. He couldn't have done that with the lock and chains from the inside. So unless he climbed over the top afterwards . . .'

'Wouldn't rule it out.'

'We'll keep our eyes peeled, just in case.'

Jane scanned the area. 'What is all this stuff, anyway?'

'A little bit of everything. Sort of like the university's version of a junk drawer.'

'I don't see Crazy Horse.'

'Over there,' Brace said, pointing toward the far left corner. 'Behind all that stuff. I hope.'

He led the way.

The statue *could* be back there, Jane realized. A Bradley tank could be tucked out of sight in that corner behind the accumulation of clutter.

So could Mog, Master of Games. Or he might be hiding anywhere along the way.

Most of the dark shapes over there were too indistinct to identify. But Jane thought she could make out a collection of park benches standing on end; at least a dozen cages of various sizes, all stacked up like castoffs from a travelling zoo; plywood trees that she imagined had served as props for a stage production (*A Midsummer Night's Dream* came to mind); and a small forest of standing Doric columns, twice Jane's height, that looked dirty gray in the darkness.

She turned sideways to follow Brace through the columns. She brushed against some, rubbed against others as she squeezed between them. They felt cool and rough like concrete.

She almost asked Brace if he knew what they were for.

But she didn't want to know. Not that badly.

Not badly enough to speak and invade the silence with her voice.

He might be anywhere.

Near enough to hear Jane whisper, close enough to touch her. She reached out for Brace's arm, but he kept moving, unaware, and her hand found only air.

Don't leave me behind!

512

She hurried after him. Her footfalls were nearly silent in the soft, dewy grass. Good. You want to be silent, she told herself. But her breathing sounded awfully loud. And her denim skirt rasped as her buttocks rubbed against the rough grain of a column. Another column thrust against her left breast as she squeezed by. It didn't hurt her and it made no more than a whisper against the fabric of her blouse, but gave a tug that popped her top button out of its hole. As she reached up and fumbled to refasten the button, the maze of columns ended.

She halted. She lowered her arms. She glanced at Brace. His head turned toward her and his hand reached out. She took hold of it, squeezed it.

In front of them stood the statue of Crazy Horse.

It loomed high over them, nearly double the size of a real horse and rider, black in a bright glow of moonlight.

Black and magnificent.

The black stallion at full gallop was stretched out long and sleek, mane afly, tail aloft, only a single hoof at the left rear grounded to the pedestal, the other three airborne as it raced through frozen time.

And on the stallion's bare back rode Crazy Horse, war chief of the Sioux. Naked except for a loincloth, lean and muscular, hunched over, hugging the mount with his knees, one hand raised in a fist, the other bearing a lance. His mouth was wide in a warcry, his long hair and the rear flap of his loincloth high up behind him, lifted by the same ceaseless wind as the stallion's mane and tail.

'What do you think?' Brace asked.

'My God.'

'Yeah.'

They moved closer together, and Jane leaned against him. He slipped an arm across her shoulders.

'Who was the alumnus, Frederic Remington?'

'A guy named Pat Clancy, class of thirty-nine. This was the only major piece he finished before the war. His plane went down somewhere over the Himalayas in forty-three.

He's up there now, near Mount Everest somewhere, always will be.'

For a while, Jane didn't trust herself to speak. She knew her voice would falter. After wiping her eyes, she took a deep breath and said, 'It shouldn't be hidden away back here. It should be where everybody can see it.'

'Yeah. Well, maybe someday.'

'I didn't even know it existed. If you hadn't brought me here . . .'

'I helped a bit,' he admitted. 'But it was your friend Mog who *really* brought you here.'

Jane gazed up at the statue of Crazy Horse. 'You're right,' she whispered. 'How weird. I've been afraid of him, and what has he done? He's given me money . . . he's led me to a copy of a great novel like *Look Homeward, Angel* . . . and he's brought me over here to see this fabulous statue. What's to be scared of?'

'Maybe nothing,' Brace said.

'Maybe plenty, huh?' Jane said. 'He might be trying to lull me into trusting him. Then *wham!*'

'It's possible.'

Jane nodded. 'Anything's possible, isn't it?'

'Pretty much so.'

'But, you know? Even if he turns out to be some vicious, bad-to-the-bone creep, I might never have seen this Crazy Horse statue if he hadn't sent me here. Might've missed getting to know you, too.'

'I know *I'm* grateful to him,' Brace said.

They faced each other.

Jane knew that he was about to pull her into his arms. Knew. Felt it. Any second, now. He wouldn't stop with embracing her, with kissing her, wouldn't stop at all.

Oh, my God. I'm not ready for this. No! It's too soon, way too soon.

We can't!

'So,' Brace said, 'where do you think he left the envelope?'

'Huh? Oh. I don't know.'

'Somewhere around the horse, more than likely. "At midnight, horse around." '

'It isn't midnight yet, is it?' Jane asked.

'Are you okay?'

'Yeah. Fine. Just a little nervous. What time is it?'

Brace checked his wrist watch. 'Only eleven-thirty. It shouldn't matter, though. If this is the right place and he did that to the chain, he's already come and gone.'

'Maybe.'

'You don't want to leave and come back at midnight, do you?'

'No. I guess we should go ahead and look for it.'

'It's probably up on the statue somewhere,' Brace said, 'but let's check the easy places first.' He started to make his way around the pedestal, Jane following. He walked slowly, crouched over, head turned toward the statue.

His trousers were gray and slightly baggy. He had a bulge in the rear left pocket. Jane supposed it was his billfold.

'This used to be on top of a huge concrete base in the middle of the quad,' he explained as he moved along, inspecting the pedestal, the horse's legs and underside. 'They kept the base where it was, at least for a while. Figured they might put a new statue on top of it to replace Crazy Horse. Problem was, they couldn't come up with any ideas that didn't have a potential for negative political ramifications. I mean, there are campus and community activists who will find something wrong with *anything*. So when somebody figured out that they could remove the concrete block and put up a tree instead of a statue, that was it. Now we've got a Sequoia growing in the middle of the quad where Crazy Horse used to be.'

'What did they decide to call the football team after all the problems they had?'

'The Chargers.'

'Oh, that's it. Couldn't think ... And their mascot is a credit card?'

He laughed. 'No, but maybe it should be. They don't have

a mascot. And we don't seem to have an envelope down here.' He stood up straight and tipped back his head. 'I'd bet anything it's up there someplace. Maybe smack on top of the chief's head.'

'Wouldn't surprise me,' Jane said.

'Okay, well, make yourself comfortable and I'll . . .'

'Oh, no you won't. If somebody has to climb the statue, it'll be me. This is *my* gig, remember?'

'Well, sure, but . . .'

'You may come up, too, if you like. But I want to go first.'

'Fine.'

Jane suddenly felt annoyed with herself, certain that she'd been too abrupt with him. 'I mean, I just don't want you doing the hard part for me. It wouldn't be right.'

'That's fine. I didn't want to climb up there. High places make me queasy.' He reached out and gave her shoulder a gentle squeeze. 'Be careful, okay?'

'Don't worry, I won't fall.'

'Glad you've got so much confidence.'

'Hey, why do you think they call me Jane?'

'Why?'

'Tarzan, Jane, Edgar Rice Burroughs?'

'You were named after *that* Jane?'

'You bet.'

Brace laughed. 'If you say so.'

'I've been a climbing fool all my life. And I swing from vines.'

'Okay. If you say so.'

'You believe me, don't you?'

'Sure.'

'You do?'

'Sure.'

'Whoo. You're sort of gullible.'

'Maybe I'd better do the climbing.'

'No. I was serious about that. I'll go up and find the envelope. Or try, anyhow. You just stand by and catch me if I fall.'

'Jane would never fall, would she?'

'This Jane might.'

She made her way to the rear of the statue, stepped onto its pedestal, and reached for the horse's tail. Stretching, standing on her tiptoes, she could just touch her fingertips to the tail's cool bronze. So she jumped. She caught hold and struggled to pull herself up.

'Give you a boost,' Brace said. Not waiting for a response, he moved in from behind, hugged her around the thighs and hoisted her.

Instead of keeping her grip on the tail, she twisted and pressed herself against the horse's hindquarters. She reached her right arm across the rear flap of the chief's bronze loincloth. Grabbing it, she gasped, 'Okay.'

Brace released her legs.

She kicked up her left leg.

Giving him a great shot up my skirt.

It's too dark, she told herself. He can't see anything.

Can't see much, anyhow.

Gasping, thinking how silly it was of her to blush at a time like this, Jane squirmed and pulled at the shelf of loincloth until she straddled the horse's back.

'How is it up there?' Brace whispered.

Like doing the splits, she thought. But she said, 'Okay, I guess.'

For a while, she remained sprawled there, trying to catch her breath. Her face trickled with sweat. The statue felt cool underneath her, but the back of her blouse and the seat of her panties, soaked, were glued to her skin.

After a couple of minutes, she brought her legs closer together and lifted herself. On her knees, she crawled forward until the flap of the loincloth went in between her thighs and underneath her skirt. She sat on it. It felt as wide as a teeter board, but wavery. The bronze was chilly against her overheated skin, and she could feel it through her panties. It felt good.

She leaned forward against the chief's cool back, and

wrapped her arms around his waist. From there, she looked down at Brace.

So far down!

'Oh, jeez,' she muttered.

Pressing her forehead against the chief's back, she thought, I'm doing this for two hundred dollars? I must be nuts.

There might not even *be* two hundred dollars!

This isn't for the two hundred, she reminded herself. It's for that, but it's also for the clue to the next step. The next step . . . if there is one . . . if the game goes on . . . might lead to four hundred dollars.

And the one after that to eight hundred.

Then sixteen hundred.

I could get rich.

If the game goes on long enough – if the Master keeps doubling the ante and if I don't quit.

Anyway, I'm already up here.

So where's the envelope?

Easing herself backward slightly, she checked to the right and left. The chief's back appeared to be nearly four feet across. From her seat on the loincloth in the middle, she might be able to take a look past one side or the other if she leaned over far enough. It would mean a major shifting of balance, though. If she should loose her grip . . .

No, I don't think so.

She leaned forward again. With much of her weight against his broad, solid back, she relaxed the grip of her thighs against his sides. She shoved her feet down against the horse and straightened her legs, raising herself off the loincloth. Her leg muscles trembled. She blinked sweat out of her eyes.

Then she was standing on the horse, clinging to the bronze sloping back of the hunched warrior chief. She rested her face against him and shut her eyes and gasped for air.

You still down there, Brace? she wondered. Sure wish you'd say something.

Maybe he decided it was time to go home.

Maybe Mog crept up on him and slit his throat.

518

'Take it easy,' she whispered to herself. 'Everything's cool.'
Get this over with!

She stepped up onto the loincloth with one foot. Pushing against it, she slid herself up the chief's back, stretched, and clutched the curved ridges of the trapezius muscles on each side of his neck.

Hanging on to them, she squirmed higher and higher.

And bashed her head. The pain slammed down through her body. Her vision flashed. For an instant, she imagined a vicious dwarf perched atop Crazy's Horse head, armed with a tomahawk – guarding the chief, gleefully whacking the heads of trespassers.

Through the pain, she felt herself slip downward a bit.
NO!

She flinched rigid, locking her arms, freezing her fingers in their grip on the bronze shoulder muscles.

'My God,' Brace blurted in a harsh whisper. 'Hang on!'

'I am,' she murmured. In a louder voice, she said, 'I'm okay.'

Sure, she thought. Just great.

What she really wanted to do was let go and rub the top of her head. The urge was almost great enough to make her try, but she told herself that a little bump on the head would be nothing next to the pain of falling from this height.

Tipping back her head, she looked up.

Just above her, a sheaf of blackness jutted out from the rear of Crazy Horse's head.

His hair, flowing out behind him.

His bronze hair.

'Do you want me to come up?' Brace asked.

'No! Please don't. I'm okay.'

By this time, the pain from the blow had faded, leaving behind a hot place on her scalp and a dull ache inside her skull.

Jane pulled herself higher, squirming over to the right and tilting her head sideways to avoid the outcropping of hair. Soon, she was able to hook her right arm over the top of the chief's shoulder.

When she looked around, her stomach seemed to fall.

Oh, man, this is too high!

She was way up in the moonlight, slightly higher than the chainlink fence, higher than many branches of the nearby trees. Through the treetops, she could glimpse bits and pieces of some university buildings. Mostly, however, the limbs blocked her views of the regions beyond the fence.

She had an aerial view of the odd clutter within the enclosure. She spotted the statue of David. Nothing else resembled a human.

Mog has to be down there, doesn't he? Why does he put me through this if he can't watch?

She sure couldn't see him, though.

Of course, she couldn't see Brace, either. She supposed Brace was somewhere behind her.

Maybe Mog, too.

She didn't dare change her position to look for either of them.

While looking about, she'd been vaguely aware that no envelope was attached to the statue below her. But she hadn't actually focused her attention on the search.

She did that now.

The way Crazy Horse was hunched over, she couldn't see much of the stallion; its head, most of its mane. To see more, she would need to climb higher and hang down over the chief's shoulder. That should give her a top view of the stallion's withers, the chief's chest and belly, the front flap of his loincloth and the tops of his legs clamping the stallion's sides. And maybe the missing envelope.

She wasn't ready to do that, though.

The less I have to crawl around on this guy . . .

She checked his right arm and the lance he carried. No envelope there.

Most of his left arm, fist high, was out of sight on the other side of his head.

Let's just check on top of his head.

Clamping herself more tightly against the chief, she twisted and reached up with her left hand.

She patted the top of his head.

Nothing.

The envelope had damn well better be somewhere up here after all this!

Halfway down the furrowed slope of Crazy Horse's hair, Jane's hand touched a papery packet. She explored it with her fingertips. It felt like an envelope folded in half, every edge taped down against the bronze.

She ripped it free.

Though her body trembled with the strain of keeping herself clamped to the statue's shoulder, she took a few moments to inspect her find.

The square was a folded envelope, all right. It looked grimy gray in the moonlight, and the cellophane tape along its edges gleamed silver. It had a comforting thickness.

In the middle of the square was one word: JANE.

'Got it,' she called down in a loud whisper.

'Yes!'

'I'm tossing it down. Ready?'

'Be careful.'

She reached across herself and dropped the envelope into the night beyond her right shoulder.

Chapter Six

Jane was drenched with sweat and every muscle in her body seemed to be twitching by the time she made her way down to the horse's tail. As she struggled to lower herself from it, Brace caught her dangling legs.

He eased her toward the ground, letting her slip gradually through his arms.

Jane felt her skirt being rucked up, felt his hands on her bare legs.

She accepted it. Brace was helping her down, and this sort of thing was probably unavoidable. Or maybe he meant to have his hands under there, the better to cop a feel. Either way, Jane didn't much care. She was out of breath, sopping wet, aching and shuddering from the exertions of the climb, still scared. She'd been so high up. She'd come so close to falling. But now she was almost to the ground. It didn't matter where Brace's hands were.

They were high on her thighs, pressing her against him, when they lost their grip. Jane gasped and dropped abruptly a few inches. She felt a soft tug between her legs. Then Brace clutched her hips and pulled her sharply, forcing her rump tight against his chest and bringing her to a halt.

He bent his knees. The moment Jane's feet touched the ground, he released her. As his right hand went away, she felt a gentle snap of elastic and realized his fingers had been inside her panties. Under the front panel. They must've gone in from the side when Brace lost his hold and had to make the quick grab.

It probably wasn't on purpose, she told herself.

Maybe he didn't even notice.

He noticed, all right. Are you kidding?

'Sorry about that,' he whispered.

Just pretend it's nothing. No big deal.

Jane turned around. She rested her hands on Brace's hips and bowed her forehead against his chest. She was too winded to talk. Good. It gave her an excuse for ignoring where his hand had been.

As she gasped for air, she realized that she could pretend *she* hadn't noticed.

'How's the head?' Brace asked.

'Sore.'

'Do you feel dizzy or anything?'

'No. It wasn't . . . that bad. Just that it . . . almost made me fall.'

'Thank God you held on.'

'Yeah.'

She felt both his hands gently caressing her back. She couldn't imagine why he would want to do that, considering the sodden condition of her blouse. The touch of his hands felt good, though. Soothing, comforting.

'About ready to get out of here?' he asked after a while.

She nodded. 'You've . . . got the envelope?'

'Sure do.' Taking her hand, he led her on a meandering route to the gates of the fenced enclosure. There, he eased one of the gates open slightly and stuck his head out. 'Coast is clear,' he told her, then opened it wide.

While Jane waited behind him, he wrapped the chain around the gate posts and hooked it together. 'I'd like to really secure the thing,' he whispered. 'Can't do it without a key for the padlock, though.'

'They'll probably fix it tomorrow,' Jane said.

'Yeah. Let's get out of here.'

They made their way through the darkness. Soon, they rounded the corner of the science building and walked toward the lights of the quad. Brace dug the folded envelope out of his pants pocket. 'We can stop under the lights and . . .' When he looked at her, his words died. 'Uh-oh.'

Jane lowered her head.

She had known that she must look a mess, but this was worse than she'd expected. Her blouse was not only filthy with a mixture of grime and bird droppings from her climb on the statue, but it was completely untucked and mostly unbuttoned. Plastered to her skin with sweat, it was twisted askew so that the wide gap in front showed the side of her right breast.

Turning away from Brace, she pulled her blouse shut and fumbled with the buttons.

'This is really the pits,' she muttered.

'Hey, you got the envelope.'

'What if somebody sees us?'

'Would you rather take the long way around? We can stay behind the buildings and avoid most of the lights.'

'Yeah. I don't want to be seen like this.'

'Might make people suspicious,' Brace said. 'Especially if we run into campus security.' Taking her arm, he led her toward the dark area at the rear of the building. 'Not that we did anything wrong.'

'They'll probably think we did. I'd hate it if you got into any sort of trouble over this.'

'It would've been worth it,' he said.

'Think so?'

'Definitely.'

She was surprised to feel a smile spread across her face. 'It has been quite a night.'

They moved through shadows and encountered no one. When they reached Park Lane, Brace hurried off to fetch the car. Jane waited near the bridge, staying out of sight in a stand of trees.

As she waited, she shivered.

The night was very warm, but her sweaty clothes felt chilly. She pressed her legs together and crossed her arms and gritted her teeth.

It isn't so much the cold, she thought. It's everything else.

Nerves and excitement.

Soon, Brace's car came along. It passed on the other side of the street, slowed down on the bridge, then made a U-turn and came back. It swung to the curb in front of Jane's hiding place. It stopped and the passenger door opened.

Jane walked quickly over to it, climbed in and pulled the door shut. 'That was pretty quick,' she said.

'I hurried along. Where to now, the library?'

'Let's see what's in the envelope.'

'Here?'

'Sure. You never know, he might send us back to the statue, or something.'

Brace dug it out of his pocket and handed it to Jane. She tore off the strips of tape and unfolded the envelope. As she ripped open its flap, Brace reached to the dashboard and the car's courtesy light came on.

'Thanks,' she said, removing the note.

The lined sheet of paper was folded into thirds, just like the others. Inside, she found a fresh pair of hundred-dollar bills. She showed them to Brace.

'Very good,' he said. 'The guy came through.'

'I'd be a mighty unhappy camper if he hadn't.'

'Well, I'd say you earned it.'

'*Worked* for it, that's for sure.'

'And he doubled it, so he's sticking to the pattern.'

'Right,' Jane said. 'The next should be four hundred bucks.'

'Maybe two's the max.'

'Oh, I sure hope not.' She set the money down on her lap and raised the handwritten note. ' "My dearest Jane,"' she read aloud, '"The game goes on. Troll for your next treasure tomorrow, midnight, under Park. You'll be glad you did. Yours, MOG, Master of Games."'

'Tomorrow night,' Brace said.

'That's a relief. I've about had it for tonight.'

'Shall we be off?'

'Guess so.'

He started driving. Jane folded the note and tucked it back inside the envelope. She picked up the money. 'How about taking one of these?'

'Nope.'

'Are you sure? I never would've gone into a place like that alone. Hey, I wouldn't have even *known* enough to go there.'

'Glad I could help. But it's your money. I don't want any, really.'

'Okay.' She slipped the bills into the envelope. Bending over, she reached down between her knees and lifted her purse off the floor. 'If you change your mind, let me know.' She dropped the envelope into her purse.

'Are you planning to go on with all this?' Brace asked.

'I guess so. I don't see why not. Will you come with me tomorrow night?'

'You bet. Want me to meet you at the library?'

She considered it for a moment, then shook her head. 'I think I'll go home first and change clothes.'

'Good idea. You messed up your blouse pretty good tonight.'

'Yeah.' She blushed at his mention of the blouse. Even though she was fairly certain that her nipple had stayed out of sight, Brace had definitely seen a lot of her breast – and he was well aware that she wore nothing at all underneath the blouse. 'I'll get into some grubbies for tomorrow night,' she said.

Soon, Brace slowed his car and swung into the library's parking lot. Ignoring the lines on the asphalt, he steered directly toward Jane's car.

'Maybe I should follow you home right now,' he suggested. 'It's pretty late. Make sure you get there safely, and it'll save me from having to hunt for your house tomorrow night.' He stopped beside her car.

He wants to go home with me. Then what?

He's okay, she told herself. He's fine. Hell, he's terrific.

Yeah, right, this terrific guy just so happened accidentally to slip his hand in my panties.

It was an accident. I was all sweaty and he lost his hold, that's all.

Yeah, right.

It wasn't on purpose, I know it.

'Sounds good,' she said.

'Fine. I'll be right behind you.'

That seemed very much like her cue to leave – but not at all like a farewell. As Jane lifted her purse and opened the passenger door, she realized that Brace intended to do more than follow her home and drive off.

He'll want to come in.

'See you later,' she said, then shut the door and went to her own car.

Brace stayed a safe distance behind her as she drove from the library to her rented house on the outskirts of town. She pulled into the driveway, and he stopped at the curb.

It came as no surprise when his headlights went dark. But it made Jane's heart pound harder, made her stomach go squirmy.

Brace strode up the driveway while she climbed out of her car. She slung the purse onto her shoulder, shut and locked her door. Then she turned to face him.

'Thought I'd better find out what time you want me here tomorrow night.'

'I'm not sure. I don't know exactly where we're supposed to go.'

'Maybe we should take a closer look at the note, see what we can figure out.'

Jane reached into her purse. She pulled out an envelope, saw that it didn't have a crease in the middle, put it away and came up with the envelope from the statue. She handed it to Brace.

He removed the note, leaving the money untouched. 'We'll need some light on the subject,' he said, and led the way toward Jane's porch.

Standing under the porch light, he unfolded the note and read it. 'That's what I thought.'

'What?'

He grinned. 'I'm here to lend help, not to do all the thinking for you.' He handed the note back to Jane. 'Take a look and tell me what *you* think.'

She gave the note a glance, then met Brace's eyes. He's a good guy, she told herself. He won't try anything.

Right. Sure.

I want to trust him, she thought. So here goes.

'Would you like to come inside?' she asked.

'Oh, I suppose so. Can't stay long, though. I'm already way past my bedtime.'

'Well, we'll have to make it quick, then.' She unlocked the door, and Brace followed her into the living room. She turned on a lamp, then tossed her purse onto an easy chair. In the bright light from the lamp, she saw that more than her blouse was filthy: her hands, her blue denim skirt, her bare legs, even her white socks and gray Reebok shoes were smudged and streaked with grime.

She suddenly wanted very badly to get out of her clothes and under a hot shower.

Not while he's here.

She dropped the note onto the coffee table in front of the sofa. 'Would you like something to drink?' she asked.

'Thanks. Whatever you're having.'

'Beer okay?'

'Beer's great.'

He followed her into the kitchen. There, she washed her hands with soap and hot water, dried them on a paper towel, then removed two cans of Budweiser from the refrigerator. She carried them to the counter, set them down and popped their tabs.

'Maybe we'd better take a look around the house,' Brace said. 'Just to be on the safe side.'

'Oh, great,' she muttered.

'You never know.'

'You think Mog might've used this little game of his to keep me away from the house – so he could be sure I wouldn't show up and surprise him?'

'Anything's possible,' Brace said.

'Yeah. When nothing makes sense, anything *is* possible.'

'Why don't you give me a tour?'

They took their beers with them and started to walk through the house. Right away, Jane found herself less worried about running into an intruder than encountering castoff undergarments or other such surprises. But the house seemed reasonably clean and tidy. The clutter wasn't half as bad as it might've been. And she hadn't left any dirty clothes scattered around.

Still, she felt a little embarrassed that Brace was getting this opportunity to see so much – the mementos on top of her dresser, the pictures on her walls, the bed where she slept, her toilet, her bath tub.

My God, she thought, this guy has already seen and touched more of me – my body *and* where I live – than the last five guys I went out with.

Finished with the search, they returned to the living room. 'It was sort of a longshot,' Brace said. 'Glad he *wasn't* here, though.'

'Me, too.' Jane sat down on the sofa. Brace sat down beside her – nearly a foot away.

Close, but not too close.

Maybe *he's* the timid one, she thought. But probably not.

Leaning forward, he reached to the coffee table and picked up the note. 'So, what's your take on this?' he asked, passing it to Jane.

She read the note to herself. 'Okay,' she said when she was done. 'At midnight tomorrow . . . or tonight, actually, since this is *already* tomorrow . . . I'm supposed to "troll" for my next treasure. Troll under Park. And Park is capitalized. So it's a proper noun, possibly the name of the street we were on tonight. Park Lane?'

'Sounds about right to me.'

'So this could mean I'm supposed to troll under Park Lane. By "troll," I don't think he means I'm supposed to go fishing or sing a song. He probably wants me to *make like a troll*. Traditionally, they dwell under bridges, right?'

In a deep, menacing voice, Brace said, 'Who's that walking across my bridge?'

'It's own-wee me,' Jane baby-talked. 'Wooddow teeny-weeny Baby Behwwy Goat Gwuff.'

Laughing, Brace rocked sideways toward Jane and gently bumped against her upper arm before swaying away. 'You oughta be in pictures.'

'That was actually my Chicken Little impression.' She took a deep breath. 'Anyway. I think what I'm suppose to do is go where the trolls are – underneath a bridge. Probably the Mill Creek Bridge on Park Lane.'

'Strange,' Brace muttered.

'I know. We were just there. Jeez, we should've gone down and checked around.'

'Want to go now?'

'Are you kidding? All I want to do is get out of these disgusting clothes and take a shower.'

Terrific. Talk to him about getting naked.

She turned away from Brace and took a drink of beer.

'If we went now,' he said, 'it'd probably be a waste of time. I don't think Mog would risk leaving his envelope down there a day ahead of time. The wrong person might find it.'

'Yeah. Good. Because I've got no intention of looking for it now. Midnight'll be plenty soon enough.'

'And you want me to pick you up here?'

'That'd be nice.'

'What time?'

She thought about it. She usually arrived home from the library by nine-thirty. If Brace came over then, they'd have at least two hours before it was time to leave for the bridge.

Two hours in the house with each other . . .

No way.

'Maybe if you come by at around eleven,' she said. 'How would that be? We could have a beer or something before we hit the road.'

'Sounds good.' He tipped his head way back and drained his can of Budweiser. Then he leaned forward and set the can on the table. Rising, he said, 'I'd better be off.'

Jane stood. She walked with him to the front door.

As he opened it, he turned and faced her. 'I'll bring a flashlight. We could've used one tonight, huh?'

'Yeah. This time, we'll have to be better prepared.'

He gave her a parting smile and nod. 'Take care of yourself,' he said, and started to leave.

Jane caught hold of his arm. 'Hey,' she said. He turned toward her. 'Thanks. I don't know what I would've done.'

'My pleasure.'

Keeping her grip on his arm, she curved her left hand behind his neck and drew his head down. She gazed into his eyes as she brought his face closer. They looked different. Gone was the sharp intelligence, the alertness, the spark of mischief that she'd grown used to seeing there. They suddenly seemed dark with longing and maybe sadness.

Then they were so close that Jane lost focus on them. She shut her eyes and kissed him.

His lips were open and warm and moist.

They didn't move. Brace seemed motionless except for his breathing.

Then he moaned into her mouth.

Then he wrapped his arms around her and hugged her hard, squeezing and kissing her until she squirmed against him, out of breath.

Can't let this happen, she thought. No. Can't let it.

As if Brace could read her mind, he eased his lips away from her mouth and relaxed his embrace. A corner of his mouth tilted up. His eyes looked normal again. 'Well,' he said.

'Well?'

'Whew.'

She glanced down at his chest. 'Now you've gotten your shirt all dirty.'

'Oh, that's okay.'

'I could wash it for you.'

'What, now?'

'Sure.'

'Thanks. I've really got to be going, though. And you need to take that shower.' He gave her a quick peck on the forehead. 'Goodnight, now.'

Jane stood in the doorway. She watched him walk out to the street, enter his car and drive slowly away.

Chapter Seven

Jane shut and locked the front door. Then she stood motionless. The house seemed very silent, now that Brace was gone. Silent and empty.

Though she was accustomed to being alone, though she *needed* to be alone now so she could shower and go to bed, she suddenly felt more lonely and vulnerable than usual. The house didn't seem as safe as usual.

Don't get spooked, she told herself. There's no reason to feel spooked.

She took the two beer cans to the kitchen, drinking from hers along the way. It was empty by the time she reached the sink. She rinsed out both cans, then tossed them into the recycling bin beside her oven.

Before leaving the kitchen, she double-checked the back door. It was almost never unlocked, and she was fairly certain that neither she nor Brace had touched it tonight, but she wanted to make absolutely sure it was secure.

The lock button in the knob was turned horizontal.

She tried the knob, anyway. It rattled slightly, but refused to turn. She pushed at it. The door didn't budge.

As she left the kitchen, she flicked off its lights. She entered the living room, prepared to turn off the lamps. But she changed her mind about that.

Not tonight.

Tonight, she didn't want the living room dark while she showered.

Silly, she thought. But so what if it's silly? I don't want it dark in here, so I'll keep the lamps on. It's what I want to do, and nobody's exactly keeping score.

With her back to the lights, she walked up the hallway and past the bathroom. She stopped at her bedroom, reached around the door frame and found the light switch.

We already searched the whole house, she told herself. There's no reason to be so nervous.

She couldn't talk herself out of it, though.

After the lamps came on, she stepped into her bedroom and looked around. She checked inside the closet. On her knees, she checked under the bed. Then she shut the window curtains.

'Nobody here but us chickens,' she muttered. '*Brawwwk brawwwk brawwwk!*'

She took off her blouse and held it up by the shoulders. It didn't appear to be torn or snagged. But the stains!

Soak it in Clorox?

The hell with it, she thought. If it doesn't come clean in the wash, I'll just buy a new one and keep this for yard work, or something.

She tossed the blouse into her hamper, then added her socks, skirt and panties. She set her Reeboks on top of the hamper, figuring she would wipe them with a wet rag in the morning.

Her bathrobe hung from a hook on the back of her closet door. She took it down, but didn't put it on. The robe was for after her shower, when she would be clean.

Leaving her bedroom lighted, she walked down the hall to the bathroom. She reached in, clicked the rheostat and turned its knob until the lights were as bright as they could be. Then she entered, shut the door, and hung her robe on its hook.

As she turned around, she saw herself in the mirror. She looked away quickly, but not fast enough to avoid glimpsing the stringy mess of her hair, her dirty face, or the thickness of her waistline.

God, what a wreck!

At least Brace saw me before calamity struck.

She knew that she normally looked pretty good. Clean, well-groomed, and the extra weight was hardly noticeable when she wore the proper clothes.

Just gotta always keep my clothes on.

I shouldn't have let myself go, she thought as she crouched and turned on the water.

Hey, the hell with that. If Brace doesn't like my looks, tough tacos. Who am I trying to impress? No one, that's who.

Anyway, I'm not all that fat. Pleasingly plump.

He can like it or lump it.

Jane smiled. Pretty obviously, Brace *did* like it. Or at least he didn't seem to be put off by anything about her.

Her smile died. *Don't get all hot and bothered. He's a guy. When it comes right down to basics, he's probably a creep like the others.*

She touched the water gushing from the bathtub spout, adjusted the flow of cold to ease the burning heat, then twisted the shower handle and stepped into the tub. Quickly, she rolled the glass door shut.

She turned to the hot spray. Eyes shut, she took it full in the face. It seemed to engulf her. It tapped her eyelids, filled her mouth, spilled down her chin. It soothed her, made her feel drowsy.

After a while, she bowed her head. The spray soaked and matted her hair, heated her scalp, but also drummed her sore bump where she'd thudded her head on the underside of the chief's bronze hair.

Enough of that.

She turned around. Now, the water hit the back of her head and neck. It splashed her shoulders, flowed heavily down her back while numerous trickles meandered down her front. It felt very good, now that it was no longer striking the bump on her head.

She stood motionless for a while, savoring the feel of the water. Then she began to soap herself.

She wondered if Brace would someday be standing here with her.

Taking a shower with a man had always been one of her favorite fantasies.

She'd never done it.

Not that she hadn't been asked.

But you don't jump into a shower with just anyone. Especially when you're a little too plump. You don't want just anyone to see your fat unhidden.

Sliding the soap over her skin, she wondered if she would allow Brace in.

Say he shows up right now, she thought. He comes into the bathroom starkers, with a boner that doesn't quit. What do I do? Squeal and try to cover up? Or slide open the shower door and say, *Come on in, honey, the water's fine?*

Forget it, she told herself. Won't happen.

But what if it *did* happen? Make it easy on yourself – say you've lost fifteen pounds, or even just ten. And you're in here all lonely and hot and bothered, and you look through the shower door and there he is, coming at you, naked as the day he was born, all huge and stiff.

Jane turned toward the glass of the shower door. It was steamed up, white except in a few places where drops of water made clear streaks.

Though she couldn't see much through the fogged glass, she could easily see that nobody was approaching her from the other side.

But maybe Brace is in the hallway now, undressing, about to come in.

With both hands, Jane gripped the aluminum runner above the door. She leaned forward until her breasts touched the glass. It felt slick, and surprisingly cold. She rubbed herself lightly against it, and watched the tips of her nipples mark clear strips across the fog.

How would this look from the other side? she wondered. What would Brace think if he saw this? Better yet, what would he *do*? What would he do if he showed up right now and saw me like this?

Come over, maybe, and lick the glass.

Then slide the door out of the way, and I would hold on up above while he does it, feeling the glass slide against me, and then feeling his mouth.

Jane let out a small moan.

Hey, let's not get carried away. He isn't here, he isn't likely to be here in the near future, if ever. And if he did walk through the door buck naked right now, you'd probably give him hell and maybe throw the bar of soap at him.

'More than likely,' she muttered.

She leaned her head against the glass, pressing it with her brow and the tip of her nose.

So much for fantasies, she thought.

She rolled her head slowly from side to side, liking the rub of the cold glass.

Of course, she thought, *I could make it come true if I wanted to. Just one telephone call.*

Why not?

Who knows?

Because it would spoil things, she supposed. One way or another, things were sure to be ruined by a move like that.

It's too soon, anyway. Way too soon. By the time I know him well enough, maybe I'll hate him.

She realized she had slumped against the glass door, was holding herself in position by her grip on the aluminum runner at the top. So she straightened up.

And her eyes came level with an oval of glass that had been wiped clear of fog by her forehead.

The door to the hallway stood open.

Okay.

Jane was certain she had shut it, had heard the clack of its latch.

Okay.

So a gust of wind hadn't shoved it open. Nor had a settling of the house. Nothing short of a major earthquake could've opened that door.

Nothing except a hand.

Someone's in the house.

Okay.

Just dandy.

Forcing herself to look away from the door, she raced her gaze across the bathroom.

Nobody. Not yet.

She again fixed her eyes on the door.

Someone's probably just on the other side.

She tried to tell herself that it might be Brace. Might be. Just like in her fantasy. She couldn't believe it, though. Brace wouldn't sneak back and break into the house in hopes of delighting her with a surprise appearance. She was sure of it.

So sure that she felt no eagerness.

She felt only fear. She was gasping for breath as her heart galloped. Her insides seemed to be shriveling and twisting. Her skin crawled.

It's not Brace.

Maybe Mog, hotshot Master of Games, showing up to do whatever it is that he does.

Or someone else.

A burglar, a peeping Tom who got carried away with his hobby, or better yet, a rapist or serial killer.

Maybe none of the above, she told herself. Maybe it's something . . . perfectly innocent. Something I'll laugh about tomorrow.

And maybe tomorrow I won't be alive to laugh about anything.

'Not if I can help it,' she muttered.

Slowly, she rolled the shower door aside. Though it made a soft rumble, she doubted that the sound could be heard by the intruder lurking in the hallway. Not over the rushy noise of the shower.

Steadying herself with one hand on the wall, Jane stepped over the edge of the tub. She stood on the bathmat, panting for breath, trembling and dripping. Her purple robe still hung from the hook on the door.

The door stood half-open, showing a small section of the hallway beyond it.

She saw nobody out there.

What's he doing?

Maybe he's gone.

Sure, fat chance.

In two seconds, he'll probably come charging in to nail me.

Her mind raced. Should she charge the door, herself, smash it with her shoulder and make a dash for safety? Or jerk the door shut, lock it, and try to escape through the bathroom window? Or wait? Or what?

Try to run, she thought, and he might get me from behind. She could almost feel a knife blade slicing down her spine.

And then she pictured herself making a brilliant escape, dashing outside in the buff, only to discover after some major embarrassment that nobody had been inside her house, at all.

Even as she thought about her options, Jane began to sidestep toward the sink. Two steps, and the bathmat was no longer under her feet. The tiles of the floor felt cool and slick. Water dribbled down her body. She blinked to keep her eyes clear, and never looked away from the door.

After a while, her rump met the edge of the counter. She moved sideways a little more, and stopped. Reaching back with a hand, she found the front of the sink.

She spun around.

Glimpsed a wild, wet Jane in the medicine cabinet mirror. Her foggy portrait darted sideways and vanished as the mirror's hinges squawked.

Most of what she saw on the narrow shelves would be of no use at all. Too many tubes, cardboard packages, bottles and jars made of lightweight plastic.

But the bottle of cough syrup was made of glass.

She grabbed it.

Then she snatched down an aerosol canister of OFF! insect repellent and struck its top against the edge of the sink. The big, plastic cap fell off. She took a moment to figure out which way the spray hole was pointing, then turned it away from her body and positioned her fingertip on the button.

Armed, she rushed the door. Though her wet feet skidded and slipped, she stayed up. She hunched low and rammed the door with her shoulder.

It flew wide. It pounded the wall behind it.

She lurched into the hallway, skidded on the carpet and

whirled herself around, ready to hurl the bottle at her assailant, ready to spray his face with bug repellent.

But no one was there.

She stood motionless. She held her breath and listened. She heard only the thumping of her heart and the hiss of the shower.

Maybe the door *had* opened by itself, she thought. If it hadn't really latched ... I suppose I could've been wrong about hearing that.

Or maybe he's in another part of the house.

She resumed breathing.

She considered what to do next. Get out of the house? Go looking for the intruder? Call the police? Call Brace and ask him to come over?

There might not be anyone here.

'Screw it,' she muttered.

She stepped back into the bathroom. Her robe had fallen to the floor, so she crouched, set down her two makeshift weapons, and picked it up. She hung it on the hook again, then shut and locked the door.

If somebody *is* out there, she thought, maybe he'll be gone by the time I come out.

She half expected to find the bathroom flooded. In spite of the open glass door, however, most of the shower's spray had stayed inside the tub. She climbed back in and began to shampoo her hair.

It was probably just a false alarm, she told herself. I bet nobody's in the house but me. The door opened on its own. They do that sort of thing all the time when the latch doesn't quite catch.

Regardless, she knew she would be compelled to search the house carefully as soon as she finished her shower.

Make your first stop at the kitchen, she told herself. Grab a good, big knife.

She certainly didn't relish the idea of searching the house all by herself. It seemed better than the alternatives, though.

After rinsing, she shut off the water, rolled the door open

and climbed out of the tub. She spent a long time drying herself.

No big hurry.

She hung up her towel. She used the bathmat to mop spilled water off the tile floor, then draped the mat over the side of the tub. She used the toilet. She brushed her teeth.

When she could think of no other delaying tactics, she went to the bathroom door. She unhooked her robe, swept it around her back and slipped her arms into its sleeves. Then she closed it around her. Holding it shut with her left hand, she reached with her right for the cloth belt dangling from its loop by her hip.

She wasn't watching her right hand.

But she looked at it fast when one of her fingertips brushed against a small corner that felt like paper.

A white envelope stood on end, a fraction of an inch protruding out of the pocket of her robe.

Chapter Eight

Brace arrived a few minutes early. Through her living room window, Jane watched him stop at the curb, climb from his car and stride toward her house. He wore dark clothes. He carried a flashlight. He walked with a light step, almost a bounce, as if he had to restrain himself from prancing like an eager kid.

She opened the front door as he bounded up the porch stairs. He stopped abruptly and smiled. 'All set for another big adventure?' he asked.

Nodding, Jane stepped backward. Brace followed her into the foyer and shut the door.

'Actually,' she said, 'more like yes and no.'

'Having second thoughts?'

'Hundred-and-second.'

'But I see you dressed for it.'

'Yep.' To blend in with the night, she wore black jeans and a navy blue chamois shirt. The shirt was too heavy and hot for a night like this. But she needed the dark color and the long sleeves, and this was the best she could do.

'You're going to be mighty warm in a shirt like that,' Brace said.

'Already am.' She led him into the living room. 'Would you like something to drink?'

'Thanks, but I'll pass. You go ahead, though.'

'Nah.' She sat on the sofa and patted the cushion at her side.

Brace took the offer. But then he scooted farther away, turned sideways until one of his knees almost touched her leg, and rested his elbow on the back of the sofa. He looked into her eyes. 'What is it?' he asked. 'Something isn't . . .?'

'We've got a little problem,' she said.

'A problem?' His eyebrows lifted slightly. 'What sort of problem?'

She leaned toward the coffee table and picked up an envelope. She showed it to Brace. 'This came "special delivery" last night. Apparently, hand-delivered to the pocket of my bathrobe.'

Suddenly, Brace looked concerned. 'Your robe? Where was it?'

'On the bathroom door.' She was blushing, but she continued. 'I hung it there when I took my shower last night. Just after you left? He must've opened the door and slipped the envelope into my pocket while I was in the shower.'

'Oh, man,' Brace muttered.

'It shook me up pretty good.'

'He was *in the house*?'

'He had to be. But the doors and all the windows were locked. After I found the note, I looked everywhere. I couldn't find him. I couldn't even figure out how he got in. Everything was still shut and locked up tight.'

'You must've been scared half to death.'

She gave a little shrug with one shoulder and tried to smile. 'It wasn't so bad. I was scared, but . . . he'd passed up a great chance to attack me. I mean, nobody else was in the house, and he'd already opened the bathroom door. He could've nailed me right there in the shower, if he'd wanted to. That's why I wasn't as frightened as I might've been. I think he was just here to deliver the envelope.'

'I *really* don't like it that he was in the house.'

'I'm not thrilled about it myself.'

'No idea how he could've gotten in?'

She shook her head. 'All I can think of is that he either picked a lock or had a door key. I mean, how else *can* you get into a house without breaking something?'

'I don't know. The police might've been able to figure out how he did it.' Brace laughed softly. 'You didn't call them, though, did you?'

'Almost. The thing is, he *didn't* attack me. And I don't think he stole anything. Except for how the bathroom door opened and I ended up with the envelope in my pocket, there's no sign that anyone was even here. I couldn't call the cops about something like that. And I'd have to show them the envelope he left, and they'd end up reading the note and finding out about the Game.'

Brace slid his arm off the back of the sofa, reached out and gently squeezed Jane's shoulder. 'So you just . . . searched the house all by yourself?'

'Me and my knife.'

He made a face. 'That little switchblade?'

'It isn't so little. But anyway, that isn't the knife I used. I grabbed me a big old butcher knife from the kitchen.'

Rubbing her shoulder, Brace shook his head and looked a bit like an exasperated but rather proud parent about to say, *You monkey, what're we gonna do with you?*

But he didn't tell her that. Instead, he said, 'I would've

come over, you know. All you had to do was call. I could've been here in ten minutes.'

'Maybe if you'd given me your phone number . . .'

His hand went rigid on her shoulder. He groaned.

'You're unlisted,' Jane said.

'So you *did* try to call?'

'Well, I got as far as a talk with an operator.'

'Damn it,' he muttered. 'I'm sorry. I had my number taken out of circulation so long ago, I hardly ever think about it anymore. If only I'd . . .'

'It's all right. I could've used some moral support, but everything turned out okay. I mean, Mog was nowhere to be seen. I'm perfectly fine. No harm done.'

Brace released her shoulder. He pulled an old, battered black wallet out of his rear pocket, opened it and found one of his business cards. 'Here, keep this. It has my office number *and* my home number.'

Jane took the offered card. It looked as if it might've been dropped onto a floor and stepped on. 'Is it an antique?' she asked.

'Pretty near. I had them printed up in a burst of naive enthusiasm when I first got hired. *Before* I started getting calls from students at all hours of the night.' He reached up and tapped the back of the card. '*Nobody* gets these anymore.'

'I'm honored.'

'I just wish I'd given it to you last night.'

'So do I.' She slipped it into a pocket of her shirt, and found a grin spreading across her face. 'I guess we'll never know what might've happened.' When the words came out, she blushed.

'We'll never know,' Brace echoed. 'And I'm beginning to wonder if *I'll* ever know what's in the envelope. Did he bring you more money?'

'Afraid not.'

'What? Or is it supposed to be a secret?'

'You aren't going to like this. I know *I* don't.' She sighed, then picked up the envelope. She opened it and removed the note. '"Jane,"' she read aloud. '"Ours is a game built for two. Three's a crowd. If you have any desire to continue with me, lose Brace. I must insist. Mog."'

She handed the note to Brace. His eyes seemed to darken as he read it. 'The plot thickens,' he muttered.

'What do you think?'

'Obviously, he wants me to butt out.'

'It also means he watched us last night,' Jane said.

'At least part of the time,' Brace agreed. 'And he knows my name. How could he know my name? Maybe he's a student. Or someone on the faculty. That'd make sense. Look where he's sending you: to the Crazy Horse statue, to Mill Creek Bridge – places on or near the campus. And there's the literary angle.'

'He could've picked up your name by listening to us last night.'

'Eavesdropping?' He frowned. 'Most of the time, nobody was close enough for that.'

'Nobody we *saw*, anyway. But someone might've been . . . when we were inside the fence, there was so much junk around.' The skin on the nape of her neck suddenly prickled with goosebumps. 'I *felt* like we weren't alone in that place. I'll bet he was there.'

'It's possible,' Brace admitted.

'And he wanted me there by myself.'

'I don't like this one bit.'

'Neither do I,' Jane said. She realized that the goose-bumps weren't just on the nape of her neck. Her forehead and arms and nipples and thighs felt crawly, too.

'I can only think of one good reason,' Brace said, 'for wanting me out of the way.'

'Yeah.' Jane slid her hands slowly up and down her thighs, rubbing them through the legs of her jeans. 'But that doesn't make sense, either. If he wanted to attack me, he could've done it last night when I was in the shower. Would've been easy.'

'Then why *does* he want me out of the way?' Brace asked.

'Who knows? Why does he do *any* of this?'

Brace shook his head, his cheeks and lips puffing out as he expelled a deep breath.

'Maybe,' Jane said, 'we need to take the whole thing at face value. Maybe it really *is* a game, and he thinks of himself as the big boss, or something, and he doesn't want anybody playing it except me.'

'Sounds like a good time to quit.'

'I know. It does. But on the other hand . . .' Grimacing, she slid her shoulders up and down. 'I sort of want to keep going with it.'

'He broke into your *house*.'

'I guess so.'

'There's no telling *what* he might do.'

'Well, you know . . . If his past actions are any indication, he'll probably give me more and more money.'

'But *why*?'

'To keep me playing his game.'

'He's up to something,' Brace said. 'He's gotta be. Up to something no good.'

'We don't know that. Maybe he's some sort of mysterious benefactor. Like that creepy guy in *Great Expectations*? The fellow who popped up in the graveyard and scared the hell out of poor little Pip?'

'Magwich.'

'Right, Magwich. Maybe it's something like that.'

'You're not going to be talked out of this, are you?'

'Nope.'

'Well, it's your call.'

'I want to go ahead with it.'

'Alone?'

She nodded.

'Well, at least I can drive you over there. Why don't I do that? If you're still absolutely sure you want to play by his rules, I'll park and wait on the bridge while you go down after the money. That way, at least I'll be close by. If something goes wrong, you can yell.'

'That'd be nice,' Jane said. 'But I don't think so.' She shrugged again. 'I've thought a lot about all this. He wants you out of it, Brace. If I let you chauffeur me over there and hang around, he might just drop me. No more envelopes, no more clues, no more money. I don't want that to happen. I want to play this out – as far as I can, anyway.'

'Why should he care if I drive you over . . .?'

'The thing is, he might.'

Wincing as if in pain, Brace shook his head.

Jane clasped his knee. 'It'll be all right.'

'I'm sorry,' he said. 'This is . . . it's none of my business. I mean, whatever you want to do. It's just that I don't want you to get . . . in trouble or hurt. I feel like I need to take care of you, but . . . crazy, huh?'

'Yeah, crazy.'

'We hardly even know each other.'

'Hardly even.'

'And you're pretty good at taking care of yourself.'

'Pretty good,' she whispered, and by now she was twisted around on the sofa, facing him, her hands on his sides. She brushed her lips against his, then murmured, 'You stay here. Okay? I'll go to the bridge, and you stay here, and you'll be here when I get back. Okay?'

'If that's what you want.'

'It might be a while. He might give me something else to do. You know? There might be more than one thing.'

'Might be.'

'But you'll stay?'

'Sure.'

Smiling slightly, Jane straddled his legs, sat on them. 'Have yourself a little party while you wait,' she whispered.

'Oh, that'll be fun.'

'Eat, drink, watch TV, read something.'

'I've got my book in the car.'

'The Wouk?'

'The Wouk.'

'If you get tired of reading, take a little nap.' She leaned into him and wrapped her arms around him. 'Only one rule.'

'Uh-huh?'

'Stay away from the bridge.'

He stiffened slightly in her arms.

'Promise. You've got to promise.'

He hesitated. 'All right.'

'That means no following me, no surveillance in any way, shape, or form. You stay completely out of this business tonight.'

He didn't say anything. Jane felt his chest rising and falling against her chest as he breathed.

'Promise.'

Brace sighed. 'But what if he tries something?'

'He won't.'

'Then why do you have your knife?'

It came as no surprise that he knew about the switchblade. Jane could feel it herself, down at the bottom of her shirt pocket, sideways just under her breast, the handle pressed tight against Brace's ribcage.

'It's just in case,' she said. 'I wouldn't go if I thought . . . you know, that I'd be in real danger.'

'The thing isn't gonna open by accident, is it?'

'Not this time. I put a good, strong rubber band around it.'

'Will you be able to get it open if you need it?'

'Sure. But I won't need it. And you changed the subject on me. I'm still waiting for your promise.'

'I promise,' he said.

'You promise what?'

'To stay out of it tonight. I won't leave your house. How does that sound?'

'Sounds perfect.'

Jane kissed him long and hard on the mouth, then eased herself away. With the back of her hand, she wiped the moisture off her lips. Then she checked her wristwatch. 'I'd better get going.'

Brace looked at his own watch. 'If you leave now, you'll get there fifteen minutes early.'

'The sooner I get there, the sooner I'll be back.'

'You don't want to break the rules, do you? He said midnight.'

'We were early last night and he didn't complain about that. It probably doesn't matter to him, a few minutes one way or the other.'

'Maybe not.'

She climbed off Brace's legs, then pulled him off the sofa. 'Come on, you can walk me out to my car.'

Chapter Nine

On the way from her home to Mill Creek Bridge, Jane saw only one car in her rearview mirror. She wondered if Brace had broken his promise, after all. But the car turned off, and the road behind her remained empty.

She parked under a streetlight near the bridge – exactly the same place, she realized, where Brace had pulled over last night to pick her up.

She removed Brace's flashlight from her purse, then set her purse on the floor where passersby wouldn't be likely to see it. Keys in hand, she climbed out. She locked the door and shut it. As she walked toward the bridge, she dropped the key case into a front pocket of her jeans.

They were good, loose jeans.

She gave the other front pocket a try, and found that it was large enough to hold the flashlight. The flashlight was a big ribbed metal job, probably a foot long, with a heft like a club. She was surprised that it fit.

It softly bumped her right leg as she walked.

And it tugged her jeans lower. She stopped walking, reached under the hanging front of her shirt, pulled up her jeans and tightened her belt.

Now, the jeans felt nice and snug around her waist.

She walked on to the middle of the bridge. Stopping there, she leaned against the concrete parapet. In the light from the nearby lamps, she could just barely make out the creek straight down below her, the rocks and bushes along its shores, and the wooded slope beyond the far side of the bridge. The footpath down the slope wasn't visible, but she knew it was there. She'd followed it once, on her first free day after moving to town for the new job.

She'd spent all that day exploring, but the path had been one of her first discoveries. She'd spotted it from about here while crossing the bridge early that morning. And it had beckoned her.

Nothing beckons like an unexplored path, she thought.

She'd followed it down to where the creek went under the bridge. On the way to the bridge, the creek was shiny with sunlight and slipped around trapped dead branches and gray rocks. Under the bridge, the shadows turned it dark and cool.

You could walk alongside the creek and go under the bridge, and come out in the sunlight on the other side.

Jane had taken only a few steps into the gloom – and was thinking how fresh and cool the air felt – when she realized that a dark shape at the foot of one of the concrete pillars wasn't a bush after all.

It was a man. He wore filthy rags. He sat with his back to the pillar, his knees up against his chest, his arms around his knees, his head pillowed on one knee but turned in Jane's direction. His head was a tangle of filthy brown hair and beard – he seemed to have no face at all.

Shocked, Jane had gaped at him for a few seconds. Then she whirled around and scampered back up the path.

She'd returned many times to Mill Creek Park and had spent hours by the shore of the creek. A few times, she had even taken a look underneath the bridge. Except for that first morning, she'd never seen anyone lurking there. But she'd stayed out from under it, anyway.

Jane pushed herself away from the parapet and continued across the bridge.

I'm really going under there by myself? At midnight, no less?

The notion made her feel shriveled and tingly somewhere low inside.

It's for four hundred bucks, she told herself. Four hundred, if Mog sticks to his routine. As much as I make in a whole week at the library.

Just hope the creepy guy isn't down there.

My own private troll.

'It's own-wee me,' Jane whispered. 'Wooddow teeny-weenie Baby Behwwy Goat Gwuff.'

She grinned and shook her head.

Cute, she thought. Real cute. Can't believe I did that in front of Brace. Lucky thing he didn't throw up.

She pictured him lounging on the sofa in her living room, *Youngblood Hawke* propped up on his lap.

Wish I was there, she thought.

I just hope *he's* there, she told herself. If he broke his promise about coming . . .

She looked up and down the street. A car was approaching from behind, but it wouldn't be here for a while. She doubted that it was Brace's car. She wanted to trust him.

Other vehicles were parked along both sides of the street. A few scattered cars, a van or two, a pickup truck. Jane was pretty sure that they'd arrived before her.

She supposed that Mog might be in one of them.

Watching her right now.

'Naw,' she muttered.

If he's anywhere, he's down below. Waiting for me under the bridge.

She ducked into the trees beyond the end of the bridge. Crouching behind a trunk, she waited for the car. Her heart gave a nasty lurch when it came into sight.

A police car.

But it didn't slow down or stop.

She watched it for a while. When it was far away, she turned her back to the street. She pulled the big flashlight out of her pocket, switched it on, and used its beam to locate the top of the path. Then she shut it off.

Without the flashlight on, she couldn't see much of the path. But she kept it off. Better to have trouble finding her way down the slope than to make herself conspicuous.

Somebody might very well be down there. Her own personal troll. Or Mog. Or God-knows-who.

She carried the flashlight dark. Ready to flick on if she had to. Ready to swing if someone should leap at her.

She moved slowly, watching the steep ground just in front of her feet, trying to stay on the vague blur of the path. She supposed that the path must have fairly regular foot traffic. Its foliage – grass, weeds, whatever – was skimpy from being trampled down.

It was probably used now and then by students from the college.

Adventurous couples seeking someplace dark and private.

She wondered how many of them fell on their asses.

Jack fell down and broke his crown . . .

The last thing I need is a good fall, Jane thought.

All day, she'd been suffering with sore muscles. Climbing on Crazy Horse had done it. Left her with an aching stiffness in her neck and shoulders and arms and back and sides and belly and butt and legs. Even in her toes.

All I did was climb on the thing. Didn't fall of it.

Did almost break my crown, though, she reminded herself.

And gasped as she planted the heel of her left shoe on the slope, started to shift her weight forward, and felt the slick ground jerk her foot out from under her.

Her rump hit the earth. It sent a jolt up her back and into her head.

She felt a quick stab *underneath* the lump on her head. With that and the sting to her rear end, she felt her throat go tight. Her eyes began to burn and spill tears.

'Wonderful,' she muttered.

She shut her eyes. She took a deep, trembling breath. With the back of her empty hand, she wiped tears from her cheeks.

No pain, no gain, she thought, and sniffed.

Small price to pay for four hundred bucks.

Then she felt cool moisture seeping through her pants.

She struggled to her feet. Standing precariously on the dewy slope, she plucked the seat of her jeans away from her buttocks. Then plucked again to nip her panties through the denim and unstick them.

Not that it helped.

They resumed clinging the moment she took her next step down the embankment.

Could be worse, she told herself. I could've sat down on a sharp rock. Or a broken bottle. Or a board with a nail sticking up.

Quit it.

She moved more slowly, more carefully. Before she reached the bottom of the slope, several muscles in her rump and legs began to shimmy. But she didn't fall again.

At last, she found her way to level ground. She leaned back against a tree near the shore of the creek and huffed for air.

Gotta get in better shape.

Do enough of this stuff, she thought, and I'll either shape up or ship out.

As her breath returned, she realized that her mouth was parched. She licked her dry lips. She looked at the creek. It was a broad, black strip, sprinkled here and there with silver bits of moonlight.

She wondered if its water was clean enough to drink.

It sure *sounded* wonderful. It blurbled and hissed and sounded icy cold.

Take a sip, and I'll probably drop right where . . .

'Jane!' A man's scratchy voice.

It knocked her breath out. Rigid, she pressed her back hard against the tree.

What'll I do? He's seen me!

552

Run?

'Huh?'

'That's what she says here. Jane. J-A-N-E.'

He's spelling, she thought. He's reading. *He's reading off the envelope!*

There're two of them and they have my envelope.

But at least they don't know I'm here, she told herself. I don't think so. The guy wasn't calling my name, just reading it.

'Jane,' he said again. 'See that? Plain as the nose on yer face.'

'Nothin' wrong with *my* nose,' said a second male voice. 'Open 'er up.'

'Don't know if I oughta. Thing's meant for ol' Jane. I ain't Jane. *You* shore ain't Jane.'

'Fuck Jane. Open 'er up.'

'Likely just a birthday card, some such shit.'

Jane bent her shaky legs. The bark was rough through the back of her shirt as she lowered herself to a squat. Getting down on all fours, she turned herself around and peered past the side of the tree.

At first, she couldn't see the men at all.

Then she found two figures under the bridge, black against the lesser darkness beyond them. They seemed to be standing. One of the men looked tall and skinny and seemed to have a horribly huge, misshaped head. The shorter man looked broad and bulky. His head looked odd, too, but Jane figured its unusual shape was due to a hat.

They were farther away than she'd expected.

That's how come they didn't see or hear me, she thought.

She wasn't sure why she'd been able to hear *them* so well. Loud talkers, she guessed. Or maybe being underneath the bridge amplified their voices.

'Shore ain't no birthday card. Strike up a match there.'

A moment later, light flared.

Jane flinched.

No!

553

It can't be him, she told herself. But of course it is him – almost had to be, huh? When it comes right down to it? Wouldn't you just *know*?

The ruddy flutter of the matchlight showed that the awful size and shape of the tall man's head wasn't caused by bulging deformities of bone and flesh. It was hair. Thick, filthy tangles that massed around his head and mingled with his eyebrows, moustache and beard so that he seemed to have no face at all.

My own personal troll.

Why him, of all people?

He stood with his side toward Jane, and the other man stood in the way, blocking much of her view. They both wore long, heavy coats.

Must be sweltering in those things, Jane thought.

Good. I hope they drop dead of the heat.

Though she couldn't see much, she was fairly sure that her own personal troll was the one opening her envelope while his short friend held the match.

'Shit,' said the short one. 'Them things real?'

'Shore look real.'

'*Four* of 'em?'

'One, two, t'ree, four. That's right, Swimp.'

'Fuck me twice. What's that letter . . . Ow!' Swimp jerked his arm and killed the light. A couple of seconds later, another match flared. 'Read me what she says, Rale.'

'Read 'er yourself,' said the tall, faceless one.

'Haw haw.'

'Awright. Here she goes. "Dear Jane, you sweet thing. This here's them C-notes you asked us for. We all chipped in."'

What? Jane thought. That can't be right. He's making this up.

Rale continued, '"Now you gotta come across with yer crack t'morra night."'

'She spose t'fuck 'em?' Swimp asked.

'Naw. They're buying *crack* off her.'

'Ain't that what I just said?'

'Ya moron.'

'Ain't no moron.' Swimp swept off his headgear – a straw cowboy hat with most of the brim missing off one side – and swatted Rale on the shoulder with it. As he did that, his second match went out. In the darkness, he said, 'This here Jane, she shore don't come cheap. Course, what you said about 'em *all* chippin' in, guess there might be a whole slew of fellows. Maybe she's fixin' to fuck the baseball team. Whatta they call 'emselves? Use t' be the Warchiefs, but . . .'

'The Chargers,' Rale explained.

'Yeah.' Swimp lit another match. 'Well,' he said, 'bad luck for them, good luck for you 'n' me.' The hat was back on his head. He nudged Rale with his elbow. 'Bad luck for ol' Jane, too.'

That's for sure, Jane thought. The idiot didn't know what he was talking about, but he was right, anyway.

Bad luck for ol' Jane.

And then some. Losing the four hundred dollars was bad enough, but losing the note could put a stop to the whole game.

If that damn Rale had just read what was there instead of making the whole thing up . . .

Maybe Rale can't read. Maybe he's as illiterate as his buddy, Swimp.

Wait, she thought. No. He read my name. If he knows Jane when he sees it . . .

'How we gonna split her up?' Swimp asked.

'You mean ol' Jane? Reckon I'll have me the front 'n' you take the back.'

Swimp snorted and gave Rale another shot with his elbow. 'Go awn. The *bread*, the *moola*. We gonna split her even-Steven, right?'

'Well, now . . .'

What if I just step out and show myself? Jane wondered. Tell them they're welcome to the money, but could I please have the note?

Brilliant idea.

'Reckon that'd be a fair split,' Rale said.

He wants my front and Swimp gets my back. Real nice.

But maybe it's just talk, she thought. Just a couple of horny, drunk bums talking big.

The match died.

I've gotta get the note!

No, I don't. I can just forget about it. Forget about the whole thing. Go home and see what Brace is up to. Consider myself lucky to be out of it three-hundred-and-fifty bucks to the good, relatively unscathed, and with a fine new friend who might be just the sort of man . . .

Swimp lit another match.

During the short period of darkness, the two had changed positions. Now, they stood facing each other, their profiles to Jane. Swimp was holding both hands toward Rale. He kept the match in his right. Jane could feel no breeze at all, but the match flame shivered and wobbled, casting a crimson glow that made the two men look ghoulish.

They aren't ghouls, Jane told herself. Just a couple of dim-witted bums. *And they're screwing up everything!*

Swimp's left hand was open, palm up.

Rale dealt him two bills.

Two hundreds.

Mine!

'All fair 'n' square?' he asked.

'Fair 'n' square,' Swimp said, his head bobbing up and down.

Rale tucked the other two bills back into the envelope, folded the envelope and shoved it into the side pocket of his long, bulky coat. Then he said, 'Let's scat.'

Swimp shook out his match. 'Spose Jane's gonna show up?'

'Shore.'

They began to walk alongside the creek. At first, Jane thought they were walking *away* from her.

Chapter Ten

'Wanta hide 'n' see her?' Swimp asked.

'Wanta get us shot dead? She ain't no whore, y'lamebrain. The gal's a *drug* pusher, and folks like that . . .'

They're coming!

Not walking away, but heading straight toward Jane. She was on all fours, the tree trunk between her and the two men.

It won't be between us for long!

Run!

But which way? She wondered. Up the slope? It's so steep and slippery! I'll fall flat on my face and they'll grab me by the ankles . . . Run up the shore? I'm probably faster than them. But what if I'm not? I'll be running deeper and deeper into the park . . .

If I try running anywhere, they'll see me and chase me and . . .

Here they come!

She eased herself down flat against the ground at the foot of the tree, and lay motionless.

They won't see me, she told herself. I'm dressed in black (well, not *really* black but close enough), and if I lie absolutely still they'll walk right on by without even knowing I'm here.

Maybe.

Please!

Their voices came closer and closer. Jane couldn't follow what they were saying; she could only think about the distance. Ten or twelve feet away. Now maybe six. Now probably just on the other side of the tree. Now coming alongside the tree.

They can see me now. If they look, they'll see me.

Don't look!

Just keep walking and don't look down over here!

'Jumpin' shit!' Swimp blurted.

The footsteps stopped.

'She dead?' Swimp asked, his voice hushed.

Don't panic!

Though her face was turned away from the two, she shut her eyes. She strained to control her breathing, to take small breaths so her movement might go undetected in the darkness.

'She don't appear real frisky,' Rale said.

Someone stepped on her. A shoe pressed against the seat of her jeans, pushed down on her buttocks and began to jerk back and forth quick and hard. She stayed limp, letting her whole body wobble with the rhythm of the shaking foot.

'Spose it's Jane?' Swimp asked.

'Might be,' Rale said. The foot lifted off her rump. 'Let's see what she's got.' He groaned and a couple of his joints crackled as he squatted beside Jane.

She felt a hand push down into the left rear pocket of her jeans. She knew it could find nothing there. But it rubbed and squeezed her before coming out and entering the other pocket. The hand stayed longer in that empty pocket, kneading her buttock.

Done, Rale said, 'Let's turn her over.'

Hands clutched Jane's left shoulder and arm and hip and leg. They pulled and lifted, rolling her onto her right side (where the pocketed flashlight shoved painfully against her wrist), then onto her back. She kept herself limp – let her head wobble, her legs flop lifelessly.

'Hey,' Swimp said, 'wanna see her?'

'Shore.'

She heard the snick of a match. A shimmery, pinkish glow soaked through her eyelids.

'Wah!' Swimp blurted. 'She's a hon. Ain't she a hon?'

'A beaut. Ain't no more dead 'n' you 'r me, but she's shore a beaut.'

'Ain't dead?'

'At's okay,' Rale said. 'Reckon she's passed out, 'r somethin'.'

She felt a tug at her waist. Her belt went loose.

'Whatcha doin'?' Swimp asked.

'Jackin' her belt.'

'No, you ain't.'

Rale laughed. Then he unbuttoned the waist of Jane's jeans and she snatched the flashlight out of her pocket and both men made surprised noises and flinched. Swimp, crouched by her arm, dropped the match. Rale, by her hip, had both hands on her zipper. Just as he let go, the flashlight crashed against his temple. The blow knocked his head sideways, spit flying. The falling match died. Swimp yelled in the sudden darkness. The hot matchhead found Jane's skin just down from her throat and she gasped, 'Ah!' Rale tumbled backward, arms flung high. Swimp, still yelling, scurried backward on his knees. Jane rammed the flashlight at his belly, but missed, so then rolled toward him, rising onto her left elbow as Rale splashed into the creek, flinging herself over and stretching as she jabbed. But Swimp was out of range. Jane sprawled facedown. She drove both hands against the ground and pushed herself up fast. Her jeans fell down around her ankles. Swimp didn't notice. Or didn't care. Whimpering, he stumbled to his feet and started to run away.

As he fled, Jane clamped the flashlight under her arm and pulled her jeans up. She fastened the waist button. She buckled her belt. Then she turned her attention to the creek and looked for Rale. Unable to spot him, she grabbed her flashlight and thumbed its switch.

Nothing.

Must've busted it when I whacked him.

Keeping the flashlight in her hand, she stepped to the edge of the creek. The water looked black except for bits of silver from the moon.

Still no sign of Rale.

I hit him awfully hard. What if I knocked him out, and he drowned?

What if he's just fine, thanks, and already out of the water? Hiding somewhere?

That can't be, she told herself. He hasn't had time to get out. And I've been right here. I would've seen him.

He hasn't had time to drown yet, either.

Jane suddenly waded into the creek. The chilly water filled her shoes, wrapped her ankles, climbed past her knees and up her thighs. Though the current was slow, she could feel its gentle push. She turned her back to it and trudged a few steps closer to the bridge.

Too slow.

She shoved the flashlight into her jeans pocket, took one big step and lunged, leaving her feet, plunging forward, diving down below the surface. Her shoes and heavy clothes dragged at her. Instead of gliding, she was almost stopped. She kicked to the surface and swam hard.

But only for a few strokes.

Then her right hand swept down and slapped a sodden tangle.

Got him!

Him or maybe a beaver.

As her blow submerged whatever it was that she had struck, her left hand collided with a sunken object that might've been Rale's chest.

With both hands, she grabbed.

By his coat lapel and beard, she raised Rale to the surface of the creek. He was limp.

Playing possum?

Jane doubted it.

She waded backward, towing him, then dragged him onto the dirt and rocks of the shore. When only his feet remained in the creek, she let go. She was huffing for air. She dropped to her knees beside him and pushed the wet hair away from her eyes.

Though Rale didn't seem to be moving, she pulled the flashlight out of her pocket. Holding it in her right hand, ready to strike him, she reached into his coat pocket with her left hand and pulled out the soaked envelope that he'd put there.

He still lay motionless.

What if I killed him?

He can't be dead. Can't be.

She needed both hands to open the envelope, so she clamped the flashlight between her thighs. She picked at the torn, wet opening at the top of the envelope, spread the edges, and fingered what was inside.

Two dark bills.

And a folded sheet of paper.

Mog's note.

Got it!

She knew that the bills would be okay, so she tucked them into a pocket of her shirt. Then she carefully unfolded the note. She thought she might have to peel the paper away from itself, but it opened easily. It seemed damp, but certainly not sodden. For the brief amount of time that it had been submerged, the envelope must've kept most of the water out. She doubted very much that the handwritten message had been ruined.

This was no time to read it, though.

She shook a few drops off the paper. Putting it anywhere on her body would be risking further water damage, so she placed it on a nearby slab of rock. She pinned it down with a smaller rock.

Taking the flashlight from between her legs, she leaned over Rale's sprawled body. With her left hand, she shook him by the shoulder.

Oh, my God, if he's dead . . .

'Rale! Hey! Wake up!'

She shook him harder.

Nothing.

Hunkering down, she put her ear close to his mouth. She heard no breathing, felt no air against her ear.

With her left hand, she fingered his thick growth of facial hair until she found his lips. They were slightly parted. She forced his mouth open wider and reached in deep with two fingers. They rubbed against the edges of his teeth, slid over the slimy flesh of his tongue.

If he's faking it and bites . . .

Nothing seemed to be blocking his airway.

She pulled her fingers out, wiped them on the shoulder of his coat, and again slipped the flashlight between her legs. With her right hand, she delved through his beard and reached his neck. She found his carotid artery, felt its beating pulse.

At least I didn't kill him, she thought.

But he isn't breathing.

She tilted his head back, pinched his nostrils shut, and held his jaw open.

What am I, nuts? He was all set to rape me. Maybe he would've killed me. And I'm gonna do this?

Apparently yes, she thought.

And took a deep breath and covered his mouth with her lips and blew her air into him. When she lifted her mouth away, the air rushed out of him, flapping his lips.

She blew into him again.

Again.

Again.

Come on, she thought. If you die on me . . .

Where the hell is your good buddy Swimp? Ran off and left you. Some friend. One of us could've gone for help.

She again blew her breath into Rale.

He puked. It happened fast. Jane had no time to get her mouth away. There was a sound like the muffled bark of a dog, and up came a belch loaded with vomit.

It filled her mouth.

She lurched back, head down, his sour fluids spilling out of her. She spit and spit. She gagged. With Rale coughing behind her, she scurried into the creek, waded out until it was knee-deep, bent down and cupped water into her mouth. She didn't swallow any, but spit it out and rinsed her mouth again and again.

Turning around, she found Rale on his hands and knees, head hanging as he coughed and gasped.

Jane rushed for the shore, kicking at the water, splashing it high.

Rale twisted his head around and looked over his shoulder.

'Don't move!' Jane snapped. 'Stay right there! Stay right there!'

He stayed on his hands and knees, still coughing but not so much as before, and watched Jane as she splashed ashore and crouched to grab her flashlight. With the flashlight in her hand, she didn't feel so vulnerable. She shook it at Rale. 'Stay right there,' she warned.

She bent down and plucked Mog's note out from between the rocks.

Anything else? she wondered. Have I got everything?

Everything but the two hundred bucks Swimp ran off with.

At least I got half the money, she told herself. And the note. The note was the important thing.

Is it? she wondered. Maybe the important thing is that I didn't kill anybody. And nobody killed me.

'Stay right there,' she told Rale again. Keeping her eyes on him, she stepped backward toward the slope. The ground began to rise behind her. She turned to the slope and started climbing. After a few strides, she looked down over her shoulder. 'Stay right . . .'

He was gone.

The shock almost knocked her breathless.

Flashlight in one hand, note from Mog in the other, she bounded up the steep, slippery hillside. Halfway to the top, she fell. She started to slide downward on her elbows and knees. Letting out a whimper of fright, she scurried and found footing and made it to the top.

She ran all the way to her car.

Chapter Eleven

Jane stopped on the front porch. Keeping the note from Mog in one hand, she used her other hand to pull off her muddy shoes. As she crouched to set them beside the welcome mat, Brace opened the door.

She smiled up at him.

Her smile seemed to require a ton of energy.

'What happened?' Brace asked.

She felt too weary to answer. So she shrugged and shook her head as she straightened up.

Brace looked ready to reach for her. She shook her head again. 'You don't wanta touch me,' she said. 'Take this.' She thrust Mog's note at him.

'So you got it,' he said, taking it from her hand. 'Are you all right?'

'Not sure.' She waved him aside. He moved out of her way and she entered the house.

'Are you hurt?'

'No. Just . . . yucky. And I don't feel too hot.' She turned toward the hallway, but looked over her shoulder at him. 'Can you stick around? I've gotta shower and change. Okay?'

'Sure.'

'Thanks. I'll tell you all about . . .' She stopped. She turned around. 'Gotta have a drink.'

'I'll get it for you. What do you want?'

'Jim Beam. It's in the cupboard by the fridge. And a glass. Want a glass. One for you, too. If you want.'

'Ice?'

Jane shut her eyes and shook her head.

'I'll be right back,' Brace said.

'I'll be in the john,' Jane muttered.

As Brace hurried toward the kitchen, Jane staggered down the hallway and entered the bathroom. She left the door open. Standing by the counter, she removed the flashlight and key case from the wet pockets of her jeans. She set them on the counter, then dug into her shirt pockets. She fished out the soggy pair of hundred dollar bills, the switchblade knife, and a flimsy, damp card.

Confused, she stared at the card.

Brace Paxton, PhD, Instructor of English, Donnerville University . . .

'Ah!'

His business card.

Jane added it to her collection on the counter, then shambled over to the toilet, lowered its lid, and sat down. Groaning, she bent low and peeled off her wet socks. Her feet looked pink, and a few bits of grass were pressed into her skin. How did *they* get there? she wondered. How'd they get in my *socks*?

'Just one a those things,' she murmured.

Then raised her head as Brace came in with the bottle and two glasses.

'Ah,' Jane said.

'A wee bit o'cure for what ails ya,' he said.

'I'm gonna want more than a wee bit.'

He set the glasses on the counter near the collection from Jane's pockets. As he started to pour, Jane said, 'I broke your flashlight for you.'

'No problem.'

'I'll fix it. Or buy you a new one.'

'Looks like you only got two hundred this time.'

'Somebody else got a share.'

He handed one of the glasses to Jane.

'Thanks. Anyway . . . a long story. Tell you later.' She filled her mouth with bourbon. She sloshed it around and held it, feeling its heat soak into her tongue and gums and cheeks. After a while, the inside of her mouth started to tingle and burn. Her eyes watered. She swallowed, and sighed.

Brace watched her. He looked concerned.

Jane filled her mouth again.

'Are you sure you're all right?' Brace asked.

She nodded. 'Just worn out. Drained.'

'You aren't going to fall down in the bathtub, are you?'

Jane fell down and broke her crown . . . and a troll threw up down her throat.

I didn't swallow any, she told herself.

Hope not, anyway.

She shook her head and took a small swallow of the bourbon stored in her mouth. It scorched her throat and slipped downward to join the heat in her belly.

'Want a refill before I go?'

She nodded and held out her glass. Brace added enough for another mouthful.

'All set?' he asked.

She nodded again.

'See you when you're out,' he said, and stepped into the hallway and shut the bathroom door.

Jane thought about locking it. She decided not to bother. Brace wouldn't try anything funny.

Might be nice if he would, she thought.

No.

Don't want any messing around. Don't even want to think about it. Too tired. Too sore. Too fat . . .

She swallowed the last of the bourbon in her mouth, then took her glass to the counter and set it down. Keeping her eyes away from the mirror, she took off her wet clothes. Then she stepped over to the tub, spread the bathmat, squatted down and started the water running.

She felt so terribly tired.

Tired all over, sore in every muscle, filthy, half numb inside her head.

When the water was ready, she climbed into the tub and shut the glass door. The strong, hot spray felt good, but it sapped away even more of her energy. Though little effort was needed to soap herself, her arms ached and grew heavy as she washed her hair. Finally, she sank down and sat on the bottom of the tub. Hot water splashing down on her, she folded her arms around her knees and hung her head.

The water felt wonderful.

So wonderful.

She could almost sleep . . .

She woke up shivering, gasped out 'Yah!' as she found herself being drenched by ice cold water, lurched forward and twisted the faucets until the shower shut off. Teeth chattering, she hurried out of the tub. Her dripping skin felt tight and hard. It was spickled with goosebumps. Shuddering, she snatched her towel off the bar. She started with her hair, and worked her way downward.

By the time she was done drying herself, the tremors had subsided. She draped the towel over her shoulders, stepped to the counter, and took a couple of swallows of bourbon.

Oddly, the mirror wasn't fogged up. The cold shower must've cleared away the steam.

Jane's reflection was sharp and clear.

She started to turn away, then hesitated, surprised.

I don't look all that bad, she thought. Not really.

Of course, the thick towel hanging from her shoulders to her waist hid plenty.

Watching herself in the mirror, she brushed the tangles out of her hair. When her short, damp hair was smooth against her head, she set aside the brush and pulled the towel away.

It's really true, she thought. I'm changing. I've already changed.

No doubt about it, the mirror showed that she looked less soft and pudgy than usual. She doubted that she'd lost much weight, but the physical exertions that had caused her to be sore and weary had apparently also tightened her muscles.

You've still got a long way to go, she told herself.

But this is pretty good for just two nights of chasing after Mog's envelopes. Pretty amazing, in fact.

Keep it up, and before long I'll look as good as I ever did.

Yeah, great. Just what I need. I was *so* happy then. Everything was *just so wonderful*.

Screw it. I oughta stay fat.

She took another drink. She turned around, gazing at her reflection.

No matter what, it felt *good* to look better. It would be great to look the way she used to – like throwing aside an old disguise that had outlived its usefulness.

Who says I don't need it any more? she wondered.

And who says it's even a disguise?

Don't think about it, she told herself. Why bother? I'm looking better, and I wasn't even trying. It's just the way things have happened. So I'll just let things happen as they happen.

Maybe Mog wants to make me slim.

She smirked at herself in the mirror.

Sure, that's it. You've been looking for his Big Plan. Well, maybe that's it. The whole point of the Game is to wear the pounds off Jane, shape her up.

Ship her out.

Play hard, die young, have a good-looking corpse.

The corner of her mouth curved higher.

Sure, she thought. That's got to be it.

She laughed softly, then frowned.

A silly idea, she thought. Interesting, though. Sort of like Hansel and Gretel in reverse. In the fairy tale, the old witch fattened up Hansel so there'd be more of him to eat. Maybe the point of the Game *is* to whip me into shape . . . make me slender and firm and more good-looking.

But why?

Some sort of Pygmalion thing? Wants to shape me into his idea of perfection?

She sighed and shook her head.

I'd better finish up and get out of here.

She swung the mirror open on its hinges. From the medicine cabinet behind it, she took her toothbrush and tube of paste. She swung the mirror shut.

She started to brush her teeth.

And suddenly remembered the feel and taste of Rale's vomit. She gagged and her eyes watered.

Stop it! Don't think about it!
Think about something nice.

Brace waiting for me in the living room. Probably wondering what's taking me so long.

Done with her teeth, she put away the brush and paste. She drank some cold water, dried her mouth and hands with the towel, then turned toward the bathroom door.

Where her robe didn't hang.

You never got it, you idiot. Came right in here, did not pass Go, did not go to your bedroom and grab your robe. Where was your mind?

Probably back by Mill Creek Bridge.

No big deal, she told herself.

She shook open her bath towel, wrapped it around her body, and tucked a corner in between her breasts to hold it up. The towel was wide enough to hang past her groin and rump. But just barely.

A terrific night, she thought. A really wonderful night. What'll be next to go wrong?

She inched open the bathroom door. The hallway looked clear. Brace was probably in the living room, sipping his drink and reading while he awaited her arrival.

The house sounded awfully quiet, though.

How much noise would he make, sipping and reading? None, that's how much.

Jane stepped out into the hallway. It was dark in the direction of her bedroom. At the other end was light from the living room. She stood motionless and stared into the light. She could see the carpeted foyer and the front door, but nothing else. She listened very hard.

Why doesn't he cough, or something?

Because he's gone, that's why.

He got tired of waiting and he went home.

She began to walk slowly toward the light.

He wouldn't just leave like that, she told herself. Something's wrong.

What if Mog got him? Mog was here last night. Maybe he came tonight, too. Maybe he snuck up on Brace . . .

Where the wall ended, Jane halted. She pressed a hand against her chest to make sure the towel didn't slip loose, and felt the quick hard pounding of her heart.

This is dumb, she thought. Brace is fine. I'm making a big deal out of nothing.

Leaning forward, she peered around the corner.

The lamp on the end table partially blocked her view down the length of the sofa. She could see enough, though. Brace wasn't there. He wasn't across from the sofa on the reclining chair, either.

Maybe he'd gone into the kitchen, or . . .

Jane saw fingertips on the floor beyond the coffee table. She shuffled toward them, sliding her feet over the carpet, trying to make no noise. The rest of the hand came into sight. And then the rest of Brace.

He lay on his back, sprawled alongside the coffee table, legs spread slightly apart, left hand curled by his side, right arm away from his body and bent at the elbow as if he'd extended it past the table to help Jane find him. His shirt was untucked. Open at the bottom, it showed a triangle of bare skin just above the belt of his dark gray trousers.

His face was covered by one of the big, blue pillows from the sofa.

Jane's mind screamed, *NO!* as she rushed toward him.

Dropping to her knees, she grabbed the pillow and hurled it away.

Brace's eyes leaped open and he gasped.

Jane's mouth dropped. So did her towel. She caught the towel and lifted it and clutched it to her breasts. 'You . . .!' she gasped. She scurried backward. 'You were *sleeping!*' she blurted, and scrambled to her feet and ran for her bedroom.

She felt like a fool as she ran.

Now I've done it!

In her bedroom, she slammed the door. Then she fingered the wall until she found the light switch. She leaned back against the door and gasped for air.

I've really done it. God! What was I thinking?

'Jane?'

She flinched. She hadn't heard him approaching. She pressed her back harder against the door, and clutched the towel more tightly to her chest.

'Jane?' he asked again. 'Are you okay?'

'I thought you were dead!'

Silence for a few moments. Then his quiet voice said, 'Why?'

'You were on the floor! You had . . .'

'I was just taking a nap.'

'On the *floor*? That's what the sofa is for!'

'It feels better for my back. I like to lie on floors sometimes.'

'With a pillow over your face?'

'Sometimes.'

'I thought you'd been *suffocated*!'

'Oh.'

'Murdered!'

'I'm really sorry, Jane. I just stretched out on the floor to rest for a couple of minutes. I put the pillow on my face to block out the lights, you know? I had no idea you might come along and think . . . anything was wrong.'

'Well, I did! I thought you were dead! I thought Mog had gotten in and killed you!'

'I'm really sorry. I am.'

'And my towel fell down,' she blurted. 'I bet you're all sorry about that, too.'

'Yeah, I am.'

'I'll just bet you are.'

'I'm sorry if you're embarrassed about it, that's all.'

'I thought you'd been killed.'

'I know.' After a few moments, he said, 'Would you like me to leave?'

'Yes! Please.'

'Okay. Well . . . I guess . . . so long, then.'

'I didn't mean *leave*! Brace? You still there?'

'Yeah.'

'I only meant you should go back to the living room. Will you? I'll be out in a few minutes.'

'Sure. Whenever you're ready.'

Chapter Twelve

When Jane entered the living room, Brace stood up in front of the sofa and smiled. 'Hey, you look great.'

'Thanks.' She knew that she didn't look great; not with her hair still plastered down flat from the shower and her eyes red from crying. But she did feel nicely dressed in her fresh white shorts, white blouse and moccasins.

She and Brace sat down beside each other on the sofa.

'I got a little crazy,' she said. 'Everything's been so weird, you know? None of this was your fault, that's what I'm getting at. I mean, you can stretch out on my floor any time you want. I promise I won't go nuts next time.'

'See that you don't,' he said.

She saw the look in his eyes, and laughed. 'Creep,' she muttered.

Turning toward her, Brace brought his knee up onto the cushion, leaned sideways and rested his arm across the back of the sofa. 'What *I* want to know,' he said, 'is what happened at the bridge. You must've had quite an adventure.'

'Maybe I could use another drink.'

'Your glass still in the bathroom?' He started to rise.

'Don't bother. We can share, can't we?' She leaned forward, lifted the bottle of bourbon off the coffee table, and started to refill Brace's glass.

'Fine with me,' he said. 'You aren't wearing lipstick, are you? I hate the taste of lipstick in my bourbon.'

She put down the bottle. 'See for yourself,' she whispered, leaning toward him.

He laughed softly, pulled her up against him and kissed her on the mouth. He kissed her for a long time. Then he eased her away and said, 'Guess you don't have any lipstick on.'

'That was quite a test,' she murmured, and rested her forehead against his shoulder.

He moved his hands softly up and down her back.

'It's okay,' he said, 'if you don't want to tell me about tonight. If you're too tired, or you'd rather just not talk about it.'

'No, it's not that. I want to tell you. But maybe first you'd better test me once more for lipstick.'

Brace laughed. Laughing, the movements of his chest and belly jiggled her. She raised her face and met his lips again.

When it was done, she whispered, 'That's a lot better. Thanks.' She took a very deep breath. 'What a night.' Turning away from Brace, she leaned forward and picked up the glass. She took a drink, and passed the glass to him.

'So anyway,' she started, 'I parked on Park Lane right at the same place where you picked me up last night.' She leaned back, sinking into the soft cushion of the sofa, and propped her feet up on the coffee table. 'I left my purse in the car, but I took your flashlight with me. Good thing I did, too.'

And she went on, telling Brace every detail she could remember about her quest for the envelope, describing Rale and Swimp, mimicking their speech, leaving out nothing.

Almost nothing.

She made no mention of Swimp's confusion over the sale of 'Jane's crack.' It was irrelevant, crude, and way too personal.

She also said nothing about Rale vomiting into her mouth.

She was afraid she might gag if she had to tell him about that. And she was afraid he might not want to kiss her again for a very long time.

Brace listened to it all, sometimes taking a sip of bourbon and passing the glass to Jane, sometimes looking very worried, but never interrupting her story.

After she finished, he remained silent. He looked very serious.

'So, what do you think?' she asked.

He scowled. 'I should've gone with you.'

'Wrong.'

'My God, Jane.'

'It worked out okay.'

'Oh, it worked out just great. You nearly got yourself raped. And they probably would've beaten you up, at the very least. They might've *killed* you. And you damn near did kill that Rale bastard.'

Jane made a weary smirk. 'Don't forget Swimp got yourself raped. And they probably would've beaten you up, at the very least. They might've *killed* you. And you damn near did kill that Rale bastard.'

Jane made a weary smirk. 'Don't forget Swimp got away with half my money.'

'That's the least of it.'

'Well, at least they didn't get all the money – or the note. It was the note that really had me worried. If they'd ended up with that . . .'

'It might've been a lucky thing if they *had* gone off with it. Maybe that would've put an end to all this.'

'I don't think so. What I think is, I would've gone after them and stayed with them and gotten it back one way or another.'

Brace blew softly through his pursed lips. 'You are *really* hooked on this thing.'

'I want to get as much out of it as I can. And find out what's going on.'

'But look at what happened tonight.'

'I know. Are you kidding, I was *there*. I was scared out of my wits. But it was just one of those things. An accident, you know? Those two bums just happened to be at the wrong place at the wrong time. It was a fluke. I could go chasing down Mog's envelopes from now till doomsday and never have anything like that happen again. You know?'

'No,' Brace said. 'First, he's sending you to lonely places in the middle of the night. You're bound to run into more trouble if you keep at it. Second, you can't be sure it was a fluke.'

'Well . . . I can't be *sure* of anything, but . . .'

'Maybe Rale and Swimp were sent by Mog. For all you really know, one or the other of them might've *been* Mog.'

She let out an uneasy laugh. 'It's possible, but I sure doubt it. I mean, I think those things are both *very* unlikely. These guys just happened to be there.'

'Maybe, maybe not. The thing is, it got bad tonight. It could've gotten a lot worse. You were lucky. One of these times, you might run into more trouble than you can handle.'

'Trying to cheer me up?'

'Trying to make you quit.'

'I'm not going to quit.'

'At least let me go with you next time. I can stay out of sight . . .'

'No.'

'Rale saw the note,' Brace reminded her.

'Yeah, but it was pretty dark. He might not've been able to make out everything it said. The stuff he pretended to read for Swimp didn't have anything to do with what was really written. And even if he *did* manage to read it all, that doesn't mean he could necessarily figure it out and remember it well enough to go there.'

Leaning forward, Brace lifted the note off the coffee table and unfolded it.

Jane sat up and looked at it with him.

The paper was dry, slightly rumpled from all the handling, a little warped and bulgy here and there where the creek had gotten to it through the envelope. A few of the ruled, blue lines had small smears – almost as if someone had wept over the note. Three or four drops of moisture had also struck the handwritten words, making the ink of certain letters dark and fuzzy.

It had still been wet when she'd read it the first time.

After racing to her car, she'd tossed the paper onto the passenger seat, keyed the ignition and sped away – eyes on the rearview mirror, watching for Rale and Swimp. Only after driving halfway across town had she pulled to a curb and stopped. There, she'd turned on the courtesy light and read the note.

She'd read it four or five times.

She read it now as Brace held it open over his lap.

Dear Jane,

Glad this wasn't a bridge too far. How far *will* you go? To the moon? To the stars? To the pits of hell? Or all the way to Paradise?

Tomorrow, when churchyards yawn, see the Babe.

Love and kisses,
The Master

'I don't think we need to worry much about *Rale* showing up,' Jane said.

'Showing up where?' Brace asked.

'Yeah. That's what I mean. He might've read this thing once – in the moonlight. He'll never figure it out. Just hope *we* can. What do you make of it?'

'I know when churchyards yawn.'

Jane grinned. 'When's that?'

'At "the very witching time of night," ' Brace said.

'Like about the time of night "when churchyards yawn and hell itself breathes out contagion to this world"?'

'That's it! Most excellent, Jane! You do know your *Hamlet*.'

'Obviously, so does Mog. But tell me this, professor – what exactly *is* the witching hour? Midnight?'

'Yep.'

'Midnight again. Okay. At midnight, I'm supposed to see the Babe. Babe Ruth?'

'Paul Bunyan's blue ox?'

'Any statues I need to know about?'

Brace shook his head. 'Not anywhere around here. I think

we're getting ahead of ourselves, though. Why don't we start at the beginning and work through from there?'

'Okay. The beginning. '"Dear Jane."' She shrugged.

'*A Bridge Too Far*,' Brace said, 'might be an allusion to the Cornelius Ryan book . . .'

'We have it in the library.'

'Maybe the envelope's in the book.'

'Check the index for a Babe?' Jane suggested.

'Doubt if that's even close.'

'Same here. I think he's just being cute about the bridge too far.'

Brace shook his head.

'What?' Jane asked.

'You don't suppose he knew you'd have a battle at the bridge? That's what the book is about, you know – a disastrous World War Two attack on . . .'

'Saw the movie. I still think it's Mog being cute.'

'Let's go on. "How far *will* you go?"'

'The jerk.'

'What?'

'Him and his innuendos.'

'Oh. Okay, how about "To the moon?"'

'Maybe the guy's a Jackie Gleason fan.'

Brace grinned. 'Think so?'

She waved her fist in front of his nose. Trying to sound like Ralph Cramden, she said, 'One a dese days, Alice! To da moon! To da moon!'

Seeing the look on Brace's face, she laughed.

'You *are* a little nuts, aren't you?' he asked.

'Maybe a smidgen.'

He bumped her softly with his shoulder. 'It's all right,' he said. 'I sort of like little nuts.'

'Ho!'

'What?'

'Never mind. "To the moon? To the stars? To the pits of hell?" Very nice. The pits of hell. I'll pass on that, thank you.'

'You draw the line at the pits of hell?' Brace asked.

'I do believe so. We should be up to eight hundred bucks for this one, right? Well, that ain't enough for a visit to the pits of hell.'

'Glad to hear it.'

'Wouldn't want to try for Paradise, either. The place has stiff entry requirements.'

Brace nodded. 'Like being virtuous and sinless?'

'Like being dead.'

They both laughed for a while. Wiping her eyes, Jane sighed. 'It's getting late. *I'm* getting giddy.'

'We'd better wrap this up.'

'I'd say the envelope will be waiting for me in Paradise. In a Paradise I can visit alive. Maybe there's a Babe at the place, and he, she or it will have the next envelope.'

'It's probably something like that,' Brace agreed.

Chapter Thirteen

At two minutes before midnight, Jane swung open the door of the Paradise Lounge and stepped inside.

It was dimly lit and smoky. The air smelled bad. Off to one side, pool balls clacked. The juke box played Mary Chapin Carpenter.

Could be worse, she thought.

She'd expected it to be pretty bad, the address being on Division Street. In an area of town known for its high crime rate, thrift shops, pawn shops, porno shops, hookers, winos and druggies, the Paradise Lounge was certain to be a dive.

'I bet it's that lounge on Division,' she'd told Brace last night after looking up Paradise in the white pages of the Donnerville telephone directory. There were only four listings: the Paradise Drive-in, an outdoor movie theater north of town; Paradise Gardens Memorial Park, a cemetery; Paradise Lanes, a bowling alley; and the Paradise Lounge, certain to be a dive.

'What makes you think it's that place?' Brace had asked.

'Tomorrow'll be Thursday. The drive-in is only open on Friday, Saturday and Sunday nights. I doubt if the bowling alley is open at midnight on a Thursday, but I'll give it a call tomorrow just to make sure.'

'What about Paradise Gardens?' Brace had asked.

'It's a bone orchard.'

'I know. Seems like just the sort of place I'd expect Mog to send you.'

'I don't want to go to a place like that.'

'Nobody does.'

'Very funny. Damn. It probably *is* the cemetery. All this stuff about hell and paradise and yawning churchyards.'

'Churchyards *are* graveyards.'

'I know, I know.'

'This one's probably got plenty of babes in it.'

'Jeez.'

'Babe is probably someone's name, though. You'll have to read the tombstones.'

'Just what I want to do.'

'Nobody's forcing you.'

'What I think I'll do is try the other places first. If I don't have any luck, I'll go to the boneyard.'

'Such is life.'

'Oh, you're awfully fine and jolly.'

'That's because I'll be back in my apartment, getting a good night's sleep for a change, while you're out in the night hunting through sleazy bars or whatever. Unless you'll let me come with you.'

'I wish you *could* come along.' After saying that, she'd kissed him and snuggled with him there on the sofa. But it hadn't lasted long.

Out on the porch, he'd said, 'Call me when you get done tomorrow night, okay? Let me know how it went.'

'You don't want me to wake you up, do you?'

'You won't wake me up. You don't really think I'll be able to fall asleep, do you?'

'You said you would.'

'I lied.'

Walking into the Paradise Lounge, Jane wondered if Brace had also lied about his intention of spending the night at his apartment.

She almost hoped so.

She would be furious with him, but she knew for certain that the cold hard knot in her belly would loosen and go away if she found Brace here at the Paradise Lounge.

She scanned the place, looking for him. She didn't see him. He wasn't sitting at one of the tables, or standing by the pool table, or perched on any of the bar stools.

Neither was Rale, the bum she had nearly killed last night.

She spotted three women. One of those was the barmaid. Two female customers, she thought. I make three. Terrific.

Maybe one of them is Babe.

Babe could easily be a man's name, though.

She didn't bother counting the men, but guessed there were at least fifteen of them.

More than a few were watching her.

Studying her.

She started for a corner table, where she could sit in the shadows and wait. Maybe Babe would come to her table and hand the envelope to her.

But what if the wrong person came over, someone who wanted to bother her? Over there at the table, a lot of things could happen without anyone even noticing.

She decided she would be safer at the bar.

She walked toward it.

She was very glad that she had decided to wear a bra. She disliked the things, and avoided them when she could. But making a midnight trip to a bar in a sleazy section of town required one. So did her tight shirt, which would've shown every jiggle.

The bra didn't stop the men from staring at her, though.

Partly, she guessed, they were staring because she was a lone woman coming into the bar at midnight.

More than that, it was probably because she looked so very out of place. There was just no way for her *not* to look out of place. Even though she wore an old shirt and faded blue jeans, she was too well-dressed.

Too well-dressed, too clean-cut, too well educated, too well employed, too young, too innocent, too pretty, too almost *everything* for a joint like this. And all of it showed, she was sure of that.

I don't belong here. They all know it, too.

Would've been better off going to the graveyard.

I'll probably end up there, yet, she thought, and imagined how Brace might laugh if she told him that.

She found three empty barstools in a row, went to the one in the middle, and climbed onto it. Leaving the strap on her shoulder, she rested her denim purse on her lap.

The bartender worked his way toward her, wiping the counter with a towel. He smiled. He was a big guy, probably no older than Jane, and had a vague look in his eyes.

Maybe he's loaded, she thought. Or naturally moronic. Or he might even be a brain. Jane had known brilliant people who appeared to go through life in a daze because their minds were always off on field trips.

'Hi,' she told the bartender. 'I'll have a beer. Do you have Budweiser?'

'Got any ID?'

Nodding, she opened her purse. She found her billfold and removed her driver's license from its clear plastic sheath. She showed it to the bartender.

He squinted at it. 'So, that'll make you twenty-six and legal.'

When he came back with her mug of beer, he said, 'Want me to run you a tab, Jane?'

'Yeah. Good idea, thanks. You picked up my name from the license, huh?'

He sniffed. 'Jane Marie Kerry.'

'What's your name?' she asked, and took a drink of beer. It was cold and good.

'Glen.'

'Nice to meet you, Glen. You wouldn't happen to know, would you, if maybe someone left an envelope here for me? It would have my name written on it.'

He shook his head, his heavy cheeks shimmying. 'You hang on a minute and I'll ask the help.' His gaze swayed away from Jane. He called out, 'Tango!'

Jane swiveled on her stool and saw the barmaid striding through the smoke. This had to be Tango. A pert blonde with pixie hair, dressed in half a T-shirt and short-short cutoff blue jeans. She walked behind a loaded tray.

Stopping alongside Jane, she slid the tray onto the counter. 'Yow,' she said to Glen.

Close up and out of the shadows, she stopped looking young and cute. She had to be at least forty-five. Her face looked long and horsy. She wore a hideous excess of eye makeup. Her lipstick had wandered past her lips. Her cheeks and chin were pitted and lumpy with old acne scars.

'What's up?' she asked Glen.

'Meet Jane Marie Kerry,' he said.

Tango slanted her eyes down at Jane. 'How's it hangin', Jane Marie Kerry?'

'Okay. And you?'

'Peachy, 'cept for I got me this fuckin' ingrown toenail givin' me hell.' She pointed down at her right sneaker. 'You ever get one a them ingrown toenail fuckers?'

'I've had 'em,' Jane said. 'Not in a long time, though.'

'Yer lucky.'

'Yeah, they hurt.'

'*Nasty* fuckers.'

'I keep telling you, honey,' Glen said. 'Let me at them with my pliers.'

Tango laughed and shook her head and snorted a few times. When she was done, she told Jane, 'Our Glen, he's a card.

Him and his pliers.' She laughed a few more times, and sniffed. Then she asked, 'Ya lookin' for a fella?'

'Well, in a . . .'

'She's looking for an envelope,' Glen explained. 'Do you know anything about somebody leaving an envelope here for her?'

'It would have my name on it,' Jane said.

'Who'd they give it to?' Tango asked.

'I don't know.'

'But yer spose to get it?'

'Right.'

'Who's it from?'

Jane almost answered, 'Mog.' But that certainly wasn't the Master of Games's real name. It wouldn't mean anything to Tango or Glen. In fact, it would probably make them wonder about Jane. Mog sounded, more than anything, like the name for a creature from outer space.

Like something lumbering out of the fog in an old black-and-white monster movie.

Jane could hardly tell them, either, that she was expecting an envelope from the Master of Games. She would just have to explain that she didn't know who it was from.

Whoa!

'Babe,' she said. 'I got a message that I'm supposed to come here and get an envelope from Babe.'

Tango stepped back from the bar, turned sideways, and swung an arm high. 'Yow! Babe! Haul yer butt over here!'

One of the pool players nodded at her, said something to a friend, laughed, and handed away his cue. A few long-neck bottles of beer were lined up on the rail of the pool table. He grabbed one and swaggered forward.

Babe didn't look old enough to be legal. He hardly looked eighteen, much less twenty-one.

Maybe that's why they call him Babe, Jane thought.

He was tall and slim, with a handsome face. Sideburns grew down to his jaw. His dark hair was drawn straight back and swung behind him in a pony-tail. He wore an earring.

His denim jacket hung open and its sleeves had been taken off. He didn't wear a shirt. He had tattoos on his chest and arms. Just below his navel, he wore a big brass belt buckle. His raggedy jeans hung so low they looked ready to drop. Their frayed cuffs brushed against black motorcycle boots with side-buckles.

His eyes roamed down Jane as he approached.

'You two met?' Tango asked.

Jane shook her head.

'This is Jane Marie Kerry,' Glen announced from behind her. 'She's looking for you, Babe.'

'Looking for me?' He took a pull at his beer. He glanced from Glen to Tango. 'She a cop?'

'I'm not a cop,' Jane said.

'She looks like a cop.'

'Whatcha worried about cops for?' Tango asked him. 'Ya better *not* be worried 'bout no cops.'

'I'm not, I'm not! Shit, get off my back!'

'I'll lay into ya.'

'I ain't done *anything*! Shit!' He was grimacing and breathing hard. 'I just thought she looked like a cop, that's all.'

'I'm not,' Jane said. 'Not even close. I'm a librarian.'

Babe smirked. 'You ain't no *librarian*.'

'I'm *the* librarian. I run the place. The Donnerville Public Library.' She raised her right hand. 'Scout's honor. So don't worry, I didn't come here to arrest you.'

'I didn't *do* nothing.' He cast a nervous glance at Tango. 'I swear to God, Mom.'

Tango made a hissing sound through her nose. 'Ya got somethin' for Jane?'

He narrowed his eyes. 'Like what, for instance?'

'The envelope,' Jane said. 'Somebody named Babe was supposed to give me an envelope.'

He frowned for a few moments.

Then he brightened. 'Oh! You're *that* Jane! Sure. I've got your envelope.' Nodding, he tilted back his head and finished his beer. 'Didn't wanta bring it in with me. Come on, let's go get it.' Reaching between Jane and Tango, he plonked the empty bottle down on the counter.

'Where's it at?' Tango asked him.

'Just out front. I forgot and left it in my saddlebag.'

'Just go out 'n' bring it on in.'

'No, that's fine,' Jane said. 'I'll go with him. I'm just here for the envelope. I'll get it and go.' She swiveled around, took a few quick swallows of beer, and set down the mug. 'What do I owe you, Glen?'

'You have to run off so soon?' he asked, sounding vaguely disappointed.

'Well, it's pretty late for me.' She took out her billfold.

'One fifty should cover it,' Glen said.

She slipped a five onto the counter. 'Keep it. And thanks. Thanks, both of you.' She smiled at Tango.

Tango smiled back, and gave Jane's arm a squeeze as she hopped off the barstool. 'Don't be a stranger, Janey.'

'So long,' she said, and hurried after Babe.

At the door, he waited for her. He held it open, and followed her outside. 'That's my Harley, over there.' He pointed at a big motorcycle on the other side of the street. They waited for a car to pass, then started across.

'How did you actually get the envelope?' Jane asked.

'What do you mean?'

'Was it mailed to you with instructions? Did somebody hand it to you?' She shrugged. 'The thing is, I don't have any idea who's sending them. If you met him, I'd sure like to know who he is, what he looks like . . .'

'I didn't meet him.'

They walked behind a couple of parked cars, and stopped beside Babe's Harley-Davidson. He patted its saddle. 'Ain't she a beaut?'

'She's a great looking machine.'

'I'm saving up, gonna get out there to Sturgis next month.'

'That sounds nice,' she said, though she didn't know what he meant.

'Ain't never been there. Spose to be about the best ol' time you can have, though. I aim to find out. You like motorcycles?'

She shrugged. 'I don't know much about them, really.'

'Wanta hop on with me?' He mounted up, grinned over his shoulder at Jane, and patted the seat behind him.

She shook her head. 'Thanks, I don't think so. It's getting awfully late. I really need to get home.'

'Aw, come on.'

'No, really. Thanks, though. Not tonight.'

He hung his head for a minute, then climbed off his bike and faced her. 'What's going on with you and your envelope, anyhow?'

'What do you mean?'

'You come in the saloon saying I'm spose to have it, and all, but you don't know who it comes from. Do you know what's in it?'

She didn't like the sound of this. 'Do you?' she asked. 'Did you open it?'

'Nope.'

'May I please have it?'

He lowered his head. 'I reckon you're gonna call me a liar and go tell on me, but I honest-to-God don't know nothing at all about no envelope.'

'What?'

'I don't know nothing at all about . . .'

'You said you've *got* it.'

He raised his head and looked at her. 'You're the one said I had it. You told Tango and Glen how I'm spose to have this envelope of yours and how I'm spose to hand it over to you. Only thing is, it's news to me.'

'You don't have it?'

'I *never* had it.'

'But you said . . .'

'That was only just to stop Tango from figuring I ripped you off. Who you think she's gonna believe – you or me?'

Jane shrugged. 'If your own mother won't believe you . . .'

'Aw, Tango ain't my mother.'

'You called her Mom.'

'Well, it's just a thing I call her sometimes. She's my old lady.'

Old lady is right, Jane thought. Tango certainly looked old enough to be Babe's mother. And the way she'd talked to him, threatened him . . .

'She's your wife?' Jane asked.

'Might as well be.'

'Oh.'

'I ain't been in no real trouble in more than a year, but she's always got her eye on me, you know? And now you come along and I'm spose to have your envelope and I *claim* I ain't got it, she's gonna tear into me. She can get awful mean when she wants to. So the thing is, I'm hoping you won't tell on me.'

'This is . . . you don't *have* my envelope?'

'Nope.'

'You *never* had it?'

'Nope.'

He seemed sincere. And worried. And sorry.

'Cross your heart and hope to die?'

Nodding, he fingered a big X in the middle of his chest. 'Hope to die,' he said.

'If you're not the right Babe . . .' She grimaced. 'I don't want to make any trouble for you. Are you going to be in trouble?'

'I don't know. Maybe not, if you don't tell on me.'

'Come on.' She took hold of his arm and led him across the street. 'Do you know of anyone else named Babe? Maybe a regular customer, or something?'

'Just me.'

'There's a chance I might've come to the wrong place – chosen the wrong Paradise.'

'If your envelope turns up, I'll sure get it to you.'

'I'd appreciate that, but I think it went somewhere else.' She pushed open the door and entered the Paradise Lounge with Babe at her side. She spotted Tango standing over a table, talking to a customer. 'Tango?'

Babe's old lady looked around and grinned. 'Howdy there, Janey.'

'Got it,' she called. 'Thanks a million for the help.' With Tango watching, she slapped Babe on the back a couple of times. Then she headed for the door.

Chapter Fourteen

Back to square one, Jane thought as she climbed into her car.

Not quite square one. We know it isn't the Paradise Lounge. At least it probably isn't. Just some sort of weird coincidence that there happened to be a guy named Babe at the place.

Or maybe not a coincidence, she told herself. Who the hell *knows* what's going on?

Anyway, Babe had seemed like a fairly decent guy. They'd all seemed like decent people. A little peculiar, but nice enough. Not at all the sort she would've expected to find in a grubby bar on Division Street.

Maybe I'll take Brace there some night, we'll sit at the bar and have a few beers and chat with Glen and Tango and Babe. Might be sort of a kick.

On the other hand, maybe not.

As nice and decent as those people had seemed, she was glad to be away from them. She could get along just fine if she never saw any of them again.

She suddenly realized that she felt uncomfortable sitting in her car this close to the Paradise Lounge. Someone might come out, come over to her . . .

She drove for two blocks, turned a corner, and parked under a streetlight. Reaching down between her legs, she found Brace's flashlight. She picked it up and tried it. With the new bulb she'd bought on her way to the library that morning, it worked fine.

Her purse was on the passenger seat. She swung it over to her lap, reached in and took out her notepad. She shone the flashlight on her brief list of paradises.

'So,' she whispered, 'which is it gonna be? The drive-in, the bowling alley, or the bone orchard?'

She sighed.

'Yeah. Just guess.'

Should've just gone to Paradise Gardens in the first place. We both knew that's where Mog was sending me. Brace knew it, I knew it. If I'd gone there, it'd probably be over with by now and I'd already be home.

Brace won't be waiting, she reminded herself. Home'll be lonely tonight.

'Just so long as Mog doesn't pay a visit,' she muttered.

Mog, she thought, is probably at the graveyard wondering what happened to me.

She switched off the flashlight and put away the list. After shifting her purse and flashlight onto the passenger seat, she checked the side mirror and swung out onto the road.

A U-turn headed her toward the cemetery.

My God. Going to a place like that at this time of night. Must be nuts.

'No big deal,' she said. 'It's not like they're gonna crawl out of their graves and come after me. Probably.'

She laughed once. It sounded a bit nervous.

She wished Brace was with her.

She turned the radio on. Garth Brooks was singing 'Friends in Low Places.'

How appropriate, she thought.

But it was a cheery, raucous song that she was always glad to hear. She turned the volume high.

By the time the song was over, she had left downtown

Donnerville behind and was driving through a residential area west of town. The houses were small, close together, and dark. Not all of them were dark. A few had porch lights on. Here and there, dim light seeped through window curtains. Some windows shimmered with a glow that came from rooms where no lights were on, where a television kept away the night.

On her radio, the Traveling Wilburys were singing 'End of the Line'. She listened for Roy Orbison's clear, melancholy voice, but didn't hear it. Travelling Wilburys had recorded this song without him, she remembered. He'd died. In the music video, there was an empty chair to show that he was gone.

She turned the radio off.

The night seemed darker than before. Jane had driven beyond the last streetlight.

Out here, there weren't so many houses. Each stood by itself among trees and sheds. Each had at least one very bright light shining on the front yard or the driveway to discourage prowlers.

The last house before the cemetery didn't have any light at all.

It wouldn't, of course.

Jane had seen the old, two-story Victorian building a few times while driving this road in daylight. A decrepit ruin, it had obviously been abandoned many years ago.

No wonder they abandoned it, Jane thought. Who could stand living this close to all those graves? My God, you'd be afraid to look out your windows at night.

Unless you were a real weirdo.

An ideal home site for a necrophile, she thought, and smiled.

Leaving the old house behind, she took her foot off the gas pedal. She gazed at the cemetery through the bars of its wrought-iron fence: gentle slopes of grass, tombstones, trees, crosses, shadows, monuments of saints and angels and children, vaults that stood here and there like small chapels.

She didn't like the looks of the place.

But at least nobody seemed to be wandering around.

I'm not really going in there, am I?

The hell I'm not. For eight hundred bucks, I'd swing naked on a vine over a pit full of rattlesnakes.

No, I wouldn't, she thought. But I'll do this.

She turned left at the corner, and followed the two-lane driveway to the main gates. They were wide, double gates of wrought iron beneath an archway of elaborate grillwork that read Paradise Gardens Memorial Park.

Once, Jane had been driving by and noticed a funeral procession entering.

Tonight, however, the gates were shut.

Shut, and probably locked.

What if I can't get in?

Fat chance, she thought. Mog wouldn't have sent me here if there wasn't a way in.

Not wanting to leave her car near the gates, she drove past them. When she spotted a thick stand of trees to the right, she eased off the road and steered into their shadows.

Her purse would be in the way, so she decided to leave it in the car. Her switchblade knife was in it, though. After shutting off the car, she found the knife. She dropped it into a pocket of her jeans, along with her keys. After climbing out, she tried to stuff the flashlight into her other pocket. It wouldn't fit. These jeans were tighter than those she'd worn to the bridge, and had much smaller pockets. So she carried the flashlight as she crossed the street and hurried to the main gates of the cemetery.

Thinking that Mog might've arranged to leave the gates unlocked, she tugged at them. They rattled slightly. They felt heavy and very secure. They were locked, but not with a chain and padlock, like the gates of the fence surrounding Crazy Horse. After studying them for a few moments, Jane decided they could probably only be opened with a key or by remote control.

She wouldn't be getting in through the gates.

Maybe I don't need to get in.

She spent a few minutes searching the area near the entryway, but found no envelope.

Of course not, she thought. He wouldn't make it that easy for me.

Wants me to climb.

The gates, topped by the arch of grillwork spelling out the cemetery's name, would make a more difficult obstacle than the fence itself. But climbing the fence wouldn't be easy. Or safe. Each of the upright bars looked like an iron spear aimed at the sky.

Standing close to the fence, Jane could reach high enough to grab the uppermost crossbar. But the points were higher still. If she managed to find a perch on the crossbar – and then fell wrong – she might find herself impaled on eight inches of iron rod. Maybe in more places than one.

One could go straight up my butt. Or worse.

Which *would* be worse? she wondered.

Thinking about it made her legs ache.

I'm not going to chance finding out, she decided. Not for eight hundred bucks.

She began to walk through the grass and trees along the outside of the fence, searching for a less hazardous way to get in.

Beyond the bars was a fairly large parking lot, dim and gray in the moonlight. No cars at all were parked there, not even a hearse. Which probably meant the grounds were deserted: no visitors, no caretakers, no grave diggers, no guards, nobody.

Great, if I can just get in.

Soon, she found the answer to her problem.

The tree branched out low and stretched a good thick limb over the tips of the fence.

Crouching near the trunk, Jane reached between two of the iron bars and set her flashlight down on the grass. Then she climbed. The tree, with its easy angles and rough surface and plenty of good places for her hands and feet, was a much easier climb than Crazy Horse. It gave her no trouble at all.

On her belly, clutching the limb between her thighs, she squirmed out beyond the spear points of the fence. When they were well behind her, she crawled to the underside of the limb, let go of it with her legs, dangled by her arms, and allowed herself to drop.

The ground jolted her, but not badly. She rolled with the impact and got to her feet. She came up with the back of her shirt wet and clinging, but the dew didn't soak through her jeans.

She looked at the fence and smiled.

Got over that hurdle without a scratch. I'm getting good at this stuff.

She hurried back to the fence and picked up the flashlight. Keeping it dark, she turned toward the cemetery.

Now, to find the envelope.

'Babe,' she whispered. 'Gotta find Babe.'

She wondered if Babe might refer to a monument – maybe a statue depicting an infant.

Might be a cupid, she thought.

Cupid? In a graveyard?

Who knows? It's possible.

She decided to keep her eyes open for statues of babies, but to concentrate on checking the names on headstones.

She hurried to the nearest grave. After a quick look around to make sure she was still alone, she shone her flashlight on the marble slab.

No Babe buried under this one.

Nor the next, nor the one after that.

This can't be right, she thought as she aimed her light at another tombstone. There must be more to the clue, or this is the wrong paradise, or something. Mog wouldn't make me go around and check every grave here. Doesn't make sense. It could take all night.

She kept at it, though.

This *had* to be the right paradise.

It won't take all night, she told herself. I'll just go row by row, take it one step at a time. Should be able to cover the whole place in a couple of hours.

She walked quickly from grave to grave, stopped in front of each, aimed her flashlight at every headstone, pushed the button to send a beam of light through the darkness, read the name of the deceased, killed the light and hurried on.

The grass was long and wet.

The beautiful, uncut hair of graves. Whitman? Had to be Whitman, *Leaves of Grass*.

The dew on the grass soaked through her shoes and socks.

The wet hair of graves.

She thought of the bodies underneath the ground. Bodies in coffins – some of the coffins maybe so old they'd fallen apart, some of the bodies nothing but bones, others in various stages of rot, some almost fresh – all around her. Nothing between her and them except a bit of dirt.

I'm walking on them.

Stepping on their faces, or maybe on their chests or bellies or . . .

Cut it out, she told herself.

And she wondered if they knew she was here.

They can't know.

She wondered if they could feel her footsteps.

Don't be ridiculous.

She wondered if they were lying there, motionless, listening to her approach, feeling her weight as she stepped on them, growling softly in the silence of their graves, hating her for walking on them and maybe hating her for being alive, maybe dreaming deadman dreams of dragging her down into the earth with them.

They're dead. They don't dream shit.

And maybe Jane would believe that, be certain of it, have total faith in it on a sunny afternoon, especially if she were with some good friends.

But this was the middle of the night in a graveyard, and she was alone, and she could *feel* them.

Feel them hating her, wanting her.

She knew it was ridiculous. The bodies beneath her feet

were completely unaware of her presence. And they were mostly – probably – the bodies of nice, decent people. Friendly folks who'd left loved ones behind.

Not fiends.

So how come they feel like fiends?

Like fiends and trolls who can't wait to get their hands on me?

If I don't stop this, she thought, I'm going to scream and run and that'll be the end of Mog and his game.

She stopped in front of a grave, shivered, plucked the damp back of her shirt away from her skin, and shone her flashlight on the stone marker. This one, a thin slab, stood at a tilt in the tall grass. It was so old and weathered that the inscription had been worn down. Only shallow valleys remained of the words and dates that had once been chiseled deep.

With a marker like this, she thought, must be nothing at all left of the body.

The chances of this being Babe . . .

The chances will be excellent if it's the only headstone I can't read. It'll be sure to be the one if I skip it. That's how things work.

So she sank to a crouch in front of the tilted slab.

Holding the flashlight in her right hand, she reached out to the headstone with her left. She traced the first letter with her fingertip.

Might be a B. But more like a P.

Am I squatting right over his face? she wondered. What if he's not really six feet down? What if he's only a couple of inches under the dirt and . . .

The tombstone fell, knocking her hand away, pounding her left knee. She yelped with alarm and pain. As she fell backward, the stone *whumped* the ground.

Missed my toe.

She landed on her back.

Right on top of him!

Sprawled on her back, arms out, legs spread, she wanted to clutch her hurting knee. But she thought, This is when he

595

gets me. Reaches up right out of the ground and grabs me . . . bites . . .

She flipped over, rolled, and scurried to her feet. After limping a few steps backward, she whirled around to make sure nobody was coming. The whirl saved her from colliding with the corner of a vault. Halting herself, she turned and gazed at the fallen headstone.

It was barely visible in the tall grass.

No cadaver was rising in front of it.

What did you expect?

Bending over, Jane rubbed her knee. It didn't hurt much, now. She supposed it would be black and blue tomorrow.

I shouldn't have touched that tombstone, she thought. Not the way it was leaning like that.

She wondered if she should set it back up.

I've got to, she thought. I'm the one who knocked it over.

Would've fallen down, anyway.

Sure, but it was me who made it fall tonight.

She muttered, 'Shit.'

She hurried to the stone, stepped behind it, crouched and leaned forward and grabbed it near the top with both hands. It felt cool and damp – a little bit slimy. Shifting her weight backward, she raised it. The slab was heavy, but manageable. She settled its base into the trench of loose soil from which it had been uprooted. When it was standing upright, she tested it by relaxing her hold. Each time she started to release it, the slab began to tip.

'Great,' she muttered.

What am I supposed to do, stay here forever?

Forever, or until morning – whichever comes first.

Being careful not to let it fall, she turned around. She sat down hard on top of the slab. It made soft noises in the soil. She raised herself and sat down again. Five times, she stood and sat, using her body to pound the slab deeper.

That seemed to be enough.

The tombstone remained upright as she made her way around it, stomping the earth to pack it firm.

She stepped back.

A job well done, she thought.

She rubbed her rump.

And she realized that she was probably standing directly on top of the buried corpse, but it didn't bother her. This grave, at least, no longer contained a fiend. In this one was the body of someone who'd needed help with a bad tombstone. He, she, whatever – almost felt like a friend.

Jane was a little winded, but her jitters were gone. She took a deep breath.

She turned around slowly, scanning the moonlit graveyard.

Though she was aware of having wandered quite far from the tree where she'd entered the cemetery, she was surprised to discover that the parking lot and fence were no longer in sight. She must've roamed quite a distance while studying the names on the tombstones.

Off to her left, through the trees, she could see a small part of the roof of the old, abandoned house by the edge of the graveyard.

Which meant that the parking lot and the front gate should be behind her. She turned around, and found herself looking at the slope of a low hillside.

What should I do? she wondered. Keep searching? Head back?

From the sweet, moist smell of the air, the night seemed very late.

She shone her light on her wristwatch.

Ten after two.

'Jeez,' she muttered.

She didn't need to be at the library until noon, though. She could sleep as late as eleven, if she had to.

Keep at it, she told herself. Babe's bound to be here someplace. Just a matter of being persistent.

She stepped to the next tombstone and shone her flashlight on it.

Somewhere not very far away, a car horn beeped.

Chapter Fifteen

From the top of the rise, Jane could see a pickup truck at a far corner of the cemetery's parking lot. It stood motionless and dark under the moonlight.

It hadn't been there before.

Jane shifted her gaze to the main gates. They were too far away and too dark; she couldn't see whether they were open or shut.

She started moving, keeping low, staying in shadows, ducking behind trees and tombstones, taking her time but steadily closing in on the pickup. Now and again, she halted and gazed at it.

Had it been there before? She was sure she hadn't noticed it. The way the small truck was tucked away in a corner, though, she might've simply failed to spot it.

It looked like one of those tiny little Japanese pickups, the kind that city people bought when they liked the rugged, man-of-the-earth image of driving a pickup truck, but had no real use for one.

It was the only vehicle in sight.

It's gotta be the one that honked.

Horns don't honk by themselves, she thought. Not usually. Which means somebody must've beeped it.

But why? Just for the hell of it? Honk in the graveyard, see if you can wake the dead?

Or was it meant to be a signal?

A signal for who?

Maybe somebody else has been here all along.

Or maybe it was meant for me.

Maybe Mog got tired of all my fooling around, looking for the envelope in all the wrong places, and he beeped to call me in.

I'll find out soon enough. Maybe.

Stopping, Jane peered around a tree trunk. Moonlight gleamed on the windshield of the pickup truck. She couldn't see into the cab.

Somebody has to be in there. Or nearby. The truck didn't get here by itself. It didn't honk by itself.

But she couldn't see inside, not even after sneaking almost to the edge of the parking lot and peering at the windshield from behind a bush no more than fifteen feet away. The moonlight still plated its glass with silver.

I can't see in, but he can see out.

Charming.

At least there can't be a whole gang inside, she told herself. No more than two people could fit in the cab. Two fairly small people.

She was tempted to stand up in plain sight and walk straight to the truck and get it over with.

That'd be a real smart move.

But what if I go in really low? she wondered.

If she squirmed on her belly, the driver's view of her would be obstructed by the hood.

Not at first.

For the first several feet, she would be in plain sight. If the driver happened to be looking in the right direction, he would probably spot her.

Once she'd made it closer to the pickup, though, she would be hidden.

Worth a try, she thought.

So she lowered herself flat onto the grass behind the bush. Dew soaked through the front of her shirt. Head up, she squirmed around the side of the bush and writhed her way toward the pickup. Dew made it through the front of her jeans. A few tips of grass tickled the bare skin of her chin and throat.

Her heart thudded.

She listened for the sound of a door opening.

If the door opens or the engine starts . . .

Then she was on the asphalt. It felt warm under her body,

but hard. Bits of gravel scraped at her ribs and belly and forearms through the thin cloth of her shirt. The bra helped a little. The jeans gave her very good protection.

She remembered the denim jacket that Babe had been wearing. If she had a jacket like that . . .

BABE!

The front license plate of the pickup truck, level with her eyes, read BABE 13.

Tomorrow, when churchyards yawn, see the Babe.

YES!

She quit belly-crawling and studied the front of the pickup: its tires, bumper, grill, headlights. No sign of the envelope.

It had to be nearby, though.

It had to be somewhere on the pickup, or inside it.

Maybe under it.

The space beneath the pickup looked slim.

I won't go searching under there, she told herself, except as a last resort.

She squirmed toward the license plate, stopped just in front of the bumper, and pushed herself up. On hands and knees, she was almost high enough to peer over the hood. But she kept her head down and crawled to the left. Past the corner of the bumper. Past the tire. At the passenger door, she turned toward the pickup. Still on her knees, she reached up to the door. Hand braced against it, she raised herself.

She moved very slowly. Inched her head higher, higher.

No matter what you see in there, she warned herself, don't make a sound.

Just get ready to run like hell.

Though her eyes were still lower than the bottom of the window, she knew that the top of her head was exposed. Anyone watching the window was sure to see it. So she raised herself high enough to peer in.

And she could see straight through the cab and out the window beyond the driver's side.

Nobody!

Now, if nobody's hiding in back . . .

She stood up straight and looked past the rear of the cab. The pickup's bed was large enough to conceal two people lying side by side. Short people, anyway. And someone *could* be lying there, cloaked by the heavy shadows.

Jane raised her flashlight and shone it in.

Nobody there.

The bed of the pickup truck was empty except for a single board: a two-by-four about five feet long. She wondered why anyone would drive around with nothing but one board. No tool box, or . . .

Doesn't matter, she told herself. What matters is, nobody's hiding in there.

The coast is clear.

She took a deep breath and blew out, puffing her cheeks. She rubbed the back of her neck.

She brushed bits of gravel off the damp front of her shirt and jeans, then began to wander around the pickup, sweeping it with the beam of her flashlight, looking for the envelope.

The vehicle was bright red, and appeared to be brand new. Its make was announced in raised, white-painted letters on the tailgate: TOYOTA. Its rear plate, like the one in front, read BABE 13.

At the driver's door, Jane found a set of keys. One dangled from a ring while the other was stuck into the door's lock.

Fine, she thought. I can get in. But where's the envelope?

Inside. That's why he left me the keys.

Jane pinched the door key between her thumb and forefinger, turned it, saw the lock button pop up, and yelped and leaped back as a growling, snapping dog sprang out at her face.

Its muzzle slammed against the driver's window.

It hit with such force that it rocked the pickup.

'Jeez!' Jane gasped.

The dog rebounded off the window, then attacked again, pounding the glass, shoving at it, snarling, trying to bite it.

Six feet away, Jane aimed her flashlight at the dog.

It looked a lot like a German shepherd, but its muzzle seemed too broad, too stubby.

A Rottweiler? That's what it is.

Its fur was black, its teeth huge and white, its tongue pink. One eye, apparently blind, was the color of phlegm.

It lunged at the driver's window, wild and drooling, as if nothing else mattered but getting Jane.

She supposed it must've been down on the front seat, probably asleep, until she'd twisted the key. The sound of the door unlocking must've awakened it.

If the dog had delayed its attack for half a second longer, she would've had the door wide open.

What's Mog doing, trying to kill me?

Booby-trapped the car with fucking Cujo!

Just my luck, she thought, the envelope's probably in there with the monster.

As she thought that, she spotted a rectangle above the steering wheel. On the windshield?

Please let it be on the outside! Please!

She hurried to the side of the pickup, leaned over its hood, shone her flashlight at the windshield and stared at the rectangle.

It seemed to be flush against the glass.

Through the glass, her named showed.

That's it!

Moving closer, she saw that the envelope was taped to the inside of the windshield. Just to make sure her eyes weren't betraying her, she ran her fingertips down the glass. Cool and slick.

'Terrific,' she muttered.

And her heart gave a kick as the dog hurled itself at her. The steering wheel stood in its way, but it shoved its head through the ring and barked and snapped.

The envelope was just beyond its teeth.

Jane stepped back, wanting some distance between herself and the dog. Then she stopped, gazed at the envelope, and wondered how to lay her hands on it.

Smash the windshield right where the thing's taped to it, she thought, and maybe I can grab it without getting myself chewed up.

She had never broken a car window, however, so she couldn't be sure how the glass might behave.

Obviously, it would break inward.

Which would obviously push the envelope closer to the dog. Not good. Worse, maybe the glass would crumble and drop the envelope to the pickup's floor. And worst of all, what if the glass *really* came apart when she broke it? Instead of making a hole the size of her hand, she might demolish it.

Making a way for the dog to get out and nail her.

'Yeah,' she muttered. 'Thanks anyway.'

Anyway, she told herself, it isn't my car. It's probably stolen, or something. God only knows how much it'd cost the owner to have his windshield replaced.

I'm not gonna wreck someone's car, not for eight hundred bucks.

So, she wondered, how do I get the envelope?

Wouldn't be any problem at all, except for the dog.

Normally, dogs liked Jane. Even if they gave a nervous growl or two at first, a few words from her would calm them down. Before you knew it, Jane would be squatting over them and they'd be swishing their tails, licking her hand, rolling onto their backs and squirming as she scratched their bellies.

She had a feeling this dog might be different.

I let it out, it'll rip me up one side and down the other.

Maybe not, she told herself. Maybe it's only acting so crazy because it's trapped in there.

Right. Sure.

She wondered, though.

She stepped close to the driver's window. The dog threw itself at her. It hit the glass, shaking the pickup. It barked and snapped. It rammed its paws against the window and worked them as if trying to dig a tunnel through the glass, claws clicking, clattering, squeaking.

'Hey, boy,' Jane said.

The dog stopped attacking the window. It looked at her and tilted its head sideways.

'Hi, there. Are you a good fella? Huh? You look like a pretty good fella to me. What's your name?'

It bared its teeth and growled.

'Aw, that's no way to behave, is it? Not if you want me to let you out of there. Do you want me to let you out? Huh, boy?'

The dog quit snarling.

'What's your name, Cujo?'

It lunged and snapped, front teeth clashing against the window.

'Maybe not. How about Rin Tin Tin? You sort of look like a mutated Rinty, you know? God, you are a spooky looking thing. Real nice eye. You look like you *belong* in a bone orchard. Spook, the graveyard hound. Is that your name, Spook?'

The dog hurled itself at the window.

Jane wished she had food for it.

She had nothing on her that she cared for it to eat.

If she went back to her car . . .?

No food in it. Except maybe some chewing gum in the glove compartment. Chewing-gum wouldn't do the trick. What she needed was a package of bologna, or a slab of steak, or a hamburger: something good and meaty that she could throw and be certain the dog would chase if she opened the door.

Maybe I can lay my hands on a corpse around here someplace – cut off an arm or something for my pal Spook.

Course, I'd need a shovel..

She smirked at the thought, and shook her head.

What I could do, she realized, is go back to my car and drive into town and buy stuff.

There were several twenty-four-hour fast-food joints and convenience stores. She could buy the dog an irresistible feast.

Only one problem with the idea; Jane didn't want to do it. Getting into the cemetery had been tough enough – physically and emotionally. To deal with the fence again and drive into town and buy the food and come back and deal with the fence again and come back to the pickup and throw the food and grab the envelope and deal with the fence again . . .

Too much. Way too much.

Besides, who could say that the pickup would still be here when she returned?

There's gotta be another way. Something quick and simple.

She stood there, watching the dog leap and snap and slobber on the window. Stood there thinking. Trying to free her mind and let it roam.

And she found a new idea.

She considered it for a while.

It *ought* to work.

Feeling a warm squirm of excitement in her belly, she twisted the key in the lock of the driver's door. The lock button sank down, then popped up when she turned the key the other way.

Unlocked.

She pulled the key out, then hurried around the front of the pickup to the passenger door. As she reached it, the dog slammed its snarling muzzle against the window.

'Oh, quit it,' she muttered.

The lock button appeared to be down. She pushed her key into the slot, twisted it, and watched the button jump up. She dropped the keys into a pocket of her jeans.

Too bad the door didn't have a real handle. She could just loop her belt through one like that . . .

This oughta work, though.

She stepped past the cab, aimed her flashlight at the two-by-four in the bed of the truck, saw that the board was near enough to reach, then leaned in over the side and dragged it closer. She would need both hands to lift it out, so she switched off the flashlight and set it on the floor behind the cab.

She hoisted out the board. Propping it up against the truck, she took off her belt. She slipped one end of her belt through its buckle, then dropped the leather loop over the top of the two-by-four. She pulled until it was cinched loosely around the board a couple of inches from the top.

Then she braced the door shut, propping the board at an angle from the pavement to just below the handle. The dog yapped and crashed against the window as she worked the handle and unlatched the door.

She tugged the board and jammed its top end under the handle.

The door lurched as the dog hit it.

The two-by-four's lower end started to scoot away.

Jane grabbed the board with both hands, put her weight on it, and kept the door from flying open.

She stomped on the bottom end, hoping to make it more secure against the asphalt.

The next time the dog struck, the board didn't scoot.

Jane grabbed the dangling end of her belt. The brace continued to hold as she took a step backward. It still held as she climbed over the side of the pickup. Getting to her feet behind the cab, she saw the dog attacking the rear window. No wonder the brace worked so well: the dog had quit hitting the door.

She stood motionless for a few seconds, trying to catch her breath, wondering if she should go ahead with her plan.

If anything goes wrong, I'm dog food.

A little bit late for backing out, she thought.

Leaning out over the right side of the pickup, she jerked her belt. It yanked the end of the two-by-four out from under the handle of the passenger door, swung the board toward her, released it. As the loop of her belt jumped up, the board dropped toward the asphalt.

The clamor of its impact reached Jane as she bounded to the other side of the pickup and leaped. Landing, she whirled around and reached for the driver's door.

Through its window, she glimpsed the dark swish of a tail as the dog sprang out the passenger door.

How smart is it? How smart is it? What if it wheels around and jumps right back in . . .?

She heard the click of its toenails, the huff of its breath as it dashed around the rear of the pickup.

Atta boy!

Jane threw open the driver's door, leaped in behind the wheel and slammed the door shut. An instant later, the dog crashed against it.

She dropped across the passenger seat, reaching for the open door.

Couldn't reach it.

This wasn't how she had figured things.

She hadn't figured on the passenger door standing wide open, so wide that she'd have trouble shutting it fast.

Where's Spook?

Jane squirmed across the seat, reaching . . .

Reaching . . .

'Damn it!' she cried out.

Her fingertips caught the inside handle. She pulled. The door swung and thumped.

It didn't thump shut.

It thumped against the broad black head of the dog, and the handle was torn from her fingers as the dog thrust its way in.

Jane was sprawled on her right side, her right arm pinned beneath her body, her left arm extended.

Immediately, she jerked her left arm to her face. She twisted onto her back and drew her knees up as the dog sprang on top of her. Though her upraised arm protected much of her face, a paw got through and jabbed her cheek. Others stomped on her shoulders and chest and belly. Toenails scratched her, dug into her.

Jane shoved her right hand down inside the pocket of her jeans and grabbed her switchblade knife.

The dog stood on her, front paws near her hips, chest against her belly, rear end high, hind paws on her shoulders, penis swinging above her face.

Jane pulled out her knife.

The dog's thick muzzle burrowed in between her thighs, snapping.

'Get outa there!' she yelled.

A paw tore at one of her upraised legs. The denim of her jeans wasn't thick enough to save her from the pain of the raking nails.

'Ow! Stop!'

She got the knife to her mouth. With her front teeth, she ripped at the rubber band she'd wrapped around it to keep the blade in. The band snapped, stinging her lips.

The dog sank its teeth into the crotch of her jeans. Jane felt them thrusting and chewing, trying to get at her through the denim.

She thumbed the button on the handle of her knife.

The blade sprang out and clicked.

She rammed it up into the dog's belly.

The animal yelped. Hot fluid spilled down onto Jane's chest and throat.

God, no, she thought. God, no.

But she stabbed the dog again, and then it twisted around and sprang off her. Sprawled on her back across the seats of the pickup truck, she heard it run away yipping and squealing.

Chapter Sixteen

She shut the passenger door, then stayed on her back, gasping for breath.

She felt as if she'd been beaten up by a thug.

The dog's paws had done more damage than its teeth. She could feel at least a dozen places where they'd probably left their marks. Only one place where the teeth had gotten her.

Damn good thing I'm not a guy, she thought.

She supposed she was bleeding here and there. Probably

nothing very serious, though. It was the dog's blood, not Jane's, trickling down her face, coating her throat, pasting her shirt to her chest. The wetness at the crotch of her jeans was probably the dog's slobber. She hoped it wasn't more than that.

She wondered if she'd killed the thing.

It might not be dead yet. It soon would be, though. *I stabbed it. I stabbed it twice.*

She still held the knife in her hand. Its handle felt slick and sticky.

She wondered if she could find the dog and bring it back to the pickup and take it to a vet. With the right kind of medical treatment, it might pull through.

Why would I *want* it to pull through? she asked herself. So it can get well and attack me again? I'm lucky I stabbed it before it had time to *really* mess me up. The thing's vicious monster. Maybe next time it'll go after a little kid. Maybe it'll kill somebody. I'd have to be nuts to try to save it.

If I want to be a good citizen, she thought, I oughta track it down and finish it off.

'Right,' she muttered. 'Give it another whack at me.'

Groaning, she swung her feet to the floor. She struggled to sit up, elbowing the seat, twisting, then grabbing the steering wheel and pulling at it. Finally, she sank into the driver's seat.

She shut her eyes and tried to catch her breath.

The blood made her skin feel itchy. She wanted to wash.

She wondered if there was a creek nearby. She hadn't noticed one, and she'd probably seen most of the cemetery during her search for Babe's tombstone.

Besides, the dog was out there. It might not be dead quite yet.

Just get home, she told herself.

Keeping the knife open, she set it on her lap. Then she wiped her right hand on the leg of her jeans, reached around the steering wheel and peeled the envelope off the windshield.

There better be eight hundred bucks in here. Went through all this. Killed a dog.

She wondered if eight hundred dollars was enough. It seemed like pretty meager pay for going through a night like this.

She ripped the envelope, spread it open, and pulled out the note. Wrapped inside the folded sheet of paper were quite a few bills. She pulled them out. In the moonlight coming in through the windshield, she saw that they were hundreds. She counted them. Eight.

She tilted the note toward the windshield. She could see lines of scribbles, but there wasn't enough light for reading them.

She couldn't get to her flashlight without leaving the cab.

She reached for the door handle, figuring to open the door and activate the interior light. But she remembered that the door had just been open – both of them had been – and no light had come on.

'The hell with the note,' she said.

It could wait. She wrapped it around the money, tucked it all inside the envelope, then folded the envelope in half. When she shifted her body to slip the envelope into a seat pocket of her pants, she felt the knife slide and fall between her legs. She finished putting the envelope away, then bent down and searched the floor near her feet.

First, she found her belt. The belt came as a surprise. She'd lost track of it after whipping it off the two-by-four, but she must've kept hold of it until she got inside the cab. She brought the belt up, undid the loop, then wrapped it around her waist. After fastening the buckle, she bent down again and found the knife.

She wiped both sides of its blade on a leg of her jeans. With the hanging front of her shirt, she cleaned off the handle. Then she folded down the blade. No rubber bands to keep it safe, but the possibility of the blade flying open by accident didn't concern her. Not after everything that had happened.

She slipped the knife into a front pocket of her jeans, fumbled around down there and brought out the pickup's keys. She tried one of them in the ignition, and it fit. She turned it. The engine kicked into life.

She considered putting the headlights on, but decided against it.

After fooling with the controls for a few moments, she made the Toyota start moving in reverse. She backed toward the middle of the parking lot, stopped, shifted, and turned toward the main gates of the cemetery.

The gates appeared to be shut.

No problem.

She drove past them, over a low curb, and onto the grass. She steered alongside the fence and stopped.

Sure be easier, she thought, than hunting for a tree to climb.

This close to the fence, she wouldn't be able to open the driver's door more than a few inches. So she moved to the passenger seat. She reached for the handle, then hesitated.

She frowned at the glove compartment.

Could the registration slip be in there? What if this pickup isn't stolen – suppose it belongs to Mog and the registration gives his name, his address?

She reached out fast and opened the glove compartment.

A light came on inside it.

No registration slip.

Nothing.

Nothing except a stainless steel pistol.

'Whoa,' Jane said. 'What the . . .?' She leaned closer.

The pistol had black grips and a small square of paper taped to its slide. On the paper was written, 'For you, my sweet. Interesting times await. Mog.'

He left it here for me.

To use on the dog?

She wondered if it was loaded and ready for action. From the size of the pistol, she supposed it must be a twenty-two. It looked like a smaller, less powerful version of her father's Colt .45 automatic. She'd never been strong enough to handle the .45, but she'd watched him with it. This weapon probably operated on similar principles.

She plucked off the note and stuffed it into a pocket of her jeans.

Keeping her finger away from the trigger, she held the pistol in the glow of the glove compartment's light. Tiny markings engraved in the steel informed her that it was a Smith & Wesson twenty-two. She tilted it and drew back its slide. Through the port, she saw a cartridge being retracted from the chamber.

He gave it to me loaded, ready for bear.

Ready for dog.

She let go of the slide, rechambering the round.

Very considerate of him.

Why the hell didn't he leave it out where I could see it?

At least I've got it now, she told herself.

She released the magazine. It felt heavy for something so small and slim. She could see cartridges through a slot in its side. Maybe five or six of them. To be sure how many, she would need to empty the magazine.

There didn't seem to be much point in that.

She slid the magazine up the handle and bumped it into place with the heel of her hand.

She located a thumb switch that was probably the safety. She flipped it up and down. The up position appeared to be what she wanted.

She shut the glove compartment. She scanned the darkness beyond the Toyota's windows. She saw nobody. She saw no dog.

It's black. It might be anywhere.

It's probably dead by now, she told herself.

Pistol in her right hand, she opened the door. She aimed at the dark grass, braced herself for the noise of a bang, and squeezed the trigger. The trigger wouldn't budge.

Very good, she thought. Now we know about the safety.

She switched the safety off. Then she climbed out of the pickup, swung the door shut and stood motionless, listening and watching.

She heard only the twitter and hoot of night birds.

The parking lot looked empty. The gentle slopes of the cemetery looked crowded.

But nothing came at her.

She thumbed the safety on, then climbed into the bed of the pickup truck. She picked up Brace's flashlight. She stuffed the pistol into a seat pocket of her jeans. On the way in, it made the envelope crackle. It felt hard and snug against her buttock.

She knew the flashlight was too big for a pocket, so she lifted her shirt, sucked in her belly and started to push the thick cylinder down under her waistband. A tight fit. And if she fell wrong with it in there, she might hurt herself. So she pulled it out.

After giving the problem some thought, she realized the solution was the belt hanging slack around her waist. She tugged it, cinching in her shirt as tight as possible. Then she unfastened a button at her belly. She slipped the flashlight in. The belted shirt held it like a hammock.

As she shut the button, the corner of her eye caught a movement. She turned her head.

She groaned.

She felt her skin start to crawl.

The dog was coming.

Big and black against the gray of the grass, paws wobbling at the sky, head and tail hanging toward the ground and swaying slightly as the dog was carried through the graveyard high above the head of a man in tattered rags.

A tall, gawky man who staggered like a drunkard.

'Oh, Jesus,' Jane murmured. 'Oh, my God.'

She scurried onto the roof of the pickup's cab. From there, she took one large upward step and planted her left foot on the crossbar of the fence. She shoved off with her right, and kicked forward.

For a moment, she was poised on one foot above the spikes at the top of the fence.

Then she was dropping fast. Clear of the spikes. The fence to her back. The flashlight leaping straight up somehow between her breasts and out the top of her shirt and striking the underside of her chin.

An instant after the flashlight hit her, the ground slammed the bottoms of her feet. Her legs collapsed. She tumbled across dewy grass.

Getting to her knees, she could feel the pistol stiff against her rump. But the flashlight was gone from inside her shirt. She twisted around and spotted it on the ground, its cylinder shiny in the moonlight.

She crawled back for it.

On the other side of the fence, the Toyota blocked her view. She couldn't see the stranger lurching toward her with the dog, couldn't tell how far away they were – or how near.

She snatched up the flashlight and ran from them.

Ran for her hidden car.

After a quick sprint that took her past the main gates and across the road, she slowed to a trot and looked back.

The stranger had stopped short of the pickup truck. He was turning around and around, swinging the dog by its hind legs. Together, they whirled in the moonlight.

The dog seemed to stretch. Its forelegs reached out like the arms of a little Superhound about to take flight.

And then the man let go.

The dog flew high into the night, coming for Jane.

It almost made it over the fence.

The spikes at the top of the fence snagged it out of the sky.

Jane heard the ringing thunk it made. And quick wet ripping sounds.

And then the laughter of the man beyond the graveyard fence.

Chapter Seventeen

After a long, hot shower, Jane went into her bedroom. She took off her robe. The air felt cool after the steamy heat of the bathroom. She looked at herself in the mirror on her closet door.

Could've been a lot worse, she thought.

The dog's paws had scuffed and scratched her right cheek, her shoulders and chest, her sides, her belly, her hips, and her right thigh. But she could find only four places where the toenails had actually drawn blood. All above her waist.

The jeans had done a good job protecting her. Her thigh was red and striped with welts where the dog had raked it with a paw, but the skin was intact. The heavy denim had also blunted the dog's attack on her groin. Through her sparse coils of hair, she saw red marks, but the two deep dents made by the lower fangs were now only shallow dimples. Soon, they would probably be gone entirely.

She had brought cotton balls and a bottle of antiseptic with her from the bathroom. She dampened cotton balls and patted them against her wounds.

The clear liquid felt chilly except when it hit raw flesh and seemed to burn her. Mostly it felt good, though. Where it dribbled down her body, it felt like ice water.

I *am* losing more weight, she thought as she watched herself. A little skin here, a little blood there – it adds up.

She made a grim smile.

Keep going with this, and I'll end up in great shape. What's left of me.

I'm a lot better off than the dog.

She felt a little sick again, thinking about what she'd done to the animal.

It attacked me, she told herself. It didn't have to do that.

But I didn't have to let it out of the pickup. I wanted the money. That's why the dog is dead.

And because Mog put it there to make life hard for me.

She was tired of thinking about it, tired of feeling the guilt. She'd gone over all of it in her mind, again and again, while driving home from the cemetery, while dealing with her bloody clothes, while taking her shower. She didn't want to think about it any more.

Done with the first aid, she put on her robe. She returned to the bathroom with the cotton balls and antiseptic, then went into the kitchen and poured herself a small glass of bourbon. In the living room, she sat on the sofa. She sipped her drink.

She stared at the money on the coffee table. She'd tossed it there, along with the note, after emptying the blood-smeared envelope. Leaning forward, she set down her glass and picked up the stack of bills. Then she reached into the side pocket of her robe and took out all the other money that she'd received from Mog since the start of the Game. She put both bunches together and counted.

Thirteen hundred, fifty dollars.

One thousand, three hundred and fifty bucks.

'Not bad,' she said. 'Not bad at all for three nights' work.'

Worth killing a dog for?

We weren't going to think about that, she reminded herself.

She started to remember how it had felt to shove the knife into the dog, so she muttered, 'Self defense,' and leaned forward and picked up her glass. She took a drink.

Self defense with Rale and his buddy, too. They would've messed me up good. And I saved Rale's life. And his pal got away with my two hundred bucks.

Was it Rale in the graveyard tonight? she wondered. Looked like a bum, the guy who threw the dog.

Looked like a goodamn zombie, is what he looked like.

But Rale had seen the note. He might've figured out where to go.

It wasn't Rale unless he'd shaved, she told herself. This guy had a face.

She'd seen it, a pale blur in the moonlight.

Creepy son-of-a-bitch. Why the hell'd he wanta do that with the dog?

It was dead, anyway.

Yeah, dead anyway. Thanks to me.

She took another drink. Then she dropped the stack of money onto the cushion beside her, reached past the arm of the sofa and lifted the telephone off the end table. She set it on her lap, reached again to the table and picked up Brace's business card.

Should I or shouldn't I? she wondered.

He did tell me to call him, she thought. And he didn't tell me not to call if it was after three in the morning.

Maybe he's wide awake, wondering how come I haven't phoned yet. Maybe he's really worried by now.

Holding the glass between her knees, she raised the handset to her ear, heard the dial tone, and punched Brace's number. As she listened to the ringing, she began to think it had been a bad idea, phoning him at this hour. After the fifth ring, she hung up.

He must've fallen asleep, she thought.

His talk about staying awake to wait for the call had been nothing but talk.

The power of Jane's disappointment surprised her.

It's no big deal, she told herself. I should've known better than to call him this late.

But he promised to stay up!

The hell with it.

She lifted the glass from between her knees. It was almost to her mouth when the phone rang. Her flinch slopped bourbon over the rim of the glass. Liquor splashed her chin and spilled off it, dribbling onto her chest, running down all the way past her navel before it was stopped by the barrier of fabric where her robe was belted shut.

Jane squirmed, set her glass down, mopped with her robe at the wet trail down her front, and picked up the handset.

'Hello?' she asked.

'It's me.'

It was the voice she wanted to hear. A calm, comfortable feeling spread through her. And so did a shimmer of excitement. 'Hi there.'

'I hope that was you who just phoned,' Brace said.

'It was. Did I wake you?'

'I was reading. You hung up before I could get to the phone.'

'I let it ring *five* times. Is your place enormous, or something?'

'Just a one-bedroom apartment. Guess the first few rings didn't sink in. I should've warned you. When I'm reading, I don't always hear the phone. You might have to let it ring ten or twelve times.'

'Ah. Your deep powers of concentration.'

'My curse. Anyway, how'd it go?'

'Not bad.'

'Rale didn't show up, did he?'

She hesitated before answering, 'Nope.'

'You don't sound very sure.'

'Oh, I saw a creepy-looking guy over at the bone orchard, but it wasn't him. This guy didn't have a beard.'

'Did he hurt you?'

'Nope. He never got close enough.'

'You had to go to the cemetery, huh?'

'Yeah. You were right about that. I should've gone there in the first place. The Paradise Lounge was sort of interesting, though.' She told him about it, and he seemed both surprised and amused by the news that she'd found a Babe there – the wrong Babe. Then she told him about her foray into Paradise Gardens Memorial Park. As she spoke, she decided to skip the part about the dog.

Why bring it up? At best, Brace would be upset to hear that Jane had gotten herself into a dangerous situation and had been injured. At worst, he might despise her for killing the beast.

I'll have to make up a story to explain the scratches on my

face. Maybe I tripped and hit something. And I'd better make sure to keep my clothes on till all the other places are healed.

'So just as I went to unlock the door,' she said, 'this huge mother of a dog leaps at me.'

I thought I wasn't gonna tell him.

'He left a *dog* in there?'

'Yeah. I think it was a Rottweiler. It was a monster. Blind in one eye . . .'

'The dirty bastard.'

'The dog?'

'Mog,' Brace said. 'What the hell is he trying to do to you?'

'Trying to keep the Game interesting, I guess.'

'The dirty bastard.'

'It's all right,' Jane told him. 'I got the envelope.'

'You *got* it?' He sounded astonished. 'How?'

'I let the dog out.'

'Oh, great.'

She explained about using the two-by-four to prop the door shut, how she'd climbed onto the truck, jerked the board free, then beaten the dog in a race to the driver's door.

'But after I got in,' she said, 'I couldn't shut the passenger side fast enough. So it jumped in on me.'

'Oh, Jesus. What'd it do to you?'

'Not much, but . . .'

'A Rottweiler?'

'I had to kill it.'

Only empty sounds came from Brace's end of the phone.

'I got it with my switchblade before it had a chance to bite me.'

'You're kidding.'

'It was so awful, Brace.' Her throat tightened. 'The way it squealed. I didn't want to hurt it.'

'You could've been torn to pieces.'

'But I wasn't. I'm okay, mostly. I just feel bad about the dog.'

After a few seconds of silence, Brace said, 'I don't like the way this is going.'

'*I'm* not exactly thrilled.'

'I mean, it's one thing when he's sending you to find money in a book. But then he had you climbing up Crazy Horse – you bashed your head and almost fell.'

'That was my own fault.'

'You wouldn't have gone up there except for Mog and his damn Game. And then last night . . .'

'I don't think he put the bums there.'

'But he put *you* there. And he must've put the dog in the pickup tonight. It's getting worse and worse. He's escalating on you.'

'Well, the stakes are getting higher.'

'If he'll put a Rottweiler between you and your money, he might do anything. Maybe next time it'll be a nut with a chainsaw.'

Why'd I go and tell him about the dog? I knew better! Should've kept my mouth shut!

'Are you saying you think I should quit?' she asked.

'Do you think you shouldn't? How far do you want to go with this thing? You've already made over a thousand bucks . . .'

'Thirteen hundred and fifty.'

'That might seem like a pretty good bunch of money, but look what you've gone through to get it.'

'I know exactly what I've gone through.' She couldn't keep the annoyance out of her voice. She took a drink of bourbon.

'Look,' Brace said. 'Suppose someone offered you that much to go out and stab a stray dog? What if someone offered you *five* thousand dollars to stab a stray dog to death. Would you do it?'

'This was different. I didn't go out and murder the thing; it *attacked* me.'

'I'm not trying to condemn you for killing the dog, Jane.'

'Well, you could've fooled me.'

'It's just that you're being dragged by this guy into some very bad situations, and each one's getting worse. He's making you *do* things. And he's doing things *to* you. God knows why.

But I don't like it. You've been lucky so far, but . . . I wish you'd quit before your luck runs out.'

She drank the rest of the bourbon. There was more in her glass than she'd expected, though. It made her eyes burn and water.

'Well,' she said. 'As it turns out, I don't need to quit.'

'What?' Brace asked.

She leaned toward the table, put down her glass and picked up Mog's most recent note.

'I would've told you earlier, but you started in on me, and . . . Anyway, listen to what his note says this time. "Dearest Jane, the fell hand of circumstance is waving farewell to your master, yours truly. I am compelled to fold my tents like the Arabs, as the saying goes. The Game is done. The rest is silence. Adieu, Mog." And then he's got a P.S. down here. Says, "It's been swell." So. I guess that's it. He isn't escalating the Game, he's calling it off.'

'Well, now,' Brace said.

'I can't say I'm delighted about it, but . . . I suppose it's just as well. Things *were* starting to get a little hairy.'

'Mog's calling it quits?' She could hear the relief in Brace's voice.

'That's what it sounds like. He must have to leave town, or something. "The fell hand of circumstance . . ." Maybe he lost his job, or got transferred . . . or the cops got after him about something? Who knows?'

'Maybe he ran out of money,' Brace suggested.

'Could be.'

'Well – whatever the reason, I'm glad it's over. The past two nights . . . Anyway, I'm sorry your bonanza has to end so abruptly, but better that than . . . whatever might've happened if the thing had kept going on.'

'I suppose so,' Jane said.

Brace said nothing.

She settled back against the sofa and put her feet on the coffee table. It felt good to stretch out her legs. She crossed her ankles.

'I'm going to miss working on the clues with you,' Brace said.

'Same here.'

'Maybe we can try collaborating on crossword puzzles.'

'Oh,' she said, 'we'll think of something to do.'

'How does tomorrow night sound?'

She moaned. 'That'd be nice, but . . . I'm feeling awfully worn out from all this chasing around. I've got to get some rest, or I'm gonna drop. What I need to do is come home tomorrow night and hit the sack early. So maybe we should wait till the weekend. How would that be? The library's closed Sunday and Monday, so . . . how about if we get together Sunday? We could make a day of it. By then, I'll be all rested up and ready for action.'

'Sunday?' He sounded disappointed.

'Is that all right?'

'It's a long time off.'

'I know. It is. I'm gonna miss you.'

'Will you?' he asked.

'I miss you right now.'

'Want me to come over?'

She closed her eyes and smiled, thinking how nice it would be to have him here. 'It'd be great,' she said, 'but you'd better not. As it is, I won't be getting enough sleep tonight. And what about you? Don't you have classes to teach in the morning?'

'Can't let a little thing like that get in the way. Besides, my first class doesn't start till nine.'

'Nine *a.m.*?'

'No problem. I . . .'

'Jeez, I shouldn't have called. Go to bed.'

'You can't give me orders,' he said. 'We're not married.'

She could almost see his grin and the mischief in his eyes. 'Very funny,' she said.

'You aren't blushing, are you?' he asked.

'What do you think?'

'Definitely. I bet you're as read as a rose.'

He's almost right, she thought, staring down at the ruddy skin exposed by her open robe. 'If you think you know so much,' she said, 'what am I wearing right now?'

'Uh . . .'

'Give up?'

'Yeah. I'd better not, uh . . .'

'Just my telephone.'

From the other end, she didn't hear anything.

'You still there?' she asked.

'Uh. Yeah. You're kidding about the phone, right?'

Now who's doing the blushing?

'Wrong,' she said. 'I've got nothing on but the phone on my lap. Goodnight, now. See you Sunday morning, okay? But don't make it too early. Maybe ten or eleven.'

'Okay. If you're sure you want to wait that long.'

'I think it'd be a good idea.'

'Okay. Well . . . goodnight, Jane.'

'Sleep tight,' she said, and hung up.

Then she picked up the note from Mog. She had only read it twice before. She read it again.

Dearest Jane,

I do hope that you prevailed over the canine with little or no injury to yourself. I should hate to see your ability to continue the Game impaired, or your loveliness diminished.

Did you find your gift in the glove compartment? Be sure to bring it with you.

Our usual time.

At the house at the edge of Paradise.

Your Master,
MOG

Chapter Eighteen

All day at the library, Jane kept expecting Brace to stop in. He was supposed to stay away from her until Sunday, but he was bound to show up. Just to say hi, maybe. Just to see her. Maybe he would ask her to supper.

And she would be glad to see him.

She might even tell him about the lie.

The lie gnawed at her. It had been a cowardly way to squirm out of arguing over the Game. She should've stood up to Brace, instead – explained that she appreciated his concern, but wouldn't quit until she was good and ready.

His response to that would've been well worth hearing. Maybe he would've lost his temper, raged, demanded obedience. Or he might've pouted. Or begged. Or simply dumped her. Or calmly accepted her decision.

The calm acceptance seemed to be Brace's style, but she'd been afraid to test him.

Afraid of getting the wrong response.

A wrong response would ruin things, so she'd avoided it by lying to him.

Stupid! Like committing suicide to avoid surgery.

During the course of the day, she made up her mind to confess.

When he shows up, she thought, I'll tell him all about it, show him the note . . . It'll be his reward for coming over.

He will show up, she told herself. He has to.

He didn't.

Nor did she find him waiting when she returned home at nine-thirty that night.

Jane put a small, frozen pizza into the oven, then popped a can of Budweiser and went to her bedroom.

'What do you wear to a haunted house?' she muttered. 'Chains. Or a sheet.' She sipped her beer. 'No, that's ghost attire. I'm not the ghost, I'm the fearless treasure-hunting heroine. Right.' She set her beer can on the bureau and started to unfasten her denim skirt. 'Make that the brainless heroine going where she knows she shouldn't. What would be the proper . . .? She laughed softly as she stepped out of her skirt. 'Running shoes.'

Then she thought, Why stop with the shoes?

She changed into the loose blue shorts and tank top that she used to wear when she went for morning runs with Ken, the filthy son-of-a-bitch, back in olden days when she was slim and fit.

The outfit felt light and cool.

She remembered how the running used to feel.

I'll start doing it again, she decided. Every morning. Get back into shape.

She stepped over to the mirror. Gazed at herself and grimaced. Not because she looked too husky; she was used to that, and the past few days had led to some major improvements. It was the condition of her skin that shocked her. In the skimpy, clingy shorts and top, a lot of it showed. Where it wasn't pallid, it was bruised or scratched. She'd looked a lot better after her shower last night, when her skin had been ruddy from the hot water and most of her injuries had been shades of red.

I can't go out looking like this, she thought. What if somebody sees me?

Who's going to see me? I'll be in my car the whole way, and then in a creepy old empty house.

Which may or may not be empty.

She imagined herself wandering through the dark rooms. Too much of her body bare and vulnerable in the running outfit. Too much skin available for sharp edges, splinters, odd debris, for dirt and webs and spiders, for mice and rats.

No way, she decided.

She would change into long pants and a long-sleeved shirt, but that could wait until it was almost time to leave.

Staying in her running clothes, she picked up her beer can

and returned to the kitchen. She waited there until her pizza was ready. Then she took her meal into the living room and tried to watch television while she ate.

She spent a lot of time staring at the bruise on her thigh. A swath of purple and red and blue and gray – lovely.

If Brace shows up, she thought, I'll run in quick and put on my robe. Can't let him see all this.

He won't show up. Not now. Not this late. He would've been here by now if he was coming over.

My own fault. I told him to get lost till Sunday, and that's what he plans to do. Probably figures it'd be a sign of weakness to come any sooner. He'll stay away just to keep his pride.

'Men,' she muttered.

Of their many faults, however, she supposed that pride wasn't as bad as most. It probably screwed things up as much as anything else, but at least it was an honorable flaw. And one that had some worthwhile sides.

He won't call me, Jane thought, but I could call him. Just tell him I changed my mind and I want to see him tonight. If he comes over right away, we'll have the better part of an hour together before it's time for me to go . . . and maybe he can stay here like he did when I went to the bridge . . .

She got up from the sofa and stepped to the end table. There, she found his business card. She picked up the handset and tapped in his phone number.

When he gets here, she told herself, I'll show him Mog's note, and explain. It'll make everything all right.

Sort of all right, anyway.

She listened to the ringing at his end of the line.

What if he asks me to stay home and forget about going for the envelope?

Depends on how he asks, she thought. Maybe if he asks in a very nice way . . .

Why isn't he answering his phone?

It must've rung eight or nine times by now. Could Brace be reading, not yet aware of his ringing telephone?

'Come on,' she said.

What if he's not there? It's Friday night. Maybe he went out.

Maybe he goes with someone, and just hasn't bothered to tell me . . .

A sickly warm feeling of jealousy spread through her.

No, she told herself. If he went out, he went out alone.

Yeah, right.

If he's like every other guy . . .

'Come on,' she said. 'Pick it up, Brace. Don't do this to me, okay?'

You've gotta be there!

She wondered if he might have an answering machine set to take messages after the fifteenth ring – or the twentieth.

Not that anyone would ever stay on long enough to hear it.

Besides, his phone must've rung at least twenty-five times by now.

More like thirty.

If he isn't there . . . If I don't at least leave a message, he won't know where I've gone.

She waited a while longer. Then she hung up.

She watched her phone. Last night, Brace had called back almost at once.

Tonight, the phone stayed silent.

For the next hour, Jane stared at the television and fidgeted. She felt abandoned and betrayed, though she knew she had no right to feel that way.

He'll call, she told herself again and again. Any second now, the phone will ring. Or the doorbell. The doorbell, that'd be great.

Right now, he's on his way over.

She hoped so, but she doubted it.

She pictured Brace in bed with a slim, gorgeous, eager woman – maybe one of his students.

Screwing the gal just to get back at Jane. Accused of it, he says, *You don't want to see me till Sunday, huh? Well, guess what, you're not the only fish in the sea.*

She imagined him eavesdropping on such thoughts, sneering, saying, *You sure must have a high opinion of yourself, thinking I'd nail some other babe just to make you jealous. Here's a news flash, Janey – you ain't that hot.*

Brace isn't like that, she told herself. He would never say things like that. Nobody but a filthy son-of-a-bitch like Ken would ever say things like that.

And Traci might've been hot, but she had the personality of a weasel and the brains of a bug.

'Not to mention a tattoo on her ass,' Jane muttered.

A butterfly. A butterfly on her butt.

Jane tried to laugh, but then she couldn't stop herself from remembering Ken's mussed black hair down there between the butterfly and the mattress of his bed.

And wondered why the memories still caused her so much pain, why she remained so bitter. Ridiculous. Absolutely. Hell, she was lucky to be rid of Ken, the filthy son-of-a-bitch. What if she *hadn't* caught him with Traci? What if, God forbid, she'd married him?

I oughta be thanking Traci every day of my life for saving me from him.

Maybe years from tonight, she thought, I'll be thinking I should thank some other bitch for saving me from Brace.

She looked at her wristwatch.

Eleven thirty-two.

Mouth dry, heart pounding hard, she made another phone call to Brace. This time, she counted the rings. She counted them up to twenty, then lost track as she wondered if she might be disturbing his neighbors. After a few more rings, she hung up.

She glared at the phone. 'Where the hell are you?'

Time running short, she hurried into her bedroom. She threw off her shorts and tank top, and searched her closet until she found an old pair of corduroy trousers. They were too tight around the waist, but they would have to do; the pants from her previous adventures had been soaked to remove the stains, but she hadn't yet run them through the washer.

She put on a long-sleeved chamois shirt.

Dressing like it's winter.

I'll melt, she thought, but at least I'll be protected.

'Speaking of protection,' she said.

She went to her nightstand, pulled open its drawer, and took out the pistol. She slipped it into the right front pocket of her corduroys. Into the left front pocket, she dropped her switchblade knife.

'Ready for bear,' she said, heading into the hallway.

Her purse was on the dining room table. So was Brace's flashlight.

She hooked the strap of her purse over her shoulder, but left the flashlight on the table.

It had given her too much trouble.

And she kept feeling guilty for breaking it.

On her way to work that morning, she had bought another bulb for the thing, and had purchased a flashlight for herself.

The new flashlight was much like Brace's, but half the size. It should fit nicely into any of her pants pockets. For now, it was buried somewhere inside her purse.

On her way to the door, she stopped beside the end table.

Try to phone him one last time?

Why bother? He isn't home.

I'm going into that awful old house and Brace won't know anything about it. If something happens, he won't know where to look for me.

She thought about stopping by his apartment and leaving a note – maybe sliding it under his door. She could get his address off the business card. But then she'd have to hunt for the place.

But what if he turns out to be there? What if he's with someone?

Another glance at her wristwatch, and Jane decided that she didn't have enough time, anyway, for a trip to Brace's apartment. She snatched up the note from Mog, folded it into a square, and slipped it into a pocket of her shirt on her way to the front door.

Chapter Nineteen

Jane stopped across the road from the old house and shut off her headlights. She could hardly believe that she actually intended to go inside.

Gray in the moonlight, it looked ancient and dead.

From the first time she had seen the place, there had always been something familiar about it. She'd assumed it reminded her of the Bates house in *Psycho*. But now she realized the memory it evoked was from a novel she'd read as a teenager. She couldn't recall the name of the book, or its author. But she would never forget the house.

It was located in a coastal town somewhere north of San Francisco. A weathered, grim Victorian structure with turrets and gables and a witch's cap, just like this one. Instead of an abandoned ruin, however, that house had been a wax museum. On display were grisly figures of men, women and children who had supposedly been ripped apart by some sort of monster. In the daytime, you could go safely through with guided tours. But people kept sneaking in at night. As Jane recalled, some pretty awful things had happened to most of them.

That was only a book, she told herself. This place won't have any monsters in it.

And it can't be any worse than the graveyard.

Oh, yes it can, she thought.

She turned her eyes to the cemetery and scanned it through the bars of the fence.

Sure, the boneyard was creepy because of all the graves and tombstones and things – you knew you were surrounded by the dead. But at least you were out in the open. You could see what was coming in time to run away.

Like that awful man who came after her with the dog and threw it . . .

God, I hope he isn't somewhere in the house.

If he is there, she thought, he'd better be careful he doesn't get shot.

She checked her wristwatch again.

Five till twelve.

Gotta get moving.

Though no other cars had come into sight since she'd left the town behind, Jane didn't like the idea of parking here. It was just too close to the house. Anyone driving by would be sure to see her car and guess where she'd gone.

No good cover nearby, either.

But a dirt track, overgrown with weeds and low bushes, led past the side of the house toward the tilted ruin of a garage in the rear.

Keeping her headlights off, Jane steered by moonlight onto the driveway. Gravel crushed by the tires made groaning sounds. Brittle limbs crackled and crunched as she rolled over them, while others scraped the undercarriage, squeaked against the sides of her car.

Hope I don't get a flat tire driving through this crap.

Should've let Brace know where I was going.

A little too late for that, now.

At the rear of the house, she shifted to reverse and swung her car tail-first off the driveway. The gravel noises ended, but the dry foliage of the desolate lawn was thick and loud.

When the house completely blocked her view of the road, she stopped. She killed her engine. For a moment, she left her key in the ignition; it would be good there in case she needed to make a fast getaway.

Then she changed her mind. Better to waste time fumbling with her keys than to come out in a big hurry and find that the key had been stolen.

Or the entire car.

She pulled the key, then removed the new flashlight from her purse. She tucked the purse underneath the driver's seat. After climbing out, she started to put the key case into the right front pocket of her cords. That's where she liked to keep it when she didn't carry her purse.

But the pistol was already there.

She wanted nothing in the way of getting to her handgun, so the key case went into her left front pocket where the switchblade was.

She eased the car door shut.

Considered locking it, but decided not to.

She might be in a very big hurry when it came time to leave.

Standing in the knee-high weeds beside her car, she wondered if she was forgetting anything.

Forgetting to be smart and get my butt out of here.

Yeah, sure. And pass up sixteen hundred bucks? Not to mention a chance at the next bundle – twice that. Three thousand, something. Over six, the time after that. If Mog comes through and if I can stick it out.

With the flashlight in her left hand, but dark, she trudged through the weeds. They rubbed at her legs, snagged the fabric of her trousers, but gave way to the force of her strides.

At the back of the house, a flight of wooden stairs led up to a small, covered porch. Jane aimed her flashlight at the darkness under the porch roof. She switched it on. The beam shot out a narrow, bright path.

She saw the remains of a screen door. The hinged frame and pull handle were there. But the frame lacked a screen.

The solid interior door was either wide open or gone. Jane's light reached all the way into the darkness of the house.

The place is wide open.

Of course it is, she thought. Mog had to get in and hide the envelope.

But maybe it had been wide open for a long, long time.

God only knows what might be inside.

Probably not the wax dummies of mutilated murder victims. Certainly not a monster. Or ghosts or goblins or ghouls.

If anything, an ordinary horror like a mad dog or wino or

druggie or rapist or serial killer or some other brand of fruitcake.

Any of which she would hate to run into.

With the gun, though, she ought to be fairly safe.

She pulled it out of her pocket. Keeping her finger away from the trigger, she started to climb the stairs. The old planks sagged a little under her weight – felt like thin ice on a river. They groaned and squeaked like ice, but much louder.

One of these is gonna bust, she thought.

Instead of continuing up the middle, she moved to the side where the treads should be less likely to give out. Her left hip rubbed the banister as she finished the climb.

Then she stood with her rump against the railing. In front of her, on the other side of the porch, was the screenless door. She shone her light through it.

Nobody came lurching out at her.

Be ready for it, though, she told herself. Don't pitch a coronary when it happens. If. If it happens.

She couldn't see much through the doorway: a floor littered with broken glass that sparkled in the shine of her flashlight; chunks of plaster on the floor, and leaves and a dark rag and the tumbled sheet of a newspaper; across the floor and off a bit to the right, the ruin of an old refrigerator; straight ahead, a doorway with more littered floor beyond it – and the rest of the house.

I'd better get in and start looking, Jane thought. This might take a while.

She hesitated. She didn't want to go inside.

It's just an old house, she told herself. Nothing evil about it.

Somebody's in there.

Somebody or something.

You go in, and you're asking for it. Why do you think Mog gave you the gun? Because he thinks you'll need it, that's why.

If you go in, things will get ugly.

But the alternative was to back down, quit, go home, never get any more prize money, lose any chance of finding out who Mog was or why he'd chosen Jane to be his player or what the point of the Game was.

Screw that, she thought.

Then she called out, 'Ready or not, here I come.'

Real smart, she thought. Announce you're here.

Why not? Maybe it'll scare off . . .

What if I get an answer?

Only silence came from the house.

'I'm coming in!' she yelled.

Reaching out with one foot, she pushed at the porch floor. It didn't feel especially solid.

If it'll hold for just a split second while I take just one step . . .

What if this is it? she thought. This might be like the dog last night – Mog's surprise for me. Maybe I'm supposed to try crossing, and the floor gives out and down I go. And maybe he's got a treat down there under the porch for me. Like broken bottles or spikes or a pitch-fork.

He doesn't want me ruined, she reminded herself. It'd spoil the Game. He wants to test me, not break me.

Yeah. That's encouraging. But he can't control everything. Like how rotten the floor is.

She shoved at it again with her right foot. It didn't fall apart, so she took a deep breath and swung her left leg forward. The floor squawked. She stepped down close to the door frame, then hurried through.

'Thank you,' she whispered. 'Thank you, thank you.'

The hardwood floor beneath her feet felt good and sturdy as she took a few strides deeper into the house. Stopping, she swept the area with her flashlight. This was definitely the kitchen. It had cupboards, sinks, an old stove, and the refrigerator she'd seen from outside.

The refrigerator door was rusty, dented, and pocked with bullet holes.

Somebody had used it for target practice.

Wonderful, Jane thought.

Maybe they put someone in it, first.

That was an especially charming thought.

Why not open it up and find out?

There isn't a body inside, she told herself. I'd be able to smell it.

Depending on how long it's been there.

I'm not going to look. No way.

But what if that's where Mog put the envelope?

She stepped closer to the refrigerator. It was the primitive type that hadn't been made for ages – the kind that had a lever handle. They'd been outlawed. Kids used to get trapped inside and die.

A dreary, abandoned house like this might attract kids. The daring ones. It'd be a fine place for playing spooky games, especially hide and seek.

What if a kid came along and hid inside the refrigerator and his friends couldn't find him?

There'd been no reports of missing children since Jane had moved into town. But someone might've gotten trapped in the old refrigerator a year ago, two years ago, five . . .

Or it might happen tomorrow, Jane realized.

Somebody should've taken this door off its hinges.

To free a hand for opening it, she tucked the flashlight under her right arm. She pointed her pistol at the door, and turned her body slightly until the beam of light also pointed at it. Then, with her left hand, she gripped the handle.

Might be something pretty bad inside. Whatever it is, don't panic. Stay cool.

Just in case, she switched off her pistol's safety. She curled her forefinger across the trigger.

Then she tugged the handle. The door swung open, hinges growling.

Nothing leaped at her. Nothing tumbled out. Nothing hideous or dangerous waited for her on any of the shelves or racks.

The refrigerator appeared to be empty except for a single white envelope hanging by a strip of tape from the edge of the center shelf. Handwritten on the envelope was her name.

The first place I looked!

Jane wanted to be elated. But she felt too nervous for that. It can't be this easy.

With her left hand, she tore the envelope free. She liked the feel of its thickness and weight.

If this is really it, I can get out of here.

But she had doubts.

She backed away from the open refrigerator. When her rump met a counter, she stopped, switched the safety back on, then bent down and clamped the pistol between her knees. She kept the flashlight pinned beneath her arm. Using both hands, she tore open the envelope.

She took out the packet.

A sheet of notebook paper, as usual, was folded around the bills. She removed the bills and fanned them out. At the corner of each was a big 100.

She counted how many. Sixteen.

She felt a warm swelling of excitement in her chest.

This was easy, she thought. This was really easy. Good thing, too. Wouldn't have taken much at this point to make me quit. Maybe Mog sensed that, or something.

She folded the money in half and slipped it down inside a rear pocket of her corduroys. The seat of the pants was fairly tight. She could feel the stiff block of the cash against her buttock.

All mine. Incredible. All it took was a little guts.

She opened the note and held it up in front of her flashlight.

Dearest,

The Game remains afoot, so carry on. Hotfoot it upstairs to the Master bedroom.

You won't be sorry.

Love & kisses,
MOG

Chapter Twenty

Jane read the note again, her elation sinking.

Not a word about the Game being over for tonight and resuming tomorrow night at the usual time. Mog was clearly telling her that it was continuing right now.

'Terrific,' she muttered.

She didn't want to go upstairs, especially not to the master bedroom. She wanted to go home.

It's supposed to be over when I get the money!

Not necessarily, she thought. On the first night of the Game, she'd gotten three payments: the fifty at the circulation desk, the hundred inside *Look Homeward, Angel*, and the two hundred at the top of the Crazy Horse statue. Only on the second and third nights had she been given single tasks and payments. From that little pattern, she'd assumed it would remain one per night.

Shouldn't go assuming, she told herself.

Anyway, Mog's the Master of Games. Which probably means he can make up whatever rules he pleases. And change them when he likes.

Doesn't mean I have to go along with it. I can quit.

She looked again at the note.

The Game remains afoot, so carry on.

Which ought to mean, Jane realized, that another envelope would be waiting for her upstairs in the master bedroom.

So far, Mog had remained consistent about doubling the amount of money.

If I carry on, she thought, I'll get twice sixteen hundred dollars. Three thousand, something.

In her mind, she doubled the sixes. They added up to twelve, making two hundred after you carry the twelves one over for the three thousand. Giving a total sum of three thousand, two hundred dollars that should be somewhere upstairs in an envelope for her.

'Man,' she whispered.

She tucked the note into a pocket of her shirt, then shut the refrigerator door.

She started to turn away, then faced the refrigerator again.

I can't just leave it this way, she thought. Someone might come along.

In the morning, she could make a few phone calls – notify the authorities. They'd send people out to remove the door, cart the whole thing away, or whatever. But what if a kid should come along tonight and climb inside and . . .

'Fat chance,' Jane muttered.

Besides, nobody was likely to suffocate in there – not the way it was riddled with bullet holes.

Still . . .

She frowned. There must be a way to make the thing safe. She opened the door and studied its hinges.

I'm procrastinating, she realized. Anything to keep me from going upstairs.

But this is important. It might save a life.

Yeah. Maybe.

She didn't have the tools for removing the door from its hinges. She supposed she could *shoot* the hinges off. That'd be awfully noisy, though, and a waste of ammo. She might be able to turn the refrigerator around, shove it door-first against the wall. Or tumble the thing forward onto its door.

Yeah, drop it onto me. Great plan.

Then she found an idea that seemed just fine. She spotted the old sheet of newspaper that she'd noticed earlier, picked it up, ripped it, crumpled it, and stuffed a thick wad into the refrigerator's latch hole. After making sure it was packed in tightly, she swung the door shut.

A soft bump, and the door swung back open again.

'Brilliant,' Jane whispered. 'If I was any smarter, I'd be a threat.' She laughed softly, then felt her bowels crawl.

Gotta go upstairs, now.

'Oh, man.'

Hey, she reminded herself, it's for three thousand, two hundred bucks. For money like that, I'd walk through Dracula's Castle blindfolded with a bloody nose and my period.

'Or maybe not,' she muttered.

Flashlight in her left hand, pistol in her right, she stepped out of the kitchen and entered an area that had probably been the dining room. Before going farther, she swept the room with her light.

She saw nothing capable of attacking her.

The room was empty of furniture. Wallpaper hung in tatters like shredded rags. In some places, the walls had been bashed and torn open. Glass from the shattered window was mixed on the floor with broken slabs of drywall and old boards of various sizes, some with nails jutting, points up. Odd pieces of clothing were strewn about: a sock here, a pair of pants there, a boot, a stiff wad of boxer shorts. She spotted a crushed cigarette pack, part of a potato chip bag.

Being careful what she stepped on, Jane walked across the room.

The air smelled like old, wet books.

What a charming place, she thought.

In the next room, she whispered, 'Ah, this one's furnished.'

The furniture consisted of one skinny, stained mattress over in a corner. On the floor near the mattress were smashed beer cans, broken liquor bottles, and dark mounds that Jane supposed were blankets and an assortment of clothing and rags.

This room smelled worse than the other. Mixed in with the musty aroma were scents of booze, urine and feces.

Jane felt an urge to gag, so she held her breath and quickened her pace.

As she rushed along, she kept her light and eyes on the dark mounds. They were probably just blankets or clothes or rags, but she worried that one of them might be covering things – things that might start to come at her.

Soon, they were behind her.

She found the foyer, the front door, and the foot of a stairway that led to the second floor. Still holding her breath, she shone her light at the top of the stairs.

Nothing coming down at her.

She turned around.

Nothing coming at her from behind.

She tested the first stair. It creaked, but felt good and solid. Those that she could see above her looked all right, so she climbed. When she reached the sixth stair, she let out her breath and filled her lungs.

The air didn't seem quite so bad, here.

She supposed that she would need to go back through that horrible room on her way out, though.

Unless she could leave by the front door.

None of the house's doors or windows seemed to be boarded up.

I should be able to get out that way, she thought. Unless it's nailed shut, or something.

She wished she had tried to open it before starting up the stairs.

Find out soon enough, she thought.

She aimed her light again at the top of the stairway.

So far, so good.

If I was in that horrible book, she thought, I'd have a monster bounding down at me. One of those slimy white ape-things with teeth in its cock.

It wouldn't take one of those to scare me witless, she thought. Wouldn't take much of anything at all.

But nothing appeared.

At the top of the stairway, she halted. She swung her flashlight this way and that, spotted no assailants coming at her from up or down the long corridor, but glimpsed plenty of shadows and debris.

What'm I doin' here? she thought.

We're here because we're here because we're here because we're here . . .

Three thousand, two hundred bucks, she reminded herself. And more after that if the Game goes on.

If I don't drop dead.

I'm too young to drop dead.

Sure.

I've probably felt worse, she told herself.

She was having a difficult time catching enough breath. Her heart was slamming. Her mouth was parched. Her face dripped sweat. Her hair felt soaked. So did the sides and back of her shirt, and the seat of her panties. Soaked and clinging to her skin.

This isn't so bad, she thought. At least I'm not getting hurt by some damn dog – or bums. Not yet, anyhow.

She just wished that she hadn't worn such heavy clothes. A long-sleeved shirt on a hot night like this? Not to mention corduroy pants?

They're cooking me.

Should've stayed in my running shorts.

But she would be grateful for the shielding clothes if things turned bad.

She glanced at the side of her pistol to make sure the safety was off. The red dot showed. All set. Keeping her forefinger straight out alongside the trigger guard, she began to search for the 'Master bedroom'.

Why did Mog use the upper case M? she wondered. He's so big on hints and clues, it must mean something.

Master is what he calls himself. Is he saying it's his bedroom?

What if he lives in this place?

She probed a bathroom with her flashlight beam, then backed away until she met the wall at the other side of the corridor. With the wall against her back, nothing could sneak up on her.

What if Mog lives here?

Maybe this is it, she thought.

She'd supposed from the start that Mog's scheme had a special purpose. She couldn't be sure what its purpose might be, but maybe the Game was designed to lead her, step by step, toward a particular destination – a place she would normally shun.

Such as a creepy old house by a graveyard.

Such as Mog's bedroom inside that house.

Envelopes of money like a trail of cheese for the rat to follow.

I'm not a rat, she told herself.

And then gasped as something scurried over the side of her neck, something with legs that tickled. Spider! Shuddering, going prickly with gooseflesh everywhere, she sprang away from the wall and swept at the creature with the head of her flashlight.

Got it!

But a moment later, she felt a tickle underneath her shirt, just below her collar bone.

God, no!

Fast as she could, she shoved the flashlight between her thighs. While she did that, the spider scampered downward onto her left breast.

She slapped it through her shirt.

Felt it crumble and squish.

After the sting from her slap faded, she could feel the body like the weight of a coin on her breast. It was stuck to her skin, mashed into the moisture of her sweat, glued there with its own juices.

The feel of it disgusted her.

She had to wipe it off. Fast.

So appalled she could hardly think straight, she tugged open the top of her shirt. She had to do it one-handed. It came undone, and a moment later a button clicked on the floor.

The barrel of her pistol would only smear the mess, so she jammed her hand down into her corduroys and brought out the switchblade knife. Tonight, she hadn't bothered with a rubber band to keep the blade shut. She'd decided to take her chances rather than slow things down – and snap her lips.

She thumbed the button and the blade sprang out.

She wished she could see what she was doing.

But the flashlight was between her legs, pointing into the bathroom. She could see nothing of her breast.

Maybe just as well, she thought. I don't want to see whatever's a left of the damn spider.

Just be careful. Real careful.

Quickly, she lowered the edge of the blade until she felt it against her skin just above where the mess was. Then she scraped. One quick stroke as if shaving the top of her breast with a straight razor. She felt the small gob skid along in front of the blade, and hoped it wasn't leaving much of itself behind.

Bending at the waist, she gave the blade a flick.

That should've gotten most of it.

She wiped both sides of the blade on a leg of her trousers. Clamping the handle between her teeth, she lifted the untucked end of her shirt and scrubbed at the trail left by the spider.

Then she took the flashlight from between her legs and inspected the damage. Her flushed skin was landscaped with countless goosebumps. The knife, however, had left no visible mark. The spider had left no trail of juice or pieces; the blade or the vigorous wiping with her shirt had gotten it all.

Except that!

It looked like a thick black whisker.

Jane knew it was part of a spider leg.

She tucked her chin down and blew on it. The leg trembled slightly, but stayed. Wincing, she brushed it away with the edge of her gunhand.

She checked her breast once more with the flashlight.

It looked as if it had been dipped in ice water.

No traces remained of the spider, so she clamped the flashlight under her right arm and closed her shirt. She kept the flashlight where it was, and took the knife from her teeth.

She held on to the knife.

Let's find that envelope and get out of here, she thought. Before we meet another spider.

Turning, she followed the pale beam of light down the corridor toward another doorway.

One more spider and I'm gone. Rather face fifteen Rottweilers than . . .

The door was shut. Jane nudged it with her knee. Squalling on dry hinges, it swung open. Her light stretched into a large room.

She caught a whiff and quit breathing.

What the hell died in here?

Doesn't matter, she told herself. This is the place.

She would find the envelope here.

Inside the dirty coffin in the middle of the floor.

She stepped through the doorway. Twisting her torso, she swept the light from side to side. She saw no human or animal. The room seemed to be empty except for the coffin.

No hidden recesses. No other doors.

Two windows on the far wall exposed the night. Some of the night came in through them, tossing crooked grimy rectangles onto the floor.

Jane bent slightly at the waist to drop the angle of her light. She turned around slowly, inspecting the floor. It looked much the same as the floors downstairs: scattered with glass and plaster, broken boards bristling with nails, leaves and shreds of paper and plastic wrappers, rags, remnants of clothing.

The coffin had been dragged across the room from the doorway, scraping a path through the debris.

Jane stepped closer to it.

The coffin was constructed of wood. Pine, maybe. It looked like a good piece of furniture that had been left out in the weather for a few years.

Underground, is more like it.

The top and sides were filthy with dried mud.

Terrific, Jane thought. He dug it up out of the neighbor's yard.

Or wants me to think so.

She started to ache from holding her breath, so she hurried

644

toward one of the windows. As she neared it, she felt a warm breeze on her face. Shards of glass snapped and crunched under her shoes.

At the window, she leaned forward carefully, ready to stop if her head should meet trouble.

Bumping nothing, being stabbed by nothing, she eased her head outside and breathed deeply. The air smelled of summer and of deep night, but was not without a vague but revolting scent of rotten flesh. She could feel the breeze sliding inside the open front of her shirt. It felt very good in there on her hot, sweaty skin.

The window gave Jane a panoramic view of Paradise Gardens Memorial Park. From this height, she could see most of it.

She found herself searching the graveyard for the stranger who'd been there last night, who'd carried the dog overhead like a barbell and hurled it at her.

She spotted a few human shapes, but none that moved. They were probably statues.

Or one might be him, standing still. Maybe gazing up at her.

A whole new swarm of goosebumps raced up her skin. They were quick and cold. They stiffened the flesh at the back of her neck and squeezed her scalp and made her nipples rise hard and achy.

He's watching . . .

Jane started to duck away, but forced herself to stop.

Big deal if someone's down there staring at me. As long as he's down there and I'm up here.

Fighting her urge to get away from the window, she took time to scan the parking area, the main gates, and the section of fence near the gates.

The Toyota pickup was gone. So was the dog that she'd last seen skewered on top of the fence rods.

Bet I know where the dog is now, she thought.

Easing herself clear of the window, she turned around.

The flashlight beneath her arm swung its beam to the coffin.

Right in there, she thought.

I'm supposed to think Mog dug the coffin up, complete with corpse.

A real test of my willpower. Do I have the guts to open it and see how a person looks after being in the ground too long? Will I go that far for my three thousand, two hundred bucks?

'You betcha,' she whispered.

But she wouldn't be finding a dead person in there. She'd be finding the Rottweiler, a day old, torn open and stinky. That's where Mog put the thing. And that's where he put the envelope.

She stepped to the side of the casket, lifted her left foot and pounded her heel against the edge of the lid.

The lid wobbled.

Not fastened down.

Jane considered putting away the knife and pistol, placing the flashlight between her legs, bending over, and removing the lid with her hands. But she wanted to keep her weapons ready. And she certainly didn't want to have her face down there when the lid came off.

No way.

Unless, she amended, it turns out that none of the other ways will work.

Like kicking.

Bending her left leg slightly for balance, she lashed out with her right. The sole of her shoe caught the coffin lid, raised it, knocked it crooked, shoved it and dropped it. The lid skidded off the far edge of the coffin, then crashed to the floor.

Jane flinched at the noise it made.

She stared into the coffin, hardly able to believe her eyes.

No stinky, mutilated dog. No human cadaver.

She felt as if she'd been tricked, but she was relieved, almost delighted.

The coffin contained nothing dead or disgusting.

With its shiny blue satin lining and pillow, it looked almost inviting.

Her envelope had been placed on the pillow. She glanced at it, then turned her eyes to the flat box near the middle of the coffin. The box, about the size of a hardbound novel, was brightly wrapped in gold foil paper tied with a scarlet ribbon and bow that gleamed in the shine of her flashlight.

'Now he's leaving presents,' Jane whispered.

At the sound of her voice, she realized that she had been forgetting to hold her breath – probably ever since coming away from the window. Without thinking about it, she'd been taking shallow breaths through her mouth.

Now, she tried a small sniff. The stench hadn't gone away, but it seemed less horrible than earlier. She was growing accustomed to it. But the source of the foul odor was obviously somewhere other than inside the coffin.

Maybe a dead rat over in a corner, something like that.

The inside of the coffin *looked* as if it should smell like perfume.

As nice as a freshly made bed.

Mog's bed? she wondered. In the note, he'd called this the 'Master bedroom'. And he's the Master of Games.

Is he nuts enough to sleep in a coffin?

The satin lining and pillow case were smooth, without a wrinkle. Jane doubted that anyone had ever slept on them.

She began to feel very nervous.

Mog got his hands on an old, weathered coffin, she thought. Maybe by digging it out of the graveyard. He fixed it up with brand new upholstery.

What'd he do with the body?

Why'd he fix it up?

She swiveled around fast to make certain she was still alone in the room. Then she thumbed her safety on and slipped the pistol into her pocket. After changing the knife to her right hand, she bent over, reached into the coffin with her left, and picked up the envelope. She slit it open with her knife.

Pulled out the money wrapped in a note.

She counted the hundred-dollar bills. Thirty-two of them.

'Man,' she muttered. 'Man, oh man.'

Her heart was thudding. Her throat felt tight. Her stomach squirmed.

She felt very odd: elated, scared.

This plus the sixteen hundred – almost five thousand just tonight.

How much does this make altogether? she wondered. She tried to calm herself so that she could remember and count.

No luck.

It's a lot. It's a real, real lot.

But she was afraid to read the note. Afraid of the gift-wrapped box. Afraid of who or what might be in the house, maybe watching her right now, maybe sneaking closer.

The note fluttered in her twitching hand as she held it in front of the flashlight.

My Dear,
   I do believe I'm falling in love. Not only are you a vision of delight, but oh! such spunk to have come this far.
   The gift is for you. Open it now. You'll be glad you did.

Kisses,
MOG

Chapter Twenty-one

Jane crouched over the coffin, set her knife on the satin-covered pad, and picked up the brightly wrapped box. Flashlight pinned between her right arm and ribs, she tore off the bow and ribbon and wrapping paper and let them fall to the floor.

Holding the bottom of the box steady on the edge of the coffin, she peeled off its top.

Inside, she found a kitchen timer, a negligee and a note. The note was taped to the timer.

Darling,

You've labored long and hard, this night. You deserve a rest.

Slip into this dainty number, set the timer for half an hour, and ease yourself down onto satin comfort.

At the sound of the ding, you may rise, collect your prize, and be off.

Your Master,
MOG

Jane read the note three times.

More times than that, she thought, he's gotta be kidding.

She was shaking very badly. She had an odd, numb sensation behind her forehead. And a strange, buzzy feeling down inside as if a low-level electrical current might be humming through her bowels.

She placed the timer beside her knife at the bottom of the coffin.

Then she let the box fall to the floor as she stood up with a shoulder strap of the negligee pinched between her thumb and forefinger. The strap looked like a slim ribbon of silk. The garment swaying below it might just barely be long enough to reach from Jane's chest to her thighs.

The beam of her light passed through the gauzy red fabric.

A dainty number?

He actually wants me to strip and put this on, she thought. And then lie down in the coffin for half an hour.

'Oh, man,' she muttered. 'He's got the wrong gal.' In a loud voice, she said, 'You're out of your mind.'

No answer came.

Not that she expected one.

Mog never answered.

But he must be here, she told herself. He promised another 'prize' if I follow orders. He has to deliver it, doesn't he? And if he isn't watching, how will he even know whether I do what I'm supposed to do?

If he isn't watching, why does he *want* me to do it?

He's watching, all right. Maybe through a hole in the wall, something tricky like that.

Wants to pay me six thousand, four hundred bucks so he can play peeping Tom.

Peeping Tom in a dark room.

If I turn off the flashlight, she thought, he won't be able to see anything.

Besides, what is there that he hasn't already seen? He must've spied on me in the shower that night. And who knows how many other times he's seen me with nothing on? He comes and goes as he pleases like some sort of invisible man.

Maybe he *is* invisible, she thought. That would sure explain a lot.

Maybe he's a ghost.

'A rich spook,' she muttered, 'with a penchant for voyeurism.'

He's making *me* rich, she reminded herself. This could be the end of it, if I don't follow orders. Am I going to let a little modesty get in the way of six thousand, four hundred dollars? Plus all the money that might come my way later on if I don't back down?

Especially since he's already seen me naked?

And since he can sneak into my house – probably sneak just about anywhere just as if he *is* invisible even if he's not, and see or do just about anything that pops into his head?

I can do it, she told herself. No big deal.

Okay, but what about the coffin part?

I can do it. I can do anything. It's all in the state of mind.

Moving her flashlight slowly, she inspected the interior of the coffin. No sign at all of dirt or bugs. It appeared to be perfectly clean.

She wondered how the satin would feel against her skin. Probably slippery and cool.

She'd been tempted, at times, to buy satin sheets for her bed at home . . .

This isn't a bed.

No? I don't see any other furniture in here, and this is supposed to be the 'Master bedroom'.

Does Mog sleep right here inside the coffin? she wondered. Like a vampire?

Maybe *that's* what he is.

'Bull,' she whispered.

If he does sleep in the thing, she thought, that's his problem. It's clean now. It looks plenty clean enough for me.

She stepped on the back of a shoe, pulled her foot out, raised her leg over the side of the coffin and lowered her foot onto the padded bottom. Holding the negligee's strap between her teeth, she reached down with her empty hand and removed her other shoe.

She left both shoes on the floor.

Standing inside the coffin, she switched off her flashlight. She crouched and placed it near her feet. Then she stood up, took the strap from her mouth, and looked down at herself. All she saw was black and shades of dark gray.

In this sort of darkness, she could prance butt-naked through a crowded room and nobody would be the wiser.

Balancing on one foot, she raised the other and peeled off its sock.

She felt the satin under her bare foot.

Oh, my God, I'm doing it.

She felt shivery all over.

This can't be happening. I can't really be doing this.

But she didn't stop.

When her socks were off, she crouched, reached over the side of the coffin and tucked them into her shoes.

She slipped her pistol underneath the pillow.

Needing both hands, she returned the negligee's strap to her mouth. It was moist from being there before. It felt and tasted like a wet shoelace, and she found herself wondering when she had ever had a shoe lace, wet or otherwise, in her mouth.

Must've been when I was a kid, she thought.

Right now, it was hard to imagine she'd once been a kid. It even seemed strange to think there had been a time before coming into this house tonight.

I had a life before all this. I'll have a life after. This is just . . . a weird interlude.

Wary of the filth on her clothes, Jane rolled her shirt and corduroy pants into bundles, crouched and set them carefully on top of her shoes. Then she stood up. She raised her arms to slip the negligee down over her head, but changed her mind and lowered them.

Just give me a couple of seconds, she thought.

Her clothes had been heavy and hot and sticky with sweat. She was glad to have them off, and not yet ready to put on something else, not even such a scant and wispy bit as the gift from Mog. The night air felt like a soft breath stirring against her bare skin. She wished there was more of a breeze. She thought about taking off her panties.

They were snug and damp, and made her feel a little itchy.

She'd intended to leave them on. Mog's note, after all, had only told her to wear the nightie – not to strip naked. Keeping her panties on wouldn't be going against any specific orders.

I'm supposed to take them off, even if he didn't come right out and say so.

She pulled them down, stepped out of them, squatted and added them to the pile on the floor beside the coffin. For a while, she remained squatting, savoring the feel of the air where she was so very hot and moist.

She was shivering so much that even her lungs seemed to tremble as she breathed in and out.

A feverish shiver.

It had nothing to do with cold. It had little to do, anymore, with fear. It had mostly to do with being naked and feeling the soft breeze, with knowing why she'd stripped, with knowing where she was.

Shaking badly, she forced herself to stand.

She looked down at her body.

She'd been wrong to think that the darkness would hide her.

Mog has to be watching, she thought.

I don't care.

She raised her arms high, arched her back, stretched and twisted, relishing the feel of her flexing muscles and how the air touched her.

Jane suddenly realized that she *wanted* Mog to be watching her.

Watching the show.

His watching made it more delicious, somehow.

What's he doing to me?

Hugging her breasts, Jane dropped to her knees.

She had a quick urge to get dressed and run from the house. And be done with it. Done with it forever.

But part of her mind wondered why.

Because he's making me do these things!

He isn't *making* me do anything. I'm doing all this because I want the money.

No no no no no.

I want the money. Of course I want the money. But it isn't just that. It's a lot more than that.

It's because I want to do these things.

Some of them, anyhow.

This, for instance.

Turned on like crazy. But not so frenzied now. Calmed at least slightly by the shame of catching herself at it.

Let's just try to get down to business, she told herself – do what needs to be done, and go home.

Still on her knees, she slipped the negligee over her head. It drifted down her body, hardly touching her at all, gliding against her here and there with a tickle so soft and subtle that she had to squirm. As expected, it didn't reach down very far. Its edge brushed her high up on the thighs.

The breeze stirred the weightless nightie, caressed her with it. Trying to ignore the sensations, she searched the dark bottom of the coffin with her hands and she found the flashlight. She thumbed its switch, then squinted as the sudden brightness hurt her eyes. When she could see again, she took a quick look around.

He can see me, but I can't see him.

She looked down at herself.

The scanty garment didn't cover much of her. Except for the slim straps, she was bare to mid-chest. There, the negligee draped little more than her nipples, stiff and jutting and plainly visible underneath. The wispy fabric concealed nothing, but gave a red hue to her skin, her scratches and bruises from the dog last night, and the small, pale triangle of hair between her legs.

Jane could hardly believe she was wearing such a thing.

What *won't* I do? she wondered.

It's no big deal, she told herself. People wear nighties like this all the time.

Yeah. Only maybe not for pay, while they're kneeling in a coffin in a cruddy old ruin of a house at the edge of a graveyard – with a stranger watching.

Anyway, she thought, this is a lot better than last night.

So far.

And so what if the whole deal's got me a little hot? That's no crime.

She slipped the flashlight between her thighs, beam up. Holding the timer in the light, she twisted the dial until it pointed to thirty.

The ticking sounded very loud.

She placed the timer on the floor of the coffin where it would be near her feet. After sliding her knife aside, she took the flashlight into her hand, turned and sat down. She stretched out her legs, spreading them so that the timer was between her ankles, then started to ease herself down. When the top of her head rubbed against the end of the coffin, she scooted forward a bit. Then she continued going down until her back met the cushion and her head sank into the soft pillow.

The satin felt cool and slick.

This isn't half bad, she thought. Just don't think about how this is a coffin.

This is a coffin.

This is what it's like to be in a coffin. Except I'm alive. Someday, I'll be stretched out in a coffin, dead, and they'll put the lid on, and . . .

A sick feeling started swelling inside her.

No! Stop it! Who's to say I'll end up in a coffin? A lot of things can happen – I might get disintegrated in a nuclear explosion, or . . .

Quit it!

Think about something else!

Now I lay me down to sleep, with bags of peanuts at my feet. If I should die before I wake, you'll know it's from a belly ache.

Die before I wake. Wonderful.

Mog is doing this to me, wants me to think horrible thoughts – that's why he's making me lie here.

She wondered how much time had passed.

No more than a minute or two, probably.

This half hour is going to take forever.

In a very quiet whisper, Jane began to sing, 'A hundred bottles of beer on the wall, a hundred bottles of beer, if one of those . . .'

She stopped, afraid her voice might hide the sound of Mog's approach. She wanted to hear him if he came.

He'll come, she told herself. He has to. It's only a question of when – and what he'll do when he gets here.

Silently set the envelope on her pile of clothes, and sneak away?

But what if this really *is* what it's all about? What if the whole point of the Game was to get me here? Here where nobody will hear my screams. Here in this coffin – Mog's bed? What if this whole thing is about raping me and torturing me and murdering me?

She suddenly remembered the pistol.

A gift from Mog himself. So lighten up, bucko. You're not here to get nailed. Not by Mog, at least.

Reaching under the pillow, she took hold of it and pulled it out.

The heavy, solid feel of the pistol made her feel safe.

Everything's just fine, she told herself.

Gun in hand, she straightened her arm down along her right side. She placed the flashlight by her left hip, searched nearby until she found her switchblade, then set the open knife onto her belly. Leaving it there so she could feel it and grab it quickly in an emergency, she lowered her left hand and gripped the flashlight.

Nothing to do now except wait.

Wait and listen to the ticking of the timer.

It didn't actually make a ticking sound. More of a tock-tock-tock.

It was the beating of his miserable heart!

Right, start thinking about Poe stories, why don't you? Wonderful idea.

Try 'The Premature Burial.' Yeah, great.

And what if Mog's idea of a good time is to sneak up while I'm in here and drop the lid on me and seal me in? Maybe there's an open grave just waiting in the neighbor's yard.

The one this coffin came out of, for instance.

He wouldn't do that to me, she told herself.

You hope.

Could she shoot him through the lid? Maybe. The pistol was loaded with .22 long rifle cartridges. They were capable of blowing a hole through an inch of wood. But a strong, hard wood might stop them. It'd all depend on the lid.

It won't come to that.

He won't do anything to me. This is just another step in the Game. The whole deal is to have me strip and put on the nightie and stay in the coffin for half an hour.

Only this and nothing more.

When the half hour is up, I'll get dressed and find an envelope full of money and go home.

Somewhere nearby, the floor creaked.

Chapter Twenty-two

The sound of the creaking board sent a shock of cold through Jane. Her body went stiff, heart slamming, hands tightening on her flashlight and pistol. She held her breath. She cursed the clock for its tock-tock-tock-tock that got in her ears and stopped them from hearing any slight disruption of the silence of the room.

Old houses make lots of sounds, she told herself. That one little noise doesn't mean someone's coming.

Wanta bet?

It's Mog, she thought. He's on his way. Maybe just to leave the envelope, or . . .

What if it isn't Mog!

What if it's Rale, or that creep from last night, or God only knows?

Shoot first and ask questions later.

Wonderful idea. And suppose it does turn out to be Mog? I've just blown away the goose that lays the golden egg. Or maybe some harmless kid or . . .

It's nobody at all, she told herself. The noise meant nothing. Nobody's here. Just relax. False alarm. God, you're so tense. When the timer goes off, you'll probably blow off a toe.

She thought about where the pistol was aimed, and figured that an accidental discharge wouldn't hit any of her toes. Instead, it would probably gouge the side of her calf, and maybe hit the knob of bone sticking out from her ankle. Not to mention scorching her thigh with powder burns.

She wondered if the safety was on.

Then she wondered how much longer before the timer would ding.

Then a brilliant light blinded her and she gasped and jerked rigid.

'Jane!'

No! Not Brace! Of all the people in the world . . . better anyone than Brace. But it had been his voice saying her name, Jane was certain of that. It was Brace, and nobody else, standing at the end of the coffin shining the light in her face.

'Damn it!' she cried out, and flung up her right arm.

'Don't shoot! It's me!'

What's he got, a headlight?

She used her upraised arm to shield her eyes. 'Get that light out of my face!'

It didn't move away, it moved down.

'Damn it, Brace!'

As she sat up, the strap fell off her left shoulder. That side of the negligee slipped down. Her breast was caught naked in Brace's beacon.

The light jumped away from it.

And came to a stop, as if by accident, aiming down at an angle between her parted legs.

Jane cried out, 'Damn it!' and threw her legs together and hunched forward, an arm across her breasts. 'Turn it off! Just turn it off!'

Instead of killing the light, he swept its beam away from her. She was no longer in its bright center, but still lit by the glow.

'How's that?' Brace asked.

'Turn it off!'

'Sorry, I can't.'

'What do you mean, you can't?'

'I mean I won't. Not in a place like this.'

'You didn't have it on when you were sneaking up on me.'

'That was different.'

'You bastard.'

'Get on up out of there, Jane,' he said, sounding very calm. 'We need to get out of here.'

'What're you *doing* here?'

'I was worried about you.'

'You followed me!'

'I know.'

'You followed me! You had no right! Damn you! What right do you think you had? You don't own me! Jesus! What the hell did you think you were doing? Just get out of here! Get the hell out! Go!'

'I don't think it's safe for you to be here.'

'So what!' Jane blurted. 'Just get out and leave me alone! This isn't any of your business!'

The beam swung back at her. She cringed and turned her face away. 'Get that off me!'

It stayed. 'I think we'd better leave,' Brace said.

'I think *you'd* better leave.'

'Not without you.'

'Ho! Not without me? Who the fuck do you think you are? Get out of here!'

'Look at yourself,' he said.

Jane didn't move. 'I know what I'm doing.'

'You do?'

'Yes!'

'You know where you are?'

'Yes!'

'You know what you're wearing?'

'Damn it, get that light off me!'

'Look what he's doing to you, Jane.'

'He isn't doing anything – except giving me a hell of a lot of money.'

'Sure looks like he's making you do a strip and sleep in a casket.'

'He isn't *making* me. I'm doing it because I want to. There's a big difference.'

'How much are you getting paid this time?'

'Maybe nothing, thanks to you.' Turning her head, she scowled at Brace through the glare of the light. 'What the hell possessed you, damn it?'

He moved the light a little so it no longer blazed straight into her eyes. 'I care about you,' he said.

'Great. I care about you, too. But what makes you think that gives you the right to screw around with my life?'

'It probably doesn't,' he admitted.

'Damn right, it doesn't! If I'd wanted you in on this, I would've told you so. I didn't *want* you in on this. That's how come I lied about the note.'

'I already figured that out,' he said.

'Obviously. But you just decided to go ahead and butt in, anyway, didn't you? God, I don't follow *you* around. I don't spy on *you*. You know why? Because I don't *do* that sort of shit. I respect people's privacy. Privacy. You know what that is? How would you like it if I did that to you? Huh? Snuck around and spied on you in the middle of the night? Do you think you'd like that?'

'I'm sorry you're upset,' Brace said. 'I'm not sorry I came here, though. Somebody . . .'

'I'll *bet* you're not. Got yourself a free show.'

'It wasn't something I expected.'

'Bet you watched, though. Didn't you!'

'Sure, I watched. Who wouldn't?'

'A lot of people.'

'Well, sorry. But I don't look away from things like that. I'm not a priest, and you're not an ugly cow. So I watched. But I can't say I enjoyed it much.'

'Oh, thanks.'

'For godsake, don't let *that* offend you. I was too damn shocked to appreciate the view. I couldn't believe you were really doing it.'

'Surprise, surprise.'

'I knew you were awfully eager to get as much money as you could from this guy, but . . . this is crazy. I never would've thought you'd stoop to it.'

'Sorry to disappoint you. But now you know. I'm nothing but a cheap slut. Nothing I won't "stoop to" for a buck.'

'I'm starting to wonder,' Brace said.

'Yeah, well, fuck you and the horse you rode in on.'

'Jane.'

'Get out of here, okay? Or haven't you insulted me enough yet? Or are you waiting around for another eyeful? God-damn it, you weren't supposed to be here! You've ruined everything! Everything!'

'Someone has to watch out for you, Jane.'

'No! My God, what do you think I am – an invalid?'

'You're not an invalid,' he said softly.

'No, of course not. I'm a woman. Same difference, huh? I'm a woman, so I'm too damn stupid and emotional and weak to take care of myself. I need a big smart guy like you to make sure I stay out of trouble.'

'This isn't trouble?'

'No,' she said.

'You're dressed like a hooker and sitting in a casket with a gun in your hand.'

'So what?'

'Ah. This is normal behavior. I see.'

'There wasn't supposed to be an audience.'

'Ah. If nobody's watching, it isn't happening? Like the tree that falls in the woods . . .'

'Exactly,' Jane said.

'Ah. But what about Mog? He's watching, isn't he?'

'I don't know.'

'Of course he's watching. Do you honestly think anybody would pay you to do these things unless he wants to watch them happen?'

'I wouldn't know. I've never seen him. Have *you* seen him?'

'No.'

'Well, why the hell not?' she blurted, almost shouting. 'You've seen everything else!'

'Take it easy, Jane. You're getting upset again.'

'I've got a clue for you, buddy! I've never *stopped* being upset!'

'Look, let's just get out of here.'

'*You* get out of here.'

'Someone might show up. What if the police come along and find us?'

'Who cares?'

'What *do* you care about, Jane?'

'I used to care about you.'

Brace suddenly kicked the coffin so hard that it jumped and scooted. The blow jolted Jane. She gasped. She felt stunned, and shaken, almost ready to cry.

'Don't!'

'Game's over, honey. Get out of there. Right now, or I'll drag you out.'

'You've got no right!'

'Who cares?' he threw back at her. 'Out. Now.'

'You bastard.'

'I know.'

'How'm I gonna get my money if I leave?'

'You won't. At least I hope not. Learn to live on your salary like everyone else. You didn't know where to draw the line, so I'm drawing it for you.'

Her right hand, pressed against her breast, still held the pistol. In her mind, she saw herself swing her arm forward and aim the weapon at Brace; she heard herself order him to leave the house. But then something went wrong. He lurched for Jane. Her finger twitched. *Bam!* Brace slumped to the floor, a bullet hole in his forehead.

I could make it happen. I could shoot him.

The thoughts slammed through Jane.

Shocked her. Killed her rage and shame and her will to resist. Suddenly feeling very tired, she lowered the pistol to her side. She stood up, leaving it at the bottom of the coffin, along with her flashlight and knife and the ticking timer. She could feel the strap still dangling against her arm. She knew that her breast was bare, and that the negligee hid nothing even where it covered her.

She was on her feet, facing Brace, totally exposed to his gaze.

She didn't care at all. She felt weary and numb.

'You'd better get dressed,' Brace said.

'If you say so.' She slipped the negligee up her body and off, and let it fall.

'Jeez.' He sounded surprised and angry.

'You said I should get dressed,' she pointed out as the nightie settled softly across the tops of her feet. It felt light and ticklish like wisps of tissue paper. 'You're the boss,' she added.

Now who's the calm one? she thought. Just look how calm I am. Very easy to be calm when everything's ruined and nothing matters anymore.

Easy as pie.

'You don't have to act crazy,' Brace muttered as he hurried around to the side of the coffin.

'What's there to hide?' she said. 'You've already seen everything.'

'It wasn't supposed to be like this.'

'It never is.'

Crouching, he set his electric lantern on the floor and picked up Jane's panties. He held them out to her. 'Put these on.'

She felt the corners of her mouth curl up. 'Are you sure you don't want to fuck me first?' she asked.

'Of that I'm certain, my dear.'

She hit him very hard in the face with her fist. The blow made his head jerk a little sideways. But he turned back to Jane and gave her a terrible look of surprise and disappointment.

The timer went off just then, dinging like the bell at the end of a boxing round.

Jane burst into tears. She took the panties from Brace and bent over to step into them and lost her balance and he caught her by the shoulders and held her steady until she had her panties on. He held her again when she had trouble getting into her corduroys.

The bastard! Why doesn't he mind his own fucking business and let me fall!

She wished she could stop crying.

When she tried to stop, however, it only got worse. She was bawling out of control by the time she'd finished dressing.

With Brace's help, she gathered her belongings.

'What about that stuff?' Brace asked, shining his light at the negligee and timer still at the bottom of the coffin.

'They . . . aren't . . . mine,' she gasped out between sobs.

'Are you sure you don't want them?'

'Leave 'em.'

'Okay. Let's go, then.'

Brace led the way. Jane followed him out of the room and downstairs and out of the house. His car was parked on the rear lawn, next to hers.

'Will you be able to drive home all right?' he asked as he opened her car door.

Jane sniffled. She wiped her eyes. 'I'm not drunk,' she said.

'You're awfully upset.'

'You oughta know.'

'I'm sorry about all this.'

'Not as sorry as me.'

'Don't bet on it,' he said.

'Yeah. Right.' She dropped onto the driver's seat and tried to shut the door.

Brace held it open. 'I'll follow you home,' he said.

'Don't bother.'

'I just want to make sure you get there okay.'

'Swell. But don't . . . don't think I'm gonna . . . let you in. I never . . . never never never . . . wanta see you again.'

He let go of the door, and Jane slammed it shut.

Chapter Twenty-three

Still half asleep the next morning, Jane rolled onto her side. The sheet beneath her body felt cool and slippery. Nice. But the mattress seemed strangely hard under her shoulder and hip. She tried to curl up. Her knees and heels bumped walls.

Uh-oh.

Her eyes sprang open. She flipped onto her back, glimpsed a stained and tattered ceiling, then snapped her head from side to side.

She was lying in the coffin.

'Oh,' she murmured.

Shoving at its padded bottom, she raised herself to her elbows. She muttered, 'Oh, my God,' at the sight of her negligee. She couldn't believe she was wearing such a thing. It had no more substance than mosquito netting. And it was twisted crooked, leving her bare below the waist.

Through the transparent red material, Jane watched her skin darken to a deep shade of scarlet as she remembered that Brace had seen her dressed this way.

Worse. I even took it off.

The memories of last night began pouring into her. Though the morning air felt cool, she soon was dripping with sweat. Bad enough that Brace had found, *caught* her in the coffin with nothing on except this poor excuse for a nightgown. But the horrid things she'd said to him! How could she have said such things? And acted that way?

I even hit him!

What was I, nuts?

None of it would've happened, she told herself, if Brace had stayed away. It was really all his fault. He followed me, snuck up on me, looked at me. Shone that damn floodlight on me and saw everything, the dirty . . .

Saw all my wounds, too. And saw me before I could get back into decent shape.

Well, that's the last he'll ever see of me.

Pushing at the bottom of the coffin, she sat the rest of the way up. She looked around the room to make sure she had no visitors.

Nobody here.

Except maybe for Mog at a peephole or something – who knows with him?

The place was a mess. It looked a lot worse in daylight.

'What doesn't?' she muttered, casting a glance at her awful nightie and all it exposed of her scratches and bruises and places that clothing was normally meant to hide.

He never should've seen me in this, she thought.

I'm the one who put it on.

But he wasn't supposed to show up, damn him!

Forget it, she told herself. Doesn't matter. It's all over.

Leaning forward, she reached to the timer between her feet and picked it up. It was silent, the pointer on the zero.

Did I forget to set the thing? Jane wondered.

No. She could remember thinking, *Here we go again*, while she'd turned the dial to the thirty.

I slept through the bell, that's all. Hardly surprising.

It had been after four in the morning by the time she'd set the timer for her second try. Four thirteen, to be exact; she could remember glancing at her wrist-watch.

After being escorted home by Brace, she'd watched him drive away. Then she'd turned off the lights and waited just in case he was only pretending to leave.

Soon, she'd decided it was pointless to wait any longer. Even if Brace *was* keeping an eye on her, he probably wouldn't dare confront her again.

So she'd hurried out to her car and returned to the house, parked behind it like before, and rushed upstairs.

This time, there'd been no hesitation.

She'd hopped into the coffin, stripped, slipped into the negligee, sat down on the bottom of the coffin, set the timer for thirty minutes, then stretched out and shut her eyes.

She hadn't fallen asleep immediately.

She could remember thinking, I might be a lot of things, Brace old pal, but I'm no quitter.

And she was pretty sure that, just before falling asleep, she had called into the silence of the dark house, 'Hey, Mog, I'm back!'

Jane put the timer down. She looked at her wrist-watch.

Nine thirty-five.

Fine. No problem. Plenty of time to drive home and shower and grab a bite to eat before going to work.

Now if I can find the envelope . . .

Jane got to her feet. Standing on the smooth satin pad, she stretched and moaned. Then she took off the negligee. She rolled it into a small bundle, planning to take it home with her, certain that Mog meant for her to keep it.

She knew that Mog might be peering at her. She supposed it didn't matter, though.

Squatting, she set down the negligee. She reached under the pillow, found her pistol and put it on top of the gown. It mashed the bundle almost flat. Her flashlight was beside the pillow. She slid it closer to the other things.

Unable to spot her switchblade knife, she remembered that she'd left it in the pocket of her cords.

That's everything, she thought, and stood up.

Again, she yawned and stretched. She felt awfully good.

Muscles a little sore, but taut. The softness of the breeze.

I ought to be feeling miserable, she thought. All that with Brace . . . But I'm okay. I feel better than okay.

Maybe because I had the guts to come back. And it's a wonderful morning. And I'm free. And I'm about to lay my mitts on gobs of money.

Hands on hips, Jane turned slowly, scanning the room for the envelope.

'I came through for you, Mog,' she said. 'I hope you held up your end of the deal.'

A few moments later, she said, 'You're gonna make me search for it, huh?'

Kneeling, she reached over the side of the coffin. She gathered the piled clothes between her arms, lifted them, turned, and brought them in with her. As she lowered them, they brushed against her thighs.

And something scratched her skin.

For an instant, she wondered if her knife had once again sprung open on its own.

She placed the bundle of clothes in front of her knees,

glimpsed the thin pale mark on one leg, then reached down and found a stiff point of something between her folded corduroy pants and her shirt.

Not the tip of her knife, at all.

The sharp corner of an envelope.

'All right!'

She slipped the envelope out. And there was her hand-written name.

This envelope felt twice as thick as the last one.

Jane tore it open and pulled out a thick stack of bills wrapped in a single sheet of lined paper.

She ignored the note.

All the bills were hundreds. She counted them.

Sixty-four!

Jane let out a whoop of joy. Which sounded horribly loud, and made her cringe.

She glanced at the two windows overlooking the graveyard. The panes of both were shattered, of course.

Her delighted shout could've carried down to the cemetery.

What if a grounds keeper had heard it? Or grave diggers?

What if a graveside funeral service is going on down there and *everyone* heard it?

Fast as she could, she slipped into her shoes. She leaped from the coffin and ran for the nearest window. Wary of being spotted, she hunkered down at the last moment. Then she straightened up, raising her head above the sill.

Nobody seemed to be down there.

But she wanted to make sure, so she stayed at the window and kept on looking. She could almost *feel* someone down there.

Maybe the creep who threw the dog . . .

It's probably just my imagination, she told herself. From this height, she could see the entire cemetery. The distant parking lot was empty. Nobody was mowing the grass, or tending to flowers, or visiting the grave of a loved one. Nobody was there at all, unless they were hidden from view behind a monument or vault or bush or tree.

Or hiding at the bottom of that hole way over there by the corner of the fence.

Not a hole, Jane thought, a *grave*. An open grave. Which must mean somebody's getting buried today.

I've gotta haul my butt outa here!

She hurried back to the coffin. She didn't step in, this time, but stood beside it and ducked down to pick up her clothes. When she was dressed, she stuffed the pockets of her corduroys with the pistol, flashlight, and thick wad of cash.

Six thousand, four hundred bucks, she thought. Incredible. Next time, it'll be twelve thousand, eight hundred.

God knows what he'll make me do for that kind of money.

Reaching into the coffin, she picked up the note and the empty envelope. She had already decided not to read Mog's message until she got home.

Whatever it might say, she wasn't ready for it.

She slipped the note and envelope into a pocket of her shirt.

Then she reached into the coffin and took out the negligee.

A souvenir of my most humiliating experience, she thought.

A souvenir of the night I lost Brace.

She was halfway down the stairs when she suddenly unfurled the garment and, making whimpery noises and grunts, tore it to shreds.

Chapter Twenty-four

Dearest Jane,

You're far better off without the insufferable lout. Who needs him? Am I right?

We have each other.

We have the Game.

Who could ask for anything more?

I will be in touch. In the meantime, rest and heal.

> Love,
> MOG

P.S.   I kissed you as you slept, my sweet,
In the casket in my lair.
I kissed you here, I kissed you there –
I kissed you almost everywhere.

She had planned to save the note and read it after her bath. Pulling out the envelope while emptying her pockets in the bedroom, however, she had changed her mind.

Stunned, she read it twice.

She thought, I can't handle this. Huh-uh. No way.

She dropped the note and it drifted to the floor.

Then she took a bath. Sprawled in the hot water, she rubbed herself thoroughly with a bar of soap.

Did he really do it? she wondered. Kiss me? Here and there and almost everywhere? Maybe he's just kidding about that. But he sure had the opportunity. He did sneak over to the coffin while I was asleep. That's how the envelope got there. So maybe he really kissed me. Here and there and almost everywhere. While I was zoned, dead to the world.

What else did he do to me!

Probably nothing else, or he would've bragged about that, too.

But it sickened her to think that a stranger's mouth had been on her while she slept.

You sure Mog counts as a stranger? she wondered. We've never met, but we've sure been in touch . . .

He's been in touch with *me*.

And touched me, unless he's kidding about that.

So we aren't exactly strangers.

Sure. Right. He's been kissing me all over the place and I don't even know what he looks like. I don't know if he's handsome or repulsive. For all I know, he might be a skulking horror with rotten teeth and runny sores.

And even if he's the best-looking, most wonderful specimen of man to ever stride the Earth, he's got no business messing with someone who's asleep.

Sick. Perverted.

Perverted? Give me a break, bucko! This is the guy who set a Rottweiler on you and made you stretch out damn near naked in a coffin that looked a hell of a lot like a USED coffin and it's coming as some sort of big surprise to you that he might be a bit of a pervert? Get real. If you're very lucky, maybe he did nothing worse than stick his tongue in you.

And I asked for it, she told herself. What does that say about me?

Says I'm either stupid or crazy.

Brace was right – I didn't know where to draw the line. Which still didn't give him any right to interfere.

'You really blew it,' she muttered.

Done with her bath, Jane considered phoning Don to tell him she was too sick to make it in for work today. This being Saturday, with the library closed on Sunday and Monday, she would be giving herself a three-day weekend.

Three whole days for doing only what she wanted.

She wanted only to go to bed and stay there.

Wanted to sleep and forget about everything that had happened with Brace and with the dog and with the bums by the creek – sleep and stop worrying that the Game might be over.

The note had said, 'I'll be in touch.' Sounded a lot like a brush-off. Maybe Mog ran out of money, Jane thought. Or maybe he got tired of playing . . . or tired of me.

Or the Game simply ended – ran its course, whatever that might've been, and came to its natural conclusion.

If it's over, why didn't he just say so?

Who knows?

It probably isn't over. 'We have each other. We have the Game. Who could ask for anything more?' That doesn't sound like a guy calling the Game off.

This is just an intermission.

He wants to give me a night or two off, that's all.

Knows I've been through a lot. Knows I need to rest and heal.

I can use it, she thought. I can really use it.

Since Mog apparently wouldn't be sending her on a mission tonight, Jane decided against calling in sick. She would go to work as usual, then come straight home after closing the library, and hit the sack, and not have to be back at work until noon on Tuesday.

She still had time for a meal before getting dressed and heading for work, so she went into the kitchen. She planned to make coffee, bacon and eggs, and toast.

She made only the coffee and two slices of toast.

The rest seemed like too much effort.

After buttering her toast, she didn't even feel up to bothering with jelly.

Without jelly, the crusts were too dry. She ate only the centers of her toast. They were soggy with butter and tasted very good.

Jane's day at the Donnerville Public Library was marked by all that didn't happen.

She didn't pull out of the daze that made her feel dull in the head and body.

A surprise envelope from Mog didn't appear.

She didn't get any sleep, even though she tried during her lunch hour, shutting the office door and closing the blinds and putting her head down on her desk.

Brace didn't phone her.

She didn't eat.

Brace didn't show up.

She didn't phone him.

She didn't ask Don to keep her company when it came time to go upstairs and close the stacks.

All alone in the gloom of the stacks, she didn't feel afraid.

* * *

On her way home from work, Jane stopped at the drive-up window of the Jack in the Box and ordered three tacos.

When she got home, Brace wasn't there.

She searched her house, looking for an envelope from Mog.

She changed into her robe, took a beer out of the refrigerator, and sat down on the living room sofa to watch TV and eat her tacos.

She could only eat one taco. It seemed dry and tasteless, and she had trouble swallowing it at all.

She doubted very much that it was the taco's fault.

She took the two remaining tacos into the kitchen and put them in the refrigerator. While there, she grabbed herself another beer.

She drank a total of four beers, and woke up to find herself sprawled on the sofa, all the lights on, a movie on the TV that she recognized as *The White Zombie* with Bela Lugosi, her neck stiff, her head splitting, her blood vessels buzzing, her bladder feeling huge and about to burst.

The way her bladder was, she couldn't stand up straight. She could hardly walk.

But she made it to the bathroom, finally, in time to save herself.

When she finished on the toilet, she found herself to be wide awake. She looked at her wristwatch as she staggered to the sink.

This time last night, she'd already been caught by Brace and was on her way home.

She wondered what Brace was doing right now.

Probably sleeping, if he's got any sense.

Maybe Mog is sleeping, too. That could be the real reason he called a stop to the Game – he needs some rest, himself. Even God rested on the seventh day.

On the other hand, this *is* Saturday night. Well, Sunday morning by now. Maybe the fellas are out on the town with dates, or something.

'Both my guys,' she said to herself in the mirror, and shook her head. 'Former guys,' she corrected. 'Brace and Moggie, gone with the fucking wind.'

She washed her face. She brushed her teeth. She swallowed two Excedrin PM tablets with a fizzy glassful of Alka-Seltzer, then made the rounds of the house to turn off the TV and lights.

Can't make a habit of this crap, she told herself as she headed for her bedroom. I'll turn into a drunken old sow.

So who cares, anyhow?

She flicked off her bedroom light. Halfway across the dark floor, she shrugged off her robe and let it fall. She crawled onto her bed and clawed the covers down.

Between the sheets, she sighed.

'Ain't life grand,' she muttered.

But she had to admit that it was good to be back in her own bed. It had no satin sheets, but it wasn't a coffin.

She woke up Sunday morning sprawled on top of the sheets with sunlight shining on her from the window beside her bed, and a breeze caressing her like feathers. She had no headache. She felt very fine until she remembered about Brace.

This was the day she and Brace had planned to spend together.

Would he do anything about it? Phone, or maybe come over?

He might.

He probably will. He'll apologize and I'll forgive him, and we'll take it from there. Maybe we'll go on a picnic.

Feeling good again, Jane got out of bed.

Her robe lay in a heap on the floor. She picked it up, put it on, then checked its pockets in the hope of finding an envelope from Mog. The pockets were empty.

So she searched through the house.

She started in her bedroom, then went out into the hallway and checked the closets and bathroom before heading into the living room. She crouched, stood on tiptoes, searched on shelves and cupboards. Looked for an envelope from Mog in the very same sorts of places where, as a child an hour's drive from here, she had searched on Easter Sundays for the treats hidden about the house by the Easter bunny.

She never failed to find loads and loads of candy eggs and bunnies.

This morning, she had no success at all in finding an envelope left by Mog.

Probably because he didn't leave one, Jane thought.

Still hopeful, she went outside. The sun felt hot, but a nice breeze was blowing and it made her robe slide softly against her skin. She hadn't put on shoes. The concrete stoop and driveway were hot under her feet. The grass was cool and still wet from last night's dew.

She walked completely around her house. Twice.

No envelope.

Back inside, she felt sad and lonely. She placed a phone call to her parents. As she listened to the ringing, she remembered that they'd planned a trip to Lake Tahoe for this weekend.

She hung up.

She stared at the phone.

Call Brace?

I can't. It's up to him. He's the one who screwed up, so he's gotta be the one to make the next move. Besides, maybe he doesn't want to see me again.

Yeah, and maybe I don't want to see him, either.

She wondered how she would feel if she had to face him.

We'll find out, she told herself. We'll probably find out pretty soon, too.

Jane spent all day waiting for Brace to call or show up at her house.

While she waited, she went about her business. She ate, did a load of laundry, read a book, watched television, vacuumed the floor. She thought about phoning some of her friends in Mill Valley, but didn't want to tie up the phone in case Brace should call. She thought about taking a walk, or driving to the mall or the video rental store, but didn't want to leave the house.

The day passed very slowly.

Night came.

By nine o'clock, Jane had lost all hope that Brace would call or arrive.

I was kidding myself, she thought, to think he might. It's over with him.

At least I've still got the Game, she told herself.

'Oh, yeah?'

I *will* still have the game, if Mog ever gets over this stupid idea of giving me a rest period. If that's really what's even going on.

'It'll be okay,' she said, nodding at the television. 'He'll come through for me. He won't let me down like certain dirty creeps I could mention.'

I've just gotta figure out how to kill the time till he gets back to me.

At midnight, she left the house.

She had no mission from Mog. She carried no purse or flashlight or weapons.

She left the house dressed in her tank top, gym shorts, crew socks and running shoes. She wore her wristwatch. A key to her house was tucked inside the top of one sock.

She walked briskly along the street for a while, loosening up, getting used to the notion of being out on her own at this time of the night with nowhere special to go.

No envelope full of money waiting somewhere up ahead. No bizarre or dangerous task, either.

Which doesn't mean I have to stay home, she told herself. Just because Mog hasn't got a mission for me, I don't have to sit home and rot.

Leaning forward slightly, she picked up her knees and began to run. She ran slowly at first, then quickened her pace, pumping her arms, swinging her legs out longer and faster until she was sprinting along the roadside. It felt wonderful. The speed, the mild night air blowing against her, the smooth feel of her muscles at work.

Too soon, the fine feelings turned to misery. Her lungs burned. Her muscles grew sore and tight and heavy. Sweat stung her eyes. The sweet night air became the breath of an oven.

She quit running and walked – grimacing, huffing, drenched with sweat.

Gradually, her body recovered. She found herself ready to run again. Instead of sprinting, however, she tried a moderate jogging pace. It lacked the thrill of an all-out dash, but it didn't demolish her. She was able to maintain a good, steady pace for a long time before succumbing again.

She hadn't started out with a destination in mind.

The idea was simply to run in the night. To run as hard and as far as she could.

Slowing down for a breather, however, she saw that she was just across the street from the university campus.

The gates of the chainlink enclosure were secured with a new chain. This chain seemed to have no broken links. So Jane climbed the high fence, dangled from its top, and dropped to the other side.

Within the enclosure were vague, dim shapes in the moonlight and darkness. Familiar shapes: the Porta-potties, the tractor mower, the bird bath, the statue of David, the maze of Doric columns off in the corner. They looked just the same as they had looked on Tuesday night when she had been here with Brace.

But there was a big difference, too.

Nothing seemed menacing or strange or dangerous.

It was a familiar, comfortable place to be.

Jane climbed the statue of Crazy Horse and sat behind the chief on the stiff shelf of his unfurled loincloth. She leaned forward against his back. Her hands held him by the sides. Her knees pressed against his hips. The bronze was hard and cool against her.

Chapter Twenty-five

Monday was easier for Jane.

Since Brace hadn't gotten in touch with her yesterday, a day they'd set aside for being together, the chances of a call or visit from him today were slim.

Worse than slim.

So she didn't wait around for him. After getting up late in the morning, she skipped breakfast and went to the Donnerville Fashion Mall.

As she wandered from shop to shop, it dawned on her that she could afford to buy *anything* she saw. I really could, she thought. There was probably nothing in the entire mall that cost as much as $12,550 – her take, so far, from the Game. She hadn't brought that much with her, of course. She'd brought five hundred of it, and left the rest hidden at home.

The five hundred dollars in her purse felt like a fortune.

What'll I do with it? she wondered.

Buy a wheelchair, maybe.

Oh, it's not quite that bad. Almost, but not quite.

With every step, Jane's body ached. The aches came from muscles that had been worked hard. They reminded her of the running. They reminded her that she was becoming stronger, slimmer.

In a sporting goods shop, she bought new running shoes, a pair of shiny blue shorts, and a gray tank top. She also bought two iron weights that looked like miniature barbells and weighed twelve pounds each.

She carried her purchases out to the parking lot, shut them in the trunk of her car, and returned to the mall.

She bought two blouses, one skirt, pajamas that were royal blue and shiny like satin, three pairs of panties that were very sexy and expensive and that she doubted anyone but her would ever see, and a bikini that she intended to wear nowhere except inside her fenced back yard.

She hurried on to the bookstore, and helped herself to eight paperbacks she'd put off buying for several weeks.

It's great to have money, she thought.

At the food court, she ate cashew chicken.

Then she left the mall and drove across the road to the Cineplex. She bought a ticket, but she avoided the refreshment stand.

By the time the movie ended, she was eager to get home.

It came as a disappointment, but no surprise, that Brace wasn't at the house waiting for her.

The mail had arrived. It didn't include a letter from Mog.

Without an answering machine, she didn't know whether Brace had called. She doubted it, though.

'Ask me if I care,' she muttered.

She wandered about the house, looking here and there just to make sure Mog hadn't left a new envelope for her. It was a casual search, however; she didn't really expect to find one.

A glance out the kitchen window showed sunlight on the patio. Jane picked the book she was most eager to start, then snipped the tags off her new bikini. She changed in her bedroom. And stared at her image in the mirror.

She supposed she had always wanted a bikini like this. Never dared, though. Afraid someone might see her in it.

After the negligee from Mog, this thing seemed downright modest. The shiny blue fabric didn't cover much, but at least it hid the little that it covered.

She wondered if she would ever have the guts to wear it to the beach.

Not till I've lost three scabs, fifteen bruises and ten more pounds.

Not even then, she admitted.

In the bathroom, she rubbed sunblock over her skin. Then she washed the goo off her hands, grabbed an old blanket, put on her sunglasses, picked up her paperback, and went out the back door.

She spread her blanket on the grass and stretched out on

it. Propped up on her elbows, she tried to read. But her mind refused to stay on the story. After a while, she set the book aside, sank down against the blanket and folded her arms beneath her face.

The heat of the sun seemed to melt the soreness out of her muscles. She thought about reaching back to untie her bikini top, but she couldn't bring herself to move. She felt too comfortable and lazy.

Oughta, she told herself. Better yet, take it off – Brace'd be *sure* to show up, then. The guy has a talent for catching me without my clothes on. I try a little nude sun-bathing, and he'll be johnny-on-the-spot.

Last thing I need. Shocked him once too often, already. Guy thinks I'm nuts and about half a rung up from being a whore.

Thanks a heap, Mog.

Hey, don't blame Mog. He didn't force me into that coffin. Or into that nightie.

Brace's fault. He should've stayed away.

Comes when he's supposed to stay away, stays away when he's supposed to come.

Like now.

The hell with him. The hell with him, anyway. If he cared about me at all, he would've come over yesterday.

Anyway, who needs him? Nobody, that's who.

Then she imagined Brace climbing over the gate at the side of her house and coming into the back yard and seeing her there on the blanket, stretched out shiny in the sunlight. She saw his smile and the look in his eyes.

'I had to come,' he says. 'I've missed you so much, Jane. I couldn't stay away any longer, I just couldn't.'

'I've been waiting for you,' she tells him.

Kneeling over her, he kisses the nape of her neck. Then he unties her bikini top and begins to massage her bare shoulders and back. His hands slide on her slippery skin.

Jane woke up. The weight of the sun seemed to be pressing her against the blanket. She was drenched with sweat. The sweat slid and ran as she rolled over and flopped onto her back.

Shouldn't fall asleep again, she warned herself. Don't wanta burn.

She tried to sit up, but felt as if all her energy had been sucked out.

In her mind, she was sprawled on a beach, the sky pale blue overhead, gulls swooping and squawking, combers washing ashore with a steady, hushed easiness. She heard the song, 'Surfer Girl.'

She woke up feeling renewed. Roasted and basted, but full of energy. She sat up, spilling sweat down her body. The dribbles made her itch. She wiped them off with slippery hands, then scurried into the house.

In the bathroom, she dried herself with a towel. Her hair was a jumble of wet coils, her skin flushed, her bikini dark with moisture and clinging.

Jane liked the way she looked.

Wild surfer girl.

It's only a start, she told herself. A couple more weeks, and there'll *really* be a difference. Brace won't even recognize me.

Forget him, will you? Just forget him.

I'm doing this for myself, not for Brace.

With the towel draped over her shoulders, she went to the living room and picked up her new weights. She carried them outside. Standing in a shaded area close to the side of the house, she began to work with them.

She'd had no training, so she used her imagination and lifted them in every way that popped into her head. By the time she finished, she was breathless, again dripping sweat, and her muscles ached all over her arms and shoulders and neck and chest and armpits.

She set the weights down, and returned to the blanket. It was still moist. She lay on it and began doing sit-ups and toe touches and leg lifts. As with the weights, she improvised.

When she was done, she couldn't move for a while.

Finally, she struggled to her feet. She wiped herself all over with the towel, then hung the towel and blanket on a line to dry.

In the shower, she kept her bikini on for a while. Then she peeled it off, wrung it out and draped it over the top of the shower doors. Her skin was slightly rosy except where the skimpy garment had kept the sun away. The pale areas looked stark. And a little sickly, she thought.

No big deal, she told herself. Who's gonna notice?

Besides, most of the color wouldn't last. It would fade, and so would the rather startling contrast.

After her shower, Jane made herself a tall vodka and tonic loaded with ice. She sat on the sofa and swung her legs up. Drink in one hand, book in the other, she boarded The Busted Flush with Travis McGee.

Who's McGee gonna nurse back to physical and emotional health this time? she wondered.

Poor bird. Whoever she is, she's bound to end up dead.

At midnight, wearing her new running shoes, shorts and top, Jane left her house.

She walked with long, quick strides. The muscles in her legs and buttocks felt stiff and sore. With every step, they seemed to bunch and slide underneath her skin.

Then she tried to run.

After a few strides, she gasped, 'Oh, my God,' and stopped. No more running tonight; her legs and arms couldn't stand it.

At least I can still walk, she told herself.

Where to?

Doesn't matter.

No orders from Mog, so it's my choice. All up to me. Free to go where I wish.

She could think of nowhere she wanted to go, but decided that she didn't need a destination. It was enough to be outside and on the move, getting exercise, wearing off calories, enjoying the sweetness and mysteries of the night.

Only now and then did a car go by. Most of the houses

along the street were dark except for porch lights. She supposed that people were asleep inside – or trying to sleep. From many of the houses came the noisy hum of air conditioning units. From a few, she heard music or voices.

People were in houses all around her.

Most sleeping. A few awake. Probably all of them strangers.

If any look out and see me passing by, she thought, they'll wonder who I am and where I'm going. Some are sure to think I'm crazy to be out alone at this time of night. Or up to no good. Some will probably envy me and wish they were doing it, too.

They might like to be out, but they stay safe in their homes.

And watch me go by. And wonder.

And know they're not as free as me.

This is so great, she thought. Why haven't I been going out every night like this?

Wouldn't have dreamed of it before Mog.

Back when I was sensible – and afraid of so much.

Look at all I was missing!

Then she heard the quick smack of footfalls coming at her from behind.

Jeez, I'm gonna get nailed! So much for a whole new life featuring midnight walks.

The rushing footsteps bore down on her. Someone running, panting.

Just a jogger?

Look and see. Maybe it's Brace.

Yeah, right, sure. More likely Rale or some other brand of demented creep. Maybe with a knife he's eager to plant in my back.

All the more reason to look.

Jane swiveled and twisted her head. The man, only a few strides away, was young and shirtless, dressed in shorts and running shoes, apparently nothing worse than a jogger. He gasped, 'Hi.'

'Hi,' she told him, and stepped off the sidewalk to make room for him to pass.

But he didn't pass. He stopped and faced her. 'Warm night,' he said. Huffing for air, he put his hands on his hips, lowered his head, and shook one of his legs. Then he raised and shook the other leg. He met Jane's eyes. 'You're the librarian, aren't you?'

Great. He knows me.

'That's right,' she said.

'Thought so. You live near here?'

He sounded friendly, but Jane didn't trust him. 'Not very far away. How about you?'

'Over on Plymouth. By the way, I'm Scott.'

'I'm Jane.'

'I've seen you at the library.'

Have I seen him? she wondered. He looked somewhat familiar, but she supposed there must be plenty of men in town with a similar appearance: average height, slim build, neatly trimmed dark hair, and a face that was pleasant but hardly memorable.

'You sure don't look much like a librarian,' he said.

'Ah, well . . .'

'Bet you get that a lot, don't you?'

'On occasion.'

'Are you going anywhere special?'

Jane shrugged.

'Well, what-say we team up for a while? Do you mind?'

'I'm not running,' she said.

'That's okay. I'll walk with you.'

She shrugged. She didn't want him walking with her, wanted to be rid of him, wanted her solitude back. But she couldn't bring herself to refuse. 'All right,' she said. 'We can walk for a while, I guess.'

She stepped onto the walkway and started out.

'You set the pace,' Scott said, matching her stride.

'Thanks.'

'You do this much?' he asked.

'Do what?'

'Go for walks. This time of night.'

Wonderful, she thought. He's hoping we can make it a regular thing. Just what I'd need.

'No,' she said. 'I'm usually asleep by now.'

'Not me. I'm a real night hawk.'

He means 'night owl,' Jane thought, but decided not to correct him.

'You don't need to be at a job in the morning?' she asked.

'Not me.'

'Oh? What do you do?'

'Sleep in.'

'Ah,' she said. Let it drop, she told herself. If he wants to be coy about his employment, if any, that's fine with me. 'So,' she said, 'I take it you're a bank robber.'

Oh, well. What the hell.

He laughed.

The sort of laugh that seemed to say, 'I did notice the attempt at humor, babe, but it dropped well short of the mark. Nevertheless, I'm quite the sport. I give you credit for the try.'

'Guess again,' he said.

'I'll pass.'

'Aren't you the least bit curious?'

'I'd be happy to hear what you do for a living, if you want to tell me. But it doesn't matter. You can let it drop, no big deal.'

He grinned. 'As a matter of fact, I don't work at all. I'm a man of leisure.'

'Ah.'

'Fabulously wealthy.'

'No fooling?'

'I kid you not.'

'Are you sure you're not a used car salesman?'

That laugh again.

'Trust me,' he said, 'I'm fabulously wealthy.'

Jane grinned at him. 'Do you know what? It's been proven by scientific studies that ninety-nine point nine per cent of the time, the words "trust me" precede a bald-faced lie.'

Scott grinned back at her. 'Are you calling me a liar?'

'No, of course not. Trust me.'

'I bet you get into a lot of trouble with that mouth of yours.'

'Oh, on occasion.'

'But do you know what? I like a girl with spirit. How would you like to come over to my place? We'll kick back and sip a little *vino*, get to know each other . . .'

'Are you serious?'

'A ten-minute walk from here . . .'

'Well, thanks anyway. But A, I hardly know you; B, it's after midnight; C, I don't go into stranger's houses.' That's a good one, she thought. 'D, all of the above.'

E, I don't like you much.

'I'm not just some fellow trying to pick you up, you know.'

'Ah.'

'I wish you wouldn't say that so often.'

'What?'

'Ah.'

'Ah.'

'It's . . . condescending.'

'I see. But what about that "spirit" of mine you like so much?'

'I don't enjoy being mocked.'

'Ah.'

'Or called a liar.'

'I never called you a liar. What I did, I mocked you for saying, "Trust me." You may very well be so rich you've got money coming out your wazoo, but "trust me" is a very annoying thing to say. I kid you not.'

'You're beginning to wear a bit thin.'

'Then you won't want me coming over to your place, will you?'

'I didn't say that. The offer stands.'

'If you don't like being mocked . . .'

'You can be trained.'

'Oh. I like the sound of that. Are you talking about whips?'

'Gentler arts of persuasion.'

'Ah. What do you do, troll the streets at night looking for gals to take home?'

'This is a first.'

'Oh, sure.'

'What do you say?'

'Not interested. Thanks, anyway.'

'I'll pay you.'

The words kicked away Jane's bluster. She stopped walking. She gaped at him. He grinned back at her.

'You'll pay me?' she asked, hardly able to lift her voice above a whisper.

'That's what I said.'

'Oh, my God.'

'Cash money. A lot of it.'

'Who are you?'

He raised his eyebrows.

'Are you him?'

'Who?'

'Mog?'

His grin stretched. 'Let's go to my house and talk about it.'

He took hold of Jane's arm, but she jerked it away. 'Not so damn fast, sport. *Are* you Mog, or aren't you?'

'That all depends, doesn't it?'

'Knock off the games.'

'Okay, I admit it. I'm him. Of course I'm him. Now, let's walk over to my . . .'

'What does Mog stand for?'

'Truth, justice, and the American way?'

'M-O-G.'

Without a moment of hesitation, he said, 'Man of God.'

Is he joking around, she wondered, or doesn't he know?

'Memories of Grandeur?' he suggested. 'Multiple Orgasms Granted? Meal of Guts?'

'Okay, cut it out.'

'Master of . . . Gonads?'

'If you're him, tell me. Tell me, or I'm leaving right now.'

'I already told you,' he said.

'Make me believe.'

He smirked. 'Forget it. If you want to leave, fine. Nobody's stopping you. I just thought you might want to come with me and have a good time and make yourself a little spending cash, okay?'

'Why me?' she asked.

'Why not?'

'Why?'

'Because you're here,' he said. 'And I like the looks of you.'

'That's all?'

'Is there supposed to be more?'

'Yeah.'

'I like your spirit,' he reminded her.

'Only not very much,' she pointed out.

'I bet you're fierce in bed. A tiger.'

'You'll never find out.'

'Five hundred dollars says I will.'

'You'll pay me five hundred dollars to sleep with you?'

'Sleep isn't exactly what I have in mind.'

'Ah.'

'Five hundred smackaroos.'

'I thought you were supposed to be fabulously wealthy.'

'Five hundred's a lot of money.'

'Not nearly enough.'

'You think you're worth more than that?'

'I'd say so.'

'You're dreaming.' He laughed at her, and jogged away.

Chapter Twenty-six

Stunned, Jane watched him run down the sidewalk. Her throat was tight and she had tears in her eyes.

'Bastard,' she muttered.

How could he say that to me? *You're dreaming*.

Bastard was cut from the same cloth as that filthy son-of-a-bitch, Ken.

As he turned the corner at the end of the block, his head swung toward Jane and he raised his arm and jabbed his middle finger at the sky.

Same to you, bud, she thought.

A moment later, he vanished down the sidestreet.

'Good riddance to bad rubbish,' she said.

She considered turning around and heading for home.

If I do that, she told herself, I'm nothing but a quitter. Why should I let a creep like him ruin my night?

So she wiped her eyes, then continued with her walk.

How come he offered me money in the first place? she wondered. Does it show? Have I got it scribbled on my forehead, 'This gal does weird stuff for cash?'

I won't do *anything*, though, will I? Guess I proved that.

Hey, Brace, there *are* some limits after all, huh? Some lines I won't cross?

But a small voice in Jane's head whispered, Maybe, or maybe the guy just didn't make the offer tempting enough. Five hundred is a pretty meager sum when you've got more than twelve thousand at home. Suppose he'd gone to a thousand? Or ten thousand?

We'll never know.

We'll never know because I'm not worth any more than five hundred bucks. I'm *dreaming* if I think I'm worth any more than that.

'What a piece of scum,' she said.

* * *

Soon, Jane found herself across the street from the university. She was tempted to head for Crazy Horse.

Not tonight, she told herself. Do it again tonight, and next thing you know, you'll be going there every night.

Why not? It's so nice and safe inside the fence, and it's wonderful to be up there high on the statue. It's like having a special tree to climb and hide in. But the statue feels so much better than a tree. It's cool and smooth.

And it's where I went with Brace.

Our special place.

All the more reason *not* to go there.

She didn't cross. Instead, she walked straight ahead, leaving the campus behind, and two blocks later came to Standhope Street.

She gazed up at the sign.

She suddenly felt shaky.

So this is where Standhope is, she thought.

As if you didn't know.

I didn't know. I had an idea it might be over here in this general vicinity, but I didn't know. And I for sure don't remember Brace's address. It's not like I came out on purpose to look for where he lives.

I'm not an idiot. I would've brought his card along. Or at least made an effort to memorize the address.

She turned her head, looking both ways. Just down the street to her right was the business district. Brace wasn't likely to reside in that direction. To her left, the street was mostly bordered by apartment buildings.

Closer to the university, too.

Jane chose that direction, crossed the road, and began wandering along Standhope.

This is nuts, she thought. What if I *do* find where he lives?

Don't worry. Not much chance of that.

Anyway, I'm not *trying* to find it. I'm just out for a little exercise and fresh air, and I happen to be strolling down Standhope Street.

I don't even *want* to find it.

Who cares where he lives?

In this section of town, there seemed to be a lot of activity in spite of the late hour. Cars went by. Quite a few young men and women were out walking. Loud music thumped from many of the apartment windows. She heard laughter and shouts.

If Brace lives in the middle of all this, she thought, how does he ever get any sleep?

How does anybody?

She checked her wristwatch. Five after one.

What time do things settle down around here, anyway?

She stepped aside to make way for an approaching threesome: a girl supported by two fellows. They were swaying, stumbling, laughing. Jane supposed they must be drunk.

The girl in the middle, arms around the shoulders of the boys, wore a big floppy hat and earrings that were peace symbols. Her T-shirt read: 'SAVE A TREE, EAT A BEAVER'. The shirt was pocked with gaping holes that showed her skin. It ended halfway down her belly. Her denim mini-skirt hung very low on her hips. She wore fishnet stockings and white cowgirl boots.

The boys under her arms didn't look nearly so flamboyant. One wore a white polo shirt and matching shorts and shoes. The other was shirtless, jeans hanging, the white waistband of his underwear on display.

'Top of the evening to you!' the girl greeted Jane.

'And to you. Could I ask you something?'

The trio halted and swiveled. 'We are at your service,' said the girl. 'Ask, and ye shall receive.'

They *aren't* drunk, Jane realized, now that she could see their faces in the lights from the apartment building. They looked too alert to be drunk or stoned. Just kids goofing around.

'I'm looking for a friend,' Jane said.

'We'll be your friends,' the girl announced.

691

'Join in,' said the shirtless guy, offering his empty arm.

'Thanks, but that isn't . . . I have a friend who's a student and I know she lives on Standhope, but I lost her address. I didn't think I'd have any trouble finding her place, but now that I'm here . . .' She shook her head. 'I was over at her place last month, but things look so different at night.'

'They do,' the girl agreed. '*Everything* looks different at night.'

'Especially the sky,' said the guy in the polo shirt.

'The sky, my eye,' the girl said. '*Most* especially, the face of reality.'

'I'm just having trouble with these apartment buildings,' Jane interrupted. 'Maybe you can tell me which one she's in. If you know her.'

'What's her name?' asked the shirtless guy.

Jane hadn't gotten to the point of thinking up a name for her non-existent friend. So she said, 'Jane. Jane Masters.'

The girl frowned. 'Masters, Masters.'

'Jane Masters.'

'I know a Jean Masterson,' offered the shirtless guy.

'This is Jane Masters.'

The girl turned her head from side to side, asking, 'Bill? Steve?' Both of her friends looked puzzled and shook their heads. She faced Jane. 'Afraid we don't know anyone by that name.'

'Well, thanks for . . . hey!' Jane blurted. 'I just thought of something. Last time I was there, she introduced me to a member of the faculty who lives in the same building. A guy. An English teacher, I think. He had a name like . . . Patton, or maybe . . .' She shook her head.

'Paxton?' the girl asked.

'That might be it! Paxton?'

'Light brown hair? Semi-gorgeous?'

'Sounds like him. His place was right next to Jane's, so if you . . .'

'I just happen to know exactly where he lives,' the girl said. 'Followed him home a couple of times. Such a cute butt.'

Steve in the polo shirt scowled. 'Men do *not* have cute butts.'

'Disgusting,' agreed Bill.

'Appalling,' added Steve.

'Wrong,' said Jane.

'Three blocks straight ahead,' the girl said. 'I can't give you the address, but the place is called the Royal Gardens. Sort of a fancy-ass name, but what're you gonna do? My name's Splendor, can't get much more fancy-ass than that.'

'What's in a name?' Jane said.

'Precisely.'

'Splendor is a splendid name,' said Steve.

'Well,' Jane said, 'thanks for the help.'

'The pleasure was ours,' Splendor said. 'Delighted we could be of service.'

'Hope you find your friend,' Bill said.

'Thanks.' She stepped around them. 'Have fun.'

'We do,' Splendor told her.

Jane smiled as she watched the trio skip off down the sidewalk. And she laughed softly when they began to sing, 'We Three Kings.'

Christmas carols in June, she thought.

Youth.

As she started walking away and heard the singing voices fade, her amusement changed to a gentle feeling of sadness. She didn't know why. Maybe because Splendor and her friends had seemed so free and happy. Maybe because she knew they would only have a few such nights.

She wondered if they knew how special it was to be skipping along the sidewalk in the hours after midnight, arm in arm with true pals or lovers, talking nonsense and singing.

I could've gone with them, she thought.

Yeah, but I would've been an outsider. It's six or eight years too late for me to be playing the wild and goofy coed.

Truth be known, it wasn't all that great at the time.

Oh, it was pretty great.

But the past always looks better after you've left it far behind. Even the crummy stuff.

A few years from now, she thought, I might look back on tonight as being magic and wonderful.

Especially if things go nicely at Brace's place.

Just within the lighted entryway of the Royal Gardens, Jane found the name Paxton on the mail box for apartment #12. She opened the wrought iron gate, walked through the passageway and found herself in a courtyard that had a fairly large swimming pool.

She heard air conditioners, and music, and voices. Nothing loud, though.

All but a few of the windows were dark.

Nobody was wandering about the pool's concrete apron or the second-story balcony.

Nobody seemed to be in the pool. Its lights were out. Much of the surface glinted with reflections of the lights from the surrounding apartments. Somebody might be hiding in one of the dark places, but . . .

No big deal, she told herself. Who cares if I get seen? I'm not here to burglarize the joint.

Or murder anyone.

But why *am* I here? she wondered. There must be a reason. I sure went to a lot of trouble to find the place.

Curiosity. That's all. I just want to know where he lives. She the building and see his door and his window and maybe catch a glimpse of him.

That's all.

Is it?

Who the hell knows?

In a corner of the courtyard near the deep end of the pool, she found a 12 on a door. The curtains of the large picture window glowed with light.

He's up! Oh, my God!

Probably reading. He stays up till all hours reading, doesn't he? He's probably stretched out on his sofa with *Youngblood Hawke* on his lap.

In the very middle of the window was a vertical strip of light where the curtains didn't quite meet. Spotting it, Jane moaned. She gritted her teeth and pressed her legs together and rubbed her arms.

You don't do this sort of thing, she told herself. You don't peek in at somebody. Just go to the door and knock.

That's what I want, anyway. To have him open the door and see that I've come to him, and watch his face, and then step in and feel him take me into his arms and kiss me.

But what if he's asleep?

So what if he's asleep?

He'll think he's dreaming when he comes to the door and there I am.

Quietly, slowly, Jane stepped to the door of Brace's apartment. She stared at it. She grimaced.

Just do it! she told herself.

And raised her fist to knock.

What if he hates me?

He doesn't. Probably takes me for a money-grabbing idiot who'll do anything for a buck, but ... He's the one who screwed up. Followed me around, *spied* on me as if I was some sort of a criminal.

Lowering her arm, she looked over at the narrow space between the curtains.

Why not? she thought. Why the hell not? Turn-about's fair play. It'd serve him right.

She crept over to the window. The gap revealed very little as she approached it. Not until she stopped and leaned forward, brow to the glass, did the opening give her a good view into the apartment.

Her heart gave a rough lurch when she spotted him – sitting on the sofa, naked, his back toward her ...

No, that's not ...

What *is* that?

And then she knew what she was seeing. The naked back

belonged to a woman, a short-haired blonde kneeling on the sofa, sitting on Brace's lap, her legs wide apart and Brace's bare legs between them, Brace's thick shiny cock sticking straight up and disappearing into her, all of it vanishing as she sank down on him, then showing again as she raised herself.

Jane felt as if she'd been clubbed in the belly.

This is what I get. Never should've looked. This is what I get. The dirty rotten filthy fucking bastard!

She wanted to run away.

But she stayed.

Let's just see what the bitch looks like. Come on, turn around. Let's get a look at you.

Maybe it's someone I know.

That didn't seem likely. Except for patrons of the library, Jane hadn't met very many people. All her friends had been left behind when she moved here to take the job.

Never *should've* come here, she thought.

Who is she? Who is this miserable damn slut . . .?

Probably one of Brace's students. I'd bet on it. A dirty thing to do, fuck your students. Happens all the time, though. And what the hell, he's a guy. It's the sort of thing guys do. They're all so horny they'd fuck the crack of dawn.

Why should Brace be different.

But I thought he was.

Yeah? Well, watch him in action – giving one of his English majors a private lesson.

Come on, bitch, turn around. Let's see what you've got, huh?

Are you prettier? You got bigger tits?

Obviously, she was slimmer. She didn't need to turn around for that to be apparent. Jane could see the way her back tapered down to a slender waist before flaring out around the hips and rump.

She's not *all* that much thinner than me, Jane told herself. And I bet I'm stronger.

Yeah, she's skin and bones. Looks almost frail.

The cock came all the way out of her. Nobody reached down to do anything about it. The girl kept hold of Brace's shoulders, and his hands stayed out of sight – probably playing with her tits. The engorged head of his cock prodded her a few times, then found its way in and she sank down, taking all its length and thickness into her.

Jane groaned.

Stop watching! Stop it!

No. I've gotta see what she looks like from the front. See what's so special.

Try knocking on the window, Jane thought. She'll be sure to look around, if I give it a few good sharp raps.

Why not? Why the hell not?

They'll catch me, and they'll know I was watching, and . . .

So what? What's Brace gonna do about it, dump me?

Go on, do it!

No. That'd be crazy.

Suddenly, Jane heard voices from the other end of the courtyard. She scurried backward away from the window and looked toward the gate. Nobody there. Not yet. But she still heard the voices.

Male and female.

Probably another prof bringing home a student to screw.

Oh my God, I can't be caught here!

She twisted this way and that, looking for a place to hide. And spotted a lounge chair she might duck behind. But it was at the far side of the pool. No chance of getting to it in time.

Nowhere else to hide.

Nowhere close enough to reach in time.

Except for the pool, only a few paces away.

Jane rushed to it, sat down quickly and lowered her legs into the chilly water. She scooted forward until the edge of the poolside pressed into her rump. Then, hanging on to the edge, she eased herself down. The water climbed her body, wrapping it with cold.

When the water reached her waist, she turned herself around so she faced the wall. She lowered herself to the chin, took a deep breath and let go of the side. She went under. Motionless and limp, she waited. After a few moments, the water began to lift her. So she blew out some of her air and stopped rising.

Her lungs began to ache.

She wondered if it would be safe to rise.

They're probably inside an apartment by now, she told herself. But even if they haven't gone in, they aren't likely to spot me over in the corner here. Probably so dark here they wouldn't see me even if they looked.

But she decided to wait.

How about half a minute? Can I hang on for half a minute?

In her mind, she started counting slowly toward thirty.

By the count of ten, her lungs felt as if they were being squeezed by vices while fires blazed inside them.

At thirteen, she came up for air. She sucked in a deep breath with a gasp.

Hope nobody heard that!

Blinking water out of her eyes, she tried to breathe more quietly as she scanned the courtyard.

No sign of the intruders.

Curling her fingertips over the edge of the pool to hold herself high enough, she peered at Brace's window.

Just as well I had to run for cover, she thought. Otherwise, I'd still be standing there.

You can't go back, she told herself. Not without making puddles and footprints on the concrete. You sure don't want to leave tell-tale signs like that at his window.

What I'll have to do is climb out of the pool at the other end – put my trail as far from Brace's rooms as I can.

Screw it.

She boosted herself up, water sluicing down her body and splashing into the pool, then pattering on the concrete. Her shorts had been tugged halfway down her rump by the pool's suction as she popped out, so she pulled them up.

Her shoes made squelching noises with each step as she walked toward the window.

She thought, Who cares?

Why am I doing this? I know better!

She stopped just in front of the window and leaned forward until her dripping forehead touched the glass.

Guess I won't need to knock, she thought.

Because the girl was facing her – off the sofa and striding straight toward her, filling her view.

All Jane could see was the girl.

Tall and slender, wet coils of hair clinging to her brow and temples, sweat speckling her face, her skin ruddy around her mouth from too much kissing, blotches on her neck and shoulders and breasts from the suck of a mouth – Brace's mouth.

It isn't her face that got him, Jane thought. I'm a lot prettier.

Has to be her boobs.

Twice the size of mine.

They bounced and swung as she walked.

Gimme a break.

She reached up and grabbed the edges of the curtain, and started to pull them together, and happened to look straight forward – straight at Jane.

Who mashed her face against the glass and bared her teeth.

The girl's eyes bulged. Her mouth leaped open.

Jane listened to the muffled shriek as she sprinted alongside the pool.

Glancing every which way, she saw nobody look out any windows at her, no doors swing open.

If I'm quick enough . . .

Then she was hidden in the passageway.

Made it!

She opened the gate, stepped out, eased it shut, then dashed across the street and ducked behind a parked car. From there, she watched the front of the Royal Gardens. Nobody came rushing out.

She started walking. As she hurried away, she kept an eye on the gate of the apartment building. So far, so good.

At the first cross-street, she headed to the right.

Got away with it!

She let out a laugh.

'Did you hear that bitch scream?' she asked herself. 'Got her! Man, did I get her!' She laughed again.

Brace might figure out it was me, she thought.

So what? He can't *do* anything about it. And who gives a shit what he thinks of me, the filthy son-of-a-bitch? And I hope I scared the piss out of his hot little teenybopper slut.

Then Jane was crying, bawling as she walked along.

Don't be a twit, she told herself.

She kicked an empty beer can. It tumbled and skidded along the sidewalk. 'Hope his fuckin' dick drops off,' she muttered. After a sniffle, she added, 'Probably will, too. Asshole never heard of a rubber?'

Chapter Twenty-seven

Jane woke up, saw that she was in her own bedroom and the morning looked sunny outside her window. A beautiful day, she thought. But a cold, hollow feeling in her belly told her that the day was about to turn foul. Something really ugly had happened, and as soon as she could remember . . .

Oh.

Brace.

The sudden memory of what she'd seen through Brace's window made her groan and roll onto her side and hug her belly and bring her knees up.

Her clothing didn't feel right.

Looking down, she found herself wearing her tank-top and running shorts.

She frowned.

What'd I do, just flop into bed last night without . . .?

That's what I did, all right.

She could remember it now: staggering into the house, breathless and crying, half-blinded by her tears, stumbling along until she came to her bed, then flopping on it face-down and burying her face in the pillow.

Ah, yes.

Didn't even so much as take a shower.

Should've at least brushed my teeth, she thought.

She ran her tongue across her teeth. They felt scuzzy.

'Great,' she muttered.

Groaning, she crawled out of bed. When she tried to stand, muscles everywhere rebelled. She groaned again. And groaned with each step as she hobbled, bent over, toward the bathroom.

The first thing I'll do when I get there – if I get there – is brush my teeth. Next comes peeing. Or should that be first? No, gotta brush my teeth first – they're disgusting and they're in my mouth.

Brush, then pee, then shower, then scoot into the kitchen and get the coffee started.

Or do the coffee first, so it'll be ready . . .?

No no no. It can wait.

In the bathroom, Jane made her way to the medicine cabinet, then forced herself to stand up straight. She gazed at her reflection in the mirror as she scrubbed her teeth.

Hair a tangle, eyes dazed, cheeks hollow, still a dim yellow bruise on one cheek where the dog had stepped on her face.

A vision of loveliness, she thought.

And spit a mouthful of foam into the sink.

Then studied her face some more as she resumed brushing.

On my worst day (and this might be it), I look better than that pony-faced whore of Brace's.

Done with her teeth, she put the brush away and bent over the sink to rinse her mouth. As she cupped up water with her hand, she saw her cleavage in the mirror.

Okay, so she's got bigger boobs than me. Doesn't mean hers are any *better*.

Jane shook her shoulders, and watched how her breasts shimmied a little inside the drooping front of her shirt.

'Oh, well,' she said.

She laughed once, then turned away from the mirror. Stepping toward the toilet, she peeled the tank-top over her head. She tossed it into a corner.

Her back to the toilet, she hooked her thumbs under the elastic waistband of her running shorts. As she was about to give the shorts a pull, she looked down.

'Huh?' she murmured. Not troubled, at first. Just confused, disoriented.

Whatever the things might be, maybe she wasn't seeing them quite right. Maybe they were something *normal*.

But she didn't think so.

What they looked like were rows of black marks across her skin between the bottoms of her breasts and the waist-band of her shorts.

Small black squiggles mixed in with tangles of horizontal and vertical lines.

She bent lower. Pressing her breasts closer to her chest, she peered over the backs of her hands.

'Oh, my God,' she muttered.

Handwriting.

Someone had scribbled a message across her skin. With a felt-tipped pen, from the looks of it.

But Jane couldn't read the message.

Even though she was viewing it upside-down, that wasn't the problem; from time to time, she had practiced reading things upside-down.

This looked like gibberish.

A foreign language? she wondered. No. That's not . . .

It's backward writing!

Just like the letters you see on the front of an ambulance when you aren't looking at them through the rear-view mirror of your car.

Jane hobbled over to the medicine cabinet. In its mirror, the jumble of black marks became letters, words . . .

My Dear,

On the tablet
of your body and soul
we script the book
of

Of what?
She tugged her shorts down.

Jane

Chapter Twenty-eight

At first, Jane felt sickened by the knowledge that Mog had come to her bedroom during the night while she was fast asleep. He'd done that sort of thing before, of course.

And left his little verse about kissing her.

Almost everywhere.

This time, he had penned his poetry (if it could be called that) on her very skin.

How could he do that without waking me up? she wondered.

A delicate touch, maybe.

What else did he do?

'Anything he wanted,' she muttered.

She stared at the message and pictured Mog crouching on the mattress, lifting her tank top, starting with 'My Dear' just below her breasts and working his way downward, line by line, the pen's felt tip sliding on her skin, the 'of' fitting in nicely between her navel and the waist of her shorts.

Ran out of room on purpose, she supposed.

Because that's how he'd wanted to finish his weird little note: by scrawling her name down where she would read it through the wispy coils of her pubic hair.

Mog's idea of a little humor, she supposed.

Or maybe he'd done it that way figuring it had some sort of major significance.

This is Jane – her essence, her center.

Or what I am to Mog, she thought.

Maybe it's just his way of calling me a pussy. Or worse.

Could be a lot of things, she supposed. It might be nothing more than his way of showing he was there.

Mog and his bizarre little ways.

Like writing the stuff backward. How the hell did he do that, anyway? Using a mirror? Better yet, why? Just to make things even stranger than usual? Trying to freak me out?

Suppose he did it just so I could read the thing in my mirror? Wanted to make it easy for me.

Maybe.

Maybe maybe maybe.

Why does he do anything?

The pervert gets a charge out of messing with me, that's why.

Tilting back her head, Jane called out, 'Hey, Mog. If you're gonna drop in and screw around and write on me and everything, how about dropping off some of that money you're so famous for? I'd appreciate it.'

Then she smirked at herself in the mirror, and gave her head a shake.

'Do you find me amusing, Mog?' she asked.

At least *he* hasn't deserted me, she thought. I oughta be grateful for that. *He* hasn't dumped me.

Faithful and rich, what more could a gal want in a fella?

Sanity, perhaps?

Laughing softly, Jane left the bathroom. She went to the kitchen and started a pot of coffee. By the telephone, she picked up a notepad and pen. In the bathroom again, she stood in front of the mirror and copied the message.

Then she read it off the note pad.

My Dear,

On the tablet
of your body and soul
we script the book
of

Jane

'Right,' she muttered.

Then she studied it, wondering if there might be hidden clues about where and when she might go off to seek another envelope.

She couldn't find anything of the sort.

Which didn't surprise her. This just didn't *seem* like that kind of message.

Not an instruction. More of a commentary.

Which, she supposed, would explain why it hadn't been accompanied by a payment.

Who says there wasn't a payment?

I'll have to look around, she told herself. Shouldn't just assume he didn't leave a bunch of money for me somewhere.

The search, however, could wait till after her shower.

Before heading for the shower, she double-checked her note against the mirror's reflection of the writing on her skin, found no errors, and set the pad aside.

She started to turn away.

What if he wrote on my back?

She whirled around and peered over her shoulder at the mirror.

Her back was slightly pink from yesterday's time in the sun. The bikini ties had left a thin, pale line across it. On her buttocks was a pale triangle with stripes that reached to her hips.

Nobody had used her back as stationery.

'Oh, well.'

She supposed she ought to be glad about that, but all she felt was mild annoyance and disappointment.

She took a long, hot shower.

The writing did not come off easily. She scrubbed at it with a soapy washcloth, rinsed, found a dim ghost of the message lingering on her skin, and had to scour it two more times before washing away every trace of ink.

After her shower, she roamed casually through the house, searching for more money but not expecting to find any.

None turned up.

So she ate breakfast, put on her work clothes and drove to the library. She arrived a little early, and got busy.

It helped, being busy.

Whenever her mind strayed to Brace or his teeny-bopper, she felt like yelling in rage. Or weeping.

Though it was awfully funny, the look on that gal's face when she saw me in the window. That was damn near worth the price of admission.

What price, a broken heart?

Sometimes, Jane smiled or chuckled quietly when she thought about how she'd shocked the girl. But her amusement never lasted long before it twisted and dropped and left her feeling ruined.

Thinking about Mog, at least, didn't cause her any pain.

It only confused her, worried her, made her blush with shame, filled her mind with countless questions, frightened her, excited her.

Like I've got a phantom lover, she thought.

That night, she thought about doing exercises or lifting weights.

But she was too tired for that, and her muscles ached too much.

What about a walk?

Yeah, she thought. Right. A, I'm way too tired. B, what if I run into that creep from last night, Scott? C, if I go out, I'll probably sneak over to Brace's place, or something, and make more trouble for myself.

D, all the above.

She wanted to do nothing except go to bed.

She put on her new pajamas. They were royal blue, shiny as satin, and felt slidy against her skin. In front of her bedroom mirror, she unfastened the top button. Then she brushed her hair.

Don't forget your lipstick, honey.

Yeah, right, she told herself. This hasn't got anything to do with Mog. If it was for him, I'd put on a see-through nightie or nothing at all. And I always brush my hair at night so it won't be knotty in the morning.

Like hell you do.

I do when I think about it!

She left her bedroom window open and lay on her bed with the covers down. Hands folded beneath her head, she closed her eyes.

She wondered what time Mog would come.

Late. Very late, probably.

Maybe I should try to stay awake, she thought.

I'd never make it. Way too tired.

What if I set my alarm to wake me at midnight?

She considered it. With a couple of hours of sleep, she could probably stay awake for hours. Play possum and wait for him. Be wide awake when he arrives.

It seemed like a good idea.

But she didn't have the energy to roll over and reach out to set her alarm clock.

In the morning, she woke up feeling wonderful. She was sprawled on her back, uncovered, arms and legs out as if she'd awakened from a dream of floating on the warm surface of a lake.

She heard birds twittering, the sputter of someone's lawnmower, the faraway sound of Garth Brooks singing 'Unanswered Prayers.' The air smelled sweet. She could feel it blowing softly across her from the window.

A great morning.

But then a shadow of unease began creeping toward her.

Brace.

Don't think about him, she warned herself. He's history. Nothing but a filthy . . .

The way the breeze felt, she suddenly realized her pajama shirt was open.

Mog came!

Shoving her elbows at the mattress, she raised her head and gazed down her body.

Except for her arms and shoulders, still covered by the shirt, she was bare to the waist.

Her skin was still slightly pink where the sun had been on it. The bruises were vague yellow-green patches, nearly gone. Little remained of the scratches.

Nobody had left a message on her chest or belly.

Sitting up fast, she popped open the snap at the waist of her pajama pants.

But found no writing.

She flung off her shirt and stood up. The pants dropped around her ankles. She stepped out of them and hurried to the full-length mirror.

She inspected her front. Turning around, she gazed over her shoulder at the reflection of her back. She even stood on one leg at a time to check the bottoms of her bare feet.

She found no writing anywhere on her body.

She found no sign of any kind that Mog had visited her overnight.

It's all right, she told herself. Maybe he had other things to do.

But she couldn't help feeling just a bit abandoned.

Done with breakfast, Jane still had a couple of hours before it was time to leave for work. She put on her bikini, took her book outside, spread her blanket on the grass, and read in the sunlight. Then she exercised and lifted the weights until she ached all over. After that, she took a shower, got dressed, and drove to work.

She tried not to think about Brace or Mog.

But she thought about them a lot.

She supposed it was partly her fault that things hadn't worked out with Brace. He'd wanted her to quit the Game, and she'd lied to him, then gone on a rampage against him when he showed up at the creephouse.

Bastard sure was quick to find himself a replacement.

We might've patched things up . . .

Still could.

Yeah, right. Forget it. Not after what I saw him doing to that bitch.

He's gone, *kaput*, outa here.

Good riddance to bad rubbish.

But what the hell happened to Mog? she wondered. Has he dropped me, too? Maybe he pulled Brace's stunt and found himself a new gal to play with.

Then where'll I be?

Alone.

Big deal. I've been alone before. I can handle it. I can get along quite nicely, thank you, by myself.

After work that night, Jane changed her clothes and went running. She ran *away* from downtown, *away* from the campus. Her muscles ached a little, but she felt stronger than ever. She poured on the speed, pumping her arms, swinging her legs out with long quick strides, feeling the caress of her shorts and top, feeling the warm breath of summer blowing against her bare skin, filling herself with the sights and aromas of the night, the freedom of fast moving.

She ran until she couldn't run any more.

Then she walked home.

She took a long, cool shower.

In her pajamas, she carried a glass of ice water into the living room and flopped on the couch. She stretched out her legs, bare feet on the coffee table. Pointing the remote control through the space between her feet, she thumbed the TV on.

The clock on the VCR showed 11:12.

Why am I even bothering? she wondered. Everything's already started.

She was sure to find movies on the higher channels, though. There would be something she'd already seen, an old film she could watch for a while until she'd fully recovered from the running and was ready to turn in.

As she made her way up the channels, she stopped at every station to take a brief look.

When she saw the front of a B. Dalton bookstore on the screen, she quit changing channels.

It looked like the one at the Donnerville Fashion Mall.

They all pretty much look alike, she thought. But it might be . . .

'. . . seen Monday night when she left her job as a sales clerk at this bookstore. Young Gail Maxwell never made it home.' The view of the bookstore was replaced by a photograph of the missing woman. A brunette, probably no older than Jane. The photo stayed on the screen as the newswoman kept on talking. 'Her car, a white Toyota, was found abandoned early yesterday only two miles from the mall where she worked.'

'She's a gonner,' Jane muttered.

And quickly left that channel behind.

I was *at* that bookstore on Monday. If that's the one at the Donnerville Mall.

Probably isn't.

But . . . No, the face in the photo hadn't looked familiar.

Hope to God it *wasn't* Donnerville. That's just what we'd need, some sort of maniac out there . . .

Jane flipped back to the station that had carried the story, but now there was footage of a protest march, the Rev. Jesse Jackson in the front row walking arm-in-arm with activists for some cause or other.

She shut off the television.

And wished she hadn't turned it on in the first place.

Switching channels at any time of the day or night, you could hardly fail to bump into a news broadcast, and the damn reporters were *always* eager to fill you in on something that you'd rather not know about.

Maybe I'd better quit running at night, she thought.

Screw that. I'll just start carrying my gun. Anybody tries to put the snatch on me, I'll blow their brains out.

Yeah, sure.

She turned off the living room lights. She made a stop in the bathroom to pee and brush her teeth. Then she went into the kitchen. She opened the 'junk drawer' where she kept a collection of rubber bands, tape, glue, paper clips, small tools, string and writing implements. After a quick search, she located her blue, felt-tipped marking pen.

She carried the pen into her bedroom.

She took off her pajama shirt, tossed it onto the bed, and stood in front of her mirror.

Carefully, glancing from the mirror to her own body, she drew a broad M underneath her right breast.

In the mirror, it appeared to be under her left.

Confusing.

While considering her plan earlier in the evening, Jane had wondered whether or not to write her message backward. Maybe Mog could only read things spelled out that way. An eye disorder, some sort of dyslexia, who knows?

But Mog most likely had a normal ability to read.

She'd made her decision to write from right to left, not reversing the letters, so her message would be legible to someone looking straight down at her while she slept.

She no sooner started to write than she discovered that the trick was to avoid looking at the mirror, keep her eyes on herself, concentrate on how the letters should look upside-down, and watch her hand guide the pen over her skin.

After finishing, she clamped the pen between her teeth and pushed in her breasts and bent down and tried to proof-read her message.

It seemed okay, but . . .

She raised her eyes to the mirror and saw crooked lines of gibberish.

Then an idea struck her.

She fetched a hand-mirror from the top of her dresser. Twisting herself and adjusting angles, she managed to find the big mirror's image of her torso in the glass of the small mirror.

Reversed twice, the message she'd scrawled on her skin was crooked and sloppy but legible.

MOG,

Please come back
and tell me
what you want
me to do.
I'm ready.

She'd had to lower her pajama pants just slightly to fit in 'I'm ready.' There'd been no room for adding her name.

I could write it where he wrote it, she thought.

No. That would be going too far.

And this isn't?

Anyway, it doesn't need to be signed. Mog is fairly sure to know who wrote this.

She decided not to bother putting her shirt back on.

She turned off the lights and went to bed. She lay on her back, arms up, hands under her pillow, and stared at the ceiling. She felt edgy, excited.

A very long time passed before she was able to fall asleep.

In the morning, she hurried to the mirror and found Mog's answer written on her back:

My Dear,
I am delighted
by your eagerness
and taste.
The Game will resume.

Not yet, butt

Soon   Soon

Mog had penned one 'soon' on each of her buttocks.

'Real cute,' Jane muttered.

And what's that about being delighted by my taste? she wondered.

Face it, the guy definitely has a crude side to him. But at least he came through. He answered. And he says we'll get back to the Game soon soon.

That night before going to bed, Jane wrote on the clean slate of the skin:

MOG,
When ? ? ?

In the morning, she found written beneath her navel:

EAGER

She tugged her pajama pants down to find the other half of his message:

BEAVER

When she saw that, she muttered, 'Asshole.'

Though not really expecting to find any more remarks from Mog, she turned her back to the mirror and looked over her shoulder.

The message there began between her shoulder blades and worked its way down:

Honey
Sweetness
Light of my life

Guess who is the
MASTER
around here

ME   MOG

'Guess we can add surliness,' she muttered, 'to your list of sterling qualities.'

When she went out to the driveway that morning, she found an envelope taped to the windshield of her car.

He came through!

But why did he have to put it there, of all places?

No doubt because he finds it amusing to remind me of the dog attack and how I murdered the thing.

'You're a real creep, Mog,' she said.

Bending down, she peered into the window on the driver's side. Then she sidestepped and looked through the back window.

She saw nothing inside her car that shouldn't be there.

She glanced up and down the street in front of her house, scanned the sidewalks and the neighboring houses. Nobody seemed to be approaching or spying on her. Nothing seemed out of the ordinary.

She took a few steps backward, then got to her knees and looked underneath the car.

Nothing there.

So she opened the trunk.

No surprises there, either.

She unlocked the door on the driver's side and stepped backward again as she pulled the door open wide. Standing motionless, she waited and watched and listened.

He *must've* booby-trapped the car somehow, she thought. That's how he operates. Wouldn't be any fun if he couldn't pull a stunt on me.

She half expected to see some small, unpleasant creature crawling on the seat or floor.

Or squirming.

She listened for rattlesnakes.

Nothing.

As a final precaution, she opened the back door and inspected the rear seats and floor.

Okay, she thought. Maybe this time he *didn't* leave me a nasty surprise.

Leaning into the driver's side, she reached over the steering wheel and dug her fingernails under the tape at the top edge of the envelope.

The envelope was *fat*.

'Oh, man,' she whispered.

She tore it from the windshield.

It seemed like a very long time since she had held an envelope from Mog in her hand.

Not since the coffin.

Stepping back a safe distance from her car, she ripped open the envelope. Inside, two sheets of lined paper were wrapped around a thick stack of bills.

She pulled out the bills.

All hundreds.

She began to count them, but her mind strayed and she lost track somewhere in the sixties. She thought about starting over.

No need to bother, she told herself.

She knew how many there would be. God knows, she had thought about it often enough during the past few days – and wondered if Mog would ever come through with it.

One hundred and twenty-eight hundred-dollar bills.

Which added up to $12,800.

Taking so much money to the library didn't seem like a good idea, so Jane went back inside her house. She put it with the rest.

For a grand total so far of $25,350.

Minus what she'd spent at the mall on Monday.

Still, a lot of money. One hell of a lot of money.

'Now, let's see what the catch is,' she muttered. With a mixture of fear and excitement, she unfolded the two sheets of paper. She read the one on top:

Surprise!
You're invited to a party, Jane!

Where: 482 Chestnut Street
When: tonight, 9:30 p.m.
Why: just because.
B.Y.O.B. (Bring Your Own Body)
R.S.V.P. not applicable. I have every
confidence that you'll be there.
Special Instructions: At the door, present
your host with the enclosed note.

Jane read the enclosed note, shook her head, and muttered, 'What the hell are you trying to do to me?'

Chapter Twenty-nine

Parked in her car half a block from the party house, Jane once again read the note she was supposed to present to her host:

My Friend,
    I will never be able to thank you properly for what you've done. Please greet my servant, Jane.
    She is yours to use as you please until midnight. Your wish is her command.
    I have already seen to her payment.
    Enjoy.

Gratefully yours,
MOG

She folded the note and dropped it onto her lap.

All day, she'd wondered if she would have the nerve to follow through. She'd never really doubted it, though.

Not much I won't do, comes right down to it.

Not with more than twenty-five thousand dollars at stake. When I get that, I'll have over fifty thousand bucks. *Fifty thousand.*

She took a deep breath. She was shaking badly. Otherwise, she felt all right: alert and strong.

This won't be so bad, she told herself. Whatever happens between now and midnight, it can't be much worse than what I've gone through before.

Anyway, she thought, nothing happens without my say-so.

Reaching into her purse, she found her pistol.

Before leaving for the library that morning, she had inspected the weapon to make sure it hadn't been tampered with: looked it over carefully, unloaded it and dry-fired it. It had seemed fine. The ammo had seemed okay, too.

Just to be on the safe side, however, she'd stopped by a gun shop on the way to work and bought a fresh box of ammunition. She'd emptied the magazine and refilled it with brand new cartridges.

The pistol went nicely into the big, loose pocket on the right front of her culottes.

She dropped her switchblade knife and car keys into the left front pocket.

After tucking her purse under the passenger seat, she picked up Mog's note and climbed out of the car. She locked the door before shutting it. Then she walked slowly up the street until she came to the house at 482 Chestnut Street.

It came as no great surprise that the place wasn't brightly lit, noisy with music and laughter, and swarming with merry-makers.

This, after all, was a party devised by Mog.

A surprise party?

With probably no one being more taken by surprise than its host.

Don't be so sure about *that*, Jane thought. The host may be none other than the Master of Games, himself.

She walked slowly toward the lighted porch.

That'd be perfect, she thought. He sends me to himself with a note like this.

But would Mog live in such a place? It looked like the modest home of a middle-income family, maybe two or three bedrooms, nicely kept up, but hardly a mansion. Not the sort of place where someone really wealthy would choose to live.

And Mog had to be filthy rich, or he wouldn't be throwing around so much money for the sake of his Game.

You never know, Jane told herself. Mog *might* live in a place like this. Or he might even live in a place like the creephouse by the cemetery – in his poem about kissing me, he called *that* miserable ruin his 'lair.'

I kissed you here, I kissed you there . . .

Shaking her head, Jane jabbed the doorbell button.

Her heart suddenly began to hammer.

Everything'll be all right, she told herself. Everything'll be fine. Whatever goes on, it'll be over by midnight and I'll get twenty-five grand.

She finched when the front door swung open.

A man gazed out at her through the screen door.

Of course, a man. She'd hoped, all day, that she might find a nice, pleasant young woman living at 482 Chestnut. But she'd known that Mog would never make things that easy for her.

This guy doesn't look too bad, Jane thought.

Though barefoot, he wore an old pair of blue jeans and a plain white T-shirt that looked almost new. He was probably only a few years older than Jane, and had a fairly ordinary appearance. Though not especially handsome, he was certainly not the sort of drooling, hideous creature Jane had half expected.

Maybe this'll turn out okay, she thought.

His expression as he stared out at her showed pleasant surprise.

'May I help you?' he asked.

Jane fluttered the sheet of paper at the screen. 'I'm supposed to give this to you.'

'Oh?' He raised his eyebrows. Then he unlocked the screen door and swung it open.

Jane handed the note to him.

The door swung back and bumped against his shoulder. He stayed where he was, keeping it half open as he read the note. After a few seconds, he frowned at Jane.

'Who's this from?' he asked, looking curious but untroubled.

'I don't know. It's signed M-O-G.'

'Hmm. I don't know anyone by that name. Funny name, too.'

'I think it's his initials.'

'Oh. You're probably right.' His frown deepened. Apparently, he liked to frown while he concentrated. 'I can't think of anyone with those initials, either. This isn't a joke of some kind, is it?'

'I don't think so. He paid me good money to come here and be your servant till midnight.'

'Well then, you might as well come on in.' He pushed the screen door open wide for her.

It swung shut after she was inside.

The man closed the main door.

Wonderful, she thought.

'Would you rather I leave it open?' the man asked.

'It's up to you.'

'The air conditioning's on,' he explained.

'That's fine.'

'You look worried.'

'I'm okay.'

'I could open it if you want.'

'Well . . .'

He reached for the handle, then hesitated and looked at her. 'You don't have accomplices out there, do you?'

Whoever he is, he's a little worried, too. He doesn't know what's going on.

Unless it's an act.

'Nobody's with me,' Jane said. 'It's just what the note says. I'm here to be your servant until midnight.'

He looked at his wristwatch. 'That gives us . . . just shy of two-and-a-half hours.'

'What would you like me to do?'

'Sit down.'

They entered the living room. Jane sat on the sofa, but the man chose an easy chair off to the side. He reread the note from Mog, then looked at her. 'You're Jane, I take it.'

'I'm Jane.'

'Do you know who I am?'

She shook her head.

'I'm Clay. Clay Sheridan.'

'Nice to meet you.'

'Would you care for a drink?'

'It's up to you. I'll have a drink if that's what you want.'

'I see.' He stared at her as if she were a strange animal that had wandered to his door.

Jane looked away. The room was cluttered, but didn't seem to be dirty. It had a rather comfortable, almost rustic feel to it. On the walls were several paintings of woods and mountains. She found no evidence of anyone trying to feminize Clay's surroundings.

What do you think, Mog would send you like this to a married guy?

And I suppose there's no chance he's gay, either.

'Do you live alone?' Jane asked.

'I'm not sure if I should answer that.'

'You don't have to worry,' she said. 'I'm not here to case the joint.'

'I hope not.'

'I'm not a criminal.'

'What are you?' he asked.

Good question, she thought. He probably figures I'm a prostitute.

'Your servant,' she told him.

'Uh-huh. According to the note here, this person feels that he's indebted to me for some reason, and he sent you to me by way of appreciation?'

'Right.'

'Very thoughtful of him.'

She shrugged one shoulder. 'I guess so.'

'The thing is, I've got no idea who this guy is and I can't think of anyone who might feel particularly indebted to me. I've helped people from time to time, but . . . I sure can't think of anything I did to warrant . . . such an extravagant display of gratitude. It's puzzling, you know?'

'I know.'

She thought about telling him, *It doesn't matter why I'm here. You'll never figure it out, anyway, so don't waste your time. Just go along with things.*

Then she realized how stupid it would be to talk him out of questioning the situation. The more time he spent at that, the less time he would have left for making use of his 'servant.'

'You honestly don't know who sent you here?' Clay asked.

'No. He mailed that note to me in an envelope with my instructions and payment.'

'So, here you are.'

'That's right.'

'Have you done this sort of thing before?'

For a few moments, she thought about how to answer. Then she said, 'I've done errands for him. Never anything like this, though. He's never sent me anyplace to be someone's servant.'

Clay fidgeted and shrugged. 'I hope you won't take offense at this, but . . .'

'I'm not a prostitute.'

'Oh? Okay. I couldn't help but wonder. This is really . . . out of the ordinary. Women just don't pop in on me every night like this and . . . You're definitely not a prostitute?'

'No.'

'But you've been sent here to have sex with me.'

So far, Jane had managed to stay calm, fairly detached. Now, she felt a hot blush spread over her skin.

'That isn't what the note says,' she explained.

'Not in so many words.'

'Not in *any* words.'

He laughed softly. 'Well, I suppose you're right about that. But the implication is there. You're mine to *use* as I please? My wish is your command? It sounds pretty obvious what he's getting at.'

'I don't think *he's* getting at anything. He's offering you my services, not telling you how to use me. That part is up to you.'

'And you've never done this before?'

'Never.'

'Has he ever . . . ordered you to have sex with anyone?'

'No. And he isn't doing that now, either.'

'But my wish is your command.'

'That's what the note says.'

'You'll do *anything* I ask?'

'Ask and find out.'

He sighed. Staring at Jane, he rubbed his chin. 'This is very strange.'

'I know.'

'If I just knew who sent you, maybe . . .'

'Knowing who sent me won't change anything.'

'Well, I'd sure feel better if I found out it was some friend behind all this – especially if he's the sort who enjoys a good prank . . .'

'If I were you, I wouldn't consider this a prank.'

'What would you consider it?'

She shrugged. 'I'm not sure. An opportunity? A challenge? If nothing else, you're about to learn quite a lot about yourself.'

'That's a pretty good bet, I guess.' Settling back in his chair, he smiled at Jane and raised his eyebrows. 'How does Clay Sheridan, who thinks of himself as a good and decent fellow, behave when offered a gorgeous young woman to use as he pleases?'

Gorgeous. He just called me gorgeous.

Hmmm.

'Are you a cop?' he asked.

She couldn't help but laugh a little at that one. 'If I am, I don't suppose I'd be likely to admit it.'

'Good point. I suppose I could search you.'

Oh, no.

'If I *am* a cop, which I'm not, do you think I'd bring along my badge for something like this?'

'I don't know. I bet you'd bring a gun, though.'

Oh, shit.

'Maybe I'd better have a look,' he said. 'Would that be all right?'

She tried to smile. 'I'm your servant. If that's what you want to do . . .'

'This isn't one of those deals where I just get one wish, is it? Or three, or something?'

'There's only the time limit.'

'Okay. Good. 'Cause if we're counting wishes, I'd hate to throw one away by asking to search you.' He got to his feet. 'Why don't you stand up and come around to the other side of the table?' As Jane followed his orders, he said, 'I feel kind of awkward about this. I'd like to be able to trust you. You seem like a very nice person, and everything. But all this is so odd.'

'I know. I understand.'

She thought, I could pull the gun now and keep him covered till midnight.

But I'm supposed to do what he wants.

If I go against him, Mog'll probably know it.

For all I know, this guy is Mog.

As Clay approached, she raised both her arms.

He let out a nervous laugh. 'I'm new at this. Guess I was supposed to say, "Stick 'em up."'

'This is a first for me, too,' Jane said. 'I've never been searched before.'

He stopped in front of her. He grimaced a little. His hands

patted the legs of his jeans a few times. Then he moved his gaze slowly down Jane's body, and up again. 'Well . . .'

'Well?' she asked.

'What've you got in your pockets there?'

'You're *asking*?'

'I don't want to put my hands in your pockets.'

'I don't bite.'

'All the same. Just tell me, all right?'

'You trust me to tell the truth?'

'Let's give it a try,' he said.

'Okay. I've got my keys, a switchblade knife and a pistol.'

'A knife and a *gun*?'

'Just in case of trouble. Do you want to see them?'

He shook his head. 'I'll take your word for it. Do you have a billfold?'

'In my car.'

'So you don't have any ID at all with you?'

'Not on me.'

'Are you wearing a wire?'

She let out a laugh. 'You've gotta be kidding. You've seen too many movies.'

'I like movies.'

'So do I. But this *isn't* one. A wire. Really.'

He looked a little sheepish. 'I'm just trying to find out what's going on, that's all. For all I know, you might've been sent in here to set me up for something.'

'I don't think so,' Jane said. 'And I know I didn't come in here with a hidden microphone. Or camera. But go ahead and search me.'

'I'm *not* going to search you. You can go ahead and put your arms down.'

She lowered her arms.

Clay stood facing her, looking into her eyes and not moving. He seemed very uneasy.

'So,' Jane said, 'what now?'

'I don't know. What do *you* want to do?'

'Don't ask me, I'm the servant. You're the one who's supposed to give the orders around here.'

'You don't have any suggestions?' he asked.

She shook her head.

'Well, I have an idea.'

Oh, God, here we go. What's it gonna be? Something sick. Mog knows what he's doing; he wouldn't send me to a nice, normal, decent sort of guy. Where would the fun be in that?

'Let's call it a night,' Clay said.

'What?'

'Look, it's been very interesting and I'm glad we had this chance to meet, but I don't have any real use for a servant tonight.'

'You're kidding, right?'

'No. Why don't you just go on home, now, and I'll go to bed, and that'll be the end of it? That way, neither one of us will wake up in the morning with something to regret.'

Jane couldn't believe at. 'You mean to say you don't want to . . . have me?'

'Not tonight.'

'What's that supposed to mean?'

'I don't know. It just wouldn't be right.' With a smile, he added, 'I don't do servants.'

'You're kidding,' she said again.

'Sorry. You're very . . . attractive, but . . . I'll have to pass.'

'Oh, man. So . . . that's it? I'm supposed to leave now?' Jane checked her wristwatch. 'It isn't even ten yet. I don't know about this. I'm supposed to be here till midnight. I *can't* leave. If I leave now, I could lose a . . . a *lot* of money.'

Clay looked concerned. 'Really?'

'Really.'

'Well, in that case, you can stay. And if you're staying, you might as well go ahead and be my servant. Come with me, and I'll give you some orders.'

He led her into the kitchen.

Jane tried to follow his orders, but didn't know where anything was, so they worked together.

When they were done, Clay carried the glasses of Pepsi into the living room and Jane carried the big plastic bowl of popcorn. He said, 'Wait, don't sit down yet.'

Jane stood by the sofa.

Clay brought her a VCR tape. 'Do you know how to load this?'

'Sure.'

'What are you standing around for! Do it! *Schnell!*'

She laughed and said, '*Ja wohl.*' She took the tape from him, hurried to the TV, crouched, and inserted it into the VCR.

Then they sat down beside each other on the sofa, munched popcorn, drank their sodas, and watched the video tape – a John Candy movie called *The Great Outdoors*.

Jane had already seen it three times before, but she didn't mention that to Clay. It was one of her favourite movies. She was glad to watch it again.

During the movie, they laughed. Occasionally, they made comments. Jane held the remote control. She used it to rewind a few times at Clay's command – particularly so they could take more time reading the subtitles that translated the awful things the raccoons were saying.

Clay never touched her.

At the end of the movie, he announced, 'We still have some fifteen minutes.'

'Why don't we take this stuff into the kitchen and clean up?' Jane suggested.

'Are you telling me what to do, servant?'

She smiled. 'So sorry.'

'Anyway,' he said, 'there isn't much. I'll take care of it after you're gone.'

'So. What would you like to do for the next fifteen minutes?'

He turned toward Jane and stretched his arm across the back of the sofa. 'I've got a great idea.'

'Shoot.'

'Tell me what's really going on.'

'What do you mean?'

'My wish is your command, right? So here's my command: tell me the truth.'

She wondered if she should.

Then she said, 'Okay. It's like a game, I guess. M-O-G stands for Master of Games. He's pays me money to go places and do things. I don't know who he is, or why he's doing it, or why he chose me to be his player. I just know that each time I follow his instructions, I end up with a new batch of money and a new set of instructions. So I keep on doing it. Why not? It's a lot of money. And I have my weapons in case anything gets out of hand.'

'Have you had to use them?'

'I had to stab a dog that attacked me. That's the only time.'

'What sort of things does he have you do?'

'Things like come here tonight.'

'What else?'

'I don't want to get into any of that. Okay? We hardly know each other. The thing is – as far as you're concerned – I don't know why he picked you for this deal tonight. Maybe he had a special reason, or maybe he just picked you at random. Or maybe you're him.'

Clay grinned. 'Mog? You think I might be Mog?'

'Are you?'

'No.'

'Can you prove it?' Jane asked.

'Can you prove I *am*?'

'If you *are* Mog, I'd sure like to know.'

'I already told you I'm not.'

'But why should I believe you?'

'Why shouldn't you?'

'Okay.'

'Anyway,' Clay said, 'I think he must be a real jerk.'

'He gives me a lot of money.'

'Only a jerk would send a young woman like you to a man's house with a note like that. Either he doesn't care what happens to you, or he's *trying* to get you into trouble. Either way, he's a jerk.'

'And am I a jerk,' Jane asked, 'for playing along with him?'

'You're not a jerk.'

'Are you sure?'

'You can't be a jerk. I like you, and I don't like jerks.'

'Thanks.'

Clay looked at his wristwatch. 'Five after. I guess it's okay for you to go now. You've been a fine servant.'

'Thanks. You've been an excellent master. And you make good popcorn.'

She followed Clay to the front door, and he opened it for her. She turned and face him. 'I was awfully worried about all this,' she said.

'You had every reason to be.'

'The chances were about one in a million that I'd actually run into a man who didn't want to . . . mess with me – or worse. Especially with Mog picking the guy.'

'He might've sent you here without knowing anything about who's in the house.'

'Maybe.'

'And I don't think it's as bad as one in a million.'

'I do. Anyway, I sure am glad he sent me to you.'

'Me, too,' Clay said.

'Hey, maybe he did know what he was doing.'

'Sent you here because he knew you'd be safe with me?'

'Yeah.'

'Don't bet on it. He couldn't know me that well. *I* don't know myself that well. I probably shouldn't tell you this, but it was never a sure thing. When you raised your arms like that for me to search you . . .' He shook his head. 'Plenty of other times, too . . . It was close. It might've gone the other way.'

'But it didn't.'

'Guess I'm a wonder of self-control,' he said, then smiled. 'You should see yourself blushing.'

'It's nice to know . . . that I wasn't easy to resist.'

'Incredibly difficult.'

'Good.' Looking into his eyes, she stepped toward him.

He gripped her upper arms and stopped her. 'You'd better go,' he said.

'What's wrong?'

'Nothing. Just ... Come back some time after you've finished your game with Mog. If you want to.'

'After it's *finished*?'

'Yeah.'

'But that might not be for ... I don't know, weeks, months. Who knows?'

'It'll only go on as long as you're willing to play.'

My God, she thought, he sounds exactly like Brace.

'The game's crazy,' Clay said. 'But you've already figured that out, I think.'

'Maybe. It might be crazy, but it's lucrative. And it gives me something to do.'

'Well, *I* don't want anything else to do with it.'

'Including me?'

'I'm afraid so. The way I see it, you're playing Russian Roulette and this Mog fellow – he's the gun. I don't want to fall for you any more than I have already and then stick around while you blow your brains out.'

'It's not like that,' Jane said.

'Well, that's sort of how it looks. Anyway, you know where to find me.'

'Okay.'

'Be careful, all right?'

'Okay.' She offered her hand. 'You can shake, can't you?'

'Sure.'

He took her hand gently, and shook it.

Jane murmured, 'See you.' Then she hurried away.

That wasn't so bad, she told herself. It really *couldn't* have gone any better. What the hell was Mog thinking, sending me to a guy like Clay?

Probably a mistake. He probably goofed with the address, or something.

Don't cry!

She could feel it coming.

Don't!

Maybe *that's* his game, trying to make me cry. Well, I'm not going to do it. Not this time. He threw me against Clay just to show me what I'm missing out on. I'm not falling for it.

Anyway, Clay's probably a bastard underneath it all. He can't be as nice as he seems. Nobody is.

Brace sure proved that.

'Who needs either one of 'em,' she muttered.

When she opened her car door, she found an envelope on the driver's seat.

'Thank you, thank you,' she said, picking it up.

She sat down and locked her door, then turned on the overhead light and tore open the envelope. The stack of hundred dollar bills seemed twice as thick as the bunch she'd received that morning.

She figured there should be two hundred and fifty-six of them.

Not bad pay for two-and-a-half hours entertaining a fellow who didn't really want anything out of you except maybe some companionship. Better than ten thousand bucks per hour.

If Mog keeps this up, she thought, I'll be able to spend my old age in the lap of luxury.

Might be the only lap I get.

'Ha ha,' she muttered, and drove away without reading Mog's note.

Chapter Thirty

My beauty,
　　Tomorrow night, 901 Mayr Heights for a gala time.
　　In the meantime, don't feel lonely. You have me. I
shall come to you tonight.
　　No need to wait up.

> Love to my lovely
> hot wet wench,
> MOG

Hot wet wench. Why did he have to be crude like that?

He wouldn't be Mog, she told herself, if he weren't such a
crude, nasty creep.

Part of his charm.

Yeah, right.

She'd first read the note after returning to her house, just
before hiding the money. Now, in her pajamas and sitting on
the edge of her bed, she read it again.

Not only crude, she thought, but arrogant. Like he's under
the impression that I just can't wait for him to show up.

'I've got a secret for you, Mog,' she said. 'It's no big deal to
me whether you show up or not. You know what I mean? I
never get to see you, anyway, so who cares?'

Maybe this time, she thought, I really should try to stay
awake for him.

Won't work. The guy's like Santa. He won't come while I'm awake.

Why don't I try leaving him a message again?

Her heart beat quicker.

I shouldn't make a habit of this, she thought.

She slipped off her pajama top and went to the dresser
where she'd left her marking pen. She stepped close to the
mirror. On the stretch of lightly tanned skin below her breasts
and above the waistband of her pajama pants, she wrote:

WAKE ME
SHOW YOURSELF
PLEASE

In the morning, Jane found written on her back:

GREAT TIME
TOO BAD YOU SLEPT
THROUGH IT ALL

'Right,' she muttered. 'What's your idea of a great time, Mog? Practicing your penmanship?'

If it'd been much more than that, she told herself, I wouldn't have slept through it.

Don't be so sure. It might've been a lot more than that.

So what else is new? she thought. He can do whatever he wants – and probably has been doing exactly that. No way to stop him.

Not that I've tried.

Pretty much the opposite, comes right down to it.

Tipping back her head, she said to the bedroom ceiling, 'The least you could do, Mog, is wake me up next time.'

Mog, of course, didn't answer.

Jane dropped her pajama pants and inspected herself carefully. The writing on her back seemed to be the only evidence of Mog's visit.

After starting her coffee, Jane took a shower to wash off the messages. As usual, they needed a lot of scrubbing. When she was done, she put on her bikini. She carried a cup of coffee and her book outside to enjoy the morning sunlight for a while.

She drank two cups of coffee. Then she brought her weights out of the house, took them to her blanket on the grass and worked out until she was dripping sweat, huffing for breath, and worn out.

Back in the house, she took another shower. Near the end,

she made the water chilly and stood beneath it, rigid, her teeth clenched. She didn't stay in the shower for long. Time was getting short, and she didn't want to be late for work.

Still dripping, she hurried out of the bathroom with her towel. She was mostly dry by the time she reached her bedroom.

As she stepped into her panties, she decided to go ahead and wear her denim culottes and a good, short-sleeved blouse – the sort of outfit she usually wore to the library – and go straight to the Mayr Heights address after work.

It's probably a house, she thought.

Mog had written about a 'gala time.' Which might mean there would be a party.

Right, a party of two like last night.

On the other hand, suppose he means it this time?

The 'Heights' in the name of the street sounded ritzy. What if this turned out to be a fancy section of town, and she was expected to participate in an actual party of some sort?

Not awfully likely.

The place might just as easily turn out to be a filthy old ruin like the creephouse by the boneyard.

It might be just about anything.

So I ought to be ready for anything, she told herself.

Ten minutes later, dressed and groomed and ready to go, Jane left the house with a paper sack in each hand. Stuffed into one were blue jeans, a chamois shirt, and a pair of running shoes. In the other sack was a pair of blue pumps and a neatly folded evening dress that the filthy son-of-a-bitch Ken had bought for her to wear to a dance at his parents' country club.

Two weeks ago, the gown wouldn't have fit her.

But she'd tried it on quickly before putting it into the sack, and the fit had been fine.

In the mirror, she'd looked smashing.

Hard to believe, though, that she had actually gone to a dance wearing a garment like this. Elegant, but terribly clingy and revealing. Of course, Ken had insisted.

He was always insisting on something.

She could remember protesting, 'I can't wear this. My God, everybody'll *stare* at me.' To which Ken had replied, 'I *want* 'em staring at you, babe. I want 'em *drooling*. What's the point in having you if I can't show you off?'

And I'm going to take this with me tonight? she'd asked herself.

Why the hell not? I look great in it.

Besides, it's my only good gown. And the chances of having to wear it are slim to none.

As she carried the two sacks out to the driveway, her purse swung by her hip. It was heavy with her flashlight, knife, pistol, and box of ammunition.

She put the sacks into the trunk of her car, then drove to work.

A dead end?

'Great,' Jane muttered, and slowed down as she drove past the sign.

The last address she'd been able to spot, some distance back, had been in the seven hundreds. Now, all of a sudden, Mayr Heights was planning to pull a disappearing act?

What the hell happened to 901?

The road seemed to continue for a while, though. Maybe she would find 901 before it ended.

No such luck.

The road curved to the left, and her headlights illuminated the barricade. She drove closer to it, wondering if this might mark an interruption, not an end.

Off beyond the barricade, the hillside seemed to drop away.

She reached for the map on the passenger seat, then changed her mind. There was no need to check. What did it matter if the road resumed somewhere else? This was the section where 901 should be.

She must've simply missed it.

She'd seen no houses at all on Mayr Heights. Apparently, they were hidden on the wooded hillside and you could only find them by venturing onto those awful little driveways.

She'd seen plenty such driveways – if that's what they were. Narrow lanes, paved but dark, bordered by thick bushes and trees. Often, they'd seemed to be unmarked. No visible mailbox or address. No clue at all as to where the things might lead.

One of them, she supposed, must go to 901. *I probably drove right past it.*

'Terrific,' she muttered.

She made a U-turn near the barricade, and drove slowly back the way she'd come.

From the few addresses she'd been able to find on the way up, she at least knew that the odd numbers were over to her right. The house she wanted would be uphill. At the top of one of those nasty little driveways.

But which one?

Check them all. Stop and get out and look.

The third time she climbed out of her car to study a small, paved gap in the roadside foliage, she found a redwood mailbox buried in the bushes. Carved into the side of the box was the address, 901, and a name, S. Savile.

'Yes!' she gasped.

She shone her flashlight up the driveway.

The concrete was cracked, crumbling in places, with small weeds growing out of the fissures. Bushes pressed in close on both sides, so that the lane resembled a very narrow tunnel – a tunnel up an awfully steep grade. Near the far reach of her flashlight, where her beam faded to a hazy glow, the driveway curved out of sight.

'Yuck,' Jane muttered.

Sure I'm gonna drive up that thing. When I get done, I'll try walking blindfolded up some rollercoaster tracks.

She felt a little cowardly as she headed back to her car.

Driving up there would be stupid, she told herself. Forget how creepy the thing looks, it's *one way*. *What if I run into another car on my way up?*

Better yet, *what if I run into one on my way down?*

I'm not gonna let myself get trapped. No way.

S. Savile might be a perfectly nice fellow – like Clay last night. But he might not be. The way Mog is into word games, it's probably significant that name has 'vile' in it.

Back at the car, she climbed into the driver's seat. She moved the car a good distance past the driveway entrance, then pulled as far off the road as possible.

Now that she faced a hike to the top of the steep driveway, she knew for sure that she wouldn't be wearing the party gown. She considered her jeans and chamois shirt. Protective clothes, but heavy. And hot. She would be a lot more comfortable if she stayed in her culottes and light blouse.

But who knows what's at the top? she thought. Maybe I'd rather cook in my jeans and shirt than end up having bare arms and legs in a bad place.

She hurried to the trunk and opened it. No cars were coming. No house was in sight. From all she could see and hear, nobody seemed to be nearby. So she undressed at the rear of her car and quickly got into her jeans, running shoes, and chamois shirt.

She shut the trunk.

Standing by the driver's door, she took what she needed from her purse. She slipped the keys and knife into the front left pocket of her jeans. The pistol went into the pocket on the right. She opened the box of ammunition, filled her hand with cartridges, dumped them into the right front pocket of her shirt, then returned the box to her purse. She clamped the flashlight under her left arm.

Then she tucked her purse under the passenger seat, locked and shut the door.

She headed for the driveway.

As she walked, she felt the weight of the extra ammo dragging at her pocket, swinging under her breast.

It had surprised her a bit when she'd decided to take more ammunition. She hadn't *planned* to do that. She'd briefly considered it earlier in the day, but hadn't made up her mind.

The business of Mog's about a 'gala time,' that's what had made her think of it in the first place.

He isn't sending me to any party.

In the library that afternoon, a bit of poetry had crossed her mind: 'Lo, 'tis a gala night.' And then it had crossed again and again. She hadn't been able to get rid of it.

The opening of 'The Conqueror Worm,' by Poe.

She knew the poem well. Too well. Back in junior high school, she'd memorized it for a Halloween presentation. She could still recite it – and often did, usually late at night, usually half drunk, and always to the annoyance of her friends. Oh God, how the language slithered and rolled off her tongue! 'It wriiiiithes! It wriiiiithes with mortal pangs! The mimes become its food!'

What a fabulous, gross poem.

But it wasn't something you wanted in your head when you were planning to visit a stranger's house late at night.

Vermin fangs, in human gore imbued.

Charming stuff.

Mog's 'gala time' had snapped it all into her mind and kept it there. And made her think that extra precautions might be in order.

Maybe take along a few more bullets?

And then to see that the resident of 901 Mayr Heights was someone by the name of Savile.

Change one letter, you've got 'So vile.'

I'm probably just going paranoid in my old age, she thought.

Better safe than sorry.

If I really think I might need the gun – much less a pocketful of extra ammo – I shouldn't be going up there at all.

The same old tune, she thought. A tune that doesn't mean a whole lot, anymore, now that the stakes are up to fifty thousand bucks.

More like fifty-one thousand, something, she corrected.

She began to trudge up the driveway. She couldn't see much of it: a strip of gray speckled only here and there by moonlight, with darkness on both sides. Though she held the flashlight in her right hand, she kept it off. Better to stumble along in the dark than to make herself conspicuous with the light.

Her leg muscles, still a little stiff and sore, ached at first. Soon, the aching faded.

In spite of the many curves in the driveway, the climb was steep, and hard work.

Gasping for air, drenched with sweat, she stopped to rest. No sign, yet, of an end to the driveway.

What if it goes on for miles?

It won't, she told herself.

She fluttered the front of her shirt, and felt cooler air from the outside come in and buffet her hot skin. The back of the shirt was clinging to her. So was the seat of her panties.

Hope the house has air conditioning, she thought. Or a pool. Wouldn't it be great to leap into a cold swimming pool about now!

She fluttered her shirt again, took a very deep breath, then resumed her trek.

And suddenly found herself at the top of the driveway.

The dim strip of moonlit pavement stretched across an open field to the garage of the house at 901 Mayr Heights. There were a few lamps on posts along the sides of the driveway. They looked like old-fashioned gas lamps. Not one was lighted, though.

The front porch of the old, two-story house was dark.

So were all the windows.

Well, Jane thought, obviously there isn't a party going on.

That was a relief. She wouldn't have to hike back down for her gown. Nobody would have to see her in it. She wouldn't need to talk her way in to the party, or mingle with strangers or try to fend off the advances of pushy, obnoxious men.

Odd, though, that *all* the lights were off.

Mog hasn't sent me to another abandoned house, has he?

Chapter Thirty-one

Instead of walking straight up the driveway, in plain sight of anyone who might be watching from one of the dark front windows, Jane stayed among the trees and bushes beyond the edge of the lawn and made her way around to the side.

Only a few yards of open space separated her from the wall of the garage.

She dashed across it.

Cupping her hands against the garage window, she peered in. Blackness. So she took the risk of turning on her flashlight. Its beam hit the dirty glass, went through, and formed a bright disk no larger than the lid of a small mustard jar.

Jane scowled.

After a few moments of studying the odd phenomenon, she realized that her light was being blocked, just inside the window, by thick, black fabric.

The fabric covered the entire window.

This is a wonderful sign, she thought. Someone wants to make sure nobody can see in.

Or maybe it's just to keep out the sunlight.

Terrific. A vampire lives in the garage.

Jane laughed quietly, nervously.

Screw vampires, I wanta know if there's a *car* in there.

Break the window?

That'd be a great move, particularly if somebody's in the house (or garage) and hears it.

Besides, she told herself, cars or no cars in the garage, you couldn't be completely sure whether someone's in the house.

Giving up on the window, Jane slipped along the side of the garage and gazed around its corner. The rear grounds were dark, just as she'd expected. She took a few strides until she could see the back of the house.

Dark, everything dark.

She was tempted to explore the area back here: it looked lush and extravagant. Trees, benches, walkways, statues, a gazebo off in the distance. She wouldn't be surprised to find brooks and waterfalls, and maybe even a fabulous swimming pool.

If everything turns out okay, she told herself, I'll take a look later. Right now, I'd better concentrate on getting into the house and laying my hands on the envelope.

Wherever the hell it might be.

She hurried to the front of the house, climbed over the railing at the end of the veranda, and crept as quietly as she could toward the front door. The huge window beside her looked black. She ached to shine her light on it, but didn't dare take the risk.

No sounds came from the house.

She tried to make no sounds herself as she crossed the veranda, but its old floorboards sometime squawked under her weight, and once she walked into something that bumped her belly an instant before she struck it with her knee. She stifled her gasp, but the thing – whatever it was – scooted loudly and thudded.

Moments later, she found it with her hand.

A chair. She felt its wicker back under her fingers.

After that, she walked more carefully and encountered no more furniture.

Turning, she faced the front door.

She took a few deep breaths. She lifted the front of her shirt and mopped the sweat off her face. Then she opened the screen door and tried the handle.

The solid oak door was locked.

She had pretty much expected that.

Now what? she wondered.

Without pausing to think, she jabbed her fingertip into the doorbell button. She listened for the sound of ringing from inside the house, but heard nothing.

Great, she thought. How am I supposed to know if the damn thing works?

She waited. She listened hard, but heard no one approaching.

So she poked the button a few more times.

Nothing.

A, she thought, nobody's home. B, the bell doesn't work. C, whoever's in the house is asleep, or doesn't hear the bell for some other reason. Or D, somebody is hearing it just fine, but *choosing* not to come to the door.

'Swell,' she whispered.

Let's at least eliminate B as a factor.

She knocked hard on the door, pounded it until her knuckles hurt. And waited some more.

Okay, she thought as she backed away from the door. Now what?

Two choices: either break in, or go home.

Midway between the front door and other end of the veranda, she found a window that looked just right for smashing; double-hung with a screen on the lower half, and low enough to climb through.

She stared at it.

Her stomach hurt.

I shouldn't do this, she thought. I should just go home. If I do this, I'm nothing better than a criminal.

It's my fifty-one thousand dollars inside!

It *will* be mine, she corrected herself, if I have the guts to go in and find it.

But this isn't an abandoned old ruin by the edge of a graveyard – this is a house where people actually live. They might be away right now, but this is still their property, their home.

If I go in, I'm a house-breaker. An intruder. They'd even have a right to shoot me.

Nobody's going to shoot me. Nobody's home.

What if there's an alarm, or something? What if the cops show up? They might shoot me. Or at the very least, I could end up in jail.

If they catch me.

She shut her eyes and muttered, 'My God, Mog, what are you trying to do to me?'

Then she bashed a hole in the upper window with the butt of her flashlight. The clamor of bursting glass made her cringe and clench her teeth. After the glass stopped falling, she waited – ready to run.

Nothing happened.

She reached through the hole and unlocked the window. With her switchblade, she cut the screen out of its frame. Then she slid the window up.

She stared into blackness.

Let's just see what the hell . . .

She switched her flashlight on.

And its beam was abruptly stopped by a heavy black shroud.

Oh, boy.

Jane killed her light. She was holding her knife in her right hand. With that hand, she reached forward. She pushed her knuckles gently against the fabric. It had the scratchy feel of a thick, wool blanket. It had very little give. Instead of hanging like a curtain, it seemed to be drawn taut across the window.

Somebody likes a lot of privacy. Or darkness. Or something.

Definitely queer.

Jane pierced the fabric with the tip of her knife. She slipped the blade in a bit farther, then drew it downward, carving a four-inch slit. A faint thread of light came through the cut.

Jane switched her flashlight off. She stuffed it into the left front pocket of her jeans to free her hand, then spread the slit apart and peered in.

The room looked like it might be a den or a study, but she couldn't see it very well. The only light came through its doorway from a hall.

She ripped the gap wide and stuck her head in and looked all around. Nobody. She listened. No voices, no music, no sound whatsoever to suggest that anyone might be home.

Great, she thought. Now what?

Shit or get off the commode, that's what.

But I don't wanta break into someone's house! It's illegal! It's wrong! It's in a whole different ballpark than the other stuff. If I do this, I'm really really crossing the line.

But it's *my* money I need to go in and get. I won't be stealing anything of theirs.

And hell, I've already busted the window. The job's half done: I've done the breaking, now all that's left is the entering.

When I find the money from Mog, I'll leave them a couple of hundred to pay for the damage.

She liked that idea. Pay for the damage. Maybe even leave them a decent chunk. If she left them quite a lot, they might even be *glad* she broke in.

How about giving them a thousand bucks?

Before she could do that, however, she would need to locate Mog's envelope.

Feeling somewhat less like a criminal than before, Jane split the fabric all the way down to the window sill and climbed into the room.

Then she stood motionless, barely breathing. It was strange to be in someone else's house without permission. It made her feel powerful, but very exposed and vulnerable.

It would be great, she thought, if you could do this sort of thing without any fear of being caught.

She wondered if that's how it was for Mog. He seemed to be capable, somehow, of coming and going wherever he pleased, never showing himself . . .

Quit dinking around, she thought. Nobody's home. But they might come tooling up the driveway any second, so you'd better get on with it and get the hell outa here.

She hurried to a lamp and turned it on.

Should've brought gloves, she thought.

Never figured I'd have to worry about leaving fingerprints. Jeez!

Just watch what you touch.

Quickly, she scanned the room: bookshelves, lamps, a desk, a couple of small tables, an easy chair, a familiar painting on

743

one wall – a print of the Goya that has a giant about to bite off someone's head.

So-vile living up to his name.

But she was looking for her envelope, not for clues to the character traits of S. Savile.

And she saw no envelope here.

This could take forever, she thought.

Holding the knife in her teeth, she slipped Mog's note out of her shirt pocket and unfolded it. She read it slowly, wondering if she might've missed a clue during the previous readings.

My beauty,
    Tomorrow night, 901 Mayr Heights for a gala time.
    In the meantime, don't feel lonely. You have me. I shall come to you tonight.
    No need to wait up.

                Love to my lovely,
                hot wet wench,
                Mog

Only the first part seemed at all relevant to tonight. 'Tomorrow night, 901 Mayr Heights' was there to tell her when and where. Could there be a clue in 'My beauty'?

It brought to mind *Beauty and the Beast*. Maybe Mog hinting that he's a beast. But what could that have to do with the location on the envelope?

Maybe a lot, she decided. Keep it in mind.

'My beauty' also made Jane think of *Sleeping Beauty*.

Interesting. A couple of fairy tales. Are they both from the Brothers Grimm? she wondered. She wasn't sure. But she did know that many different versions of the old tales had been published, and that Disney had made animated feature movies of both stories.

Maybe the envelope's inside a book of fairy tales. Or in a Disney book. Maybe it's hidden in a Walt Disney section of Savile's home video collection, if he's got such a thing.

Keep an eye out, she told herself.

Now, what about 'a gala time?' Maybe the guy has a Poe book. Hey, maybe this big old house has a ballroom or a dance floor.

Anything else in the note?

Nothing that seemed to pertain to tonight.

She returned the note to her shirt pocket, took the knife from her mouth and hurried over to the bookshelves. As fast as possible, she scanned the titles.

No book of fairy tales. Nothing about Disney. None by Poe, or any that appeared likely to contain poetry. Most of the books were nonfiction works and they seemed to cover only two subjects: police procedures and true crime.

'A real good sign,' Jane muttered. 'Splendid.'

She turned off the lamp. At the doorway, she leaned out and glanced up and down the hall. Nobody there. She stepped forward. To her left were a few doorways. But she could see the foyer and the foot of a stairway to her right, so that's the direction she chose.

Where would Mog put that envelope?

He wants me to find it, so he probably hid it somewhere fairly obvious. But he wants to make me work for it.

Upstairs.

Upstairs in a bedroom. That's where he made me go in the creephouse. And it'd tie in with *Sleeping Beauty*. And that's where he'd like to put me, up where I'll have a hard time escaping in case S. Savile comes home.

Hell, maybe he's got a coffin waiting for me.

The foyer was lighted by a rustic chandelier made from a wagon wheel. The candle-shaped bulbs gave off a weak, yellow glow so murky that Jane felt as if she were viewing the front door through a pool of cider. For a moment, she couldn't find the windows. She knew they should be there: long, narrow windows on both sides of the door. She'd seen them from outside, but . . .

Oh.

Masking the windows, on this side, were black rectangles framed like works of art and nailed in place.

Somebody went to a lot of trouble, Jane thought. This is looking worse and worse.

But she noticed a good sign – the guard chain for the front door hung from its mount. Normally, if people were home at night, they would secure that sort of chain.

They probably *aren't* home, she told herself.

Maybe S. Savile took his wife to the movies. If there is a Mrs Savile. Which Jane was beginning to doubt. Like Clay's place last night, S. Savile's home showed no signs (so far) of a female influence.

So maybe he went out for a night on the town by himself. Or with a significant other of the male persuasion.

Maybe he went on a business trip. That's something to hope for. Gone, not due back for days.

Unless he's back already, just now steering his way up the driveway.

Jane opened the door, mostly to see if she could.

It opened easily.

She looked out toward the area where the driveway slanted down out of sight.

I oughta get out of here right now, she thought. Any second, there might be headlights and it'll be too late.

Sure, boogie right outa here and kiss fifty-one thousand bucks goodbye. What I'd better do, instead, is find out where the back door is. That way, if I need to make a quick exit . . .

What I'd better do is go upstairs and find the envelope and haul my butt outa here!

She shut the door, turned around and gazed up the stairway. There were no lights on at the top. She grimaced.

Maybe I'd better look around down here for a . . .

Just do it. Get it done!

She slipped her right hand into the front pocket of her jeans and wrapped it around the grips of her pistol. She started to pull the weapon out.

And just who am I planning to shoot, the owners of the house? Terrific.

She left the gun inside her pocket. As she began to climb

the stairs, she thought about putting her knife away, too. She shouldn't have a knife in her hand if the man of the house suddenly appears at the top of the stairs.

But she couldn't bear the thought of having no weapon ready.

Reaching behind her with both hands, she lifted the tail of her shirt and slid the blade down between her belt and the back of her jeans.

By the time she'd finished doing that, she was almost to the top of the stairs. She thought about taking out her flashlight.

No, better to sneak through the darkness.

She was one stair from the top when a woman screamed.

Chapter Thirty-two

A quiet, muffled scream that came from somewhere nearby and felt to Jane like an icicle stabbing her low and deep.

Oh, Jesus! Oh-my-God-oh-Jesus, what was THAT?

When the scream ended, Jane unfroze and climbed the final stair and hurried to the right. She knew she was making too much noise. Someone was in the house, after all – a woman in enough trouble or pain to make her scream like that – and Jane wanted to be silent but she needed to hurry and her shoes thumped on the carpet of the upstairs hall – *Christ, I sound like a stampede!* – and she threw open the first door that she found.

The skinny young woman sitting in the middle of the bed looked up and grinned. Her lips and chin were bloody. A finger pointed at Jane from between her teeth. On the plate on her lap was the rest of the hand.

A right hand.

Her right wrist was a bandaged stump.

So was her right thigh.

She wore a sleeveless T-shirt. It had an arrow pointing to the left and read, 'I'M WITH STUPID.' It was spattered with dried brown blood and wet red blood. She didn't have on any pants. The plate with the severed hand covered her groin.

Jane could only stare at her, shocked.

With her remaining hand, the woman took the finger from between her teeth and nibbled skin off its side.

Jane gagged and looked away.

'Hi,' the woman said. 'I'm Linda. Who are you?'

She sounded cheery.

'Jane.'

'Haven't seen you around here before.' She dropped the finger onto her plate. It made a bad sound landing. 'Show me your arm?'

'What for?'

'Just because.'

Jane unbuttoned the cuff and slid the right sleeve of her chamois shirt up her forearm. When her fingers touched her arm, they felt like ice.

'Mmmm,' Linda said. 'You've got meat on you.'

Jane took a step backward, swallowed hard, and said, 'What's going on here?'

Linda grinned. Her front teeth were bloody. 'I'm eating myself, what does it look like?'

'Why?'

She shrugged and smirked. 'They let me.'

'They *let* you?'

'Yeah. They wouldn't let me eat nothing, you know? Just kept me here and fucked around with me and wouldn't give me nothing to eat. I got hungry. I got *real* hungry. I begged and begged for something to eat. So finally, Steve goes, "Okay, I'll get you some food. And what'll you have?" he asks me. So then I go, "Anything, anything." So then he cuts off my right foot and lets me eat that. Not much to a foot, but it was better than nothing.'

Jane took a deep breath. It didn't feel deep enough. Her heart seemed to be pounding too hard to let her breathe properly.

'I only just wish I hadn't of gone on my diet last year. You wanta stay away from diets, Janey. I dropped *thirty* pounds and wasn't I proud of myself! Biggest mistake I ever made. Shoot, I was only just skin 'n' bones when I got here, and things've gone downhill ever since. You're lucky you've got some meat on you. Take off your shirt for me, will you?'

Jane shook her head. 'No thanks.'

'Oh, come on.' She grinned.

'Look, I'll help you get out of here.'

'Oh, really? Do you really think so? Whoo! You'd better think again, Janey. Nobody gets out of here.'

'Are there others?'

'Why, sure. Me and Marjorie and Sue . . . woops, no more Sue. Poor girl just dwindled down to nothing.' Linda laughed. 'There's the new girl, too. She's a skinny thing already, and hasn't been here more'n a few days. I danced with her last night, 'n' I could feel her rib bones poking me.'

'Danced?' Jane heard herself murmur.

'Why, sure. The boys throw dances for us all the time. Steve plays himself a killer fiddle, and . . .'

'But your leg . . .?'

She laughed. 'I get around real good for a crip. Just lift up your shirt, okay? All I wanta do is get a look at how much meat you got on you.'

'Forget it. Who else is here? You, Marjorie, and the new girl.'

'Gail.'

'And Gail.'

'Not *and*. Gail, she's the new girl.'

The name suddenly pounded her.

A gala time.

'Where's Gail?' Jane asked.

'Where do you think?'

'Hey, come on.'

Linda batted her eyelids. 'You know what I want.'

'Okay, okay.' Jane lifted the bottom of her shirt, baring her midriff.

'Nice. You look good 'n' firm. You been working out?'

'Tell me where Gail is. Come on.'

'Higher.'

'Hey.'

'Do you wanta know where she is?'

Jane did as she was told.

Linda said, 'Oooo, nice. Come here so I can feel.' She reached out her hand.

Jane didn't move.

'Okay, be that way. Wanta see mine? I already had one of 'em, but . . .' She pulled up her T-shirt to show Jane.

Jane looked away fast and jerked her own shirt down so hard it made a soft *whap* as it went taut.

'Mighty tasty, but Sue's was better. Not that I got enough of it. They're all such a bunch of pigs around here, and poor Sue didn't have that much to go around in the first place, if you know what I mean.'

Jane whirled around and ran for the door.

'Don't you wanta know where Gail is?' Linda called.

Jane staggered into the hallway. She glanced both ways. Nobody.

As she ran toward the next door, she dug into her pocket and pulled out her pistol. She thumbed the safety off. With her left hand, she flung open the door.

This had to be Marjorie on the bed.

Apparently, Marjorie had been here longer than Linda. Too much was missing. She had leather harnesses holding her up.

'Heh-lowwww,' Marjorie greeted her. 'Come in, come in.'

Jane shook her head. Then she threw up.

'Well,' Marjorie said as Jane vomited, 'Isn't this a fine

how-do-you-do? All that wonderful grub going to waste on the floor. How am I supposed to get to it? Tell me that?'

This can't be happening. This just cannot be happening.

When her stomach was done erupting, she turned away from Marjorie's door. She stumbled down the hall.

'Bring me some in a cup!' Marjorie suggested, and giggled.

Jane stopped at the next door. She grabbed the knob, but hesitated.

This can't be as bad, she told herself. Gail's new.

She opened the door.

The woman flat on her back looked very pregnant. She still had both of her legs. They were spread wide apart and tied at the ankles to the corners of the bed frame. She suddenly sat up. She still had both her arms.

Nothing of this woman seemed to be missing. But she was naked and she looked as if she'd been worked on by people trying to make her scream.

'You've gotta get me out of here!' she blurted. 'They want my baby! They want my baby!'

'Are you the one who screamed?'

She nodded.

'Are you . . . starting labor?'

'Huh-uh, no.'

'That isn't why you . . .?'

'They wanta eat my baby.'

'Nobody's going to eat your baby.'

'Promise?'

'Yes. Are you Gail?'

'I'm Sandra.'

'Where's Gail?'

'You've gotta help me!'

'Shhh. I'm looking for Gail.'

'Please.'

'Don't worry. I'll get you out of here. Where's Gail?'

Sandra nodded her head to the left.

Jane rushed down the hall to the next room and threw open the door. The woman standing against the wall by the bed gazed at Jane with bulging eyes. She had a broad strip of duct tape across her mouth. Though her dark hair was a tangled mess and she looked haggard and terrified, she didn't appear to be badly hurt. A few bruises, many minor wounds that trickled blood – but none of her body parts had been removed. She stood with legs apart and arms outstretched, a human X fixed to the wall by tight strands of barbed wire. The blood came from places where the barbs had pierced her skin.

Wires crossed her ankles, her thighs, her waist, her ribcage, her breasts, her neck and forehead. They looped across her raised upper arms, and they looked very tight where they crossed her wrists. Thin streamers of blood from her wrists ran down her arms and armpits and sides all the way down past her hips.

Jane glanced around to make sure nobody else was there. Then she scanned the room more carefully, looking for the envelope.

This is Gail's room. The place to have a 'gala time'. This might just be where Mog put the envelope.

Jane suddenly wondered how she could even *think* about the envelope at a time like this.

Fifty-one thousand bucks, that's how.

Right, and what about self-preservation? I've gotta get out of here! I've gotta get these poor wrecked women out of here before these fucking lunatics come along and catch me and . . .

I'll shoot myself, she thought, before I'll let them do this shit to me.

Don't shoot yourself, shoot them.

'It's gonna be all right,' she said. 'I'll get you out of here.'

As she stepped closer, she could see that the woman was standing rigid, trying not to move, but having trouble breathing through her nostrils. Each time she inhaled, her breasts, her ribcage and her flat belly pressed against strands, sinking half a dozen barbs into raw bloody holes already there.

Jane walked up close to her and stopped. She glanced over her shoulder.

So far, so good.

She switched the pistol to her left hand, and used her right to rip the tape away from the woman's mouth. The mouth sprang open and the woman gasped – and whimpered as her wild breathing drove barbs into her skin.

'Take it easy,' Jane whispered. 'Easy. You're hurting yourself.'

The woman shut her eyes. Tears spilled down her face.

'Just take it easy and I'll get these wires off you.'

Jane studied the hook-up. Each strand seemed to be attached at both ends to swivel eyes in brass plates screwed into the wooden wall. This was no make-shift rig that had been thrown together in a few minutes. Each plate took four screws.

'Was this already here?' Jane asked.

'Uh. The things here in the wall?' Her voice sounded high and shaky. 'Yeah.'

Jane started to untwist one end of the wire that crossed the woman's breasts. 'Are you Gail?'

'Yes.'

'You're in a lot better shape than the others.'

'They . . . they only got me . . . Monday.'

Monday. Gail.

Jane looked at her face. It did seem a little familiar. Was this the face she'd seen on the TV news? 'You're the one from the mall.'

'They got me . . . on the way home.'

With a final twist, the wire loosened its grip on the brass eye. Jane pulled it through and shoved it aside. She started to work on the strand across Gail's ribcage. 'Who's doing this stuff?'

'I don't know . . . who.'

'How many?'

'Three? Maybe more but . . . I've only seen three . . . together. When they got me. And at the dances. There could be more. I don't know. They have masks they wear.'

'Where are they now?'

'I don't know.'

She got the second wire loose, drew it out through the brass eye, let it swing away, and started on the strand across Gail's waist. 'Did they leave the house?'

'I don't know.'

'Did they drive away? Did you hear a car?'

'No. I don't know where they are. They don't tell me what they're doing. They don't tell me much. They just come in and do things and go.'

'What things?'

'A lot of stuff.'

'Do they come in very often?'

'It seems like . . . all the time.'

Jane finished the wire at Gail's waist, started on the one across the girl's left thigh, then decided it would be better to free her arms before starting on the legs. That way, maybe Gail could lend a hand. She wished she'd thought of that earlier.

Straightening up, Jane started to untwist the wire beneath Gail's upper arm.

'What about tonight?' she asked. 'Have you seen any of these guys tonight?'

'One came in a while ago.'

'How long ago?'

'I don't know. Maybe an hour. He's the one . . . He put me here with the wires. He raped me on the bed, and then he made me stand here and he wired me and then he raped me again. He did it really rough that time, and made the wires stab me. It really hurt, and that's when I bit him. So then he taped my mouth.'

'You bit him, huh? Good for you.'

'But I couldn't breathe. I thought I was gonna suffocate.'

'You'll be fine.' Jane reached high and began to work on the wire under Gail's wrist. 'I'll have you out of here in just a minute.'

'Who are you?'

'Jane.'

'Are you with the police?'

'No.'

'I don't . . . how come you're here?'

'A very long story.'

'You saw the others, didn't you?'

'How many are there? All together?'

'Four. Including me. That I know of, anyway.'

'I saw the other three,' Jane said.

'They're really fucked up.'

'Yeah. So I noticed. Except Sandra. She's pretty much okay and she isn't nuts like the others. Maybe because they haven't started cutting her up yet. What sort of asylum is this, anyhow?'

She freed the wrist, and Gail lowered her arm.

'I'll get your legs,' Jane said, crouching. 'You get the wires up there. And keep an eye on the door. Anyone shows up, yell.'

'They . . . maybe they're in the show room?'

'What?' Jane looked up at her. Gail was unwinding an end of the wire across her throat.

'They've got a special room downstairs. It's like a movie theater. They've got one of those giant-screen TVs in there. They took us in and we watched *Saturday Night Fever* last night before the dance.'

'Downstairs?'

Jane thought about all the noise she'd made at the front of the house: ringing the doorbell, pounding the door, breaking the window.

What if they'd heard her and come to the door and let her in and pretended to be friendly and then had taken her by surprise and brought her to one of these rooms and . . .?

Didn't happen. Don't think about it.

I could've ended up like . . .

Don't!

She finished with the wire across Gail's left thigh, then reached down for the ankle wire.

'Is it soundproof?' she asked.

'What?'

'That viewing room downstairs. Is it soundproof?'

'I don't know. Maybe.'

'Must be. If that's where they are.'

'It might be where they are,' Gail said.

'It would explain why nobody's shown up yet,' Jane said. 'Unless they went somewhere. God, I hope they went somewhere. If we can just get out of here before they come back . . .'

'Just the two of us?' Gail asked.

'No, we'll take Sandra.' Finished with the ankle, Jane shifted sideways and started to unfasten the wire at Gail's right thigh.

'She's awfully pregnant.'

'All the more reason to take her,' Jane said.

'She'll slow us down.'

'I'm not going to leave her.' Glancing up, she saw that Gail was done with the wire across her forehead and was busy with the one pinning her right wrist to the wall. 'You don't have to help.'

'That's okay. I'm sticking with you. Whatever you want.'

'Thanks.' Jane worked at the ankle. 'We'll have to leave the other two. I don't see how we could take them with us.'

'Anyway, they're crazy.'

'Yeah,' Jane said. 'Maybe it makes you crazy when you eat yourself. What we'll do, we'll try to make it to my car and we'll go somewhere and call the cops.'

'Let's call them from here.'

'If we have to. It'd be better to get away first. The sooner we're out of here, the better.' She drew the ankle wire out through the brass eye and looked up in time to see Gail shove the arm wire aside.

'That's it?' she asked, rising.

'That's it.' Gail stepped away from the wall and suddenly wrapped her arms around Jane and squeezed her hard and began to sob. Jane kept her gun hand down. She put her other hand on Gail's back and stroked her gently. The skin of Gail's back felt slippery.

'It's all right,' she whispered. 'It's all right.'

'You ... you saved me. I'll never forget ... Oh, God, you'll never know ...'

'We aren't out of here yet, Gail. Come on.' She eased Gail away from her. 'We've still gotta get Sandra.'

'I can't leave like this.' Sniffling, she wiped her eyes.

'Where're your clothes?'

'I don't know.'

'Just grab a sheet.'

Gail sniffed and nodded and stepped toward the bed. Where she'd been standing a moment ago, Jane saw the rough, body-shaped outline of the brass plates on the wall, the strands of barbed wire sticking out every which way.

Midway between the two brass plates that had held the wire across Gail's ribcage, a thick white envelope was tacked to the wall.

The sweat from Gail's back had smeared the ink of Jane's name.

Chapter Thirty-three

Jane tore the envelope from the wall. It felt soggy. She plucked the thumb-tacks out of each end, and tossed them aside.

'What's that?' Gail asked, wrapping a bedsheet around her shoulders. 'I felt something back there ...'

'It's what I came for.'

The envelope was sealed, and seemed at least two inches thick.

'What's in it?'

Jane shook her head. Clamping the pistol between her knees, she folded the envelope to make a tight package around the money. Then she reached up beneath the hanging front of her shirt and shoved the envelope down the front pocket of her jeans.

Taking the pistol in her right hand, she rushed for the door. She crouched before peeking out.

The hallway looked clear.

'Let's go.' She walked quickly, watching the hall ahead, twisting around to check the rear.

Gail hurried along behind Jane. The bedsheet was wrapped around her shoulders, held together in front with both hands and trailing behind her like the train of a child's makeshift wedding gown. She had a very frightened look on her face, but she tried to smile when Jane glanced at her.

Sandra was braced up on her elbows when they entered her room. She gazed at them over the huge mound of her belly.

'We're getting out of here,' Jane said.

Sandra started to cry.

'What should I do?' Gail asked.

'Watch the hall,' Jane said. On her way to the bed, she switched the pistol to her left hand. With her right hand, she reached under the back of her shirt and pulled the knife from her belt.

She slipped the blade underneath the rope that stretched from Sandra's right ankle to the bed frame. Her hand was shaking very badly. The blade of her knife jittered under the taut rope.

'Anyone coming?' she asked.

'Not yet,' Gail said from the doorway.

Jane tried to sever the rope with a single quick upward tug. The rope jumped and jerked Sandra's foot off the mattress, then slipped off the tip of the knife and dropped Sandra's foot.

Jane saw the shallow cut and muttered, 'Shit.'

She started sawing at the rope.

She pictured herself a long-time prisoner here, a ruin like Linda, eating herself and wondering how it ever came to this. *It came to this because I didn't sharpen my knife. I could've done it so easily, too. If only I'd bothered.*

The rope parted. She leaped sideways and started on the other rope.

'Just a few more seconds,' she said.

'It's okay here,' Gail told her.

As she sawed at the rope, she looked up at Sandra. 'Will you be able to walk?'

'I don't know.' Sandra snuffled. 'My legs . . . I can't feel them.'

'They look okay – probably just asleep. Once you're up and moving, you'll be fine.'

Sandra bobbed her head. Her eyes were red and shiny, her face dripping. She had stopped crying, though. 'What about Marjorie and Linda?'

'We'll have to leave them.'

'Good.'

'Good?'

'They're so horrible.' She took a deep breath, making a high whiny noise that trembled. 'They're after my baby. They call out at night and say . . . awful things about eating it, like which parts they . . .'

'Got it!' Jane blurted as her knife popped up through the top of the rope. 'Let's move, let's go!'

Sandra pushed at the mattress. She sat up and stared at her legs. Then her lips stretched thin and twitched at the corners. 'I can't move them!'

'Don't worry.' Jane said. She called over her shoulder, 'Give us a hand.'

Gail nodded and hurried over.

Quickly, Jane slipped her knife under the belt at the back of her jeans. She set her pistol on the mattress by Sandra's right foot. She scowled at it. She hated not having it in her hand.

Gail had to let go of her sheet, and she let out a quiet little whimper as it slipped off her body.

They each took hold of an ankle.

Together, they swung Sandra's legs sideways and off the bed and lowered her feet to the floor. Then they took her by the upper arms and hauled her up. After she'd been standing for a few seconds, Jane said to Gail, 'You got her?'

'Yeah.'

'Right back.' She let go and hurried to the end of the bed. With Gail and Sandra both watching over their shoulders, she picked up the fallen sheet, took out her knife again, and cut a straight, two-foot slash in its center.

'Neat idea,' Gail said.

'You want one, Sandra?'

'I guess. My legs are starting to . . . Oooo . . . Pins and needles . . . ow!'

Jane yanked the sheet off the bed and cut a slit for Sandra's head. She put her knife away, picked up her pistol, and carried the sheets to the women. One-handed, she helped Sandra and Gail into the garments.

With Sandra in the middle, her arms across the shoulders of Gail and Jane, they hurried across the room and into the hallway. Jane had taken the right side to keep her gun hand free, but now she regretted it; she was nearest the bedroom doors.

Though she kept her eyes forward, her peripheral vision saw into Marjorie's room, saw the remnants of the woman swaying in her harness above the bed.

'Hey!' Marjorie yelled, suddenly twisting and lurching.

'We'll send help for you,' Jane called. And took one more step that put Marjorie out of view.

'No! You can't take 'em! Hey! Sandra! Sandra, you get back to your room! Gail! Come back!' Then she shrieked, *'They're getting away!'*

With every shout from Marjorie, Sandra flinched rigid against Jane's side as if she were being lashed.

'It's okay,' Jane whispered.

'Help! They're getting away!'

'Make her be quiet!' Sandra begged.

Sure thing, Jane thought. 'We'll be out of here in a minute,' she said.

'*Linda! They're getting away!*'

Linda, at least, was staying quiet so far.

That's all we'd need, Jane thought – both of them yelling like a couple of maniacs.

At Linda's doorway, Jane looked in.

The bed was empty except for the plate and the gnawed hand. Jane swiveled her head to scan the room as she hurried by with Sandra and Gail. She saw no Linda.

'Where'd Linda go?' Gail asked.

'Who knows? At least she isn't yelling.'

Jane realized that Marjorie had stopped yelling. From the room down the hall came growls and snarls of rage, mixed in with squeaks and creaks and groans from the leather harness, and buckle sounds that clinked and jingled.

'Marjorie's going ape-shit,' she muttered.

Sandra gave her a quick, frantic grin, then looked back and yelled, 'You won't get my baby now, you crazy bitch!'

'*That's what you think!*'

Sandra faced front. She quickened her pace, rushing Jane and Gail along with her outstretched arms. In an odd, very high-pitched voice, she said, 'Shit?' as if asking a question.

'Should've kept your mouth shut,' Gail told her.

Realizing that Sandra had recovered the use of her legs, Jane said, 'I'll go first.' She dropped her arm from across Sandra's back, slipped free and hurried ahead.

The two seemed to get along fine without her.

At the top of the stairs, she studied the area below. She saw the foyer and the front door, dimly lighted by the wagon wheel chandelier.

She saw nobody.

She considered a quick dash down the stairs and out the door. Such speed would be noisy, though. In spite of all the noise so far, she wanted silence now.

Besides, Sandra was enormously pregnant. Even with her legs recovered, she wouldn't be capable of much speed.

So, Jane made her way slowly down the stairs, treading lightly, sometimes glancing back. Sandra and Gail, just behind her, seemed to be doing fine. In their bedsheets, they looked like overgrown urchins dressed as angels for some sort of skid-row Christmas pageant. Battered, wingless angels who were sweaty and haggard and scared.

And I'm leading them to safety, Jane thought.

Did Mog send me here to save them?

Nobody's saved yet.

At the bottom of the stairs, Jane hurried to the door and opened it and looked outside. The grounds looked the same as before: dark and empty.

She stepped back, swinging the door wide for Gail and Sandra. Then she followed them out onto the veranda and eased the door shut. 'My car's all the way at the bottom of the driveway,' she whispered. 'It's pretty far away. We'd better hurry. You go first, I'll cover the rear.'

She waited, watching them climb down the veranda stairs.

Hurry!

At any moment, headlights might push a pale glow into the darkness at the top of the driveway. Or the door might be flung open behind them.

Who knows where the bastards might come from!

And chase us down.

And take us back inside.

And oh God I don't want to think about it – just let us please make it to my car and get out of here – don't let 'em get us, please, please – as if God gives a rat's ass anyhow or He wouldn't let scum like these filthy bastards ever get born in the first place to do these things to people – or if they have to get born at least He should stop them and save all the poor innocent . . .

'Wait,' she said, and stopped at the bottom of the veranda stairs.

Gail and Sandra looked back.

With her left hand, Jane dug into the front pocket of her jeans. She brought out her car keys. 'Catch.' She tossed them to Gail. 'You two go on ahead. But watch out and hide if a car comes along. Get off the driveway fast. Hide in the trees. You'll be all right as long as you aren't seen. My car's off to the right when you get to the bottom of the driveway. A Dodge Dart. Get in and wait for me, but if somebody else comes along, just take off – then get the cops out here as fast as you can. I shouldn't be more than five minutes, though.'

'What're you *doing*?' Gail asked.

'I lost my necklace.' She touched her neck. 'I think I know where it happened.'

'Forget it,' Gail said. 'Don't go back in there.'

'Not for a necklace,' Sandra added. 'They might get you if you go back in.'

'My name's engraved on it.'

Gail moaned. 'I'll come with you.'

'No. Do like I said, okay?'

'I think they're in there,' Gail said. 'Their movie might be ending any second . . .'

'Then we'd all better hurry. Get going.' Jane turned away. At the top of the veranda stairs, she looked back and saw the sheeted women heading for the driveway. She hurried to the front door.

Locked.

Of course.

So she entered the house through the window she'd used before. There was no longer a need for silence. She wanted to be quick about this, get it done and catch up with Gail and Sandra.

Either they're here or they're not.

She raced through the ground level of the house, checking doors.

In the living room, she found a black door to left of the fireplace. She turned its knob, eased the door wide enough to see the darkness on the other side, then opened it a bit wider and slipped in and gently shut it.

She stood with her back against the door.

She wished her heart would slow down. She wished she could get a big enough breath. Gasping for air, she used a sleeve to wipe the sweat out of her eyes. This room seemed even hotter than the rest of the house.

On the giant-screen TV at the end of the room, Barbara Streisand was belting out a song in a movie that looked like it might be *Funny Girl*. The volume was terribly high, the voice blasting.

No wonder the guys hadn't heard anything. Whether or not the room was soundproofed, the noise from their show would've been sufficient to overwhelm every other sound in the house.

Jane saw the silhouettes of three heads above the seat-backs of the front row.

Hail hail, the gang's all here.

They took up the center three seats of the first row, leaving an empty seat at each end. Jane counted six rows. Seating for an audience of thirty.

But the Show Room appeared to be empty except for these three.

So-vile and his buddies, she supposed.

In the light from the TV screen, Jane could see that the heads were facing the front. They had short hair.

Clean-cut fellas.

None turned around as she walked down the aisle.

When she got closer, she saw that their shoulders were bare.

No wonder, it's so damn hot in here.

She entered the second row of seats and crept in. From here, she had a fairly good side view of the three. They looked young, not much older than twenty. They looked ordinary. Though she could only see the left side of each face, she was fairly sure that she didn't know any of these men.

Each had a can of soda, and they took turns reaching into a big bowl of popcorn on the lap of the man in middle.

She shot the middle one first, the muzzle of her pistol an inch from the back of his head.

The shot came at a quiet place in the movie.

The heads of the two other men started to swing around.

She shot one in the temple. She aimed for the temple of the other but his head was still turning and her bullet punched through his left eye.

It was over very fast.

The one in the middle was still pitching forward by the time Jane finished her third shot. He wasn't wearing any pants. His soda can rolled toward the TV, flinging sudsy fluid. Somehow, the popcorn bowl positioned itself just right, so the top of his head jammed into it and he stayed that way on his knees with his butt in the air and his head in the bowl.

The one who'd taken the bullet in his temple simply slumped sideways as if to lean on an invisible companion in the neighboring seat. His can, up-ended on his lap, burbled soda onto his half-erect penis.

The one who'd been shot in the eye fell to the floor and landed on his side next to his friend. He looked as if he might be down there for a special perspective on his friend's stunt with the popcorn bowl. He still held onto his drink. He suddenly spasmed, crushing the can so it shot out a gush of soda.

Jane was pretty sure that all three men were dead.

She shot each of them one more time, to make sure.

Then she thumbed the release and slid the thin black magazine out of her pistol. She clamped the pistol between her thighs. With the empty magazine in her left hand, she used her right hand to scoop cartridges out of the pocket of her shirt.

Both of her hands felt cold and tingly. So did her face.

She tried to thumb a fresh cartridge into the top of the magazine. She dropped it, and tried with another. This one slipped from between her thumb and forefinger, and she jabbed her thumb on a sharp metal corner of the magazine.

'Ow!' She stuck the thumb in her mouth.

Forget it. They're all dead, anyway. I don't need the gun.

So she dumped the ammo into her pocket, the .22s tumbling against her breast and dropping to click against the others at the bottom of the pocket.

She took a last look at the three men.

Did I really do that?

Then she said, 'Fucking perverts,' turned away from them and walked to the aisle. There, she broke into a trot. She hadn't been very long at this. She might be able to overtake Gail and Sandra before they could reach her car.

At the rear of the Show Room, she shouldered the door open. While wiping the knobs on both sides with the loose front of her shirt, she wondered if there were other places where she had left fingerprints.

Probably.

My prints aren't on file, anyway.

What about hairs and threads and . . .?

The only sure way to destroy every bit of physical evidence would be to burn the place.

No way, she told herself.

Finished with the door knobs, she rushed toward the foyer.

Burning the house might be a great idea, but she'd need to take Marjorie and Linda outside first, and she never wanted to *see* either of those women again, much less touch them, try to carry them . . .

And then she *did* see Linda.

Linda stood on her one leg, her back to the front door, and grinned at Jane. In her only hand, she held a big, shiny meat cleaver. 'Hi-dee ho,' she said.

Jane stopped. 'What's going on?'

'I've got the hungries.'

'It's all over, Linda. I'll be sending help for you and Marjorie as soon as . . .'

'We don't need no help, Janey. We get along jusssst fine. Fact is, I was about to help *myself* to Marjorie, but she's slim pickins at this stage, so . . . *HAPPY TRAILS!!!*'

As she shouted, she bumped her way off the door with her bare rump and lunged at Jane, hopping, hoisting the meat cleaver high.

Jane aimed the pistol at her face. '*FREEZE!*'

Though Linda couldn't know the gun was empty, she

squealed with delight. She kept hopping forward on her single leg, bouncing closer and closer to Jane, swinging her cleaver in circles overhead, flapping her arm stump up and down, kicking her leg stump back and forth, giggling as she hopped, her one breast bobbing and swinging under her grimy 'I'M WITH STUPID' T-shirt.

Jane threw her pistol at Linda.

It seemed like such a dumb move. In every shoot-out she had ever seen on the screen, the bad guy who runs out of bullets throws his gun at the hero. The hurled weapon sails by. Or bounces harmlessly off the hero's shoulder.

Jane's pistol smacked Linda in the face. The blow knocked her head sideways and gashed her cheekbone. As the gun caromed off her face, her giggle changed to a cry of pain and she went backward – hopped a couple of times, waving her arm and swiping at the air with her stump. Then she slammed the floor with her back.

Jane leaped across her body and kicked her hand. The cleaver skidded away.

Linda flopped over onto her belly. She started to push herself up.

Jane kicked the arm out from under her.

Linda dropped hard, face striking the floor.

'Stay put!' Jane shouted.

Linda lay sprawled on the foyer floor, gasping and sobbing. Jane snatched up her pistol, then ran to the front door and jerked it open. As she used her shirt to wipe the inside knob, she said, 'I'll send help.'

She shut the door, wiped its outside handle, and raced for the driveway.

Chapter Thirty-four

She was huffing and sweaty by the time she reached her car. She found Gail behind the steering wheel and Sandra stretched out across the back seat. Gail swung the door open for her, then scooted over. Jane climbed in. The pistol in her back pocket pushed hard against her buttock, but she didn't feel up to doing anything about it. She fluttered the front of her shirt to stir some air against her hot skin.

'How'd it go?' Gail asked.

The engine was quietly idling. She shifted, and swung onto the road before answering. 'Okay.'

'You found it all right?'

Found what? she wondered. Ah! My non-existent necklace. 'Yeah. It was where I thought it'd be.'

'Did you run into anyone?' Sandra asked from the back seat. She sounded nervous.

'No. Thank God. Maybe the guys went out to a movie, or something. This *is* Saturday night.'

'Date night,' Sandra muttered. She sounded bitter.

'Like those bastards needed dates,' Gail said. 'They had a houseful of fucking slaves. You gonna turn your headlights on?'

'Oh.' Jane put them on. 'If we see a car come along, you'd better duck out of sight.'

'Don't let 'em get us again,' Sandra said.

'I won't.'

'They wanted my baby. That's why they took me. They were gonna dig a fire pit in the yard and do it like a pig – like . . .' She sobbed. 'Like a . . . Hawaiian thing . . . a luau. Steve . . . that's what he wanted to do, and Linda said she knew how, she'd lived on Maui and . . .' Then Sandra gave up trying to talk.

Jane glanced back at her, but quickly returned her gaze to

the road. 'I never heard any news reports about you.'

'They grabbed her in Reno,' Gail said. 'That's why. It didn't make the news out here. They got Linda in Oregon and Marjorie in New Mexico.'

'You're the only local gal?' Jane asked.

'Yeah. One of them got the hots for me. He used to watch me at the store, he said. The B. Dalton at the mall?'

'Yeah.'

'He said that's why they picked me.'

'Are you all right back there, Sandra?'

The high, uncertain voice answered, 'Yeah.'

To Gail, she said, 'Where do you want me to take you?'

'Home?'

'Where do you live?'

'On Standhope.'

Brace's street.

She was vaguely surprised to find that she could feel pain and loss through the heavy daze that seemed to muffle her mind.

'Do you know where that is?' Gail asked.

'Yeah. I used to have a friend . . . Maybe I should take you to the hospital. You could both use some medical care.'

'I don't want a hospital,' she said.

'I wanta go home, too,' Sandra said.

'Do you have people in Reno?'

'My . . . husband.' She resumed crying hard.

Gail looked around at her. 'You can phone him from my place, if you want.'

'Phone the police first,' Jane told Gail. 'They've gotta get up to the house for Linda and Marjorie. Do you know the address?'

Gail shook her head. 'You can call the cops, okay? You'll come in with us . . .'

'I can't.'

'What?'

'I'm going to drop you two off and disappear. I can't get mixed up with cops and stuff.'

'You can't? How come?'

'Any sort of attention, and I'm . . . I ran away from my husband a few months ago. He used to . . . do terrible things to me. He'll kill me if he finds me. And I know he's looking. He even has private investigators searching for me. They check the newspapers . . . even a general description of me, and they'll figure it's a lead and come looking. If they have any idea where I am, they'll tell him and . . . God only knows what he'll do to me. I might be better off with Savile and his pals.'

'No, you wouldn't,' Gail said.

'I have to be kept out of this.'

'You saved our lives.'

'Looks that way.'

'I'll never do anything to hurt you.'

'Me neither,' Sandra said from the back seat, and snuffled.

'Why don't you say it was a guy who saved you?' Jane suggested.

'If that's what you want.'

'Sure,' Sandra said.

'But why were you there?' Gail asked. 'Why, really?'

'I went in to find the envelope. It has money in it. I was just after the money. I had no idea about any of the other things.'

'You didn't know we were there?'

'Nope.'

'So . . . you just found us by accident?'

'I'm not sure how much of an accident it was,' Jane said, 'on the part of whoever put the envelope there. You didn't see who put it there?'

'I felt it behind me, that's all. I didn't see it until you showed it to me.'

'The guy who wired you to the wall must've known it was there,' Jane said.

Or put it there, himself.

'Guess so.'

She suddenly wondered if Mog was one of the men she'd shot. She had always suspected that a mission would eventually bring her face-to-face with him, but . . .

If one of those guys was Mog, what was he doing butt-naked in the Show Room with his buddies watching a Streisand movie and stuffing his face with popcorn when he knew I'd be coming?

That didn't make any sense.

But the envelope had been in plain sight on the wall. The guy who wired up Gail couldn't possibly have missed it.

He had to be Mog.

No, not necessarily. The guy who put it there might've been following Mog's instructions.

But he might've been Mog.

'What did he look like?' Jane asked.

Gail shook her head. 'He wore a mask. One of those leather masks with zippers. Red leather. It covered his whole head. It made him look like . . . an executioner.'

'What about the rest of him?'

'He was big. He was awfully big. Maybe six-four. And he was all muscles. His . . . he had a huge *thing*. I mean, it was terrible. It was way too big, but he . . . he managed.' Gail turned her head away and stared out the window.

'Are you sure about his size?'

'Are you kidding?'

Jane felt an odd tightness in her throat.

Even though she hadn't seen any of them standing up, she was certain that none of the three guys in the Show Room had been over six feet tall.

The man who'd fixed Gail to the wall with barbed wire was nobody Jane had shot.

I do believe that I'm about to scream.

Cut it out, she told herself. Whoever he was, wherever he might've been, you're away from him now. You're safe. We're all safe. No call for panic, here.

She stopped for a red light, and realized she was only a block or two away from Standhope Street. She looked over at Gail. 'Was there anything else about him? Tattoos, a birthmark, any sort of scars . . .?'

Gail nodded.

'What?'

She looked at Jane and frowned. 'He didn't have any tan at all. None. A guy like that, you'd figure him for a sun-worshipper, you know? But he was white all over. It gave me the creeps.'

From the back seat, Sandra said, 'I never saw a guy like that.'

'I didn't either till tonight,' Gail said.

'He wasn't at the dances?' Jane asked.

'No, he sure wasn't. Or if he was, he must've been somewhere out of sight. I never laid eyes on him till he came into my room . . . a couple of hours before you showed up.'

'Man,' Jane muttered. 'He's *gotta* be the one who put the envelope there.'

'I just hope to God I never see him again.'

Slowing as she approached Standhope, she asked, 'Which way?'

'Go right.'

Right. Away from Brace's apartment. Thank God.

'It'll be a few more blocks,' Gail told her.

'Do you live with somebody?'

'My folks. They're probably out of their minds. They probably think I'm dead. Look, couldn't you come in and meet them? I mean, you saved my life. They'll really want to meet you.'

'Not tonight. The fewer people who see me . . . Maybe I'll get in touch with you sometime after all this has blown over.'

'That'd be great.'

'Remember about saying I'm a man, okay?'

'I won't forget,' Gail said.

'Me neither,' Sandra said.

'And don't tell what kind of car I drive. Say it's some other kind. How about a Jeep Cherokee?'

'That sounds good. What color?'

'Black.'

'Okay.'

From the back seat, Jane heard, 'A black Jeep Cherokee.'

'Do we know your name?' Gail asked.

'No. The fewer things you need to lie about, the better. The cops'll ask you what I look like, so maybe you should just describe me the way I am – except turn me into a male.'

The sound of a small laugh came from Gail. 'That's pretty good. Do you do this sort of thing a lot?'

'Not really.' Jane slowed and turned a corner.

'Hey.'

'I know.' She swung to a curb in front of a dark house and killed her headlights. 'I want to let you off here.'

'We're still two blocks . . . Oh. Yeah. I get it. This'll be fine.'

'I'd like to drop you off at your door, but . . .'

'No, this is great.' She turned toward Jane. 'I think . . . I'd like us to be friends. It isn't just what you did. There's something about you that . . . hell, you're gonna start thinking I'm a lesbian or something . . .'

'Not that there's anything wrong with it.'

Gail laughed. 'Right. But I'm not. But I really like you. I sort of feel like we might have a lot in common, or . . . I don't know.'

'I know. And I think you're right.'

'So . . . is there a way for me to get in touch?'

'I'll get in touch with you. Don't worry, I know your name and where you work. And almost where you live.'

'Okay, then.'

'Okay.'

Gail reached over and squeezed Jane's wrist. 'Take care.'

'You, too.' She looked over her shoulder. 'You, too, Sandra.'

'Thanks. And thanks for getting me out of there.'

Gail climbed out of the car and opened a rear door. As she helped Sandra out, Jane said, 'Remember to lie for me, gals.'

'You bet,' Gail said.

'Yeah,' said Sandra. 'And thanks again.'

'My regards to the hubby.'

Sandra laughed in a way that sounded almost happy.

Then Gail shut the door.

As they started across the street, Jane swung away from the

curb. She watched them in the side mirror. In the white bedsheets, they looked like a couple of overgrown trick-or-treaters out in ghost costumes on the wrong night.

Chapter Thirty-five

Back on Standhope, she drove in the direction of the Royal Gardens apartment complex.

I won't even stop, she told herself. I'll just take a look at the place, just to . . . Why? Just to torture myself? Just to rub it in how I lost him and now when I really need someone – not *someone*, Brace – now when I need him, I can't go to him?

I don't need him. Hope he rots, the filthy son-of-a-bitch. Him and his cute little teeny-bopper slut.

As she drove along, she realized that her right buttock hurt from the imprint of the pistol. Shifting her weight, she reached back, pulled the weapon out of her pocket, and sighed. She tucked it between her thighs.

Could always reload and pay them a visit, she thought. Blow 'em both away. No big deal, just running up the score a bit.

It made her feel sick to think about it, even in a joking way. *I don't want to shoot anybody!* It was bad enough shooting those three . . .

A block from the Royal Gardens, she turned off Standhope and headed for home.

She supposed she ought to get rid of the gun. If she kept it, she might end up using it again. Besides, she was in danger from the law as long as she had the murder weapon in her possession. *The Godfather* movie had taught her that. And the lesson had been reinforced by plenty of other movies, and scads of crime novels. It was a physical link to the shootings. Being caught with it could mean real trouble.

But what if I need it?

I won't need it, she told herself.

So how do I get rid of it? she wondered. Throw it off the bridge? Right, so Rale or Swimp or some kid can fish it out of the creek and use it on someone? Toss it in a dumpster? Bury it? Gotta think of a way to dispose of the thing so nobody'll have a chance of ever finding it.

Best way to make sure nobody gets their hands on it, she thought, is to keep it myself.

I don't want it! What if I use it again?

I won't, she told herself. I'd just better keep it. That way, I'll know who has it.

Besides, no telling how Mog got the pistol in the first place. What if he went to a gun shop and bought it under my name? Could he do that? Hell, why not? He gets into my locked house and writes on me whenever he gets the urge, shouldn't be any big trick putting my name on a few government forms.

I'd damn well *better* hang on to the thing.

If I get rid of the ammo . . .

Up the street, a car was parked at the curb in front of her house. It looked very much like Brace's old Ford.

Even before she spotted Brace, she knew that it *was* his car. It had to be his. He'd come to see her, and she was about to face him and she suddenly felt squirmy and hot deep down.

I don't need this. Oh, God. What does he want? Why tonight? I don't need this. I don't!

As she steered into the driveway, her headlights swept across Brace. He was sitting on the front stairs, leaning way back with his elbows on the stoop.

Jane moaned.

To find Brace here seemed almost more strange and dreamlike than what had happened back at the house on Mayr Heights.

She climbed out of her car and approached him. She felt

sick with despair and hope. Brace stood up as she walked toward him.

'What do you want?' she heard herself ask as she stopped in front of him. Her voice sounded far away and cold. She felt as if her whole body were trembling, inside and out.

Brace stepped forward and put his hands on her upper arms. His touch made Jane flinch.

'Don't,' she said.

Instead of letting go, he held her and moved up close against her.

'Damn it!' She shoved him away.

This time, he did let go. He took a step backward and frowned at her. 'I don't care about your game,' he said, his voice soft. 'You can run around chasing Mog's envelopes from now till hell freezes over, I'll go along with it. I'll worry like crazy every time you step out of the house for one of your missions, but I won't get in your way. I won't let it come between us. The past week has been . . . I was fine before I met you, but . . .' He shook his head. 'I can't get along without you – not now, not any more.'

They were the sort of words she would've longed to hear – before watching Brace with the girl. Now, they seemed like a mockery.

'You looked like you were doing just fine Monday night,' she said.

He looked confused.

'You and your cute little teeny-bopper slut.'

'What?'

'You're not the only one who can sneak around and spy on people.'

As he shook his head, a corner of his mouth turned up. 'You spied on me, huh? Well, I suppose I deserved it. But what is it that you saw?'

'You know damn well what I saw.'

'Me and my "cute little teeny-bopper slut"?'

'You got it, pal.'

'When was this?'

'Oh, come on. You don't remember? What is it, an everyday occurrence, slipping it to your students?'

'Is that what you think you saw?'

'It's what I did see.'

'I don't see how.'

'It was easy. You should've been more careful about closing your curtains.'

Brace's jaw suddenly dropped.

'Ah. You do remember.'

'This was Monday night, around one or two in the morning?'

'Now you've got it.'

'*You're* the one she saw in the window.'

Jane sneered. 'Yeah, me.'

'You scared the hell out of half the people in the building. You're lucky the cops didn't get you.'

'You called the cops?'

'I didn't, personally. Dennis made the call.'

'Dennis?'

'Lois's husband.'

'Lois?'

'The one who saw you. You *really* gave her a scare. I went down to their place just after it happened, and she was hysterical. She thought you were a guy, for one thing. And she said you looked insane.'

Jane shook her head. 'What're you trying to . . .?

'They were . . . actually going at it when you looked? No wonder she was so upset. But how could you mistake Dennis for me? We might be about the same size, but the resemblance sure stops there.'

'You trying to say it wasn't you?'

'Of course it wasn't me. You didn't see what you thought you saw, Jane.' He smiled slightly. 'So you thought it was me "slipping it" to Lois. That's what you get for spying.'

'I saw you.'

'Not my face, obviously. Or, if you did, your mind must've been playing tricks on you.'

Jane gazed at him. 'I know it was you,' she said. She *had* seen his face. True, the girl's back had been in the way most of the time, but . . .

'They *were* in my old apartment. We traded when they got married, so they could be down by the pool.'

'You traded?'

'It was all on the up and up.'

Jane blinked.

What is going on? she wondered. What is this? Has everything gone crazy?

'Oh, man,' Brace said. 'I gave you that business card, didn't I? It still shows me living in number twelve, so that's where you . . . I'm in twenty-two now. I'm directly above twelve. It never occurred to me that you might come over on your own, especially not after you'd dumped me.'

She heard herself say, 'What about your mail boxes?'

'What about them?'

'Did you trade mail boxes?'

He frowned and tilted his head a bit like a curious dog. 'You were going by the mail boxes. Ah. Well. We thought it'd be a lot easier all around if we just kept our same mail boxes. We didn't feel like getting into that whole change-of-address hassle . . .' Brace's smile returned. 'See what happens when you go sneaking around and you don't really know what's going on?'

'I'm supposed to believe this?'

'Yes.'

'Why?'

'Because I would never lie to you.'

'How do I know that?'

'Take my word for it.'

'Yeah. Sure.'

'Let's take a little drive. I'll introduce you to Lois and Dennis.'

'Are you kidding?'

'Or you could just look in the window at them.'

'Very funny.'

He checked his wristwatch. 'They're probably still up. Let's give them a call on the phone.'

'Okay.'

Brace followed her to the front door. She unlocked it and entered. As she let him in, she thought, Why bother calling? I didn't see his face. It happened the way he said, and I know it.

But she led the way to the end table and stood by the phone.

He picked it up and dialed for directory assistance.

'You mean you didn't trade phone numbers while you were at it?' she asked.

Boy, I can be such a bitch.

Yeah, and you should see me with a gun.

'Donnerville,' he said into the phone, and smiled at Jane.

'I'd like a number for a Dennis Dickens.' He nodded, then punched the cut-off button and dialed. 'Hope I don't catch him in the middle of "slipping it" to her.'

Jane snarled.

Brace chuckled. 'Hi! Dennis! . . . Yeah. Hey, sorry to bother you at this hour . . . Good. Look, remember your peeping maniac a few nights ago? . . . Wanta talk to her?'

'No!' Jane blurted.

'No,' Brace said into the phone, 'I'm not kidding. Remember when I was telling you about Jane? . . . Yeah, the librarian . . . No, I'm not kidding. She thought she was spying on me. And she's been mighty upset to think that whatever you were doing to Lois was what I was doing.'

How can he be telling all this to some guy I don't even know?

Because he doesn't lie, that's how.

'Would you talk to her?' Brace nodded and grinned and reached toward Jane with the handset.

She shook her head wildly from side to side.

Into the phone, Brace said, 'She's pretty embarrassed about all this.'

'Give it to me,' she muttered, and snatched away the handset. 'Hello?'

'So you're the one who caused all the excitement, huh?' The voice of Dennis sounded amused.

'I guess so. I'm awfully sorry.'

'Well, it sure perked things up around here.'

Things were mighty perky before I got there, she thought.

And she felt herself blush, remembering what she'd seen through the window.

That was this guy.

This guy, not Brace.

Apparently.

'What apartment number *are* you in?' she asked.

'Twelve. I used to be upstairs, and Brace had this place. He sort of traded with me for a wedding present.'

'How long have you lived there?'

'Still checking up on him, huh?'

'I guess so.'

'Don't bother. The guy is crazy about you. He's been a basket case for the last week. If you've got any sense, you'll get back together with him.'

'What're you, his PR man?'

'I know him, that's all. He's such a good guy it makes the rest of us look like shit, if you'll pardon the expression.'

'So, how long *have* you been living in apartment twelve?'

'It'll be exactly a month, tomorrow.'

'Would you tell me . . . I'm sorry, but . . . I've been through so much weirdness lately, I just hardly know what's going on any more.'

'I'll help any way I can. You know, I wanta see Brace happy, and . . .'

'What was going on in your place when I looked in the window?'

He hesitated. 'For starters, we were bare-ass naked. We'd been . . . fooling around, you know. And we no sooner got done than Lois realized the curtains weren't shut all the way. That's when she got up to pull them shut. She was right up there at the window and there you were . . . It was you, huh?'

'Yeah. I'm afraid so.'

'She said you snarled like a maniac.'

'I was pretty upset. I'm awfully sorry, though. Will you tell her how sorry I am?'

'Want to talk to her?'

'No, that's all right. Thanks. I've gotta go, now. Goodnight.' She hung up.

Brace raised his eyebrows. 'Well?'

'How do I know you didn't coach him?'

'It's possible. Anything's possible. Didn't you once say something like, "When anything's possible, nothing makes sense?" '

'Did I?'

'I believe so. But the thing is, I had no idea the Peeping Tom might be you.'

'Maybe you saw me.'

He shook his head. 'I didn't see you. I had no idea who it was until you told me about it a few minutes ago – which didn't give me much of an opportunity to coach Dennis.'

Jane stepped away from him. She slumped on the couch, kicked off her shoes, and put her feet on the coffee table. She rubbed her face. 'I'm so wasted,' she muttered.

'Maybe I should leave, now – give you some time by yourself to figure things out. You can give me a call later, if you want . . . or drop by and see exactly who is living where.'

Still rubbing her face, she said, 'No. Don't go.' She raised her head. 'Everything's . . . don't leave me. Okay?'

He sat down beside her and reached an arm across her shoulders.

'I'm such a mess,' she muttered. 'It's good to have you back, though.'

'I *am* back?'

'As far as I'm concerned.'

He gently squeezed her shoulder. 'So what else has been going on? You're still playing along with Mog?'

She reached into the front pocket of her jeans, clutched the thick block of paper and pulled. It was in there very tight against her thigh, but she felt it move a bit. Slowly, she was able to drag it out.

'Is that money?'

'I think so.' She unfolded the envelope and tore it open, revealing a small brick of bills wrapped in a sheet of paper. She tossed the paper aside. With her thumb, she riffled the bills.

'Good Lord,' Brace said.

'More than fifty thousand bucks,' Jane told him.

'What'd you have to do for it?'

She hesitated, then said, 'Break into a house.'

'An abandoned place like . . .?'

'No. A big expensive place up on Mayr Heights.' She watched him. 'Do you know where that is?'

'Mayr Heights? Yeah. The head of the English department lives up there.'

'His name isn't Savile, is it?'

'Ketchum.'

'Well, that's where I had to go tonight. To a house up there. But I didn't think anyone was home. I rang the doorbell, and knocked, and everything. Nobody heard any of that – luckiest thing that ever happened to me, probably. Anyhow, I had to break in through a window. I planned to pay for it, leave a few hundred bucks behind to make everything all right.'

She saw the look on Brace's face.

'I know, I know, the money wouldn't have *really* made everything all right. But at least it would've paid for having the window fixed.'

'True. So what happened next?'

'If you're bothered by a little matter like breaking a window, I'd better stop right there.'

'It gets worse?'

'I'd say so, yeah.'

He looked into her eyes as if studying them. Then he said, 'You don't have to tell me.'

'I don't think I can. Not right now. Is that all right?'

'It's fine,' he said, rubbing her shoulder.

'The thing is, I'm done with it all. It went . . . way too far. So you won't have to worry about me going out to strange places in the middle of the night. Never again.' She stuffed the thick stack of bills back inside the envelope and tossed the envelope onto the coffee table. It landed near her feet with a solid *whop*.

'Let's just find out,' she said, 'where I *won't* be going.' She picked up the note, spread it open, and held it over to her right so that Brace could see it, too.

She started to read it.

And felt heat rush through her body.

I must be nuts letting Brace read this!

My dear Jane,

No pain, no gain, as the body-builders say. Your body, I must say, is coming along splendidly.

I can think of some sweeties who would give an arm and a leg to be in your condition. Ho ho ho ho ho.

Please don't think too unkindly of their keepers. Boys will be boys, you know.

Hope you get out of here in one piece.

Tomorrow night, take a refreshing dip in John's pool. You'll feel like a new woman.

Love and kisses
and licks
MOG

She smashed it into a tight, hard ball and hurled it across the room.

'What's this stuff about women with keepers?' Brace asked.

Jane shook her head. 'I just don't feel up to . . . it'll probably be in the papers, tomorrow. And on the radio and TV news . . . the whole nine yards. Why don't we wait and talk about it then? Okay? I'm just too wasted. I'd probably go haywire if I had to talk about it tonight. But it's over. It went too far.

There's not enough money in the world to make me go to that pool tomorrow night. Wherever it is.'

A corner of Brace's mouth curled upward. 'Bet I know where it is.'

'Well, don't tell me. It'll make it easier not to go there if I don't know where I'm supposed to go.'

Brace laughed softly. 'I won't tell.'

'Good.' She swung her legs off the coffee table and leaned forward, elbows on her thighs. 'I'd better get out of these,' she mumbled, and let her head droop. 'A nice shower.'

She felt Brace's hand roaming over her back, rubbing her gently through the heavy fabric of her shirt. Then he was rubbing the nape of her neck. She moaned.

'In a little while,' she mumbled.

Feeling almost too weary and comfortable to move, she turned sideways and lifted her legs onto the sofa and sank backward. Head on Brace's lap, she stretched out her legs.

'Were you . . . going somewhere?' she managed to ask.

'No,' he said. 'It's all right. You're fine right here. Just rest.'

Jane woke up and tried to scream, but her mouth wouldn't open. The scream became a siren muffled inside her head as she searched the black night with eyes sealed shut, as she writhed on her back unable to move her arms or legs, as she felt the blade slicing her, the blood spilling.

What's happening? What's happening?

Where am I?

Where's Brace?

Why isn't he stopping this?

Maybe he's the one doing it!

She willed herself to stop screaming. And fought to suck in air through her nostrils. And tried not to think about the blade carving trails of raw pain in the space between her ribcage and navel.

Chapter Thirty-six

'JANE!' The agonized bellow startled Jane awake. She opened her eyes. The bedside lamp was on. Squinting against its brightness, she saw Brace rush toward her.

She had never seen him looking so terrified.

It scared her.

He stopped beside the bed and gazed at her, gazed at the area below her chest where she felt strangely stiff and burning. He was shaking his head. His hands were raised in front of him. He looked like a guy who had just dropped a priceless vase, watched it explode on the floor, and couldn't come close to believing he'd been so clumsy and lost so much.

Wanting to see how bad it was, Jane propped herself up with her elbows.

And joined Brace in staring at her body.

It came as no surprise that she was naked. But she'd expected to find her torso coated with blood. The cutter had obviously mopped up after himself; her skin was clean except for the handprints and the word.

He must've dipped his hands in her blood, then placed them on her breasts and hips and thighs – being careful to leave clear, unsmeared prints. They were extremely large hands.

The word across her midriff was no longer bleeding. Its four big letters were made of slits that looked juicy inside but not very deep. The only letters she recognized at first were those at each end – the Y beneath her right breast and the O beneath her left.

Her mind reversed all four letters, and she understood Mog's message.

She almost told Brace that he needed to turn the letters around in his head. If she told him, though, he might figure out that she'd learned the trick by studying previous messages. She didn't want him to know about any of that.

'What does it say?' she muttered.

Brace, frowning, shook his head. 'I don't . . . I can't think. This is . . . Who *did* this to you?'

'Mog. It has to be Mog.'

'God!' he cried out.

'Take it easy, okay?' She tried to smile. '*I'm* the one who got cut up around here.'

'The bastard!'

'Shhh.' She frowned down at her word. 'It looks sort of . . . backwards.'

'We've gotta call the cops.' Glancing about the room, Brace muttered, 'Do you have a phone in here?'

'No cops,' Jane said.

'We *gotta* call the cops.'

'No, we don't.'

'He butchered you! The bastard butchered you!'

'I'm not butchered. I'll be all right. This was just a warning . . . whatever it says.'

Brace stepped out of the way as Jane sat up and swung her legs off the bed. She felt shaky. She walked slowly past him until she was standing in front of the full-length mirror. The first thing she noticed was the blood on her neck and face. More prints from Mog. Her stomach gave a nasty little twist. These weren't fingerprints.

Mog must've kissed her a dozen times with lips that he'd dipped in her blood.

Brace came to her side and she saw him looking at her reflection. She turned her own eyes to the word carved across her midsection:

OBEY

Brace was looking at the word, but also shifting his gaze up and down.

He's checking me out, she thought.

Don't be an idiot, he's inspecting the damage.

In the mirror, she saw that his shirt was untucked. It draped the front of his gray trousers. She quickly lifted her gaze to his face.

It was slack, flushed.

Is he shocked or turned on? she wondered. Or maybe both.

'How could he do this?' Brace asked, his voice husky and quiet.

'I'm sure he enjoyed it.'

'But I was just in the other room. I never heard anything.'

'I screamed.'

He shook his head. 'I didn't hear you. God, I'm sorry. If I hadn't fallen asleep . . .'

'That's okay,' Jane said. 'It wasn't much of a scream.' She turned away from the mirror. Bloodstains on the sheet formed a general outline of her body. Off to one side were a couple of wadded silvery clumps. 'Duct tape,' she said. 'My mouth and eyes were taped shut. My hands and feet must've been tied – I couldn't move them.' The only foreign articles on the mattress were the wads of duct tape. She looked at her wrists. No sign of having been bound.

Walking slowly around the bed, she looked for other indications of what might've happened.

She found no ropes, no cords, nothing that might've been used to bind her.

She did find her royal blue pajamas on the floor at the far side of the bed. She picked them up. The buttons were missing from the front of the shirt. From the neatly sliced appearance of the thread clusters, she guessed that buttons had been shaved off – no doubt by the same blade that had scribed OBEY on her skin.

As she slipped into the shirt, she asked, 'Was I wearing these pajamas?'

Brace shook his head. 'I don't know.'

'Must've been. But I thought I fell asleep on the sofa.'

'Yeah. You zonked right out. But then you woke up at about two o'clock and went to your room. You were still in your jeans and that big heavy shirt when you left.'

Stepping into her pajama pants, she tried to remember. Couldn't. 'What else happened?'

'You were really out of it,' Brace said. 'You know, disoriented. Like you didn't know what you were doing on the sofa. You don't remember?'

'Not really.'

'Actually, I thought you were planning to come back. You mumbled something about getting comfortable, and went staggering off. I stayed on the sofa. I heard your bedroom door shut. But I kept thinking you'd come back in a few minutes. Then I must've dozed off, myself.'

'And you didn't hear anything at all?'

'No,' he said. He looked miserable. 'God. I slept right through it.'

Jane felt herself grimace. 'I slept through some of it, myself. I guess the pain when he started cutting woke me up. I couldn't move. I could hardly breathe.' She found herself gasping now, as if the memories were robbing her of air.

Brace came around the bed and put his arms around her. He pulled her gently toward him. Jane wrapped her arms around him. They embraced, his body pressing solid and warm against her, but not quite touching the sore area where Mog had sliced his command. Jane pressed her face into the curve of his neck. She felt his hands glide slowly up and down the back of her pajama shirt.

After a long time, he murmured, 'I'll never let anyone touch you again.'

She knew he meant it. But she doubted that Brace – or anyone else – would be able to protect her from Mog.

'Don't think about it,' she whispered.

'You could've been killed.'

'I wasn't. He just wanted to hurt me.'

'He doesn't want you to quit the game.'

'No shit, Sherlock.'

Brace laughed softly, blowing a few small puffs of breath through her hair. She kissed the side of his neck.

'Maybe you'd better do what he wants,' Brace said.

'No. It has to end.'

'But he'll keep at you. He won't stop at this. If he's nuts enough to sneak into your room and cut *words* into your skin, he's . . . he'll keep at you until you cave in and do what he wants.'

Jane eased backward a bit and looked up into Brace's eyes. 'I've got news for Mog,' she said. 'I don't cave. The Game's over.' In a loud voice, she said, 'Do you hear that, Mog? The Game's over. You can whittle on me from now till Hell freezes over – I'm done with following your orders.'

'Do you think he can hear you?' Brace asked.

'Wouldn't surprise me. The way he comes and goes.'

Narrowing his eyes, Brace stared past the top of Jane's head as if studying the far corners of the ceiling. 'We'd better call the cops,' he said. 'Maybe they can find him.'

'No.'

'Yes. Look what he's done to you, Jane. It was different when he was just sneaking around and giving you money . . . he's committed a real crime now. It's gotta be at least assault with a deadly weapon. They can put him away for that.'

'They can put me away for murder,' Jane said, and watched Brace's eyes react.

They might look the same way if she suddenly shoved her switchblade into his belly.

She stepped away from him. 'But go ahead and call the cops, if that's what you want. I have to take a shower.'

He stood there, stiff and hunched over slightly, and watched her walk out of the bedroom.

The strong hot spray of the shower made her cuts burn, but it felt wonderful everywhere else. With a bar of soap, she scrubbed away the bloody handprints and rubbed her face to take off the marks put there by Mog's lips.

She wondered if Brace would call the police.

She doubted it.

Such a damn straight arrow, though, he just might do it.

She could hear him now. *As much as I care for you, Jane, I can't condone murder. You left me no choice but to turn you in.*

Her back to the spray, she blinked water out of her eyes and looked down. The scratches and bruises from the dog attack had finally gone away, just in time to leave her skin unblemished for Mog's assault with the blade. She saw, however, that she'd gotten all the handprints off. Her skin looked shiny and clean except for the raw, carved letters.

I look pretty good, she thought. *Pretty* good? Better than ever. Thanks to all that exercise and some sunlight – and several days with almost no appetite at all thanks to Mog and Brace.

She supposed she had been thinner, years ago, but she had never been in such good shape.

Now, if Mog'll just quit cutting on me . . .

She set the bar of soap in the small tray by the side of the tub, then took a step, bent down, and reached for her plastic bottle of shampoo. As she wrapped her fingers around the slippery sides of the bottle, the door behind her skidded open.

She gasped. Letting go of the shampoo, she straightened up fast and turned around.

Brace stepped halfway into the tub. He looked at her and raised his eyebrows. 'Just say the word, and I'll leave.'

Jane didn't say the word.

He brought his other leg into the tub and slid the glass door shut. His body blocked the spray.

Jane went to him.

She halted when her belly met his erection.

His hands cupped her shoulders, and a smile fluttered at the corners of his mouth. 'I decided it wouldn't be wise to let you out of my sight. No telling where the enemy might be lurking.'

'Did you hear what I told you?' she asked.

'You killed someone,' Brace said.

'Aren't you going to turn me in for it?'

'Not a chance.' He put his hands on her breasts.

She took a quick, shuddery breath.

'I know you,' he said. 'If you did it, it was the only thing to do.'

'Oh, God.' She moved in, feeling him prod her and slide upward. She winced as one of her cuts was rubbed – part of the E, she guessed – but she didn't back away. She pressed herself more tightly against Brace. In spite of the slight pain from the pressure against her slit skin, she liked how she could feel the whole length of him straight up against her belly and know that he was this hard and this thick because of her.

Then she had the hot spray in her face and Brace was crouched, hands everywhere on her buttocks and the backs of her legs while he kissed and licked and sucked her breasts.

She pushed her fingers through his hair. She squirmed.

At the end, he had her back pinned to the slick tile wall and only the tips of her toes were touching the bottom of the tub. He was all up inside her. His thrusting jolted her, lifted her off her toes. The tiles slid up and down against her back and rump.

When they climbed out of the tub, Brace spread a towel over the bathmat and helped her to lie down on it.

OBEY was bleeding.

Parts of it had been bleeding for quite a while. A few times, Brace had gasped, 'We'd better stop,' and, 'We'd better take care of that.'

But she'd told him, 'It's all right.' She hadn't wanted anything to be stopped, or even interrupted.

She supposed she must've said, 'It's all right,' about one thing or another ten or twelve times while they'd been in the tub.

Now, he said, 'Is it okay to use the washcloth?'

And she said, 'It's all right.'

Up on her elbows, she watched Brace spread a white washcloth across OBEY. He was squatting by her side, naked and dripping. On the cloth, specks of blood began to appear.

Brace shook his head. 'The washcloth'll probably be ruined.' Water falling off his chin tapped Jane near the hip.

'It's all right,' she said. She smiled.

Brace met her eyes and smiled. 'Is that all you know how to say?'

She nodded.

'We should've stopped. It's my fault you're bleeding again.'

'It's all right.'

He returned his gaze to the washcloth. 'I don't know what got into me,' he said.

'I know what got into *me*.'

'Funny.'

'That's me.'

'Not to mention I didn't . . . use anything.'

'It's all right,' she said.

'That's what you kept telling me.'

'It's still true.'

'You don't believe in . . . practicing safe sex?'

'I haven't been practicing *any* sex.'

'Well, that makes two of us.'

'So,' she said, 'the worst that can happen is we get a baby.'

'A baby?'

'You know. One of those little people.'

'Oh.'

'It's not terribly likely, though. I think we're safe . . . for now.'

She looked down at the washcloth. The specks had grown into bright red dots, but the dots formed only small bits of lines and curves.

'Doesn't look like you're in any danger of bleeding to death,' Brace said. He peeled off the washcloth and studied the wounds. 'We ought to put some disinfectant on here. And bandage you.'

'In the medicine cabinet,' she told him.

The hydrogen peroxide felt chilly when he poured it on her middle. It gave her goosebumps. It went white and fizzy wherever it touched her cuts.

She sent Brace into her bedroom for the bandage. He came back with a big red bandanna from her dresser drawer. Folded lengthwise into thirds, it formed a pad that completely covered OBEY. Brace fixed it in place with long strips of adhesive tape.

By the time they left the bathroom, the sun was up. Jane gave her robe to Brace. It fit him fine. She wore a big, loose T-shirt. They made coffee, and took their mugs into the living room. They sat on the sofa, close enough together so that their sides touched.

'I guess I'd better tell you about last night,' she said.

'If you want to.'

'You want to know about it, don't you?'

'I want to know *everything* about you.'

'My favorite color?'

'Everything.'

'Right now, I'd better stick with the stuff about last night.'

She began to tell him about it. When she came to the part about the women, he went pale and stopped drinking his coffee and kept turning his head to look at her. Finally, she told about sneaking into the Show Room and shooting the three men.

Brace gave her thigh a gentle squeeze. He kept his hand there, caressing her. 'I don't know how you could do something like that.'

'It was easy.'

'Jane, the jury.'

'Yeah. Me and Mike Hammer. But I had to do it. I had to make sure they wouldn't come after us. That was part of it. And it was partly to protect the two we had to leave behind. Once the guys knew there'd been an escape, no telling what they might've done to Linda and Marjorie. Anyway, they didn't deserve to live. Not after what they'd done.'

'I don't know,' Brace said. 'I'm just awfully sorry you had to do it.'

'You and me both. But if I'd just left ... everything

would've been my fault from then on. You know? They would've gotten away, I'm sure of it. And it would've all been on me, everybody they hurt or killed from then on.'

'I hope you really believe that,' Brace said.

'I do.'

'Because it's a big thing, killing someone. Maybe it's the biggest thing there is. To carry with you.'

'Have you done it?'

'No. I'm not sure if I could.'

'You could.'

'Probably.'

'I bet you would've killed Mog if you'd caught him carving on me last night.'

'I bet I sure would've tried.' His hand tightened on her thigh. 'We've got to figure out how to protect you tonight.'

'Yeah. I know. Are you hungry?'

'Are you kidding?'

Chapter Thirty-seven

Together in the kitchen, they made themselves breakfast. While bacon sizzled in the skillet, they leaned against counters across from each other and sipped coffee. Sunlight coming in through the window above the sink cast a glare on the linoleum floor and lit Brace to the knees. Where the sunlight touched him, it made his hair glint golden. Most of his left leg showed because of how the robe hung away from it. But only the bottom part was sunlit.

Jane stared at his legs as she drank coffee and told about how Linda had attacked her on the way out of the house last night.

'My God, you saved her and she did that!'

'I think she's warped in the head. Who wouldn't be, you know?'

'What do you think she did after you left?' Brace asked, and sipped his coffee. The kitchen smelled wonderful because of the bacon.

'I don't know. I suppose the police have her, now. She's probably been hospitalized, don't you suppose? She and Marjorie?'

'If she didn't . . . do something to Marjorie.'

'I know.'

'You thought about that?'

'It's crossed my mind. I didn't want to kill her, though. If she went back upstairs for Marjorie . . . I hope she didn't, but . . . I don't know. I just don't know.' She turned away and checked the bacon. It looked ready, so she lifted the skillet off the stove and carried it over to the counter by Brace and forked out each strip of bacon onto a paper towel.

Waiting for the bacon grease to cool down, she helped Brace get started with the toast. Then she put him in charge of it. She took four eggs out or the refrigerator and cracked them on the edge of the skillet. None of the yolks broke. The clear jell surrounding the yolks grew white and solid quickly from the bottom upward without a crisp brown rim forming around the edges, so she knew the grease was right. She stood over the eggs, using her spatula to flip grease over their tops until the yolks turned creamy yellow and nothing on the whites looked like phlegm anymore.

By the time the eggs were done, Brace had finished with the toast. Two buttered slices on each plate.

Jane slipped an egg on top of each slab of toast. Brace added the bacon strips.

They carried their plates to a small round table at the end of the kitchen. Then they scurried about, gathering utensils and napkins, salt and pepper. With fresh mugs of coffee, they sat at the table.

They ate for a while without talking.

When half his breakfast was gone, Brace said, 'This is great.'

'Yeah,' Jane said.

'It doesn't get any better than this.'

'Are you talking about the bacon and eggs?'

'Yeah. And the toast and coffee. And how you look. And what we did in the shower. And just being here with you like this on a Sunday morning. I wish it could be like this every morning.'

'We'd get a terrible cholesterol problem.'

'Yeah. I suppose.'

She smiled. 'We could do it once a week, though.'

'A Sunday morning ritual.'

'Let's just leave out the blood sacrifice.'

'Good idea,' Brace said.

'Do you think it'll leave scars?'

'No. I doubt it.'

'It isn't very deep,' Jane said.

'It won't leave much. Probably nothing.'

'It'll be a long time before it goes away, though.'

'I'll be able to read you like a book – Madame Librarian.'

'Shut up and eat.'

Brace laughed.

They stared at each other as they ate the rest of their breakfast. Afterwards, they cleaned off the table.

'I'll wash and you dry,' Brace said.

'I can take care of the dishes, if you want to go in the living room and relax.'

'I'd rather stay right here.' He filled the sink with sudsy hot water and began to scrub a plate with a sponge.

'I'll find a towel,' Jane said. She walked away from him. By the breakfast table, she took off her T-shirt. She draped it over the back of a chair, and crept toward Brace. When she stepped on the sunny place, the floor was hot on the bottoms of her feet.

She eased herself lightly against Brace's back. He must've expected her, because he didn't seem startled. He wiggled, the robe sliding cool against Jane. She could feel the heat of his back and rump through the thin fabric.

Reaching around him, she spread the robe apart. She roamed his bare skin with her hands.

'You're destroying my focus,' he said.

'How much focus does it take to wash a few dishes?'

'Plenty. Maybe I should take a break.'

'No, no, you're doing fine. Let's see you do them all. Let's see if you've got what it takes. It'll be a test of your willpower.'

Though squirming and moaning, Brace worked his way through the plates and coffee mugs and silverware and spatula. But as he lowered the skillet into the sink, Jane squatted and reached under the back of the robe. She came up with one hand between his legs. As she grasped him from below with that hand, her other took him from the front, lightly encircling him and sliding downward.

'No fair!' he cried out.

Then he was on his back on the kitchen floor, Jane straddling him in the warm brightness of the sunlight that came through the window.

After that, they got dressed. Together, they removed the sheets from Jane's bed. She put the bloody bottom-sheet into a tub in the utility room to soak. Then they made the bed with fresh sheets.

When the bed was done, Brace sat on it. He looked up at Jane.

She stepped between his knees and caressed the sides of his face. 'Shall we give it a try?'

'What?'

'The bed, the bed.'

'Nope,' Brace told her.

'What do you mean, nope?'

'It's time for you to pack.'

'Pack?'

'A suitcase. Then we'll stop by my place and I'll grab a few things. Then we'll take off.'

'Where to?'

'The walls have ears.'

'Ah.'

'We'll decide along the way. The thing is, we'll pull a little disappearing act. See how good Mog is at cutting orders on you when he can't find you.'

'I hope he can't.'

'We'll find out.'

'How long will we be gone? I have to be at work on Tuesday. *You've* got classes to teach tomorrow.'

'I'll get someone to take them for me. Just bring enough for a couple of nights. We should know very fast whether or not it works.'

'By tomorrow morning,' Jane said.

'Probably.'

'It's worth a try.'

Brace sat on the bed and watched Jane while she hurried about her room, gathering clothes for the trip. He stayed with her when she went into the bathroom to stock her toilet kit. Smiling over her shoulder, she said, 'What if I need to use the john?'

'I'm looking forward to it.'

'Hey!'

With a quiet laugh, he stepped into the hallway and pulled the door shut. 'Yell if you need me,' he said.

When Jane came out of the bathroom, she had to search for Brace. She found him on the living room sofa, the *Donnerville Morning Times* in his hands. A coldness spread through her stomach. 'Terrific,' she said. 'The paper came.'

'Better take a look,' Brace said.

She sat down beside him. He passed the newspaper to her. The headline stunned her:

INFERNO CONSUMES HOUSE OF HORRORS

'Oh, my God,' she muttered. She read the first few lines of the story. 'It *burnt*!'

'You didn't know?'

'Somebody must've started it after I left. Linda, maybe. Or the big guy.'

'Big guy?'

Jane took a deep breath. She was trembling. 'Gail said there was a big guy,' she explained. 'Six-four. He was the one who wired her to the wall. But nobody I shot was that size. I never saw him. He might've been Mog, I don't know. But if somebody started a fire on purpose . . .' Shaking her head, she began to read the story.

Fire units, last night, arrived to find the Mayr Heights home of Steve Savile engulfed in flames, even as bookstore clerk Gail Maxwell, missing since Monday night, phoned the police emergency operator with a tale of escape from the Savile house, where she and several other women had allegedly been kept as prisoners.

Ms Maxwell's ordeal, the details of which have not yet been fully disclosed, came to an end last night when she and a second female captive, Sandra Briggs of Reno, were rescued by an unnamed young man. The rescuer is believed to be an intruder who entered the house to commit burglary, but happened by chance upon the prisoners and chose to set them free.

'Nice touch,' Jane said. 'A burglar.'

'They took you for a guy. Were they blinded by their ordeal?'

'That was my idea. They really came through for me.'

Jane returned to the news story.

According to police sources, two other women, as yet to be identified, were also being held against their will at the time of the rescue. Subjected to severe abuse by their captors, however, they'd been rendered incapable of escape. It is now feared that they may have perished in the blaze.

'Are you okay?' Brace asked.

Jane grimaced. 'Just . . . My God.' She pictured Marjorie writhing and screaming in her harness as fire climbed her bed. 'Can you imagine being a multiple amputee in a burning house? *God.* It sounds like the punchline for a really sick joke.'

Brace nodded. 'What's worse than sliding down a banister that turns into a razor blade?'

'Yeah. Exactly.'

'Maybe they got out.'

'Maybe Linda. Not Marjorie, though. I should've taken her out when I had the chance. It's just . . . I thought she'd be okay. I mean, I'd killed the guys. And I didn't know about number four. So i thought she'd be okay. Unless Linda did something, but . . .'

'Don't blame yourself,' Brace said. 'You did what you thought was right. You saved two of them. If you'd tried to take out Marjorie, there's no telling what might've happened. Maybe *none* of you would've made it. You just never know.'

'It's so awful,' Jane said. 'She was just supposed to be left there for a while, you know? Till the cops could show up and take care of things. I thought she'd be all right.'

'Things happen,' Brace said.

'Yeah,' Jane muttered, and went back to reading the story.

The four women, and possibly others, are said to have been abducted from various western states during the past year by three or more male Caucasians in their early twenties. The identities of the alleged kidnappers are unknown at this time. However, authorities suspect that the ring-leader may have been Steve Savile, present owner of the house where the victims were being held.

Steve Savile inherited the property four years ago following the brutal slaying of his parents, Dr and Mrs Harold Savile, and the rape and murder of his two sisters. Steve, away from home at the time of the crimes, was initially considered a suspect. No charges were filed, however, and the matter has remained a mystery to this day.

At this time, authorities believe that the captors may have fled the house upon detecting the escape of two of their prisoners. An all-points bulletin has been issued for Steve Savile.

Police indicate that the women, while held prisoner, were subjected to starvation, torture, numerous sexual assaults and other forms of abuse.

No information has been made available concerning the cause of the fire that totally consumed the Savile residence. Arson, however, is suspected and investigation is pending.

Police are hoping to identify and locate the young man who freed Ms Maxwell and Mrs Briggs from captivity, in hopes that he may be able to shed some light on the events of last night.

'Yeah, I can shed some light,' she muttered. 'Try looking in the ashes.' She folded the paper and tossed it onto the coffee table.

Before leaving the house, Jane dropped her switchblade knife into a pocket of her culottes. She reloaded the pistol and put it into her purse, along with the box of ammunition and five thousand dollars of the money she'd gotten from Mog.

They left her car in the driveway, and took Brace's car over to the Royal Gardens. He parked on the street in front of the building.

'Maybe I should wait here,' Jane said.

'It'd be better if we stay together. Besides, don't you want to see whether or not I live in apartment twelve?'

'I believe you. But I'll come.'

'It's not even nine o'clock, so I don't think you need to worry about running into Lois or Dennis. Or anybody else, for that matter. This place is dead on Sunday mornings.'

Side by side, they went to the front gate. Brace opened and

shut it slowly, so that it made little noise. They walked toward the swimming pool. A bright plastic beach ball floated in one corner.

Jane saw nobody.

She heard nothing from the surrounding apartments except for the hum of a few window air-conditioning units. The only other sounds came from birds.

Brace led the way upstairs and along a balcony. They both walked quietly. Near the end of the balcony, Brace stopped in front of a door marked twenty-two. He unlocked it, eased it open, and gestured for Jane to follow him inside.

He stepped around to the front of the sofa, bent down and lifted a thick book off the coffee table. Showing it to Jane, he raised his eyebrows. The book was *Youngblood Hawke*.

'I believe you,' Jane whispered.

'No need to whisper,' Brace whispered.

Laughing softly, she turned around. The walls of the room were hidden behind heavily loaded bookshelves. Books, magazines, file folders and scattered papers littered every table in sight, and half the sofa. Only the easy chair in the corner was free of junk.

'You're sort of a slob,' Jane said.

'Oh, you'll probably cure me of that.'

'Not unlikely.'

'Maybe you should wait here,' he said.

'No no no – we'd better stick together.'

He made a grumbly noise, then led the way to his bedroom. Apparently, his bedroom doubled as a study. His desk, facing the only window, held a computer and pounds of written material. Bookshelves stood against two of the walls. A few shoes were scattered about the carpet in odd places, as if they'd been kicked in the dark. But Jane saw no dirty clothes on the floor or furniture. Brace's bed was unmade, but the sheets looked reasonably clean.

She sat on the edge of the bed.

Brace gave her a crooked smile.

'It's not so bad,' she said.

'You're very kind.'

She laughed, and Brace stepped up to her. She tipped back her head. He kissed her on the mouth. Reaching up, she caressed the sides of his face. Reaching down, he cupped and rubbed her breasts through her blouse.

Soon, he whispered against her mouth, 'We'd better quit.'

Jane whispered back, 'Quitters never prosper.'

'We've gotta get out of here.'

'I know.'

'There'll be plenty of time later.'

'I hope so,' Jane said.

He released her and stepped away. She sank down on his bed, sighed and closed her eyes.

Plenty of time later. Sure.

It's nothing, she told herself. It's not as if he's abandoned me. He's being practical, that's all. It's only because he's worried about me and wants to take me somewhere far away and safe.

But it hurt. It hurt anyway, even though she knew it shouldn't.

Don't be an ass. This is the best I ever had it.

She sat up. Brace swung a suitcase onto the bed and opened it beside her.

'It's weird, isn't it?' she said. 'That this is all because of Mog.'

'Yeah.'

'We wouldn't even know each other if he hadn't started the Game that night. You wouldn't have run into me in the stairwell . . .'

'Maybe not,' Brace said, looking over his shoulder as he opened a drawer of his dresser. 'We might've met, anyway. In fact, I'm sure of it. But his little game is what got us together. No way around it.'

'Do you suppose he *meant* it to be this way?'

'No.' Brace turned around and came back to the bed with socks and underwear. He tossed them into his suitcase. Then he met Jane's eyes. 'I think Mog is a very sharp and tricky guy, with maybe a bit of Houdini in his blood. But he's not invisible. He's not superhuman. He doesn't have any Big Plan. He never intended for the Game to bring you and me together – that was just an accident. And it's an accident that probably doesn't please him at all.'

'But a lot of good things have come out of all this,' Jane said. 'If he hadn't sent me to that house last night, Gail and Sandra would still be there . . .'

And Linda and Marjorie might still be alive, she thought. *But I saved the ones who were savable.*

Yeah, sure.

'He might've sent you there,' Brace said, 'hoping that *you'd* be taken prisoner. Don't go and give him altruistic motives for any of this. He's using you, that's all. The Game is nothing but a gimmick for manipulating you. And now that you won't go for his bribes, he'll do whatever it takes to make you obey.'

'I don't know if he'll do *whatever* it takes.'

'If he'll cut words in your skin, he'll do anything.'

Jane sat silent, thinking. 'I don't know,' she finally said.

'You don't know what?'

'Maybe I oughta just go ahead and do what he wants. You know? The money . . . should be more than a hundred thousand. And whatever happens, it can't be worse than at Savile's house last night. And it might be a *lot* better than what he'll do to me if I refuse.'

'It's up to you,' Brace said. 'I'll stand by you, either way.'

She felt a corner of her mouth turn up. 'Of course, I threw away the instructions. I wouldn't know where to go, even if . . .'

'"Take a refreshing dip in John's pool. You'll feel like a new woman."'

'So I have to find a guy named John with a swimming pool?'

'I might be wrong, but my guess is that he wants you at the Calvary Baptist Church.'

'Ah,' Jane said, 'John the Baptist. A dip in the pool. Baptists practice immersion, don't they? And baptism supposedly changes you into a new person, so I'd "feel like a new woman." Very good, Brace. So where *is* this church?'

'Over on Park Lane. You can see it from Mill Creek Bridge.'

She met Brace's worried eyes. 'Why would Mog be sending me to a Baptist church?'

'Maybe he wants to see you do the Dance of the Seven Veils.'

'Think he'll bring me a head on a platter?'

'What do you think?' Brace asked.

'I ain't goin' to no Calvary Baptist Church at midnight, honey. No way.'

Chapter Thirty-eight

In the living room of his apartment, Brace searched the shelves and pulled out a telephone directory. He sat down and opened it on his lap.

'I don't need the address of the church,' Jane said.

'I had an idea. It'll take a few minutes, though. Do you want a drink or something?'

'No, thanks. What's your idea?'

'We're taking a taxi.'

'Huh?'

Smiling, he held up a hand. Then he made the call. After he'd hung up, Jane said, 'Why are we taking a taxi?'

'Mog probably knows my car. And he's rich and nuts. For all we know, he might have access to some sort of high-tech equipment.'

'Ah. Like homing devices.'

'Yep.'

'Good thinking.'

'We'll take the taxi to a rent-a-car outfit.'

'Excellent. Make things tough for the son-of-a-bitch.'

'If we *really* wanted to make it tough for him, we'd steal a car. Anything short of that, there'll be a paper trail he can follow. But . . . I'd like to get through this without breaking any laws.'

'Oh, you're such a stick in the mud.'

He grinned. 'That's me.'

'Hell, *I'll* steal a car. Laws mean nothing to me.'

He laughed and shook his head.

'I'm a regular Bonnie Parker.'

'I think renting a car should be enough to throw him off our track. We'll save your criminal talents for emergencies. Who knows, we might need to stick up a bank.'

'Are you kidding?' Jane said. 'I *am* a bank.'

Less than forty-five minutes later, Brace stopped the Mazda rental car at the exit of the agency parking lot. 'Which way?' he asked.

'Right's the quickest way out of town,' Jane said.

'Right it is.'

He made the turn.

Jane studied the road behind them. The only approaching car swung to the curb two blocks away. As she watched, the female driver climbed out and hurried across the street.

'The coast looks clear in the rear,' Jane said.

'Mog never got as far as the rent-a-car place. If he'd been trying to follow the cab, we would've spotted him.'

'Yeah. The guy pulling five Us behind us.'

'Five?'

'Something like that. The cabbie was having a ball. He should've tipped *us*.'

'I might try a few Uies myself.'

'Don't bother unless there's another car in sight.'

* * *

Two hours later, Brace swung onto the gravel shoulder of a two-lane road. On both sides, onion fields stretched into the distance.

Turning her face to her open window, Jane took a deep breath. 'Smells great, doesn't it? Makes me want a hamburger.'

'We'll have to stop for lunch in a while.'

'Why are we stopped now?'

'Mostly, I want to see what comes along.'

Jane stared forward, then back. 'Nothing's coming.'

'We'll see.'

They waited.

After a few minutes, Jane climbed out of the car. She stretched, sniffed the scented air, tilted back her head to feel the sun on her face. The sky was cloudless. She heard nothing except birds and the soft hiss of the breeze.

Turning to the car, she ducked and said into the window, 'No sign of any helicopters. He might have some sort of high-altitude spy plane, though. What do you think?'

'I think we're probably safe.'

Jane's stomach suddenly fell as she heard the faint, distant grumble of an engine.

Down the road, something dark came around a curve.

'Someone's coming,' she said.

'Maybe you'd better . . .'

'Climb in?' she asked, swinging the door open. 'Good idea.' She dropped onto the passenger seat and shut the door. Looking over her shoulder, she saw that the approaching vehicle was a black pickup truck.

The driver wore a western hat. He had a thick red face and white eyebrows.

He slowed his truck. He stopped it beside them on the road. He leaned toward the passenger window and rolled it down. He wore an old, plaid shirt. Around his neck was tied a red bandanna just like the one taped across OBEY beneath Jane's shirt.

'You folks got trouble?' he called through the window.

'We're fine, thanks,' Brace told him. 'Just stopped to rest and switch drivers.'

'Well, that's all right, then.'

'Thanks for asking,' Brace said.

'No trouble. You folks have yourself a good day, now, y'hear?'

'You, too.'

'Thank you,' Jane called out. The old man smiled at her and touched a finger to the brim of his hat. Then he drove away.

'I don't suppose that was Mog,' Brace said.

Shortly after four o'clock that afternoon, they came upon a roadside sign that pointed to the right and read, Emerald Pines, 32 mi.

'What do you think?' Brace asked.

'I've never heard of Emerald Pines.'

'Neither have. I Sounds like just the place.'

'If they have a motel.'

'Every town has a motel.'

'You think so?' Jane asked.

'Maybe not *every* town.'

'Let's give it a try.'

The narrow, bumpy road to Emerald Pines took them into an evergreen forest where trees crowded the edges of the pavement. The shadowed road was very dark. Now and then, gaps in the trees allowed sunlight to reach down – long, slanting pillars of dusty gold.

Jane had her elbow out the window. The afternoon air blew against her arm and up inside the short sleeve of her blouse, hot and dry. It rubbed her face and tossed her short hair. It smelled rich and sweet and made her think of Christmases when she was very young.

'It's wonderful in here,' she said.

'Maybe we should've brought camping gear.'

'Not that wonderful.'

'Do you want to stop and look around?' Brace asked.

'I'd rather come back some time when all the bad stuff is over – when we don't have to think about Mog,'

As she spoke, she felt a cold little tremor.

This might be the only time we get.

Jane waited for Brace in the car. After a few minutes, he came out of the office of the Lucky Logger Inn and smiled at her. 'All set,' he said as he climbed in behind the wheel. 'We're in lucky number twelve.' He drove to the end of the gravel parking lot, and parked in front of the door to their room.

They went in together.

'Twin beds?' Jane asked.

'It's all they had.'

'Do you think we can both fit on one?'

'We'll have to stack up,' Brace said. Grinning, he swayed sideways and bumped against her. 'Not a bad room, though.'

'It's fine.'

The room looked very rustic: pine walls, beams across the ceiling, several framed paintings of woodland scenery. The lamp on the stand between the beds sported beavers on its shade.

Beavers.

The sight of the animals triggered a flutter in Jane's stomach.

EAGER BEAVER

Penned on her skin by Mog in the good old days when he'd done his writing with a marking pen instead of a blade. And what'll he write on me tonight? she wondered.

Nothing.

He won't find me tonight. Not here.

No way.

Everything will be fine. At least till we have to go back home.

Please.

* * *

They dined that evening on a pitcher of beer and a Winky's Special pizza at a saloon called Winky's that had sawdust on the floor and Randy Travis on the jukebox. The beer was so cold it made Jane's teeth ache until she got used to it. The Special had a thin, crunchy crust. It dripped grease and loops of melted cheese down their fingers and chins. They went through a small stack of napkins.

By the time they left Winky's, the sun had gone down behind the forest. Everything was tinted gray. The town had no sidewalk, so they walked along the road on ground that changed with every few steps: sometimes solid dirt, sometimes gravel, occasionally shin-high weeds, grass now and then, and areas of pavement. It made for tricky walking, especially in the dusk. Brace held Jane's hand.

'Are you going to let me up?' Brace asked.

'No,' Jane said.

He was pinned beneath her on the narrow bed.

Earlier, she had been hunched over him, clutching his shoulders, gasping and sweating, squirming on him and sliding herself up and down while he caressed and squeezed her breasts. That had been a while ago. Afterwards, she had eased herself down and stretched herself out on top of him.

They were bare against each other except where the pad of Jane's bandage made a soft, moist barrier between their bellies. He was hot and slippery under her.

Jane wasn't gasping, now. Neither was Brace. His heart no longer pounded so hard against her chest. But he was still big and hard and buried deep inside her.

'I'm never going to let you get up,' she said. 'I'm gonna keep you right where you are.' She tightened herself around him. 'I've always wanted one of these things – now I've got one.'

His hands glided down her back and gently rubbed her buttocks.

'My "lucky log,"' she said.

He laughed. The laughing bounced her. She felt him twitch inside her. And grow.

'What's happening?' she asked.

'You.'

'Aren't you worn out yet?'

'Pooped,' he said.

'Me, too. I don't think I can move.'

'That's okay,' he said. 'Just lie still.'

Kneading her rump, he writhed under her. He eased up against her, lifting her slightly. He delved from side to side. Then he was pushing up harder at her, then harder, thrusting, twisting, shoving, bucking, clutching at Jane to keep her from being thrown off.

She stayed limp, letting it happen, not trying to hold on or help, savoring every sensation of the strange, wild ride.

Before it ended, he threw her onto her back. She started to fall off the bed, but he caught her behind the shoulder and swept her to the center of the mattress. Obviously not wanting to bear down on her wounds, he propped himself above her as if doing a push-up. Jane flung out her arms. She spread her legs as wide as she could.

They touched nowhere.

Nowhere except at the center where he pounded and plunged.

'I don't want to hurt you,' Brace said.

'It'll be all right.' She pulled at his arms. 'Please.'

So he lowered himself onto her, but she could feel that he was holding himself up enough to keep most of his weight off her body.

'Relax,' she said.

'I don't want to mash you.'

'You won't mash me.'

'Your cuts . . .'

'Obey,' she said.

'All right,' he said. 'But just for a minute.'

She felt him sink heavily onto her. The weight of him pushed her into the mattress, and felt good and safe. It made her feel sore where he pressed against the cuts, but that was fine. It was the rest of it that mattered.

She could feel his hot wet face against her cheek. His whiskers felt scratchy. His breath tickled her ear. She could feel the thudding of his heart, and how his torso seemed to swell every time he inhaled. His penis lay against the side of her thigh, heavy and sticky.

After a while, Jane flexed her leg muscles beneath it, 'Is it dead?' she whispered.

'Comatose.'

She laughed. Then she wrapped her arms around his back and hugged him as hard as she could.

Brace groaned.

When she relaxed her hold, he said, 'What was that, your bear hug?'

'I'm pretty strong, huh?'

'Superwoman.'

'I've been working out a little.'

'I know.'

She raised her eyebrows. 'You been spying on me again?'

'Nope. I can just tell. It's how you look and feel.'

'How do I feel?'

'Firm and smooth. And I know I've gotta be crushing you.' He started to rise.

'No, come on.'

He kissed her softly on the mouth, then pushed himself up and crawled backward. Jane lifted her head.

Brace, kneeling between her legs, was frowning at her mid-section.

OBEY was bare. The bandanna bandage hung at her side, dangling by a single strip of tape. She wondered at what stage of things the bandage had come unstuck.

The letters of the word were thin, red slits. Only the leg of the Y seemed to be bleeding at all.

'Guess you need to be repatched,' Brace said. 'Lie still, I'll take care of it.'

812

He climbed off the bed and headed for the bathroom. He walked unsteadily, limping a little.

After he shut the door, Jane shut her eyes. She stretched and moaned. The sheet beneath her body was damp. In places, it felt cool and sticky. She thought about trying to scoot away from the gooey areas. But she felt too lazy and good to move, and she decided she liked being on them.

Soon, Brace returned with Jane's bottle of hydrogen peroxide, her spool of tape, and a neatly folded white handkerchief that didn't look familiar.

'Your hanky?' she asked.

He nodded. 'It's clean.'

'It'll be ruined.'

He shook his head and grinned. 'Improved.'

'Right. So what does that make you, a hopeless romantic or a vampire?'

'A guy without much use for handkerchiefs.'

'Ah. That's begging for a quip, but I'm not gonna be sucked in.'

'Afraid you'll blow it?'

'Oh, oh!'

'Were you considering a barb about the way I keep my nose clean?' He trickled the cool antiseptic onto her wounds. She flinched. 'Or how I stick it into other people's business?'

'It's not your nose you've been sticking in.'

'It's not?'

' 's not.'

'A few more days like today,' Brace said, 'and we might have to resort to it.'

'Maybe,' Jane grinned. 'Who knows?'

Shaking his head and laughing softly, Brace spread his folded handkerchief across OBEY. Jane felt it stick to the moisture there.

Brace came out of the bathroom wearing faded blue gym shorts. Jane, already washed and in bed, lifted a side of her sheet for him. She wore a fresh white T-shirt that hung low enough to cover the panties that she'd bought at the mall on Monday.

'Join me?' she asked.

'You gotta be kidding.'

She grinned. 'Just to sleep.'

He came to her, but didn't climb into bed. Instead, he bent down and kissed her. Reaching up, she stroked his chest. His kiss seemed too brief.

'I think I'll stay up for a while,' Brace said.

'Aren't you *tired*?'

'Never too tired to read.'

He went to his suitcase, which was open on the dresser, and lifted out *Youngblood Hawke*.

The book he'd chosen the night they met.

The night the messages from Mog had started.

And Brace hadn't finished reading it yet. His bookmark, a small crescent of white paper, jutted out like a torn banner a quarter inch from the back of the book.

When was it due? Jane wondered.

A two-weeker.

He hasn't renewed it, so the thing must be way overdue by now. Wait. No.

My God, she thought. It isn't due till Tuesday. Day after tomorrow.

Not even two weeks since all this started!

It seemed incredible that so much could've happened in such a short span of time.

Jane rolled onto her side. Propping herself up with an elbow, she watched Brace walk past the other bed, set the book on the table by the curtained window, and turn on the nearby lamp.

'Are you going to be done by Tuesday?' Jane asked.

'With the book? I'll probably finish it tonight.'

'Well, we can always renew it for you. But I'm surprised you're not done with it by now.'

'I'm no speed-reader. And there've been a few interruptions.'

'You're not including me, are you?'

He turned up a corner of his mouth. 'I had a bad time for a few days. I was too screwed up to read. Couldn't concentrate on the words.'

'I thought your concentration was supposed to be all-powerful.'

'It kept straying to you.'

Jane felt her throat tighten.

Instead of sitting down to read, Brace lifted her purse off the table. 'I'd like to borrow your gun,' he said.

'Oh, God,' she muttered, feeling a little sickened by the reminder that Mog might be coming for her.

'I'm sure he won't find us here, but . . .'

'Yeah. You must be *real* sure, since you want my gun.'

'Just a precaution.'

'I know. I know.'

'May I?'

'Help yourself.'

He spread the purse open wide and peered in. Then his hand went inside and he came out with the pistol.

'Do you know how to use it?' Jane asked.

'I'm a guy, am I not? It's in my genes.'

She laughed, then saw him drop the magazine, look it over, knock it back into place with the heel of his hand, draw back the slide far enough for a glimpse of the round being retracted from the chamber, and let the slide snap forward.

'In your genes, my eye.'

He flashed her a grin. 'I am a man of many parts.' He set the pistol down on the table beside his book, then sat down.

'You're planning to stay up all night, aren't you?'

'Yep.'

'I should be the one who stays up,' she said. 'You should sleep.'

'Why is that?'

'Suppose he *does* show up? You're planning to shoot him, aren't you?'

'If I have to.'

'I don't want you killing someone for me, Brace. You said yourself, it's the biggest thing there is. I don't want you to have it on your conscience. If shooting needs to be done around here, I should be the one to do it.'

'No.'

'Hey, I already shot three guys dead in cold blood. What's one more?'

Even though the length of the room separated Jane from Brace, she could see how his eyes narrowed and went cold. 'Mog got you into this,' he said, his voice hard. 'He made you do things. He *cut* you. So this killing's on me.'

Jane felt an icy swarm of goosebumps racing up her skin.

After a few moments, the look of Brace softened. 'Anyway,' he said, 'Mog won't find us here. This is just in case. Okay?'

'Okay,' Jane said. She reached out to the nightstand, picked up her glass of water, and took a sip. The ice had melted, but the water was still very cold. She drank it all, then set down the glass.

'Would you like a refill?' Brace asked.

'No, that's all right. I don't want any more. I'm going to sleep.'

'Okay. Goodnight, honey.'

'Night.' Jane slid her elbow out from under her and settled down in the bed. She tucked her arm under the pillow. She watched Brace.

He picked up the book, crossed one leg over the other, and rested the thick volume against his upraised knee. He opened it to the bookmark. Then he looked up at Jane. 'Does my light bother you?' he asked.

'How would you read in the dark?'

'It wouldn't be easy. But I don't have to read.'

'Yes, you do. The thing's due day after tomorrow.'

'But I've got an "in" with the librarian.'

'That you do.'

'I'll turn off the light.'

'No. Don't. The light's fine. I want it to stay on. I want to be able to see you if I wake up.'

'I'll leave it on,' he said.

'Thanks.'

But the room was dark when Jane woke up.

Chapter Thirty-nine

Her heart slammed like a door kicked shut.

Flinging herself sideways, she shoved herself up on an elbow and stretched her other arm up through the darkness. Her hand bumped the lamp. She fumbled, found the switch, and thumbed it. The light came on.

Brace was gone from his chair. The book and pistol lay side by side on top of the small, round table. The other bed was empty, its covers smooth.

'Brace?'

Her voice sounded choked.

She tried again. 'Brace?'

No answer.

He wouldn't just leave!

She swung herself sideways, pushed at the mattress and stood up. And looked down at her front because something felt oddly stiff there.

Her T-shirt hung loose past her groin. A little wrinkled. But not bloody. It looked fine. And she could feel that she still had her panties on.

Quickly, she lifted the T-shirt up to her chin.

She hadn't been written on. She hadn't been cut. Everything seemed fine. Brace's folded handkerchief was still taped in place across her OBEY. It dropped a little near the middle, but still looked secure. It showed no traces of blood.

Nothing's happened, she told herself, and lowered her shirt. False alarm.

She stepped past the end of her bed, turned to her left, and walked toward her reflection in the mirror over the sink. A section of wall stretched along the far side of her bed. Moving past it, she saw a strip of light along the floor to her left. The light came from under the bathroom door.

It's *all* a false alarm.

He's just in there using the john. Maybe Winky's Special pizza hadn't agreed with him.

With one knuckle, Jane lightly rapped on the door.

From behind it, she heard the hum of the ventilation fan. 'You okay?' she called softly.

He didn't say anything.

'Brace?' She knocked harder. 'Are you all right in there?' She waited.

Heart thumping hard again, she grabbed the knob and turned it and pushed the door open.

Brace wasn't sitting on the toilet.

He wouldn't be taking a bath at this hour! Not when he's supposed to be guarding me!

The tub, off to the right, was hidden by the open door. Jane pushed the door out of her way. As it swung back toward the wall, she saw bright red spatters on the tile floor. They led toward the bathtub. The shower curtain was shut, and hanging inside the tub. Jane couldn't see through its heavy white plastic.

But she knew . . . *knew* . . . what she would find on the other side of the curtain, sprawled at the bottom of the tub.

Whimpering, she ran for the tub.

Her feet skated on the blood.

She flapped her arms. Her rump slammed the floor. The blow sent a shockwave up her spine and into her head. She slid, falling backward, and skidded on her back until the bottoms of her bare feet slapped softly against the side of the tub.

She flipped herself over. Got to her knees. Scurried to the tub and flung the curtain aside.

Brace's dead, mutilated body was not sprawled in the tub.

The tub was empty, and looked clean – but its bottom was wet.

Where is he?

Maybe he's okay, she told herself.

Maybe this doesn't have anything to do with Mog.

Like hell! Like fucking hell!

Sobbing, she held the edge of the tub and started to get up. She raised her right knee; planted her foot on the slippery tiles, leaned forward to put weight on it, and heard a crackly, papery sound.

It came from where the top of her thigh was pressed against her body – pressing the front of her T-shirt against the right side of the bandage covering OBEY.

And what's that stiff feeling in there?

Paper?

Swinging herself around, Jane sat on the cool enamel of the tub's edge. Her T-shirt was pasted to her back with the blood from the floor. She peeled it off and dropped it into the tub.

The makeshift bandage of Brace's handkerchief was fixed to her midsection with criss-crossing strips of tape.

She started to pick at them with her fingernails.

They stuck tightly to her skin. Finally, gritting her teeth and growling, she ripped them away.

The bandage came off with them.

So did the long, white envelope that had been sandwiched between the bandage and her skin. The envelope fell away from Brace's handkerchief and dropped onto her lap.

Hanging the mass of cloth and tape across one thigh, she picked up the envelope.

It had her name on it.

She tore it open.

When she pulled the folded sheet of loose-leaf paper out of the envelope, she knew it contained something. Not a stack of money, but something.

Something that had leaked a few spots of blood.

She didn't want to think about what it might be – something

gross, for sure. But she didn't quite suspect a body part.

The ear fell out when she unfolded the paper.

Yelping, she clamped her legs shut to catch it. She didn't want to let it hit the floor. The tiles were bloody and dirty and it was Brace's ear – had to be Brace's, didn't it?

It landed on the bit of gauzy black fabric at her groin, slid down the slope there, and was halted by her shut legs. She could feel its weight.

She picked it up carefully by the rim.

With hands that shook very badly, she wrapped it in Brace's handkerchief.

A guy without much use for handkerchiefs.

Till now, Jane thought.

Her crying got worse.

Holding the wrapped ear gently against her chest, she stood up. She slid her feet over the tiles. Outside the bathroom, the carpet felt safe. She knew she was leaving prints on it, but she didn't care.

She hurried over to the table and started to put Brace's ear into her purse.

What good is it? she wondered.

Well, shit, I'm not gonna throw it away.

Maybe it can be reattached.

Gotta put it on ice, she thought.

She ran toward the ice bucket. She could see it at the far end of the room, next to the sink. And she could see the tear-blurred image of herself running toward it. She looked like a madwoman in the mirror: hair wet and stringy, wild eyes spilling tears down her face, breasts bobbing and jumping, the slits of OBEY just above where her hands were cupping the hanky-wrapped ear.

She stopped at the sink. With one hand, she reached for the ice bucket.

Instead of ice, the plastic container held a few inches of water. Jane dipped her fingers in the water. It was still chilly, but not ice-cold. She dumped it into the sink.

'Gotta have ice,' she sobbed. 'Gotta . . .'

It all began to seem a little absurd as she hurried into her robe and found the room key and lurched into the night (the rental car still parked in front of the door) and raced barefoot down the motel's walkway toward the ice machine, the plastic bucket clutched to her belly, the cloth-wrapped ear sliding around the bottom of it.

Trying to save Brace's ear when, for all she knew, the rest of him might already be dead.

No!

Or she might not be able to find him for hours – or for days.

Or the ear might already be ruined.

She knew almost nothing about what was required for putting someone together again. Only that it could be done if the conditions were right, and you needed to keep the severed part on ice until you got it to the surgeons.

So maybe it's absurd, she thought. Maybe it's a waste of time. But I've gotta try, at least.

Earlier, she'd been to the ice machine with Brace. She knew where to find it. She knew how to use it.

As she ran, the belt of her robe loosened. She used one hand to hold the robe shut, though she saw nobody anywhere and supposed that everyone at the motel must be asleep.

At the ice machine, she took the ear out of the bucket. She set the bucket onto a grate beneath the dispenser's spout, held a red button down with her thumb, and waited while chunks of ice rumbled down like a tiny avalanche.

When the bucket was full, she didn't know what to do.

Unwrap the ear? Though the handkerchief seemed protective, it might increase the risk of contamination, or something. She just didn't know. She hated the idea of putting Brace's ear into the ice bare.

But that seemed like the right way to go.

She scooped out some ice, removed the ear from Brace's hanky, and gently set it down in the depression.

A small grave.

It's not a grave!

821

Sobbing, she covered the ear with chunks of frosty white ice.

Then she ran with it back to the room.

She set the ice bucket on the table.

Rubbing her eyes, she sniffed. 'Everything'll be fine,' she muttered. 'Everything . . . fine.'

But now what?

Gotta figure out how to find Brace, that's what.

She remembered the sheet of paper that had been wrapped around the ear.

Probably a note from Mog.

But she didn't have the note with her. She couldn't remember what had happened to it after the ear fell out.

So she hurried back to the bathroom and spotted it on the floor by the tub – a pale rectangle through the blur of her tears.

Heading for it, she slipped on blood-smeared tiles. This time, she managed to stay on her feet. It had been close, though. Too close. She didn't want to fall and hurt herself again. And a fall onto the blood would ruin her robe.

She took off the robe. A towel bar was within reach. She tucked the garment securely over the bar, out of harm's way. Then she lowered herself slowly to the floor and crawled the rest of the way to the note.

On her knees, she spread it open. She wiped her eyes again, and began to read.

Friends, Romans and Jane.

Guess who should've played along. Does the word OBEY mean anything to you? Which part of OBEY don't you understand?

In case you might be wondering, the ear belongs to your dear one. I hope you appreciate my kindness in sparing your favorite part – for now.

The rest of him will be waiting for you, intact until midnight. I have every confidence that you will not fail him . . . or moi.

Any further disobedience from you will be rewarded with an additional part. Perhaps you'll be able to rebuild him one piece at a time, but I doubt it.

Until midnight in the pool . . .

Yours forever,
whether you like it or not,
MOG

Chapter Forty

On her hands and knees, Jane scrubbed the bathroom floor. She used her T-shirt, since it had been ruined anyway by her slide through the blood. When the tiles looked clean, she did the best she could to clean the stains out of the carpet. Only her first few steps had made footprints of any consequence. She was able to scour away most of the blood.

Done with the floors, she tossed her T-shirt and panties into the wastebasket. She pulled her robe off the towel bar and looked at it closely. It had a few minor stains inside from when she'd worn it on her trip to the ice machine. It looked salvageable, though.

She took the robe into the shower with her and scrubbed its stains with soap and a washcloth. She lifted it close to the nozzle to rinse it. Then she turned and reached up to drape it over the shower curtain rod – and felt a stir of cool air against her back.

Looking over her left shoulder, she saw the window. She knew that she must've seen it before; it hadn't *grown* there. She couldn't recall it, though.

The sill was level with her chin. There was no screen.

She approached it, walking carefully toward the back of the slippery tub.

The window, with side hinges, had been cranked wide open. She couldn't see its frosted pane until she peered out into the darkness.

A voyeur could have a field day, she thought.

She took hold of the crank and started to turn it.

And stopped.

And gazed at the tall, narrow opening.

A tight fit, but even a big man could probably squeeze through if he really worked at it – came in on his side . . .

That's how!

Mog squirmed his way in and waited in the tub. Probably with the shower curtain shut.

The curtain had been open when Jane had used the toilet just before going to bed.

Mog must've climbed in later, while she was sleeping and Brace was reading the book. Climbed in and waited in the tub. Eventually, Brace had set down his book, left it on the table with the pistol, and paid a visit to the john. That's when Mog jumped him. Subdued him somehow – very fast and silently. Then cut off his ear. And paid his visit to Jane.

Leaning forward against the cool tiles of the wall, she gazed out the window.

She could make out a clearing back there. Vague, black shapes of trees not far away.

What if he's out there now? she wondered.

He couldn't have taken Brace out through the window.

Don't count on it. How the hell do I know what *Mog can't do?*

Unlikely, though. He probably carried Brace out the front door. Stopped the bleeding first, then hauled him through and took him outside and drove him away.

Except maybe they *haven't* left yet. Mog might want to stick around and watch the fun.

Jane scanned the darkness beyond the window.

He's probably out there right now, she thought. Looking back at me.

He's always watching, isn't he?

Suddenly, Jane's heart was slamming. She cranked the window. It swung toward her, its frosted glass shutting out the night.

Shutting her away from Mog's sight.

If he's out there.

If he's out there, hasn't left yet . . .

Brace!

Maybe locked in a car trunk, or . . .

She snatched her robe down off the curtain rod and whipped the curtain aside. Water spilling off her body, she slipped and slid her way across the bathroom. When she had carpet under her bare feet, she ran. She struggled into her robe. At the table, she grabbed the room key and pistol.

Then she stepped outside.

Here we go again, she thought.

She hurried along the walkway – the same route that she'd taken to the ice machine – lighted doors and dark windows to her right, the fronts of parked vehicles to her left.

What am I even looking for?

Mog.

A big guy, six-foot-four.

He was probably around back till I shut the window and wrecked his view. Might be coming around the corner of the building any time now.

Yeah, sure. He isn't going to let me see him. I've *never* seen him.

Not likely to see Brace, either. He's probably hidden away in a car or something.

At the ice machine, she stopped. Her back to the machine, she turned her head and studied the vehicles in the motel lot. Most were lined up in spaces adjacent to the rooms where their owners were apparently spending the night.

As she peered at them, she fought to catch her breath. Her wet robe felt like a clinging layer of clammy skin. Water dribbled down between her legs, tickling – and making a puddle on the pavement. She rubbed her legs together.

Where do I even start? she wondered.

She could look them all over, one at a time, but getting into their trunks would be a pretty good trick.

And Brace might *not* be in a trunk. He might be in one of the motel rooms.

Start with the cars, she decided.

The nearest car was an MG.

Mog with an MG?

But both the front seats were empty, and a full-sized person wouldn't fit anywhere else in the vehicle. Jane walked past the rear of it. The trunk looked big enough, maybe, to hold half a man.

On the other side of the MG was an old Jeep Wagoneer. It had no trunk, but plenty of room inside. Jane stepped close to its rear window, bent over, and cupped her hands to the glass.

The cargo space wasn't empty.

Along one side, she saw a dark, bulky shape – a man covered by a blanket?

About the right size for that, but . . .

Jane heard an engine.

She whirled around.

The car rolled slowly toward her, headlights off, as if sneaking past the rear-ends of those that were parked for the night. It looked very big and very black.

When she saw it was a hearse, her bowels went icy.

She stood rigid at the back of the Wagoneer, struggling to breathe.

As the hearse kept coming, she eased her right arm backward slightly and pressed the pistol against the side of her buttock. She thumbed the safety off.

It won't run me over, she told herself. Not unless it suddenly swerves.

It didn't swerve.

When the passenger door was directly in front of Jane and no more than one large stride away, the hearse stopped.

Oh, Jesus! Oh, sweet Jesus! What's he DOING!

She heard a quiet buzz as the window slid down.

Bending her knees, leaning forward, Jane looked in.

She saw the driver.

He was blackness, huge in his seat, topped with a cap like a chauffeur.

'Care for a lift?' he asked, his voice no more than a whisper.

Jane wanted to run.

She felt frozen.

He's got Brace.

'Care for a lift?' he asked again.

'Yes.'

'Try wearing high heels,' he said, and chuckled, and stepped on the gas. The tires whirred, spinning, throwing up smoke and gravel.

In the instant before they caught hold and hurled the hearse forward, Jane dived through the open window. She made it past her waist. Then the car clubbed her left hip and she cried out. Her shoulder punched the cushion of a seatback. Her head jerked quick and hard. As she rebounded off the cushion, the momentum released her. She dropped. The windowsill rammed her. She folded, head dropping toward the empty seat.

With her left arm, she shoved at the seat.

She raised her right arm. Tried to lift her head, but couldn't. But knew where the driver was, didn't need to see him. Pointed her pistol. Cried out and dropped the pistol and wondered if her hand was broken and wondered why she had pulled such a stupid stunt in the first place as to dive through the window.

Ain't the movies, stupid.

Now I'm gonna be sorry.

She didn't think her wrist could bend any further, but it did. She hissed and shuddered with the pain.

'I like your guts, honey,' the driver whispered. 'You're not always so smart, but you've got spunk. Yer chock full o' spunk.' He chuckled.

Releasing her hand, he grabbed the nape of her neck. He thrust her down, pushing her forehead into the car seat.

'Yes,' he hissed. 'Your dear one is here in the hearse with us. All but his ear. Doing his Van Gogh routine in our coffin.'

Our coffin? The one she'd used in the old house by the graveyard?

'And yes, you will keep your rendezvous at midnight as planned. Yes?'

'Yes,' Jane grunted.

'For now,' he said, 'enjoy the ride.'

Keeping her head shoved down with one hand while he apparently steered with the other, he made a quick turn that hurled her legs sideways. The force threatened to fling her out of the hearse. She gasped with alarm – then with pain as the fingers dug into her neck.

When the turn ended, she felt as if she'd been released from a tug-o-war. Her legs fell against the side of the door. They swayed as the hearse sped along.

Where is everyone?

Someone has to be up!

Someone has to notice if a goddamn hearse is tooling through town with half of me sticking out its window!

But the town didn't last long.

Jane knew when they had left it behind; the seat cushion went dark under her eyes and somebody seemed to turn up the volume on the night-time wilderness soundtrack of bird and bug noises.

In spite of her discomfort and terror, she noticed the strong, piney aroma of the trees. The slipstream flapping her robe felt cool and moist where it rushed over her bare skin.

'Are you enjoying the ride so far?'

'Fuck you,' she said.

'How rude,' the driver said, sounding amused.

He slowed almost to a stop and turned right. The tires made crunching sounds. Then the engine noise swelled and the hearse lunged forward.

Not on pavement, anymore.

On a rutted, pitted gravel road.

The windowsill pounded Jane. She bounced on it, slid on

it, bumped against one side then the other as her face was shoved harder into the seat. Her legs, hanging outside, crashed against the door and flew up and about, thrown every which way by the bounding hearse. Sometimes, they were hit by bits of rock spit backward by the front tire. Bushes or saplings growing close to the roadside jabbed her and whipped her.

'Midnight, darling. Be there or be square.'

The hand clutching the nape for her neck let go.

Chapter Forty-one

Jane woke up.

Her head ached. She felt a little nauseous.

High above her, leafy green branches were motionless against the blue of the sky. Beneath her, most places felt springy and soft but she could also feel hard knobs and pointy things.

It took her a few moments to remember about the hearse.

Midnight, darling. Be there or be square.

An instant later, the back of her head had crashed against something – the top of the door? – and out she'd gone. She had a vague memory of the falling, the impact, the tumbling down a rough slope. She might've been knocked out, but she didn't think so. She thought she could recall trying to stand up afterward, but feeling too tired and ruined for such nonsense, and sinking back down to the ground.

Couldn't have been very long ago.

A couple of hours?

From the look of the sky and the feel of the air, she guessed that this was early morning. Maybe seven?

Got till midnight to get to the church.

Jane raised her head, groaning as the pain swelled. She propped herself up with her elbows.

She hadn't lost her robe, but the right sleeve was torn so it drooped off her shoulder, and the front was wide open. Her legs had caught the worst of things: they were cross-hatched with patterns of welts and scratches, gouged and bloody in a few places, scuffed with abrasions, filthy. She had a few pine needles in her pubic hair. Her midsection, though better off than her legs, was mottled with blood and dirt, battered and scratched so that she couldn't find more than a few traces of OBEY. Her breasts were dirty, but looked okay except for a thin scratch on the top of her right breast. It was two inches long, and ended at the edge of her nipple. It didn't look as if it had bled much.

On the tablet of your skin, we write the book of Jane.

Is that how it went? Close.

Then she thought about Brace's ear.

My fault. All my fault.

And now Mog's got him in a coffin, *our* coffin.

I was in it and wearing that nightie, and Brace found me in it and got so upset, and now he's in it himself. Except for his ear.

Doing his Van Gogh routine.

She didn't want to think about such things.

Stop thinking, she told herself. Just stop it and get moving.

She sat up, wincing and groaning as the pain in her head swelled. Her neck felt almost too sore to hold her head up. She ached everywhere.

Yeah, she thought, and what else is new? Been a wreck ever since Mog started in on me. Bumped my head on Crazy Horse's hair, that was the first ... no, that wasn't the first. The first was when my switchblade popped open on the library stairs and caught me in the boob.

Been a damn pain-fest from the get-go.

As she struggled to stand, she squeezed her eyes shut. She felt herself swaying slightly. And felt a heavy weight swinging the right side of her robe.

Her hand went into the pocket.

And lifted out the pistol.

He gave it back to me?

Checking her other pocket, Jane found the key to her room at the Lucky Logger Inn.

Must've come down here after he threw me out . . .

She staggered over to a tree. Leaning back against it, she eased back the pistol's slide for a glance at the chambered round. It hadn't been removed. She checked the magazine. Still fully loaded.

Should've shot while I was diving in at him, she thought. Leaped and started pulling the trigger.

He who hesitates is fucked.

'Next time,' she muttered. 'Just wait till next time.'

Talking made her head hurt worse.

She slipped the pistol back into her pocket, then closed her robe and tied its cloth belt. With a thrust of her rump, she shoved herself away from the tree. She took a few slow, wobbly strides, then began to trudge up the slope.

On her way up, she found plenty of evidence that this had been her route to the bottom: furrows in the ground cover of dead pine needles; saplings with fractured limbs, white inside; moist, dark pits of various sizes where her passage had uprooted rocks.

At the top, she found the narrow, rutted lane.

Gotta follow it, she told herself. But which way?

To the left? Of course. I went out the passenger window and ended up on this side, so the hearse was heading to my right. I want to go back the way we came, so . . .

Left, it is.

She walked and walked. She longed for aspirin to soothe the tight, cold pounding in her head. She longed for a hot bath to ease the stiff soreness of her muscles. And she longed for shoes. With every step, she seemed to land a foot on something either hard or sharp that made her gasp and hobble.

Often, she found her mind straying to thoughts of Brace.

In the coffin in the hearse.

His ear in the ice bucket in the motel room.

Had the ice melted yet?

It'll be all right, she told herself. Everything'll be all right. Well, maybe not the ear. But we can get by without his ear – he can grow his hair long . . . The ear won't matter. It's the rest of him that counts. I'll go to that Baptist church tonight and do whatever Mog wants, and he'll give Brace back to me and everything will be all right except maybe the ear.

How long *is* this road?

At last, she staggered around a bend and saw two lanes of smooth, dark asphalt in the shadows ahead.

When she was standing on the asphalt, she balanced on one leg at a time and brushed the clinging gravel and twigs and pine needles off the bottoms of her feet. She found a few minor cuts. Patches of sticky sap. And a large black spider mashed against her right heel.

She wrinkled her nose at that.

Said, 'Yuck.'

It looked awfully fresh, though flat. She must've nailed the thing with the last step she took, or it would've rubbed off.

She found a twig and scraped the crushed body away.

A single black leg remained, clinging to her heel like a stray whisker.

Just like the spider at the old house by the graveyard. It, too, had left a leg on her as a token of its death.

Jane rubbed her heel against the asphalt.

Looked again.

'Gotcha,' she muttered.

And heard a feeble, whinnying sound. A car engine?

She tensed.

Thought about making a dash for cover.

'Screw that,' she said. Instead of trying to hide, she stepped to the edge of the road, checked her robe to make sure it was shut, and slipped her hand into the pocket. She held her pistol, but didn't take it out.

Around the bend came an old VW bug being driven by a teenaged girl. The VW was a convertible. The girl's long, blonde hair blew behind her.

No passengers.

Leaving the pistol in her pocket, Jane waved.

The girl looked worried.

Can't blame her, Jane thought. I must look like I wandered away from a lunatic asylum.

Before reaching her, the car stopped. Jane didn't move.

Careful, she told herself, or this gal's gonna pull a Uie and head for the hills and I'll have a long and painful hike back to the motel.

'My boyfriend beat me up last night,' she called to the girl. 'He threw me out of the car and beat the crap out of me and left me in the woods. "Let's see if your feet work as good as your mouth, you damn bitch." That's what he said.'

'Golly,' the girl said. She didn't look worried any more. She looked, instead, rather befuddled. 'What'd you do to him?' she asked.

'I called him a name.'

'Yeah? What'd you call him?'

'Shit-for-brains.'

The girl smiled. 'How come you wanted to call him that?'

'He tried to run over a dog last night. It was crossing the road, you know? And he swerved and tried to hit it, but it got out of the way in time. That's when I called him shit-for-brains. I hate it when somebody pulls cruel stuff like that.'

'What sort of a dog was it?'

'A Rottweiler.'

'No fooling? I had me a Rottweiler once.'

Oh, God, Jane thought. Don't tell me . . .

'Name of Randy, but it bit my kid sister's face and so my daddy beat it to death with a shovel.'

'Anyway, my friend – Roy? – he tried to run down that dog last night, so I yelled at him. Then he pounded me and left me out here.'

The girl wrinkled her face. She had a very pretty face when

she wasn't busy contorting it, but mostly she kept it looking crooked and a little freakish. 'You want a ride, or something?' she asked.

'That'd be great,' Jane told her. 'I need to get back to my motel. The Lucky Logger?'

'Sure. That ain't far.'

Jane expected the girl to drive closer, but the car stayed put. So she limped toward it. The girl watched her approach, studying her, wide-eyed and mouth drooping.

Jane opened the passenger door. She sank onto the seat, and sighed at the good feel of being off her feet. She pulled the door shut.

'This is awfully nice of you,' she said.

'Yeah.' The girl started to turn her car around.

'My name's Jane.'

'How come you're out here in your robe?'

How come *you're* in a long-sleeved sweatshirt and jeans? Jane wondered. Must be baking inside all that.

'It's what I had on,' she said. 'Roy wanted me to go with him in the car. I'd just taken a shower, and all of a sudden he wanted me to go with him for a drive in the woods.'

The girl made a huffing sound. 'That's a guy for you.' Done changing direction, she stepped on the gas. She shifted into higher gears as the car picked up speed. 'Won't take long now,' she said.

'I sure do appreciate this.'

'Bet you do.'

'What's your name?' Jane asked.

'Rhonda.'

'Rhonda. That's a nice name.'

'It's kind of frippy. Mostly, I just go by Ron, least with my friends. My daddy hates it – Ron. He says if he wanted himself a Ron he would of had a son. And I tell him how they shouldn't of stuck me with such a frippy name. Which goes over like a lead balloon, seeing as how they named me after Grandma. Grandma Rhonda. I call her The Old Vick. That's 'cause she smells like Vick's Vapo-Rub.'

'Sounds like you've got an interesting family,' Jane said.

'Yeah, they're all a bunch of losers.' She glanced over at Jane. 'Speaking of losers, whatcha gonna do about yours?'

'Huh?'

'Your guy. What's his name?'

Jane had to think for a moment. 'Roy?'

'Yeah, him. He staying at the Logger with you?'

'He was.'

'You gonna dump him, or what?'

'I don't know.'

'Better make up your mind, 'cause here we are.'

Looking forward, Jane saw the Lucky Logger Inn just ahead. Most of the spaces in front of the rooms were empty, now. The rental car in front of room twelve looked like an old friend. 'I think everything will be fine,' she said.

'Yeah?' Rhonda swung into the motel's parking lot. 'Where do I go?'

'Right up here by the gray Mazda, that'd be fine.'

'That's your car?'

'Yeah.'

'Spose Roy's in the room?'

'Guess so.'

Nodding, Rhonda swung her VW sideways and stopped it beside the Mazda.

Jane opened the door. 'Thanks a lot for the ride. I really needed it.'

'Sure.'

She climbed out. As she swung her door shut, Rhonda swung her door open. Then the girl stepped out of the car and smiled. The smile made her look a bit moronic.

Jane smiled back at her.

Oh, boy.

'I can come in, can't I?' Rhonda asked.

What is going on, now?

'Might not be a good idea,' Jane said, making her way slowly toward the door to her room – Rhonda coming after her. 'Roy's probably inside, and . . .'

'Wanta meet him.'

'What on earth for?'

Rhonda made a lopsided smile and shrugged. 'Just because,' she said.

'Because why?'

'Gonna lick him for you.'

Jane put her back to the door and tried to keep her smile. 'You want to beat him up?' she said.

'Sure. Betcha I can, too. I can lick most anybody.'

'Well,' Jane said. 'That really doesn't sound like . . .'

Off to the right, a door opened and an elderly man stepped out, a suitcase in one hand.

Quickly, Jane dug out her key. She unlocked the door, threw it open and hurried inside.

Rhonda followed, and shut the door.

Oh, boy.

She's probably not dangerous, Jane told herself.

Look who's talking.

'Where is he?' Rhonda asked.

'Roy!' Jane called. 'Roy, you here?'

No answer. As expected.

Jane shook her head and tried to look perplexed.

'Where y'spose he went to?' Rhonda asked.

'I don't know.'

'I'll pound him till he can't see straight. You just watch and see if I don't. I got scars. I got scars all over me. Fellas, they been at me with knives and busted bottles and everything else. You just name it. But they're the ones who get whipped. This Roy of yours, I'll whip his ass. Teach him to go around whacking on you.'

'Well . . .'

Rhonda headed across the room.

'He must've gone away,' Jane said.

Ignoring her, Rhonda kept walking. She called, 'Roy, you in there? I'm talking to you, fella. You deaf?'

Deaf!

Jane jerked her gaze to the left – to the ice bucket on the

table beside her. Brace's ear was submerged, but plainly visible beneath the clear water and floating bits of ice.

Almost to the sink, Rhonda called, 'You hiding in the toidy, Roy? Come on outa there.' She stepped out of sight.

Jane's left hand splashed into the icy water. She snatched out the ear and plunged her dripping hand into the pocket of her robe.

A moment later, Rhonda reappeared. She came back toward Jane, shaking her head.

'Too bad,' Jane told her. 'I would've enjoyed watching you whip his ass.'

'That's okay, I'll just wait. He's bound to come along.'

'I have to pack up and get going,' Jane said.

'That's okay. Don't mind me.'

Jane opened the door and stood beside it, holding the knob. 'I really think you'd better go, now, Rhonda. If you stay, I'm afraid somebody might get hurt.'

'And I know who. Roy, that's who.'

'Would you like a hundred dollars?' Jane asked.

Rhonda narrowed an eye. 'What do I gotta do for it?'

'Nothing. Just go on ahead wherever you were going before you stopped and picked me up – and forget about fighting Roy. I don't want you getting hurt.'

Rhonda waved a hand. 'Oh, I sorta *like* that part.'

'Getting hurt?'

'Sure. Don't you?'

'No. Not really.'

Rhonda smirked. 'Yeah. Right.'

Jane picked up her purse. Holding it to her belly, she walked past Rhonda, reached in, fingered her stack of money, and pulled out a bill.

She took it to Rhonda. 'It's all yours.'

'That's a *hundred*!'

'Yeah.'

'Holy smoking Judas!' She plucked the bill from Jane's fingers. She held it close to her face. 'It is real?'

'It's real, all right.'

'Never seen me a *hundred*.'

'Well . . . Thanks for the help.'

'How about I give you a hand with your packing?'

Jane sighed. 'I need you to leave, now. Okay? I have a lot of things to do, but I've got to be alone. Please?'

Rhonda folded the bill in half and shoved it down the front pocket of her jeans. Then she rubbed her nose. 'Tell you what. You're an okay gal in my book. Any time you need me, just give a holler. My daddy's in the phone book, name of Dodge. Ed Dodge. You call, and I'll come running.'

'I appreciate it. You're okay in my book, too, Ron.'

Rhonda stuck out her hand.

Jane shook it.

'*Adios amigo*,' Rhonda said. '*Via con Dios*.'

'You, too. And thanks again for the ride.'

Chapter Forty-two

Jane drove away from the Lucky Logger just before its ten o'clock checkout time.

She wore culottes and a fresh, white blouse. In the front pockets of the culottes were her pistol and switchblade knife. On the floor in front of the passenger seat – where she could keep an eye on it – was the plastic bucket from the motel, full of fresh ice and Brace's ear.

She'd left a ten-dollar bill in the room to pay for the bucket, though she doubted it was worth more than about eighty-nine cents.

She didn't want anyone taking her for a thief.

Driving along, she felt very strange.

The opening of *A Tale of Two Cities* ran through her mind: 'It was the best of times, it was the worst of times.'

The strange part was that she felt so good.

The woods were lovely; the warm morning breeze felt good; she was clean from her shower; her car seat was comfortable; her nicks and scrapes and bruises and sore muscles didn't bother her very much; aspirin had vanquished her headache; she was acutely aware that she loved Brace and that she intended to spend the rest of her life with him; she was on her way to rescue him.

'Or die trying,' she said. Then, in a low and somber voice intended to mimic some old Indian chief about to go into battle (though not Crazy Horse, she was pretty sure), she intoned, 'It is a good day to die.'

Her Indian chief, she decided, sounded a lot like Bela Lugosi.

So she tried, 'I vahnt to suck your blood.'

'Horrible,' she said, and softly laughed.

And glanced at Brace's ear, and felt guilty.

It didn't seem right to feel good, considering the circumstances.

This sort of thing had happened to her before, though.

Maybe it's a gift, she thought. Nature or God or whatever tosses some nice stuff your way – like sunlight or a good smell of trees or a bit of silliness – to help you get through the really bad stuff. Maybe because without it you'd just crumple and quit.

Throw in some love and hope, too. You gotta have those.

You don't gotta, she thought.

You can probably get by on how a forest looks, a good song on the radio, the taste of fried eggs with bacon and buttery toast . . .

Which made her think about the breakfast she'd had with Brace in the sunny kitchen of her house.

Which made her start to cry.

She'd eaten nothing since her Winky's Special pizza last night. Though she had an empty feeling inside, she had no appetite. She didn't *want* to eat.

By one o'clock in the afternoon, however, she was beginning to get a sickish feeling.

At a gas station, she filled the car and bought a can of Pepsi and a long brown stick of Teryaki jerky and a cellophane package containing a dozen orange-colored crackers, each pair pasted together by a thin tan layer of peanut butter.

She drank and ate as she drove.

The meal was delicious. It made her feel, at first, as if she were on a holiday trip. But then she glanced at the empty passenger seat, and she went hollow inside. She looked down at the ear, and the food went tasteless.

Everything will be okay, she told herself. I'll do whatever Mog wants me to do, and he'll let me have Brace back.

Until next time I disobey.

'Like fuck I'll do what he wants,' she muttered.

I'll take Brace back, and blow that bastard to Kingdom Come.

'I'll kill his ass,' she said, and smiled.

What remained of her Pepsi and jerky and peanut crackers suddenly tasted a lot better.

She plotted.

I'm supposed to be at the church at midnight, she thought. In the baptismal pool, or whatever they call it. Brace'll probably be somewhere close by.

It's all a question of how to rescue Brace.

And nail Mog.

Gotta do both.

What about calling the cops? Have them go in with a SWAT team. They'll need to know everything. That'd be okay, though. Better if they don't know anything at all about any of this – cspccially about killing those guys at Savile's house – but if that's part of the price for saving Brace . . .

Who says they'll save him?

They'll go into that church thinking Mog's just some everyday scumbag. Doesn't matter what I tell them. They'll figure I'm a nut case if I start in on how it's almost supernatural the way Mog can operate.

They'll underestimate him.

And some of them might die, and Brace might die.

Nobody knows Mog like me. It'll take me to take him down.

Alone?

'The big stuff,' she said, 'you always do alone.'

And she grinned.

She wondered if she'd picked up that one from Hemingway. It sounded like Hemingway . . . or Mickey Spillane.

Tough talk, but not necessarily true. You don't always have to do the big stuff alone. Sometimes, you can use help.

So, how about going back to that town and finding Rhonda? Take her with me tonight. She'd love it – and hell, according to her, she can lick near anyone.

And how about Babe, the motorcycle boy from the Paradise Lounge? He acts tough and he owes me one. He'd probably be glad to help, too.

Maybe take along that Clay fellow who was so nice to me the other night – all we did was eat popcorn and watch *The Great Outdoors* and he didn't try to bang me. I bet he'd help, if I asked him.

Gail would probably do anything I asked, too. Hell, I rescued her from Savile and those other lunatics. And she probably has family and friends we could bring in.

We could throw together quite a gang.

Storm the church . . .

But Jane knew that she didn't have time to return for Rhonda. Even if she did have the time, she wouldn't do it. She wouldn't ask any of these people for help.

Brace had gotten involved, and look what had happened to him.

'It's just me,' she said. 'Li'l ol' me.'

She smiled. 'Me and Travis McGee,' she added. 'Me and Mike Hammer. Me and Steve Carella and Bert and Cotton and Meyer Meyer. Me and Matt Scudder. Just me with a little help from my friends.'

How would they handle a situation like this?

Splendidly.

* * *

'A,' Jane said, 'show up early. B, have some surprises up your sleeve. C, don't play fair. D, all of the above.'

Jane stopped at a convenience store and bought a bag of ice. A few minutes later, she pulled off the road and stopped beside a tree. She went behind the tree with the bag of ice and the plastic bucket. There, she plucked Brace's ear out of the nippy water.

It was looking a bit gray.

This isn't going to work, she thought. This thing's a gonner.

She couldn't simply toss it away, though. Brace might still want it.

And if he doesn't, I do.

So she dumped the bucket of cold water on the ground behind the tree, filled it with clumps of frosty ice, and gingerly added Brace's ear.

Half the bag of ice remained.

She placed the bucket on the floor in front of the passenger seat, the bag of spare ice on the floor behind it.

Later in the afternoon – having plotted until she was weary of plotting, and not wanting to think anymore about anything – she turned on the car radio.

Music played for a while. Then news came on. The woman read with a mild, pleasant voice. Jane didn't pay attention to the first story or two. Then she heard this:

In a shocking new development, a total of eleven bodies, including . . . uh . . . including several partial bodies, have now been removed from the Donnerville home of Steve Savile, which burned to the ground late Saturday night.

The bodies, charred beyond recognition, are believed to include those of Savile and possibly two other men suspected of abducting and committing brutal atrocities against an unknown number of women whom they held captive prior to the fire.

Authorities fear that a total of eight . . . that's eight . . . of the bodies found in the rubble may belong to victims of the three men.

Due to the intense heat of the fire, autopsies will be required in order to determine the causes of death – and even the genders – of all eleven bodies. Identification, if possible, will be based on dental and medical records.

On a happier note, Senator Ellis Jones is expected to make a full recovery from the gunshot wounds he received Sunday morning . . .

Jane turned the radio off.

Eleven bodies!

She couldn't believe it. The three she'd shot in the Show Room, plus Linda and Marjorie, only made five. Where had the other six come from?

If Gail and Sandra had known about other prisoners, they would've mentioned them. Wouldn't they? Of course.

Maybe the six had been kept separate from the others.

Maybe they'd already been dead.

Who knows? Who the hell knows?

Probably Mog.

I'll never find out, Jane thought. If Mog's the one with the answers, they'll stay in him because I'm not gonna ask him any questions. I'm gonna kill his miserable ass the first chance I get, so help me God.

By the time she reached the city limits of Donnerville, much of the ice was melted, water sloshing about in the bucket. But she wasn't ready to return home. Not quite yet. So she pulled off the road.

By the side of the car, she scooped out Brace's ear and dumped most of the water on the ground. A fair amount of ice remained. And she found several good unmelted chunks in the bag she'd stowed behind the seat. She added those, then added the ear.

Then she went to the mall.

She glanced into the B. Dalton book store as she walked by, but didn't spot Gail. Maybe Gail was taking time off to recover from her ordeal. She hadn't come to the mall, however, for a visit with her friend.

She paid a visit to the sporting goods store.

At the mall's food court, she had a supper of cashew chicken and fried rice.

Then she drove over to Division Street. Babe's Harley-Davidson was parked in front of the Paradise Lounge, so she knew he wouldn't be hard to find.

She was right.

Babe seemed very glad to see her, and eager to help.

Shortly before eight o'clock that night, Jane arrived home. On her first trip in from the car, she carried the ice bucket. She took it into the kitchen, plucked out Brace's ear, shook off the excess water into the sink, gave the ear a little sniff (not bad), then sealed it inside a small, pink Tupperware bowl and placed it on a shelf in the freezer compartment of her refrigerator.

Then she set about making her final preparations.

Chapter Forty-three

There was something creepy about being in an empty church at night.

Every deserted building, Jane supposed, was creepy at night. Simply because of the silence and darkness. And you know that nobody should be there, but you're never quite sure what might lurk in the dark with you or who might be sneaking toward you, unseen.

This place seemed worse than others.

Because it was a church, she guessed. God's house, if there is a God. (Sometimes she doubted it; other times, she couldn't help but believe.) Maybe He didn't appreciate trespassers in his house.

Especially armed trespassers hoping to kill someone.

But regardless of what God might or might not appreciate, Jane didn't enjoy being in a place where people came every Sunday to hear sermons about such matters as death and Heaven and the eternal punishments waiting for sinners in Hell. Not to mention that an occasional funeral service was probably held in here.

And especially not to mention the cross.

The enormous wooden cross hung from the ceiling by chains directly above the baptism pool.

It looked ready for action.

Jane had been in Catholic churches. Catholics had Jesus hanging on their crosses, looking miserable and bloody and pretty gross for Jane's taste. At least this cross here didn't have *that*.

Thank God, she thought.

And smiled.

And looked up at the cross looming above her head. It was a dim, vague shape in the darkness – lit only by whatever moonlight and street lights might be coming in through the stained glass windows.

It'd be *really* freaky with a body hanging on it.

Well, maybe not.

Maybe as long as you're sure it's only Jesus . . .

Might even be nice, in a way.

A little company.

Sure hope that thing doesn't fall on me.

At least I don't need to worry about vampires.

She looked at her wristwatch, but couldn't read its face in the dark. She knew better than to turn on her flashlight; that'd give away the whole deal.

Why haven't they shown up yet? she wondered.

It must be at least eleven, by now.

She'd arrived at nine, which *had* to be at least two hours ago. And Mog was bound to come early. He would need time to set up, wouldn't he?

Put the envelope somewhere interesting?

She wondered if there would be $102,400 in it. But more than that, she wondered if Mog would bring Brace here to the church.

She knew that part of the note by heart: 'The rest of him will be waiting for you, intact until midnight.'

Which seemed to mean he would be here.

This better be the right place, she thought – and remembered that it was Brace who'd put the clues together and said to come here.

Hope you weren't wrong.

This has to be the right place, she told herself.

Even if it is, the note didn't actually say he would be here. Just that he would be waiting for me. Maybe waiting somewhere else.

She might need another note to tell her where to find him.

Or maybe ten more notes.

Maybe I'd better *not* shoot Mog, she thought. At least not till I've found Brace.

Not that he'll give me a chance to plug him, anyway. He's too slick for that.

Yeah? We'll see.

Come on, Mog, where are you?

Might be anywhere.

After arriving, Jane had made a thorough search of the church. The parking lot outside had been empty, but that was no guarantee that someone wasn't inside. She, herself, had parked more than a block away and walked back. The main doors at the front of the church had been locked – a good sign. But she'd found a side door that opened easily – leading her to think that Mog might've arrived ahead of her.

Her search had turned up nothing, though.

By the time she'd finished roaming every corridor, searching every room, looking into every nook and under every pew – looking *everywhere* – she'd been sure that nobody else was in the church. Fairly sure.

You could never be completely sure.

Especially with Mog in the Game.

But Jane had gotten to the church *three hours* early, which certainly ought to be early enough to beat Mog.

For quite a while now, she had been sitting on the tiles at the back edge of the baptism pool. Waiting and keeping watch.

If Brace was right about the message, this was where she belonged. At the pool.

But it also seemed like a very good place to be.

With a wall at her back, nobody could sneak up behind her. The wall had a large, stained glass window that let in a dim mist of moonlight – not much, but enough to let her see if anyone was sneaking toward her.

Elevated at the rear of the sanctuary, the pool gave her a height from which to look down at the back of the pulpit, the altar, and beyond to the nave with its row upon row of dark pews.

Only the choir loft, at the far end of the nave, provided a higher vantage point than Jane's place by the pool. The loft had drawbacks, though. The way its balcony jutted out, you couldn't see what might be going on underneath it. And for the best view, you had to be in the front row. If you kept watch from there, your back was vulnerable because of entryways at the rear of the loft. Someone could sneak up on you. Throw you over the railing . . .

Here by the pool was a much better place to be.

But her rump was starting to go numb from sitting on the hard tile edge.

Uncrossing her legs, Jane scooted forward. She eased herself down into the water. It was lukewarm, and deep enough to soak through the underside of her bikini top. Leaning back, she pressed her elbows against the top of the ledge and let her legs rise.

She would want to have the water warmer if this were a spa.

It's *not* a spa. Don't be sacrilegious.

A lot *like* a spa, though, she had to admit. But spas were usually round or square, whereas this was fairly long and narrow, with stairs at both ends.

A short distance beyond each set of stairs was a door. Like stage doors, they led into a network of corridors and small rooms. Dressing rooms, Jane supposed. Some of them, anyway. Where you'd go to change into whatever you wear to get baptised in.

Probably not a bikini, she thought.

Unless maybe you wear something over it, like a choir robe.

Those doors had her a little worried.

She looked at them now. They were way off to the sides, so she had to turn her head as if looking both ways before crossing a street. She could only see one door at a time.

When Mog comes, she thought, he'll probably come through one or the other of them.

They were several yards away, though.

They both had hinges that squeaked.

I'll have a second or two, at least . . .

Jane gasped as a door swung open.

Not one of the side doors, though. This was farther away – and straight ahead. It swung with a *whoosh* that was probably very quiet, but swept like a hollow gust through the stillness of the church.

Jane snapped her gaze straight forward.

She couldn't see the double-doors at the end of the center aisle; they were shrouded by the black shadow of the overhanging choir loft. But she was almost sure that one of those must be the door she had heard swing open.

Lowering her feet to the bottom of the pool, she stood up.

Out from the choir loft's shadow lumbered a black thing that didn't look like a man.

A bulky, cross-shaped oddity that walked on two legs.

Coming down the aisle toward Jane.

What the hell is it?

It *is* a man, she realized as it strode closer. A big man, a monster of a man, carrying someone across his shoulders.

Carrying Brace?

That *must* be Brace.

Jane ached to grab her flashlight and shine it on them – see Mog's face, at last – and make sure this was truly Brace. But she didn't move. Didn't go for the flashlight.

Gotta take him by surprise. My only chance.

She bent her knees slightly, lowering herself until her eyes were just high enough to see over the front side of the pool. Her shoulders were submerged. She felt warm water licking her under the chin.

Better, she thought. Nothing for him to see but the top of my head. And its very dark here. He probably won't see me.

As he came closer, Jane had an urge to submerge.

Disappear from sight.

But she had to keep watching.

A low railing stretched across the front of the sanctuary.

He stepped over it, took a few more steps, halted, swung the body off his shoulders and dumped it onto the altar.

The meaty sound of the impact was followed quickly by a grunt.

He's alive! Brace is alive!

You hear one grunt and you know it's Brace?

Yes! Damn straight! I'd know that grunt anywhere.

She heard a click. And had to squint as a lighter suddenly flared in the darkness. For an instant, she couldn't see anything except a shock of brightness.

Then she could see just fine.

The fire, the size of a candle flame, cast a glow like a golden mist.

Brace was stretched out on the altar.

He lay on his back. The eye that Jane could see – his right – was open. That side of his head looked dark and messy. It was where he had lost his ear. A silver patch of duct tape sealed his mouth. His arms appeared to be strapped down straight against his sides with duct tape that encircled his body. One band of tape crossed his chest. Another crossed him at the hips. His shorts were gone. His public hair shimmered in the firelight. His penis hung limp against his left thigh. More duct tape wrapped him around the thighs and ankles, strapping his legs tight together.

From what Jane could see of Brace, he looked unharmed except for the side of his head where his ear should've been.

The other man peeled a small strip of tape off the bottom of his lighter. The flame died. But the darkness didn't last long. When it came back, he was taping down the thumb-tab at the top of the lighter.

He pushed the bottom of the lighter into the crack between Brace's legs.

To free his hands, Jane realized.

Nothing more ominous than that.

With both hands, he took hold of straps at his shoulders.

He was wearing a backpack.

As he removed it, Jane studied him. She supposed that he must be at least six-four, just as Gail had described him. Not only tall, but powerfully built. His leathers, skin-tight and shiny bright red, encased a body that was packed with mounds and slabs of muscle.

There were many zippers on the outfit – mostly at odd angles, some in places where zippers didn't belong. They might have been put there to relieve strains on the outfit in case he should bulge too much.

The zippers looked like shiny scars.

Made him look like some sort of Frankenstein monster/outlaw biker/sado-masochistic freak.

And executioner.

The sort of executioner who used to wear a hood over his head.

This wasn't a hood, though. This was a red leather mask. It covered his entire head. His eyes, hidden behind round holes, caught specks of light from the flame. A red flap protruded, pushed outward by his nose. His mouth was out of sight behind a three-inch zipper. The zipper was straight, but higher at one end. The pull tab dangled at the high end, gleaming in the light.

He swung the pack off his back. Holding it by one strap, he bent down. Jane couldn't see much of him. Just the zippered back of his red mask and the leather stretched taut across his back.

Certain that she couldn't be seen by him, she slowly turned around. The water rubbed her softly. It made some quiet, slurpy sounds, but nothing loud.

From the tile floor near where she'd sat before entering the pool, she picked up her flashlight and her .22-caliber pistol.

She knew the pistol would work.

Aware that it had been in Mog's possession after he'd thrown her out of the hearse, she hadn't trusted it. So she had checked it carefully before leaving home tonight. And she'd replaced the ammo in the magazine with fresh rounds. She had even tested it, taking it into the back yard and firing it once into the ground.

The pistol in her right hand, the flashlight in her left, she turned herself around.

A black candle now stood on the altar just above Brace's left shoulder.

Black.

What are you, Mog – a Satanist?

He lit another black candle on the flame of the lighter between Brace's legs, and placed this one above Brace's other shoulder. Then he lit two more. He stood them upright by Brace's ankles, then retrieved his lighter, killed its flame, and bent down again.

To put it in his pack, Jane supposed.

The four candles made things very bright.

Jane hoped she was beyond the reach of their glow. She slipped forward a bit, and lowered both hands to the cool tiles in front of the pool.

Realizing that her pistol might be pointed straight at Brace, she turned its muzzle to the left.

She thought, Why don't I just go ahead and shoot when he stands up? We're not here to play by Mog's rules. Don't need to wait for midnight. Just go ahead and . . .

But he came up holding a thick, white envelope. It made a soft *whop* as he slapped it against Brace's chest. He let go of it. It was tilted, lifted slightly at one end by the slope of Brace's left pectoral muscle.

It didn't look thick enough to be holding a hundred and two thousand, four hundred dollars.

Not in hundreds, anyway.

Maybe Mog's switched to thousand-dollar bills.

Or maybe he . . .

He rammed the ice pick down very fast.

It was on its way down before Jane even noticed he had it.

'NO!' she yelled.

As she jerked her pistol up to take aim, the shiny steel spike of the ice pick jabbed through the envelope and plunged into Brace.

Chapter Forty-four

Jane fired.

Brace jerked.

Mog whirled and dropped, falling as Jane snapped off two more shots. Through the ringing in her ears, she heard him crash to the floor.

Out of sight.

Brace and the altar in the way.

She hurled herself out of the pool, scurried on knees and knuckles, leaped to her feet and raced for the altar.

Brace's head turned to watch her.

She skidded to a stop against the altar, against Brace's arm, leaned over him and aimed down past him at the floor . . .

Nothing there but the backpack.

She thumbed her flashlight switch. Caught a shape of fleeing red leather halfway down the center aisle. Fired but he didn't fall or even flinch. Took careful aim and fired fast, emptying the pistol at his back.

But he didn't go down.

He smashed through the double doors at the rear of the nave.

And was gone.

She cried out, 'Shit!'

Then she realized that she could feel Brace's arm against the wet skin below her navel.

She set her pistol and flashlight on his belly.

'You'll be all right,' she whispered. 'You'll be fine. Everything'll be fine.'

Pressing her left hand gently against the envelope on his chest, she squeezed the shaft of the ice pick between her middle and index fingers. With her right hand, she gripped the wooden handle of the weapon. She pulled straight upward. Brace flinched and made a quick sniffing noise. The steel spike slid up out of him, warm where it was caught between her fingers.

She pushed the envelope away and grabbed her flashlight.

The wound was bleeding, but not much.

She shoved the heel of her hand through the blood, smearing it away, and found a small hole. A couple of inches above his left nipple, and over to the side.

'Mm! Mmmm!' The moans sounded urgent – or frustrated. Jane tore the duct tape off Brace's mouth.

He gasped for air.

'I'll get you out of here,' Jane whispered.

He kept gasping.

'I didn't shoot you, did I?'

'Nuh . . . No.'

'Don't think I shot Mog, either.'

'Get . . . outa here.'

'Yeah.'

She looked for something to use as a bandage. It wouldn't take much of a bandage to cover such a small hole.

Setting the flashlight on his chest, she picked up the envelope. She shook the stack of money down to one end, and tore off two inches from the top. She let the rest of the envelope fall. It came to rest in the crease between Brace's right arm and Jane's belly.

With shaking fingers, she folded the piece of envelope. Made a small, square pad of it. Placed the paper bandage against Brace's hole and fixed it there with the wide strip of duct tape she'd taken from his mouth.

'We'll get you to a hos . . .'

'JANE!'

The boom of the voice made her jump.

Brace's head jerked sideways.

'Up here, Jane! In the choir loft.'

She spotted his dim, dark shape up there.

And lowered her eyes to the pistol on Brace's belly. Its slide was locked back. Empty.

'You tricked me, you sly bitch.'

'I tried,' she called.

'Not hard enough. But the money is yours.'

'I don't want any of your fucking money!'

'That's no way to talk.'

'Fuck you!'

'I suggest that you read the note.'

'I suggest you eat shit and die!'

'Read the note, or you'll both die. I'll count to three. One.'

She grabbed the flashlight and swung its beam toward him. 'Two.'

He stood in the front row of the choir loft, aiming a strange device her way.

A crossbow?

'Okay, okay!' she shouted. She grappled blindly down by

her belly, clutched the envelope and raised it. 'I've got it! Don't shoot!'

'Read your instructions. Read them out loud. I'm sure Brace will be amused.'

'Okay. Okay.' She fumbled the sheet of paper out of the envelope, leaving the money inside. She set the envelope on Brace, next to the pistol.

She unfolded the note. With one hand, she held it over Brace. With the other, she shone her light on it. '"My Dearest One,"' she read. Though she didn't speak loudly, her voice seemed to resound through the church. '"It is unfortunate that you chose to make life difficult for me – and impossible for your dear one, Brace. I blame him, in part, for your insurrection. He simply must go. But all is not lost. Far from it. After you've dispatched him, you and I shall resume the Game. With your combination of wit and spunk, my love, you stand . . . you stand to earn a fortune."'

She glared up at the indistinct figure in the choir loft. 'I'm not "your love", you bastard. And the Game is over.'

'Read on, Jane.'

She scanned the page, located the place where she had left off, and continued reading. ' "Inside the back-pack, you will find the proper instrument for the job. Use it on Brace's neck. After you've done that, place his head on the silver tray – also to be found in the backpack – and . . ."'

Crumpling the note, Jane yelled, 'You sick bastard, there's no way . . .'

'Four hundred thousand dollars, Jane. Four hundred thousand, and change. All yours. Tonight. All you need to do is chop off his head and . . .'

'Fuck . . .!'

'Refuse and I kill you both!'

She shone the flashlight at him. The crossbow seemed to be aimed directly at her.

She suddenly had a very hard time catching her breath. Her heart was slamming. She felt dribbles of water or sweat running down her sides and back and legs.

'I'll put a bolt right through Brace's temple. Then it'll be your turn. But I won't kill *you* with a single, clean shot. I'll cripple you first, then come down and work on you. I'll cut you up a little bit at a time. And I'll fuck you till you can't see straight. Been wanting to do that for a long time, now. Oh, we'll have loads of fun.'

She shut her eyes. She felt herself swaying slightly from side to side.

'You can't ask me to kill him,' she said.

'Either way, he gets killed. If *you* do the honors, you'll earn yourself a fortune and you'll walk out of here alive.'

She opened her eyes. She looked down at Brace. His eyes were shiny in the candlelight and staring up at her.

'This,' she whispered, 'is where you're supposed to tell me to do what he says and save myself.'

'You think I'm nuts?' he whispered back.

Jane almost laughed, but her throat got thick and tears came to her eyes. Blinking them away, she raised her head, 'Okay,' she called. 'I'll do it.'

'Thanks a heap,' Brace whispered.

Jane took a deep breath, then stepped around the altar. In front of it, she squatted down and shone her flashlight into the backpack. It was half-full. But the meat cleaver was at the top, cushioned by a coil of rope. The silver tray was tucked down the back. She pulled out the tray, first, and set it down by her foot. Then she lifted out the meat cleaver.

Its big, gleaming blade looked heavy enough to whack off a head with one blow.

She switched off her flashlight, and left it on the floor beside the tray.

The cleaver in her right hand, she stood up straight.

Her back felt very much like a target. A huge target, bare all the way down to her rump – except for a couple of bikini strings.

Not turning around, she called, 'You promise you'll let me go?'

'If you follow orders.'

'I don't wanta die!'

'You won't be killed. That would put a crimp in the Game, you know.'

'Okay,' she said. 'You'd better keep your word.'

'I'll keep my word. Count on it.'

In a whisper to Brace, she said, 'I love you, don't move.'

She raised her arm high and swung the cleaver down in a silver arc toward his neck. And then she turned it in midair. As she lopped off the tips of the candles by Brace's shoulders, snuffing them, she heard the sound of a *thwung*.

She chopped down hard into the top of the altar beside Brace's ear.

Go for the temple!

As the blade chunked into the wood, the bolt struck with a noise like a hammer clanking an iron skillet. She felt the shock of the impact through the cleaver's wooden handle.

And then she let go of the handle. Grabbing Brace by the shoulders, she flung herself up and sideways. She dropped onto him, kicking at the two candles by his feet, hugging him to her body and rolling, tumbling him off the altar.

They seemed to fall through the darkness for a long time.

When they hit the floor, Brace was on the bottom. He let out a grunt.

'Sorry,' Jane whispered.

She pushed herself up to her hands and knees.

'Cut me loose.'

'Stay here and be quiet.'

'Jane!'

'Shhh!' She crawled off him. Keeping low, she scampered to the front of the altar and patted the floor until she found her flashlight. 'It's you and me, Mog!' she shouted.

No answer.

On her feet, she made her way through the darkness to the front of the sanctuary. She bumped into the railing. Climbed over it. Stood on the other side and switched on her flashlight. She aimed its beam at the choir loft.

He'd disappeared.

'I'm here, Mog,' she called. 'I'm here, and I want to play. So come on.'

She heard nothing.

'You aren't afraid of me, are you? What's to be afraid of? Look what I'm wearing.' She shone the light on herself, moved it up and down the front of her body. 'You can see I don't have a gun.' Turning around, she held the light over her shoulder to illuminate her back. 'See?' She turned toward the loft. 'I don't have any weapon at all . . . except my good looks.'

She heard a single, quiet huff of laughter. It came from somewhere in front of her. From the loft? From among the pews near the back of the nave? She couldn't tell.

She took a few slow, careful steps up the center aisle. After passing the first row of pews, she halted. 'What are you scared of?' she called.

'Let's see you take it off, honey.'

'Let's see *you* take it off me. Honey. If you've got the guts.'

She swept the front of the loft with her flashlight. No sign of him.

But she jerked with alarm when the double doors crashed open. She brought her light down and caught him in it.

Striding down the aisle, coming straight at her. Red and glossy in his leather suit and mask, zippers shiny as gold. He'd left his crossbow somewhere else. In one hand, he carried a very large hunting knife. His other hand held a long, black bullwhip.

Jane heard herself let out a groan.

'Whips and knives?' she muttered.

'All's fair in love and the Game, honey.'

Jane took a quick sidestep, reached in between two hymnals in a trough on the back of the pew, and pulled out a Smith & Wesson .357 Magnum long-barreled revolver she'd bought from a grinning fellow named Gatsby that afternoon with the help of Babe.

She cocked its hammer as she swung the muzzle, yelling, 'All's fair, Mog!'

He dived sideways as she pulled the trigger.

The blast stunned Jane. The recoil kicked the gun out of her hand. As she ducked and tried to catch it, she heard the clamor of Mog crashing down on a pew.

The revolver hit the floor. She crouched and lit it with her flash and picked it up and ran to the place where she'd last seen him.

She expected him to be gone.

She was wrong.

He looked as if he had stretched out on his back for a nap. But the seat of the pew was too narrow for him. He had one foot planted on the floor to keep himself from falling off.

Jane pointed the flashlight and revolver at him.

He didn't move.

She wondered if she had hit him, after all.

Where's the blood? Where's the hole?

'Just freeze right there,' she said.

She could see him breathing. Other than that, he remained motionless.

Both his hands were out of sight – one hidden between his side and the wooden back of the pew, the other down beneath the seat.

'Let me see your hands,' Jane said. 'They'd better be empty.'

Even as she spoke, she thought, This isn't a good idea. I should shoot him. This is stupid!

But she had shot three men in the back of the head at the house on Mayr Heights while they were watching a Barbra Streisand movie and having Pepsis and popcorn.

Shooting three men dead in cold blood, even though they had deserved it, was three too many for Jane.

Now that the choice was upon her, she didn't relish the idea of making it four.

Besides, this was Mog.

Master of Games.

The Answer Man.

His hands were still out of sight.

Jane thumbed back the hammer. 'Show me your hands

right now or I'll blow your fucking heart out your back!'

Then came the splash.

A heavy, thumping collision with water – the water of the baptism pool?

Brace!

Trussed in duct tape.

Jane jerked her head sideways. 'Brace!' she yelled.

Should've cut him lose, damn it, why didn't I cut him lose before . . .

At the edge of her eye, she saw Mog bolt upright.

She faced him. The hunting knife had already been launched at her chest. With a yelp of surprise, she batted her revolver at the huge, tumbling blade.

Slammed it aside with her barrel.

As the weapons clashed together, Jane's gun went off. Part of the knife-handle disintegrated. The rest of the knife jetted off into the darkness behind the pew and disappeared.

Like before, the recoil tore the gun from Jane's hand.

This time, it pounded her hip. As it bounced off her body, she caught it.

But she jerked with a sudden spasm of pain, cried out and lost the gun as the bullwhip slashed a streak of fire across her arm and back.

In the glow of her flashlight, she saw the revolver bounce off the edge of the seat, fall between the pews, and vanish. She started to crouch and go after it, but heard the whistle of the whip.

Flinging up her arms to protect her face, she whirled away. The whip lashed her like a tentacle, cutting across her back and wrapping around to rip her belly. But then she was running. Sprinting up the center aisle toward the sanctuary.

Toward the baptism pool.

'Brace!' she yelled.

He didn't answer.

She heard only her own hard breathing, the slap of her bare feet on the church floor, the heavy pounding not far behind her back – and the whistling sound of the whip.

She glanced over her shoulder.

In the darkness, he was coming. One arm, held high, twirled the whip above his head.

Jane leaped the railing in front of the sanctuary. The flashlight was still in her hand. In its wildly prancing beam, she saw the altar ahead.

She raced for it.

And the whip came down over her shoulder, lashing down the front of her body all the way to her hip. Squealing, she fell to her knees and clung to the altar.

The backpack seemed to be gone.

The voice behind her said, 'Get up.'

She still had the flashlight.

She didn't even try to get up.

'Would you like another taste of the lash?'

Bastard sounds like a pirate movie.

'No,' she murmured. 'Just . . . give me a second.'

Wincing with pain, shivering and twitching, Jane struggled to her feet. She bent over the altar, hands on its top to keep herself steady. In her left hand, she still held the flashlight.

Its beam pointed toward the place where she had buried the cleaver in the wood of the altar.

The cleaver was gone.

This is good news, she thought. This could be very good news. Brace must've . . .

'Turn around.'

She turned around and leaned back against the altar. Its edge pushed into her buttocks. As she gasped for air, she felt fluids trickling down her skin everywhere.

Blood, tears and sweat.

Brace'll be popping up any second . . .

Unless he's dead at the bottom of the pool.

'You will do exactly what I say.'

'Don't count on it,' Jane said. She raised her flashlight and shone it on him.

He held the bullwhip by his side. 'Watch,' he said.

'I'm watching.'

A pair of zippers at the crotch of his red leather suit formed a big V. He raised one zipper, then the other. The wedge of leather was lifted high by a massive erection.

'I'm impressed,' Jane said.

'You'll be shrieking with delight. Now, strip.'

'You take off your mask first, and . . . then maybe I'll strip for you.'

'I'm the one who gives orders around here.'

'I don't follow them anymore.'

'We'll see about that.'

He gave the whip a quick snap.

Jane yelped and clutched her belly. Trying not to cry, she gasped, 'I want to see what you look like, okay? That's all. I mean, my God . . . After everything we've . . . Show me your face. Come on.'

After a few moments of silence, he said, 'Sure. Why not?'

With one hand, he reached behind his head. Jane heard the quiet buzz of a zipper. The smooth red front of the mask rumpled. A cheek of it sank in.

He peeled the mask off.

Jane shone her light on his face.

He had very short blond hair, blue eyes, broad features. She supposed that many women would consider him terribly handsome.

She had never seen him before.

'Who are you?' she asked.

He smiled. He had striaght, white teeth.

'Tell me,' she said.

Where the hell is Brace?

'Who am I? Bradford Langford Crawford. My friends call me Ford. What else would you like to know before we proceed with the fun?'

'Why me?' she asked.

'Why not?'

'What's it all about? The Game?'

'Playing.'

'That's all?'

'Playing to win.'

'Ah.' She hurled the flashlight at his face. It tumbled end over end. She didn't wait for it to hit him or miss him; she flung herself around. Heard a thunk and a gasp. Vaulted the altar. Hit the floor on the other side – where she'd landed with Brace not very long ago (Where is he?) – and raced for the pool.

'NOW I'M REALLY GONNA HURT YOU, YOU FUCKING CUNT!!!'

Now it was dark.

It had gone dark at the same moment she'd heard the thunk and gasp.

She could only see dim shapes of gray and black.

The floor dropped out from under her.

She fell forward sprawling into the darkness.

Into the water.

Into the water where she had started out and where she had thought all the action would be, Mog having instructed her to 'take a refreshing dip in John's pool.'

She slammed down through the warm water, dug for the bottom, and grabbed the center post of the twelve-pound hand weight that she had put there. The weight lifted, but only slightly.

Where's Brace?

Jane kicked her legs about, stretched out with her free arm, but couldn't touch him.

Where, damn it?

Maybe at one end or the other. But Jane doubted it. The pool didn't seem large enough.

Doesn't matter.

Gotta nail Mog.

Holding the weight, she swept a hand down under one end and snatched up the knife that she had pinned underneath it earlier.

Not her little switchblade.

A hunting knife with a heavy, twelve-inch blade.

She'd bought it that afternoon at the sporting goods store

at the mall. At home, she had slipped the sheathed knife onto a belt, and buckled the belt.

Now, fast as she could, she pulled the looped belt down over her head.

With the knife suspended from her neck, she peeled a plastic bag off the other end of the weight. The tape came off easily. She didn't bother to remove the .357 from the bag. Gripping it through the filmy plastic, she let go of the weight.

The revolver and knife were enough to keep her submerged. She turned herself around. Squatting, she gazed up through the water.

Saw nothing.

Come on, Mog. Come on. Any time, now.

She waited.

Her lungs were starting to hurt.

What's taking you so long?

It had been very lucky that he hadn't leaped on her back while she was trying to get her hands on the knife and revolver. But now she was ready for him.

With surprises.

Come on, Mog. Jump in. The water's fine.

She wouldn't be able to stay under much longer.

Can't just pop up and start blasting away in the dark. If he isn't right there . . .

Should've picked up some kind of underwater flashlight.

As if her wish for light were a prayer that had been heard and granted, lights suddenly bloomed around her.

Pool lights.

What the hell?

Startled, she gazed up. The water looked very clear. She saw the shiny, rippled underside of its surface. She saw the front wall of the pool, its submerged panel of light, its side above the waterline.

No sign of Mog looming over her.

Nothing but darkness above the edge.

She glanced to both sides.

No sign of Brace.

Nobody else in the pool, either.

Just me.

Jane looked down at herself. The bright lights and water gave her skin an eerie, pale shimmer. Made her look as if she were already dead, drowned. OBEY was hardly visible. Her bruises, scratches and gouges from last night's encounter with Mog were stark and vivid – but the lash marks from tonight were worse – long, thick trails of raw flesh.

So much for having a good-looking corpse.

I'm not dead yet, she told herself.

Just look that way.

She wondered if Mog was looking down at her. If so, he could probably see every detail: how she squatted on the floor of the pool, a huge revolver in a plastic bag in her right hand, a knife dangling like an enormous pendant from the belt around her neck.

If he *is* looking down, she thought, I've already lost any chance to surprise him.

Maybe Brace nailed him.

Maybe it's Brace who turned on the lights.

I should be so lucky, but . . .

Jane could no longer hold her breath.

Gripping the revolver with both hands through the plastic bag, she shoved at the floor of the pool and thrust herself upward. She blasted through the surface, huffing, blinking water out of her eyes as she raised her arms.

Mog – Ford – stood just beyond the edge of the pool, swinging his whip overhead.

Jane pulled the trigger three times very fast.

Each time, the hammer dropped with a solid clank.

She felt no recoil, heard no gunshots.

She heard herself yelling, 'YAHHHHH!'

And she kept on pulling the trigger and yelling, thinking that this was simply not possible – she had bought the revolver herself from Gatsby and the ammo *had* to be good because the other .357 had been loaded from the same box and had fired as it should – she had *definitely* loaded it, had double-checked the cylinder just before sealing the gun inside the plastic bag and taping the bag to her hand-weight and placing it at the bottom of the pool.

This can't be happening!

Could water have gotten into the bag and ruined the ammo?

No chance. That sort of thing doesn't happen in real life – only in fiction written by people who don't know guns.

Why isn't it firing?

Through the keening noise of panic and disbelief coming from herself and the clanking of her hammer and the whistling of the whip, she heard laughter. She saw a big grin on the face of Bradford Langford Crawford.

He seemed to be very happy laughing and swinging his whip overhead. Happy and excited. His erection was still jutting up high through the gap in his leather pants.

He must've seen her looking at it.

He bumped his pelvis forward.

'We're gonna have a hot time, baby.'

She lowered her arms into the water.

She let go of the revolver.

'Take it off,' he said. 'Take it all off. Or I'll rip it off you with my whip. I can do that, you know. But I might nip off a bit of tit in the process. Wouldn't want that, would we?'

'Don't do that,' she said. 'I'll . . . just let me get out of the water, okay?'

'Climb on out. All the better to see you, my dear.'

Jane waded forward, boosted herself out of the pool, and stood on its edge.

'Get rid of the knife.'

With both hands, she lifted the looped belt over her head.

'You sure came prepared. Must be an old Boy Scout, huh?'

'Girl Scout.'

'Yes. You are a girl, all right. And you'd better drop the knife, now.'

She didn't drop it.

She clutched the handle of the knife and tugged. The long, broad blade came out of its scabbard.

'You must be kidding.'

She tossed aside the belt and sheath.

'Don't even think about it.'

'Who said anything about thinking?' she asked.

And then she went for him. She rushed in low, left arm up to shield her face. The whip lashed her arm and licked a trail of fire down her back. The pain made her muscles feel watery, but she stayed up and kept moving, backing him away as he struck her again and again with the whip.

She heard herself yelling with pain.

I'm not really doing this, she thought.

Oh, yes, I am! Oh, Jesus!

Kept lurching at him and he kept backing away and kept whipping her and she wouldn't let herself quit.

Because quitters never prosper.

And because sometimes it has all gone too far.

And sometimes tricks aren't enough.

'Stop it!' he yelled so loudly that Jane could hear him through the whistle and crack of his whip and her own cries of pain.

And, 'Are you nuts?'

And, 'Damn it, I'm gonna kill you if you don't stop!'

And, 'Last chance.'

And, 'Now you're in for it.'

And then, 'Fuck!' as he stopped abruptly.

Jane supposed he must've backed into something. She supposed his retreat was blocked.

The lashings stopped.

He struck her across the face with the handle of his whip.

She drove her knife at him in an upward sweep toward his belly. He caught her by the wrist.

'Now,' he whispered, 'you're really gonna get it.'

He twisted her wrist. She cried out. The knife fell from her numb fingers.

'BRACE!' she shrieked.

Her wrist was jerked upward. Higher and higher until her arm was stretched as high as it would go – then higher. Her feet left the floor.

As she dangled in front of him, Ford tossed his whip aside to free his right hand. He grabbed the front of her bikini top. He ripped it off her.

His huge hand began to fondle her breasts. 'Ooo. Yes. Nice.' He squeezed one. He pinched the nipple or the other. 'Very . . .'

Her left fist punched him in the nose.

The nose made a crackle sound.

He growled like an outraged dog. Still holding Jane suspended high by her right arm, he stopped toying with her breast. He smashed his fist into her belly so hard that it started her swaying. He punched her two more times, then rammed his hand between her legs.

Clutching her groin, he lifted her. His other hand released her wrist and grabbed her by the throat.

And he raised her above his head.

He turned in circles, spinning her.

Then he hurled her across the darkness of the sanctuary.

She crashed against something – the pulpit? – and knocked it over.

Things fell on her.

A book dropped onto her face, crunching her nose.

Papers fluttered down.

This *must* be the pulpit.

And that was probably a *Bible* that hit me.

Her body rang with pain.

She didn't think she could move. She *knew* she couldn't breathe.

But her mind seemed strangely alert.

She thought, When the going gets tough, the tough get going.

She thought, I oughta kill whoever said that.

She thought, Brace or the Cavalry or some damn thing had better come to the rescue pretty fast, or I'm in very deep shit.

Nobody seemed to be coming except Ford.

Backlit by the glow of the pool, he looked like a giant.

'Rough landing?' he asked.

Jane concentrated on trying to get some air into her lungs.

He knelt in front of her. He didn't need to spread her legs; they were already thrown wide apart and she couldn't bring herself to move them.

He tore off her bikini pants with such a rough yank that her rump was jerked up off the floor for a moment. Then the fabric tore and her buttocks fell with a smack.

Her tailbone pounded against something hard and cool.

She wondered if she might be able to move her hand.

Maybe.

'Time to rock and roll, honey.'

Leaning way forward, he grabbed her shoulders.

Yes.

He thrust and went in deep, big and hurting.

She cried out, 'NO!'

Oh yes.

Oh yes oh yes.

As he pumped and she whimpered (*yes*) she tugged the Colt .45 automatic out from under her rump (*yes! yes!*), the .45 she had bought from Gatsby that afternoon (*yes!*) along with four .357 magnum revolvers and three other .45 automatics and four .38 revolvers all of which she'd placed strategically about the church (*yes! yes!*) – the .45 on the bottom shelf inside the small wooden stand of the pulpit (*oh, yes!*) – because toughing it out was good but being tricky was better (*ha!*) – and because God helps those who help themselves (*amen!*) – and as Ford thrust and grunted and Jane shrieked with the pain and horror of his invasion she shoved the muzzle against his ear and pulled the trigger.

The crash of the gunshot deafened her.

(*YES! YES! YES!*)

Chapter Forty-five

For a while, Jane thought she might not be able to get out from under the body.

He wasn't just on top of her.

'Bastard,' she gasped.

Summoning all her strength, she twisted and bucked and shoved at the body, and was finally able to squirm free.

She picked up the Colt.

She was sure that Ford must be dead.

But she fumbled through the darkness until she found his face. His mouth was already open. She thrust the muzzle inside until it wouldn't go any farther, then pulled the trigger twice.

All these shots, she thought, and no cops.

Not yet, anyway.

Just as well.

It was a long time before Jane was able to stand.

She found Brace stretched out motionless on the floor across the sanctuary from the demolished pulpit. He was still bound with duct tape.

When she put her face against his chest, she heard his heartbeat and felt the rise and fall of his breathing.

'Brace?'

He didn't answer.

Leaving him, she wandered the sanctuary. She found her hunting knife on the floor by the altar. She also found Ford's backpack. She staggered, carrying it through the darkness, and sat down beside Brace.

Feeling her way inside the backpack, she found a lighter and a few candles. She lit a candle, dripped it on the floor near Brace, then set it upright in the patch of melted paraffin. She did the same with two more candles.

By the light of the three burning wicks, she used her knife to slice the bands of duct tape around Brace.

He woke up while she was ripping the tape from his skin. His first word was, 'OW!' Then he squinted up at her. He looked as if opening his eyes all the way might be too painful. In a voice that sounded squeezed, he said, 'Jane?'

'Are you okay?'

'God . . . what happened to you?'

'It's all right.'

'You're . . . all torn up.'

'You don't look so hot, yourself.'

'What happened?'

'He's dead,' Jane said. 'I shot him. It's all over.'

'Thank God.' Brace lifted a hand off the floor. He lowered it onto Jane's thigh. His fingers tightened slightly, holding her.

She stroked his head. His hair felt wet. By the light of the candles, she could see that the wetness wasn't blood. Not up there. Sweat, probably. Or water.

'Did you fall in the pool?' she asked.

'Pool?'

'Under the cross.'

'No, I don't . . .'

'I heard a splash. I thought you fell in.'

'I don't think so.'

'What happened to you? You're not where I left you, and . . .'

'Don't know. I . . . I remember you getting me off the altar. Hit the floor a good one, and . . . and you went after him . . . by yourself. Why didn't you let me . . .?'

'Didn't have time. But you must've gotten up. Did you go for the cleaver?'

'Don't remember.'

'It's gone. I figured you'd gotten it. For a while there, I thought you were gonna sneak up on the bastard and give him forty whacks.'

'Don't know. Maybe.'

871

'Guess you fell,' Jane said.

'Wish I could remember.'

'Do you think you can get up?'

'Sure hope so.'

'Or should I get an ambulance?'

'No ambulance. If we can get out of here . . .'

'We can try.'

'Or we'll be in trouble.'

'A shitload,' Jane said.

'Yeah. Let's see if we can't scram.'

Squatting beside Brace, she helped him to his feet. Then she put an arm around him. Side by side, hanging on to each other, they made their way out of the sanctuary. Brace's body was slippery against her.

'You okay?' she asked.

'I don't feel . . . like I'm gonna drop. It's just my shoulder and . . . he cut off my ear. And I feel like I got my head caved in, but . . . what about you?'

She wondered if she should tell him about the rape.

Yeah, she thought. I should.

But I can't.

Just can't. Not right now.

Maybe never.

No, I'll have to tell him. Have to tell him before we make love next time. Have to warn him.

'Jane?'

'Huh?'

'What did he do to you?'

'Beat me up pretty good.'

'Did he . . . did he *whip* you?'

'Yeah. He had one of those big old bullwhips.'

'Jesus.'

'But I had a gun. He's deader than hell.'

Brace looked over his shoulder. As he peered backward down the aisle, he stumbled. Jane staggered with him, holding on, and swung herself around and caught him. They clung to each other, gasping.

'Sorry,' he said.

'It's okay.'

'Am I hurting you?'

Her raw, lashed flesh burned where he was pressed against it, but she said, 'It's fine.'

'Should've watched what I was doing.'

'No problem.'

'I wanted a look at the bastard.'

'Can't see him from here. He's over to the side where it's dark.'

'We shouldn't leave . . . the candles burning.'

'It's okay. I have to come back. Right now, let's just get out of here.' She eased him away from her body, moved again to his side, and slipped her arm across his back. She felt his hand curl against her hip. As they walked toward the rear of the nave, his hand glided upward. It caressed the side of her breast.

'You must be feeling better,' she said.

'Awfully glad we're both still alive.'

'Yeah. Me, too.'

'Can we go to your house?' he asked.

'We'd better visit an emergency room.'

'Better if we get cleaned up first. And . . . we oughta make up a story. To account for stuff.'

'Yeah. You're pretty smart . . . for a guy.'

He groaned, then asked, 'Where's your car?'

'By the bridge. You know where you picked me up after Crazy Horse?'

'That far?'

'Yeah.'

'You got any clothes? 'Cause I don't.'

'I noticed. Don't worry. I'll get the car and bring it back for you.'

'What about you?'

'I've got stuff.'

At the back of the nave, they pushed their way through the double doors and entered the narthex. 'Do you want to wait here or outside?' Jane asked.

'Better not go out like this.'

'You can claim you're Adam.'

'That'd go over big.'

'Wait here,' Jane said. 'I've got a few things to do, but I'll hurry. Would you rather sit or lean?'

'Lean. So I won't have to get up again.'

'Okay.' She guided him across the dark narthex to the space between two of the doors to the outside. 'Is here all right?'

'Fine.'

He sighed as he leaned back against the wall.

Jane moved in close to him. 'I won't be long.' She kissed him gently on the mouth.

Two rows from the back of the nave, she found her nylon satchel underneath a pew. She dragged it out, lifted it onto a seat, and searched its dark contents until she found the backup flashlight she'd bought that day at the mall.

She switched it on.

The satchel, which she had carried into the church loaded with guns, now held only her purse and the clothes that she had worn over her bikini.

She stepped into the soft, denim skirt, then pulled a T-shirt down over her head. Though the T-shirt was big and loose, its touch set fire to her wounds. Trembling, she pulled it off.

Save it for when I have to go outside.

Feeling a little better, she sat down and put on her running shoes.

Then she picked up the satchel and began to hunt for the handguns that she had hidden about the church. She knew just where she had left them. She gathered them quickly, but stayed away from the sanctuary until the end.

There, she picked up the .45 that lay on the floor beside the red-clad body of the man who had beaten and raped her. Near his feet, she found the torn remnants of her bikini pants. She put them into her satchel.

She found the little .22 that had done her no good tonight, but had been so effective against the three men at Savile's house.

On the floor near the altar, she found the envelope that had been pinned to Brace's chest with the ice pick. It was spotted with blood. She glanced inside to make sure the money was there.

She found the note nearby.

The note telling her to cut off Brace's head.

It was wadded into a ball.

She tossed the envelope and note into her satchel.

She left the ice pick on the floor.

And she decided to leave the silver tray. She quickly wiped both its sides with her T-shirt to take care of her fingerprints. Not that her fingerprints were on file anywhere. And not that she wasn't certainly leaving prints throughout the church. But the tray was right at her feet and such a shiny surface and so obviously connected to tonight's mayhem that she thought it would be tempting fate *not* to give it a couple of quick swipes.

As she tossed the T-shirt back into her satchel, she remembered her handweight at the bottom of the baptism pool.

She placed her satchel on the edge of the pool. Not bothering to take off her shoes or skirt, she jumped into the water. She waded toward the dark shape of the miniature barbell, then ducked down. The lukewarm water felt cool and soothing against the heat of her wounds. She stayed under for a few seconds, savoring it. Then she picked up the weight.

Her skirt felt heavy and clinging when she boosted herself out of the water. Her shoes made squelching sounds when she walked, lugging the heavy satchel and searching the area with her flashlight.

What else do I need to take care of? she wondered.

Once I'm out of here, I'm not coming back.

And the cops will find whatever I leave behind.

So let's do this right.

The beam of her light fell on a revolver inside a clear plastic sack.

Her .357 magnum.

The gun that she'd counted on to drop Mog.

The gun that had failed her.

The gun that got me raped, she thought. And almost got me killed.

Her satchel thunked against the floor as she set it down. She crouched and picked up the revolver.

Flashlight clamped under her arm, she ripped away the flimsy plastic covering.

Even if water got in, it shouldn't have . . .

She swung out the cylinder.

Empty.

Empty?

It couldn't possibly be empty.

Jane remembered punching the big, magnum rounds into each of the cylinder holes. She'd done it in her kitchen only a few minutes before leaving for the church.

She had loaded it.

She had slipped it inside a plastic bag, and taped the bag shut.

And then later, at the baptism pool, she had taped the bag to the side of her hand weight and submerged it along with the hunting knife.

This revolver simply could not be empty.

But it is.

She shut the cylinder. As she lowered the gun into the satchel with the others, she remembered the heavy sound of the splash she'd heard during her showdown with Mog in the pews.

She'd been afraid that Brace had fallen into the pool.

She'd feared he might drown.

But he'd denied falling in.

Had he jumped into the pool? To unload the magnum?

Why the hell would he do a thing like that?

Ask him.

Jane stood up and strained to lift her satchel.

Maybe he's been in this from the start, she thought.

No. That's crazy. Mog cut off his ear, stabbed him with an ice pick.

Some sort of double-cross?

No, she told herself. You can't make Brace part of this. If he's part of it, there's nothing left – nothing to believe in, no one to love.

I can believe in myself, she thought.

I can love myself.

Love myself. Big deal.

'Damn it, Brace,' she muttered. 'You've gotta be a good guy. Gotta be.'

As she lugged her satchel through the sanctuary, the swinging beam of her flashlight revealed Mog's backpack.

'Thar she blows,' she said.

She'd been promised four hundred thousand dollars (and change) for chopping off Brace's head.

She hadn't played along.

But Mog must've brought the money with him. Probably in the backpack.

She hurried over to the pack, set down her satchel, and knelt on the floor. She dumped the pack upside-down.

The coil of rope fell out. So did one black candle, a couple of Bic lighters, a hammer and several nails, a screwdriver with its tip filed to a point, a pair of pliers, a road flare, a straight razor, a white envelope with JANE written on it, and a second white envelope.

A second envelope?

She clamped the flashlight under her arm and picked it up.

On one side of the envelope was written FORD.

She ripped it open.

No cash inside.

She pulled out a single sheet of lined notebook paper and unfolded it.

And glimpsed a handwritten message.

Her eyes darted to the bottom of the page.

Where three gleaming gems were fixed to the paper with cellophane tape.

Diamonds?

They sure looked like diamonds.

Big ones.

In the white beam of her flashlight, she read the message.

My dear lad,

Enclosed is an envelope that you may give to our lovely friend Jane after she has completed her assigned task.

If she follows through, three cheers!

She is a spunky lass, however. Be prepared for trouble.

If she refuses to play, you have my permission to dispatch her lover-boy in any way you see fit. Then you may have Jane for yourself.

Enjoy her to the hilt, so to speak.

But be careful. She might be hazardous to your health.

Your buddy,
MOG

Stunned, Jane tried to read the message a second time.

She couldn't. The paper shook too badly in her hands, making the handwriting blur.

Can't be, she thought. No.

Then the bullet hit her in the head.

Chapter Forty-six

She cried 'Ow!'

As she reached up with one hand, the flashlight fell from under her arm and the cartridge dropped like a stone onto Mog's note. It smacked the paper down. The flashlight bumped the floor by her right knee, but didn't go out. Jane clutched the top of her head. The magnum rapped the floor in front of her knees and rolled.

Tears flooded her eyes.

The second cartridge struck her right breast.

Like getting flicked hard by a bully's finger.

It bounced off and clattered to the floor.

Jane looked upward, blinking tears.

Someone laughed.

She snatched up her flashlight.

Aimed it high.

Aimed it toward the quiet, mean laughter.

The beam made a path upward through the darkness to the huge wooden cross suspended by chains above the baptism pool.

She saw the man up there.

The sight of him made Jane go loose and shivery inside.

She suddenly felt as if a tub full of live spiders had been dumped onto her head and she was naked and the creatures with their thousands of tickling feet were racing all over her, scurrying into every orifice.

She knew that the man on the cross was Mog, Master of Games.

So white his skin seemed to glow.

White – and shiny wet.

Skin and bones.

Hairless.

With a face like a grinning skull, but a skull that had full red lips and big pale eyes.

Perched atop the cross-beam, legs dangling, left arm hugging the upright, the cleaver gleaming in its hand. Right arm high and cocked, ready to throw another round at her – then throwing it.

The tumbling brass glinted in the light of Jane's flashlight.

Coming down toward her face.

With her left hand, she snatched it out of the air.

She shoved her flashlight between her knees.

Reached into her satchel for the .357, clutched the first gun she touched, realized most of them were already loaded *except* for the magnum, dropped the revolver and found an automatic and grabbed up her flashlight with her left hand.

Aimed flashlight and pistol at the top of the cross.

The huge cross was swinging slowly back and forth, groaning on its chains.

Abandoned.

Chapter Forty-seven

Jane slammed shoulder-first through the double doors. She staggered into the narthex, .45 in one hand, her ponderous satchel in the other.

'Brace!' she gasped. 'Brace!'

'Yeah?'

She spotted his dim figure against the wall. 'Let's go!'

'What?'

'*Let's go!*'

At the nearest door to the outside, she swung around. She slammed her rump against its crossbar and the door flew open. She backed her way through it and stood there to hold it wide for Brace.

He lurched out, one hand cupping his genitals, and glanced at Jane with frantic eyes.

The front of the church was well lit.

'Let's go, let's go!'

Rushing down the concrete stairs, Jane scanned the area ahead. Nobody in sight. The road empty. The wooded park across the road dark.

Brace stayed by her side.

She twisted her head around and glanced over her shoulder at the doors.

So far, so good.

At the bottom of the stairs, Brace blurted, 'What is it?'

'Mog.'

'You said he was dead.'

'I was wrong. It wasn't Mog I shot.'

'What?'

'He's after us.'

Brace glanced back. 'Where?'

'Don't know. He was up on the cross. But he . . . vanished. Could be anywhere. Just don't know. But he's got that cleaver.'

Side by side, they raced across Park Lane.

'Which way?' Brace asked.

'Into the trees.'

'Your car.'

'No point. He'll just . . . Can't run away from him.'

Jane ducked into the trees beyond the border of the park. She dropped her satchel to the ground and fell to her knees.

Brace knelt beside her. 'What're we doing?' he asked.

Jane slapped a pistol into his hand, then reached into the satchel for another. She gave it to Brace, too.

'Jane?' he asked.

'Yeah?'

She filled both her hands with guns.

'What're we doing?' Brace asked.

'We can't run away from him,' she said.

Brace looked at her. Light from the streetlamps came in through the foliage, making his eyes glint.

'I love you,' Jane said.

'Hey . . .'

'Are you with me?' she asked.

'You name it,' he said.

'We make our stand here.'

'You don't sound very optimistic,' Brace said.

'I'd feel a lot better if we had silver bullets.' Jane turned on her knees so that she was facing the road and the front of the church. Beyond the bushes and tree trunks, she could see the doors at the top of the concrete stairs.

Brace, on his knees next to her, eased closer until the warm skin of his side touched her.

'Tell me he's not a werewolf,' Brace said.

'I don't know what he is. Some sort of spook.'

'I'm not sure I believe in spooks.'

'I do.'

They never saw the church doors open.

They never saw Mog at all until he lurched out of the trees behind them. The only sound he made was a quiet, mean laugh.

The cleaver whistled on its way to Brace's neck.

But Jane had heard the laughter and swung around, both guns blazing.

A slug bashed Mog's arm aside in time to save Brace's neck.

Another punched through his cheekbone.

Brace, too, swung around.

Together, they filled the night with thunder and muzzle flashes and full metal jackets that pounded Mog backward and made him dance like the marionette of a madman until he slammed against a tree trunk.

The trunk knocked him forward.

He pitched facedown on the ground.

They stood over the torn, motionless body.

'Is it *him*, this time?'

'What?' Jane asked. Her ears were ringing from the gun blasts.

'Mog? Is this him?'

'Yeah. I guess. He's the guy from the cross.'

'Still think he's a spook?'

She wrinkled her nose. 'He looks pretty dead. I don't know.'

'We didn't even need silver bullets.'

'Keep an eye on him, okay?' Jane turned her back to the corpse and squatted over the satchel. She set her two empty guns inside. Then she tugged out the T-shirt.

She tossed the T-shirt to Brace. 'You can wear it to the car.'

'What about you?'

'I'll say I'm Eve. If anybody asks.' Bending over, she searched the ground and found the cleaver.

She picked it up.

From Brace, she heard a gasp. Then he blurted, 'Jane!'

She whirled around.

Mog got to his knees, grinning.

This can't be happening. Cannot. No.

Yes.

I knew it

knew it

knew it

a fucking spook!

Brace kicked him under the chin.

Barefoot.

And cried out with pain.

Mog's head snapped backward. The kick lifted him off his knees, sent him sprawling until the back of his head slammed the tree trunk.

As Brace hopped, clutching his toes, Jane leaped past him.

She heard herself whimpering.

She dropped and skidded on her knees through the litter of dead leaves between Mog's spread legs.

Stopped just short of his crotch.

Forced herself not to look at the huge white thing jutting up from there like a pike.

Jammed the heel of her left hand against his slippery forehead.

Chopped through the side of his neck with the cleaver in her right.

Chapter Forty-eight

People must've heard the gunfire. If not the shots inside the church, at least those that had crashed through the silence of the park.

Jane expected police cars to swarm in from all sides, lights aflash and sirens screaming.

But no cops showed up.

On the way back to the car, she saw nobody.

Except Rale.

Rale, the bearded and faceless wino, stepped out suddenly from among the trees on the far side of the bridge, held out a filthy hand and grumbled, 'Spare me a . . .' Then he made a choking sound.

Jane doubted that Rale's stunned reaction had much to do with confronting a young man who wore nothing except a T-shirt that was not quite long enough for decency.

It probably had little to do with encountering a torn and bloody young woman dressed only in a skirt and shoes.

Maybe he recognized her as the one he'd tried to rape.

More likely, though, the shock came from seeing what she carried upside-down beneath her left arm – the severed, hairless head of Mog.

Instead of finishing his request for a handout, Rale squealed and fled into the wooded darkness of the park.

Nothing else happened on their way to her car.

Early the next morning, clean and bandaged and nicely dressed, Brace presented himself to the emergency room of Donnerville's hospital.

He explained that he had tripped in his garage while carrying a window. He had plunged through the window, its shattered glass slicing off his ear. Then he had fallen on a board that had a jutting nail.

Two hours later, he returned to Jane's house with a new puncture from a tetanus shot, fresh bandages, and two prescriptions that would require a trip to a pharmacy.

According to the news reports that day, Satanists were believed to be responsible for the brutal slayings of two unidentified males found in and near the Calvary Baptist Church.

Nothing was mentioned about the missing head.

They buried Mog's head at midnight in the weed-choked back yard of the creephouse next to Paradise Gardens Memorial Park.

'That oughta keep him down,' Jane said, stomping the ground flat.

At dawn the next morning, they buried Brace's ear in Jane's back yard.

It was still frozen.

Jane wanted to leave it in the Tupperware bowl for the ceremony, but Brace objected. 'We don't wanta do that,' he said, peeling off the lid of the bowl. He handed the lid to Jane. Crouching, he placed his ear into the small hole. 'Ain't biodegradable.'

'You're right.'

'Besides, you might wanta use it again.'

Jane wrinkled her nose. 'You've gotta be kidding. Not that I've got anything against your rotten old ear, but I don't think I wanta put *food* in the bowl.'

'You women are all so squeamish.'

She laughed softly. 'That's me.'

With the edge of his shoe, Brace pushed dirt into the hole. 'So long, ear.'

'So long,' Jane said to it.

Gently, Brace rubbed her back. Already, he seemed to know

where the worst of her wounds were – and he stayed away from them as he caressed her.

In a somber voice, he said, 'Nothing will ever be able to take us by surprise again.'

She grinned at him. 'Don't tell me.'

'Don't tell you what?' He raised his eyebrows, oh so innocent.

'Because,' Jane said, 'you'll always have your ear to the ground?'

Brace laughed. '*I* didn't say it,' he protested.

'You were gonna.'

'If I'm so damned predictable, what am I going to say next?'

'That's not fair. If I get it right, you'll just deny it.'

'I never lie, remember?'

'You lied to the doctor, and . . .'

'Never to you.'

'Oh, okay.' Jane grinned. 'So, what is it that you were planning to say next?'

'You're supposed to tell *me*,' he reminded her.

'Oh. Okay. Here's what you're going to say.'

'What?'

'"Jane, you're the most gorgeous babe in the world and I can't get enough of you."'

Brace laughed and shook his head.

Then he looked her in the eyes. His smile vanished. 'Jane, you're the most gorgeous babe in the world and I can't get enough of you.' Suddenly, his eyes bulged. His mouth fell open. 'My God!' he blurted. 'How did *you* know I was about to say that?'

'I can read you like a book,' Jane said.

Then he kissed her.